Maybe It's About Time

Maybe It's About Time

NEIL BOSS

Matador
Unit E2 Airfield Business Park,
Harrison Road, Market Harborough,
Leicestershire. LE16 7UL
Tel: 0116 279 2299
Email: books@troubador.co.uk
Web: www.troubador.co.uk/matador
Twitter: @matadorbooks

ISBN 978 180313 503 8

British Library Cataloguing in Publication Data.
A catalogue record for this book is available from the British Library.

Printed and bound in the UK by TJ Books Limited, Padstow, Cornwall
Typeset in 11pt Minion Pro by Troubador Publishing Ltd, Leicester, UK

Matador is an imprint of Troubador Publishing Ltd

To Mena

You have been next to me for every single word of this book.
That's why it's dedicated to you.
Truly, this man's best friend.

Chapter 1

Points Failure

The concourse at Waterloo Station was rammed as Marcus Barlow emerged from the warm cocoon of the Underground like a pupating moth. Thousands of Monday evening commuters were awaiting their fate at the hands of South Western Trains. He took his AirPods out of their case. For years he had resisted, insisting they looked like hearing aids. Now they were as much a part of his uniform as his Cartier cufflinks and Ferragamo tie.

His smartphone came to life. A picture of his family taken the previous year on holiday in the Maldives. Four tanned bodies, squinting into the sun waist-deep in a turquoise ocean. A happy picture taken at a happy time.

Marcus started The Sequence, a ritual he performed multiple times a day, checking his collection of apps grouped in labelled folders. If a new app didn't have a folder, he created one. Outlook told him he had twenty-five new emails. He inhaled deeply and rolled his eyes. He would read them on the train.

He opened Stockwatch and checked the closing price of the FTSE 100. Green days were good, red days were bad. Uncertainty over Brexit meant there had been a lot of red days recently. Everything was green and it made him feel less anxious. WhatsApp pinged. A message from Alice.

Hi M. U on time? Lmk if u going 2b late. Pick u up at stn. Veg lasag 2nite.

Lots of smiley, yellow faces. His wife liked yellow faces, smiling ones, laughing ones, crying ones, ones with their tongues sticking out. Along with her fondness for text speak, he loathed them and wondered WTF had gone wrong with her? He opened the last app in The Sequence, Spotify. Marcus believed that music only existed in physical form, vinyl and CDs but Sonos and Spotify had changed that.

'You should sell the lot on Discogs,' said Andy, his AV man, scornfully. 'Now you've got Spotify, you'll never listen to another CD. Trust me.'

Marcus found it hard to trust a man who boasted he had been in the SAS, had lost two fingers in Operation Desert Storm and been a personal bodyguard to Dodi Al Fayed. Installing high-end AV equipment in the plusher neighbourhoods of Surrey seemed a bit of a comedown for an ex-war veteran with an ego problem. But Andy was right. Spotify now ruled Marcus's life with its powerful search engine and massive back catalogue. He selected his 'Classic Punk' playlist and turned up the volume. The thudding drums of the Damned's 'New Rose' pummelled his eardrums.

He looked up at the iconic, four-sided clock, made famous in the classic 1945 film *Brief Encounter*. He wondered what would have happened if Laura Jesson and Dr Alec Harvey had started their love affair in 2020?

South Western Trains' incompetence would have given them a bit more time to nip round the back of the station for a snog and a grope, he thought.

The commuting congregation was staring up at the departures board like pilgrims outside St Peter's Basilica at Easter. He half expected the Pope to appear on the balcony to bless the frustrated hordes, but all he got was a row of 'delayed' signs and a tannoy announcement. Points failure at Clapham Junction. Groans of despair, a mass shaking of heads and rolling of eyes. The crowd continued to stare at the screens hoping it was a cruel hoax. But it wasn't.

Having commuted in and out of Waterloo for the best part of twenty-five years, Marcus had heard every excuse. 'Points failure' was up there with 'signal failure' and 'an incident on the line'. The latter was railspeak for a suicide, attempted or successful, and would mean at least a couple of hours' delay to clear up the mess. Years of commuting had numbed his senses, making him intolerant of human tragedy.

The option of going to his pied-à-terre flat in Queensway was scuppered by not having a clean pair of underpants for the following day. Marcus was fastidious about his underwear and berated himself for not having sufficient clean clothes at the flat. There was no alternative but to sit it out. With a bit of luck, Network Rail would fix the problem before he resorted to dossing down with a tramp who was happy to share his soiled sleeping bag, a bit of stale croissant and the warmth from his dog.

Alice's news that dinner would be 'veggie lasagne' filled him with dread. With the Christmas turkey barely cold, his daughter, Olivia, had persuaded her mother that the consumption of red meat accelerated the onset of colon cancer. Sunday roasts and steaks were now history. His son, James, had buggered off to university leaving him to fight his own battles. He had been happy to compromise on chicken and fish, but as soon as Olivia had shown Alice videos of battery chickens and turtles with plastic straws up their noses, they were off the menu too. He knew dairy was on death row too when he saw the carton of oat milk and packets of vegan cheese in the fridge.

His thoughts about food were distracted by 'London Calling' by the Clash. It was one of his Desert Island Discs, although he accepted he was unlikely to be invited to share them with the programme's listeners. Marcus worked in corporate finance and nobody was interested in that. If he had discovered a new species of tree frog or been the latest winner of *Strictly Come Dancing*, Lauren Laverne and the BBC might have come knocking, but he knew they wouldn't. He let the final words of the Clash's masterpiece fade out before calling Alice.

'Hi Al. It's me.'

A photograph of Marcus looking pompous and self-important appeared on her phone like it did every time he called.

'Hi Marcus, I know it's you. Everything okay?'

'Not really. Shit day at work, boring meetings and too many emails. South Western Trains have fucked up again. Points failure! Fuck knows what time I'll be home.'

His liberal use of the word 'fuck' was one of the many things that had irritated Alice throughout their twenty-three-year marriage.

'Marcus, why do you have to swear every time something doesn't go your way? I know it's frustrating but I'm sure they're doing their best.'

Her lack of empathy annoyed him. The only frustration in Alice's day was discovering her Pilates class had been shifted from the tranquility of the 'Be the Best You' room to the 'Let it Rip' suite immediately after the spinning class had ended and its walls were dripping with sweat and pheromones.

'Any idea when you'll be home? I can hang on with the veggie lasagne? Or you can warm it up when you get in?'

'Not a clue. Go ahead and eat and I'll get a cab from the station. That's assuming I get to the fucking station before Easter.'

'Why don't you go to the flat?'

'I don't have any clean underpants.'

'Can't you wear the same ones for another day? Or have you crapped yourself or something?'

'That's disgusting. You know I never wear the same pair two days running.'

'Fine. I'll leave the veggie lasagne out. See you later.'

'Fine' meant that it wasn't fine.

A decision on food was becoming urgent, he was getting hungry. Expensive lunches, usually charged to a client, had become a thing of the past. A series of corruption scandals and accounting frauds had put a stop to them. Now anything more than a sandwich and a few cold samosas was seen as bribery. He reviewed his options.

A sit-down meal wasn't feasible if Network Rail got its act together and he had to move quickly. Yo Sushi, with its continually moving conveyor belt, didn't appeal to him. Marcus was not a decisive man. By the time he had made a selection, somebody further up the food chain had stolen it and he was back to square one. The only option was fast food.

He had often been tempted by the intoxicating aromas wafting from the little booth of the West Cornwall Pasty Company. He approached the warm glass cabinet. He was instantly horrified. Next to the row of traditional pasties was an array of other fillings that would make a Cornish tin miner turn in his grave. Marcus had eaten enough 'fusion' meals to know what worked and what didn't. Mince, carrots, potatoes and spices worked. Thai green chicken curry didn't. He was greeted by Craig, a young man in an over-washed, black shirt.

'Yes bruv? What can I get you?' he said in an urban slang accent.

'Where in West Cornwall are your pasties made?'

'Dunno,' said Craig with a baffled look. 'All we does is heat them up.'

'So it's not Penzance then?'

'Where's Penzance? Na, what can I get you?'

Craig's lack of product knowledge had disappointed him. There seemed little point in discussing menu options.

'Thank you very much, Craig. Perhaps another time?'

Marcus turned and walked back into the crowd, which was still waiting for an update on the points failure. Behind him, Craig made a gesture.

It came down to Burger King. Growing up in an era when a trip to the Wimpy Bar in Staines was the highlight of his school holiday, he had witnessed the demise of Wimpy at the suffocating hands of the ubiquitous McDonalds. When Burger King entered the market, he hoped the new underdog would give the bully a bloody nose. He preferred a flame-grilled Whopper to a Big Mac. It had more in common with a Wimpy. He also thought Ronald's 'special sauce' tasted like puke.

He was greeted by a smiling, enthusiastic girl in a crisp, well-pressed, blue uniform. Her name was Britney.

'Are you named after Britney Spears?' said Marcus, trying to build rapport. She nodded.

'It's American,' she said, proudly.

'Although you don't sound very American,' he said. She laughed.

'I ain't. I'm from Balham.'

Marcus thought that in fifty years' time, there would be a whole generation of pensioners called Britney who could be carbon-dated by their name back to the year 2000.

'What would you like?' said Britney.

'I'll have the Double Whopper with bacon and cheese, large fries and a portion of onion rings, please. A bottle of water, some extra ketchup and salt.'

She tapped his order into the keypad using her recently manicured nails, which resembled a vulture's talons.

'That'll be £12.80, please?'

He reached into his breast pocket, took out his Mulberry wallet and gave her a twenty-pound note. Marcus still used cash, convinced that the overuse of credit cards was a major cause of cybercrime. Two years earlier, he had returned from a family holiday in Acapulco to be informed by American Express that someone had been running wild in Miami with his credit card and had run up a bill of £7,500. It turned out it had been cloned in a beach taco bar. Amex refunded the money, but it was three weeks of stress he could have done without.

He sat down at one of the tables on the concourse in a good position to hear any tannoy updates and run to the platform. The previous occupants had left the remnants of their meal, and he cleared away the half-eaten chicken burger, some cold, limp chips and two fried mozzarella sticks. He hadn't noticed them on the menu, and made a mental note. They looked great, if a little greasy.

From the side pocket of his Tumi laptop bag, Marcus took out his bottle of melon-scented hand sanitiser, squirted a blob on his hands and rubbed them together. Taking the Underground or 'the Drain' on most days, he was paranoid about germs. Nobody in his office sanitised their hands as frequently as he did. He carefully laid out his food in front of him. Everything was going well until he leant forward and dipped the cuff of his white Turnbull & Asser shirt in his extra pot of ketchup. Despite plenty of spit and wiping, it had left a stain.

By the time he finished his Double Whopper, it was 7.35. Still no news from South Western Trains. What to do next? Check his emails, read the *Evening Standard* or update Alice? Calling home wasn't a good idea. The 'veggie lasagne' would be at a critical point and the last thing he needed was being blamed for a burnt bechamel.

He checked his email. There were thirty-one unread emails in his inbox. Twenty were from Mason Sherwin, all with the same title: 'Project Spearmint – URGENT'.

Fuck it. It can wait, he thought, *Sherwin is a bellend*.

Marcus disliked Mason.

He took out his copy of the *Evening Standard* from his laptop bag and unfolded it.

'WE'RE ROYAL DISRUPTERS', said the front-page headline.

The nation was in a state of hysteria over the decision by the Duke and Duchess of Sussex to step away from public duties and seek independent lives away from the royal family. Questions were being raised about the survival of the monarchy. Marcus didn't understand what all the fuss was about. If Harry and Meghan wanted to bugger off to Canada, he wouldn't stand in their way.

He turned to the back pages which, for once, weren't covered by a full-page advert for a mobile phone operator. His phone was paid for by The Firm, and data usage or iCloud storage meant nothing to him. Marcus supported Crystal Palace, one of the capital's less fashionable clubs, whose ground was in a dingy part of South London. Newspapers rarely devoted column inches to the Eagles, unlike the club's swankier and wealthier London neighbours. Tonight was no exception, bugger all news.

He returned to the body of the paper and was attracted by a headline.

LONDON WATERLOO NAMED UK'S BUSIEST STATION FOR SIXTEENTH YEAR IN A ROW.

Apparently, 94.2 million passengers had used the station in the past twelve months. *Poor suffering bastards!* he thought. *Suckers for punishment.*

With time on his hands, he read more of the newspaper than usual. On *Love Island,* Mike had dumped Jess, and the Mayor of London's latest campaign to stop knife crime in the capital was going nowhere. Marcus looked up. The departures board hadn't changed, a clean sweep of 'delayed' signs across every destination. Platforms of backed-up trains, lights out and doors closed as if they had gone to sleep for the night.

'World News' was a part of the paper he rarely read. If there was anything important, he would see it on television or online. He flipped from 'Londoner's Diary' to global events. The bushfires raging in Australia dominated the pages.

Koalas are cute, thought Marcus. *Getting public support for an ecological disaster is much easier with a picture of a toasted koala.*

It was a headline tucked away in the bottom right-hand corner that caught his eye.

CHINA REPORTS FIRST DEATH FROM MYSTERIOUS OUTBREAK IN WUHAN

A 61-year-old man in the Chinese city of Wuhan had died from an unidentified pneumonia-like virus and seven other people were in hospital. Forty-one people had been diagnosed with the pathogen. Chinese health officials were ruling out common respiratory diseases, such as influenza and bird flu.

Marcus didn't know where Wuhan was but, as China was a big place with a massive population, forty-one people getting the flu didn't seem such a big deal. The station tannoy crackled into life. The points issue had been fixed and services would be starting in fifteen minutes.

He looked at his watch, it was 8.30. He stared up at the departures board and saw that the train to Weybridge was leaving from Platform 5, directly opposite his table. He stuffed the newspaper in his laptop bag, buttoned up his Burberry raincoat and made his way to the platform. It was already three deep and his train would be making additional stops. As a first-class season ticket holder, he would get a seat, as long as there were no gate crashers from second class. The doors opened and he squeezed his way into the carriage. It was almost full but he got a seat by the window, facing forwards. Facing backwards gave him motion sickness. At least he had a double seat to himself.

He saw him coming down the gangway. A squat, fat man wearing decorator's overalls and a hoodie was squeezing his way through the narrow gap between the seats, bumping his ample backside into people's heads. He had a large, square head with a navy-blue cap with 'NYY' in white letters on the front. The adjustable strap was on its last hole and was cutting into a roll of pink fat on the back of his neck. His face was a blood red, purplish colour, like Sir Alex Ferguson's nose and he was sweating profusely, little rivers of salty juice running down his cheeks into his chins. Marcus prayed he would find a seat before he reached him but his luck ran out. Beetroot Man swivelled and plumped his sizeable buttocks on the seat next to him, squashing Marcus against the window and sitting on his raincoat.

'I'm very sorry!' said the man, wheezing and out of breath. 'I had to run for the train.'

Marcus thought the man hadn't run anywhere in years. He tugged at his trapped raincoat and the man lifted his left cheek to release it.

'Sorry again!' said the man, still panting.

'No need,' said Marcus, being polite 'We all just want to get home. It's been a long wait. You're here now.'

Marcus wished he had been kinder. Perhaps the man had Type 2 diabetes and couldn't help his obesity? Maybe it was congenital and he had always been fat, the kid who was last to get picked for the football team? The strong smell of turpentine vaporising from the man's paint-stained overalls was making him feel queasy and he decided to call home.

'Hi Al, I'm on the train now. I'll be getting into Weybridge around 9.40. How's everything with you?'

'Not good. I've got a splitting headache and I've taken two Nurofen. I'm going to bed soon.'

Since the menopause, Alice had started to suffer from regular migraines which HRT had failed to alleviate. He tried to lighten her mood.

'Sorry to hear that. Are you sure it wasn't the veggie lasagne that brought it on?'

It was a daft thing to say and he regretted it instantly, but it was already out there.

'Oh fuck off, Marcus! I don't need your sarcasm right now. I feel like shit.'

Alice could swear like a trooper when a bad mood caught her. Now wasn't the time to point out her hypocrisy about swearing.

'Sorry, it's been a long day. I was only trying to cheer you up. Don't worry about picking me up from the station. I'll get a taxi.'

'That's big of you, thanks very much. Have you eaten?'

'Yes.'

'What did you have? KFC? Nando's?'

Marcus felt guilty so he lied, saying he went to the Natural Kitchen and had a halloumi salad with quinoa and spinach. He suspected she knew he was lying but didn't have the energy to interrogate him.

'I've left the veggie lasagne out for you. You can microwave it if you want. Don't leave it out, put it in the fridge. It will do me for lunch tomorrow.'

'Thanks. I'll see if I'm hungry when I get home. How's Libby?'

'She's fine. In her room, revising for her mocks. I hope she's working and not spending all her time chatting on WhatsApp or Instagram.'

There was little chance. Olivia was a model student. Deputy Head Girl, fiercely competitive, academically bright and captain of the First XI hockey team. Her ambition was to be a vet and she was studying hard for her A levels to win a place at Bristol University in the summer. Apart from the occasional glass of wine, drugs, boys and Jager bombs hadn't distracted her from her objective.

'She'll probably still be up when you get home,' said Alice. 'Honestly, Marcus, I'm really not feeling great. See you later. Glad you got the train in the end.'

Beetroot Man lifted his giant buttocks and got off at Surbiton giving Marcus ten minutes to recover from the smell of turps and re-inflate his squashed body. The train pulled into Weybridge and around twenty people got off. He and Alice had moved to the area seventeen years earlier, just after Olivia was born. Weybridge had a Waitrose, which was important to Marcus. He called it The Temple.

Like most nights after nine, the exit barriers were open. He wondered if having a season ticket was worth it and why he didn't simply dodge the fare? However, being charged with fare evasion by a Revenue Protection Officer in front of one of his neighbours would definitely be an item on the agenda for the next Neighbourhood Watch meeting. If the shame wasn't enough, Alice's position as Treasurer would become untenable.

He approached the dingy cabin next to the station with its flickering neon sign, 'Ace Cars – 24 Hours'. There was nothing 'ace' about Ace Cars. Parked outside was a row of Toyota Prius cars and Marcus wondered if minicab drivers drove anything else. Ace Cars had none of the technical gimmickry of Uber. It was cash only, no accounts and no credit cards. He went into the cabin and stared through the little window into the control centre. The temperature in the cabin was stifling as two fan heaters circulated warm, stagnant air.

Sat in front of him were three drivers all eating home made food out of Tupperware containers. The sofa they were sitting on looked like it had been reclaimed from the local recycling centre. Sagging, frayed and dirty, it contained enough human DNA to keep Dr Nikki Alexander from *Silent Witness* busy for a month. Marcus had a secret fancy for Emilia Fox, beauty and brains. He peered through the hatch where the controller was staring at multiple screens and speaking into several telephones simultaneously. He could have been guiding a Boeing 747 into Heathrow. He looked up.

'Yes mate. Where do you want to go?'

'Twin Gates, Brooklands Avenue.'

The controller looked straight past him and yelled into the aromatic smog.

'Kareem, Brooklands Avenue!'

Kareem levered himself out of the collapsed sofa, took a spoonful of rice, wiped his mouth and his beard with his sleeve and gestured Marcus outside to his white Toyota Prius. Inside, the car smelled of pine air freshener. They pulled away from the cabin silently.

'It's very quiet isn't it?' said Marcus making 'taxi chat'.

'It's a hybrid electric,' said Kareem proudly. 'Very economical.'

The driver turned up the volume on the car radio. Smooth FM, not one of Marcus's favourites.

'Celine Dion is great, isn't she?' said Kareem, as the pointy-chinned warbler belted out the theme tune from *Titanic*.

'Not really my taste,' said Marcus. 'More of a Sex Pistols man myself.'

'Never heard of them,' said Kareem.

Not on Smooth FM, you wouldn't, thought Marcus.

Kareem turned into the driveway and pulled up outside the front door. Marcus and Alice had bought their house before he became a partner at The Firm and Alice was working as a corporate lawyer at one of the City's Magic Circle firms. Although it was a stretch for two incomes, they had embarked on a major renovation project which saw them living amongst rubble and debris for the best part of a year. Now they had one of the nicest houses in the road. On the drive was Alice's black BMW X5 and Olivia's Fiat 500. She was learning to drive.

'Nice place,' said Kareem, looking up at the façade of the house.

'Thank you. How much do I owe you?'

'Eight pounds, please.'

Marcus handed him a ten-pound note.

'Keep the change.'

The Prius departed silently as Marcus turned the key in the lock of the immaculately painted double doors, still adorned with the Christmas wreath, which Alice ordered every year from their local florist.

Eighty pounds for some old cinnamon sticks, pieces of dried orange peel and twigs! Better take that down at the weekend before it brings us bad luck, he thought.

He walked into the kitchen and inspected the 'veggie lasagne' left on the large granite island. The bechamel had congealed to the consistency of wallpaper paste and the broccoli had disintegrated to a mush. Alice had a flair for including a random ingredient in every meal, so the addition of diced cornichons was no surprise. Still full from his Double Whopper Meal, he sealed the dish and put it in the fridge.

The fridge was full of boxes of meat substitute products with names such as 'Like Meat Soya Based Chicken Bites'. He had recently read an article in *Metro* which revealed that men who regularly consumed soya in preference to meat had a lower concentration of sperm. Staring into the fridge, he imagined veganism was a plot by women to take over the planet by eliminating fertile men. In his mind, he role-played confronting Alice with his theory.

'Marcus,' she would say patronisingly, 'we're quite capable of surviving on this earth without men.'

'But even with IVF and turkey basters, you're still going to need some sperm to fertilise your eggs. Or are you planning to clone women so they all look identical? Droids with tits and fannies?' Marcus could see the appeal of a world full of Emilia Fox clones. 'So whose jizz are you going to keep? Gary Lineker's?'

Alice had a not-so-secret crush on the *Match of the Day* frontman. It was the only reason she watched it, peering over the top of the *Daily Mail* when he was summing up. Marcus had suggested growing a small goatee beard like Gary's but Alice dismissed the idea, saying he would look ridiculous.

'And what are you going to do when your spunk stocks run low and Gary's balls have dried up?'

'We'll keep a few fertile men fed solely on wagyu beef to top up our stocks. And then we'll kill them!' Alice laughed maniacally.

'A bit like mayflies? Born, fly, mate and die?'

'Exactly!'

The beeping alarm from the open door snapped him out of his fantasy. He closed the door and took a mug out of the cupboard. He put a spoonful of coffee in the mug and turned to the Quooker, the instant hot water tap that every designer kitchen had to have. Marcus hadn't seen the need for one, but Alice had insisted. Now he wouldn't be without it.

He sat down at the oak kitchen table and stared out of the bifold doors into the garden. It was glistening with the night frost. He took his phone out of his pocket. Outlook was now up to forty-eight emails. Mason Sherwin was still working.

Oh, piss off, Mason, thought Marcus as he closed his phone.

He took out the crumpled copy of the *Evening Standard* from his laptop bag and returned to the page he had read earlier.

CHINA REPORTS FIRST DEATH FROM MYSTERIOUS OUTBREAK IN WUHAN

The word 'mysterious' was playing on his mind. Flu happened everywhere, every year, so why was this mysterious? He closed the paper, put his empty mug in the dishwasher and turned off the kitchen lights. As he climbed the stairs, he could see the light on in Olivia's room. He knocked gently. She was sitting at her desk, lamp on, surrounded by open textbooks.

'Hi Libby. How's it all going?'

As a toddler, her older brother hadn't been able to say her name properly, and Libby had stuck ever since.

'Hi Dad. Not too bad. Got my Biology mock exam tomorrow. Up to my eyes in parasites at the moment.'

'Bit like working for The Firm,' said Marcus, and he laughed.

She got up and came over to him. She put her arms around his neck and kissed him on the cheek. She had recently showered, her hair was still damp and he could smell the perfume of her moisturising cream.

'How was your day at work? You're home late. South Western Trains fucked up again then?'

In spite of Alice's best efforts and a public school education, Olivia had inherited her father's flair for expletives.

'Yes. Wankers, I fucking hate them! Work was okay, same old, same old.'

'How's Project Spearmint going?'

Olivia was always making fun of his projects and the lack of originality in their names. Usually colours, gods or planets.

'It's fine. Mad client doing mad things.'

'You love it!' said Olivia, winking and tweaking his cheek.

'Maybe, maybe not. Don't work too late. If I don't see you in the morning, good luck tomorrow. You'll smash it.'

'Thanks Dad. You're a star.'

The bedroom was dark and Alice was asleep. Apart from when he was drunk, he could navigate his way to the ensuite in his sleep. He switched on the cabinet light and looked at himself in the mirror. His fifty-fifth birthday was looming but everyone said he looked forty-five. He didn't feel it.

He slid under the duvet next to Alice, feeling her warmth as she stirred. Her shoulder-length hair draped across the pillow and she snuffled. He wanted to spoon up to her, to feel the curve of her body next to his but waking her with a migraine would start a row. He turned on to his back, pulled the thin duvet up to his shoulders and stared at the ceiling. The menopause had given Alice flushes and she was always hot, even in winter. Marcus now had to make do with a four-tog duvet in the middle of January.

He set the alarm on his phone for 6.20 and plugged it into the charger by his bed. One last check on Outlook. His inbox was now up to fifty-five emails. He was still awake. He thought about going downstairs and doing some work but instead he lay on his back, breathing quietly through his nose, feeling his heartbeat in the tips of his fingers.

'*First death from mysterious outbreak.*' The words kept going around in his head.

It was Monday, 13 January 2020.

Chapter 2

Every Little Helps

The security guard glanced along the fruit and veg aisle at the young woman pushing a buggy towards him. She stopped to pick up a bunch of bananas and some apples. Andrew Coates' days in Tesco Express in Ladbroke Grove were usually dull. Apart from petty theft from Beers, Wines and Spirits and the occasional 'runner' from ready meals, there was little action. Most of his day was spent telling shoppers where to find things and explaining the self-service checkouts to pensioners who couldn't get the hang of them.

He had wanted to be a policeman in the Met but failed the medical due to a severe allergy to peanuts. He thought it was unfair. The chances of a suicide bomber strapping jars of Sun-Pat Crunchy to his chest and blowing himself up, causing Andrew to go into anaphylactic shock, seemed low. Being a security guard in Tesco Express was a step down, but it came with some perks. The odd nicked chocolate croissant here and a pain aux raisin there.

Andrew looked again at the woman with the buggy. She was about twenty-five and wearing a black, quilted puffer jacket with a fake fur hood. It seemed too big for her and came down to her knees. She was wearing dirty trainers with no socks. Her short, brown hair was tied back revealing that she wasn't wearing any makeup. The little girl in the buggy was happily eating raisins from a small box. Holding on to the buggy was a boy, and Andrew guessed he was about five or six. He was wearing a blue Spiderman hoodie and seemed more interested in the contents of his nose than the shopping.

The woman turned past Andrew at the chiller cabinets, smiled and stopped to pick up some packets of mince.

Four seems a lot? he thought.

He was on the lookout for suspicious shoppers and she seemed to be shopping for an army. Pasta, baked beans, sweetcorn, tinned tomatoes, frozen peas, turkey dinosaurs, chicken nuggets, burgers, oven chips, toilet roll, tissues. After poking around in his nostrils, the little boy was getting fractious.

'Can we have Haribo, Mummy?'

'Just wait Kyle, we'll see.'

'I'll get some!' said the little boy and he started to run.

'Kyle, just wait I said!'

The woman grabbed the little boy by his hood and dragged him back to the buggy.

'Just do as you're told,' she shouted as she shook him by the arm.

The little boy's lip quivered and he started to cry, tears mixing with the snot. He wiped his nose on his sleeve and wiped his sleeve on Spiderman. The little girl looked up and continued eating her raisins. The woman put two bottles of sugar-free Ribena in her bag and moved along the aisle to the sweets. They got to the Haribo display and she stopped. She felt bad for shouting at her son.

'Okay, what do you want then?' she said, looking down at him.

The little boy's face lit up and he pointed to a bag of Haribo Milkshakes. She took a bag, opened it and gave him a banana milkshake. He was happy and quiet now. She approached the self-service checkouts. They were all busy and she waited until one became available.

'Please scan your first item,' said the voice.

She scanned two packets of mince, the machine emitting its little 'boop' noise.

'Please place your items on the shelf.'

She put the packets of mince in one of her bags, took out the two remaining packets and put them directly into her bag. She repeated this process until her shopping bag was empty.

Two for you, two for me, she thought. *Every little helps.* The electronic display showed the total, £42.65.

'Please scan your Tesco Clubcard,' said the voice.

She scanned her Clubcard. Tesco knew a lot about her shopping habits, but not everything.

'Please select payment type.'

She opened her purse, just over two pounds in loose coins. By the middle of the month, there was little left of her Universal Credit to feed her family. There was only one payment type, her credit card. She had extended her credit limit three times and would soon be extending it again. She entered her PIN, held her breath, said a prayer and waited.

'Payment accepted. Would you like a receipt?' said the voice.

The machine regurgitated a roll of paper and she stuffed it into one of the plastic bags. Kyle was chewing on another banana milkshake, and he held her arm as they walked to the door. The security guard stood in front of her, arms folded, barring her way to the exit.

'Excuse me. Would you mind if I took a look in your bags?'

'Why? Is there something you want?' she said, flippantly.

'Is this your shopping?'

'Well, whose do you think it is? Angelina Jolie's?'

She could feel her heart starting to race, her breathing becoming heavier.

'Don't get smart. Just open your bags. Do you have your receipt?' said the security guard.

She shrugged her shoulders, opened her arms and gestured for him to take a look. He unfurled the crumpled receipt and poked around.

'Mmm … it seems you haven't scanned everything in your bags, have you? In fact, you seem to have forgotten quite a lot.'

'Have some items not gone through?' she said. 'Those machines are quite unreliable, you know?'

'Come off it. Just admit it, you were nicking. I've had my eye on you the whole time. I'm calling the store manager. Don't move an inch!'

He unclipped the walkie-talkie from his lapel and spoke into it loudly.

'Security to Lester. Security to Lester. Come in Lester. Major incident at the front of the store. Back up needed. Please support.'

She thought the security guard had been watching too many crime dramas. The store manager, who was standing in the next aisle next to 'cooked meats and dips', heard his voice and came running.

Lester Primus was a small, chubby man. He had started to go bald in his early twenties and now shaved his head. Coming down the aisle, he looked like a bowling ball in a badly fitting suit. The son of Jamaican immigrants from the Windrush generation, he had grown up locally in Harlesden and had worked his way up through the management ranks.

'What seems to be the problem, Andy?'

The security guard hated it when Lester called him 'Andy', which he did all the time.

'Big case of "shop and rob" here, Lester,' said Andrew. 'Over eighty quid's worth of shopping and she's paid for just over half of it. We'll have it all on camera, she's nailed.'

The store manager turned to the young woman. She was starting to cry, and it wasn't because the Haribo had run out.

'What's your name, love?' he said gently.

Lester had recently attended a two-day course at head office to ensure all managers embraced diversity. Being black and growing up in Harlesden in the days of skinheads and the National Front, he understood racism better than most. Having a breakout discussion about gender neutral toilets wasn't going to fix diversity. He called everyone 'love' out of habit and none of the employees had a problem with it.

'Claire. Claire Halford,' said the woman in a soft Midlands accent.

'Let's talk about this in my office shall we, Claire?' said Lester. 'It'll be a little more private.'

Andrew moved to follow them. Lester obviously needed him to be bad cop.

'That's fine, Andy, thank you. I'll take it from here. If you would just like to follow me, Claire?'

The security guard begrudgingly stepped aside as Claire, Kyle and the buggy followed Lester down the aisle, through the plastic doors leading to the warehouse and the back of the store. He showed her into his dimly lit office. Some cheap, chipped veneer furniture, a couple of threadbare chairs with torn seat cushions, a desktop PC with a grimy monitor and a metal filing cabinet. On one wall was a year planner with multi-coloured stickers all over it. It looked like a painting by Jackson Pollock. Only Lester understood it. On the other wall was a notice board covered with paper from head office which spewed out memos and product updates by the gallon. Sometimes, not every little helped.

To brighten things up, Lester had invested in some soft-focus posters of beaches and mountains with motivational quotes on them.

BELIEVE & SUCCEED – Courage does not always roar. Sometimes it is the quiet voice at the end of the day saying, I will try again tomorrow.

He had often stared at the quote, wondering if the person who said it was real, or if they only existed in the make-believe world of management bollocks.

'Claire, please take a seat. And who do we have here?' he said, looking down at the children who looked up at him nervously.

'This is Kyle and this is Alexa,' said Claire, pointing to her two children. 'Say hello to the man, Kyle.'

Kyle turned inwards and wrapped his limbs around her legs like a shy python.

'Don't worry. Even Spiderman gets shy sometimes. Would you like a sweet?' said Lester.

Kyle uncoiled himself from his mother's legs, looked up at him and nodded. Out of his trouser pocket, Lester produced a packet of Starburst and opened it.

'You're very lucky. Strawberry. They're the nicest.' He unwrapped one and gave it to Kyle, who popped it into his mouth and started chewing.

'Shall we give Alexa one too?' said Lester, passing a swee[...]
mother.

She was shaking and he could see she was fragile.

'Please don't get upset. I'm not calling the police or any[...]
do want to understand what's just happened and why. I can't have pe[...]
into my store and stealing food. You do understand that, don't you? Tesco isn't a
food bank.'

From the moment the security guard had stopped her, panic had put its
foot down hard on the accelerator of her imagination. Escalating consequences.
Police, social services, a magistrate who would want to make an example of her,
a lazy single mother sponging off the state and shoplifting. Then prison, and her
kids sent to foster parents who didn't love them, and who didn't know that Kyle
loved Buzz Lightyear and Alexa was sick if she ate eggs.

'I'm just trying to feed my kids. I'm really sorry. My Universal Credit has gone
until next month and my credit card is on the limit. Our electric is on pre-pay
and I can't even afford to buy myself some new knickers. What am I supposed to
do? I'm so sorry. I've never done anything like this before.'

Everything she said was true, apart from the last bit. Of course, she had done
it before, she had to. She started to sob and reached into the pocket of her puffer
jacket for a tissue. She didn't have a clean one, but pulled an old one apart, blew
her nose and wiped her eyes. She took an inhaler out of her pocket, squirted two
puffs and breathed deeply. Lester looked at her. She didn't seem to fit the mould
of a professional shoplifter or opportunist thief. He couldn't see her meeting up
with her dealer and scoring some crack in exchange for turkey dinosaurs and a
couple of tins of sweetcorn.

'Can't your parents help you out?'

She shook her head.

'They live in Walsall. It's in the Midlands. We don't talk much and I haven't
seen them for over a year.'

Old copies of *Tatler*, *Vogue* and *Harper's Bazaar* found in charity shops had been
a window on a different world. While her classmates were wearing leggings and
UGG boots, she was wearing a Jean Muir crêpe de Chine dress and a Jaeger jacket.
With three good A levels in Art and Design, English Literature and Photography,
she had won a place at Central Saint Martins in London to study Fashion. It was
meant to be her way of escaping a depressing housing estate in Walsall.

'I understand,' said Lester sympathetically. 'I'm sorry you're having to cope
on your own. What about social services or single parent organisations? Can't
they help?'

.ve got a social worker, Gavin. He's been great helping me with my Universal edit and my bills. I've let him down so badly.'

She started to cry again and Kyle cuddled her.

'Well, I'll leave it for you to tell him. I don't think there's any need for me to get involved. What about food banks? Have you tried those?' said Lester.

'Around here? Are you taking the piss?' said Claire scornfully. 'Those rich bitches in their four-by-fours wouldn't give you the fluff from their belly buttons.' He paused.

'I've got an idea?' Lester said enthusiastically, sitting upright in his chair. 'How about if I put aside some of the dented tins, short shelf life stuff, mark downs? I'll keep it back for you. I can't promise you fillet steak, and it might be a pretty random selection, but it's better than nothing. What do you think?'

She expected him to say 'every little helps' but he didn't.

'Why would you do that for me?' she said.

'It's not really a big deal. We throw away so much stuff at the end of every day. It's better it goes to you than ending up in a skip. Just something between you and me. Head Office doesn't need to know. How about Tuesdays and Fridays?'

'That's amazing, it's so kind of you. I don't know what to say.'

Lester levered himself out of his chair and walked around the desk to Claire. He put his hand on her shoulder and ruffled Spiderman's hair.

'I'll see you out. You can take your shopping with you. I hate those self-service checkouts and I'm not going through the hassle of what you have and haven't paid for. I won't tell if you don't?'

Claire could smell his aftershave. Old Spice like her father wore. One of the few things she liked about Arthur Carter. She had been in his office for thirty minutes and hadn't even noticed his name badge.

'You're a saint, Mr Primus.'

He escorted them along the dingy corridor crowded with warehouse trolleys and into the fluorescent lights of the store. It was already dark outside when they reached the front door. Claire zipped up Kyle's hoodie and tucked Alexa into the buggy. The security guard was showing an elderly gentleman how to pay for two lemons at the self-service checkout.

'No chance of an Uber home then?' said Claire, turning back to face him and grinning.

'Not this time, maybe next week,' said Lester smiling.

Claire pushed the buggy into the air of the cold January night and turned left towards Kensal Green. Lester walked back into his store where Andrew Coates had sorted the problem with the old man and the lemons.

'I hope you threw the book at her, Lester? Thieving little bitch. No police involved then?'

'Probably a bit excessive, Andy,' said Lester. 'I was going to waterboard her but don't worry, she fessed up to everything.'

It took fifteen minutes for Claire to walk from Tesco Express to Kensal Mansions. There was more than a hint of irony in its name. A red brick Lego box of a building, built in the 1950s to house the working class of London made homeless by Hitler's rockets. It had nothing in common with the rows of Victorian terraced houses and white stuccoed mansions in the surrounding areas of Notting Hill and Holland Park. It was like a missing tooth in a perfect smile. Bolted to the walls outside almost every flat was a satellite dish, architectural acne delivering Sky. Prozac for the poor. Claire couldn't afford Sky.

Kensal Mansions had four floors and she lived on the second. It wasn't easy with two small children, but beggars couldn't be choosers. Less than half a mile away stood Grenfell Tower, the twenty-four-storey tower which went up in flames in June 2017, killing seventy-two people. She could see it from her kitchen window. Shrouded in a white sheet, a corpse of a building, with a large green heart and a poignant message, 'Grenfell, Forever in our Hearts'. Except everyone had forgotten now.

The narrow alleyway that opened into the courtyard was clear of the usual debris of used wraps, fast-food packaging and the occasional needle or condom. Mr Mahoney, the caretaker, had swept that day. He was one of Claire's few friends. A stocky, ruddy-faced man from Cork who had worked for Clancy, one of the big Irish construction firms which had rebuilt London after the war. His wife, Sinead, had died five years earlier from pancreatic cancer. Claire and Mr Mahoney shared each other's loneliness. They were on first-name terms in every way, except she didn't know his first name and he had never told her. He was happy being Mr Mahoney.

She could see the light from the television in his ground floor flat. Her detention in Tesco Express meant she had missed their daily appointment. He would be watching The Chase on his own. He liked The Chase because the show's host, Bradley Walsh, was funny and kind to the contestants, most of whom Mr Mahoney thought were stupid. He also had a thing for The Governess, one of the 'chasers'. Watching The Chase together was an hour of respite and solace in their lonely lives.

Before commencing their climb to the top of their Mount Everest, Claire took two puffs on her inhaler. It was the same routine every day.

'Are you ready?'

Kyle and Alexa looked up at their mum and nodded.

'One … two … three … four.'

It was thirty-six steps to the second floor, four flights of nine. The three mountaineers turned right at the top of the fourth flight and walked along the balcony. Claire's flat was the third one along, past the Hassans at No. 9 and Judith at No. 10. Her neighbour on the other side at No. 12 was Ian. He was thirty-seven and suffered from motor neurone disease. His condition was getting worse. He had a maroon mobility scooter which he kept at the foot of the stairs in a little shed, built for him by Mr Mahoney. Sometimes, Ian would let Kyle sit on it and take him for rides around the courtyard. Kyle thought it was a spaceship and Ian was related to Buzz Lightyear, living on Morph in Gamma Quadrant, Sector 4.

Claire turned the key in the lock and opened her front door, stepping into the narrow hallway and switching on the light. The kitchen was first on the right, and she dropped the shopping bags on the floor. The handles had turned to razor wire and were cutting into her hands. Her fingers were locked in a curl as if she had arthritis. Coats were taken off and slippers put on before the children ran to the living room and switched on the television. It was *Kazoops*, the cartoon adventures of Monty and his pet pig, Jimmy Jones, who only had one tooth. Kyle said that Jimmy was like Mr Mahoney.

Her social worker, Gavin, who had contacts in the house clearance business, had found Claire a decent second-hand sofa and a couple of beds. Mr Mahoney had some friends in the building trade who had got her some knock-off paint in a neutral colour, and she had turned the flat into a home. The paint had covered up the previous tenants' yellow walls, which made her feel like she was living in a tub of Lurpak. It wasn't Farrow & Ball, and it had taken a few coats to cover the previous colour, but she had made the place cosy, apart from the rising damp and black mould around the heating vents. With a flair for interior design, she had trawled the market stalls and charity shops of Portobello Road and Notting Hill to buy furniture for pennies.

Her prized possession was a black leather Arne Jacobsen egg chair, which she had found dumped in a skip outside a house on Cornwall Crescent. The builders and the owners had no idea of its value. Mr Mahoney had carried it back to the flat for her. The back was scuffed but she had renovated it and, against a wall, nobody could see the flaw. When times were desperate, she had thought of selling it. It would probably fetch over £500, which would buy a lot of turkey dinosaurs, but it was her safe place, a haven.

She started to make dinner. Spaghetti bolognese to use up some of her stolen mince. It was an easy dish to make, 'one-pot chemistry' as her mum used to call it. Claire was a decent cook in a generation which lived off takeaways and ready meals. She thought it was ironic that Britain was obsessed with cookery programmes but spent most of its time watching them while eating Domino's or McDonald's. She was more a fan of Nigel Slater than of *MasterChef*. She thought Gregg Wallace was a jerk, a jumped-up greengrocer who had got a lucky break and now got to eat Michelin-star food for nothing.

She called the children to the kitchen.

'What's for dinner, Mummy?' said Kyle.

'Spaghetti bolognese,' said Claire.

'Scetti belaise,' whooped Alexa, who ran around the tiny kitchen in circles like she had scored the winner in the Cup Final.

'And how do we know if our spaghetti is cooked?' said Claire.

'Throw it at the wall!' shouted Kyle at the top of his voice.

Claire knew the spaghetti was cooked. It was already strained and steaming in the colander but she gave them some pieces to throw at the wall. Kyle threw his first.

'Mine sticks, mine sticks!' he shouted excitedly.

'Me too!' said Alexa, always keen to copy her brother.

Claire spooned the spaghetti on to two plates and into Alexa's *Monsters, Inc.* bowl and poured the sauce over the top. She chopped Alexa's spaghetti, but Kyle liked his long so he could suck it between his lips flicking tomato freckles all over his face. The children had Ribena and Claire had water, tap not sparkling. Both children cleaned their plates, neither were fussy eaters. Some kids their age would only eat jellybeans with a cocktail stick.

After dinner it was bath time and Kyle went through his full repertoire of songs. The children splashed around, pretending to swim in the bath, little bodies wriggling like pink prawns in the shallow water. Claire lifted Alexa out of the bath and wrapped her in a towel. She put her face against her daughter's neck and inhaled. There was nothing quite like the smell of freshly bathed child.

If the manufacturers of air fresheners could replicate that smell, they would make a fortune, she thought.

Kyle flaunted his willy in Alexa's face before putting on his *Toy Story* pyjamas. He had lots of pyjamas, but Buzz Lightyear was his hero. Claire had grown up with the *Toy Story* films, and would never have guessed that her children would like it in the same way. Woody and Buzz were timeless.

Kyle ran off to his tiny box bedroom. A swinging cat would feel cramped, but it was just about big enough for him. He jumped on his bed.

'To infinity and beyond!' he cried and thrust his arm in the air to simulate his hero's laser.

'Kyle, come back … you haven't done your teeth,' shouted his mum. 'Even Space Rangers need to clean their teeth.'

He returned to the bathroom and took his toothbrush out of the mug. As usual, he squirted too much toothpaste out of the tube.

'Put some of that on your sister's brush!' said Claire. 'Don't waste it.'

Claire finished drying Alexa and brushed her hair.

At least it's one good thing you got from your dad, she thought.

Alexa had beautiful hair, long, thick, brown hair, just like her famous namesake, Alexa Chung, the model she was named after. Alexa could easily have been the face of L'Oréal Kids. She would be filmed walking along Ladbroke Grove, swinging her shining tresses from side to side. She was worth it in every way.

Claire carried Alexa into the bedroom they shared together. She had managed to squeeze a small cot-bed alongside her double bed. Sharing a bedroom with a restless three-year-old wouldn't do much for her chances of a sex life, but she had given up on sex. Once in two years, a one-night stand with an old friend from Saint Martins. He came around the Christmas before last to see her and the kids with a bottle of cheap pinot grigio. It was probably a sympathy shag for old times' sake but it boosted her ego to know someone other than Mr Mahoney enjoyed her company.

Claire tucked Alexa under her duvet. It would be cold in the flat that night without the heating on.

'What story would you like tonight, sweetie?' said Claire. She knew the answer.

'Dumpling, please Mummy?'

Claire picked up the Dick King-Smith book *More Animal Stories*. It was Alexa's favourite book. She opened the front cover and read the inscription. 'This Book Belongs to Claire Louise Carter.' It was written in pencil in a child's handwriting. It was one of the few things she had taken with her when she left Walsall at the age of eighteen. Alexa listened and nodded as her mum read the story of Dumpling, the chubby dachshund. She knew the words off by heart and as Claire turned the final page, Alexa finished the story.

'"No," said Dumpling. 'But as a matter of fact, I'm quite happy as I am now. And that's about the long and the short of it!"'

Claire closed the book and put it back on the bedside table.

'Goodnight my little princess. Sleep well. It's nursery tomorrow, you'll see Zoe and all your friends.'

Alexa threw her arms around her mother's neck and gave her a full smacker with her Cupid's bow lips.

'Night Mummy.'

Claire left the night-light on and pulled the door behind her, leaving it slightly ajar.

Kyle was kneeling on his bed, his back to the door, playing with his heroes. He pulled the cord on Woody's chest and joined in. He knew all of Woody's best lines.

'Reach for the sky!'

'There's a snake in my boot!'

Claire sneaked up behind him, grabbed him around the waist and tickled him. He screamed.

'Come on, you. Bed time soon. What do you want to read tonight?'

The other love in Kyle's life was Captain Underpants, the obese superhero principal at George and Harold's school in Piqua, Ohio. Claire wondered if Mrs Lindsay, the overweight headmistress at Kyle's school had superpowers too? Claire had bought ten Captain Underpants books for £3 from a stall in Portobello Road. Someone's child had obviously outgrown them. They had everything a small boy loves: bogies, poo, pants, toilets, farts. She read a few pages of *Captain Underpants and the Attack of the Talking Toilets* before Kyle started to fall asleep.

'Do you need to go to the toilet?'

Kyle shook his head.

After his father left them, Kyle started to wet the bed, his little mind wrestling with questions he shouldn't have needed to answer. Why had his daddy not come home? Did his daddy love him? It had been a year of getting up in the middle of the night to change wet pyjamas, bedsheets, mattress protectors. None of it was Kyle's fault.

'No, I'm okay, Mummy. I did a wee-wee just now.'

'Okay then. Snuggle down. Sweet dreams my love.'

She returned to the kitchen, filled the stainless steel sink, did the washing up and left it on the draining board. The children had clean clothes for the morning, so she didn't have to iron anything. When she wasn't stealing food, she did the washing and ironing on a Monday. Apart from Gavin's visit on Tuesday and her daily appointment with Mr Mahoney to watch *The Chase*, doing the laundry was the highlight of her week. Her clothes, once the most important things in her life, had been dumbed down to comfort and functionality. She called it 'Smew' which stood for Single Mum's Uniform. Once she had dreamed of owning her own shop selling her designs. Now she pressed her nose against the windows of the boutique shops in Westbourne Grove, her breath condensing on the glass in misty droplets of envy.

She made a cup of tea and took it into the living room, placing it on the small glass and chrome coffee table. She went over to her turntable and flicked through her record collection. She had acquired a lot of old vinyl from second-hand stalls in Camden Market, long before it became trendy. There was something tactile and organic about a record. It touched every one of the senses.

It had been a traumatic day, but she wasn't feeling depressed enough for Samuel Barber's *Adagio for Strings*. That was her suicide music. A handful of diazepam, a bottle of vodka and Samuel Barber. The perfect recipe for an exit. There was very little in her life to thank her bigoted father for. One of the few exceptions was Frank Sinatra, played on a Bush stereogram which dominated their living room in Walsall. She flicked through the vinyl. Four LPs in was *Frank Sinatra: The Ultimate Collection*, a double album. She looked at the picture on the cover.

Ol' Blue Eyes was a handsome fucker, she thought.

The trilby hat and sharp grey suit simply oozed style and charisma. She eased the black, shiny, grooved dinner plate out of its sleeve and put it on the turntable. She lifted the arm and carefully placed the stylus on the first track, 'Strangers in the Night'. It popped and crackled with loneliness. Claire wasn't exchanging glances with anyone, let alone Frank. She sat in the Arne Jacobsen chair, curled her legs underneath her and wrapped a blanket around her shoulders. She picked up her tea and cradled the mug in both hands. Arne and Frank made her feel safe. Three tracks in came her favourite, 'That's Life'. Frank must have been a glass-half-full kinda guy because every time he fell flat on his face, he picked himself up and got back in the race.

It was only January and a day she had been caught shoplifting. If it hadn't been for an angel in the form of Lester Primus, she could have been on her way to a magistrates' court, and possibly prison. Her life had to change or there was no chance of her ever riding high in April. Or May. Or June. Sometimes, she just wanted to roll herself up in a big ball and die.

It was Monday, 13 January 2020.

Chapter 3
Performance Anxiety

The alarm on his iPhone went off at the usual time and Marcus carefully peeled back the duvet. It had been a restless night, deprived of Alice's warmth and a duvet which was too thin for January. He walked naked into the bathroom, turned on the light and closed the door. He sat down to have a wee. Standing first thing in the morning was something men only did up to the age of forty.

He took his George Trumper razor and badger bristle brush out of the cabinet. The brush had seen better days. Marcus had calculated that he had spent 157,000 minutes shaving. That was three months of his life, a quarter of a year. Nowadays, beards and stubble were trendy. His son, James, had a beard, but that was because he was too lazy to shave.

He pressed the button on the shower and waited for the light to stop flashing to tell him it was the correct temperature and stepped in. He squirted some Dove 'deeply nourishing nutrition intense' shower cream from the pump dispenser into his hand and showered. He liked Dove. Alice used it too. It was a gender neutral shower cream.

He folded his towel neatly and hung it over the heated towel rail and 'squeegeed' the shower screen. Alice said he was anally retentive, cleaning the shower every time, but he hated dirty showers, especially ones with pubes in the plughole. He combed his hair and brushed his teeth. Only one more decision: the choice of aftershave. He chose Mont Blanc Explorer, recommended to him by Gavin, his neighbour at the flat in London. He returned to the bedroom where Alice was waking.

'Morning Al. Feeling better?'

She rubbed her eyes and joined the morning. 'For goodness' sake, Marcus, put some clothes on, will you? Seeing your genitals flopping around when I wake up isn't a great start to my day.'

'Any chance of a lift to the station? My car is still at the flat. It looks cold out there this morning?'

'Marcus, I'm not even up yet, not dressed and haven't done my hair. I've got to take Olivia to school and then get to tennis. You can walk, the exercise will do you good. Why didn't you mention this last night?'

'Because you were asleep, that's why. If I'd woken you, you would have been grumpy. And now, when I am asking you, you're grumpy. Perhaps I should leave a note by your bed next time? "Dear Al, please can you take me to the station in the morning and not be fucking grumpy? Lots of love. Marcus."'

It was just over a mile from Twin Gates to the station. Walking would boost his daily step count on his health app. Ten thousand steps a day was a tough target for someone who spent most of his life in an office or a taxi. His New Year's resolution had been to walk at least one leg of his daily commute. Two weeks into January and he was already failing miserably.

'Marcus, don't be pathetic. You've got loads of time. Walk.'

Because, of course, you've got so much to do today haven't you? thought Marcus.

Compared to his life, Marcus thought his wife's was a breeze. One big jamboree bag of 'me, me, me'. Tennis club (two mornings a week), Pilates and yoga (two afternoons a week), bridge club (Friday lunchtime) and art class (first Monday every month). Throw in a daily dose of *Escape to the Country*, *Loose Women* and *Cash in the Attic*, and he wondered how Alice found time to breathe, let alone work.

She was continually reminding him.

'Marcus, I'm the one who keeps this show on the road while you're having boozy lunches and flying round the world. Who do you think looks after Jacinda, tells the gardeners what to do, books the Ocado delivery, makes sure our children don't develop drug habits and ensures you have enough clean underpants? I don't think it's you, Marcus!'

He'd played it all wrong. Alice could have made a killing as a lawyer and retired at fifty. Marcus could have been the stay-at-home house husband. After getting the breakfast and the school run over with, it would have been 'Marcus-time'. Round of golf, lunch at the club, bit of *Countdown* in the afternoon to ogle at Carol Vorderman, pick the kids up and cook a nutritious dinner that wasn't devoid of meat and didn't contain random ingredients. Instead, Marcus was Breadwinner-in-Chief and Alice was Breadspender-in-Chief, supported by the army of helpers who made her life the blissful existence that it was. For a long time, he had been content with the arrangement. Now he hated working at The Firm and was resentful she had it so much easier than he did.

'Fine, I'll walk then. Better get my skates on. I might have to work late so I think I'll stay at the flat tonight and probably for the rest of the week. That okay with you?'

'Suits me fine. I'd better check on Libby to make sure she isn't having a panic attack. It's her biology mock today.'

'Yes, I know. I spoke to her when I got in. She was still revising. Parasites.'

There was something else he had to remind her about, but it had gone.

Alice got up and wrapped herself in her Missoni bathrobe, leaving Marcus alone in the bedroom. Dressing had a sequence too, routine was important. Underpants first, Calvin Klein briefs, never boxers. Socks, navy or black. He disliked the trend towards wearing loud, multi-coloured socks at work, like they were a gesture of corporate sedition. He took a shirt out of the wardrobe, double cuff, blue or white or a combination of both. He put his silver Asprey collar bones in, a pair of cufflinks from Thomas Pink and his favourite Ferragamo tie. Most of the men at work didn't wear a tie anymore and he resented the slide towards 'business casual'. For the £1,500 an hour The Firm charged its clients for his limited talents, wearing a tie and looking professional was the least he could do.

Marcus never wore the same suit on consecutive days. Only the poor, over-worked associates had only one suit. He picked a grey birds-eye from Henry Poole & Co. in Savile Row, put the trousers on and tightened them at the waist. He had lost a stone in the past year and felt good. He took a pair of black brogues out of the wardrobe, removed the shoetrees and carried them downstairs with his jacket and an overnight bag of clean clothes.

'Do you want a cup of coffee or an orange juice?' shouted Alice from the kitchen. He could hear the Quooker in full swing, dispensing instant boiling water on to her rooibos and rhubarb teabag.

'Just orange juice please,' he said. 'I'll get a coffee at work. I'm trying to cut down on caffeine.'

Like the Whopper the previous evening, this was another fib. He would have at least three double macchiatos before lunch.

'Well done you,' said Alice in a slightly patronising tone.

He put on his shoes and jacket and checked himself in the full-length mirror. He was ready for another day at The Firm. He walked into the kitchen and downed his orange juice in one.

'I'll call you from the flat tonight,' he said. 'What are you up to today?'

'Tennis this morning. Then I'm meeting Theresa at Pilates. Afterwards we're going for coffee. She wants to talk about her and Mike.'

Marcus admired Mike, Theresa's husband. He had built his telecommunications business from scratch and sold out for squillions. Mike's wealth meant that Theresa's days were even less hectic than Alice's. The previous

November, she had undergone a series of 'procedures', and now looked like she was permanently surprised, or had been electrocuted. Marcus thought she was a bad influence on Alice.

'Would you like me to have better boobs?' Alice had asked him recently.

'How do you mean, "better"?' he had said. 'I didn't realise there was a rating scale for boobs. How would you score yours? Tolerable?'

'Don't be sarcastic, Marcus. I don't make fun of your bits, do I? Since having the kids, my boobs have lost their shape. My nipples now point at my feet. I wouldn't mind getting some implants, like Theresa.'

Marcus knew cosmetic surgery would be on the agenda for later in the day. He also knew that 'I wouldn't mind' meant 'I would like you to pay for'. He had never had a problem with Alice's boobs. They ticked all the right boob boxes for him.

'Okay, I've got to dash. Have a good day and I'll call you later. By the way, was there anything on the news last night about some mystery disease in China? Some new type of flu?'

'I didn't see anything, I was in bed by nine.'

Marcus pursed his lower lip and shrugged his shoulders. It was probably something and nothing. He put on his raincoat, picked up his laptop bag and shouted up the stairs to Olivia who was getting ready for school.

'Good luck with the exam! Text you later to find out how it went. Bye.'

Olivia didn't respond. He guessed she had her headphones on, listening to Chris Brown, the R&B artist, singing about performing a sexual act on someone. It relaxed her. Marcus liked Chris Brown too. Not that he would admit to it. Chris's morals were a bit dubious, possibly misogynistic, but he could certainly sing and dance.

Marcus walked down the gravel drive and turned left into Brooklands Avenue. It was a desirable road to live in, mansions for the middle classes. Many of the original Edwardian houses had been demolished to make way for new-build, mock-Georgian 'lumps', as Marcus called them, inhabited by dentists and software designers. Mature gardens sacrificed for hot tubs, decking and patio heaters. Lawns paved over to provide parking spaces for fleets of cars protected behind electric security gates.

Marcus took his phone out of his pocket and checked The Sequence. Outlook was up to eighty-four emails. More from Mason Sherwin on Project Spearmint, the first one sent at 5.38 in the morning.

Does that wanker never sleep? he thought.

The Firm called it 'commitment'. He had been like Mason, feeding the host twenty-four hours a day, seven days a week with his 'commitment'. Now the host was killing him. His inbox was the usual tsunami of guff that The Firm rained down on its people. More compliance, more regulation, more control. RAPID, The Firm's all-powerful software brain told him he hadn't completed his online 'Embracing Diversity' training and a non-compliance would be sent to the Chief Risk Officer unless it was completed by the end of the week. It also informed him that his declaration of personal independence was due at the end of January, that he had eighteen sets of expenses to approve, that his timesheet was late and he had to sign up for the upcoming partner conference 'Ethics and The Firm: Living and Breathing Our New Values'.

Before he became a partner, work used to be fun. It gave him the energy and good humour to survive the long days and nights. Now he was a slave to RAPID and the army of faceless apparatchiks who ran The Firm. And they were running it into the ground.

Emails carried The Firm's new branding and tag line. Hundreds of thousands of pounds had been spent commissioning a branding agency to change the font and colour palette and put a meaningless squiggle over the company name. The Firm said its new branding 'resonated and aligned with our core values as a business'.

Of course it does. Because nobody has a fucking clue what our values are. What a waste of money. We would have been better off giving the staff a better Christmas party, thought Marcus.

He didn't have a problem with the new tag line, 'Doing It With You'. He agreed with it. The Firm was like a hooker. Clients got to screw it, for a fee. Just lie back, stare at the ceiling and count the fees.

The markets hadn't opened so he went straight to Spotify. Marcus walked to the station listening to 'Axemen of the 70s'. He looked at his watch. It was 7.33. Five minutes until his train arrived. He picked up a copy of *Metro*. As usual, it was picture heavy and content light. He would have read it by Surbiton. The front page was dominated by the rift in the royal family. Coming hot on the heels of the scandal surrounding Prince Andrew's relationship with a convicted paedophile and a catastrophic television interview, Marcus thought it had been a tough few weeks for the Queen.

All families have a few skeletons in the cupboard, he thought, *but the House of Windsor seems to be like a mass grave.*

The rest of the paper was given over to Storm Brendan, which was ravaging the country, and the usual fluff over what was happening on *Love Island*. He wondered if there had ever been a Storm Marcus? His eponymous turn to wreak meteorological havoc was certain to come.

The 7.38 to Waterloo arrived on time and he was relieved to get a forward-facing seat opposite a sweaty man wearing Lycra with a plastic helmet between his feet. His tight cycling shorts did little to flatter his anatomy and Marcus averted his gaze. It was probably the man's Brompton that was clogging up the doorway to First Class. Ingenious as the design of the Brompton bike was, Marcus hated them. Their self-righteous owners always took them on the Underground during rush hour, freely maiming the ankles and legs of other commuters, convinced their low-carbon mode of transport gave them free licence to injure others. The cyclist was reading a copy of *Wolf Hall* by Hilary Mantel. Marcus had bought it at the airport and tried to read it on holiday but had given up after fifty pages and turned to the latest David Baldacci thriller instead.

He suddenly remembered the thing he had forgotten to tell Alice. It was nearly eight o'clock and she would be doing the school run. He took out his phone, put Eric Clapton's guitar solo on pause and called her. He could tell by the background noise that she was on Bluetooth in the car.

'Hi Al. It's me.'

'I know it's you Marcus. What's the matter?'

'Hiya Dad,' said Olivia, cutting in.

'Hi sweetie. Good luck today. Al, is Jacinda coming today?'

'It's Tuesday, of course she is. Why?'

'The shirt I wore yesterday, the white Turnbull & Asser one?'

'What about it?'

'It's got a ketchup stain on one of the cuffs. I think it's the left one. Or it might be the right?' He knew he was running the risk of revealing his clandestine visit to Burger King but he pressed on. 'Can you remind Jacinda to use Vanish on it? And maybe put it on a hot wash too?'

Alice's patience was running low, especially on a school run in rush hour, with a hyperventilating teenager with exam anxiety sitting next to her.

'Is that why you called me? To tell me about a bloody stain? For Christ's sake Marcus, haven't you got anything else to think about?'

'It's a very expensive shirt. You will tell her won't you?'

'Yes, I will. Goodbye Marcus.'

He knew that somewhere between Weybridge and Olivia's school in Chertsey, a woman driving a BMW X5 wanted him dead or seriously maimed. He skimmed the rest of the paper. No mention of the mysterious virus in China, but it did have one interesting story which captured his imagination.

MAN SUFFERS THREE-DAY ERECTION AFTER TAKING STIMULANT USED FOR BREEDING BULLS.

The train pulled into Platform 9 at Waterloo at 8.22. Marcus got up from his seat as the cyclist was putting on his helmet, complete with GoPro, and adjusting his high-vis body condom. He squeezed past him, not wanting to have his suit soiled by grease from the Brompton's chain, or his ankle fractured as its rider attempted to assemble the bike in the gangway.

The Firm's new offices, tucked behind Bloomberg's architectural masterpiece next to Bank, had been open for almost two years. It had spent millions on the refurbishment of its shiny steel and glass palace. Open workspaces, play spaces, breakout areas, Collaboration Pods, Communication Zones, Chilling Eggs, six in-house restaurants and luxurious client meeting rooms. It had everything, apart from one thing. Offices for partners.

The new policy of open-plan hot-desking hadn't gone down well with The Firm's pampered hierarchy. Gone were the sporting memorabilia, purchased for vastly inflated sums at charity auctions, and the cheesy black and white photographs of the families the partners never saw. Hot-desking was meant to be the way forward but it hadn't worked out that way. Partners got their secretaries to block book desks in areas reserved for other partners. They could all sit together like a pride of endangered Kalahari lions.

The new building, on fourteen floors, was emblazoned with The Firm's new branding, along with pictures of young and ethnically diverse teams doing worthy things for charity. Running up and down the Three Peaks, kayaking along the Amazon and painting the stable doors at a donkey sanctuary. The Firm was making so much money, doing a bit of charity work assuaged its guilty conscience. Giving a few maltreated donkeys higher self-esteem cost it nothing.

He entered the building through one of the six revolving doors and said good morning to Michael, the security guard. He took out his Oyster card wallet containing his security pass. Keeping it in his wallet was a violation of the new security policy at The Firm. Risk and Compliance had made it compulsory for all staff to have their passes on display in new brand-compliant lanyards. Marcus had rebelled against the oppression, forcing his boss, Kelvin McBride, to summon him after yet another warning.

'Marcus, I've had a complaint from Risk. Apparently, you're one of a handful of people refusing to wear the new lanyards? Just fucking do it will you?'

JFDI was one of Kelvin's favourite phrases.

'Sorry Kelvin. Why do I have to have it on display? I carry it with me at all times if anyone wants to check who I am. I'm not wearing one of those hideous lanyards.'

'Why not? I do.'

'Because it makes me look like someone who works in IT. It's pathetic.'

Marcus made a lot of money for The Firm. Faced with an easy choice between lanyard compliance and hitting budget, he knew which way Kelvin was going to swing.

'I wish you would grow up sometimes, Marcus, and be a bit more of a team player. Just fuck off and get out.'

Marcus took his place in the queue at OnYouGo, The Firm's in-house coffee bar, and was greeted by Fernando, one of the team of baristas. He and Marcus were on first-name terms.

'Good morning, Marcus. The usual?' he said in a strong Spanish accent.

'Yes please, Fernando. Double macchiato and a porridge with raisins and honey.'

Marcus ordered the same thing every morning and Fernando was ready.

'Three pound eighty please, Marcus.'

Marcus took out his OnYouGo loyalty card. Nine little coffee beans had all been stamped. Today's coffee would be free. Marcus took it as a sign that it would be a good day.

'Not so fast, Fernando,' said Marcus, sounding like a gunslinger in a low-budget Western.

Like a cowboy drawing his Colt 45 from its holster, Marcus presented his loyalty card.

'Only £1.80 for the porridge this morning.'

With the dexterity of a circus juggler, Marcus carried his coffee in one hand and his porridge in the other, whilst simultaneously attempting to swipe out through the security barrier. In his pocket, he could feel his phone vibrating. It would be Mason Sherwin. He would have to wait.

Marcus joined a throng in the lift lobby. At busy times, he could wait up to ten minutes for a lift. He hadn't calculated how much of his life had been spent waiting for a lift. It was, at the very least, equivalent to a long weekend. He looked around at the people in the lobby. Probably over sixty people, and he didn't know one of them. He got out of the lift on the fifth floor and scanned his security pass again, nearly dropping his porridge. Marcus cursed. It probably wasn't that long before some bright spark in Risk and Compliance suggested retinal scanning at all entrances.

At least you won't have to wear your eyeball on a lanyard, he thought.

With fifteen minutes before his first meeting, Marcus sanitised his hands and took a seat in the staff area, away from his fellow partners. He wanted to eat his breakfast in peace without overhearing their conversations about second homes in Provence or why the delivery of their new Aston Martin had been delayed. He was eating the last spoonful of porridge when he felt a tap on his shoulder. It was Mason Sherwin who had sneaked up from behind.

'So you're alive then?' said Mason, sarcastically. 'When you didn't reply to my texts or emails, I thought you were dead.'

'No, I'm very much alive, thank you. I was simply ignoring you.'

Mason laughed nervously. He had the hide of a rhinoceros when it came to sarcasm. He didn't get it and carried on.

'Project Spearmint?'

'What about it?' said Marcus, being deliberately obstructive.

'Jim Ibbotson is pushing us to get the draft report to them by next Monday morning. I know we agreed next Thursday, but they have an exec meeting on Tuesday so he wants it by Monday.'

'What have you said to him?'

'I told him I would speak to you first and we would call him later today. I think we have to do it. There's a lot of fees at stake for the next phase, probably four or five million.'

Marcus knew Mason was lying and had already agreed to the client's request. When the piper calls the tune, the dancers dance. Except it wouldn't be Mason doing the dancing, it would be the staff forced to work late into the night and over the weekend.

'Let's speak after the pipeline meeting,' said Marcus.

The pipeline meeting took place every Tuesday morning at 9.00 in Communication Zone 1. Partners were expected to attend in person or join via a conference call. It was the stage for them to show off in front of Kelvin, pretending they were doing a lot even when they weren't. Today's meeting had been extended to include the interim performance review for staff. It was the opportunity for the partners to sit in judgement over the careers of the underlings.

He took his usual seat next to his secretary, Chloe Bulmer, whose main responsibility was to prepare the papers for the meeting. The papers were laid out neatly on the table and the other partners took their seats and waited for Kelvin. The room was filled with pompous banter. Marcus looked at his colleagues. He felt he had little in common with most of them.

The Firm's widely publicised agenda to increase diversity at senior levels had bypassed the team. Eleven partners: ten men, all white, all aged between thirty-eight and fifty-five. Only four had a body mass index which wasn't 'obese'. Fat Lives Mattered. There was one woman, Vanessa Briggs. Clothed in a low-cut, purple, figure-hugging dress, Marcus thought she was like a busty plum. Loud, gobby and inclined to use the C-word liberally, she was an alpha male in a Lycra dress. The Firm loved female partners like Vanessa.

To distract himself, Marcus wrote the initials of his fellow partners on his pad, ranking them on a scale of one to ten, based on likeability and capability. Only Tyler Payton (American, Oil and Gas Partner, forty-three) managed a nine. Ex-McKinsey, witty and with a healthy disregard for Risk, he was the closest thing Marcus had to a friend.

Kelvin arrived and took his seat at the head of the table. In a perverse way, Marcus admired him, even if he didn't like him. Kelvin was living proof of the adage that talent doesn't get you to the top but being good at politics does. Kelvin was a Glaswegian hard man. Thick-set, freckled and balding, and with an addiction to Nicorettes to combat a serious smoking habit, he ran the team with an iron fist with no velvet glove. At forty-nine, Kelvin had made enough money to retire years ago, but loved confrontation too much. He scored seven out of ten for being nothing more than a straightforward thug.

On either side of Kelvin sat Mason and Vanessa. If Marcus tolerated Vanessa for her toilet humour and liberal use of profanities, he disliked Mason with a vengeance. Slipperier than a greased eel, he was certain about everything and right about nothing. Like the British entry in the 2003 Eurovision Song Contest, Mason scored *nul points*.

Each partner gave an update on their projects, potential fees and timings. It was an exercise in hyperbole, a chimera wrapped in smoke and refracted in mirrors. Secret project names that nobody understood, meetings that never happened and fees that never materialised. To prove a point, Marcus had once created Project Helios, a fictitious opportunity, which, for reasons of commercial sensitivity, had to remain secret. So secret he couldn't even tell Kelvin. It remained in the pipeline for over a year, perpetuated each week by a different update.

'Marcus, can you give us an update on Project Helios?' said Kelvin.

This would be met with any one of the following responses.

'Client has requested an outline proposal. Will send to them at the end of the week.'

'Got a meeting with the CFO next week.'

'CFO got fired, waiting for the new CFO to be confirmed.'

'Meeting with the CFO and CEO next week.'

'CEO gone on sick leave. Stress. Deal on hold at the moment.'

The twists and turns of Project Helios went on for almost a year until Marcus finally closed it down.

'Bad news. The deal is dead. You can take it off the list now, Chloe.'

Nobody said a word.

Mason Sherwin had a long list of opportunities. If they all materialised, he would hit the team's budget on his own. Except they wouldn't, because they existed in some fantasy world inhabited by Mason on his own. That's why Project Spearmint was so important.

'And lastly, Project Spearmint. This is now at a delicate stage with the conclusion of Phase 1. Our draft report is due next Monday. If all goes well, I expect Phase 2 to kick off pretty soon afterwards. Much bigger team and projected fees of six to seven million pounds.'

It was typical Mason. The projected fees were a work of fiction. He had stuck his middle finger up his backside and come up with a random number depending on how much shit was on it.

Marcus interrupted.

'Just three points to make, Mason, before you drive head first into fantasy land. Firstly, we haven't agreed the deadline for the Phase 1 report. Two, there's no certainty that the transaction will go ahead. And three, we have no idea of the scope for Phase 2 or the potential fees.'

Mason scowled down the table as if Marcus had spat in his coffee. He hated confrontation, especially over anything that bore a fleeting resemblance to the truth. Truth was something that was manipulated and distorted in corridor meetings, in a bar or on an out-of-hours phone call. The truth never existed in broad daylight.

Kelvin suggested they take a comfort break and the partners trooped off to the toilets. Despite his worries over the early onset of prostate cancer, Marcus had the bladder of a camel, and stayed behind in the room with Chloe. She was one of thousands of young women who streamed into Liverpool Street Station every morning to keep the offices of the City running smoothly. Marcus looked down at her notes in her childish handwriting.

Project Zoose.

'I think you'll find that's Project Zeus, after the king of the Greek gods,' he said, trying not to be patronising. 'Z ... E ... U ... S.'

'Oh! I was wondering about that. I thought it sounded like "moose". Thanks

Marcus. I'd be lost without you. Can I get you a top-up?' said Chloe, gesturing towards the refreshment table.

'No, it's okay thanks. I had a double macchiato earlier.'

The partners were returning to the room. Mason had his arm around Kelvin's shoulder and was laughing.

Slimy little fucker, thought Marcus.

Kelvin introduced the next part of the meeting.

'Next item on the agenda, resourcing and financials. Izzy, do you want to take us through this, please?'

Izabela Majewska was the team's Operations Manager. Thirty-eight, tall and blonde, Izzy was from Krakow in Poland, but had moved to the UK with her husband, who was an investment banker at Goldman Sachs. Impeccably dressed in a beige Armani suit, she was more talented than most of the people in the room. Hired by Kelvin two years earlier to 'get control over the numbers', she knew them better than he did. Behind the scenes, Izzy was running the team and Kelvin was the frontman. Marcus liked her a lot. She was intellectually sharp, much sharper than the other blunt knives in the drawer. There was only one flaw in her formidable armour: her use of words. In the world of professional services, which generates volumes of meaningless nonsense, Izzy Majewska had a vocabulary all of her own. She removed her Dolce & Gabbana glasses and looked around the table.

'Thanks Kelvin. I've touched base with all of you over the past week to build a picture of what our resourcing landscape looks like over the next three months. I've done a deep dive into a number of critical areas and built some strawman scenarios. It's only a helicopter view and I need to loop back with each of you again, run the numbers FTF but on the 80/20 principle, it's probably pretty close.'

Izzy continued.

'We have a lot of bandwidth in a number of areas after January. We are keeping people busy and focused on business development but, ideally, we need them to be chargeable in the marketplace. In the last quarter, we picked most of the low-hanging fruit but there needs to be something big to shift the dial in Q3.'

In his head, Marcus tried to translate what Izzy had said.

'After January, we're in the shit. We've got lots of people wasting their time on crap that doesn't make us any money. We need to sell something big in the next few weeks.'

Izzy put her glasses back on and stared around the table.

'I'll be looping around with each of you over the next week to get more granularity on our position. We all need to be singing from the same hymn sheet here. We need a paradigm shift in the way we're doing things and this has to be on everyone's radar now. I think that's everything I wanted to say, Kelvin.'

Marcus knew what was coming next. Kelvin looked down the table.

'I think Izzy's made our position crystal clear.'

The vacant look on most of the faces suggested they were completely lost.

He continued.

'Let's get one thing straight here. There's no fucking way this team is missing plan. Do you all understand me? I've never missed a target in my life and I'm not starting now. I want every member of this team to be a hundred per cent focused on clients, clients and more fucking clients. This time next week, I want a plan, signed in your blood, that's going to address this situation. Clear?'

One of Kelvin's strengths was he left very little room for ambiguity. Unfortunately, Grant Bremner-Walker didn't read his mood well. More used to working in the rarefied, tea-dance atmosphere of strategy consulting, he hadn't encountered Kelvin in his 'Saturday Night's Alright for Fighting' frame of mind.

'Kelvin, please may I get clarity on one point?' said Grant.

Grant was everything Kelvin disliked. Posh, the pretentious signet ring on his left pinkie, his public school education, Oxford, and, to cap it all, a former strategy consultant. Grant brought out all of Kelvin's worst insecurities and prejudices.

'And what point is that then, Grant?' snapped Kelvin.

With his pinkie finger raised, Grant waved his pen like he was conducting an orchestra.

'Have we factored in the uncertainty surrounding Brexit and the downside risks to the M&A market in our plan this year?'

He had a point. The UK's exit from the European Union had caused a lot of businesses to put expansion plans on hold, and the market had slowed. But Kelvin wasn't in the mood for 'factors'. Having sold less than any other partner, Grant was skating on thin ice and with afterburners on his skates.

'Grant, correct me if I'm mistaken, but so far this year you have sold a total of £400,000 against a target of £3 million. Now, unless David-fucking-Blaine is going to come up with some new illusion and find a big pile of cash sitting on top of Big Ben in a glass box, I suggest you stop looking for excuses and come up with some fucking answers! Back here in ten.'

Marcus was joined on the walk to the toilets by Tyler Payton.

'What did you make of that?' said Tyler in his Texan drawl.

'Kelvin's coming under pressure from above, it's obvious. They kick him, he kicks us. It's the way it works, we all know that. Mason makes me vomit the way he's always kissing Kelvin's arse. Half the stuff he talks about is never going to happen.'

'Grant was right about Brexit,' said Tyler. 'Just a total dumbass for saying it!'

'In good times, leaders manage, and in tough times they lead,' said Marcus. 'Unfortunately, Kelvin is a fair-weather leader. Great when things are going well but hasn't got a clue when the chips are down. I've seen it all before, this is nothing new.'

The two partners walked back through one of the Collaboration Pods, complete with white boards, stress balls, beanbags and soft cushions. It was empty, nobody in The Firm was collaborating. Back in Communication Zone 1, Simon Loder, Tom Irons and Jacob Mauser, the three fattest partners, were discussing lunch.

'They do these fantastic pork crackling encrusted foie gras bonbons,' said Mauser loudly.

'Last time I went there, I had the deconstructed truffled guinea fowl done three ways,' said Irons. 'It was bloody amazing.'

'Great, Les Trois Cochons it is then. I'll book it for one o'clock. We should be done here by then.'

Marcus wondered how you could deconstruct a guinea fowl, being so small. The foie gras bonbons sounded good but tucking into the liver of a force-fed goose would be guilt on a level he couldn't live with.

Kelvin entered the room and the partners quickly put their phones away like adolescent boys hiding their porn mags.

'Alright everyone. I've got a hard stop at 12.30 so let's press on with the last item. Interim team performance review. Does everyone know Jenny from HR?'

Jenny Moffatt was the team's HR Business Partner. Her title was an oxymoron, there was no partnership between the team and HR. HR did what it was told to do. As long as the staff didn't sexually assault each other or habitually snort cocaine in the Relaxation Zone, the principal role for HR was running the performance review process.

Jenny was the latest in a long line of Business Partners. Her predecessors had left to have children or been signed off with stress by Occupational Health, never to return. With her bob haircut, heavy-rimmed glasses and rosy complexion, she looked like Thelma from *Scooby Doo*. She wore a mustard-coloured cashmere, turtleneck jumper accompanied by a chain of large purple beads and a black leather skirt which was too small for her. She had multiple ear piercings and a snake's head tattooed across the back of her neck, which was just visible above her collar. The partners speculated Jenny might be a dominatrix outside The Firm, a backlash from having to be submissive in it.

'Okay, Jenny. Over to you,' said Kelvin.

'Thanks Kelvin. Firstly, I want to remind everyone that today is only an interim review and a quick update on people. The full review will be in June.'

Jenny confirmed the assessment criteria to the group. They were different from the previous year, just as they were different every year. The process was known as 'the black box'. Stuff went in and stuff came out, but nobody ever saw inside. That was its beauty, it was never designed to be transparent. By changing it every year, HR perpetuated its own existence in The Firm.

It was Vanessa Briggs who intervened first, leaning forward on the table and resting her cleavage on her folded arms.

'I'm sorry, Jenny, but why have we changed the criteria from last year? What's this third criteria, 'internal innovation'? That's new isn't it?'

'Internal innovation' was a new criteria. The Firm had made 'innovation' one of its strategic priorities, investing heavily in a raft of internal initiatives. To be considered for promotion, people had to be involved in several internal projects that delivered zero benefit to clients but made the partners look good.

The debate over the process, criteria and ratings took the best part of two hours. Kelvin wasn't fussed. The team was an ever-changing pool of warm bodies to be deceived by false promises and compromised into sacrificing their personal lives until they either burned out or left. With his hard stop looming, he intervened.

'Thanks a lot Jenny. Great work by you and the HR folks, as always. I think we probably need to refine the process a bit. Why don't you and Izzy get together and update the deck, taking on board the comments made today? If you could then circulate the deck around to everyone? Let's put this on the agenda in two weeks' time? Thanks a lot everyone.'

Kelvin stood up, popped a couple of Nicorettes in his mouth, collected his papers and left the room. Simon Loder, Tom Irons and Jacob Mauser were happy. They had gained an extra half an hours' scoffing time and headed for the elevators. The foie gras bonbons were in for a bashing at Les Trois Cochons. Marcus looked at Simon Loder who was tucking his overhanging gut into his trousers. A button on his shirt was missing, revealing a hairy belly-button. One of the three ways for the deconstructed guinea fowl was likely to be down his tie. The meeting had finished early and the rest of the partners returned to their secure enclosure away from everyone else.

Marcus returned to his desk and checked The Sequence. Stockwatch was green, not by much, up only three points. He looked at his health app. The walk to the station had broken the back of his daily target. Only 3,000 steps left to go. The walk to the flat from Queensway station would take care of that. He checked WhatsApp. Messages from everyone, including Olivia.

Biology went well. Parasites came up!

He knew she would be fine. She deserved all of her success and would make a good vet. He opened the message from Alice.

Off 2 yoga sn and then t with T. J has dun yr shrts.

More smiley emojis. He hoped Jacinda had managed to get the stain out. He opened a message from James.

Hi Dad. Dropped a can of beer on my laptop last night and have bolloxed the keyboard. Had to pay £95 to get it repaired. Any chance you could transfer some wonga? Ta. J x

Marcus loved his son to bits but had major doubts about his readiness to be an adult. He thought of asking for the receipt as proof of payment for the repair. It wouldn't have been beyond James to fake the accident in order to fund his recreational drug habit.

He opened Outlook. Ninety-six unread messages and little time to read them. Prioritisation was needed. Fifteen messages from Risk and Compliance were instantly deleted, more reminders to complete his 'Embracing Diversity' training. He would do his timesheet and approve expenses in the afternoon. Over twenty of the messages were from The Firm's Insight Marketing Team which had grown exponentially in the previous two years, from a small unit to a cast of thousands. The Firm had a 'point of view' on everything and it all came with 'insight'. He looked at some of the titles.

How blockchain is redefining the consumer products sector.
Managing cyber risk in evolving commercial ecosystems.
When the Internet of Things changes your paradigm.
What a complete load of bollocks, though Marcus.

The rest of his inbox was dominated by Project Spearmint and messages from Mason who rarely wrote anything of importance. He merely tagged words on to someone else's email, 'FYI, let's discuss', 'We should catch up on this', 'What's your view?' Mason simply moved crap around, he didn't clear up any himself. Marcus marked them all as read and dumped them in the Project Spearmint folder. It had taken him fifteen minutes to clear his inbox and it was time for lunch.

Fernando was waiting for him at the salad bar in OnYouGo.

'Same as always, Marcus? Large pesto salmon and quinoa salad?'

'Yes please, Fernando. Not so much coriander today.'

Marcus returned to his desk to eat his pimped-up salad. It almost passed the vegan test and made him feel less guilty about last night's Double Whopper. He loaded the BBC News website and trawled around for reports of the mystery virus. The news was dominated by Harry and Meghan's imminent departure and the impact of Storm Brendan, which had ripped the roof off a building in Slough.

Wouldn't have been a bad thing if Storm Brendan had flattened Slough, he thought.

He scooped up the remains of his lunch and walked towards the EcoPod recycling zone with its multiple bins for food waste, cutlery and utensils, cans, plastic waste and paper. It took him five minutes to sort everything. Standing next to the photocopier was Mason Sherwin.

'Ah, Marcus. Was just coming to see you. I've set up a call with Jim Ibbotson at Espina for 3.30 this afternoon to discuss Spearmint. We need to be aligned on the new deadline for Phase 1 and to position ourselves for Phase 2. I've asked Kelvin to sit in as well? There's a really big prize at stake and, after this morning, we both know how much we need it. Why don't the two of us get together to make sure we're aligned on this one? How about 2.30?'

Another of Mason's little tricks, roping in Kelvin to add some muscle. That's why they'd been so chummy coming out of the toilets. 'Alignment' was a big thing in The Firm. Everyone had to be 'aligned'. Disagreement and different points of view were frowned upon.

'Sure, let's get together at 2.30,' said Marcus. He wasn't in the mood for a fight by the EcoPod.

'I'll send an Outlook invite,' said Mason.

'It's okay. I don't think I'll forget in the next hour.'

With an hour to go before aligning, Marcus logged on to RAPID, The Firm's SAP brain. The system had gone live twelve months earlier and had brought The Firm to its knees. It was anything but rapid. With the promise of *'finance at your fingertips'*, its implementation had been a catastrophe. Salaries didn't get paid, expenses weren't reimbursed, clients didn't get billed, supplier invoices went missing, and that was only the basics. As giant clusterfucks go, RAPID had set the bar high.

He opened the tab marked 'Expenses for Approval'. Before the botched deployment of RAPID, partners checked physical receipts. It was a manual, paper-based process but at least they could see who was taking the piss when it came to abusing the policy for client and staff entertainment. RAPID's automated receipt scanning system, linked via a cloud to an outsourced processing centre in Bangalore, meant it was open season on abuse. Lunches, dinners, team drinks and celebrations were charged to clients who never checked, or who were never given the chance to check. Marcus had given up caring, everything was now invisible and it wasn't his money. He clicked 'approved' against every claim.

People were returning after lunch and he looked up to see Loder, Irons and Mauser taking off their overcoats and laughing loudly. They had only been gone for two hours.

Maybe the restaurant ran out of foie gras bonbons? he thought.

Tom Irons had the complexion of a man twenty years older, blotched and dried by a daily diet of red wine and rich food. True to form, one of the 'guinea fowl done three ways' had ended up down the front of Simon Loder's shirt and he had smeared it with his napkin. It looked like a giant skid mark.

In the distance, Marcus saw Mason approaching along the corridor, picked up his Spearmint file and joined him in one of the Idea Bubbles.

'Did you read any of my emails on Spearmint?' he said with a heavy hint of annoyance that Marcus hadn't responded immediately. Marcus lied.

'Yes, I did. All forty of them. From what I'm hearing, we're on track to meet the deadline of next Thursday. Aren't we all getting together on Monday to review the first draft?'

Mason shook his head impatiently.

'That's exactly the bloody point I was making in my emails, if you'd bothered to read them, Marcus! Jim Ibbotson wants the draft report by Monday lunchtime, latest. He was pretty punchy on the phone like he always is. The team will need to work late all this week and the weekend to get it done. I suggest we aim for a first draft by close of play on Thursday or Friday at the latest.'

'We could always say "no" and stick to the agreed deadline? Espina hasn't given us all the data yet. We can't make it up. I don't think Jim is being reasonable,' said Marcus.

Saying 'no' to Jim Ibbotson hadn't entered Mason's head. He had built his career on agreeing to clients' unreasonable demands at the expense of everyone around him. To Mason, it didn't matter a jot if people had to give up their weekends and evenings to meet the revised deadline. It was a toxic mix. An unreasonable client who wanted things yesterday and a partner who rolled over like a playful spaniel at the first sign of trouble.

'Marcus, you heard Kelvin this morning? Do whatever it takes to get some money in. There's no other option, we have to agree and take one for the team.'

Mason had a point. Kelvin had been very explicit. Marcus decided to test Mason's resolve to take one for the team.

'So you'll be in at the weekend too, will you? Working with the team?' Mason's eyes opened wide and looked horrified.

'Err, I can't, I'm down in Sussex this weekend, shooting. It's my last chance before the season closes.'

'Looks like you'll have to cancel then? I'm sure the pheasants of Sussex won't mind too much if you take the weekend off. You'll probably be doing them a favour. We should both be here, doing our bit to "take one for the team" as you say.'

Mason's wriggle room was shrinking fast. Marcus had called his bluff and he started to become agitated.

'But cancelling the shooting will cost me over £1,500. Do you realise that?' he spluttered.

'I wouldn't worry too much, Mason. I'm sure you'll find a way to expense it.'

And this was the truth. It was an hour of Mason's time billed to a client who would never check.

'Fine. If that's what it takes for you to be aligned, Marcus. I don't know why you're being like this. It's not very "teamy", is it? We all had to sacrifice our weekends to get where we are, didn't we?' he said resentfully.

It was the best result Marcus was going to get. The client would get what he wanted, but he had screwed Mason's weekend as well. They were aligned on something.

Marcus returned to his desk and flicked through his Spearmint file before the call with the client. Espina had been created three years earlier by the merger of two businesses, Safewear and TuffTogs. Safewear made protective clothing and equipment for hospitals, clinics and care homes, mainly in the public sector. Its head office and factory were on the outskirts of Manchester. With a strong brand and a loyal customer base, Safewear made a steady, if not spectacular, profit every year. It was like many of the UK's medium-sized businesses, well run and profitable, with a loyal workforce.

It had been bought by Leeds-based TuffTogs, which made workwear for the construction and industrial sectors. Buying Safewear gave TuffTogs a more balanced product portfolio and access to Safewear's stable cashflows. Two years down the road, everything had gone to plan. Both businesses had continued to grow, and the staff and customers were happy. This all changed when Jim Ibbotson arrived as Espina's new Chief Financial Officer.

Recruited by TuffTogs' weak and ineffective CEO, Derek Bentley, Jim Ibbotson was a blunt, plain-speaking Yorkshireman, a bruiser who hadn't made the grade in a larger business. He had taken a step down to be a bigger fish in a smaller pond. Soon after his arrival, the best people in both businesses started to leave, intolerant of his confrontational management style. Inept as a CFO, Jim had expanded his incompetence into all areas of Espina's business. Even the bland, meaningless new corporate name was down to him. The rebranding exercise had cost the business over £3 million, money it couldn't afford.

In his twelve months at the financial helm, Jim had presided over a 50% fall in the share price, and the Board and shareholders were getting restless. In an act of desperation, guided by his 'gut feel', Jim had persuaded Derek to sell Safewear to focus exclusively on TuffTogs. He said a slimmed-down business would have 'a stronger strategic and operational rationale' and a 'more persuasive value proposition for its customers'. Marcus thought the idea was a madness. It would be like someone amputating one of their legs and hoping they could hop quicker than they could run.

Spearmint created an ethical dilemma for The Firm. Telling a client the truth caused a conflict of interest. Without a problem, a risk or a downside, there would be no fees. It was the role of The Firm to convince its clients there was always a problem, even if there wasn't. And when it all went tits up some way down the road, it wouldn't be The Firm's fault. Marcus picked up his file and returned to the Idea Bubble where Mason was already waiting, hovering over the speakerphone.

'Hi Marcus. I've just dialled us in. Still waiting for Jim to join.'

The speakerphone beeped.

'Jim Ibbotson. Espina.'

'Afternoon Jim. You've got Mason and Marcus on the line. How's your day going?' It was a feeble attempt to build rapport with the irascible CFO.

'Hi. I've only got half an hour before a call with the banks so we need to wrap this up quickly. How's the work on Phase 1 going? I haven't seen anything yet. When am I going to see something?'

Mason rushed to tell Jim the good news.

'Going really well, Jim. We know you want the draft report by next Monday morning and we're a hundred per cent committed to getting it to you by then. Our team will be working late this week and over the weekend to meet your deadline.'

'That's great,' said Jim. 'At least you lot are earning your money for once. About bloody time. And don't forget, we're doing this work as a fixed fee, so I don't expect any unexpected overruns. I know you lot. Every time you go for a piss it costs me money.'

'Of course not, Jim,' said Mason obsequiously. 'No chance of that.'

Jim had little regard for The Firm. In his mind, they were a necessary evil. It was meant to be about relationships and shared objectives but it was only about the money. Once in a while, a client appreciated The Firm's efforts, but they came around less frequently than Halley's Comet.

'Provided you get the outstanding data to us on time,' interjected Marcus. 'We're still waiting on a lot of information from your Finance and HR teams. Unless we get it in the next day or so, we won't meet the deadline. We have sent a number of emails to your team chasing it.'

Mason shot him a look of panic.

'What fucking information?' said Jim. 'First I've heard of it.'

This was a lie. Jim had been copied in on all the emails but had probably ignored them or pressed 'Delete'.

'Headcount data, org charts, product cost breakdowns, SG&A costs ...' said Marcus. 'There's probably more.'

Jim snapped back. 'You'll have it by Thursday morning.'

Marcus knew he had just thrown someone in Espina to the lions. By the end of the day, Jim would have someone's head on a spike. Probably multiple heads, like a cheese and pineapple hedgehog at a 1970s cocktail party.

Mason tried to smooth things over.

'Actually, I'm sure there's a lot we can be doing in the background until Jim gets us the data, isn't there, Marcus?'

Marcus had spent the whole day sniffing bullshit of one perfume or another. His patience was wearing thin.

'Actually Mason, no we can't. Unless we get the data by Thursday morning, we will have to revert to the original deadline. Simple as that.'

'You'll have it,' said Jim, and the speakerphone went dead.

Mason threw his pen on the table, shook his head and stared at Marcus.

'Well, that was just brilliant, Marcus, well done. What did you do that for, putting Jim on the spot like that? We didn't even get a chance to discuss Phase 2.'

'Sod Phase 2, we need the bloody data now! What do you suggest we do, make it up? Pluck some numbers out of a hat or scatter some rune stones on the table?'

'Sometimes, Marcus, I truly wonder if you're playing for a different team to the rest of us?'

Marcus gathered the Spearmint team in one of the Collaboration Pods. The team was like most teams at The Firm. A mixture of enthusiastic graduates, aspirational managers, battle-scarred senior managers and a couple of weary directors who had seen it all before. Marcus updated them on the latest news and the accelerated deadline. He looked into their eyes and read their minds. What followed would be a series of telephone calls and conversations with spouses, friends and children, informing them that plans for dinners, family events, trips to the theatre and school plays were now compromised, if not cancelled altogether. He knew the conversation off by heart. He had done it many times.

'Let's regroup in the morning to see if we can spread it around so we can all get some time off this weekend. I'm sorry to ask this of you but you all know how it is?'

Steve Pettigrew, one of the directors, put up his hand.

'Marcus, we still haven't got all the data from Espina. We can't make much progress until we get it. What do you want us to do?'

'I get it completely, Steve. Jim has promised to get it to us by Thursday morning. Let's spend tomorrow getting a draft pack together and formulating a plan. See what we get back from them on Thursday.'

By the time Marcus had returned to his desk and checked his email, Mason had already sent three emails: 'Spearmint – Next Steps', 'Spearmint – Revised Timeline' and 'Spearmint – Your commitment to this project'.

Fuck you, thought Marcus.

He stepped out of the building into the chill of a January night. It was already dark. He had only seen daylight for a couple of hours.

I bet I'll start suffering from a Vitamin D deficiency soon, he thought.

He opened Spotify. It had been an awful day and there was only one choice, the Ramones. Their three-chord, nihilistic simplicity captured his mood. He turned the volume up to maximum as 'I Wanna Be Sedated' punched his eardrums. He checked his health app.

Last week you averaged less walking and running distance than the previous week.

He felt guilty and decided to walk along Queen Victoria Street until it joined Cannon Street, around the back of St Paul's Cathedral to St Paul's Tube station. Another 2,000 steps at least. The City was buzzing at rush hour, black cabs, buses, crowded pavements, noise, lights. Marcus loved the City. It was working in it that he hated. He wished he could have it all to himself, like Will Smith in *I Am Legend*, driving through deserted streets laid waste by a global pandemic. Marcus would be the only survivor, free to have as many Double Whoppers as he wanted.

He looked up at the illuminated dome of the cathedral. Amid the steel and glass towers of London's ever-changing skyline, it remained a magnificent constant. It reminded him of the iconic photograph, taken at the height of the Blitz in 1940, undamaged as all around it was on fire. A nation's defiance embodied in a single building. He felt privileged to see it every day.

He walked around the back of the courtyard and approached the steps to the Underground. 'Sheena is a Punk Rocker' was taking its toll but the Ramones had done their job, helping him to forget Mason and Spearmint. He opened Spotify again. Time for a change of mood and he looked through his playlists. *Motown Classics* felt right and he pressed 'Play'. It was eight stops from St Paul's to Queensway on the Central Line. Enough time to get through Marvin Gaye's 'I Heard It Through the Grapevine' and 'Standing in the Shadows of Love' by the Four Tops.

He picked up a copy of the *Evening Standard*, descended the steps, swiped his Oyster card and got on to the escalator. At six o'clock in the evening, the westbound platform was three deep. If South Western Trains suffered from trains that didn't run on time, the Central Line suffered from severe over-crowding. Little red sausages crammed with human meat squeezed into their metal skins. He walked along the platform, stopping at the same point every night when he stayed at the flat. He was in no rush. His regular Tuesday night dinner with Gavin wasn't until eight.

He looked up at the billboards on the curved tunnel wall. Adverts for superfast broadband, mobile networks, organic home delivery meals and a picture of David Gandy promoting vitamins. He stared up at David who was looking straight at him.

'*I've been taking Wellman since my twenties. I never compromise on my health,*' proclaimed David from the wall.

Marcus disliked David for no good reason other than his full head of hair, his chiselled jawline (complete with stubble), his tanned, unblemished skin, and his piercing blue eyes. David was wearing a suit and tie, another thing in his favour. A train thundered into the station. It was already full. People bent like bananas inside the curved walls of the carriages. A few people got off and more squeezed in. The Four Tops faded out as 'Dancing in the Street' by Martha Reeves and the Vandellas started.

It was not until the fourth train that Marcus finally got on. Reading the newspaper on a packed train was futile, so he folded it up and put it away in his laptop bag. The usual exodus at Oxford Circus freed up a seat but he couldn't be bothered to read. He would look at the paper when he got home.

The Tube pulled into Queensway station and Marcus got off directly opposite the exit, climbed the small flight of stairs and made his way to the lifts. Queensway was bustling with early evening diners in the district's many Chinese restaurants. He had walked past them hundreds of times, thinking about going in, but there was something about the rows of bronzed Peking ducks hanging by their necks that put him off.

The complexion of the area had changed in recent years as more Eastern European and Middle Eastern influences had taken root. He loved the area and its cosmopolitan 24/7 life. Something was always going on, mostly legal, but sometimes not. There was usually some dodgy-looking group hanging around the bars and street corners, puffing on hookah pipes. It was different to leafy, suburban Weybridge, and it was the contrast that he loved most.

He had bought the flat in Kensington Gardens Square just over a year earlier. Feeling drained by his daily commute from Weybridge and persecution by South Western Trains, he had persuaded Alice that a pied-à-terre in London would be good for both of them. They could stay there on nights out when they went to the theatre or for dinner with friends, but it hadn't turned out as he had intended. Alice had been to the flat twice in twelve months. It offered her nothing. It didn't have a Quooker, an Aga or a walk-in shower.

For him, the flat fitted the bill perfectly. It was part of a new development overlooking the recently demolished Whiteleys department store at the end of Queensway, where it joined Westbourne Grove. It had taken over a year to clear the Whiteleys site of rubble and twisted metal. On her second visit, Alice had looked out of the dust-encrusted balcony window of the flat.

'Marcus, it's like looking out over Beirut. It's like a war zone. I don't know how you can live here. Look at all those rubbish bags, don't they ever collect them? It stinks of curry too.'

But that was its charm. A bit grubby, noisy and sometimes smelly too, but it was living, breathing and pulsating. From then on, it was always known as Beirut.

'It's got a Waitrose just across the road and a very good coffee shop nearby, so it's not all bad, Al,' he said defensively, but she wasn't listening.

It was a one-bedroomed flat with a single-roomed living space, kitchen, small dining area and living room all in one. The entire flat would have fitted into the living room at Twin Gates. The developers had fitted it out well with new appliances and fixtures. It was ideal for Marcus, whose DIY skills extended no further than picture hooks and a spot of painting. A couple of trips to John Lewis in Oxford Street and it was ready to live in. It had become his sanctuary, his bolthole from the rest of the world. Marcus loved living in Beirut.

He entered the lobby where he was greeted by an immaculately dressed man who was almost as broad as he was tall. He was Eric Blair, the concierge for the block. Eric stood up from his desk, as if he were standing to attention. He almost saluted.

'Good evening, Marcus. Great to see you back. How was your weekend? Good day at work?'

'Good evening, Eric. Yes, everything is fine at home. Alice and the children are well. Work today was pretty shit, so pleased to be back. Everything okay here?'

'Apart from the noise and dust from the building site, I can't complain. Are you here for the rest of the week?'

'Yes, I'll probably head back to Weybridge on Friday.'

The two men had become good friends, bonded by a shared love of plain chocolate digestive biscuits. Always McVitie's and never milk chocolate. Eric had been a regimental sergeant major in the Paras, seeing action in the Falklands and Northern Ireland. He was about ten years older than Marcus and considerably tougher. After leaving the army, Eric had joined the Corps of Commissionaires, opening the door and greeting visitors at the offices of an international bank, until it moved out to Canary Wharf and replaced ex-servicemen like him with effete young men in roll-neck sweaters. Now Eric was signing for Amazon deliveries and making sure people didn't put their food waste in the recycling bins. It was a cushy number, much easier than dodging bullets on the Shankhill Road in Belfast.

Marcus walked through the lobby to the lifts and went up to the second floor. He walked along the corridor to Flat 2.3. He heard classical music coming from Gavin's flat as he passed the door. He was probably cooking their dinner. He turned the keys in both locks and opened the door. He could immediately smell the Orla Kiely diffuser in the hall. It had been a Christmas present from Gavin. He walked into the living room, switched on the lights, threw his laptop bag on the sofa and took off his raincoat. He slumped into the sofa and threw his head back to stare up at the ceiling.

It was Tuesday, 14 January 2020.

Chapter 4

The Chase

Memories of the events in Tesco Express had kept her awake all night. Alexa was still asleep, short breaths coming out of her tiny nose and a little thumb in her mouth as a comfort. Claire stroked her cheek, skin as smooth as glass.

'Come on Alexa, time to wake up. It's nursery today.'

Alexa stirred, slowly opening her eyes. Claire loved her sleepy face. She picked her up and cuddled her. Alexa's head fitted into Claire's neck like a violin.

'Let's go and wake Kyle up.'

She squeezed through the narrow gap between the bed and the wardrobe. She had lost count of the number of times she had stubbed her toe on the leg of the bed and tried not to swear. Kyle was sprawled across his bed like a snow-angel. Buzz and Woody were embraced on the floor.

'Wake up Kyle,' said Claire as she shook him gently.

The little boy jumped up as if he had been injected with adrenaline. He looked around.

'Where's Buzz and Woody?'

Claire picked up Kyle's soulmates and handed them to him.

'They must have been playing together in the night,' he said earnestly.

'Probably on an adventure to Planet Zurg,' Claire said with equal sincerity. 'Now, let's get on. It's school and nursery today! Go and do a wee-wee and start getting yourself dressed. I'll come back and check on you.'

'I want to do a wee-wee as well,' protested Alexa.

It was always a three-way race to the toilet. Claire would have given anything to have an ensuite bathroom, to have a wee in peace. A hotel room on honeymoon in Rome was the only time she had had one.

One day I'll end up pissing myself or going in a saucepan, she thought.

She dressed Alexa and brushed her hair before checking to see how Kyle was getting on. It was a good effort. One sock on inside out and he had forgotten his underpants.

'How did you forget your underpants?' she said laughing.

'I couldn't find them,' he said seriously.

With the missing underpants found, she shooed the children off to the kitchen.

'Get your cereals out of the cupboard and I'll be right there. Mummy's got to go to the toilet as well.'

Kyle had peed on the seat.

Just like his father, she thought as she wiped it. *Too lazy to lift it up.*

A few stray drops of pee hadn't caused the breakdown of her marriage to Jack. His affair with the Senior Eveningwear Buyer at Fenwick had done that, but a wet loo seat every morning hadn't helped either.

She switched on the kettle and the radio simultaneously in an ambidextrous movement. She heard the reassuring voice of Nick Robinson on the *Today* programme. Jack's introduction to Radio 4 was one of the few things from her marriage that had survived. Her wedding and engagement rings had been sold to feed her family, but Radio 4 remained. Tensions between the US and Iran were escalating. It looked like conflict was getting closer.

Trump is a bloody lunatic, she thought.

Claire checked Kyle's school bag to make sure he had a change of underpants. There hadn't been an accident for a while, but it was better to be safe than sorry. Inside was a note from his teacher informing parents of the school trip to Hounslow Urban Farm on the twenty-sixth of March. The £15 deposit was to be paid by the end of January. She didn't have the money, but she wanted Kyle to go. There weren't that many sheep in Ladbroke Grove and it would be good for him.

Claire and the children stepped out on to the balcony. It wasn't a cold morning and, from the second floor, she could look across the skyline towards West London. The shroud around Grenfell Tower billowed in the breeze. As she closed her front door, the door to No. 10 opened and her neighbour, Judith, stepped out. It was a 'coincidence' that happened frequently.

'Hi Judith. How are you?'

'Hi Claire. Hi kids. I'm great thanks. Nice morning, at least it isn't too cold. I normally hate January and February. Always grey. How have you all been keeping?'

'We're okay. Same old, same old. Alexa has nursery this morning so we're in a bit of a rush.'

'I'll walk with you on my way to the station. I bet you could do with a bit of adult conversation, couldn't you?'

Judith was right. Claire did miss conversation with grown-ups. There was only so much Dumpling and Captain Underpants she could take. But, offered the choice between Woody's rip cord taglines and Judith's suffocating political dogma, she would take a 'snake in her boots' anytime. A state of the nation chat with Judith at eight in the morning wasn't appealing.

Judith Green was thirty-five and worked in the Communications and PR Department for the Labour Party at their offices in Victoria. She joined the party at Oxford and, after a number of corporate jobs, took up her role after Jeremy Corbyn won the leadership contest in 2015.

Claire found Judith overwhelming. Standing almost six feet tall, Judith had the physique of a bricklayer and an opinion on every cause that wafted past her flared nostrils. Women's rights, animal rights, green issues, social issues, NHS cuts, Brexit, Tory pricks, Tory press, Tory donors. She was keen to share her views on everything with Claire, knowing she would always listen. A week after Labour's heavy defeat in the 2019 General Election, Claire had bumped into Judith on the balcony.

'I'm sorry things didn't work out for you and Mr Corbyn,' said Claire.

'It was the Tory gutter press that won it for that philandering fucker, Boris,' said Judith alliteratively, almost retching with disgust.

'Maybe you didn't get your message across well enough?' said Claire innocently.

Judith didn't speak to Claire until Christmas.

At the foot of the stairs, Mr Mahoney appeared from the cupboard where Ian's mobility scooter was kept.

'Good morning my little ones!' said Mr Mahoney in his soft Irish voice. 'Morning Claire. Morning Judith.'

He had once made the mistake of calling Judith, 'love'. She had berated him for ten minutes over his use of 'toxic, patronising, masculine dominant vocabulary'. He had always been certain to call her Judith after that.

Kyle got excited when he saw the mobility scooter.

'Can Ian take me for a ride on his spaceship, Mummy? Please?'

'No sweetie. Ian isn't up yet but maybe later after school? Say goodbye to Mr Mahoney.'

The children waved goodbye to 'Mr Moany', as Alexa called him.

'See you later for *The Chase*. Could be The Governess tonight?' said Claire.

'No. She was on last night, on last night,' said the caretaker. 'She won't be on two nights running. Never two nights running.'

Mr Mahoney often repeated the same words. He popped a mint imperial into his mouth where it bounced around his few remaining teeth like a pinball.

Judith left them at the Little Acorns Nursery and headed to the station and another day holding the 'Tory filth' to account. The nursery was a prefabricated building adjoining St Peter's and All Saints Church. It had space for twenty-four children aged between two and four. Gavin knew the vicar and had put in a good word to get a place for Alexa. Most of the mothers were dressed in Smew. Three mothers were huddled together outside the entrance having a fag; the stress of the morning routine was taking its toll.

Alexa ran into the arms of Zoe, a shy, nineteen-year-old girl, dressed in a light-blue tabard and matching trousers. She looked like a trainee nurse in *Holby City*. Alexa loved Zoe and Zoe loved her back. Apart from Claire, only Zoe knew that Alexa would be sick if she ate eggs. Claire looked at her and remembered herself at nineteen, loving her first year at Saint Martins, dreaming of becoming the next Stella McCartney. Zoe scooped Alexa up in her arms and swung her around. Alexa squealed.

'Hello! My little angel. How are you?'

Alexa kissed Zoe full on the lips. Another smacker.

'So what's on the menu for today?' said Claire.

'I think it's shepherd's pie,' said Zoe. Sometimes, Zoe wasn't on the same wavelength as everyone else.

'No, I meant what are the children doing today?'

Zoe raised her eyes and shook her head.

'Sorry! We'll probably do some painting until break and then it's computer studies. Alexa's mouse control is really improving.'

Claire thought of her little girl. Two years ago she was learning how to walk. Now she was improving her mouse control.

'Sounds fantastic. Maybe I should stick around? I might learn something.'

At school, Claire hated maths and computers but loved art and literature. Every part-time job she had applied for required some proficiency with a computer. Any skills she had lapsed years ago and she was accustomed to rejection. There weren't many jobs offering flexible working hours for flunked out, undergraduate dress designers with a passion for Jane Austen and Frank Sinatra. While Alexa was improving her mouse skills, she would be washing towels and watching *Loose Women*.

Claire crouched down to toddler level. Alexa flung her arms around her neck and kissed her. Then she let go and ran off to join the other children who were hurtling around the nursery like demented flies. Kyle had been waiting patiently at the doorway, and Claire stroked the back of his head as she guided them back out to the street. She looked up at the front elevation of St Peter's with its beautiful spire, stained glass windows and the figure of the crucified Christ on the wall. Kyle had asked her why the man looked so sad. It wasn't easy convincing a five-year-old that, although Jesus had superpowers, they didn't involve lasers.

Beechwood Infant and Junior School was an urban primary in the classic Edwardian style. Built in yellow London brick and standing on three floors, it had a high surrounding wall with separate entrances for boys and girls and a small playground on either side. Its walls had been gouged with the graffiti of its pupils going back almost a century. Thousands of pupils had passed through its segregated gates, and Kyle Halford was part of the latest generation. It was the type of school that should have been bombed by the Luftwaffe but was fortunately spared. Under the dedicated leadership of Mrs Emily Lindsay, the school's rotund and committed headmistress, and her team of enthusiastic teachers, Beechwood had been turned around and gained an 'outstanding' rating from Ofsted. So outstanding that wealthy, professional parents had moved to fall within its catchment area. They were easy to spot. Dropping their children off in Range Rovers or Audi Q7s, that's if the nanny didn't do it in her BMW.

'Typical fucking Tories!' Judith had said to Claire. 'Stealing places at good state schools from working-class kids like Kyle and Alexa. It's a disgrace.'

Claire hadn't understood what Judith meant until Kyle got an invite to Sebastian and Desdemona's Space Station-themed birthday party at Kidzania in Westfield. It probably cost more than Claire's Universal Credit for a month.

Kyle's teacher, Miss Helena Mistakidis, was on playground duty and she waved to them.

'Good morning Kyle. How are you this morning? Hi Claire. How are you?'

'We're both fine, aren't we Kyle?'

Kyle nodded shyly. When his father left two years earlier, he became withdrawn when he wasn't with Claire or people he knew.

'That's great! Looking forward to a fantastic day?' said the teacher enthusiastically.

Helena Mistakidis was small, just over five feet tall, a height enhanced by shoes with three-inch crêpe platforms. She had a collection of her unique footwear in multiple colours. She resembled an astronaut moon-walking across the playground. She was thirty and had moved to the UK from Cyprus. Beautiful and blessed with an olive skin and a faultless complexion, she had dark, piercing eyes concealed beneath the fringe of her curly, black hair. Claire imagined she was a modern day Helen of Troy, a beauty who sparked the Trojan War.

She had been Kyle's teacher since September. He had difficulty with her name when he came home from school on the first day of term.

'So what's your new teacher's name, Kyle?' said Claire.

'Miss Takidis,' he said confidently.

'I think it's Miss Mistakidis, isn't it? You have to say the "miss" bit twice.'

'That's silly,' said Kyle, now becoming confused.

It had taken a lot of practice before he got it right.

Kyle ran into the playground and Claire approached the teacher.

'Miss Mistakidis, please can I have a quick word?'

'Claire, please call me Helena. No need to be so formal. What can I do for you? Is something wrong with Kyle?'

'No, not at all. He's absolutely fine, really happy. It's about the school trip to the urban farm and the deposit. It's £15 isn't it? By the end of January?'

'Yes, it is. Is that a problem?' she said with concern. The teachers all knew which children got free school meals.

'If it could wait until the start of next month and my next Universal Credit payment, it would really help? Things are pretty tough at the moment.'

Helena gave her a smile that would have melted the heart of any man, let alone a Prince of Troy. She touched her on the arm.

'Don't worry, we'll find a way. Kyle will definitely be going and it will be a great day out for everyone. Leave it with me. Got to go now, breakfast club is finishing soon.'

As Miss Mistakidis defied gravity and bounced across the playground, Claire swallowed her tears. It was her second humiliation in two days. Yesterday, it was shoplifting, today it was a school trip to stroke piglets. She hated Jack for what he had done to them.

It was 8.30 and Gavin would be arriving at ten. He was very punctual. It took her twenty minutes to walk back to Kensal Mansions. The morning rush hour was in full swing and Claire looked at the drivers in the queue of traffic. A man was speaking in an animated way on his mobile phone and staring out of the side window. In the car in front, a woman was staring into her rear-view mirror and applying her mascara.

If that wanker hits her up the arse, she could be blinded by a mascara brush, she thought.

She turned in to the alleyway. Tuesday was bin day at Kensal Mansions and Mr Mahoney was preparing for the arrival of the dustmen. The bins used to be emptied twice a week. Now, due to council cutbacks, it was once a week and they had rats the size of small dogs.

'Hi Mr Mahoney. Bin day today then?'

'Oh yes, oh yes. Always busy, always busy.'

'See you for *The Chase* tonight?'

'Of course. I've made us a new cake. It's a coffee and walnut.'

'Can't wait. Look forward to it. I'll have the kettle boiled.'

'That's grand, that's grand,' said Mr Mahoney, wheeling a bin to the front of the alley.

Claire took a puff on her inhaler, climbed the thirty-six steps and walked along the balcony. Even at nine in the morning, Mrs Hassan was cooking, the smell of onions frying and dhal being prepared for her family. Nick Robinson was giving the closing headlines on the *Today* programme. Trump, Iran, Brexit, Prince Harry and Meghan. Nothing that affected her. She tidied the flat and put the musty towels in the washing machine. She didn't want Gavin to think she wasn't coping.

Just as Jenni Murray was about to announce the agenda for *Woman's Hour*, there was a knock at the door. It was Gavin, the Louis Theroux lookalike from social services. Standing almost six feet tall and filling the door frame, he had the build of a rugby player, although Claire doubted he had ever played the game. Dressed in a black Ralph Lauren cashmere and wool overcoat and an Armani scarf, he looked like an upmarket catalogue model. On his shoulder was a Paul Smith satchel bag. He was smiling as she opened the door.

'Good morning Claire. Ready for another enthralling session with Dr Douglas? So, what's on your mind this week? You can trust me, I'm a doctor!'

He said the same thing on every visit, making her laugh and immediately putting her at ease. His skin was glowing, a shine like Alexa's. When he told her he had spent £250 on a pot of La Prairie moisturiser, she had nearly pissed her pants in shock. All she had was a pot of Nivea, half price in Superdrug. Gavin always smelled nice. Today it was Mont Blanc Explorer, one of her favourites.

'Morning Dr Douglas. Bit concerned about the early onset of the menopause and a developing case of toenail fungus. Apart from that, I'm all good.'

'Okay, step into my surgery and let's discuss this over a cup of tea.'

Gavin Douglas didn't need to work. Born into a wealthy Scottish family with an estate complete with shooting and fishing rights, he had inherited a small fortune upon the death of his grandfather, who was a baronet of the realm. When his father died, he would become Sir Gavin Douglas, although he was certain that the aristocratic line would end with him. A cocaine habit in his early twenties had burnt its way through part of his septum and most of his inheritance. Therapy and abstinence had left him with enough money to leave the family estate, change his life and become a social worker in London.

Claire and Gavin walked into the kitchen and she switched the kettle on and turned Jenni Murray down. She took two mugs out of the cupboard.

'What tea would you like? Lemon and ginger, green or builders?'

'Lemon and ginger, thank you.'

Gavin had a taste for nice tea and good coffee. He bought his cappuccino every morning from a little Italian shop in Westbourne Grove which ground its own beans and sold amazing cakes. He called it 'the Panettone Palace'. He had almost been sick the first time she had made him a cup of tea.

'What is this?' he had exclaimed, spitting the contents back into the mug.

'Tea,' said Claire indignantly.

'Really? What sort of tea? And what is this brown scum on the top?'

'I don't know. Typhoo. PG Tips.'

On his next visit, he arrived bearing gifts in the form of Tea Pigs Lemon & Ginger teabags and green tea from Mariage Frères, which came from Selfridges in a beautiful black box. Even the teabag looked expensive.

He sat down at the small kitchen table as Claire put two of the deluxe teabags in the mugs and added boiling water. The next two hours were the highlight of her week, adult conversation and a chance to laugh. It was the first time she had seen him since Christmas.

'So, how are things? How are Kyle and Little Miss Sunshine?'

'The kids are great, doing really well. Alexa is very happy at nursery and Kyle is becoming more confident at school.'

'And what about you?' he said sympathetically. 'How are you doing?'

She stared straight at him. Like a waxwork in a fire, her face started to melt and tears flowed. She picked up a damp tea towel and covered her face. She told him what happened in Tesco Express the day before.

'I messed up so badly, Gavin. January is always a tough month and I've already spent my Universal Credit. We needed food, we had to eat for fuck's sake. I'm already going without so much. I just thought I would add a few things to my trolley and they wouldn't notice. It wasn't really stealing. I just wasn't paying for everything.'

'Well, I'm not sure a magistrate would see it that way but carry on!'

'It was so humiliating being stopped at the door by the security guard. He was a complete prick. Went through all my shopping in front of everyone. People were staring at me like I was some sort of junkie. He called the store manager and I was taken to his office. All I could think about was letting you down, police, magistrates, the children being taken into care, me going to prison. I could have lost everything, Gavin.'

He listened to the rest of her story. It took her fifteen minutes to finish, by which time he had drunk his tea and hers was cold.

'Exciting day. Probably not something to be repeated in a hurry! Mr Primus sounds like a decent man. It's going to be like having your own private food bank.'

'But what if it hadn't turned out like that? What if he had called the police and the kids were taken into care. It was such a dumb thing to do.'

'Bit dramatic. I think the police have got bigger problems than a single mum nicking some chicken nuggets. Can you imagine the newspaper headlines? "Food Giant Bullies Single Mum Into Prison." *The Sun* would have a field day.'

She drank her cold tea. Gavin continued.

'I think getting through the rest of the month is the bigger issue. I'll make some calls when I get back to the office, see if we can get an interim payment. Look on the bright side, February is a short month!'

'Thanks, those few days will make all the difference! I desperately need to buy myself some new knickers? Mine are so threadbare, I'm scared to fart in case I rip them.'

'Any luck finding a job?'

'Only those few days before Christmas in the gift shop. Watching yummy mummies buying cards "To the One I Love at Christmas" made me feel ill. Their husbands were probably shagging their secretaries while they were buying them.'

'Now, now. No need to be bitter. No news from Jack then?'

'Bugger all. Didn't bother to ring the kids or send a card. It's been over a year now. And nothing from his parents either, the stuck-up wankers. Kyle and Alexa are their grandchildren for goodness' sake.'

After graduating from Central Saint Martins, Jack had got a job as a junior buyer at Fenwick, the department store in Bond Street. After his degree, taking a job in retail was selling out, but it provided them with a steady income. His parents blamed her for getting pregnant and keeping the baby. It was her egg, and not his sperm, that had ruined his life. Except, it was Jack who wanted to keep the baby. By the time Alexa was born, he was having an affair with his boss, a forty-five-year-old cougar with an insatiable taste for younger men. Their relationship was consummated on buying trips while Claire was breast-feeding and potty training.

The secret came out eventually and it destroyed her world. The cougar had been backing more than one horse in the bonking stakes, and had given Jack an STI, which he dutifully passed on to Claire on one of the rare occasions they had sex. An itchy discharge, a trip to the GP and some swabs revealed the sordid truth. He went through the charade of blaming her, calling her a slag, the usual protests from the guilty. At least he hadn't blamed the toilet seat. Eventually he confessed to the truth. Without professional support, they tried to pull their marriage back from the brink but, in the end, they fell over the edge and Jack moved out to live with his parents in Sevenoaks. Unprotected sex had changed her life twice in ways she had never envisaged.

Jack kept in contact for a few months, occasionally coming to visit the children at their one-bedroomed flat on the Holloway Road, but his enthusiasm for being a dad had died along with Claire's love for him. Before she had the chance to get a divorce or agree maintenance, Jack had buggered off to Australia on some long overdue gap year to fill the gaps in his life he had made all by himself. A couple of phone calls in two years, probably made in a melancholy moment, and that was it.

'So, apart from a minor shoplifting incident and some money problems, everything's all good then?' said Gavin flippantly.

He had a knack for making the important seem trivial, and he made her laugh. He was the sort of man she had always thought she would end up with. Kind, good-looking, stylish, charming. He had never mentioned a girlfriend in any of their conversations. He hadn't mentioned a boyfriend either. Maybe he was in love with himself and his moisturisers? Claire put the kettle on again.

'Another tea? Mine was cold.'

'No, I'm okay thanks. I had a coffee in the Panettone Palace before I came here.'

For the next hour, they talked about the usual stuff to take her mind off things. Kids, school, good programmes on TV, fashion, favourite films, favourite music. They finished their debate on the best Robert De Niro film; Gavin had gone for *Raging Bull* and Claire had chosen *Taxi Driver*. Then it was time for 'surgery' to close.

'I must be going. I'm glad you've calmed down a bit. Try to stay positive. I'll look into getting an emergency payment for your Universal Credit when I get back to the office.'

'Where are you off to now?'

'The Osman family. They're Sudanese. Grenfell Tower residents. They've been in temporary accommodation for over two years now. I've got them into a maisonette on the other side of the Harrow Road but it's not ideal. Six of them in two bedrooms. It's not good for the children, sleeping in the same room as their eighty-year-old grandmother.'

'Makes me grateful for what I've got here,' she said.

'Well, it's not Mayfair but it's certainly not the Old Kent Road either!'

'Probably somewhere like Pentonville Road then?'

'Don't be too hard on yourself. This place is Pall Mall at the least. Could have been the Strand if it wasn't for the damp. Try to stay out of jail before the next time I see you!'

He took his overcoat and scarf from the back of the chair, picked up his satchel and threw it across his shoulder.

'Okay, see you next week? Give Kyle and Alexa a hug from me.'

She walked him to the front door and opened it. Her two hours of escape were over but she wanted it to continue. The words came out on their own.

'Are you doing anything this evening?' she said nervously.

He took a step back from the threshold and leaned against the open door. He looked surprised. He turned his head to one side and pushed his glasses on to the bridge of his nose with his index finger, just like Louis Theroux did. She had never asked him a question like this.

'Are you making me an offer I can't refuse?' he said, doing an impression of Marlon Brando in *The Godfather*.

'Well, I'm asking if you would like to have dinner with me and the kids tonight? It's only chicken and pasta bake.'

'The proceeds of your crime?' He laughed. 'I'm not sure I should be handling stolen goods. That's very kind of you, but I have a dinner date of my own tonight.'

She smiled with embarrassment and flushed.

'I'm sorry. I wasn't being nosey.'

She stepped back into the kitchen doorway, wishing she hadn't asked.

'No worries, not nosey at all. I'm having dinner with Marcus, my next-door neighbour. I've mentioned him before, the big cheese in the City? We take it in turns to cook for each other on Tuesdays. It's my turn tonight. Two lonely blokes keeping each other company. I'll have to call in to The Temple on my way home.'

'What the hell is The Temple?' said Claire, still embarrassed by her clumsy proposal.

Gavin laughed out loud.

'Sorry, it's Marcus's name for Waitrose. He won't shop anywhere else. He's a supermarket snob. Luckily for us, there's one in Westbourne Grove.'

'So what are you cooking tonight?'

'Tuna steaks with a sumac crust, with a herbed bulgur wheat and courgette salad with pomegranate seeds. It's very healthy.'

Claire had never heard of sumac. It sounded like tarmac.

'Bit more exotic than chicken and pasta bake.'

'I'm sure the pasta bake will be delicious. Perhaps another night?'

His words offered her some hope. He'd said yes in a way, and he hadn't said no either. Gavin waved from the balcony. She closed the door and inhaled deeply.

Well, that went well! Another humiliation, she thought to herself.

She made lunch. Cheese on toast and a cup of Typhoo tea and put the towels in the tumble dryer. At least they didn't smell like mushrooms now. She took her lunch into the living room and switched on the TV. Fifteen minutes of *Bargain Hunt* before *Loose Women*. The same routine every day. She liked *Bargain Hunt*. It was like *Antiques Roadshow* for the couch potato masses, but without the class of Fiona Bruce. Today's red team had paid £150 for a pair of art deco wall lights, which turned out to be repro and had barely scraped £65 at auction. A big loss but at least they got to keep their sweatshirts.

Claire collected Alexa from nursery. Her daughter came running to greet her, clutching her latest creation, a picture in the shape of a hedgehog with penne pasta spines. She thrust it into Claire's hand proudly.

'His name is Spiky,' said Alexa.

'That's a great name for a hedgehog, sweetie. We'll put it on the wall when we get home. Say goodbye to Zoe.'

The afternoon pick-up at Kyle's school was like a presidential visit from Donald Trump. A fleet of black four-by-fours with tinted privacy windows were parked in the road. As Claire stood in the playground, a well-dressed and elegant woman approached her.

'Hello. You're Kyle's Mum aren't you? Miss Mistakidis pointed you out to me. I'm Beverley Cheng, Bruce's Mum.'

Claire remembered Kyle telling her about the new boy in his class who started after Christmas. She usually forgot most of the things Kyle came out with. He said Bruce was Chinese. The woman extended her hand politely.

'It's good to meet you. Bruce talks about Kyle a lot. I think your little boy has been very kind to him.'

Claire shook her hand. It was warm and her skin was soft.

'Hi, nice to meet you too. Kyle said there was a new boy in his class. How is Bruce settling in?'

'He's doing fine. The first few days were hard. His English isn't so good. Moving to England has been a big change for all of us.'

'Why? Where were you living before?'

'Hong Kong. My husband works in banking. With all the political unrest going on, we decided to leave. Both our families are still there.'

'And you picked Ladbroke Grove as a better option?' said Claire.

Beverley laughed.

'We're renting an apartment in Elgin Crescent. It's not too bad. Anyway, I'm glad we've met. Maybe Kyle would like to come and play with Bruce one afternoon after school? Or maybe have a sleepover at a weekend? I'm afraid our flat is a bit of a mess.'

Parties and sleepovers made Claire feel anxious. What could she offer in return. A damp, poky flat on an estate that should have been condemned years ago. Every invitation added to her feelings of inferiority. She replied politely.

'That would be nice. Good to meet you, Beverley.'

Claire liked her, she seemed genuine and kind. Led by Miss Mistakidis, the children in Kyle's class were emerging from the building, running around frenetically like little tadpoles. Claire waved to the teacher and Kyle ran to his mummy and little sister.

'How was school today?' said Claire, giving him a hug.

'It was great,' said Kyle. 'Miss Takidis said we can take it in turns to look after Biscuit at weekends.'

'Who's Biscuit?' said Claire, forgetting to remind him of his teacher's name.

'He's our pet hamster in our classroom. He has a very big house.'

Claire had always wanted a pet when she was a child but her father had refused. She had once been allowed to look after Janine Prescott's guinea pigs when she went on holiday, but he made her keep them in the garage.

'They're just like rats. They're not coming in the house,' said her father.

And that was it. End of conversation.

'Well, let's wait and see when it's your turn,' she said to Kyle. It was tough enough feeding three humans let alone a fourth mouth that would probably want something different to spaghetti bolognese.

The alleyway to Kensal Mansions had been swept and the grass courtyard was free from litter. Claire didn't like the children playing on it because people let their dogs poo on it. The council had put up signs threatening fines but nobody took any notice.

Ian's mobility scooter was parked by its little shed, waiting for Mr Mahoney to lock it away. They climbed the stairs and walked along the balcony. The kitchen of No. 9 was in full swing, aromas of cumin, turmeric and coriander billowing out of the open window. Occasionally, Mrs Hassan would bring Claire a little plate of samosas. They were always delicious and the children liked them too.

Claire paired the little shoes in the hall and hung coats on hooks. She made two glasses of Ribena with two malted milk biscuits for Kyle and Alexa. The children called them cow biscuits. She had an hour until *The Chase* and Mr Mahoney's arrival. Alexa came into the kitchen.

'Can we put Spiky on the wall please, Mummy?'

Some of Spiky's pasta spines had fallen off, as if he had developed hedgehog alopecia. As she only had curly fusilli in the cupboard, she decided to avoid 'spine confusion' and leave Spiky with bald patches.

'Let's put him here next to Father Christmas.'

Spiky joined the art gallery next to a picture made of pieces of red felt and cotton wool glued to a card which said, 'Happy Christmas Mummy'. Alexa ran back to the living room to be with Kyle, who was watching *Andy's Wild Workouts* on CBeebies. Andy wore a bright pink sweatband and wristbands. He looked like a throwback to a Jane Fonda fitness video. Kyle copied Andy, and Alexa copied Kyle.

The chicken pasta bake was ready to go in the oven when she heard footsteps outside on the balcony. It would be Mr Mahoney. He knocked on the door and she let him in. He was carrying a Tupperware container.

'Hello,' said the caretaker. 'I hope I'm not too early?'

'No, not at all. Bang on time as usual. Cup of tea?'

The caretaker sat down at the kitchen table. Although he was not very tall, he was stocky and looked like the Hulk sitting on a children's chair. It looked like it could buckle at any moment. She made him a cup of Typhoo, stewed with three sugars. Builder's tea.

'Would you like a cow biscuit?' she said, offering him the packet.

'No, thank you. You're very kind, very kind. I've bought you some cake. Coffee and walnut tea loaf. It was one of Sinead's favourites.'

The Great British Bake Off had been his wife's favourite TV programme and, inspired by Mary Berry, she had baked a fresh cake every week. When she became too ill to bake, he picked up where she left off. For a man who had spent most of his life knee-deep in mud and bitumen, he had mastered the challenge of a well-turned-out Bakewell tart, without a soggy bottom. With fingers like fat pork sausages, he opened the lid of the plastic box and placed the cake in front of Claire like one of the Magi offering a gift to the infant Jesus.

'Wow! That's impressive, Mr Mahoney!' said Claire looking at the immaculately risen sponge cake, iced with butter cream and decorated with walnuts. 'I could never do that in a million years.'

'Sure you could, sure you could. It's just a little love and some patience. Get two plates and we'll go and see what those morons on *The Chase* are up to today.'

Claire sat in the Arne Jacobsen chair and Mr Mahoney squeezed himself between Kyle and Alexa on the sofa, the prime viewing spot. The children cuddled into him. He was the closest thing they had to a dad and they found comfort in the warmth of his chunky hand-knitted cardigan with holes in the elbows. It had the smell of old man. He put his arms around them and smiled. It was like being hugged by a gap-toothed bear. The intro music started and Bradley Walsh introduced the day's four contestants.

'Hi, I'm Barry and I'm a bricklayer from Dunstable.'

'Hello, I'm Katie and I'm a retired credit control clerk from North Shields.'

'I'm Nigel and I restore pre-war classic vehicles.'

'Hi there. I'm Annette and I'm a nurse working for the Blood Transfusion Service.'

Claire and Mr Mahoney introduced themselves to Bradley in the same way they did every night.

'My name is Claire and I'm an unemployed single mum with two kids and no prospects so the odd ten grand would come in very useful.'

'And I'm Mr Mahoney, a retired road digger from Cork who cleans up other people's crap in West London.'

Mr Mahoney had been right, it wasn't The Governess. Tonight's chaser was The Beast. A man only slightly smaller than Mr Mahoney took his seat at the top of the illuminated ladder. He looked menacing.

'Oh, he's very good, very smart,' said Mr Mahoney. 'I think The Beast might be the cleverest of all.'

And so he was. Soon Barry, Nigel and Annette were all eliminated, returning penniless to their bricks, cars and haemoglobin. With every wrong answer, Mr Mahoney shouted at the screen, giving the right answer in most cases. It all depended on Katie to pocket £8,000 but the Beast hunted her down mercilessly and she went home with nothing.

'Another cheap show,' said Mr Mahoney. 'The Beast earned his money tonight. I suppose I'd better be going. You've got these little ones to feed and get ready for bed and I have a dinner to put in the microwave.'

'You're always welcome. The cake was delicious, one of your best.'

The chicken pasta bake turned out well. Not as impressive as Gavin's 'tarmac' encrusted tuna but all the plates were clean. Claire put the children to bed, read them their stories and kissed them goodnight. She sat in her chair and turned on the television. *Holby City* was on. It was the same plot every week. Jac Naylor, the waspish cardiothoracic genius, was putting someone's heart into someone else to save their life. She did it every week, so there wasn't much point in watching, and Claire switched off.

She flicked through her record collection. It wasn't a night for Frank and she didn't know what to choose. Nothing seemed to fit her mood. Eventually, she pulled out *Madame Butterfly*, Maria Callas and Herbert von Karajan. She didn't have much to thank Jack for. Two kids and an STI was about the sum of it. But he had taken her to Covent Garden to see *Madame Butterfly* when they were students and, although they were seated in the gods, the beauty of the venue, the music and being in love with Jack had been enough to light a fire inside her. That night, she felt like Julia Roberts in *Pretty Woman* when Richard Gere flies her to the opera in his private jet and she cries. Jack hadn't given her a diamond necklace, and they had caught the number 29 bus home, but her feelings that night were the same as Julia's. The stylus clicked and Maria Callas began to sing in the way that only she could. Pain in every groove.

Apart from the children and her record collection, only two other things survived from her marriage. Her wedding album and her portfolio from Saint Martins. They were kept under the glass coffee table as instruments of torture to be used in moments of self-flagellation. She took out the black portfolio binder, its covers tied with red satin ribbon. She undid the bows, opened the folder and flicked through the pieces of fabric and the pencil sketches of her designs. She was halfway through her second year when she became pregnant with Kyle. Despite chronic morning sickness, she managed to complete the year before getting married in the summer. She was on course for a First and was considered one of the best students in her class by her tutors. Miles better than Jack. Three of her designs made it into that year's catwalk show and two had been bought by someone from *Made in Chelsea*. The money went towards their wedding.

Although she returned for her final year, she only lasted two months before dropping out in November to give birth to Kyle at University College Hospital. Saint Martins said she could return at any time to take her final year and graduate, but she never did. She looked at the sketches, the lines, the curves, the detail. Everything had come out of her head, her imagination, her brain. The future she had planned for herself was in every line and every thread. It now sat in a tatty folder in a damp flat in Kensal Mansions. Maria started to sing 'Un bel dì vedremo' ('one fine day, we shall see') and Claire started to sob. Opportunity and hope had gone. There weren't many fine days now.

It was Tuesday, 14 January 2020.

Chapter 5

DINNER IN BEIRUT

Marcus checked his inventory of clean clothes. If he had to work the weekend, he would need to go to Selfridges. The flat had a washing machine but it had never been used. He put on his slippers. Marcus was a big fan of slippers.

The doorbell rang and he looked through the peephole. A distorted image of his neighbour filled the lens and he opened the door.

'Hi Gavin. Everything okay?'

'Evening Marcus. You haven't forgotten dinner tonight, have you? I hadn't heard from you so thought I would check. You're still coming, aren't you?'

'Fuck me. I'm so sorry. I meant to text you but I've had an absolute shitter of a day. Of course I'm coming. Highlight of my week!' He felt guilty. All the crap with Mason Sherwin had distracted him. 'Normal time? Eight o'clock? Just give me time to ring Alice and freshen up?'

'No problem. Come over when you're done.'

Marcus closed the door, sat on the sofa and picked up his phone.

'Hi Al. It's me. Everything okay at home?'

'Hi Marcus. Things are all fine here. Tennis and Pilates were good and then I went for coffee with Theresa. She's not great at the moment.'

'Oh really? Why's that?'

Marcus wasn't really interested in Theresa. She was the one putting daft ideas about body enhancements into his wife's head. One day, he would get home and Alice would look like Donatella Versace.

'She's convinced Mike's having an affair. She found another phone in the boot of his car. She hasn't confronted him yet. And they haven't had sex for over three months.'

'Well, he did own a telecommunications business. Finding a phone isn't the most incriminating piece of evidence is it?'

Marcus was shocked to learn of his wife and Theresa discussing sex lives. He hoped Alice was more discreet about theirs. The last thing he wanted was Theresa and Mike knowing about his handcuffs and ice cream fantasy.

'Yes, that's what I told her. Anyway, how was your day?' said Alice.

'Pretty grim. Those partners are just the biggest bunch of wankers. They don't care about anything but themselves. And my client is a bullying wanker too. I think I'll have to work this weekend, or at least part of it.'

He heard Alice yawn at the end of the phone. He knew what she would be thinking: that she'd heard it all before, just another typical 'Marcus day'.

'So, will you be staying in London for the rest of the week?'

'Don't know yet. I'll let you know. Perhaps you would like to come up and stay at the flat? We could do something together on Saturday evening? Dinner? Theatre?'

'I don't think so, Marcus. There's a lot here that needs doing in the house. Anyway, we shouldn't leave Libby on her own.'

Her feeble excuses annoyed him.

'She's eighteen for fuck's sake and it's only one night! I don't think a serial killer is on the loose in Weybridge. Why don't you just come out and say it? You hate the flat, don't you? Just because it hasn't got a fucking Quooker or an Aga. Anyway, I've got to go soon, I'm having dinner with Gavin. He's cooking.'

Alice only knew Gavin by name, but thought he sounded better company than her husband's work colleagues. She had met them a few times and shared her husband's dislike of them. Their partners were even worse.

'Oh, that's nice for you. What are you having?'

'I don't know but I'm sure it will be good. He's a very good cook. I'd better go then. Bye.'

He looked out at Beirut. Even in the dark of winter, he could still make out the silhouettes of the cranes and diggers. Nothing changed from one week to the next. Earth was moved from one side of the site to the other and then back again. It wasn't worth changing out of his slippers, Gavin's flat was only ten feet across the carpeted hallway. He took a bottle of wine out of the fridge and closed his front door behind him. He walked across the hall and rang the bell. From inside, he could hear classical music. He guessed it was Mozart.

Gavin opened the door with a smile. He was immaculately dressed as always. Cashmere V-neck pullover, black Armani jeans and a pair of navy suede Tod's driving slippers. Not the typical attire of an underpaid social worker.

'Hi Marcus. Come in.'

Gavin's flat was immaculate in a minimalist style. Nothing was out of place. It was probably inhabited by pixies and goblins who tidied it when he was out. It was expensively furnished from Roche Bobois and designer shops in the Kings Road. Marcus and Gavin had moved in at the same time, just as the flats were being finished by the builder. Gavin had the fitted kitchen ripped out and a new Poggenpohl one installed, complete with a Quooker. His flat was bigger than Marcus's, with a separate living room and another bedroom. Marcus had never known Gavin to have guests to stay. The living room was big enough to accommodate a baby grand piano complete with photographs of his family in silver frames. Marcus had often heard him. He was very accomplished.

They walked into the open-plan kitchen, where all the ingredients were laid out in little glass bowls, meticulously prepared as if it were a TV cookery programme.

'What can I get you to drink?' said Gavin. 'Gin and tonic? Wine?'

'A white wine would be great,' said Marcus. 'Thank you.'

Gavin poured two glasses and set about slicing and dicing as Marcus sat on one of the chrome bar stools at the island. The table was already laid. Villeroy & Boch glasses, Robert Welch cutlery and Vista Alegre plates.

'Mozart?' said Marcus, motioning to the background music.

'Chopin,' said Gavin. 'Unmistakeable. You don't mind if I cook while we talk, do you?' he said politely.

'No, not at all. You'll make someone a lovely wife one day.'

Watching Gavin gave Marcus an inferiority complex. He chopped things rapidly like a professional and did that tossing thing with a frying pan that all the best chefs could. Whenever Marcus attempted it, bits went all over the hob.

'Have a cheese straw and some harissa hummus,' said Gavin.

'Homemade?' said Marcus.

Gavin laughed.

'No! Straight from The Temple, I'm afraid. Didn't have time to make the puff pastry! The hummus is homemade though. How was your day?'

Marcus sighed and took a slurp of wine.

'Usual crap. People fighting over fees like dogs with a bone. It's hard to imagine a more dysfunctional group if you tried.'

'Aren't you supposed to be a partnership?'

Marcus took another slurp of wine and gagged.

'Are you fucking joking me? That's the last thing we are. When times are tough, like they are now, it's every man for himself. Shit on someone before they shit on you.'

'But you must be good at it or you wouldn't have lasted this long. You must be doing something right? Who are you shitting on then?'

'Nobody, I hope. Believe me, it's not much fun going to work every day knowing you're only doing it for the money. I'm like a hooker in a suit.'

Gavin seared the sumac-crusted tuna steaks, put them on the plates and carried them to the table where the herbed bulgur wheat, courgette and pomegranate salad was waiting. He always used linen napkins, another small touch of refinement. Over dinner, Marcus confessed how he had fallen out of love with The Firm. Gavin listened and nodded in the right places. Another bottle of Sancerre was opened.

'How old are you now, Marcus?'

'Fifty-five on the twenty-second of March. What's that got to do with it?'

'Give it up if you hate it so much? Do something else instead. Maybe it's about time you did something different?'

'Like what? What can I do? The Firm steals your soul and pays you back with expensive dinners, second homes in Provence and a new Range Rover every year. It's like a drug. Once you start taking it, you can't stop, even though you know it's killing you.'

Gavin butted in.

'Marcus, stop being melodramatic! Some of the people I see every day are real drug addicts or former drug addicts. Just like me. Getting yourself off heroin is a bit different to not having the latest Range Rover. You're living in a different world in your little cocoon of overpaid privilege!'

'Says the social worker living in a million-pound apartment with a baby grand piano! Bit hypocritical, don't you think?'

Marcus regretted his sniping comment instantly.

'Don't be crass, Marcus. My personal circumstances have got nothing to do with my job or why I do it. All my cases want me to do is listen to their problems, help them and make their shitty lives a bit better. They couldn't give a monkey's arse about where I live or how much money I have or don't have. They just want some care and kindness.'

His response jarred. The only thing The Firm gave him was money. Caring and kindness weren't in his job description.

'So, who have you helped today then?' said Marcus, lowering his voice. 'I'm genuinely interested, not being flippant. Honestly.'

Marcus looked across the table at his friend. He was smart, charismatic, charming and cooked like a god. The tuna was outstanding, pink and cooked to perfection. Gavin could have been successful at anything. He looked relaxed, comfortable in his own moisturised and glowing skin. What did he have that Marcus didn't?

'Well, if you really want to know, I visited a Sudanese family made homeless by the Grenfell Tower fire and helped them complete their third application for rehousing. I had an appointment with a family whose sixteen-year-old son has just been released from a youth detention centre about getting him back into school. He's a bright kid who got mixed up in a bad crowd. He did six months in Feltham Young Offenders Institution.'

'For doing what?' said Marcus.

'Joy riding expensive cars! Nothing too shabby either. Porsches, Ferraris. Got done for doing 135 miles per hour down the M40 in a BMW M5. It was his third offence too. He has to wear a tag now.'

'Lucky my M5 is in the underground car park. Good taste in cars though. Will schools take him back?'

'We hope so. He's not stupid, far from it. Then I visited a single mum who, this time last year, wanted to commit suicide, and nearly got herself into trouble for shoplifting in Tesco Express yesterday. She has spent her Universal Credit for the month and is struggling to raise two small kids on her own in a damp flat where she can only afford to have the heating on for a few hours a day. So, that was my day!'

Marcus's thoughts turned to James and Olivia, raised in the safe, leafy comfort of Weybridge, benefitting from all the benefits of a private education and every support from their parents. Their only worry was whether they had two foreign holidays a year or three.

'Must be pretty hard, trying to raise two kids on your own?'

'It is, and she's doing an amazing job. She's only twenty-five, her kids are five and three and she's doing everything she can to bring them up in the right way. I really like her. She invited me for dinner tonight. If I hadn't been having dinner with you, I would now be having chicken and pasta bake.'

'Maybe she fancies you?' said Marcus. 'Probably better company than me. At least she doesn't continually moan about her job.'

'I don't think she's my type,' said Gavin. 'And your company isn't so bad. I told her about you today, I said you were quirky. She's very sweet. Come on. Let's clear away.'

Within minutes, everything had been put in the dishwasher and the surfaces wiped with Mr Muscle. The midnight pixies would adjust anything that wasn't in its right place. Marcus looked at his watch. It was 10.30.

'Would you like a coffee or tea?' said Gavin.

'That's kind of you, but I'll have to say no. I've got an early start in the morning. I'll probably have to answer a few emails as well before bed. Mason Sherwin, the man who never sleeps.'

Marcus walked along the hall to the front door and stopped.

'Just one thing? Have you seen or read anything about a mystery bug in

China? I read about it in last night's *Evening Standard*. It's some new strain of flu or pneumonia virus they don't recognise. It's been on my mind since yesterday.'

Gavin shook his head.

'No, I haven't seen a thing. The Chinese are always getting things like this.'

He placed a reassuring hand on Marcus's shoulder and opened the front door.

'See you next week. No need to go mad, something plain and simple will do. Seared foie gras with apples poached in Sauternes will be fine. Try not to worry too much about work either. I'm sure it will be okay.'

'Thanks. Food tonight was delicious and the chat was really helpful. You might want to add me to your case list? Sad, middle-aged, corporate fucker losing the will to live!'

Gavin laughed as his friend took the ten steps across the hall in his slippers and opened his front door. He turned and waved. Marcus double locked the door, went into the living room and slumped into the sofa. Eight more emails from Mason, a timesheet reminder, three lots of 'value-driven insight' and another warning of non-compliance for not completing his 'Embracing Diversity' training.

He checked WhatsApp. A message from Alice.

Hi M. If u r wrking this wknd, might go 2 PHP wth T. Libby going 2 stay wth frnd.

Lots more smiling yellow faces. Marcus misread her text and thought it said, 'if you're wanking this weekend'. That was the problem with text speak. It didn't matter if he was working or wanking, Alice and Theresa now would be having volcanic mud smeared on their bodies at PHP, which was Alice-speak for Pennyhill Park, the luxurious spa and hotel a few miles away from Weybridge.

He stared out of the balcony window on to Beirut. An urban fox was slinking stealthily across the ground, feeding off scraps left by the construction workers. Another animal living on its wits in the city. His thoughts turned to Claire, the single mother, alone in her damp flat with her two children, trying to keep her head above water. Was she that different to him? Her dreams hadn't come true, while his had become tarnished and dirty.

He went to the bathroom and stared at himself in the mirror. He was looking at the face of a stranger, a person he didn't recognise. He lay down on the bed, staring up at the red lights on the top of the cranes. If he stared at them for long enough, he would fall asleep.

It was Tuesday, 14 January 2020.

Chapter 6

THE ETHICAL DILEMMA

The rest of his week was spent locked in a project room. Unlike the lavish client suites in The Firm's new offices, project rooms were the equivalent of solitary confinement in a Gulag. No windows, cheap furniture and the suffocating atmosphere of stagnant air, warmed by the exhaled breath of consultants, their overheating laptops and the smell of last night's Deliveroo. In the middle of the central table was a bird's nest of power and network cables connecting the team to each other and to the outside world, a world they couldn't see.

The Spearmint team had regrouped on Wednesday morning to re-plan the timetable to meet Espina's accelerated deadline. The team wore a washed out look that said they would rather be anywhere else but there. The missing data had arrived on Thursday morning. Marcus knew someone's career at Espina was over or in terminal decline. He split the team into two, one for Safewear and one for TuffTogs, and fired the starting gun to commence the analysis of tables of data, testing hypotheses, developing conclusions and building insights. There was only one objective, to give the client the answer he wanted.

The team agreed the storyboard, the number of 'insight' slides they would need, who would do what, and by when. It didn't require much creativity. The Firm had a prescribed template for its reports. It was simply a case of filling in the blanks with new numbers and drawing new conclusions. For the inflated fees, clients expected a made-to-measure Savile Row suit. Instead, they got an off-the-peg from M&S. The team worked around the clock, starting in darkness and finishing in darkness.

Marcus received his final reminder to complete his mandatory 'Embracing Diversity' training or face retribution from Risk and Compliance. He logged on to SCORE, The Firm's cloud-based, online training tool and selected the module. Five scenarios with a multiple-choice exam at the end which had to be passed. He pressed 'Start' and the module opened. Bad soft rock music and flashing images of The Firm's new logo and tagline set against a backdrop of its diverse workforce, young, athletic and photogenic. Marcus contrasted it with the team's partner group, older, white, male and very unfit.

He watched each of the scenarios designed to test his awareness of diversity and how The Firm was embracing it. The scenarios were acted out by professional actors and he felt sorry for them. For every Dame Helen Mirren and Sir Ian McKellen appearing in *Macbeth* at the Old Vic, there were thousands of other jobbing actors trying to make ends meet, playing lead roles in mini-dramas like 'Biased Interview Questions to BAME Candidates' or 'Encroaching on Personal Space at Social Events'.

I suppose it pays the bills, thought Marcus as he watched one actor nodding empathetically at another actor's request for four weeks paternity leave in the module 'Family and Co-Parenting: Demonstrating Our Flexibility'.

It took him three attempts to pass the multiple-choice exam. All the options were ambiguous. The team giggled at his cursing and eventually had to step in to help. It may have been a collective effort but he had passed, keeping the wolves from the door for another year. He booked his place at the mandatory 'Ethics and The Firm: Living and Breathing Our New Values' conference for partners in March and closed SCORE.

While the team was busy poring over historical and projected revenues, direct cost ratios, overheads and cost allocations, he checked The Sequence. Stockwatch was green, up by fifty points on the week, which made him feel good. His health app informed him,

Your average headphone audio levels were loud today.

Of course they were, he thought, *I was listening to the Sex Pistols. What did you expect?*

On WhatsApp, there were messages from Alice and James.

Hi M. Def going to PHP with T. 2 ngts. Back Sun. Sig not gr8. Call u l8er. Love u.

Yellow faces blowing kisses. He was resentful she was spending the weekend with her best friend having her body pampered while he was imprisoned in a smelly box reviewing PowerPoint slides. He opened Alice's WhatsApp profile, a picture taken on safari in Botswana two years earlier. She looked so happy. It had been two weeks away from The Firm and they had rediscovered some of the things they loved about each other.

He opened the message from James. His profile picture was taken at a festival, one arm draped around his best friend and the other around the waist of a girl he had probably never met before nor since.

Hi Dad. Hope all ok with you. Running a bit low on funds atm. Any chance you can send me the £95 for the keyboard? Any extra gratefully received!! Hahaha!!

Marcus opened his banking app and transferred £150. He replied.

Hi James. Have transferred £150. Buy some food. Hope you are working hard. x

His reply was written in hope. James would probably end up spending the extra on drugs and was unlikely to be working hard.

He closed his phone and looked around at the team. None of them had ever worked in a real business, sold anything, built anything or developed anything, but were trying to bring 'insights' to clients who had.

He received a meeting request from Izzy Majewska.

Hi Marcus. Want to set up a deep dive session with you to discuss financials and metrics, to get more granularity on next phase of Spearmint. We need a rapid build out on this if we can. Something needs to move the dial quickly. Looping in Kelvin end of next week. Have a great weekend. Izzy.

Still haven't got a fucking clue what she's on about, he thought. He pressed 'Accept' with a shake of his head.

His phone rang. It was Mason.

'Hi Marcus. Just ringing to see how things are shaping up with the report? Any early thoughts, major showstoppers, red flags?'

Mason never wanted detail, just the headlines.

'Well at least we have some data from Espina now. Probably won't be in a position to have any conclusions until tomorrow afternoon. But you'll be here anyway, won't you?'

There was a silence before Mason's reply.

'I'm hoping to be, but if I'm not we can have a conference call towards the end of the day to go through everything, can't we?'

Marcus had seen it coming a mile away. Mason would be killing pheasants in Sussex while he and the team sacrificed their weekend. He wanted to shoot him with both barrels.

'Why? I thought we agreed we would both be here to support the team? It's a fucking tight deadline, Mason.'

'Unfortunately our nanny has had to go back to Italy. Family crisis. Left us a bit in the lurch with childcare this weekend. I think I'm going to need to lend a hand with running kids around to parties. I'm sure you and the team have got it nailed? You can call me anytime. I'll set up a call for 5 p.m. tomorrow.'

Marcus knew it was a lie. At 5 p.m., bird-slaughter would be over for the day and Mason would be getting drunk in the pub with the other avian murderers. He couldn't be bothered to have it out.

'Fine, we'll speak then.'

Marcus opened Google and entered 'virus deaths in China'. It spat out a list of web pages and he opened each of them in turn. A second man had died in Wuhan and a case of the virus had appeared in the US, a man returning to Washington from Wuhan. Laboratory tests had confirmed it as a new form of a coronavirus. And it had a name, 2019-nCov. Cases had been reported in Thailand and Japan, and the number of cases in China had risen to sixty-two. The World Health Organisation had put out a statement saying, 'It is very clear right now that we have no sustained human-to-human transmission'.

Marcus interrupted the team.

'Sorry everyone, but has anyone been following this mystery virus in China? It's spreading to other countries in South East Asia and there's a case in the US now. Anyone read about this?'

The team looked at him with the blank stares of people who hadn't slept in days. There was a universal shaking of heads. All they were concerned about was filling out templates and formatting tables. They returned to their screens.

At eight o'clock, Marcus called 'time out' as the Deliveroo order was phoned in. Two pad thais, two tandoori mixed grills, two Lebanese hot mezes, two pepperoni pizzas (one with mushrooms), and three crispy ducks with extra hoisin sauce and pancakes. He wanted to add a KFC Family Bucket for himself, but opted for an extra pad thai and a bottle of Peroni. An hour later, the order arrived and the team stopped typing and opened plastic containers, handing out chopsticks and shredding duck with plastic forks and spoons.

At 11.30, the team wearily started to close down their laptops and unwind the cable spaghetti. Most of them would be working into the early hours of the morning at home. The debris from the Deliveroo order was crammed into a couple of bins. One of the young managers spooned a blob of congealed hoisin sauce on to a dried out pancake together with a few duck crumbs, rolled it up and stuffed it into his mouth in a single bite.

'See you all tomorrow,' he mumbled and walked to the lift.

By the time Marcus got back to Beirut, it was past midnight. Alice was probably discussing Theresa's next cosmetic procedure or more evidence to prove Mike's infidelity.

He was greeted by George, Eric's deputy, who did evenings and weekends. George was Bulgarian and spent the night watching YouTube videos on his iPad. He took the lift to the second floor and walked along the corridor. Gavin's flat was silent, not even a soporific sonata disturbing the peace. He lay down on the sofa and kicked off his shoes. His thoughts were dominated by the mystery virus. At least it had a name now.

* * *

He woke at the usual time, made a coffee and sat at the breakfast bar in his dressing gown, staring out at Beirut. The windows were cloudy from the dust, like they had cataracts. The traffic on Queensway was already busy, delivery vans dropping off fresh supplies to restaurants and fast-food outlets. It was still early on Saturday morning and he decided to take a walk in Kensington Gardens to clear his head and get his step count up. After walking around the pond twice, he walked back to the Bayswater Road and entered the Underground. Twenty minutes later, he was outside Bank station and walking to the office. The City at weekends was a ghost town. Pubs, bars and restaurants which throbbed during the week, noisy with conversations about money, were closed and silent. It had an eerie feel, as if everyone had died.

He walked through the revolving doors. OnYouGo was closed. For once, he didn't have to wait ten minutes for a lift. One was waiting and he took it to the ninth floor. The air in the project room was still thick with the smells from last night's takeaway and he took the litter bins and propped the door open. Two members of the team were already in, laptops powered up and keyboards being tapped by nimble fingers. Early morning insights.

Gradually, the rest of the team shuffled in with differing interpretations of smart casual and an ambivalence to shaving. Weekend stubble was acceptable. Marcus gathered the team and agreed a plan for the day. Multiple heads nodded simultaneously like the dog in the Churchill Insurance ads. They all knew the drill and the wheels of the machine started to crank. Slowly at first, but by lunchtime output was building and the shape of the report was forming.

For the next few hours, Marcus reviewed outputs, marked up pages, suggested changes and cracked the odd joke to lighten the mood. In mid-afternoon, Steve Pettigrew approached him.

'Have you got a second, Marcus?'

'Sure. Pull up a chair.'

'I've been going through the cashflows for Safewear and TuffTogs. In the past twelve months, there have been three intercompany transfers from Safewear to TuffTogs. Ten million pounds each time. TuffTogs has been running out of cash. I think the business has more problems than they're letting on. Without Safewear, TuffTogs would be going tits up.'

Steve laid some slides out in front of Marcus and continued.

'So why does Espina want to sell Safewear when it's already propping up TuffTogs? The TuffTogs systems are outdated, it's dependent on Safewear for most of its back office support. It would cost a shedload of money to get TuffTogs to stand on its own two feet. What do you think?'

Marcus looked at the graphs and the tables of data that the team had prepared. The director's conclusions were sound.

'This is all about politics. If they sell Safewear, they'll return some money to shareholders which will get them off their backs. They can use the rest of the cash to invest in TuffTogs. Don't forget Jim Ibbotson and Derek Bentley are both from TuffTogs. They're not going to admit the part of the business they're from is shit, are they?'

'But it's a big heap of shit!' said Steve.

The Ethical Dilemma was starting to take shape. Jim Ibbotson wanted The Firm to confirm selling Safewear was the right thing to do. In return, The Firm would get more fees helping Espina to sell Safewear. Everyone would be winners.

One hour before the call with Mason, the team took Marcus through the draft report. The conclusion was the same. Espina was like the runaway train in the film *The Taking of Pelham 123*, running headlong towards the buffers at 100 miles per hour, with a madman at the controls. At 5 p.m., Mason joined the call. In the background, they could hear the guffawing of bellicose men downing their beers, celebrating a good day's killing.

'Sounds like quite a kids' party, Mason,' said Marcus sarcastically. 'I hope they're not drinking alcohol with their jelly and ice cream?'

'Hahaha! No. It's just the magician. So how's everything going with Spearmint?'

'Making good progress. I've sent you a copy of the draft report as it stands, but I expect you haven't had time to look at it if you're playing musical chairs?'

'No, I haven't, but I will do,' said Mason defensively. 'I'll look at it tonight. So what's our elevator pitch to Jim?'

'Elevator pitch'. Marcus hated the nonsensical phrase that was used liberally throughout The Firm. He went for the one floor answer.

'Don't fucking do it. How's that for an elevator pitch?'

The team all looked at each other and grinned. There was no better spectator sport than watching two partners butting heads.

'What do you mean, don't fucking do it?' said Mason.

'Exactly as I said, don't fucking do it. Selling Safewear is a colossal mistake. TuffTogs is a crock of shite and it's only Safewear that's keeping it afloat. Something doesn't smell right here and I'm guessing Jim Ibbotson is behind it.'

The team talked Mason through their analysis. It pointed to one thing. TuffTogs was a crock of shite.

'So what do you think?' said Marcus.

There was a long silence before Mason replied.

'I think we're going to need to manage our stakeholders very carefully. Very carefully indeed.'

'And what do you mean by that?' said Marcus rhetorically.

'Do I have to spell it out to you, Marcus? Right now, Spearmint is the only show in town. There's somewhere between five and ten million pounds for The Firm if this deal goes ahead. Jim Ibbotson wants it to happen, Kelvin and I want it to happen and you should want it to happen too, Marcus.'

'By doing what? Not telling the truth?'

'No, by being a little more creative with the truth. Build some different scenarios, give Jim some options, put some sensitivities on the numbers. Let's have another call tomorrow to flesh this out. In the meantime, I'll drop Jim a note to start managing his expectations.'

'Managing expectations' was more bollocks. It was 'consultant speak' for preparing the client for the shock of not getting the answer they wanted while offering some hope that they might.

'Fine. You do that. We'll continue working the numbers, but it's not going to be easy putting a shine on this turd.'

Over the next six hours, the team redrafted the report, building different scenarios and shifting numbers. Smoke and mirrors in action. An exhausted team left the project room at midnight, taking cabs and Ubers home to loved ones who were already asleep. Marcus took a black cab through the bright lights of the West End, pavements thronging with Saturday night drinkers, diners and theatregoers. Everyone else was having a great time. Marcus couldn't muster the enthusiasm to talk to his cab driver. He paid the fare, collected the receipt and walked into reception. George was watching YouTube, his face illuminated by his tablet like Boris Karloff in *Frankenstein*.

'Late night again Mr Barlow?' said George, looking up from his screen.

'Too late George. Good night. See you tomorrow.'

He didn't set an alarm but was woken by a message arriving in his inbox. He reached for his phone and opened Outlook. It was 7.20. The message was from Mason.

The Creep that Never Sleeps, thought Marcus. He read the message.

Ref: Spearmint. M, spoke with Kelvin last night. He is very concerned we are not positioning ourselves well for the next phase. Wants a call at 09.00 this morning to discuss. Will send an invite. Regards M.

His day was off to a bad start and he hadn't put his slippers on yet. He made a bowl of porridge with honey. The honey had crystallised in its little squeezable bottle and he had to scoop out the crystals with a teaspoon. It annoyed him the way honey did that. Millions of years of evolution and bees couldn't produce long-life honey. Maybe cows were smarter than they looked?

He rang Alice. It had been two days since they had spoken. She was getting ready for breakfast after her sunrise yoga class. She listened sympathetically.

'When are you coming home? Tonight?' she said.

'I don't think so. Could be another late one. What about you? Having a good time?'

'Yes, all good. I have a Swedish massage booked after breakfast. We'll probably go for a swim and a sauna, have lunch and then head back.'

He was tempted to say something sarcastic about the strain of her Sunday compared to the colonic irrigation he was likely to suffer at the hands of Kelvin McBride but, with few friends in the world, pissing off his wife wasn't going to help.

'Okay. Enjoy the rest of your day then. I'll try to call later.'

There was a pause before she spoke.

'Marcus?'

'What?'

'You're our rock, you know? You keep us all going. Don't let this stuff at work drag you down. It's not worth it.'

He had enough time to make another coffee before joining the call. Mason would be having kedgeree and a glass of champagne before another day of killing and Kelvin would be at the golf club. He joined the conference call. A conversation was already in progress.

'Morning Marcus,' said Mason. 'Kelvin and I were just sharing our thoughts on Spearmint, weren't we Kelvin?'

'Hi Marcus. Mason's given me the heads-up on this but you're closest to it. What do you think?'

Kelvin's interest in his view was a smokescreen. He had already made up his mind and was going through the motions.

'As I explained to Mason last night, everything points to Espina making a colossal mistake if they sell Safewear. Derek Bentley and Jim Ibbotson are leading the Board up the garden path and they want us to rubber stamp it for them.'

'So what would you recommend?' said Kelvin. 'I'm playing devil's advocate here, keeping an open mind.'

Like fuck you are, thought Marcus.

'We should write the report showing the facts as they stand. If they sell Safewear, Espina will be dead in the water within two years, if not sooner.'

Marcus could hear Mason's sighs of exasperation in the background.

'Perhaps it's not as black and white as you're making it sound, Marcus? Couldn't we be more creative and give Jim some scenarios which would give him more options?' said Kelvin.

'Fudge the numbers, you mean?' He knew what Kelvin meant. 'Don't you think it's about integrity and telling the truth, Kelvin? "Doing It With You" and all that good stuff?'

Kelvin's temper snapped like a nine-iron hitting a tree trunk.

'Don't give me all that "integrity and values" bullshit. Get fucking real, Marcus. There's potentially £10 million on the table here and we're not exactly flush with work right now. So, I suggest you, Mason and the team start getting creative with the truth!'

There was little point in arguing. Kelvin probably had a tee-off time in fifteen minutes and wanted to practise his putting. The discussion was over.

'I get the message. We'll restructure the report to make it less specific and provide Espina with a series of options.'

Having got his own way, Kelvin tried to smooth things over.

'Look Marcus, if Espina does fuck up, that's down to them. We don't make the decisions, we just give them the options. Clients are always fucking up because they're stupid. That's why we're in our business and not in theirs. Mason, anything you want to add?'

Mason had been silent throughout the call. He had already done his talking to Kelvin offline.

'No Kelvin, nothing to add. Great call. I think we're all aligned now. You and I can speak later Marcus when we have a new turn of the deck.'

Hope someone shoots you in the back, you little weasel, thought Marcus.

In the project room, Marcus briefed the team on his latest conversation. They all knew the score and set about moving numbers around to tell the story Jim Ibbotson wanted. By five o'clock, Marcus had an eighty-page report in front of him. A work of art and fiction. The Firm made fiction look like art. Immaculately formatted tables, charts and graphs, and a narrative written in six-point font, making it impossible to read without a magnifying glass. All decorated with meaningless icons like baubles on a Christmas tree.

An hour later the team gathered around the star-phone. It was Mason who spoke first.

'Hi everyone. The updated deck looks really good. Much more in line with what Jim is looking for.'

The team walked Mason through the report, explaining how and where they had been creative with the truth.

'I'll send through my mark-ups in the next hour. I really think we're in a great position to help them get this over the line.'

'Mark-ups' were the way partners added value. Scrawly writing in red or green ink indicating, along with numerous arrows, the re-ordering of bullet points and the changing of words to best deliver 'the story'. Mark-ups never added new content or fresh insights, they simply re-ordered the ones already there.

'Okay, let's make these final changes and send it to DP to work on overnight. We'll send it to Jim Ibbotson at lunchtime tomorrow. We should be done here by ten and we can all go home,' said Marcus.

Document Production, or DP, was The Firm's in-house printing and report production centre. It was the most profitable part of the business. For highly inflated costs, DP would make sure bullet points aligned, meaningless icons were inserted and 'Doing It With You' was emblazoned on every slide. The report would look great and that's what clients paid for. Very expensive smoke and mirrors. At 10.15, Steve Pettigrew sent Marcus the final version, 'Project Spearmint Phase 1 Draft Report v.93.6 FINAL'.

'That's it, Marcus,' said Steve, closing down his laptop. 'Nothing more we can do tonight. DP will send it back in the morning and we can have one final look. It's a real work of art.'

The team made their way out of the office and into a fleet of waiting Toyota Priuses, the Uber Armada taking them home to their loved ones. In a little over seven hours, the City would be a bustling hive again. Thousands of worker bees ready to turn their PowerPoint pollen into financial honey.

* * *

Marcus was at his desk in the pool area eating his porridge with raisins and honey. It was the normal Monday morning chatter, people talking about their weekends, skiing trips, breaks in the Cotswolds, Sunday lunches with their families. Words of commiseration were given for the Spearmint team, who had been locked in a project room. If it was the Spearmint team this weekend, it would be another bunch of poor souls the next. Marcus watched the other partners joking and laughing. Mason was simulating shooting pheasants to Tom Irons and Jacob Mauser.

Like hell you were running your kids to birthday parties, you slimy fucker, he thought.

Document Production returned the finished report at 9.30 a.m. It looked so impressive, it seemed a shame to open it. Marcus sent an email to Jim Ibbotson attaching a PDF copy of the report.

Subject: Project Spearmint – Phase 1 Draft Report
From: Marcus Barlow

Dear Jim
Hope you had a good weekend. Please find attached copy of the Project Spearmint Phase 1 Report (Draft) for your review. Mason and I look forward to discussing it with you on our call.
Best regards
    Marcus

He disliked the 'best regards' sign off, it was hypocritical on both sides. Jim Ibbotson had no regard for The Firm and it had no regard for him.

With fifteen minutes before the call, Marcus checked the latest news about the mystery virus. Further cases had been identified in China, and new cases in Malaysia, Singapore and South Korea. The China National Health Commission had confirmed two medical staff had been infected in Guangdong province and the virus could be transmitted by humans. Marcus put down his biodegradable cutlery and stared out of the window. Flu outbreaks were always happening in Asia, but it was the first time the word 'epidemic' had been used.

The call with Espina was imminent, so he closed Google.

He put his unfinished salad in the EcoPod's recycling bin and walked to the Idea Bubble that Mason had booked for the call. A copy of the report was open on the desk. It had red pen all over it.

'Hi Mason. Ready to go?'

'Yes. I can't see any of the mark-ups I made last night. Any reason they haven't been included?'

'Well, it's nothing personal, if that's what you mean. We felt the report tells a better story as it stands. More creative with the truth, as you put it.'

The report did look better and it was personal. Marcus resented Mason for lying about his shooting weekend.

'How do you want to play the call?'

'I'm happy to top and tail but you're closest to the detail,' said Mason. 'Oh, Marcus, just one more thing?'

'What's that?'

'Try to remember the bigger picture, what we discussed with Kelvin yesterday? There's a lot of money on the table. Don't blow it by saying something dumb.'

'Like the truth? I know what you mean, I get it.'

The star-phone beeped announcing Jim Ibbotson's arrival. Mason 'topped' with the usual pleasantries, a mixture of sycophantic arse-kissing and scene setting, listening carefully to the client's needs, working flat out against a tight deadline and combining quality and creativity to achieve the right outcome for Espina. Fluff. Mason handed over to Marcus for the detail.

'Afternoon Jim. I doubt we're going to get further than the exec summary so I'll take you through the key findings. Happy to have a follow up with your team after this?'

Jim grunted his approval.

'Well, the report certainly looks good but that's what I'm paying you people for,' he said begrudgingly.

Jim Ibbotson didn't want detail, he just wanted the right answer. For the next forty-five minutes, Marcus explained the key findings, exploring different options and scenarios to give Espina maximum flexibility. The CFO asked the occasional question but nothing Marcus couldn't answer. He covered all the financial and operational implications of selling Safewear before Jim interrupted him.

'So, do you think it's a good idea to sell Safewear?'

Mason shifted nervously in his chair and twiddled with his pen. Marcus thought it was a good time to throw him a hospital pass.

'I think Mason is best placed to answer that one, Jim. He's on top of the strategic angle.'

Mason scowled at him. He knew Jim Ibbotson would press him for an answer and played for time.

'Well, I think Espina has a range of scenarios to consider. Each of them comes with their own opportunities and risks,' said Mason.

It was the sort of answer The Firm trained its partners to give. Lots of nice words which didn't answer the question. But Jim Ibbotson was a dog with a bone.

'Yes, I can see that, but the report doesn't tell me if selling Safewear is the right thing to do or not? What do you actually think?'

Mason nervously started drawing three-dimensional boxes in his Smythson notebook. He looked across the table and returned the pass.

'Well, I'd like to bring Marcus back in here. I'm not sure this is about strategy, more about the numbers?'

Inside, Mason was panicking. He had passed the baton. If Marcus dropped it, a large pile of fees could evaporate with one slip of a candid tongue. The Ethical Dilemma was out of his hands.

'Jim, I have to be honest with you …' said Marcus. Mason's heart started to palpitate. '… when we did the initial analysis, everything pointed to the logic of retaining Safewear. It's a stable business generating steady cash flows which can be used to invest in TuffTogs, which does have its challenges, as you are probably aware.'

Jim Ibbotson grunted again. Mason was feeling very uneasy and drew more boxes on his pad.

Marcus continued.

'However, selling Safewear could provide significant funds which could be returned to shareholders, as well as providing investment in TuffTogs to build a stronger and more resilient position in its market. Our report makes these points pretty clearly. I think there is sufficient clarity for you and Derek to make a recommendation to your exco tomorrow.'

Marcus's answer was enough for the irascible CFO. He hadn't said Espina shouldn't sell Safewear and he hadn't said it should either. His ambiguity was convincing. Feeling calmer that Jim hadn't exploded and Marcus hadn't dropped the baton, Mason stopped doodling and did some 'tailing'.

'So, Jim, I think this call has been very helpful to everyone? In terms of next steps, what is the timetable for Spearmint?'

Jim knew exactly what Mason meant and took sadistic pleasure in making him squirm. It had cost Espina £500,000 to get this far and he wanted to let them know.

'You mean, what's the opportunity for you to earn more fees?'

'Well, it's not just about the fees, Jim,' flustered Mason.

'What is it then?'

'Is there anything we can be doing in the background to support you and Derek?'

It was a bullshit answer and Jim knew it. Of course it was about the fees.

'Our exco meeting is tomorrow. The Safewear MD won't take it well, but Derek and I are completely as one on this. We have a board meeting on the fourth of February. If that goes well, the next phase will be a big piece of work which will go out to competitive tender. I'll let you know after tomorrow.'

'Competitive' and 'tender' were two words Mason didn't want to hear. It would all come down to the money. The call ended with the usual pleasantries. Phase 1 of Project Spearmint was over. There had been no collateral damage and a big prize was still on the table. Mason looked up from his notepad.

'I think that went pretty well. Jim seemed happy enough?'

'Yes, he got what he wanted. He and Derek must have another agenda, wanting to sell Safewear but I can't work it out.'

'Shame about the competitive tender bit. Maybe we should start getting a pitch team together to prepare for Phase 2. What do you think?'

Mason's suggestion made sense, but it filled Marcus with dread. The pitch process was one of the most time-consuming activities within The Firm. The merest whiff of fees brought out the worst excesses in its partners.

'Yes, we probably should. Good idea.'

It was starting to get dark outside and he wanted to get home to Twin Gates. He had been away for almost a week and he missed Alice and Olivia. He closed his laptop and slid out of the building into the cool January air, before descending into the warmth of the Central Line and emerging in Queensway.

Eric, the concierge, was back on duty, arranging the Assouline coffee-table books in the foyer with military precision. Nobody ever touched them for fear of disturbing their symmetry. Marcus took the lift to the second floor. No sound from Gavin's flat. He cleared the fridge of its out-of-date contents, a shrivelled lemon, crispy ham, a jar of pesto three weeks past its sell by date and some decomposing salad. The tomatoes would last for another week. He put the dishwasher on and wiped all the surfaces. He packed his bag with his dirty laundry. There was certainly enough to keep Jacinda busy.

He disposed of the rubbish and the recycling. Someone in the flats had thrown their food waste in the bin for glass and plastic recycling. If Eric discovered the culprit they would be punished. His navy-blue BMW M5 was parked in his space next to Gavin's purple Nissan Micra. He had never understood why Gavin had such a small car for such a big man.

The M5's in-car information system lit up, bombarding him with data which meant nothing to him. He scrolled through his playlists, selecting 'Classic New Romantics'. The synthesised, metronomic beat of 'Wishing' by A Flock of Seagulls pulsated through the car's fourteen-speaker sound system.

He called Alice from the car.

'I'm on my way home now. Depending on rush hour, I should be home before six.'

'Would you mind picking up Libby from school, if you're coming that way? She had one of her chemistry mocks this afternoon? I'll text her and tell her to wait for you.'

He had forgotten to wish Olivia luck and he felt awful. She had texted him the previous evening but, with all the nonsense with Spearmint, it had slipped his mind.

'Yes, sure. Text her and let her know. I haven't been to the school for ages.'

It was another page in the book of Being a Crap Dad along with missing Parents Nights, taking calls in the middle of Speech Day, missing James scoring a century or Olivia's solo of 'A Nightingale Sang in Berkeley Square' in the School Concert. Forgetting her exam was another compromise.

'Great, thanks Marcus. See you when you get home.'

The usual traffic jam on the Chertsey Road wasn't too bad and he felt good singing along to Duran Duran's 'Girls on Film'. He remembered dancing to it at a street party in Staines in July 1981 on the day Prince Charles married Lady Diana Spencer. He was sixteen. He wondered where the thirty-nine years had gone and if he had aged better than Simon Le Bon?

He waited in the car park at Olivia's school, looking up at the main building. Twenty thousand pounds a year in fees buys an impressive façade, well-manicured grounds, and turns out charming, confident and gregarious young ladies, fully equipped to deal with the modern world. Olivia was no exception. Marcus looked at his beautiful daughter as she emerged from the main entrance, tall in her navy school uniform, her long blonde hair falling below her shoulders, smiling and laughing with her friends. He got out of the car to greet her and she threw her arms around him.

'Hi Dad, great to see you! This is a nice surprise. How come?'

'Just decided to leave the office early and get home to see my family. It's been a tough week.'

She put her bags in the boot as he opened the passenger door, walked around and got in. 'Don't You Want Me Baby' by the Human League was starting. Olivia looked across at him.

'What's this you're listening to?'

'The Human League. They were massive in the eighties.'

She shook her head and laughed.

'You're such a dinosaur, Dad!'

In the twenty minutes it took to get home, Marcus indulged his daughter's pessimism and listened to all the reasons she had failed her exams. She got it from him. He knew she would have passed with flying colours. The car swung on to the drive and he parked next to Alice's X5. Her tennis bag was still on the back seat. Marcus took his bags out of the boot and went inside. Alice was spiralising courgettes and looked up. She wiped her hands on a tea towel and went over to hug him.

'How was the spa weekend, Al? You look great by the way.'

Marcus looked his wife up and down, not in a pervy way, but simply to check her body was the same as it had been a week ago. Alice did look great, her skin was glowing as if it had been polished with Mr Sheen.

'Thank you, Marcus. That's very kind of you. Sharing a room with Theresa was an experience, for sure. She spends over thirty minutes every night going through her moisturising and cleansing routine. It was like being away with you. And if I have to listen to any more about Mike's alleged affair, I think I'll strangle her.'

'What's the latest on that one? Has he got some twenty-five-year-old Lithuanian bimbo on the side or not?'

'I doubt it. You know how fat Mike is. Nobody's going to let him jump on top of them, not even for a British passport.'

Alice had made a good point. Mike's blubbery girth would crush even the most robust Eastern European physique.

'Maybe it's an affair based on doggy or reverse-cowgirl sex?' he said, trying to be helpful.

'I'd rather not think about it, thank you.'

She returned to spiralising courgettes.

'What's for dinner?'

'Courgetti with lentil ragu,' she said. 'It's one of my *Women's Health* recipes this month.'

'Sounds great.' He had wanted her to say 'lamb chops, chips and baked beans'. On the positive side, Alice did look pleased to see him.

'I'll go upstairs and change then.'

They sat down to eat at 7.30. It was early for him, but Alice liked to get everything washed up and cleared away before 8.30 to give her time to relax. After surviving on a diet of Deliveroo for most of the past week, a tin of cat food would have gone down well. To his surprise, the courgetti with lentil ragu was both appetising and filling. Even Alice's inclusion of enoki mushrooms hadn't spoiled it.

Olivia went upstairs, leaving her parents to clear away. Alice was stacking the dishwasher and Marcus was wiping the granite island.

'Al, have you read any of the stuff about this virus in China? It's spreading rapidly across South East Asia. It's in Japan, Malaysia, Singapore. There's even a case in the US. It's called 2019-nCov. People are dying from it.'

'You asked me this the other day, Marcus. No, I haven't. Why are you obsessing about it?'

'Because I think it's bloody serious and nobody seems to be paying any attention.'

2019-nCoV hadn't made it on to the pages of *Femail*, the *Daily Mail's* women's section, which was much loved by Alice. She was more likely to be well informed about pelvic floor incontinence than a global epidemic.

They switched off the lights in the kitchen and walked into the living room. It was a big room, dominated by a large, stone fireplace. On the rare occasions when they lit the fire, it looked like a scene from a Christmas card. It was a room for the four Barlows, but it could have accommodated fourteen.

Alice switched on the TV. It was a police crime drama with the usual plot. Quirky, rebellious female detective with loyal but dopey male sidekick in pursuit of a psychotic, serial killing paedophile.

In the advert break, Marcus said, 'I think I'm going to work from home tomorrow. I need a break from the office. Lots of people do it now, working from home.'

Alice put down her newspaper and looked across at him.

'But you never work from home, Marcus. You always go into the office or to a client. You've always maintained that it was "skiving from home". What's brought this on?'

'I can't face South Western Trains and those awful people at work. There's a break in my project, so I thought spending some time at home would do me good? See if I could get used to it?'

For the majority of their marriage, Alice and Marcus lived in separate orbits. It suited both of them. The last thing she wanted was a meteorite in the shape of her husband crashing into her planet. She returned to watching a hysterical parent identify their murdered child.

At the end of the crime drama, Alice switched over to BBC One to watch the news. There was nothing new. Brexit tensions, conflict between the US and Iran, Prince Harry leaving for Canada to be with Meghan and Archie. Marcus thought he could have been locked in a time capsule for a week and nothing would have changed.

He looked around the living room and its twenty-five years of memories. Wedding photos, pictures of James and Olivia as babies, toddlers, children, adolescents. Mementoes and artefacts from family holidays. He lay back on the sofa and stared at the ceiling. He was approaching fifty-five years of age. Possibly most of the best years of his life had gone? The Firm had stolen them and he hadn't noticed. And now, there was a killer bug running loose in the world.

He pulled a cushion to his chest and hugged it.

It was Monday, 20 January 2020.

Chapter 7

Skiving from Home

Marcus had pressed the snooze button several times before Alice rolled over. 'Bloody hell, Marcus, are you getting up or not? Make your mind up.'

'I'm working from home today, remember? I don't need to get up early.'

'Then go back to sleep or get up but switch your bloody alarm off.'

His slumber had been broken and now Alice's had too. He got up. It was getting light when he went into the kitchen and looked outside. It was a beautiful garden and the hellebores were flowering. He made a cup of coffee and switched on the television. *BBC Breakfast*. He thought Dan Walker and Louise Minchin were a bit lightweight to give politicians a serious grilling.

The programme was the usual mixture of news, fluff and topicality. Nothing to make the nation choke on its breakfast. Until they showed the scenes of the growing epidemic in China. Thousands of people wearing masks, cities going into lockdown, queues on roads, and at railway stations and airports. It was like a Hollywood disaster movie. The show's presenters didn't seem to be taking it seriously.

'And here's Sally with the sport,' said Louise, smiling.

Stoke City had won at West Brom the previous evening. The country was safe. Marcus ran upstairs to the bedroom where Alice was putting on her dressing gown.

'Have you seen the scenes in China? They're locking down whole cities! It's pandemonium out there.'

Marcus got excited about lots of things. Brexit, the cost of his season ticket, the quantity of duck in a Pret wrap and the demise of ties in the workplace. Alice usually ignored him. This was another thing to be ignored.

'Not since I went to sleep last night, Marcus, no,' she said dismissively and left the bedroom.

He shaved, showered and dressed. He poked his head into Olivia's room. Still in her pyjamas, she was surrounded by piles of textbooks and Post-it notes. She was listening to Chris Brown singing about pussies.

'Bit early in the day for him, isn't it?' said Marcus.

'He relaxes me when I'm stressed.'

'Why are you stressed? What's the next exam?'

'Maths, and I've always been crap at Maths.'

She had achieved an A* in her GCSE and was one of the brightest students in her class. She was fretting for no reason.

'You'll be fine. I'll bring you up a coffee.'

She looked him up and down.

'Aren't you going to work today, Dad?'

'Yes, but I'm working from home. New thing. Maybe we could go for a walk later if you take a break from revising?'

'Sure Dad. That would be nice.'

He took his breakfast into the office. He opened his laptop and went through the numerous layers of security to access the network. The Firm took data security very seriously since a junior employee had got drunk in a lap dancing bar and had his laptop stolen, along with files containing details of a major redundancy programme for a big client. It was now easier to hack into the Pentagon than log on to The Firm's network. His computer greeted him with a blue screen.

Your computer is undergoing a series of critical updates. Please close down all open applications. Please restart your computer at the end of the updates.

Updates to applications he had never heard of or used happened at least twice a week. He spooned some porridge into his mouth and watched the percentage completion counter creeping up glacially. Fifteen minutes later, his machine blinked, pinged and restarted, by which time he had licked the bowl clean and finished his coffee.

His to-do list for the day was in his head. He rarely wrote anything down and never forgot anything. His colleagues wrote endless lists of frivolous tasks merely for the purpose of striking a highlighter pen through them to make themselves feel better. He opened Outlook. Forty-three new emails. Nineteen from Mason, two from Kelvin, one from Izzy Majewska and two from Jenny Moffatt plus the usual slurry of reminders and insights. He sent an email to Chloe to let her know he was working from home and would be dialling in to the pipeline call. He sent a text to Gavin.

Hi Gavin. Thanks for dinner last week. It was great. Staying in Weybridge this week so won't be at the flat tonight. Can we postpone until next Tuesday, 28th?

One of the emails from Kelvin came with a 'Read Receipt' and a 'High Importance' tag. He hoped it wasn't another reminder about wearing a lanyard.

Subject: Spearmint – Sell On
From: Kelvin McBride

Marcus
Understand Phase 1 meeting with Jim went well? Great stuff! We really
need to land the next phase. Suggest we bring the full resources of The Firm
together on this one. Starting to get pressure from above on our numbers so
Spearmint is a 'must win'. No pressure! Let me know what you need from
me?
    Kelvin

Someone was rattling Kelvin's cage so he was rattling his. Pressure in The Firm only went one way, downwards. At 8.30, his phone rang. It was Mason. He decided to answer. It would mean he could delete the nineteen emails.

'Morning, Mason.'

'Morning, Marcus. Sorry to catch you on the train—' Marcus interrupted him.

'You haven't. I'm working from home today. What can I do for you?'

It took a few seconds for Mason's brain to recalibrate.

'Oh, I see. Bit unusual for you isn't it, working from home?' He paused again. 'I'm mobilising the team to plan the next phase of Spearmint, storyboard the proposal, gather insights, agree who will attend orals, get our best creds, CVs. You know, usual stuff? It's a must win.'

'A must win'. The same words Kelvin used.

Preparing a proposal came with the pain threshold of a tooth abscess. It was like throwing a cow into a swimming pool of sharks. Anyone and everyone wanted to be involved.

'I've booked out one of the Collaboration Pods for the next few weeks and started reaching out for insights, case studies and CVs. I've copied you in on all the emails. When are you going to be in the office?' said Mason.

'Maybe tomorrow, maybe Thursday. Haven't made my mind up yet.'

His ambivalent reply caused Mason concern.

'You do want to win this, don't you, Marcus? You don't seem very committed.'

'Yes, of course I do.'

'Okay, see you in the office when you decide to come in,' he said sarcastically. 'I'll set up a meeting for Thursday. Hopefully, we'll hear back from Jim with some good news.'

Marcus stared into the garden. He used to be like Mason. Hungry, ambitious, a desire to win driven by the addictive drug of more partner units, more money to spend on more things he didn't need. Now he couldn't give a toss.

Marcus dialled in to the pipeline call. Izzy Majewska was in the chair. Marcus went on mute and checked The Sequence as she started to speak.

'Good morning everyone. Kelvin sends his apologies. He had to attend an urgent meeting with the top bods on the roll-out of the new "Living Our Values" programme. Been a few hiccups apparently. Anyway, let's start with the numbers. Up to last Friday, we were showing a negative variance against plan, on a week-by-week basis, of 25.36%. With two weeks to go, we are forecasting to mitigate this to a negative 12.31% variance. On a year-to-date basis, up to the end of January, we are showing a shortfall of £4.67 million, which represents a negative variance of 7.61%. On a like-for-like basis, removing exceptional items, year on year, our growth is flat or possibly slightly negative. Any questions?'

Nobody had any questions because they hadn't understood a word. Marcus guessed the team was behind target. Izzy presented a series of graphs which modelled scenarios for revenues, costs and overheads to the end of the year. They all pointed to the same thing. The team was behind target.

'I'll be looping back round with each of you to get a really good handle on the numbers. It would be good to look at things through a number of different lenses.'

Perhaps you should have gone to Specsavers? thought Marcus.

The partners gave their updates, which Chloe dutifully captured in her unique style. He knew she would struggle with Project Oedipus. It came to his turn.

'Hi, it's Marcus. Mason's already given an update on Spearmint. We'll have to see what Espina comes back with.'

Izzy was about to move on when Marcus interrupted.

'Sorry Izzy. I've got a question?'

'Yes, Marcus?' She was impatient to get on.

'Have we considered any disruption in our scenarios due to what's happening in China with this virus outbreak? It looks pretty serious to me.'

There was a stony silence. He imagined the bemused looks on the faces of his colleagues, all thinking he had gone mad. Tom Irons scoffed in the background.

'As 90% of our revenues come from the UK and Europe, I think that's a bit of a red herring to be throwing in, don't you, Marcus?'

'Fine, just asking,' he said.

At lunchtime, he got a text from Gavin.

Hi Marcus. Not a problem. Sorry if the excellent sumac tuna forced you to back out! Look forward to next week then. No pressure!

'No pressure'. Second time that morning someone had said that. Pressure was exactly what he was feeling. He went upstairs and knocked on Olivia's door. She was poring over her books, chewing on the end of a biro.

'Do you fancy that walk now?'

'Sure, Dad. I could do with a break. Not sure what quadratic polynomials have got to do with being a vet. Give me ten minutes and I'll see you downstairs?'

He waited in the hall, coat and shoes on with a cashmere scarf around his neck, when she came bouncing down the stairs like an excited puppy.

'You're keen?'

'Yes. We don't get to do this very often, do we?'

Father and daughter held hands, walked down the drive and on to Brooklands Avenue. One hundred yards up the road was a turning which led on to a bridleway and open farmland.

'Your hands are always so warm, Dad. They're like radiators.'

'Good circulation,' he said.

They walked along the path through the fields on either side. A few bored-looking horses in winter coats nibbled on grass. He pointed.

'One day, you might have to put your hand up the arse of one of those.'

'Something to look forward to,' she replied, 'provided I get the grades. It's going to be fucking hard to get in to Bristol. I'll need three As for sure. And then there's all the other stuff on top.'

Olivia had wanted to be a vet since she was eleven. The past seven years had been dedicated to achieving her burning ambition. For the past two summers, she had worked at a local vet's practice to gain experience, and had a good reference to accompany her UCAS application.

'If I get in, you'll have to subsidise me for another five years.'

'No matter how long it is, it'll be a lot cheaper than your brother,' said Marcus.

They continued walking along the path, talking about a lot of things, giving way to dog walkers, cyclists and ramblers. At a junction in the path, next to a large oak tree that had been struck by lightning, she stopped and squeezed his hand.

'Are you alright, Dad? You haven't seemed yourself since Christmas, bit flat? You used to be so full of it. The Firm, the deals. Flying all over the world. And now, you never talk about it. At least, not in a good way.'

He wondered if she had chosen the wrong vocation. She would be a great therapist.

'Has it been that noticeable?' he asked.

Olivia nodded.

'When your mum and I got married and we had James and you, it was all about providing for everyone, giving you the opportunities we didn't have. Working at The Firm paid for all that. I've been very well paid for what I do.'

She looked straight at him.

'And you've been a brilliant dad too. James and I wouldn't have had half of what we've had if it hadn't been for you. So, what's up?'

He raised his eyes, looking through the blackened, splintered branches. He sucked in air through his teeth.

'Because it means nothing to me. This deal, that deal, none of them really matter. In ten years' time, nobody will remember that it was Marcus Barlow who did those deals. And for what? A big house, foreign holidays, ski trips, cars. None of them mean anything.'

She took his other hand in hers and looked at him.

'But they do mean something, Dad. You've given me and James, and Mum too, every opportunity to be happy, and we're all really incredibly grateful to you for that.'

'Has it changed me, Libby? Have I become a horrible person?'

'Changed you in what way, Dad?'

'I look at people at work, the way they behave. Selfish, arrogant, disrespectful, unkind people. Always thinking about the money and screwing everyone else. I don't want people to see me like that.'

'We don't see you like that. You've always been Dad to us. Funny, kind, giving. A bit weird with some of your OCD habits maybe, but nothing to beat yourself up about!'

'I'm not sure I can cope with it for much longer. Every day, it gets worse. The politics and all the shit that goes with it.'

'Then don't do it Dad, simple as that. We have everything we could ever want or need. You still have some great years ahead of you. It's your life and maybe it's time for you now?'

She put her arms around him and hugged him, inhaling the familiar smell of her father. She kissed him on the cheek and they started their walk back.

'Thank you sweetie. That means a lot.'

Marcus microwaved the leftovers from last night's lentil ragu but he wasn't hungry. He checked The Sequence. Stockwatch was red, but it was only down a little. The walk with Olivia had been helpful. His health app told him he had walked 12,382 steps, and it made him feel good. He had hit his daily target for the first time in weeks.

He sat down at his desk and answered a few emails. Steve Pettigrew had sent through the outline proposal to Espina. It was already ninety slides long excluding appendices. At 5.00 p.m., his email pinged. It was a message from Jim Ibbotson at Espina.

Subject: Project Spearmint – Update
From: Jim Ibbotson

Marcus, Mason
Exco went well. Report was helpful. Some resistance from Safewear MD, but rest of the exco onboard. Just got to get this through the board on 4th February. Expect it to go through. Anticipate Phase 2 RFP this week. Provisional date of Monday, 10th February for presentations. Will be in Manchester.
All the best
   Jim

'All the best'. Jim was in a better mood. He had got what he wanted. It was a done deal before the meeting took place. The Safewear MD would be okay but most of the employees would get screwed and probably lose their jobs in the name of 'synergies'.

Two minutes later, Mason called him.

'Hi Marcus. Have you seen Jim's note?'

'Just read it.'

'Looks like it's game on. When are you back in the office?'

'Tomorrow.'

'Awesome. Let's get together first thing and work out who's going to do what. I've already spoken with seven partners who want to get involved. See you in the morning.'

Marcus couldn't understand what was 'awesome' about his return to the office, but everything was 'awesome' now. At 6.30, he switched off his laptop and closed the door to the office. Alice was putting away some shopping from The Temple. She was still dressed in her yoga leggings.

'Hi Al. How was your day?'

He went over to the cupboard and kissed her on the cheek. He could smell Hypnose, her favourite perfume. It was his favourite too.

'It was okay. We won at tennis, went to a deciding set. Had lunch at the club and then met Theresa at yoga. She's driving me mental with this "Mike and his affair" thing. I've told her to ask him outright. She's thinking of getting a private detective.'

Marcus laughed.

'Pretty boring assignment for a private detective. Went to golf club, went to pub, went to restaurant. What's he going to do, take grainy pictures of Mike from behind a bush on the thirteenth as he's putting? Mike isn't having an affair unless it's with a big bowl of chicken tikka masala and five pints of Guinness. It's all in her mind. I miss out on all this gossip when I'm at work. I should work from home more often!'

Alice was trying to stack three packets of gluten-free pasta shells on top of each other. She looked across the kitchen at him.

'Anytime you want to swap roles is fine with me, Marcus. I'll go back to being a lawyer and you can listen to Theresa moaning about why she and Mike don't have sex anymore. When are you going into the office anyway?'

'Tomorrow.'

'Awesome. We've got tofu stir-fry tonight. That okay with you?'

He went upstairs to lay out his clothes for the morning and switched on the television in the bedroom. It was the Channel 4 evening news. He liked Jon Snow, both for his intellect and his collection of vibrantly coloured ties. The first item was the spread of the virus in China and other countries across Asia. He ran along the hall to Olivia's room and opened the door.

'Libby, come and watch this. I want you to see it. This could get serious.'

Olivia got up from her chair, put down her chewed biro and followed him into the bedroom. They sat on the end of the bed together as the correspondent reported the scenes from Wuhan: eleven million people placed under lockdown, hospitals overwhelmed, transport links closed. Cases of the virus were spreading to other countries and the World Health Organisation was refusing to confirm it as a pandemic.

'Do you think it will come to the UK, Dad?'

'It's inevitable. With international travel, this could spread very quickly. I'm amazed the Government isn't doing more. Nobody seems to be paying any attention to it. More concerned with Brexit and Prince Harry.'

Olivia went back to her revision and Marcus laid out his clothes for the morning. He joined Alice in the kitchen where she was chopping tofu into cubes and adding them to the sizzling wok of vegetables and tonight's random ingredient, yuzu juice.

'You know Al, I'm really worried about what's happening in China. Then again, I'm worried about a lot of things, to be honest.'

She looked up from the wok, put down the wooden spoon and walked across to where Marcus was sitting at the kitchen table. She cupped his face in her hands.

'Marcus, you're always worried about things you can't control. You get anxious finding forks mixed with the spoons in the cutlery drawer. Try not to let things get on top of you. It would make life so much easier for all of us.'

Alice went back to the wok and her stir-fry. She had temporarily eased his anxiety about the virus, but that was only half the story. Now wasn't the time to talk about what was really on his mind, and so he laid the table for dinner.

It was Tuesday, 21 January 2020.

Chapter 8

GOOD THINGS HAPPENED TODAY

Tuesday. It was bin day and Mr Mahoney was up early to pull out the large, circular aluminium bins into the alleyway. It was a sunny morning but the overnight frost hadn't melted on parts of the courtyard. Crystallised coils of frozen dog poo glistened on the grass. He was wearing his black donkey jacket with a dayglo orange insert across the shoulders, a remnant of his days working on the roads.

Judith had already left for work. The election of a new Party Leader was creating a lot of extra work for the Communications Team. She said that one of the candidates, Sir Keir Starmer, was, 'Just another Tory posh boy with a red rose on his lapel' and wanted a Rebecca Long-Something to win. Claire didn't care less who won. She had never voted, which Judith had said was 'a dereliction of her democratic freedoms won through the historic suffering of women.' As far as Claire could see, women like her were still suffering.

Ian Dixon, her neighbour at No. 12, was standing at the foot of the stairs leaning against the wall. She stroked him on the arm as she passed. Ian walked with a limp on his left side and his speech was impaired. His illness was getting worse.

Apart from trips to the shops and the park on his mobility scooter, Ian locked himself in his flat, playing *Call of Duty* or *Grand Theft Auto* with strangers across the globe, who knew him as the Kensal Warrior. He was a hoarder, keeping everything from newspapers to plastic bags and empty bottles of Pepsi Max. If Ian's world was already small, it was getting smaller by the day as he barricaded himself from within.

Mr Mahoney came over to them, beads of sweat on his ruddy brow.

'Morning Claire, morning my little ones. Right Ian, let me get your scooter out for you.'

The caretaker opened the padlock to the little shed and reversed the maroon scooter on to the path. Unsteady on his feet, Ian shuffled across from the stair rail and slid on to the seat. Kyle ran over to him.

'Ian, please can I ride on your spaceship?' he said excitedly.

'Kyle, Ian has to go shopping and we have to get to school. Maybe another time?' said Claire.

'But we never see Ian!' said the little boy.

Ian put his shopping bags in the little basket, sat back and made space for Kyle to sit on his lap, his little hands underneath his on the handlebars.

'Come on Space Ranger, let's go!' he said in strangled words, which the little boy barely understood.

Ian turned the accelerator handle and the scooter set off around the courtyard at a little over walking speed with Kyle, arms outstretched like his hero. They did three laps. It wasn't to infinity and beyond but, to Kyle, it was close. He gave Ian a hug, jumped off and ran back to his mum.

'Bye Ian, thank you.' Kyle waved.

Claire dropped Alexa at Little Acorns and walked with Kyle to school. The headmistress Mrs Lindsay was on morning duty. Her bottom, swathed in a green paisley skirt, was moving independently from the rest of her body, like a hippo, as she walked around the playground, ushering excited children inside. Claire saw Beverley Cheng kissing Bruce on the cheek.

'Hi Beverley, how are you?'

Beverley was immaculately dressed for 8.30 in the morning. Her raven black hair tied back in a bun, full makeup, angora roll-neck sweater, skinny jeans and tan-coloured suede ankle boots. Claire felt inferior in her Smew. Beverley smiled, a pixie with bright red lips.

'Hi Claire. I'm okay. Really busy trying to get the flat and my work sorted. We've had problems with our boiler. No hot water this morning!'

Claire wondered how she could look as good as she did with a faulty boiler.

'How about you? How's Kyle?'

'We're all fine thanks. Kyle is always talking about Bruce. I think they get on well. Can I ask what work you do?'

'I work for myself. I had a business in Hong Kong sourcing fabrics for the clothing industry. I'm trying to set it up here using my old contacts at home. It's not as easy as I thought it would be. What about you, what do you do?'

It was a simple question, but one Claire found hard to answer. 'Housewife', 'single mum', 'downtrodden useless bitch', 'unemployable failed fashion student'. She went for the easiest option.

'I don't work, I'm afraid.'

Beverley smiled warmly. It was enough to make Claire say more.

'I studied fashion and design at college, but I got pregnant with Kyle in the middle of my second year. Had to give up and never finished the course. But I loved it, it was the happiest time of my life. Then came Alexa. Their father left us and the rest is very dull and boring.'

'What a pity you had to give it up. You obviously loved it?'

'Best time of my life. I was at Central Saint Martins in London. It's quite famous. I've still kept some of my designs, I get them out occasionally to torment myself with what could have been!'

She shrugged her shoulders and laughed.

'I'd love to see them sometime. Why don't we meet for coffee one morning after dropping the boys off?' said Beverley.

Nobody invited Claire for coffee or refreshments of any sort. Her invitation took her by surprise, and it took a while before she could reply. There was something about this woman that was different.

'Thank you. I would like that.'

'Let's make it soon. I've got my in-laws coming to stay at the end of February, if they can get out of the country. Have you seen what's happening in China? They are shutting down cities out there.'

'Yes, I heard it on the radio. Aren't you worried?'

'I don't know if I'm worried or not. I don't trust anything that comes out of China. They'll cover it up whatever it is.'

They said goodbye and left the school in opposite directions. She passed Tesco Express where Andrew Coates was wearing his high-vis jacket, helping the driver unload cages from the tailgate of a delivery lorry. He didn't spot her and she passed him by.

Mishal Husain was reading the closing headlines on the *Today* programme as Claire opened the front door. The main headline was the news Prince Andrew was refusing to cooperate with the FBI over his links to Jeffrey Epstein. She had watched his interview and thought it was a car crash. She couldn't imagine Prince Andrew had ever set foot in a Pizza Express. The virus outbreak in China was one of the smaller headlines, much less important than Prince Andrew.

She saw Gavin walk along the balcony and knock on the door. She opened it and tapped her imaginary watch.

'You're late Dr Douglas. I could be dead by now.'

'You look fine to me,' he said. 'Sorry I'm late. I had to drop something off in the office and got delayed. I've got my annual review next week.'

She could smell his aftershave. It was Eau Sauvage, another of her favourites.

'Feedback from me? Punctuality, poor. Choice of aftershave, outstanding,' said Claire, teasing him.

They took their usual seats at the kitchen table. He removed his overcoat and hung it on the back of the chair. He was wearing a navy cashmere V-neck jumper with a pink shirt and jeans. He always got the balance right.

'Tea? Coffee?' she said.

'Would you mind if I had a green tea? I'm on a detox at the moment. Trying to avoid caffeine.'

'Blimey, things must be bad. No Panettone Palace then? Their profits will slump.'

Claire took two Mariage Frères teabags out of their stylish box, put them in mugs and added hot water. Gavin squirted hand sanitiser on his palms and rubbed them together.

'I do wish you wouldn't always do that. Makes me feel like my flat is dirty. Like you're scared you might catch something nasty.'

'Force of habit. Sorry. Some of the places I have to visit are pretty dreadful. They should give us facemasks.'

Doctor and patient went through the usual health check. Contemplation of suicide, kids, money, schools, Universal Credit, school meal vouchers, damp treatment, loneliness.

'Something nice happened to me this morning,' she said.

'Really? Tell me and I'll put a stop to it immediately,' he said teasing her.

'The mum of a new boy in Kyle's class, Beverley Cheng, spoke to me in the playground. Her son, Bruce, and Kyle are best friends. She and her husband have moved here from Hong Kong. She runs her own business importing fabrics from China. I told her that I studied fashion and design and she's invited me for coffee. What do you think of that?'

Claire put the mugs on the table with a flourish.

'Wow, look at you! Coffee mornings. You'll be joining a tennis club next. Seriously, I think it's great. You must go. Promise me you will?'

'Yes, I really like her, although I'm not sure about going. I'm not very confident meeting new people. How about you? How's your friend, Martin?'

'Marcus? He's okay. I haven't seen him for a couple of weeks. He's been busy working on some mega-project. He's having a tough time, as it happens. Midlife crisis and all that.'

'What crisis? You said he earns a fortune. Worried about running out of things to spend his money on, is he? I wouldn't mind having a midlife crisis like his.'

Gavin put down his mug.

'It's not about money, it's deeper than that. It's about feeling valued, about making a difference. I think he's questioning himself, probably for the first time in his life.'

'Are you worried about him?'

'Not in the sense that he's going to top himself. But he's certainly a bit of a lost soul right now.' Gavin changed the subject. 'You know a couple of weeks ago you asked me to dinner? Chicken and pasta bake, if I recall?'

'Yes, I'm sorry about that,' said Claire sheepishly. 'Didn't mean to put you on the spot.'

'Is the offer still open?'

'Why?'

'If it is, I'd like to accept but with two changes.'

Claire paused before replying.

'I suppose so. Depends on the changes?'

'How would you feel about having dinner with me and Marcus, and we do the cooking? You won't have to worry about babysitters. We'll have it here.'

She looked at him, wondering if it was another of his teases but he looked deadly serious. She slipped back into defensive mode.

'But this place is tiny. Your posh friend Marcus wouldn't set foot in a place like this. He'll probably get a nosebleed once he reaches Ladbroke Grove. It's just about big enough for me and the kids. There's no way that—'

Gavin cut her off in mid-sentence.

'It's big enough for the three of us. The kitchen has everything we need and what it doesn't have, we'll bring with us. And, by the way, Marcus isn't posh and he doesn't suffer from nosebleeds either. Not that I know of anyway.'

'And what does he think of this crazy idea?'

'I haven't asked him yet, but I think it would be good for all of us. Sometime in the next couple of weeks, I'll let you know. Assuming your new social diary isn't too full of course?'

Gavin's idea was certainly crazy but she trusted him.

'I suppose so. If Marcus is happy?'

In their remaining time, they debated who was the best ever winner of *X Factor*. They agreed it was Leona Lewis although One Direction had probably made the most money. Neither of them could remember who won last year and, after Little Mix, it had been a pile of crap, and *Strictly* was much better.

At midday, Gavin stood up to leave as Claire turned up the volume on the radio. Zeb Soanes was reading the news headlines which led with the crisis in China.

'This is what Beverley was talking about this morning,' said Claire. 'She said the virus is really bad in China and it's spreading quickly. Are you worried about it?'

'Marcus mentioned it too. I've been following it but I don't know enough to say

I'm worried. To be honest, I've got plenty of things closer to home to worry about. Like the Osman family and finding a roof to go over their heads that doesn't leak.'

She followed him to the front door.

'See you next week. Say hello to the kids for me. Good news about Beverley. I'm really pleased for you. I'll speak to Marcus, see what he thinks about my idea. I think he'll enjoy meeting you. Bit of slum living will do him good.'

Gavin winked at her and stepped out on to the balcony.

'Hope you catch something nasty on the stair rail on the way down!' she called after him.

Claire put the mugs in the sink and made cheese on toast. The fridge was looking bare but she had her appointment with Lester Primus later. She plonked herself in front of the TV. The *Bargain Hunt* team were in Anglesey and the presenter was dressed in Welsh national costume to let the couch potatoes know where Anglesey was. Claire already knew. Her father had taken the Carter family to Butlin's in Rhyl for a week when she was eleven and they had been on a day trip to Conway Castle and across the Menai Bridge to Anglesey. The blue team were smart. They bought a load of junk which buyers in the auction room were willing to pay over the odds for and ended up with a £95 profit. The presenter almost wet herself. It was gripping television.

At nursery, Alexa handed Claire her latest creation, a picture of Kyle and Ian on his mobility scooter, a memory from the morning. Kyle was bigger than Ian, whose matchstick body leaned at right angles at the hip. The anatomy was correct even if the perspective wasn't. The paint on the picture was still wet and her little fingers smudged Ian's purple face.

'It's Ian and Kyle on his spaceship,' said Alexa proudly.

'Yes, I can see. It's beautiful sweetie. Maybe we can give it to Ian? He would like that, wouldn't he?'

Alexa nodded.

They walked hand in hand to Kyle's school, talking about the random thoughts flitting through her daughter's brain.

'Why doesn't my daddy come to my nursery like Imogen's does?' said Alexa.

Three-year-olds always asked the hardest questions. Claire didn't have an honest answer, so she did what adults do best. They lie.

'Daddy went to a special place far away because it was very important. I don't know when he'll be coming back.'

Pandora's Box was now open.

'Why did my daddy have to go away to a special place? Will he come back?'

'Because your daddy is a selfish prick who left us on our own and couldn't give a fuck about you,' was what she wanted to say. Instead she lied again.

'Maybe, one day he will come back, sweetie. Until he does, it's just you, Kyle and me. We all love each other, don't we?'

Alexa nodded and ate a raisin from her little box.

At school, the four-by-four armada was parked in the road with no respect for yellow lines or safe crossing zones. Barbarians at the gates. Helena Mistakidis was on duty in a pair of metallic, lilac 'moon shoes' paired with a lemon pleated skirt. She stood out from the greys and greens like a highlighter pen.

'Hi Claire,' said Helena. 'I've had a word with Mrs Lindsay about the deposit for the school trip?'

Claire felt her neck starting to flush, another humiliation was looming.

'We've agreed you can take until the end of February to pay the deposit. Is that okay?'

Claire felt the wave of relief.

'Of course it is. That's very kind of you. Kyle's really excited about it. He really wants to see piglets. I can't think why?'

The teacher smiled.

'See you tomorrow, Kyle. Bye Claire.'

Claire got to Tesco Express, put Alexa in her buggy, much to her annoyance, and walked into the shop, looking for Lester Primus. She couldn't see him but caught the eye of Andrew Coates who was patrolling the self-checkouts. He looked at her and curled his top lip with disgust. It had been two weeks since his 'bust' was aborted and hadn't forgiven her for getting off lightly. She asked another member of staff who was putting reduced stickers on some cherry tomatoes and she went off to find the store manager. Lester Primus emerged five minutes later from the plastic flap doors to the warehouse. He had little beads of sweat on his balding head, bubbling like cheese on toast under a grill.

'Hi Claire. I'm sorry if you've been waiting. I was on a call to HQ talking about February promotions. Valentine's Day, Pancake Day, that sort of thing,' he said, rolling his eyes to the sky.

'That's okay, I don't think I'm going to be needing any red roses or a three-course meal for two. Baked beans always come in handy though.'

'Please, come with me,' he said, beckoning her inside.

In his dingy office were two bags of dented tins, broken packets and limited shelf life food. Her visits were starting to look like the opening scenes from *Ready Steady Cook*. It was lucky that neither Alexa nor Kyle were fussy eaters. There weren't many children in Kensal Mansions that had tasted chipotle and coconut cream before they were six.

'Sorry if some of this stuff is a bit weird,' said Lester. 'A lot of it would have been chucked in the bin, so I hope you'll get some benefit from it? The best before dates are only a guide. You won't die of food poisoning if you use it this week.'

He picked up one of the bags and handed it to her.

'This one doesn't need to go through the checkout. All the stuff in here would have been thrown away.'

He pointed at the other bag.

'This one will have to go through but all of it has been discounted. I hope it helps?'

Every little did help. She had a ten-pound note in her purse, but that was it until the end of the month. With a bit of luck, the nights wouldn't be too cold and the pay-as-you-go meter wouldn't need topping up. She took a look inside the bag of freebies. Some squashed croissants, two packets of wholemeal pitta bread, some dented tins of tuna in olive oil, chopped tomatoes, two broken packets of rich tea biscuits and some smoked mackerel fillets. Kyle and Alexa would be dosed up to the eyeballs on omega-3.

'It's really kind of you, Mr Primus. Nothing goes to waste, I can assure you.'

The store manager gave Kyle an orange Starburst and Alexa got the strawberry one. Nimble little fingers eagerly took off the wrappers and gave them to their mother.

'I'll see you on Friday then?' Claire said.

'Yes, take care of yourself,' said Lester.

He looked forward to the days when he saw her. He and his wife would have liked a daughter like Claire. They would have liked grandchildren even more.

She finished her shopping, deciding that Veet was a luxury that could wait. Nobody saw her untended bush anyway. There was a queue for the tills so she ran the gauntlet of Andrew Coates who was still loitering around the self-checkouts. She got out her bags and started scanning the items, praying they were priced correctly and he wouldn't throw her to the floor and put his knee on her throat.

'I hope you're gonna pay for everything this time,' he said sneeringly.

She turned towards him and looked him straight in the eye.

'Why don't you piss off and patrol the freezers?'

She rarely swore in front of her children, but they were preoccupied with the Haribo display and didn't hear her. The security guard recoiled and stepped back into a display of Pringles which were on special offer.

'It was only a joke.'

He sloped off down the aisle past 'oils, pickles and preserves' before grabbing a stale pain au chocolat from the pastries and stuffing it into his mouth in one. Then he went to the warehouse to lick his wounds and his lips.

At the foot of the stairs to the flat, Mr Mahoney was putting Ian's mobility scooter away in its mini-garage and he greeted them.

'Hi Claire. Hi my little ones. Let me help you with your shopping,' he said kindly.

The caretaker wrapped the plastic handles of four heavy bags of shopping around his meaty hands and started the climb, as Claire shepherded Alexa and Kyle up the stairs and paused at the top to use her inhaler. The caretaker dropped the bags outside her front door.

'There you go. No trouble, no trouble at all. I'll pop up just before five. It's an orange layer cake today. It was one of Sinead's favourites. Mine won't be as good as hers but it still looks grand.'

'Why don't you go and get the cake and come straight back up? I'll only be putting the shopping away and getting the kids some tea. You can sit with us, if you like? The children love having you with us, don't we kids?'

Alexa danced around in circles, her arms outstretched like a little helicopter.

'We love Mr Moany, we love Mr Moany.'

He smiled his toothy grin, an IMAX of gaps and cavities framed by greying stubble.

'Okay, if it's no trouble, no trouble.'

Claire took Alexa's picture from the buggy and rang the doorbell to No. 12. It didn't work so she knocked several times. From inside, she could hear rustling, boxes being moved, papers being shifted. It took Ian three minutes to open the front door to a crack.

He looked tired, pale and dishevelled. Six hours in a darkened room killing terrorists in the remains of a simulated bombed-out town did little for the health of the Kensal Warrior. In the background, Claire could hear the noise of automatic gunfire and stun grenades.

'Hi Ian. Alexa has something for you. She did it at nursery today. It's a picture of you and Kyle on your scooter. We thought you would like it?'

Alexa held up the painting. Ian's purple face was now dry.

Ian took the painting from her and held it up to the dim bulb in the hall. He looked at his distorted body seen through the eyes of a three-year-old.

'Thank you so much. And is that me?' he said, pointing to the angled torso.

Alexa looked up and nodded.

'Well, it's lovely. I'll put it on my wall.' Claire knew Ian would struggle to find a wall that wasn't obscured by boxes of crap.

'See you soon, Ian.'

Most of the shopping was put away by the time Mr Mahoney arrived. She made two cups of builder's tea, put the slices of cake on two plates and carried them into the living room where normal seating positions were taken. The children snuggled into his warm, ursine body.

Bradley introduced the four new contestants on *The Chase*, and Claire and Mr Mahoney introduced themselves to Bradley in their usual way.

'Hi Bradley. I'm Claire Halford, unemployed single mum from the arse end of Kensington with nothing better to do right now than watch you.'

'And I'm Phelan Mahoney, amateur cake maker, lonely widower and an expert with a pneumatic drill.'

It came out, just like that. It took Claire fifteen seconds to realise what had just happened. She had known him for almost two years and they had been 'Chase Buddies' for more than one. Bradley was introducing The Sinnerman as today's Chaser, but it was lost on Claire.

'Whoa, stop right there! What did you just say?' she shouted across the room from her chair.

'What?' he said, disappointed that The Governess wasn't on tonight's show.

'You just said your name. Phelan? You've never said it before. Two years of being Mr Mahoney and then you come right out with it. Just like that! Are you feeling okay?'

'I just felt like saying it, that's all. I've never liked it much. Too many jokes, "Phelan good", "Phelan bad", "Phelan stupid". Don't make a big thing of it. Anyway, hush now, the questions are starting.'

The show passed by in a blur. Maggie, a bookkeeper from Huddersfield and Les, a bus driver from Norwich, walked away with £9,500 but Mr Mahoney said they could easily have won more. Claire walked with Mr Mahoney to the front door.

'So, do I call you Phelan or Mr Mahoney from now on?' she said with a cheeky grin.

'Mr Mahoney has done us just fine, just fine up to now. And now Bradley Walsh knows too. If I don't see you through the week, I'll see you through the window.'

The caretaker squeezed her shoulders and walked along the balcony.

She shouted after him.

'The orange layer cake was great. Mary Berry and Sinead would be proud of you.'

He waved without turning around.

She turned on the radio to listen to the *Six O'Clock News* on Radio 4 as she cooked dinner. Tuna (in olive oil, dented tin) with pasta, sweetcorn and broccoli. She thanked Lester Primus under her breath.

Jane Steel read the news headlines. The Government had announced it was going to repatriate 200 Britons trapped inside Wuhan and was advising against all non-essential travel to mainland China. A number of airlines had cancelled all flights in and out of China. The entire province of Hubei had been placed in lockdown. The number of cases worldwide was now estimated to be 30,000.

By eight o'clock, Kyle and Alexa had been bathed and put to bed with their favourite bedtime stories. Exhausted, Claire turned off the main light and switched on the reading lamp, collapsing into her chair with a cup of tea and a blanket. It had been a really good day, the best in ages. She had made a new friend who had invited her for coffee, Gavin and his friend Marcus were coming for dinner, Lester Primus had been a saint and Mr Mahoney had told her his name.

It was Tuesday, 21 January 2020.

Chapter 9

GLADIATORS

Working from home for one day had been enough. He stared out of the window at the houses backing on to the railway line. People getting ready to start their day. He wondered how many of them were worried about the virus too?

He decided not to take the Drain and walked the mile from Waterloo to Bank. He collected his double macchiato and porridge from Fernando, sat at his desk and opened his laptop. Forty-three new emails. He dealt with them instantly, highlighting them in a single block and pressing delete.

Above the recycling area in the EcoPod was a new poster publicising The Firm's latest milestone in its sustainability journey. A Shutterstock image of two hands clapping proclaiming the great news.

Well done team! Abolishing paper and plastic cups has reduced consumption by 84%. This is a fantastic achievement. Another landmark in our quest to lead the world in sustainability.

Removing plastic cups from the vending machines and water stations had seemed like a good idea until one of the staff had fainted in the Tranquillity Zone. It had taken fifteen minutes to get her a glass of water as people rushed to rinse out the dregs from their reusable coffee mugs. And only 84% reduction? Was there a subversive cell concealing a secret stash of plastic cups so they could use them in defiance of the policy? Like most of the things The Firm did to enhance its public reputation, it came with the sour taste of hypocrisy. Its buildings were lit up like Christmas trees late into the night, wasting energy like a burning oilfield.

He walked into Collaboration Pod 3, which Mason had reserved for the next three weeks to 'hothouse' the preparation of The Firm's pitch to Espina. Collaboration Pod 3 came with white walls for 'brain eruptions', yellow beanbags for 'contemplation and reforming' and an electronic white board for 'idea fusion and synthesising'. An entire wall, the length of the room, had been given over to the storyboard, a rehash of something done before for another client, but with different logos and a new date.

Over ninety sheets of paper were pinned to the wall with little green magnets. And this was just the start. To this would be added an executive summary (what the client might read), appendices (irrelevant material that didn't make it into the main pack), case studies (something faintly similar done for other clients years before), CVs (photos of people who may or may not be doing the work) and fees (the bit the client would certainly read).

Marcus greeted the team. Steve Pettigrew walked him through the new storyboard, which was much the same as other storyboards. They carved up responsibilities, agreed deadlines and created a workplan for the next couple of weeks. Just after eleven o'clock, Mason arrived with someone Marcus had never met. A small, skinny young man with a trimmed goatee beard wearing tight, purple velvet trousers and a multi-coloured tank top. Marcus thought he looked like Geoffrey, the presenter of the 1970s children's show *Rainbow*.

Mason slumped into one of the beanbags and introduced his guest.

'Morning Marcus, morning everyone. Can I introduce you to Gerard Cornelius from the Client Ideation Centre? Gerard will be helping us with the pitch to Espina over the next few weeks. Over to you, Gerard.'

Mason had pronounced his name with a hard 'G' and Gerard immediately corrected him in a slightly effeminate tone.

'Sorry Mason, it's G-erard,' he said.

With the record set straight, Gerard continued in a theatrical fashion.

'Good morning Spearmints! I'm Gerard Cornelius and I work in Client Ideation. It's my job to help you win in this competitive market. Mason has given me a briefing and how important it is that we win this next phase of work. And that's exactly why I'm here, to help you WIN!'

Gerard took a low bow in front of the team who were staring at him in disbelief.

Mason cut in.

'I spoke with Kelvin last night and we think Gerard and his team can add a new dimension. I briefed him yesterday and his team have come up with some brilliant ideas already. Do you want to continue, Gerard?'

'Thank you Mason.' Gerard looked around Collaboration Pod 3 and waved his hands dismissively at the paper-lined wall. 'So old-fashioned and so boring. We hate this stuff in CIC.' He pronounced the initials of his department as 'sick', making it even more distasteful. Gerard continued. 'In CIC, we believe that business is theatre, it's a play. You and your clients are actors in this drama. Our job is to bring theatre into your world, to write the script with you, rehearse your lines, give you the props and produce a play that will get you a standing ovation. And WIN!'

Pairs of eyes shifted nervously around the room. Steve Pettigrew looked at Marcus and opened his eyes wide, Marcus averted his look.

Mason prompted Gerard further.

'Do you want to give the team a flavour, Gerard?'

'Absolutely, Mason. I see Spearmint as a drama in two acts. The death of dull, boring Safewear and a triumph for exciting, dynamic TuffTogs. To win, we have to show Espina that we are on their side, like gladiators, ready to enter the Colosseum and slay the beast of failure.'

Images of Mason as Maximus in *Gladiator*, all leather and sweat, fighting off Jim Ibbotson with a trident, flashed through Marcus's mind.

Gerard continued.

'So, we have to change the dynamic. Show we're on their side, part of their team. We have to show that we are all actors in the same drama. Doing it with them.'

'Tell them what you're thinking of, Gerard,' said Mason excitedly, goading him on.

'Our proposal has to reflect their business and be different. Truly differentiated. A real drama acted out right in front of them.'

Marcus looked around at the team. Blood was draining from their faces at a rate of knots.

'Our proposal will be based on a series of key words, printed on wooden bricks. At the pitch, our team will assemble the bricks into a wall, a "Wonderwall", right in front of them. When it's built, it will be a scale model of how we are going to support them. And that's not all ...'

As if turning a multi-million-pound opportunity into a combination of Scrabble and Lego wasn't enough, Gerard wasn't finished.

'... the team which delivers our pitch will be wearing hard hats with our logo and the TuffTogs logo on, and high-vis jackets with the key words printed on them. Our pitch will blow them away and we're going to WIN!'

From his beanbag, Mason beamed like a father who had just witnessed the birth of his first child.

'Truly awesome stuff, Gerard. Thank you. CIC's dynamic and innovative approach really gives us a framework to build our proposal around. We're truly looking forward to working with you.'

'Yes, me too Mason. Thank you for getting CIC involved. I can't wait. I'll be in touch.'

He gave a theatrical wave to the team and left the room. Hurricane Gerard had just blown through leaving devastation on the faces of the team like a flattened shanty town. They looked at Marcus but he was too stunned and was staring into space. Finally, he assembled enough words to speak.

'And you said Kelvin was right behind this, Mason?'

'A hundred per cent. There's a lot riding on this. We have to use every resource at our disposal. He thinks Gerard is great.'

'You don't think this is slightly risky?'

'We have to differentiate ourselves from the competition, Marcus. We need a fresh angle.'

'Hopefully, not an obtuse one,' said Marcus. 'Maybe we should still produce the normal proposal, just in case Gerard's drama isn't ready for opening night? You know, belt and braces?'

'Agree, although he seems pretty set on what we need. Have faith.'

Mason left the room, leaving the team dazed and confused. PowerPoint and Excel didn't require faith. A Greek tragedy was going to be a stretch.

'Probably a good time to have lunch?' suggested Marcus.

After lunch, the team regrouped to digest what had happened in the morning. Some direction was needed and Marcus tried to provide it.

'Well, I'm sure we're all a little stunned by what we heard earlier? As none of us are experienced in writing dramas, I think we should do what we always do. Let's start getting some content down on paper and we can worry about how we put that on to bricks, paving slabs or road signs further down the road.'

The team all nodded. Back to familiar territory and set about populating the ninety-page storyboard, filling in the blanks with recycled materials from other clients. Marcus walked back to his desk and passed Simon Loder on the way. He had the remnants of a Madeira jus on his shirt.

As their paths crossed, Loder started singing, 'Bob the Builder, can we sell it? Bob the Builder, yes we can.'

Loder laughed. The humiliation had already started and it was only going to get worse. For the next few hours, Marcus's inbox was flooded with memes and videos showing collapsing buildings and earthquakes.

Hopefully, something will end this fucking madness, he thought.

On Thursday morning, Marcus had his 'deep dive' with Izzy Majewska to discuss the team's financial position. He was curious to know why she had forecast the next phase of Project Spearmint at £1.5 million per month for the next six months.

'So how did you come up with these numbers, Izzy? Based on what? They look very unrealistic to me.'

'I sat down with Mason and Kelvin earlier this week. We think there's a great opportunity to really deliver The Firm here. We looked at the number of people we could put on it, applied weightings and risk factors, assessed the commercial and strategic rationale and came up with a forecast of £9 million.'

'How much do we need to hit target, based on our current situation?' he asked.

'£9 million,' said Izzy.

'I get it.'

* * *

Marcus's worst fears were realised on his journey into the office on Friday morning. The front page of *Metro* carried the headline, 'CHINA VIRUS ON THE WAY HERE'.

Except the virus wasn't 'on the way'. He guessed it had already landed, cleared immigration, checked in to its hotel and was lying on its bed with a map of London wondering where to create mayhem next. He tore off the front page and put it in his bag.

He spent the day working with the team, assembling the patchwork of materials into something resembling a coherent proposal. There were a large number of contributions from Subject Matter Experts, all desperately keen to ensure their area of expertise was brought to the attention of Espina. The sharks could smell blood.

He left the office in time to catch the 6.05 from Waterloo. He decided to take the longer route along the Embankment, crossing the river at Waterloo Bridge. He wanted easy listening, nothing too stressful or depressing, and scrolled down his playlists to '1970s Americana'. He had forgotten the first track was Neil Young's 'The Needle and the Damage Done'. He skipped forward immediately to 'Hotel California'.

The Embankment was busy, black cabs ferrying passengers from the City to a Friday night out in the West End. The pavements were crowded with walkers and runners, all keen to fit in some last-minute exercise before a weekend of indulgence. It was dark and the South Bank was lit up. The distinctive red neon of Oxo Tower stood out. He paused halfway across Waterloo Bridge. The Thames shimmered in the night. A river taxi passed underneath the bridge on its way to Westminster and, in the distance, a couple of small tugs were chugging downstream.

He looked at the City's skyline. It had changed dramatically since he started working for The Firm as new, iconic buildings were added every year. The

Gherkin, the Cheesegrater, the Shard, the Walkie-Talkie. Every new building had a nickname but they were impressive illuminated against the dark January sky. And to the left was St Paul's, standing like a greying stone grandad next to a new generation of glass and steel grandchildren. He loved the City. It was the powerhouse of the country's economy and he was a tiny cog in the machine. Except all the other cogs were turning in the opposite direction and something would break soon.

He walked up the steps and under the stone arch at Waterloo Station, a dedication to the dead from the First World War, and picked up a copy of the *Evening Standard* which carried a headline about the escalating levels of knife crime in the capital. The cheapness of human life depressed him and he looked up at the departures board. Platform 4, only a ten-minute delay tonight. He had got off lightly.

His call to Alice was brief. She was coming down with another migraine and there was a broccoli and Roquefort quiche from the Organic Delivery Company to go in the Aga. She and Olivia had already had pumpkin and cardamom soup.

'I'm sure you can warm it up and make yourself a salad can't you, Marcus? My head feels like it's splitting. I might go to bed early.'

At Weybridge Station, he entered the smoggy atmosphere of Ace Cars. The fan heaters were on full blast, circulating the smells of microwaved food like a giant diffuser. The controller recognised him immediately.

'Twin Gates, Brooklands Avenue, mate? Kareem, Twin Gates, Brooklands Avenue,' he shouted through the hatch.

Kareem ushered Marcus to his parked Toyota Prius. He started the car which started Smooth FM. *The Smooth Sanctuary* with Gary Vincent was playing a medley of hits by the Bee Gees. Marcus tried to engage Kareem in conversation.

'Do you know why they're called the Bee Gees?'

'No, I don't,' said Kareem.

'It stands for "the Brothers Gibb". That was their name. Barry, Maurice and Robin Gibb.'

'I like them, but not as much as Celine Dion,' said Kareem.

It was evident, nothing was going to usurp Celine in his driver's musical affections, so Marcus remained silent for the rest of the journey. Kareem pulled on to the drive and Marcus looked up at his bedroom window. He could see the light was on. Alice was already in bed. He hung up his coat and walked upstairs. The light in Olivia's room was on. He knocked and she beckoned him in. For once, she wasn't at her desk. Instead, she was lying on her bed swiping through Instagram.

'Hi Libby. Everything okay?' he said.

'Hi Dad. Yeah, just chilling out. Only one more exam to go. Biology practical on Tuesday. Probably a dissection and there isn't much I can revise. I hope it's a rat and not a worm. Worms are quite fiddly.'

Marcus found his daughter's recent conversion to veganism to be at odds with her desire to cut up dead animals and invertebrates.

'How was your day, Dad? All going okay on Spearmint?'

'Yes, it's fine. A bit mad but I'm glad it's the weekend.'

He closed the door behind him and walked along the landing to the bedroom. Alice was sitting up in bed, reading *Femail*.

'Hi Al. How are you feeling?'

He leaned over and kissed her on the cheek. On her forehead was the sleep mask from one of his British Airways business-class traveller sets. She was the only one who used them.

'I can feel a migraine coming on. I tried to watch a bit of TV but it was hurting my eyes.'

'Have you seen this? It was in *Metro* this morning, I kept it for you.'

He handed her a piece of folded newspaper from his bag. He turned to take off his suit and tie.

'Marcus, why have you given me some tatty voucher for a £1.99 meal deal in Burger King?'

He turned around quickly and snatched the cutting from her hand. He reached into his bag and pulled out another cutting.

'Sorry, this is what I wanted you to see. You see? The killer virus is coming soon, if it isn't here already. I told you so.'

'Yes, Marcus. I know. I've been reading about it as well. I'm sure we're safe here in Weybridge and, unless you're planning a trip to Wuhan any day next week, you're probably safe too. You're in more danger of getting stabbed walking home to that flat of yours.'

She was right on the first count. There hadn't been a case of the virus in Weybridge although Marcus suspected the cabin at Ace Cars could become a hub for 'superspreaders'. As he got to the bedroom door, she called out to him.

'And what are you doing with that voucher for Burger King? You're not still eating that shit are you?'

'No, of course not. I cut them out for the team.' Sometimes, if we're working late, people grab a burger. Saves them a few quid.'

He put the quiche in the Aga and checked 'The Sequence'. James had posted photographs of himself on the family's group chat, in various nightclubs and bars in Manchester, arms around his friends, a drink in one hand and sometimes in both. Marcus wondered if his son was ever going to post a picture of himself in the library doing some work?

* * *

Marcus spent most of the weekend on Project Garage. Twin Gates had a double garage which was used for every purpose apart from sheltering cars. Instead, the cars sat on the drive while the garage housed a pile of old furniture and junk, toys the children had grown out of, rusting patio heaters and most of the contents of his parents' house. It filled the garage from floor to ceiling.

His father, Graham, had been a carpenter, a good tradesman, capable with his hands and adept at fixing things. He had left school at fifteen with no qualifications apart from being good with wood and the tools needed to shape it. He had always pushed Marcus to do well at school, believing that a good education was important. And he had been right. Without it, there would have been no job at The Firm for Marcus, no Twin Gates, no private education for his children.

He sat in his mother's armchair looking at the boxes of tools that belonged to his dad. Planes, saws, chisels, hammers. If he had inherited the hard-working gene from his father, the one for DIY had mutated. He could barely use a screwdriver. When his father died six years earlier of a heart attack while digging the vegetable patch in the garden of their home in Staines, Marcus couldn't bring himself to sell his tools or give them away. The handles were stained with the sweat, and sometimes the blood, of his father's hands. But they had to go. He had found a young apprentice in a local building firm through a neighbour and the tools were going to him. He was happy they were going to a good home.

His mother, Hilary, stayed in the family home for four years after her husband died, until she passed away after a long and painful battle with cancer. She didn't leave much. Just some jewellery, which went to Olivia, and some furniture, most of which ended up in a house clearance. Marcus looked around him. It was like being in a time capsule. Fifty-five years of memories covered in dust, cobwebs and mouse droppings. It was time for it to go. Clearing the garage would take his mind off Spearmint, killer viruses and what he wanted to do with his life.

He returned from his third trip to the dump and was tying a knot in another black plastic bag of junk when his phone rang. It was James.

'Hi Dad. How are you doing?' he said in a sleepy voice.

'Hi James. I'm okay. Just clearing some of your grandparents' rubbish out of the garage and taking it to the tip. How's everything going in Manchester?'

'Yeah, all good Dad. Bit of a big night last night. Didn't get in until five this morning. Feeling a bit hungover. Thanks for the money for the keyboard and the little top-up by the way. How's everything at home?'

'Your mum and your sister are on the verge of renouncing dairy, which will be the kiss of death for scrambled eggs and cheese on toast. Life will then become a total misery. Vegan cheese is shit. Apart from that, work is manic. Mad project, mad client, usual crap.'

'Maybe when I come home, you and I can go down the pub, have a few beers and a steak and watch the football together? Get our meat fix!'

Marcus felt better knowing his son was still a carnivore and hadn't been brainwashed by Olivia and Alice.

'Yes. That would be great. I might be in Manchester in February for a meeting with a client. If the dates and times work, fancy meeting up for lunch or dinner? Unless you fancy cooking for me?'

He instantly regretted saying it. A year earlier, he had visited James's student house in Rusholme before a client meeting at The Firm's Manchester office. James lived in a four-bedroomed, semi-detached house with three other boys, none of whom had the inclination to wash their dirty dishes or their clothes. It smelled like the cabin at Ace Cars but on a bigger scale. On the kitchen worktop stood a red George Foreman grill which had the rancid smell of stale fat.

'What do you use that for?' he said to his son.

'Pretty much everything. Burgers, sausages, chicken, pizza, leftover curry. It's great.'

'Do you ever clean it?'

'No need. When it heats up, all the old fat runs into the little tray. You just give it a scrape, shove the new stuff on and it's fine.'

'Maybe we'll eat out then?' suggested Marcus.

James had taken his father to his favourite Indian restaurant on Rusholme's infamous Curry Mile, an all-you-can-eat dinner for £10 per head, including a pint of Cobra. It had given Marcus food poisoning and spoiled his overnight stay at The Lowry Hotel. One year later, one year wiser, Marcus took control of plans.

'I'll pick the restaurant this time,' he said.

'Fine with me, Dad.' A slap-up meal on his father would sustain him for a week. 'Just let me know when. Got to go now, meeting some mates down the pub to watch the football.'

'You are doing some work, aren't you? Final year and all that?'

'Of course, Dad. Don't worry. Love you.'

The phone went dead leaving Marcus to fill a few more black bags. He looked around. This was a real project, a labour of out-of-date love. He walked into the kitchen where Olivia and Alice were preparing dinner.

'What are we having tonight?' he said.

'Vegan paella,' said Olivia. 'It's just like normal paella but the chicken, chorizo, prawns and squid are replaced by artichoke hearts, broccoli and sun-dried tomatoes.'

A neutered paella wasn't that appealing, but it wasn't worth arguing with two zealots so he picked up the *Sunday Times* from the island.

'I'm going upstairs to have a shower and get changed. I stink from the garage.'

'You're not going to read the paper sitting on the toilet, are you?' said Alice. 'I hate it when you do that. It's really unhygienic.'

'Scared it might give you the killer virus?' he said sarcastically.

'Anything's possible from your arse, Marcus. Go and have a shower.'

After his shower, he sat naked on the toilet and opened the newspaper. It had a full double-page feature on the unfolding epidemic in China, its spread to other countries and the airlifting of British citizens from Wuhan. It had an artist's image of the virus. A little purple golf ball with hundreds of trumpets stuck to its surface. It could have been a Disney character; it almost looked cute. He read until the toilet seat left a ring around his buttocks and they had gone numb. His anxiety was increasing.

Olivia called upstairs from the kitchen and he quickly dressed in tracksuit pants and a T-shirt. He went commando; no point using up another pair of underpants and adding to Jacinda's workload. The vegan paella wasn't great, it was bland and tasteless. The artichoke hearts were a poor substitute for big chunks of oily chorizo. It was like going to the opera to see Pavarotti, only to discover he was sick and that Michael Bublé was the stand-in.

'What are you doing this week, Marcus?' said Alice, loading the dishwasher.

'Flat and office all week, back on Friday evening. I'm having dinner with Gavin on Tuesday night. I'm cooking.'

'You can have the recipe for the vegan paella if you like?' said Olivia.

'That's kind of you, sweetie, but I'm not sure Gavin likes artichokes. What about you two?'

'Last exam on Tuesday. Woo-hoo!'

'Good luck with that. Hope you don't get worms,' he said.

'Usual stuff for me,' said Alice with a sigh. 'Keeping the home fires burning. Nothing too important,' she said wistfully.

With Olivia going to university in September, James unlikely to return permanently and Marcus continuing to sell his soul to The Firm, Alice could foresee her role as homemaker coming to an end. Empty nest syndrome would create an even bigger void in her life. Later, they were sat in bed. Marcus was reading the *Sunday Times* business section and Alice was reading the magazine. He put down the paper, reached across and put his hand in hers.

'I know what you meant earlier when you said, "nothing too important". You gave up your career to look after us. Me, the kids, the house, schools. You're the one who's kept us all together.'

She put the magazine on her lap, took off her reading glasses and looked at him. She squeezed his hand and kissed it. Then she reached over and stroked his cheek with her other hand and looked at him.

'The world I've known for twenty years is coming to an end. I don't want it to but there's nothing I can do to stop it. It's time, but it's scary.'

A tear rolled down her cheek. He leaned across and kissed her.

'All of our worlds are changing, Al, and, you're right, there's nothing we can do to stop it,' he said. 'Any chance of a lift to the station in the morning?'

'Piss off, Marcus. Now go to sleep.'

They switched off their reading lamps and spooned together until Alice got too hot and made him roll away.

He picked up Monday morning's edition of *Metro* at the station. 'TRAPPED IN VIRUS CITY', was the headline. It was a simpleton's version of what he had read in the *Sunday Times*. The Chinese were building two new hospitals to cater for 2,500 patients, erecting them in two weeks from foundations to roof. It had taken Surrey County Council over a year to repair the potholes in Brooklands Avenue. Apparently, the virus could be spread before any symptoms appeared. Across the aisle, a man in a black puffer jacket coughed against the window, the warmth of his breath condensing in a cloud against the cold pane. Marcus took his melon hand sanitiser out of his bag, squirted a blob on to his hands and rubbed them together.

By 8.35, he was sat at his desk going through his emails. He opened one from Gerard Cornelius, sent to him and Mason.

Subject: Project Spearmint – Biographies
From: Gerard Cornelius

Marcus, Mason
Great to meet you both last week. Have given some thought to how we sell

our team to Espina. Please see attached template for team bios. Am going to bring in a professional scriptwriter to bring life to them. Her name is Arabella Ffoulkes and she will be in touch. Have given her your contact details. Will need new pics too. Working on the other stuff as well. Speak later. Let's WIN!

G

Marcus opened the attachment. It was a new CV template superimposed on an image of a house brick. He stabbed his spoon into his porridge and accidentally flicked a raisin on to his keyboard.

'Sweet Jesus!' he muttered under his breath. 'This place is going insane.'

It wouldn't matter a hoot if the CVs were written on a brick or the Turin Shroud, nobody would read them. They were only there for the vanity of the partners who lied and overstated their achievements.

Jenny Moffatt had put a date in his diary for the next round of the performance review process, and Chloe had sent him an email regarding a meeting to discuss 'Project Eedipuss'. He overheard Vanessa Briggs talking in a loud voice about her weekend. She was speaking loudly so everybody could hear.

'Yeah, I pulled an all-nighter on Friday night, worked most of Saturday as well and was completely knackered for most of yesterday. Slept the whole afternoon. Second time this month. Lawrence looked after the kids, fed them and took them to the cinema. He's been a saint.'

Marcus felt sorry for Mr Briggs. All-nighters and weekends were the campaign medals pinned to Vanessa's breast to demonstrate her commitment to The Firm. He put in his AirPods and selected 'Driving Anthems'. First track was Bryan Adams 'Summer of '69'. He was four in 1969, playing happily in the garden of the house in Staines. His mother hanging washing on the line and his father planting runner beans in the vegetable patch. He checked Stockwatch. It was down by over 100 points already, a big red day was looming.

Marcus took the Central Line to the flat. The bars and restaurants on Queensway were busy with early diners and drinkers. He took the lift to the second floor and walked along the corridor. He could hear Gavin playing the piano but decided not to disturb him and opened the door to his flat. He dumped his bags and left, taking the rear entrance leading on to Westbourne Grove to see the reassuring green sign of Waitrose.

The fish counter at The Temple had an impressive display, a proper fish counter manned by someone who knew how to skin and fillet. Even at six o'clock in the evening, there was plenty of choice. Clams were on special offer and he decided to make linguine vongole. He bought the ingredients for a starter, bruschetta with burrata, pesto and Parma ham.

Within twenty minutes, he was back home and putting away the shopping, staring out at the wasteland of Beirut. Nothing had changed in a week. He put a Charlie Bigham's beef bourguignon in the oven. The label said it was a meal for two.

Only if you've got the appetite of a six-year-old, he thought.

After dinner, he checked The Sequence. As he had predicted, it had been a red day on Stockwatch, down by almost 200 points, the biggest fall for weeks. It made him feel anxious, and he rang Alice.

'Hi Marcus. What's wrong? I only saw you this morning. You must be anxious about something?'

'Nothing's wrong. I just wanted to check you're okay, that you had a good day. Is something wrong with that? And no, I'm not anxious.'

He was lying.

'Yes, we're all fine here. Tennis was good. We're through to the quarter-finals. Have you eaten?'

'Yes, I have.'

'What did you have?'

'Wholemeal pasta with Quorn, peppers and tomatoes.'

Two lies in two minutes.

'Sounds great, Marcus. No need to worry about us, we're fine. Try to get a good night's sleep.'

The call ended and he stared out at Beirut. The urban fox was scavenging the building site for leftovers. He wondered if foxes had a gastronomic hierarchy of scraps. He imagined a group of them meeting in a darkened alleyway, discussing their fast-food tastes.

'KFC, Nando's, Pizza Hut, Burger King? What's your favourite?'

'I came across the remains of a Nando's ten-wing Chicken Roulette last week. Hardly been touched. It was absolutely to die for.'

He made a cup of green tea and watched the *BBC News* in bed. The reports from China made him feel more anxious. Latest estimates suggested that 100,000 people worldwide now had the coronavirus.

A Wembley Stadium full of potential killers, he thought. It was his last thought before he fell asleep.

* * *

Marcus took his usual seat next to Chloe in Communication Zone 1 for the pipeline meeting. He took the pipeline sheet and corrected her spelling of Project Eedipuss. She wrote 'thank you' on her notepad and nudged his arm in gratitude.

The rest of the partners trickled in, followed by Kelvin. He opened the meeting with an update on performance which Izzy Majewska had prepared for him, the key points were highlighted in yellow.

'Okay everyone, with four more billing days, we're forecasting to miss plan this month by over £1.5 million. Anyone got anything to say about that?'

Pairs of eyes darted nervously around the table, ears were rubbed and bottoms shifted. Nobody wanted to say anything. Kelvin looked around the table and drummed his fingers.

'Fine. Let me give you a little more help. If we carry on at this rate, we will miss budget by somewhere between five and six million pounds this year. Anyone got anything to say about that?'

It was like a gunfight in a Spaghetti Western, except Kelvin had an Uzi automatic and they all had peashooters. The team's youngest partner, David Prince made a break for it.

'Obviously, it's not a good situation to be in, Kelvin—'

It was as far as he got before Kelvin pulled the trigger and sprayed the room with verbal bullets, plastering blood and guts all over the walls.

'You're damn fucking right it's not a good situation, David! It's a very bad situation, actually. I've been looking at some figures Izzy has prepared for me and, out of the ten partners in this team, five of you are currently 25% or more down against your target. Now, I'm not going to name names in public but ...'

People started to relax and breathe more easily.

'... Tom, Simon, Oliver, Grant and Mason, you had better start finding some serious money to save your arses this year. I'm talking unit reductions and, if necessary, a reduction in partner numbers if this business can't sustain them. Am I making myself clear?'

No two words struck fear into the heart of a partner more than 'unit reduction'. Beads of sweat started to appear on the chubby foreheads of Tom Irons and Simon Loder. Kelvin finished giving his update.

'So, let me be crystal clear. If this ship is going down, some of us will be in a fucking lifeboat and some of us won't. And I'm not going to be drowning with anyone. Clear?'

The rest of the meeting was a muted affair. It was clear to everyone except Kelvin that the market was softening and the appetite for deals was slowing. It wasn't the right time for Marcus to raise the potential impact of the worsening crisis in China. Global epidemics weren't Kelvin's strong point. After the meeting, Mason grabbed Marcus and pulled him into a Chilling Egg, one of the yellow sound-proofed foam shells that dotted the floor.

'I thought it was bloody unfair of Kelvin to single me out in that meeting. Spearmint's been a team effort so far, hasn't it? You and me together, Marcus?'

Mason wasn't his normal arrogant, over-confident self. Facing Kelvin's wrath and retribution, 'I' had quickly become 'we'. They both knew Kelvin would throw Mason under a bus to save his own skin, and his units. Mason's hands were shaking.

'You know Kelvin hates failure. It's simply not in his vocabulary. It just means we've got to win Spearmint. Somehow,' said Marcus.

'You're lucky, Marcus. You've had a good year. I need Spearmint to come in or I'm screwed.'

Marcus put his hand on Mason's shoulder and stepped out of the Chilling Egg and returned to his desk. Chloe had left a packet of plain chocolate-covered rice cakes on his desk with a double macchiato and a note.

Thanks Marcus. You're a star.

The rest of the day passed quickly. He received a text from Gavin in the afternoon.

Hi Marcus. See you around 8pm? Have some exciting news to tell you about our next dinner! We have a mystery guest! Tell you more later. G.

Marcus didn't like surprises, they made him anxious. He wondered who the mystery guest could be? Eric the concierge? One of Gavin's relatives?

His curiosity was disturbed by an email which pinged into his inbox.

Subject: Project Spearmint – Bios
From: Arabella Ffoulkes

Hi Marcus
Gerard from CIC has e-troduced us. I'm writing the bios for Spearmint and would like to set up an interview later this week. I want to peel back the layers of the onion to find out who is really at the heart of Marcus Barlow. I want your bio to touch Espina's hearts as well as their minds. Let me know a day/time that suits? Will do the photoshoot at the same time.
    Can't wait to meet you
    Bella

He had never been 'e-troduced' to anyone and hated the bastardised construct. Being compared to an onion, and one that was going to touch the heart and mind of Jim Ibbotson, was even worse. And what did she mean by a 'photoshoot'? Maybe they were going to make him look like David Gandy? All he could do was reply.

Thursday, 9.30. On YouGo. See you then.

He answered a few more emails, signed off more potentially fraudulent expenses and did his timesheet. Risk and Compliance had sent another email regarding 'a small number of people who were not yet fully lanyard compliant'. He was still holding out against lanyard tyranny.

He left the office at 5.30 and walked to St Paul's Tube station. The front page of the *Evening Standard* carried a picture of a distressed Chinese woman in Wuhan wearing a facemask. He descended the escalator and took his normal place on the platform, looking up at David Gandy smiling down on him from the Wellman billboard.

Why are you so fucking handsome? he thought.

He let three trains go before he got on, and twenty minutes later he was in the lift at Queensway. Ten minutes later, he was in his flat. He changed and went into the kitchen to prepare dinner. His dining table wasn't as big as Gavin's, it would seat four at a push. He laid it with a white linen tablecloth and napkins. He put some music on the Sonos, Bach's Brandenburg Concerto No. 4. At precisely eight o'clock, the doorbell rang.

'Hi Gavin, come in.'

Gavin was wearing a lilac turtleneck jumper with a pair of skinny denims. Marcus wondered how he always looked so good.

'Hi Marcus, good to see you.'

Gavin gave him a shoulder squeeze. Somewhere between a kiss and shaking hands. He showed his friend into the kitchen and Gavin sat on one of the stools at the breakfast bar. He handed Marcus a bottle of wine. Meursault, already chilled. Gavin got everything right.

'What would you like to drink?' said Marcus, opening the door to the fridge.

'A Campari with ice, please.'

Marcus stopped in his tracks and stared at Gavin who remained poker-faced.

'I'm sorry but ...'

Gavin's face broke into a smile.

'Just teasing you. It's like Domestos. A gin and tonic would be good. Thanks. So how have the last couple of weeks been? It's been a while.' Gavin recognised the background music immediately. 'Bach, Brandenburg Concerto No. 4 in G major. Hope you're not playing this just for me?'

It was typical of Gavin to know the key as well.

'You can have the Clash if you'd prefer? Guns of Brixton in F sharp.'

'No thanks. Bach's fine.'

Marcus made the drinks and prepared the starter. He liked handling the orb of creamy burrata. It was like a little white breast implant. He gave Gavin an update on Spearmint, Gerard, the Wonderwall and Arabella, by which time the bruschetta had been made. He put the plates on the table, and the two friends took their seats opposite each other. Gavin opened the Meursault and poured.

'Sounds horrific, Marcus. Can companies do that? Sell a perfectly good business to invest in a bad one? I'm just a social worker, so what would I know?'

'Probably a lot more than the idiots running these businesses,' said Marcus. 'If the Board says they can, they can. Shareholders rarely say no to anything.'

'And what if you don't win it? Sounds like the "shit-or-bust" option. Is that going to be bad for you?'

'To be honest, I really couldn't give a fuck if we win or not. We should have walked away weeks ago, but we won't because of the fees. It's just about the money, like it always is.'

'Are you still thinking about giving it up or has the temptress lured you back into her bed for another session of passionate money-making? Come on darling, give it to me, just one more year of megabucks!'

His image hit the G Spot. Working at The Firm was like a seduction. Except now the earth didn't move for Marcus. He was going through the motions, faking an orgasm for a few more partner units. He cleared away the plates.

'So, tell me, who is this mystery dinner guest you've lined me up with then?'

'Lined us up with, Marcus, us! You'll have to wait, be patient. Ask me another question?'

Marcus strained the linguine and let it stand.

'Being a bit mysterious, aren't you? Bit Secret Squirrel. What's your view on what's happening in China? It's starting to really freak me out now.'

'Yes, on the surface, it does seem bad. But less than 1,000 people died of SARS so I don't think we should worry too much. Most of the people I deal with every day have bigger problems than the flu.'

Marcus served the main course and opened another bottle. It wasn't as good as Gavin's Meursault but it was a decent Albarino from The Temple. Their dinner conversation was as varied as usual. Will there be a no-deal Brexit? (Probably.) Is Emilia Fox sexy in *Silent Witness*? (Definitely.) Should Marcus get a Twitter account? (Absolutely not.) As he was clearing away, Marcus returned for a second bite.

'So, come on then, who is our mystery dinner guest?'

Gavin finally relented.

'Do you remember at our last dinner, I told you about the single mum, Claire, the one with the two great kids, who I call on every Tuesday?'

'Yes, the suicidal fashion student? The one who fancies you?'

'Inviting me for a chicken and pasta bake doesn't constitute a "fancy", and yes, her. I called on her today, told her about our Tuesday dinners. I've offered for us to cook for her one night. She can't get a babysitter so we're going there. I thought it would be a nice thing to do.'

'Oh right. And where is "there"?' said Marcus curiously.

'Kensal Mansions. A council estate just off Ladbroke Grove. Don't worry, you won't get mugged or need a police escort.'

In the year since he moved into Kensington Gardens Square, Marcus had never ventured further west than Portobello Road, and he hadn't set foot on a council estate since his vacation job as a dustman when he was a student.

'And what are we cooking for Claire. Turkey dinosaurs, chicken nuggets?'

'Don't be a snob, Marcus. We're cooking for her, not her children, although you will get to meet them. Kyle and Alexa are nice kids, you'll like them. It might do you good to see how real people live. That life isn't all about massive bonuses and expensive lunches. Probably in two weeks' time, which should give us plenty of time to organise something.'

'And what does Claire think of your idea?' said Marcus, putting the cutlery in the dishwasher basket.

'A bit hesitant but I'm sure we'll have a nice evening. Just go with it. I'll confirm the date next week.'

Gavin declined some ice cream but accepted a green tea, and the two men carried on their discussions. They finished the second bottle of wine around eleven, and Gavin got up to leave.

'Fantastic meal, Marcus. Well done. Loved it. Anything half as good as that will make Claire happy. Really good night, although we probably drank too much. Enjoy the rest of your week and I hope Gerard doesn't do anything too mad. My turn next week.'

Gavin turned back from the front door and hugged Marcus again. Marcus locked the front door, returned to the kitchen and finished tidying up. Waking up in the morning to a messy kitchen would ruin his day.

He brushed his teeth for three minutes, moisturised and got ready for bed. He was feeling slightly drunk. He got into bed and stared at the ceiling. His day at The Firm had been mad but his thoughts were all about meeting someone new, someone from a different world to him. Claire.

It was Tuesday, 28 January 2020.

Chapter 10

WONDERWALL

The drivers of the articulated lorries parked outside Beirut were sitting in their cabs, windows open to the cold January air, smoking and drinking coffee from paper cups. Marcus wondered what time they started.

He stopped at the front door. The Central Line during morning rush hour would be crammed. The thought of someone's halitosis in his face put him off and he returned to the sofa and stared into space. He was in no mood to be in early and eventually arrived in the office at ten. All the desks in the pool area were taken, so he set up camp in a vacant Chilling Egg and logged on. Blue screen. It would be fifteen minutes before he could use his laptop, so he checked Outlook on his phone. Gerard had gone into hyperdrive, spewing out emails. More sick from 'CIC'. He scrolled up to the final email.

Subject: Project Spearmint – Building the Drama
From: Gerard Cornelius

Marcus, Mason
Can we get together this afternoon to discuss the narrative for Spearmint?
I've had my team working on this 24/7 and now we have some real flesh on the bones. It's looking totally awesome. Really want to share our ideas with you. Meet in Collaboration Pod 3 at 16.00?
* Let's WIN this thang!*
*   Gerard*

'Win this thang!' God, *spare me*, thought Marcus.

He joined the team in Collaboration Pod 3. Insights from across The Firm were flooding in, burying them under paper. He said good morning and received muttered replies from faces which didn't look up from their screens. Three walls were covered in paper stuck by little green magnets. Someone had arranged some spare magnets into the outline of an ejaculating cock and balls. Nobody had the enthusiasm to remove it.

'How's it all going, Steve?' he said.

'Oh, usual fun and games, Marcus. Everyone wanting a piece of the pie, wanting to get in on the action. Nothing new really.'

If winning work in a competitive marketplace was tough, the internal battle was even harder. An unlicensed bare-knuckle fight fought with politics, back-stabbing, arm-twisting and, in some cases, vendetta.

'How many slides do you think we can get it down to?' said Marcus.

'Excluding appendices, CVs, case studies, commercials and all the insight crap? Probably around sixty,' replied the director. 'All the other stuff is probably going to double it.'

Putting together a proposal was like finding the winner of the *X Factor*. Firstly, the net was cast far and wide, a collection of materials gathered from previous proposals from around the world. Thousands of slides. It was a giant audition, everyone turning up with their favourite song and given two minutes to impress the judges. Irrelevant stuff was sorted from the stuff which 'possibly could make it'. The team had spent the last week preparing a giant PowerPoint 'Boot Camp'. And now Marcus and Steve were going to do 'Judges' Houses', whittling the three hundred hopefuls down to the final sixty to decide who went to an exotic location to sing for their place on the live show. Or, in the case of a PowerPoint slide, make it into the final deck. There would be tears of joy for the slides that made it and sorrow for those that went in the recycling bin. For those that made it, 'It was my destiny. I owned it.'

After hours of moving pieces of paper around in a giant jigsaw puzzle, they were almost there. At four o'clock, Gerard arrived in the room with Mason. He was wearing embroidered, flared denim loon pants and a tie-dyed cheesecloth shirt with open-toed sandals. He had obviously taken his time getting back from Woodstock. He was carrying a large plastic crate.

'Afternoon Spearmints!' he said excitedly.

He stopped in his tracks, put down the crate and wiggled his fingers in the air.

'Is it just me or is anyone else getting a breeze of negative energy passing over them? It must be all this paper soaking up the positivity. I'll sit down here, it might be less suffocating.'

Gerard sat cross-legged in the middle of the floor. Mason sat on a beanbag, beaming at his love child. Marcus thought it might be a good time to assert some control.

'Perhaps Steve and I could take you and Mason through the proposal as it stands right now, Gerard? Bring out some of the key themes, core messages and USPs.'

Gerard remained preoccupied by the contents of his crate. Marcus and Steve 'walked the wall', explaining how each slide delivered the key messages to Espina.

Gerard suddenly sprang to his feet like an electrocuted elf.

'This stuff really doesn't do it for me,' he said, dismissively. 'Same old, same old. Do you really believe Espina is going to read any of this stuff?'

It was the first time Gerard had said something Marcus agreed with.

'It doesn't excite me, doesn't create theatre, doesn't create magic. We need our sixty minutes with Espina to be ones which build dreams. They need to believe we are magicians with special powers!'

He picked up his plastic crate and emptied the contents on to the table. Thirty or forty rectangular wooden blocks spilled out. Gerard started to turn the blocks to face the team, assembling them in a specific order.

'Each one of these blocks is a little piece of magic. Together, they create a spell. That's what we are going to cast on Espina on opening night. A spell.'

It was turning into a scene from Harry Potter. Marcus looked at Gerard to see if he had a lightning bolt scar on his forehead. Gerard assembled the wall in front of the team, each block containing a single word printed on the face.

'Inspiration', 'Capability', 'Sharing', 'Mindful', 'Emotional', 'Proven', 'Trust', 'Empathy', 'Giving', 'Ambition', 'Feelings', 'Delivery', 'Innovative', 'Magic', 'Warmth'. And, right at the top, 'Wonder'.

Marcus turned to look at Mason. He was already under Gerard's spell and was gazing in awe. The rest of the team looked like they had been possessed by a flock of Dementors. Marcus read the words again.

'I can't see any mention of money, or value, or profit, Gerard? Do you think this might be an omission?'

Gerard gave him a dismissive wave of an imaginary wand that he had bought in Diagon Alley.

'Old hat, Marcus, old hat. Espina knows we want to help them make money. That's just the "what"? This is about the "how"? Bringing this wall to life is what's going to help us to WIN!'

'So, how do you propose we turn this,' said Steve Pettigrew, pointing at the walls of paper, 'into that?' He pointed at Gerard's wall of bricks.

'Easy peasy, lemon squeezy,' said Gerard. 'My CIC team will go through each slide with you and identify one word which encapsulates everything on it. That word will become a magic brick in the Wonderwall that we will build in front of the client.'

'And what about the proposal?' said Marcus.

'Send it to them if they expect it. What they won't be expecting is the magic we will unleash at the presentation. This will put them under our spell.'

Marcus turned to Mason. 'You're very quiet, Mason? Any thoughts?'

Mason leaned forward in his beanbag and put his head in his hands.

'I'm just really sad,' he said, shaking his head.

Gerard looked concerned. A wave of relief came over Marcus. Mason had finally come to his senses.

'Really sad to think of all the wasted opportunities, the bids we've lost, the fees we've missed because we couldn't shift our paradigm. We should have been doing this stuff years ago. This is fucking brilliant.'

Gerard beamed and started to put the blocks back into the crate.

For the second time in a week, Hurricane Gerard had blown everyone away. Gerard left to re-join the magicians in CIC and Marcus returned to the Chilling Egg. Mason walked past and poked his head into the foam capsule.

'What did you think? Happy?'

Marcus looked up from his laptop.

'You realise this could all go tits up, don't you? This is a massive risk, letting Gerard and his lunatics loose on Spearmint.'

'Come on, Marcus, be bold. Fortune favours the brave.'

'And stupidity has a knack of getting its way. Your balls are sitting on a chopping board and Kelvin is holding a very large knife. It's not too late to change, you know? We just tell Gerard to piss off.'

'No can do, I'm afraid. Kelvin has already told the top bods that we're using CIC, that we will win Phase 2 and £9 million is coming our way.'

'And who's going under the bus if we don't?'

Mason smiled and shrugged. For all his bluff, inside he was a scared little boy like the rest of them. He walked away.

Marcus was back in his flat by seven and sat on the sofa reading the *Evening Standard*. The situation in Wuhan was getting worse. Countries across the world were closing their borders to flights from China. The airlifting of stranded Brits out of Wuhan was turning into a fiasco.

Just after eight, Alice called him. He told her about Gerard and the Wonderwall. She giggled.

'He sounds brilliant, Marcus. Right up your street. What are you doing at the moment? Getting ready for a game of Quidditch?'

'You're funny. Actually, I'm reading the paper. Everything okay at home? How's Libby?'

'All fine. Exams are over so she's happy. I've got my art class next Monday and I haven't done a thing since the last lesson, so I've been doing some work on it.'

'Work on what?'

'My picture. It's a life class.'

Marcus had only ever seen Alice's depictions of bowls of fruit, random kitchen objects and local scenery in watercolours.

'What's a life class?'

Marcus had never been a big devotee of 'The Arts', although he did know who Banksy was.

'We have a model sitting for us and we paint him. It's our third sitting next Monday.'

'Him?'

'Yes, him. Tony. He's a sixty-three-year-old ex-fireman. Great muscle tones. And before you ask Marcus, yes, we do see his cock, although I'm painting him from the side so I don't have to look at it. He gets £75 for a three-hour sitting.'

'Maybe I could do something like that if I get fired from The Firm?' he said.

Alice laughed out loud.

'I love you Marcus but your body is so nondescript. You wouldn't cut it as a life model, I'm afraid.'

He thought about his meeting with Arabella the next day, how she was going to make him look like David Gandy.

'Well, we shall have to see about that,' he said defiantly.

He was hurt, she had never described his body as 'nondescript' before.

They said goodnight to each other. He would be home on Friday.

In the morning, he went straight to OnYouGo where he was meeting Arabella. He ordered his double macchiato from Fernando, who was his normal, cheerful self. He looked around the open meeting area and saw two spotlights and an impressive camera on a tripod set up in a corner. The decor of the meeting area was like the set of *Dragons' Den*, bare brick walls and wooden floorboards.

Sitting at one of the tables was a young woman with frizzy hair and small, round spectacles perched on the end of her nose. She was wearing a parka which was open and a chunky-knit, roll-neck sweater which made her look like a tortoise. Next to her sat a man in a leather jacket and a denim shirt. Marcus assumed she was Arabella and walked up to the table.

'Arabella?'

She looked up from her phone.

'Bella is fine. You must be Marcus?'

She introduced her colleague, Leo, who would be taking the photo to accompany his bio. She spoke with an accent that suggested she was born with a silver spoon in her mouth.

Probably a decent public school and Oxbridge, he thought. He took off his raincoat and sat opposite Bella, who had her notepad and pen at the ready.

'It's great to meet you, Marcus, and thanks for making time. Gerard has given me all the background on Spearmint. I'll be writing the bios for the team to meet Espina. Everything clear so far?'

She hadn't said anything not to be clear on.

'Bit of background on me first. Left Cambridge, double first in French and History, early part of my career in corporate PR, five years at the BBC in production, wrote a couple of screenplays, set up my own business and ended up back in the corporate world helping organisations like yours.'

Marcus was bang on about the Oxbridge bit.

'So how can I help you?' said Marcus stiffly.

'Well, I'm coming from the position that the traditional CV is dead. Clients don't care what you've done before and who for.'

Marcus thought if he were a client, those would be exactly the sort of things he would be interested in, particularly if he was paying £5,000 a day for it.

'So what *are* they interested in, Bella?' he said.

She replied quickly.

'In one word, Marcus. Empathy. Is there an emotional fit between you and them? Do you connect on a level that goes much deeper than a contract? Everything clear so far?'

Everything she had said so far had only made things more opaque. He nodded and took a sip of his coffee.

'So, as I explained in my email, what I need from you is to find out what makes you tick, what gives you a hard on about what you do, what makes you think you're the king of the fucking universe and makes you piss your pants when you win?'

The only thing becoming clear was Arabella and Gerard were both mad and The Firm had lost its marbles letting people like them take over the asylum. He capitulated and, for the next thirty minutes, did his best to answer her questions.

'What was the happiest moment in your life?'

'What makes you cry?'

'What has been your biggest disappointment?'

'How would you describe your relationship with your wife?'

'In three words, how would your clients describe you?'

'Rank these in order of importance: sex, integrity, money, love, recognition, faith, trust.'

Bella took copious notes, creating a spider's web of mind maps across the pages. Finally, she put down her pen and stared at him over the rim of her glasses.

'Wow, that was bloody amazing, Marcus. Truly amazing. Thank you so much. Espina are going to love you once I've finished your bio. Now, let's do your photo.'

Leo stood up and walked across to the camera. For the first time, he spoke.

'Great. If you could take your jacket and tie off, Marcus, and sit on this stool?'

'Why?'

'Because everyone's picture will be taken looking relaxed on a stool?'

'No, why do I have to take my jacket and tie off?'

'Oh, I see. Because they symbolise barriers between you and your client. Ties are authority symbols, not helpful for building relationships and displaying empathy.'

'But it's only a jacket and tie and I happen to like them. They don't make me look like a member of the SS.'

'Sorry, Gerard wants a more informal look. No ties,' said Leo. 'Take them off and put these on.'

He handed Marcus a red builder's hard hat with the slogan 'Doing It With You' emblazoned across the front and a yellow, high-vis jacket saying the same. Reluctantly, Marcus removed his jacket and tie, put on the industrial-wear and sat on the stool. Leo adjusted the lights and fiddled with the dials and lens on the camera.

'It's a pity you've shaved this morning,' said Leo. 'A bit of stubble would have worked well with the image we want to create.'

'I shave every day, even at weekends,' said Marcus, growing more irritated with Leo by the second.

'Maybe we leave it for today and do this tomorrow with some stubble?'

Marcus's patience ran out.

'How about taking the fucking picture and let's get this over with.'

Leo snapped the camera out of the tripod and proceeded to take pictures from every angle, even the 'up the nostrils' shot, the motor drive whirring with every press of the shutter. Eventually, Leo was done.

'That's great, thanks Marcus. I'll go through these with Bella and Gerard and send you the best ones.'

Marcus put his jacket and tie back on and shook hands with Leo. He saw Chloe in the queue in OnYouGo with her sustainable plastic mug.

'Hi Marcus. Can I get you a coffee?'

He quickly weighed up the benefits of remaining in the asylum.

'That's very kind of you Chloe, but no thanks. I've got to go out again. See you later.'

He walked up to the revolving doors where Michael, the security guard, was standing.

'Have a good day, Michael,' he said.

He passed through the revolving doors out on to the pavement where the City's worker bees were busy buzzing. It had started to rain. He crossed the road to Poultry and looked up. The rooftop garden of Coq d'Argent, one of London's fashionable restaurants, was a favourite spot for suicides. The sky was free from falling bodies and he walked along Cheapside until he reached St Paul's and entered the garden. All the benches were taken; office workers were drinking coffees, checking their emails, talking into their phones.

At the end of a bench sat a man in a stained overcoat and dirty trainers with holes in the toes. His grey hair was long and dishevelled and he had a patchy beard which concealed the broken veins on his face. He wore a floppy, brown trilby hat with a frayed brim. Between his legs was a large bottle of cider, the screw top was on the bench next to him. He swigged from the bottle.

'Do you mind if I join you?' said Marcus, approaching the other end of the bench.

The man stared up at Marcus and looked him up and down. His blue eyes were sunken and cloudy.

'Feel free,' said the man, gesturing to the space next to him. 'Have you got a spare fag?' he said, taking another swig from the bottle.

'I'm sorry. I don't smoke anymore.'

The man shrugged and took another swig. Marcus took his laptop bag off his shoulder and put it between his feet. The man gazed up at the dome of the cathedral, turned and spoke to him.

'It's beautiful isn't it, St Paul's? Do you come here often?'

Marcus laughed.

'Are you hitting on me? Yes, it is beautiful and I wish I did come here more often.'

The man smiled to show a set of decaying teeth and extended his right hand. His skin was stained by the grime of the City and his dirty nails were long and cracked.

'I'm Colin,' he said. 'Nice to meet you.'

Marcus turned to his right and shook his hand.

'Marcus. Nice to meet you, Colin.'

He was tempted to reach into his bag for his melon hand sanitiser but thought it would be rude. Colin had made the first gesture and, in a city where people never spoke to strangers, that meant something. The two men stared up at the dome until Colin broke the ice again.

'You obviously work in the City? Covert coat, double-cuff shirt, silk tie, Windsor knot, nice suit, brogues, probably Church's or Barkers.'

The last thing Marcus expected was Colin to know the make of shoes he was wearing. They were Church's.

'Yes, I do,' he said. 'Although nowadays, I'm seen as old-fashioned. It's all open-necked shirts and jeans. How come you know so much about City attire …?' He stopped in mid-sentence, realising his question could be taken the wrong way, that he had made an assumption about the man. 'I'm sorry, please don't take that …'

Colin waved his hand to indicate that no offence had been caused or taken and took another swig of cider, which dribbled down his stubbly chin.

'I used to work in the City. I was a trader for Merrill Lynch. Survived the crash in 2008 and then got made redundant. A "restructuring", they called it. They didn't want people like me anymore. I lost more than a job. Wife, kids, house, sanity, self-respect.'

'Didn't you make enough? What about getting another job?'

'Nobody was hiring after The Crash. Not people like me. I sat at home for months applying and getting rejected. I even did some work mini-cabbing, but it wasn't the same. The City is like a drug. Fourteen-hour days, living on adrenaline and cocaine. It seduces you, consumes you and then spits you out when it's finished with you. Eventually, my marriage broke up and the ex got most of it. She's remarried now. Lives in Cambridge. My kids are grown up but I never see them.'

'And where do you live now?'

Colin laughed. 'Where do you think?' he said, looking down at his dirty sleeping bag. 'So, what about you then, Marcus? What brings you to be sitting here?'

For the next hour, Marcus told Colin about his career and life at The Firm, how it had changed him to the point where he no longer knew who he was. Apart from Gavin, it was the first time he had talked openly about how he was feeling. Colin was a complete stranger, but one who seemed to understand what he was saying better than anyone.

'It sounds to me, Marcus, like you're fast approaching the end of the road. Maybe it's about time you took some decisions before someone makes them for you?'

Colin offered Marcus his bottle of cider which was now almost empty. Marcus stood up, picked up his laptop bag and threw it over his shoulder.

'I think I've taken too much of your time already, Colin. I should be going. It was a pleasure meeting you. Really.'

'It was a pleasure meeting you too, Marcus. Good luck.'

Marcus reached into his inside pocket, took out his wallet and removed a twenty-pound note. He offered it to Colin who put up his grimy palm in refusal.

'Please take it Colin. Buy yourself some cigarettes and another bottle of cider. It was the best counselling I could have got for £20.'

Colin begrudgingly took the note and stuffed it in his coat pocket. He looked up at Marcus.

'Maybe see you here again sometime?'

'Maybe,' said Marcus. 'I'll look forward to it.'

Eric the concierge wasn't around when he got to the flat. He opened the door, locked it behind him and walked into the living room. He took off his coat and threw it over the back of the armchair and removed his shoes. He went into the bedroom, laid on the bed in his suit and stared up at the ceiling. The words Colin had said to him were still going around in his head.

'Maybe it's about time you took some decisions before someone makes them for you?'

* * *

On Friday morning, Marcus got into the office early. The front pages of the newspapers were heralding the UK's exit from the EU. Evoking Winston Churchill's famous speech, the prime minister had said, 'This is not an end but a beginning.'

Yes, the beginning of the bloody end, he thought. *Stupid Little Englanders and their fucking blue passports.*

Marcus had been a Remainer and believed that the Brexit result had been achieved by misinformation-fed bigotry. He had fallen asleep on the bed the previous evening and hadn't eaten. He needed extra sugar and bought a pain aux raisins to go with his porridge and coffee. Outlook was full, and he spent two hours reading, replying, filing and deleting. He did his expenses and timesheet and registered for the mandatory online training course 'Cyber Attacks: Protecting Our Data', due for completion by the end of February.

Apart from David Prince, Marcus was the only partner on the floor. Everyone else was either on leave or working from home, as they did every Friday. He walked to Collaboration Pod 3 where the team was busy adapting slides to fit Gerard's new template. Gerard and two of his CIClets were grouped around the storyboard with Steve Pettigrew and another member of the team. They were all deep in thought.

'Morning everyone. How's it all going?' said Marcus.

'Fantastic,' said Gerard. 'I think we're really getting to the essence of our proposal now. We've probably got twenty of the thirty-six bricks nailed.'

Marcus glanced at Steve, who closed his eyes. The past couple of days had obviously been painful.

'So what are we looking at now then?' said Marcus, staring at a slide titled 'Complexity of Separating IT Systems'.

'I was just explaining to Gerard the difficulty of separating IT systems. It can be very complex. Gerard needs a single word to encapsulate this,' said Steve.

'What's wrong with "complexity"?' said Marcus, innocently.

'Already used it. We can't use it twice in the Wonderwall,' said Gerard. 'Describe it to me again, Steve.'

'All the different systems, servers, data and applications are all mixed up together. It's like a giant ball of spaghetti.'

Suddenly, Gerard jumped up and down and started clapping his hands.

'That's it, that's it! The word is "spaghetti". Spaghetti! Bloody brilliant. We'll use that, for sure. Love it.'

One of the CIClets wrote 'spaghetti' on the slide in black marker pen.

'When do you expect to have this all wrapped up?' said Marcus.

'Probably early next Monday. Into production on Tuesday and Wednesday. Rehearsals Thursday and Friday, opening night on the tenth assuming everything goes to plan. How did it go with Bella yesterday?'

'A fulfilling experience for both of us I would say.'

'Fantastic.'

Marcus returned to his desk just after midday. The floor was busy with people eating pizza. He had forgotten it was 'Pizza Friday'. To boost morale, Kelvin had arranged to order in twenty large thin-and-crispy pizzas with a variety of toppings on the last Friday of the month. The best topping of all would have been if Kelvin had been there to enjoy it with the team, but he was on a long weekend's skiing in Val d'Isère.

He texted Alice to say he was leaving the office and took the long walk to Waterloo via Embankment. His step count was low and his audio levels had been too high. He listened to *Blue*, in his opinion the best album by Joni Mitchell. It was warm for January and wished he hadn't worn his overcoat. By the time he got to Blackfriars Bridge, he was too hot carrying his overnight bag and laptop. The station concourse was already busy and he picked up a copy of the *Evening Standard*.

The first cases of the virus in the UK had been identified. Two Chinese nationals staying in a hotel in York. He started to feel anxious and not even Joni Mitchell was calming him. The 17.10 was delayed by ten minutes, but he was more worried about other things. He looked into Burger King and saw Britney smiling as she handed over bags of flame-grilled goodies. She didn't seem anxious about anything.

When he got home, most of the lights in the house were off, apart from the kitchen and the office. He dropped his bags in the hall and walked through the kitchen into the office. Alice was at the end of the room, sitting on a stool in front of an easel, surrounded by little coloured tubes with their lids off. The room smelled of oil paint and turpentine.

'Hi, Al. What are you doing?' said Marcus.

'Playing tennis, Marcus. What does it look like I'm doing?'

Her snappy reply put him on the back foot. After a nightmare week, he wanted some small talk to ease him into a conversation.

'Sorry, dumb question. I can see you're painting. How's it going?'

He walked behind her and stared at the canvas. He could make out the shape of a man standing naked on a blue sheet.

'So that's the fireman?' he said.

'Ex-fireman,' said Alice. 'Tony, he retired eight years ago. I'm struggling with his thighs. I can't get the proportion with his calves right.'

'His buttocks look good. I think you've got those right. Very firm. Certainly not nondescript. Oh, by the way, the virus is in the UK now. Just thought you'd like to know? I'll leave you to Tony's thighs then?'

He went upstairs, put his dirty washing in the basket and started to get changed. He paused in front of the dressing mirror in his Calvin Klein underpants, pulled them down to his knees and stared at his bottom over his shoulder.

'Maybe not as good as Fireman Tony's, but still pretty good. Not too much sag,' he said to himself.

Olivia was staying at a friend's house, leaving Marcus and Alice on their own. Six bedrooms, six toilets, four reception rooms and an office. They were rattling around in the house like pinballs. After dinner, they sat together on the sofa. He put the television on. *Question of Sport* was just ending with its familiar theme tune. The show was almost as old as Marcus.

'I bet Sue Barker will still be presenting the show from her care home,' he said to Alice. 'She still looks pretty good though.'

The television flipped from one familiar theme tune to another. *EastEnders*. If there was ever a plot to lose, Marcus had lost it after Dirty Den and Angie. The only thing he liked about the show was when the characters took a break from their East End drudgery and headed 'Up West', as if a trip to Regent Street was like going to Mars. He scanned the rest of the channels and they agreed to switch off. She turned to him and pulled her legs underneath her.

'So how was the rest of your week with Gerard?' she said with a smirk.

'Completely insane. The guy is a lunatic. The worst part is that Kelvin and Mason think he's a genius. I think The Firm has lost the plot.'

He told her about his interview with Arabella and the photo session with Leo.

'But it's always been mad and all about the money, Marcus. You knew that when you joined. Maybe it's you that needs to change, because The Firm won't? Maybe you need to decide what you want?'

They were almost the same words Colin used. It prompted him to tell her his conversation with Colin in the garden at St Paul's. He started to rub his palms on his thighs, like he always did when he was anxious.

'Well, maybe Colin has a point, Marcus. Sounds like good advice to me,' she said.

'I didn't drink his cider. His teeth were awful.'

She cupped both his hands in hers and kissed him on the lips. She stood up, pulled him out of the sofa and led him to the stairs.

'I haven't got a migraine tonight. Are you sure you didn't drink any of the cider?'

It was Friday, 31 January 2020.

Chapter 11

Grand Designs

The start of a new month brought fresh funds from Claire's Universal Credit and she felt better for being temporarily solvent. It had been a nice weekend. She had taken the children to Kensington Gardens, walked around the pond and fed the ducks. Friday's goodie bag from Lester Primus contained a half leg of lamb, reduced by 50%, and she had made a Sunday roast. Kyle loved roast potatoes and she had let him stir the gravy, standing up to the cooker on a chair. She had bumped into Judith on the stairs. She was off to a meeting to hear two of the Labour Party leadership candidates speak and couldn't stop to chat. That was her weekend, the isolation of being a single mum.

She was greeted in the playground by Helena Mistakidis.

'Hi Claire, hi Kyle. Did you have a nice weekend?'

Kyle nodded and looked up at his teacher.

'We went to Kensington Gardens and fed the ducks, didn't we Kyle? said Claire.

'That sounds lovely. How about you, Claire? How are you doing?'

'Fantastic, living the dream. Cocktails at Claridge's on Saturday night, followed by dinner at Le Gavroche.'

That was her night with Jack after they got engaged. A present from his parents. They were the only two fancy places she had been to in London. Helena smiled and raised her eyebrows.

'Really?' she laughed.

'And what about you?' said Claire.

'Probably as good as yours. Akis was working so I made stuffed dolmades, had a glass of wine and did some marking. Living the dream too.'

Claire didn't know what dolmades were but felt better knowing she wasn't the only one on her own on Saturday night. Beverley had arrived with Bruce, who ran up to Kyle and hugged him.

'Still on for coffee this week?' said Beverley enthusiastically.

Claire had been dreading the conversation. Although Gavin had urged her to go, she felt she had little in common with the elegant woman from Hong Kong. But it didn't seem she was going to take 'no' for an answer.

'Sure, when were you thinking of?'

'Your daughter goes to nursery on Thursday mornings, yes?'

Claire nodded.

'How about Thursday morning then? We can go back to the flat from here. And bring whatever you've kept from college. I'd love to see your designs.'

Apart from Gavin, and Judith, who had pointed out that nothing Claire had designed would suit her, nobody had shown any interest in her ideas.

'I will. That's great, thank you, Thursday it is then.' Secretly, she was excited, but her insecurity didn't stop her from adding, 'If something comes up and you're too busy, I won't mind if you have to cancel.'

'Thursday morning it is. See you then,' said Beverley confidently.

By the time she got back to the flat, the *Today* programme was almost over. The closing headlines were dominated by a Jihadi terrorist attacker who had stabbed two people in Streatham before being shot. The death toll in China was now at 200, with 10,000 cases identified. She was more worried about the virus than being stabbed by a terrorist.

She was having lunch with Alexa, sausages with some leftover roast potatoes and alphabetti spaghetti, when her daughter turned to her.

'Mummy, who is your best friend? Mine's Zoe.'

Alexa was searching for an 'A' in her pasta letters with a spoon. Friends? Claire had left her school friends behind in Walsall and most of her friends from Saint Martins now lived in completely different worlds. Single, enjoying their lives in London, living in boho flats in Shoreditch or Camden. Their paths would never cross again.

'Probably Gavin and Mr Mahoney, sweetie,' she said. 'They always look after us, don't they?'

'Gavin smells nice. And Mr Moany tickles me.'

Her world had shrunk after Jack left. Her social circle was now a slightly effeminate and well-dressed social worker and an ex-navvy with tooth decay and a talent for baking. She was never going to make it on to the front pages of *Tatler*.

Kyle was excited on the way home from school. His name was still in the draw to look after Biscuit, the class hamster, over the half-term holiday which was only two weeks away. The winner would be announced the following week. For Kyle, it would be like winning EuroMillions.

Mr Mahoney arrived for their daily appointment with Bradley Walsh. He had stretched himself at the weekend and brought a small Tupperware box containing twelve multi-coloured macaroons.

'Wow, these look amazing, Mr Mahoney,' said Claire, impressed his sausage fingers had produced something so delicate.

'They're the third batch,' said the caretaker. 'The first two were like rocks. I over-baked them. Had the oven on too high. Not bad for a first attempt though, not bad at all.'

On the show, The Vixen destroyed the hopes of Brian, a carpet fitter from Dorset, who was looking to win £7,500 to pay for his daughter's wedding in Las Vegas. It was a quick kill, all over in ninety seconds. Brian was a lamb to the slaughter and his daughter would have to make do with mushroom vol-au-vents and a church hall to celebrate her nuptials.

After putting the children to bed, Claire settled into her chair with a blanket and a book, *My Brilliant Friend* by Elena Ferrante, a Christmas present from Judith. Tomorrow was her favourite day of the week, Gavin's visit and Lester Primus's goodie bag. Better than being on her own.

The weather was warm and climbing the four flights of stairs had caused Claire to wheeze. She puffed on her inhaler. Childhood asthma had been a curse. At school, PE and Games lessons had been spent sitting on the side-lines cutting up the half-time oranges for the other girls.

Susan Rae was reading the news headlines as she opened the front door. Recriminations over the weekend's terrorist stabbing and a political row over the forthcoming climate change summit. Thirty thousand Britons stranded in China in the centre of the virus outbreak had been told to leave with no help from the Government. She opened the door to Gavin, dressed in a camel-coloured, cashmere jacket with a sky-blue scarf, his Paul Smith satchel bag swung across his shoulders. He was carrying two cups of coffee in a cardboard holder.

'Morning Ms Halford!' he said in a chirpy voice. 'Dr Douglas brings you gifts from the Panettone Palace. I took an Uber so they're still hot. I got you a cappuccino. Hope that's okay?'

He crossed the threshold and walked into the kitchen. It was an Eau Sauvage day.

'The Panettone Palace indeed! I'm honoured. Your caffeine detox lasted a long time then?' she said.

'Detox is officially over. My first decent coffee for over a week. And to celebrate the occasion …' He reached into his satchel and took out a brown paper bag containing two triangular segments which he proudly placed on the table. '… their famous and exalted panettone. Don't worry about plates.'

He tore open the bag and removed the lids from the coffees. They were still frothy and, for the next ten minutes, they indulged themselves in the buttery sponginess of the panettone. Gavin turned to her.

'I've got more good news for you.'

'Oh yes, what's that then? Kensington and Chelsea are going to rehouse me in a garden flat in Holland Park?'

'Not exactly, even better. Try again.'

'Victoria Beckham texted you and asked if you knew of any suicidal single mums with a fading flair for designing who might want a job?'

'She did but I forwarded it on to someone better. Think harder. Come on!'

'Don't worry, I'm not offended. Her designs are shit and I'd have turned the job down anyway. Come on, spit it out! What's so great that I have to guess?'

Gavin puffed himself up. 'Marcus and I are going to cook for you next week, here in your flat. I spoke to him last week and he thinks it's a great idea. He can't wait to meet you.'

It was only a small fib. Claire started to become anxious.

'I only said "yes" because I didn't want to upset you at the time. I didn't think you'd go through with it. Are you sure? He will hate it in this poky flat, I know he will.'

'It'll all be fine, trust me. He's not posh at all. How about next Tuesday evening?'

He was smiling and there was something about his smile that made her trust him. The last time she had had two men in her flat was when the council sent two men round to treat the damp.

'Okay, if you insist. So what are you going to cook?'

'Don't know yet. Three courses for sure. Obviously, you've got a food processor, haven't you?' he said.

'Don't take the piss. I've got a potato masher, if that's any good?' she said, starting to feel embarrassed.

He laughed again, he liked teasing her. There was a feistiness to her that he'd always admired.

'Do I need to dress up for the occasion?'

'Maybe a Balenciaga ball gown?' he replied. 'Failing that, the usual leggings and a sweatshirt will do.'

She had always wondered how he was so well informed about fashion. Always too well dressed for a social worker who grew up on a country estate in Scotland.

'Unfortunately, my ball gown is being altered at the moment, so it might have to be the leggings.'

Gavin picked up the empty coffee cups and the brown paper bag and put them in the bin. He looked around the kitchen.

'Do you have any Mr Muscle? The surface cleaner?'

'Sorry, no. I only have Tesco's. I have to buy the cheapest.'

'A poor and ineffective substitute,' said Gavin. 'You shouldn't skimp on surface cleaner. It's important.'

For the rest of their time, Gavin did what he was paid to do, checking on her wellbeing and her children.

'By the way,' he said, as he got up to leave, 'when are you having your coffee morning with the Chinese lady? You are going, aren't you?'

She hesitated momentarily. 'Yes, on Thursday.'

'Excellent. It will be good for you. Make sure you don't turn into a recluse like your neighbour. I should drop by and pay him a visit one day, just to make sure he's okay?'

'He'll probably be killing terrorists and won't answer the door,' said Claire.

Gavin frowned.

'*Call of Duty*. It's a video game. You wouldn't understand, far too lowbrow for you,' she said.

They walked to the front door and he gave her a hug.

'See you next week. I'll text to confirm dinner. Good luck with the coffee morning. Just go and be yourself.'

He walked along the balcony. As he got to the stairs, Claire called after him.

'By the way, I don't eat offal. Kidneys smell of wee and liver is disgusting. Anything else is fine with me.'

Tesco Express was empty and the menacing presence of Andrew Coates was absent too. Lester Primus was at the front of the store, rearranging sandwiches, crisps and meal deals, and saw her approaching. He stopped lining up the bottles of water and went over to her.

'Hi Claire. Everyone okay?' he said looking down at the children.

Alexa and Kyle both nodded.

'Hello, Mr Primus. Yes, we're all fine, thanks. Where's your attack dog today? Has the RSPCA taken him away to be put down?'

Lester Primus looked baffled until he finally tuned in.

'Oh, Andy you mean? Yes, he's off sick today, bit of an incident yesterday. A customer at the self-checkout breathed on him and he had a minor seizure. She was chewing a piece of nut brittle and he's very allergic to peanuts. I had to inject him in the thigh with his EpiPen, it was quite scary. We thought it best he had today off.'

She feigned concern. 'Oh dear, that's unfortunate. Give him my best.'

'Come through to the back. I've got a couple of bags for you. Bit of a mix this week.'

It's a bit of a mix every week, she thought.

Claire looked inside the bags. The mince, chicken thighs and pork steaks were reduced and the pasta was always useful. The jar of pickled cucumbers would go to Mr Mahoney. The store manager said goodbye with his usual gift of Starburst sweets, warm and soft from his trouser pocket.

She completed the rest of her shopping and entered her PIN at the self-checkout with some confidence, it was only the fourth day of the month. They were back in the flat in good time for Mr Mahoney's arrival. The children were in the living room and he walked straight into the kitchen and sat down. There was something wrong.

'Sorry, no cake today, I'm afraid. After the dustmen, I cleared the courtyard, let an electrician into No. 34 and went back to my flat to make a Bakewell tart. I never got that far, never got that far. The frangipane is still sitting in the fridge.'

The chair squeaked under his weight. Claire was making builder's tea.

'What happened, Mr Mahoney? Do you feel ill?'

'Sinead and I would have been married forty years today, forty years. We were married in Willesden Registry Office, had our reception in a room above The Greyhound pub, just us and a few friends from home. I looked at her photograph today. She looked so beautiful. I haven't been able to do much. I just miss her so much, so much.'

The big man looked down at the table and his shoulders started to shake. Claire turned, put the kettle down and put her arm around him.

'It's okay, Mr Mahoney, you're with us now, we're your family too. You're not on your own, we love having you here. Bradley and The Governess have brought us all together.'

He took a chequered handkerchief out of his pocket, wiped his eyes and blew his nose. Only old men used hankies. The thought of being united by Bradley Walsh made him laugh and the tension was broken by Alexa coming in for a glass of Ribena and a cow biscuit. She looked up at the caretaker who was putting his hankie back in his pocket.

'Is Mr Moany sad?' she said, pointing with a small finger.

'He was, but he isn't anymore, sweetie,' said Claire. 'Let's go and watch *The Chase*.'

* * *

Thursday morning was sunny and cold. The previous evening, she had sorted through her portfolio, raking over memories of nights in the flat with Jack, paper strewn across the kitchen table, designs being drawn and redrawn, fabric being cut and sewn on the second-hand sewing machine she bought from a charity shop in Archway. Her designs stood out from the poor imitation Alexander McQueen copies created by the other students. A new life away from Walsall was calling her. That voice was silent now.

She searched in her wardrobe for something to wear. She chose the best from her collection of cast-offs from the affluent women of Holland Park and Notting Hill. A pleated skirt from Reiss, a white shirt from Monsoon and a burgundy, angora cardigan from Missoni. She couldn't remember the last time she had worn a skirt. Even her best pair of black tights had a hole in the crotch but would have to do.

She got up early to wash and blow-dry her hair. She couldn't afford to go to a proper hairdresser so her hair was cut by Sylvie, the sister of a German woman who lived at No. 43. Sylvie did home visits and was cheap. Results were variable depending on the steadiness of Sylvie's cutting hand, which was dependent on when she last had a drink. Appointments in December during the festive season could be a lottery.

A bit of mascara and lipstick were the finishing touches to her look. She dropped Alexa at nursery and walked with Kyle to school. Beverley was talking to Mrs Lindsay. She looked like she must have got up at 4.30 a.m. to look that good. Claire thought Beverley was a Supermum, a woman who worked out, showered, moisturised, dried her hair, did her makeup while helping Bruce with his homework, made breakfast at the same time as answering her emails, and still had time to contribute to the latest thread on Mumsnet. Claire felt like handing in a sick note, going back to Kensal Mansions and sitting in front of *Homes Under the Hammer*, but unfortunately Beverley had seen her. Her face broke into a smile.

'Claire, hi. You look beautiful. I love the skirt.'

Mrs Lindsay looked at Claire with astonishment. It was rare for Claire's ankles to see daylight.

'Hi Beverley. Hi Mrs Lindsay,' she smiled shyly. 'I'm ready to go whenever you are.'

The two women walked across the playground together and exited through the Boys' entrance.

'Is that your portfolio?' said Beverley, looking down. 'I'm looking forward to seeing it.'

'It's part of it. I've left quite a lot at home and some has got lost during moves. I've brought the things I'm most proud of.'

Her voice choked and Beverley placed a reassuring hand on her shoulder.

'Come on, let's walk. It's only ten minutes away.'

They turned into Elgin Crescent, a road lined with plane trees in front of imposing four-storey Victorian houses. Towards the end of the crescent, Beverley stopped and tugged Claire's arm, indicating they had arrived.

'Is this your house?' said Claire, looking up, her eyes wider than saucers.

'It's only the ground floor and basement. We're only renting it.'

They walked up the steps to the front door with its pillared portico. The external walls were rendered in a fashionable grey, with white sash windows and shutters. She opened the door and invited Claire in. The entrance hall was long and the wooden floor was cluttered with packing crates.

'I'm sorry, but you'll have to excuse the mess,' said Beverley. 'I'm still unpacking stuff. There's more arriving next week.'

She walked along the hall, speaking as she walked. Claire stopped at the front door and took off her shoes. Beverley paused and looked back.

'Oh, don't worry about that. It's a wooden floor. Any dirt will sweep up.'

'Sorry, force of habit. My place is so small, a dead fly makes it look untidy.'

In the basement was a large kitchen which opened out on to a small, terraced garden. Claire's entire flat would have fitted inside the kitchen. It was clean and neutral, fitted wall units with lines that weren't disturbed by handles. A grey, granite island in the middle was punctured by a double sink and a hob with an extractor hood that looked like an appliance from a science fiction film. Four tall chrome stools were set at the island, which was free from clutter, apart from a glass bowl containing bright green apples and lemons. It was like a feature spread from *Interiors*, house porn for people who got off on soft furnishings and Farrow & Ball eggshell.

'Please, sit down,' said Beverley, gesturing to one of the stools, 'what can I get you, coffee or tea?'

'Coffee would be great, thank you. Milk, no sugar.'

Claire stared up at the ceiling. She counted twenty-eight downlighters, all of them were on. Her pre-pay meter in Kensal Mansions would be spinning like a top in this house. Beverley spooned coffee into two mugs and turned a tap by the side of the sink which immediately dispensed steam and boiling water.

'What's that?' said Claire, pointing to the tap.

'It's a Quooker. Instant boiling water. Very quick and efficient.'

'Don't you have a kettle?'

'No, this does it all. Did you say you took milk?'

'Yes, please.'

Claire stared at the magic tap as Beverley pressed an invisible handle and the door to the fridge opened silently. She stirred milk into both coffees and pressed another door, which opened silently. She put the spoon inside. Claire assumed it was the dishwasher, but it could just as easily have been the microwave or an ice cream maker. Beverley sat on a stool next to her and touched her hand.

'I'm so pleased you came this morning. I was worried you wouldn't.'

'I was worried too. It was Gavin, my social worker, who forced me to come. Said he would be disappointed in me if I didn't!'

For the next two hours, the women swapped histories. Beverley had grown up in a working-class neighbourhood in Kowloon, across the harbour from Hong Kong. Her parents ran an upholstery business and were fanatical about their children's education. The original Tiger Parents. She won a scholarship to the University of Hong Kong to study Economics and Business Management. It was there she met her husband, Edward. Both of them had careers in large corporates until she gave up when she had Bruce and set up her own business. With the worsening political situation between Beijing and Hong Kong, they took the decision to leave. Through a series of contacts, networks and some bribes, they had been able to transfer money into offshore accounts. They had come to London for a month the previous September and had made all the arrangements, before returning in December.

'I'm sorry, I didn't know your husband wasn't here with you at the moment. You must get lonely too?' said Claire.

'Yes, it's not easy living in a new country on my own especially with the virus situation in China getting worse every day. Everyone knows the authorities are lying about the real numbers. I don't know when Edward will be able to get back to England. Bruce is very upset and misses him.'

Kyle and Alexa missed their father too. At least Bruce's dad was coming back. Beverley listened to Claire's story. Walsall, her father, Saint Martins, Jack, pregnancy, leaving college, pregnancy, affair, STI, rows, separation, loneliness, poverty. She iced the misery cake with the recent shoplifting episode in Tesco Express. Claire felt at ease talking to her, she had nothing to hide.

'And, at that point, I didn't think things could get any worse. If it hadn't been for Mr Primus and support from Gavin, who knows? I'm not out of the woods yet, but I'm not ready for Samuel Barber either.'

Claire laughed and Beverley looked at her.

'Samuel Barber?'

'Yes, *Adagio for Strings*. If I ever top myself, that's what I'll play as I swallow the pills and the booze.'

Beverley squeezed her hand. 'Let's hope it never comes to that. You've got a friend in me.'

Claire immediately laughed out loud and Beverley withdrew her hand quickly, looking shocked.

'Did I say something wrong?'

Claire grabbed her hand back.

'No! That's what Woody sings to Buzz in *Toy Story*. Sorry, I wasn't being rude, honestly. It was a really kind thing to say. It just made me laugh, that's all.'

Beverley smiled politely but didn't get the joke.

'Perhaps we should take a look at your designs then? I'm really interested. Another coffee?'

Claire untied the stained ribbon on the battered portfolio and laid out some papers and fabrics on the island. It was lunchtime before the two women finished talking.

'Some of these designs are amazing. So beautiful. Such a waste they're sitting in this portfolio doing nothing. Was there nothing you could have done to finish the course? It's such a waste of a talent.'

'At the time, it was just Jack, Kyle and me. We had no support. My parents didn't want to know and Jack's parents hated me. Thought I'd ruined their little boy's life, getting myself pregnant. We couldn't afford childcare and Jack wanted his career, so I gave mine up.'

'Maybe, you could go back and finish the course? How old are you?'

'I'll be twenty-six in September.'

'Hardly too old to start again! Talent like yours doesn't care about how old you are, you could pick it up again easily.'

Claire looked at the kitchen clock. It was almost 12.30. She stood up and started to put the drawings back into the portfolio.

'It's getting late and you probably have a lot to do. I've taken up your whole morning, listening to my tales of woe and misery. I really should be going.'

Beverley stood up and looked straight at her.

'How would you like to come and work with me?'

'Sorry? I don't know what you mean.'

'Come here and work with me. Help me get my business up and running. It will be mainly admin initially but, once we get everything working, it will be emailing suppliers, customers, answering the telephone, helping me to source fabrics. Can you use a computer?'

'To say I'm a bit rusty would be an understatement. I've never had a good reason to use one. It's why I've not been able to get a temp job.'

'Then perhaps it's time you learned? Don't worry, I can show you, it's quite easy. What would you say to working two mornings a week? Nine until one. You could fit it around the children and we'll be company for each other. At least you understand fabrics and design.'

'Even if I don't understand computers!' said Claire, laughing.

Eight hours work a week would be perfect, she thought. Beverley came straight to the point.

'How about £10 an hour and I'll pay you in cash. Wednesdays and Thursdays? And in the school holidays you can bring Kyle to play with Bruce. He would love it.'

Claire smiled and nodded. Beverley extended her hand and Claire admired her beautifully manicured and painted nails. Her skin was soft and she shook her hand.

'Thank you. That would be wonderful. It's really kind of you, Beverley.'

They climbed the stairs to the living room and walked along the hall to the front door. Claire opened the door as Beverley stooped down.

'I think you might be needing these?' she said, handing Claire her shoes. 'Tods. I love them.'

Claire shrugged her shoulders and smiled. 'Portobello Market. Five pounds.'

She slipped on her shoes, tucked her portfolio under her arm and skipped down the steps on to the path. She looked back at her new employer.

'See you at school in a few hours. Thanks for a lovely morning. It was amazing.'

Beverley waved goodbye and closed the door. Claire walked along Elgin Crescent and on to Ladbroke Grove. The sun was shining and she could feel it on her face. It was the first time in years she felt like a living, breathing human being. It would be a Frank Sinatra night. *Adagio for Strings* could wait.

It was Thursday, 6 February 2020.

Chapter 12

Pitch Darkness

Marcus was disappointed that sex on Friday night hadn't counted for anything on his health app, so decided to walk to the station. More sex at the weekend would have meant less walking, but Alice had a migraine on Sunday. Most of his weekend had been devoted to Project Garage and more trips to the dump to dispose of his parents' decaying chattels.

He listened to his 'Trance Anthems' playlist, compiled by James, probably under the influence of some recreational substances. *'Levels'* by Avicii came on and it made him feel good. James had told him that Avicii had died at the age of twenty-eight, leaving a fortune which his parents had inherited. Marcus was envious that Avicii had probably lived more in his final ten years than he had done in his entire fifty-five.

Metro was always thin on a Monday morning. News of the virus from China was on the inside pages, overshadowed by the stabbing incident in Streatham. Four hundred and eighty people who had flown into the UK from Wuhan had gone missing. The Lycra-clad cyclist with his collapsed Brompton bike sat opposite him. He was reading *Wolf Hall*.

He'll still be reading that drivel at Christmas, he thought.

He checked his emails. His place at the mandatory 'Living Our Values' conference in March had been confirmed. It was being held offsite at the Mandarin Oriental hotel in Knightsbridge, followed by drinks and dinner at 'Dinner', Heston Blumenthal's two Michelin-starred restaurant. The invitation proudly announced that the purpose of the day was 'to build a spirit of oneness and *esprit de corps* within the partner community'.

Spending lots of money on partners must be one of our new values, he thought.

He was about to close Outlook when a new email appeared. It was from Arabella Ffoulkes.

Subject: Project Spearmint – The Dream Team
From : Arabella Ffoulkes

Hi Marcus
Hope you had a great weekend. Loved meeting you last week. It was a great
interview, your honesty and integrity really shone through. It truly touched
me in places. Here is your new bio, hope you love it? We need to get these
finalised today. Also attached is the photo Leo and I think is best.
Speak soon
  Bella

Marcus hadn't even opened the attachment but was already worried. He
didn't want to touch Arabella in any of her places. His vanity overcame his
indignation and he opened the photo attachment, impatient to see if Leo had
made him look like David Gandy. He hadn't. Rather than Wellman, he looked
like 'Cock-man'. Leo and Bella had chosen the 'up the nostrils' shot. The red hard
hat was too small and made him look like a penis, a shiny bellend perched on top
of his chinless head. He looked like a minor politician on a day trip to a factory.
He opened the Word attachment.

Marcus Barlow, Partner
The Real Deal

This is not just a man who lives for the deal. Every breath he takes, every
move he makes, it's always about the deal. Deals are his drug and he needs
to score. He brings twenty years of experience to the table and slams it right
down in front of you!
  It's always about relationships. Close, warm and intimate but never
scared to challenge, pushing you to levels you only dreamed of. Working
with you to build the new future for TuffTogs. Marcus is Marmite, you
either love him or hate him. 100 of the world's largest and most iconic
corporations have loved him.
  He is a family man and Espina becomes part of that family. A family
that goes through everything together. Honesty and integrity are at his core.
That's what makes him special, so special.

He closed the attachment and stared out of the window.
'Fuck me,' he muttered under his breath.

He opened the attachment again but a second reading didn't make it any better. It got worse.

Did Arabella spend her weekend on LSD, stealing lyrics and mashing them together? he thought.

He recognised the Police, Roxy Music and Radiohead. At least she had stopped short of saying he was 'so fucking special'. His journey into the office passed him by. He was still in a state of shock by the time he got to OnYouGo.

'Usual, Marcus?' said Fernando cheerily.

Marcus took a few seconds to respond.

'No, not this morning, Fernando. I'll have a double sausage sandwich on white bread with lots of HP sauce and a flat white with an extra shot.'

Fernando gave him a bemused look but made the order and handed it to him. The other people in the lift were carrying their green smoothies and stared at Marcus holding his greasy sandwich. The smell of the sausages was pervasive in the confined space. He scanned his pass and walked on to an empty floor. Most of the desks were vacant. He took one next to the window and bit into his sausage sandwich. Melted butter and HP sauce ran down his fingers, but it calmed his anxiety. He saw Kelvin approaching the pool area with a sunburnt, panda-eyed tan from his long weekend in Val d'Isère. He looked stressed, went straight into an empty office and closed the door without speaking to anyone.

Marcus opened Outlook and the latest version of the proposal from Gerard. He opened the attachment, 'Project Spearmint DRAMA Latest 020220 v57.7_DRAFT'. Apart from the two 'How we touch Espina' slides, the main pack was thirty-six pages long, one for each brick in the Wonderwall. All the pain had been worth it. Steve and the CIClets had done a great job. Fresh, dynamic and different, just as Gerard had said it would be.

He turned to his bio. Once his picture had been shrunk to the size of a postage stamp, his resemblance to a penis was less obvious. He turned to the section on fees to see what size trough Mason and Kelvin had built to accommodate all the greedy partner snouts. It was a £10.3 million pound-sized trough, big enough for all the little piggies to get fat on, and with some space leftover for a slap-up celebration dinner.

He saw Kelvin throw his phone on his desk and take two Nicorettes out of a packet. Something had obviously upset him. He decided to enter the dragon's den, knocked on the glass door and opened it. Kelvin looked up. He had forgotten to use SPF on the slopes and his nose was pink and peeling.

'Hi Marcus. What is it?'

'Have you got a few minutes to discuss Spearmint?'

'I've got five. What do you want?'

'It's about the fees in the proposal. I think they're way off the mark. Jim Ibbotson will eat us for breakfast. He's expecting somewhere between £2.5 million and £4.0 million.'

'Not ambitious enough,' said Kelvin with a dismissive wave of his hand. 'This is a great opportunity and we have to deliver The Firm on this one, Marcus, bring our full suite of capabilities to Espina. Anyway, we need £9 million to hit fucking plan. Any other bits in the proposal you have a problem with?'

'Apart from a photo that makes me look like a penis and a CV that makes me out to be a cross between Sting and Pablo Escobar, nothing else really.'

'I liked the CVs, Marcus. Anything else?'

Kelvin was showing his frustration, clicking the lid on and off his fountain pen. It was a signal his time and patience were running out.

Marcus couldn't resist one parting shot.

'Only to say that, after full consideration, I am sticking to my position on lanyards. I'm not wearing one.'

'Oh, just fuck off, Marcus.'

Marcus spent the rest of the morning fine-tuning the proposal with the team and the CIClets. He was checking Stockwatch when Tyler Payton approached his desk. He had the tan of a man who had spent two weeks working in Dubai by a pool.

'Fancy lunch today?' he said in his Texan drawl.

There was an urgency in his tone which told Marcus that he should accept.

'Sure,' he said, 'Where do you want to go? The Apprentice?'

The London Apprentice was a backstreet boozer tucked behind the Bank of England. Its lunchtime menu was limited to pies, which came with mash and gravy. Chips and vegetables (peas or carrots) were extra. It had a cosy atmosphere, served decent Guinness and didn't require booking in advance. It wasn't a gastropub, it was just a pub.

'Great, see you in reception at 12.45?'

The two men stepped out into the February sunshine. It was warm, and neither wore a coat. Tyler was wearing a plaid jacket with an open-necked shirt, beige chinos and oxblood penny loafers. A white vest was visible at the neck. Marcus wondered why Americans still wore vests in adulthood. He had stopped wearing vests after primary school.

They made small talk on the way to the pub and entered through the side entrance. It was almost empty apart from a few hardened lunchtime drinkers.

They took a table in the corner and ordered two pints of Guinness and two pies, chicken and leek for Marcus and venison and mushroom for Tyler.

'So, what's news?' said Marcus, sensing his friend wanted to talk.

He got a response immediately.

'I'm leaving. I'm going back to the States. I've been approached by Exxon to take a job in Houston. The money isn't quite as good but I've persuaded Michelle to go back as well. She's happy here in the UK, but she knows I'm not. Now is the right time if we're going to make the move with the kids' schools.'

Marcus took a sip of Guinness, the creamy head left its moustache on his upper lip and he licked it off.

'But I thought it was your wife who wanted to come back to the UK in the first place? I thought you had settled really well here.'

'We love it here. It's a lot smaller than Texas and we really like it. No, it's not England at all. It's that place, The Firm. It didn't quite work out how I thought it would.'

'Why?' said Marcus.

The pies arrived, perched on islands of mashed potato surrounded by a sea of thick, steaming brown liquid.

'I'm sick of all the politics and fighting. I thought I was joining a team. It's tough enough competing against other firms, but I spend most of my life fighting people on my own side. People are only in it for themselves, they'll stab you in the back if it's in their interest. I'll be sad to leave England but not sad to leave that place.'

'Yes, I know. It's a nest of vipers. It grinds you down to the point where you start to question yourself, what you stand for and what's important. Let me tell you something that happened last week.'

Marcus told him about his meeting with Colin in the churchyard at St Paul's. Tyler listened closely, hardly touching his pie.

'Wow! That's impressive Marcus, taking lifestyle advice from a hobo. Sounds like he made quite an impression. Are you close?'

'I'd never met him before in my life.'

'No, are you close to leaving? Retiring? What's stopping you?'

'Oh, I see! Fear, I suppose. Fear of the unknown, fear of what I would do instead of this stuff. Scared of unplugging myself from the life-support machine and finding I can't breathe on my own.'

'Strength comes from dealing with the things that make you uncomfortable, Marcus. Have you told Kelvin about how you're feeling?'

'Are you joking?' said Marcus. 'All he's concerned about right now is his budget and whether Spearmint will save him? He doesn't give a fuck about me. Have you told him yet?'

'No, and I'm not looking forward to it either. It will have to be soon though. Keep this to yourself, you're one of the few people in that place I can trust.'

Marcus joined the team in Collaboration Zone 3. Mason was sitting on a beanbag talking to Gerard, who was wearing black drainpipe trousers with sky-blue crêpe-soled shoes. He was like an anorexic Elvis with goatee beard. The thirty-six slides that made up the Wonderwall were pinned to the whiteboard with the green magnets. The cock and balls had gone. Gerard jumped to his feet.

'Afternoon Spearmints. I just want to say a massive thank you from me and my colleagues in CIC for helping us get to this point. It's been brilliant working with you. The play is now written. It's time for the characters to learn their lines. Everyone happy with that?'

'Just one small thing, Gerard?' said Marcus. 'I'm a still little uneasy about the new style bios and photos. Great that we're trying to empathise with our client, but I'm not sure describing me as "Marmite" does it. Could we go back to the old-style CVs before we look silly?'

Gerard looked across at Mason who was typing an email on his phone. He paused and looked up.

'I'm afraid that's not going to happen, Marcus. They've already been signed off by Kelvin. He approved them from a chair-lift in Val d'Isère at the weekend.'

For the next hour, the team went through each of the bricks in the Wonderwall, making minor adjustments to the proposal, adding arrows and re-ordering bullet points. As each slide was approved, Gerard assembled another brick in the wall, a single word of truth painted on it in a graffiti style font. It was all going well until slide nineteen. It was one of the junior analysts, Angela Rust, who noticed it.

'Excuse me? I think we need to alter a couple of the slides or at least change the order.'

Marcus stared at her. It was the first time she had spoken in three weeks.

'Why?' said Gerard. 'We've been through the "wall words" a hundred times. I thought we had agreed them all?'

'Because, from this side it says, "Commercial Suicide".' She pointed to the wall.

Gerard ran around from behind the wall and shrieked in horror. On their own, the individual 'wall words' meant something. Combined, they meant something completely different. Gerard wilted and slumped to the floor with his head in his hands.

'What's the matter Gerard?' said Marcus.

'I'm so sorry. This is a catastrophe!'

One of the CIClets consoled her distraught leader, who was now prone on the floor. Marcus helped him to his feet.

'We can change the words. Don't worry, we'll get around it somehow. We can fix it.'

By 6.30 on Monday evening, the proposal was ready to send to Document Production. The illusion was almost ready.

* * *

A heavy morning lay ahead. The pipeline call, followed by three hours for the reconvened interim performance review. With half an hour to kill, Marcus opened RAPID, looked at some numbers and made notes.

The partners took their places in Communication Zone 1 and waited for Kelvin. Tyler looked across the table and winked. Kelvin bounced into the room. He was in a better mood than the day before, and he called the meeting to order. Vanessa Briggs stroked his arm as he sat down.

Probably had a shag this morning, thought Marcus. *That's why he's in a good mood.*

Izzy Majewska gave her customary update which pointed to the same thing, the team was on course to miss target. Kelvin remained calm and smiled.

'Please carry on, Izzy,' he said.

'We have had to take immediate steps to address our adverse profit forecast. All non-salary costs that can't be charged directly to clients will be stopped immediately. Retrospective costs incurred this year will now be held on the balance sheet as a provision and phased back into the P&L over a three-year window. This should help to bring our profit forecast this year back in line with plan.'

Kelvin beamed. The pain of failure had been deferred by kicking the can down the road. Izzy had found a lifeboat to save him and his units. The meeting broke and the other partners left the room. Tyler and Marcus were left alone. Tyler poured two coffees and turned to him.

'Well, that was pulling a rabbit out of the hat. I was expecting another meltdown from Kelvin.'

'He's a bloody smart operator, he can play the game as well as anyone. In three years' time, he'll be gone or moved upstairs and it'll be someone else's shit to clear up.'

The other partners filtered back into the room. They were joined by Jenny Moffatt from HR and her assistant, who connected a laptop to the network ready for the next session. Jenny was wearing a collarless shirt which revealed more of her snake's head tattoo.

'Okay everyone,' said Kelvin. 'We've got three hours put aside for the interim performance review. I want to get through this as quickly as we can, so let's press on. Jenny, over to you.'

'Thanks Kelvin,' said Jenny, opening her presentation. 'Thank you for returning the assessment spreadsheets. A 100% response, which is great. We've entered your ratings into PeopleBuild, our firm-wide skills database and now have a full read across by grade for everyone in the team. Can I stress again, this is only an interim review and it doesn't guarantee any future promotion or reward?'

The partners all nodded their agreement. Jenny was merely setting the scene. She put up a succession of slides all showing the same picture, a tight cluster of dots in the top right corner of a matrix.

'So, looking at the charts by grade, we can see that almost everyone in the team is performing really well. Against a maximum possible rating of 50A, we don't have anyone who isn't at least a 36B.'

Marcus waited for Tom Irons or Simon Loder to crack a joke about breasts but they remained silent. They were still working out how to interpret the pictures. It was the same picture every year, different criteria, same results. Everyone in the team was rated 'Outstanding', except some were more outstanding than others. Someone had to break the consensus. It was Kelvin.

'So, are you honestly telling me, Jenny, that we don't have any shit people in our team?'

Jenny stood her ground.

'No, Kelvin, I'm not saying that at all. What I am saying is that nobody has been assessed as "shit" by the people around this table. I'm sure there are some underperformers, but not according to the ratings the partners have submitted.'

And this was the flaw in the system. Nobody wanted to tell the truth or give feedback that wasn't positive. People found out where they stood in the pecking order by osmosis, when they didn't get promoted or got a crap bonus.

Kelvin fired the first cannon.

'Well, that's bollocks. I asked an assistant manager to help me with a presentation the other week, and what I got back was crap. Absolute rubbish. I had to get someone else to redo it for me.'

'Who was it?' said Oliver Rankin, meekly. 'Maybe they have development needs?'

'I don't know his fucking name!' shouted Kelvin. 'What I do know is that he was absolute shit, so let's all get real here. Most of the people on those charts need to take two big steps to the left. So, can we get on with it now?'

The battle had started. For the next two hours, partners fought and bickered like children at a nursery. As they moved through the grades, individual careers were advanced, placed on hold or destroyed by a toxic cocktail of anecdote, favouritism and self-interest. The only things missing were facts. By the time the process had got to the director grade, there was blood on the carpet and up the walls. Some partners were licking their wounds, knowing they would have to deliver bad news to some people. More likely, they would lie and say, 'You were "Outstanding". Everything's on track. Nothing to worry about.'

Anytime Jenny Moffatt tried to mediate or intervene in the fighting, she was overruled. That's why she was the HR Business Partner.

Up to this point, the junior grades were only minor skirmishes. The real fight, which directors would be given the chance to chase The Golden Carrot, the path to becoming a partner, was about to begin. Kelvin drew up rules of engagement.

'Thanks everyone. The last two hours were really productive. At least we've now got some fucking realism in these ratings. Now, shall we turn to the Directors?'

Everyone knew what was coming. Only two Directors were ready for promotion, Steve Pettigrew and Laila Saetang. The others were too junior or had been put out to pasture years ago. Marcus rated Steve highly. Laila had been recruited two years earlier from an investment bank by Vanessa Briggs. They were always together, socialising after work and at weekends. Kelvin continued.

'Given this year's dismal performance, I can't see us putting more than one candidate through. So, I guess it comes down to a choice between Steve or Laila? What does everybody think?'

Vanessa brought her guns up to the front line and fired off the first salvo in a pre-emptive strike designed to neutralise any debate.

'It's got to be Laila. She ticks all the boxes. Fantastic with clients, they absolutely love her. Great at managing her teams and she's done a huge amount of internal innovation this year. She's also got a great network in The Firm. She's a 50A rating all the way and simply has to go through.'

She leaned back in her chair and folded her arms. The debate was all over, the enemy's forces were in disarray. The cavalry arrived in the form of Mason.

'I completely agree with Vanessa. Laila's a hundred per cent dedicated to the job. Late nights, weekends. She gives her life to The Firm, total and absolute commitment. I definitely think she deserves to go through. I like Steve a lot but Laila is a couple of notches above him.'

Marcus watched and listened as other partners contributed verbal evidence in support of Laila's case. Vanessa thought the battle was over and everyone could go to lunch. Marcus waited for the guns to go silent then, from left field, fired his first shot.

'Sorry, before we all get too carried away, Vanessa, can I ask why five members of project teams that have worked for Laila have left us in the past twelve months. Any connection?'

She returned fire immediately.

'None whatsoever. Laila sets extremely high standards and some people simply fail to meet them. They were just not up to the job. They probably did us all a favour by leaving.'

She thought her armour plating was bullet-proof and his next question would bounce off, but it was all the more penetrating for being based on facts.

'Well, that's not entirely true, is it? Several termination interviews have specifically cited her bullying management style as the key reason they left. Looking at some of her upward feedback, it's not exactly glowing is it?' Marcus held up some papers. Facts and evidence, powerful weapons.

Vanessa unfolded her arms and sat up to the table. The enemy had regrouped, re-organised its forces and was fighting back. Marcus brought his artillery up from the rear.

'And what are these "internal innovation" projects Laila's been involved in this year? Have they led to any additional revenues or value to our clients?' he asked innocently.

'She led the team which developed the new interactive and collaborative cloud-based report-writing tool.'

'Has it been used on a client engagement yet?'

'It's still in prototype form.'

'Has it been used on a client engagement yet?'

'Well, no.'

Under heavy fire, Vanessa's nicely arranged armies were starting to look a bit in disarray. Marcus unleashed his tanks which came in the form of more facts.

'Before this meeting, I took a look at RAPID and these are the headline numbers. Laila's sales year to date are £1.5 million. Steve's are £2.7 million. Laila's utilisation year to date is 48%, Steve's is 69%. His upward feedback scores are significantly higher and nobody has resigned because of him. I have emails from clients saying how highly they rate him. I don't know a partner around this table who has ever had a problem working with Steve?'

Although her forces were taking a pounding, Vanessa wasn't in the mood to retreat.

'I think you're forgetting one really important thing in all of this, Marcus.'

'What's that?'

'Laila is a woman and The Firm has diversity targets to meet. Now I don't give a flying fuck whether Steve goes through or not, just as long as Laila's name is on that ticket to The Golden Carrot.'

Mason re-entered the fray.

'And there's also the positive impact she will have on our ethnicity targets too.'

'What the hell are you going on about, Mason?' said Marcus.

'Her parents are from Thailand.'

Marcus threw his hands up in the air in frustration.

'They run a fucking fish and chip shop in Portsmouth! She was born and brought up in the UK. How does that help our ethnicity targets?'

'Dual nationality. According to The Firm's guidelines on ethnicity, Laila counts. Double bubble being a woman too,' said Mason.

Diversity and inclusion had changed the rules of performance management, just as nuclear weapons had changed the rules of warfare. Marcus had been playing under the old rules of 'best person for the job' when Vanessa had an H-Bomb all primed and ready to fire. She left it to Kelvin to press the button.

'Vanessa and Mason do have a point, Marcus. This isn't the most diverse team and I do have targets to meet, that's the fact of the matter. We don't have to make a final decision now, and we still have a few months to go. But unless Laila has a colossal fuck-up between now and then, she'll be going forward to The Golden Carrot.'

Marcus slumped back in his chair.

So, that's why Vanessa stroked his arm. This was probably all stitched up in a hotel room this morning.

Kelvin closed the meeting, thanking HR for their hard work and the partners left the room in clusters. Irons, Loder and Mauser were off to lunch at The Guinea Grill in Mayfair. Big steaks and red wine. Guaranteed stains on the shirt. Marcus and Tyler left the room together and found an empty Chilling Egg.

'What did you make of that?' said Marcus.

'Just another reason to head back to Texas. This really is a shit-show. Steve would make a great partner. I really like working with him. Laila is from the same mould as Vanessa. As we both know, it's never about the facts.'

'I'm going to get some lunch,' said Marcus. 'When are you heading back to Dubai?'

'Sunday. I'll probably tell Kelvin before the end of the month when I'm back.'

'Good luck with that one. Let me know how it goes.'

Marcus collected his quinoa salad from Fernando. He sat at his desk and opened Outlook. There was an email from Jim Ibbotson.

Subject: Spearmint – Board Meeting
From: Jim Ibbotson

Marcus, Mason
Had our Board meeting this morning. All went well and Spearmint has been approved. NEDs were a bit bolshie but the Chairman had them under control. Procurement will be in touch later today to confirm presentations next Monday, 10th. Will be at the Safewear offices in Manchester. It will be you and three other firms.
Jim

Before he had a chance to eat his salad, Mason appeared at his desk.

'Have you seen the latest email from Jim Ibbotson?'

'Yes, I've just read it.'

'Great news they've got it past the Board. All to play for now. Who do you think we're up against?'

'Probably the usual suspects.'

'Let's see what comes back from Procurement later. In the meantime, I'll let Gerard know and we'll set up rehearsals for Thursday and Friday. We need to bring our A-game to this one, Marcus.'

Although he disliked Mason, Marcus admired him in a perverse way. He had real enthusiasm, a belief in The Firm and a burning ambition. Just after 4.30, an email from Espina's Procurement Team arrived.

Subject: Project Spearmint – Phase II Support (Supplier Presentations)
From: Sarah Appleberry

For the attention of: Marcus Barlow, Mason Sherwin
As part of Project Spearmint, Espina Plc is inviting proposals from interested parties to support us with the next phase of work. Please see attached templates for completion by interested parties which should be returned to the email address above by no later than 17.00 on Thursday, 6th February 2020.

Technical and commercial proposals have been requested from four parties. Your slot will be at 9.30 on Monday, 10th February 2020.

Presentations will be held at the offices of Safewear Ltd (see address below). Please confirm your availability to attend at this time?

Due to space limitations, attendees from supplier firms will be limited to no more than five, and the duration will be no longer than 75 minutes (45 mins presentation + 30 mins Q&A).

We draw your attention to Schedule 1 (Commercial Terms) which must be completed in full, providing details of headline day rates by grade, and with any discounts applied. The number of days proposed for each member of the supplier team, their grade and proposed rate must also be provided. We look forward to receiving your submissions and seeing you on the 10th.

Best regards

> *Sarah Appleberry*
> *Chief Procurement Officer, Espina Plc.*

The email confirmed Marcus's worst fears. From his experience, once Procurement got involved, relationships went out the window. It would be all about the money. Furthermore, a 9.30 meeting in Manchester would mean an early train, and Avanti West Coast were little better than South Western Trains, even if they could lean over around bends. He sent James a text.

Hi James. Looks like I will be in Manchester next Monday morning for a meeting. Will come up on Sunday. Would be good to meet up if you are around? Let me know. Dad. Xx

He rang Mason and asked to meet him in one of the Chilling Eggs.

'You've seen the email from Procurement then?' said Marcus.

'Yes. Nothing out of the ordinary, I'll get the team on to it immediately. Gerard reckons on having the proposal back from DP by tomorrow night, giving us two full days to rehearse. Being first up is a bit of a bummer. Always the risk they'll forget what we said by the end of the day.'

'Better to be first than last. They'll probably be bored stiff by the afternoon. Four firms all saying the same thing.'

'So, what's on your mind, Marcus? You never ring me.'

It was true, Marcus never rang him.

'Two things. Who goes to the pitch and the fees? I'm uncomfortable about both. You know there will be a cast of thousands wanting to attend and they've limited it to five?'

Mason started to count possible attendees on his fingers.

'Well, there's you and me, obviously. Simon Loder to cover the Technology piece, Brian Snelling on Cyber, Carole Parker for People and Culture, Richard

Davis for Data Solutions…' Mason reeled off the names of twelve people who had a claim to be involved before he stopped. 'Mmm … I see what you mean,' he said pensively. 'And then there's Gerard. I think he has to go.'

'Are you fucking mad, Mason? I can deal with all the internal politics and shit that will go with getting it down to five. But Gerard? Are you serious?'

'I know he's a bit bonkers but he understands how clients think. Plus, he's the only one who understands how all the bricks fit together. We definitely need him there.'

Mason had a point. Although Gerard was on another spectrum, he was the only one who could work the Wonderwall.

'Okay. I see your point. So, you, me, Gerard and two others. Who else?'

'Loder and Carole Parker,' said Mason.

'Don't agree. Jim Ibbotson couldn't give a rat's arse about people. He calls HR "lady science", so probably not Carole. Who else?'

'Snelling for the Cyber piece then? We've got two to three million pounds riding on that, so he has to go. Kelvin wants that in there. What do you think?'

Marcus leaned backwards against the curved, foam wall of the yellow Chilling Egg and looked up.

'Probably the best compromise. You and I will have to cover everything else. I'd feel more comfortable if it was just our piece. I think that's what Espina wants and not all this other crap Kelvin wants in there.'

Mason had the worried look of a man whose testicles were resting on a block just as Kelvin was sharpening a large blade.

'I'm in a really difficult situation, Marcus. Spearmint is the last roll of the dice for me. I'm a dead man if this doesn't happen. We have to aim for the stars and we might get Venus.'

'Or we explode before we've left the earth's orbit? Maybe we need to be a bit smarter about how we present the fees? Let's think about it. There's more than one way to skin a cat.'

Marcus left the office and walked to St Paul's. He stopped to look in the garden but Colin wasn't there. He arrived home just after seven and rang the bell to Gavin's flat. It took a while for him to answer, his music was loud.

'Hi Marcus, how are you? You're a bit early.'

'Just got back from work so thought I would let you know. See you at eight then?'

'Come whenever you're ready, everything's under control. Bit of one-pot chemistry tonight. Coq au vin with dauphinoise potatoes.'

Gavin always made entertaining seem easy. Nothing fazed him.

'Sounds great. See you just before eight. Looking forward to catching up, it's been quite a week. I'll tell you all about it later.'

He changed, lay on his bed and checked The Sequence. James had replied to his text.

Hi Dad. Great news. Sunday is fine. We can watch the football down the pub, have a few beers and go for dinner. Hope all well. J xx

He wanted his son to reply saying he was trapped in the library revising and could only manage a sandwich, but it was a familiar story. He took a bottle of Pinot Noir out of the rack, left the flat and rang Gavin's doorbell. He could see his eye through the spyhole and the door opened. Gavin looked him up and down.

'Marcus, good to see you. Come in. Glad you've got your slippers on.'

Marcus walked into the living room, which was pristine as usual. Classical music was playing and Marcus took a guess.

'Chopin?'

'Schubert. Nice try but completely different.'

'Not *Trance Anthems* then?'

'Not tonight.'

As always, Gavin was perfectly dressed. Dolce & Gabbana sweater, faded Armani jeans and Tods. No socks. Two freshly made gin and tonics were bubbling on the island and Gavin offered him one with a small plate of crostini and tapenade.

'Sounded like you might need one. Cheers,' said Gavin.

Marcus gave his host the bottle of wine and sat on a stool as Gavin stirred something in a large Le Creuset casserole dish and returned it to the oven. Marcus took a bite from one of the crostini.

'Tapenade from The Temple?'

'No, homemade actually. Thanks for the compliment. I finished work a bit earlier and had time to make it. Olives are from The Temple though.'

Gavin laughed and his smile showed off his perfect teeth. Marcus admired him. Comfortable in his moisturised skin, always relaxed and never anxious. He was like David Gandy with a social conscience. He wished he was more like Gavin.

'So how have you been this past week? What's the latest on Peppermint?' said Gavin.

'Spearmint. Totally out of control, completely insane. Kelvin, my megalomaniac boss, thinks it's a £10 million job, Gerard is turning the pitch into a gameshow and Mason is on the verge of having a nervous breakdown. Oh, and they've made me look like a penis. Apart from that, all good.'

Gavin laughed out loud.

'What do you mean, they've made you look like a penis?'

Marcus picked up his phone and opened the attachment from Arabella.

'I wanted to look like David Gandy. Instead, they've made me look like a cock. Look at the top of my head, for fuck's sake!'

Gavin enlarged the image with his fingers.

'Well, David Gandy it isn't, for sure. But it's not that bad, Marcus. At least you don't look like some boring corporate wanker.'

'Now you're sounding like bloody Gerard,' said Marcus, showing his frustration.

Marcus gave his friend an update on the rolling insanity of Project Spearmint until it was time for the first course. Gavin brought two bowls of mushroom soup, garnished with chives and cream, to the table and poured the wine.

'So, next Monday is the big day then? The Spearmint Superbowl!'

'Don't take the piss. If we don't win this, there'll be some serious fallout at work. It will make Chernobyl look like a house fire. Guess what else happened last week?'

'You've decided to come out as a cross-dresser and now wish to be known as Pamela?'

He told him about his meeting with Colin in the churchyard.

'Just goes to show how our lives hinge on one or two critical events. Take a wrong turning and the next minute, everything's gone. We shouldn't take things for granted,' said Marcus.

Gavin nodded, taking a sip of soup from his spoon.

'I agree to a point. Events can and do change our lives, but it doesn't mean we're complete hostages to fortune. Look at me. I had a cocaine habit, suffered from depression, anxiety, suicidal thoughts. You name it, I had it. Three spells in expensive rehab clinics before I got myself together.'

'So what changed things for you?'

'Realising the only person who could change my life was me. But to do it, I had to leave Scotland and start again. I'm better now but I struggle from time to time. It might look like I'm in control, but I have my wobbly moments too.'

'So what would you do if you were me?'

'Listen to what homeless men tell you. They speak from experience.'

It broke the tension and the two men laughed. Gavin stood up from the table, cleared away and brought the main course to the table. The golden crust of the dauphinoise potatoes bubbled gently, ploopily releasing its cheesy aroma.

'Looks amazing as always. How has your week been?' said Marcus.

Gavin did the clever silver service thing with two spoons.

'Pretty much the same as any other week. Helping people navigate their way through a system designed to add to their problems. I've got one Grenfell family into permanent accommodation. It's in Brent but at least it can accommodate them all. But I do have some big news for us!'

'What's that then?'

'I saw Claire today. All set for next Tuesday. We need to come up with a menu, three courses minimum. You can do starter and dessert and I'll do main. Or we can swap. Up to you. She's really keen.' Gavin told the fib again.

'Does she really have all the facilities we'll need?' said Marcus, expressing concern.

'Don't be a snob, Marcus. She's got an oven with a four-ring hob and a working fridge. She might not have a melon baller or a lemon zester but she has plates, knives, forks and spoons. It doesn't need to be anything fancy. It will take your mind off Spearmint, Gerard and tramps. I'm thinking it might be nice for both of us to go in black tie as well?'

'Are you serious? What for?'

'A hundred per cent serious. Make it more of an event, something special. She has so little excitement in her life. I think it would be a nice thing to do.'

Marcus's immediate thoughts turned to logistics. He would need to take his dinner suit to Manchester on Sunday, which would mean it would get creased if he took it in his luggage on the train. He decided to drive to the flat on Sunday and leave it there. Gavin interrupted his thoughts.

'Are you okay with that? Gets you out of our dinner rota for a week as well!'

'I'm fine if you say it will be fine. Tell me about her again?'

Gavin served second helpings and topped up their wine. Marcus learned how Claire's life in Kensal Mansions was a world away from his. A life changed by a single event. A determined little sperm had turned her life upside down. His life had been planned to the last detail: loving parents, good education, lucrative career, relatively happy marriage, nice kids. Nothing had gone wrong. Over dessert, he raised the virus again.

'Have you seen the virus is here in the UK now? I'm very worried. Nobody seems to give a toss.'

'I agree. It hasn't been discussed much at work. I think everyone's waiting to see what happens. Too much other crap going on. Coffee?'

The two friends talked more over their coffee, and by eleven o'clock Marcus stood up to leave.

'Thanks Gavin. Dinner was amazing as usual. I always look forward to our dinners. An oasis of sanity in a desert of madness.'

'A dessert of madness?'

'No, I said a desert. A desert? Oasis?'

Marcus got irritated and Gavin laughed.

'Lighten up, I was just teasing you! Good luck next week with the Spearmint Superbowl. I'll text you with some menu options. If I were you, I'd brush up on *Toy Story* before Tuesday. Claire's little boy, Kyle, is obsessed with Buzz Lightyear.'

'To infinity and beyond!' said Marcus, impersonating the Space Ranger. 'Some things you never forget.'

They walked to the front door.

'Goodnight, Marcus. Have a good week.' His hand held Marcus's bicep and squeezed. It wasn't a pat or a stroke, it was definitely a squeeze.

* * *

The temperature had dropped overnight and Marcus could see frost on the windscreens of the diggers in Beirut. The lorry drivers were already parked, clouds of smoke billowing out of the cabs. He took the Central Line to St Paul's and was at his desk by 8 a.m. The office was almost empty. An email from Kelvin arrived.

Subject: Project Spearmint – Pitch Attendees
From: Kelvin McBride
To: Marcus Barlow, Mason Sherwin

Chaps
Getting a lot of flak from around The Firm about attendees for next
Monday's pitch. Appreciate we are limited to five. I don't need to remind
you that 'Delivering The Firm' and diversity are critical. Can you give this
some thought? Try to be creative.
Kelvin

It was a typical Kelvin email. A polite introduction followed by a mild threat. Marcus took a spoonful of porridge and considered how best to respond. He remembered his conversation with Gavin the previous evening and replied.

Kelvin
Fully appreciate the problems this is causing you internally. Agree it's
not ideal. If it were not for the bloated scope and fees you have been
instrumental in pushing for, this would not be a problem. Mason and I
have agreed the strongest team for Monday. We could always go in drag if
that helps diversity?
    Marcus

He knew Kelvin wouldn't respond well. He considered the worst outcome. He pressed 'Send'.

Chloe had arrived in the office after her commute from Gants Hill and Marcus went up to her desk. She looked up at him and smiled. She was always happy, grateful for having a job.

'Can you book me one night at The Lowry Hotel in Manchester for Sunday, 9 February? A standard room will be fine.'

Chloe nodded.

'Sure, will do.'

'Do you want to write that down? Just in case you get busy and forget.'

She picked up her notepad and pen and wrote it down in her large handwriting.

'*Marcus. Sunday, 9th Feb. Lowree Hotel. Manchester. One night.*'

The first rehearsal had been moved to Collaboration Pod 2 with its Amazonian rainforest theme, complete with waterfall and soundtrack of cicadas playing through the ceiling speakers. Mason was sitting on a chair shaped like a log. He looked like a child who had just been told that Christmas was cancelled.

'Morning Mason. Everything okay? You don't seem your normal, chippy self?' said Marcus.

'Kelvin's just grabbed me in the corridor. He read your email and wasn't happy. That wasn't helpful. Told me in no uncertain terms that we have to win this. Maybe we need to change the team? You can dip out if you really want to?'

Marcus looked at him. He had seen a change over the past couple of days. Less confident, the look of a man who was truly worried. Although he was a snide little weasel, Marcus felt sorry for him. Kelvin was doing what The Firm did best, natural selection by bullying and intimidation.

'It's a bit late for that now. We've just got to make the best of it. We've got a one in four chance and we do have Gerard as our star striker!'

Marcus laughed and Mason looked up at him and smiled.

'You love him really, don't you?'

'No, he's fucking bonkers and I've never come across anyone like him in twenty years of doing this stuff, but let's give it our best shot. We've got two days to get this right. Come on!'

Gerard and the rest of the team arrived, along with one of the CIClets, who was carrying a large box. Gerard was already in character. Chunky work boots, tight denim shorts, white T-shirt, the TuffTogs high-vis jacket and hard hat. He looked like a member of the Village People.

'Morning Spearmints. I hope we're all ready to WIN!'

The only person in the room Marcus didn't know was Brian Snelling, the partner in Cyber. He was very tall, well over two metres, and it seemed he hadn't eaten for six months. He was gaunt with thin lips and a pair of rimless glasses balanced on his angular cheekbones. Marcus knew him by name but not by face. He wouldn't forget him in a hurry, he was like a ghost. People took their seats around the table. Marcus noticed that Simon Loder had a smeared brown stain on his shirt.

Must have had the double sausage sandwich this morning, he thought.

Gerard instructed the CIClet to open the box and started taking out the bricks from the Wonderwall, along with more branded props. The copies of the presentation were printed and bound in the shape of a house brick. DP had done a great job.

'We've over-ordered a bit on the props and copies of the proposal. That's hit the budget a bit, but no need to worry about that now. It's all about winning this thang,' said Gerard.

'Just out of interest, Gerard,' said Marcus, 'how much has all of this cost? The props, the presentation, et cetera?'

'Including design, prototypes, drafts and—'

'Including everything,' said Marcus curtly.

'Seventy-five thousand pounds. But it's mostly wooden dollars, internal recharges, that sort of thing.'

Marcus looked across the table at Mason whose face had gone white. Once the charge hit the team's P&L, Izzy Majewska would see it and flag it to Kelvin who would go into a rabid frenzy. Marcus moved things on.

'Okay, not helpful, but let's press on? How do you want to play this Gerard? What's the format for today? Is there an agenda?'

'I think that's being a bit formal, don't you?' said Gerard dismissively.

'No, I think it's helpful. Brings structure and is proven to work. It doesn't matter, we can write one up here.' Marcus moved to the lime-green board, which was shaped like a giant banana leaf, and picked up a marker pen. 'Where should we start? Scene setting and objectives?' he said, looking around at the group for consensus.

Gerard immediately cut in.

'I think we should start with props. I'm feeling a lot of negative energy already and I think it's because we're not all in character.'

Gerard jumped to his feet and started handing out the high-vis jackets and hard hats. Someone in CIC hadn't been diligent with the measurements. The sleeves on Brian Snelling's jacket ended just past his elbows and Simon Loder's jacket stopped either side of his gut. After some mixing and matching, the team had the appearance of children on their first day at school; the uniforms didn't quite fit but they might grow into them. Gerard looked pleased.

'So, back to the agenda,' said Marcus. 'Scene setting and objectives?'

'Perhaps we should deal with logistics, travel arrangements and who is attending from Espina?' said Mason.

Marcus put down the pen. He was starting to get frustrated.

'Fine. Let's deal with that then. I'm going up on Sunday afternoon as I'm meeting my son for dinner. I'll meet you at the Safewear offices at 9.15 on Monday. It's not far. What about everyone else?'

Marcus hoped nobody had the same travel plans as him. He hadn't seen James since Christmas and was looking forward to seeing his son. Fortunately, everyone else was taking the 6.15 from London Euston to Manchester Piccadilly on Monday morning and would take taxis to the Safewear office.

'I'll drop Jim Ibbotson a note and find out who's attending from their side. It's probably him, Derek and Sarah Appleberry, plus the Safewear and TuffTogs MDs? I'll try to get a steer on what they're looking for on the day,' said Mason.

'Just a small point, Mason,' said Gerard. 'I think we need to shift our mindset from using outdated phrases like "our side" and "their side". It implies confrontation and I don't think that's helpful.'

'Good point,' said Simon Loder who was taking a bite out of a nutrition bar. 'Nice build.'

'Great. Now we're all in character, we know how we're getting there and we've changed our mindset. Can we get on with the bloody agenda now?' said Marcus impatiently.

The CIClet handed around copies of the presentation. They landed on the desk with a thud, the most expensive bricks in the world.

'Okay, why don't we do a page turn, agree who is going to say what, emphasise the key points on each slide, how they link together and how this addresses what Espina wants from us?' said Marcus.

It was an approach that had worked before. It was what clients expected and was usually what they got.

'I'm sorry to cut in again, Marcus, but that's totally the wrong approach. It has no drama, no theatre and, most importantly, no impact. It's a recipe for lose, lose and lose. We have to start with the Wonderwall and work backwards. Let me show you,' said Gerard.

He stood up and took out the first brick from the box and placed it on the table in front of the team. It said 'Pride' and he began to speak.

'Good morning everyone. Thank you for giving us the opportunity to demonstrate just how proud we are to be considered as your partner for this exciting project. We are proud of ourselves for the skills and experience we bring to you as your partner. Proud we have supported you with the first phase of this project, and proud of the relationships we have built with you. But most importantly we are proud to know that we are here, right at the start of a bold and brilliant future for TuffTogs.'

Gerard sat down, opened the first page of the presentation and waved his hand at it.

'Everything on that page, the sales messages, the USPs, our differentiating factors, logos from other clients, the boxes, the arrows, the circles, the icons, all summed up in one word. Pride.'

The room went quiet. Everyone knew Gerard was right. Pitches were usually an exercise in grinding the client into submission with endless slides. His approach had real appeal, if they could get it right. The silence was interrupted by Simon Loder.

'What's that infernal noise?'

'Cicadas,' said Mason. 'They're part of the rainforest theme.'

'Can't we turn them off?'

"Fraid not. They're programmed into the room's climate and ambiance software located in the basement.'

For the next six hours, under Gerard's direction and a soundtrack of mating insects, the team built a script around each brick in the Wonderwall. Marcus was impressed by Brian Snelling who delivered his three bricks, 'Security', 'Unhygienic' and 'Confidence', with the chilling authority of Hannibal Lecter. Even Jim Ibbotson might be terrified he would eat his liver with some fava beans and a nice Chianti. By four o'clock, they had completed three full rehearsals and had honed it down to a slick 50 minutes. Just a bit more tweaking and it was there. Marcus returned to his desk and Chloe came to see him.

'We've got a bit of a problem with The Lowry booking. It ain't on Travel Centre's approved list apparently. Too expensive.'

'How much is it per night?' said Marcus.

'A hundred and sixty-five pounds, and the limit is a hundred and twenty. You can stay at the Holiday Inn or the Renaissance instead.'

'But they're hideous. Tell Travel Centre to book it and I'll pay the difference. Forty-five pounds isn't going to kill me.'

Chloe shook her head.

'They won't book it unless it's on the approved list. And it ain't. What do you want to do?'

'Stick a burning hot poker up my fucking arse, that's what.'

Bureaucracy was strangling The Firm and nobody seemed to give a toss.

'Don't worry, Chloe. I'll book it myself online. Thanks a lot and sorry I swore just then.'

'It's okay. Marcus. My dad says far worse at home.'

Marcus booked his room at The Lowry online. He liked the hotel. He always stayed there when he was in Manchester, it was close to Deansgate and Chinatown. José Mourinho lived there when he was the manager at Manchester United. You didn't see the Special One slumming it at the Holiday Inn.

By the time he got to his flat, he was exhausted. It had been an arduous day. All he wanted to do was relax and watch Netflix. He changed into some track suit bottoms and a polo shirt, put his slippers on and picked up his copy of the *Evening Standard*.

'CHINA FAILING TO HALT RAPID SPREAD OF VIRUS,' SAYS MINISTER.

The number of cases had reached 10,000 and the health minister, Matt Hancock, had questioned whether China was doing enough to stop its spread. Marcus wondered who Matt Hancock was. He had never heard of him. There was a third case in the UK, a man in Brighton who had returned from a trip to Singapore and France. Brighton was only 60 miles from Weybridge. He called Alice immediately.

'Hi Marcus. You okay? You sound anxious, what's the matter? Bad day at work?'

'Well, that too. But it's the virus. There's been a third case now, have you seen? In Brighton. It's getting closer, it's on the South Coast now. And the NHS has been told to set up isolated zones to deal with new cases. It's coming Al, just like I said it would. Are you okay?'

'Marcus, stop panicking will you? Libby and I are both fine.'

'I think we may need to think about letting Jacinda go. She could be a risk, bringing the virus into the house. We don't know where she goes or who she meets.'

Jacinda was indispensable to Alice and integral to her hectic week. The suggestion of letting her go brought an abrupt end to their conversation.

'That's enough, Marcus. You're working yourself up over nothing. Nobody in the UK has died and we're not getting rid of our trustworthy and loyal cleaner because of your anxiety about something that hasn't happened. I don't know who you mix with half the time but I don't stop you seeing them, do I?'

He told her about his trip to Manchester and his plan to meet James. She was pleased they would be spending some time together. He was unsure about telling her about the meal with Gavin and Claire. It would take more explanation and he had already upset her.

'I'll be home early tomorrow. Probably sometime in mid-afternoon.'

'Great. I might be out having tea with Theresa when you get home. She's still having problems with Mike. I'll see you when I get back.'

He wanted to tell his wife that he loved her, but she had already gone. He put a Charlie Bigham's fish pie in the oven and ate it watching episodes of *Fast & Loud*. A bunch of talented Dallas rednecks turning pieces of scrap into muscle cars. He wished he looked like the show's frontman who had a goatee beard which was much better than Gary Lineker's. He stared out at the crane lights over Beirut and fell asleep thinking of bricks and viruses.

It was Thursday, 6 February 2020.

Chapter 13

Mushroom Management

Alice put a bubbling veggie lasagne on the kitchen table for Sunday lunch. Marcus had been in the garage filling more black bags. He came into the kitchen through the utility room.

'Wash your hands thoroughly, Marcus. Mouse wee carries diseases,' said Alice.

For a man who used hand sanitiser several times a day, he thought she was being patronising.

'I'm not a six-year-old,' he said snappily. 'Anyway, what diseases can you get from mouse wee?'

'Leptospirosis,' said Olivia, who had come into the kitchen. 'Also known as Weil's disease. Quite nasty. A good dose of antibiotics will usually sort it.'

'See, you should listen to your daughter. Now come to the table, this is ready.'

Alice sat at the head of the table with Marcus and Olivia on either side.

'So what do we have here?' said Marcus.

'Vegetarian lasagne. You said you liked it, so I've made it again. Vegan mozzarella and parmesan, oatmilk bechamel, soya mince and gluten-free lasagne.'

Sunday lunch. He remembered the days when the four of them would tuck into a rib of beef with Yorkshire puddings or a leg of lamb with mint sauce, all with roast potatoes and vegetables.

'Looks delicious,' he said, wondering what today's mystery ingredient would be.

'And probably adding years to your life too,' said Olivia, smugly.

'Where are you going for dinner with James tonight?' said Alice, spooning portions of gloopy lasagne on to the plates. Marcus had booked a table at Hawksmoor, the top-end steak restaurant in Deansgate, close to his hotel.

'A small vegetarian tapas bar in the centre of town. James booked it. I can't remember the name. We're supposed to be having a drink first and watching the football in some grotty boozer.'

'I'm sure the two of you will have fun,' said Olivia.

The mystery ingredient in the lasagne turned out to be juniper berries. Alice had made a bean curd panna cotta for dessert. He passed on dessert and went upstairs to pack for the week ahead. He decided on two suitcases, one for Manchester and another for the rest of the week. Alice came into the bedroom.

'What's this?' she said, picking up the hard hat and luminous jacket.

'My props for the Spearmint pitch tomorrow. Gerard's idea to make us all feel part of their team.'

'Ooh! How sexy. Put it on for me, Marcus, go on! Let me see how rugged you look.'

Reluctantly, he put the props on and waited for the sarcasm.

'You look—'

'A total bellend. Yes, I know that, thank you,' he said, cutting her off and throwing the hat on the bed.

'Before you butted in, I was going to say you look quite horny. I think it's a great idea. I'm not taking the piss, honestly. What time is your train?'

'Three thirty. Gets me into Piccadilly around six. I'm still waiting for James to let me know where we're meeting. He probably isn't even up yet.'

Alice saw the dinner jacket lying on the bed.

'Do you have a work event this week?'

There was always a dinner going on at The Firm. Awards dinners, industry dinners, client dinners, charity dinners. It could have been any one of them. He wanted to tell her the truth but he didn't have time so he made something up.

'Yes, some charity dinner. Prostate Cancer Awareness. Three hundred arseholes looking like penguins and talking about making a killing investing in bitcoin.'

'Sounds hideous,' said Alice.

He put his cases in the boot of the M5 and returned to the house. Alice was sitting in the living room behind the *Mail on Sunday*. Paul McKenna, the hypnotist, was on the front page promoting himself as he always did.

My Seven Steps to Guarantee You a Happy Love Life

Marcus hated Paul's over-simplified, 'do what I tell you and you'll be fine' crap. And why were there always seven steps? Not four or twelve, always seven. He thought Paul McKenna would do well at The Firm, selling crap to people who could sort their lives out much better on their own. Alice loved Paul McKenna, almost as much as she loved Gary Lineker.

She paused her reading, took off her glasses and looked up.

'Good luck tomorrow. You do look sexy in the hat.'

He still thought she was taking the piss, but he accepted the compliment.

'Thanks a lot. Call you later. Love you.'

'Love you too.'

It took him forty-five minutes to reach the flat. His anxiety started to kick in at Hammersmith and was peaking by the time he reached the entrance to the underground car park. The ramp was narrow and he pressed the electronic button to open the gate.

The car inched forward down the slope. It was like landing the space shuttle on the moon. Narrowly avoiding the wall to his left, he felt the front right tyre bump the kerb. He put his foot on the accelerator. There was a loud popping sound followed by an expulsion of air.

'Pppppsssshhhhhhhhh!'

Oh, that's just fucking brilliant, he thought, slamming the car into reverse. He inched the car down the ramp and into the car park as the dashboard flashed up its neon warning message.

Low Tyre Pressure Detected. Proceed With Caution.

'I think I knew that already!' he shouted in frustration.

He parked next to Gavin's Nissan Micra and got out to inspect the damage. The low-profile tyre was already flat. A replacement would cost £250. He would have to call the RAC when he returned from Manchester. He removed his luggage from the boot and took the lift to the flat. Inside, it smelled like someone had died. He had forgotten to empty the bin and the remnants of Thursday night's fish pie were rancid.

He hung up his clothes and opened a window to clear the smell of rotting fish. He picked up his case for Manchester along with the rubbish, left the building via the rear entrance and hailed a taxi in Westbourne Grove. Fifteen minutes later he was at Euston Station and printing his ticket to Manchester.

He took his seat by the window in First Class near the front of the train. The Firm had a two-tier policy for train travel. Partners could travel first class, everyone else couldn't. The carriage was empty apart from a well-dressed and heavily made-up young woman with a fluffy shih-tzu dog which sat on the seat next to her. The train stopped at Watford Junction and he checked for news from James. A message, sent ten minutes earlier.

Hi Dad. No footie on tonight. No point in going to pub. See you at hotel at 7.00.
J x

It was the first piece of good news he had all day. No back street boozer in Rusholme crowded with students spilling their pints of Carling Black Label down his trousers. He replied and sat back for the rest of the journey staring out at the houses along the way. More families with different accents going about their lives on a Sunday afternoon. He checked Outlook. One email from Mason and one from Gerard.

Subject: Project Spearmint – Espina Attendees
From: Mason Sherwin
To: Pitch Team

All
Spoke with Jim Ibbotson late on Friday. Wouldn't give anything away. It will be him, Derek, Sarah, Gary Chambers (Safewear MD) and Tony Bampton (TuffTogs MD). See you at Euston at 6.00 tomorrow. Have a nice night with your son, Marcus.
    Mason

Marcus thought it was a nice thing for Mason to say. He opened the email from Gerard. It was typically over the top but equally well meant.

Subject: Project Spearmint – The Final Act
From: Gerard Cornelius
To: Pitch Team

In a few hours, the curtain will go up and our drama will begin. Some of you may be getting stage fright but we must be brave and bold. We have rehearsed this until we know our lines off by heart. Spearmint is our Henry V, cometh the hour, cometh the men. Let's build our own Theatre of Dreams in Manchester and WIN!
    Gerard

The quote isn't from Henry V and the man is clearly insane, he thought.

The train pulled into Stockport at 17.45, ten minutes outside Piccadilly Station. He started gathering his things together and moved towards the front of the train. He liked to get off quickly.

His taxi took a route through the back streets of Manchester, past boarded-up Victorian warehouses, reminders of the city's industrial heritage. Ornate red-brick buildings, ripe for conversion into the new flats and apartments that were springing up all over the booming city. Marcus loved Manchester.

He wheeled his luggage into the reception at the Lowry where he was greeted by Renata. Her badge indicated she also spoke Polish and Italian.

'Good evening, sir. Are you checking in? Can I have your name please?'

'Yes, good evening. It's Barlow, Marcus Barlow. A standard room for one night?'

Renata tapped away furiously on the keyboard. His name only had six letters and he wondered what she was typing.

'I'm sorry Mr Barlow but I can't find a record of your booking. Did you do it online or through an agent?'

'I did it myself on Thursday. I have the confirmation here on my phone.'

Marcus searched for the email and opened it. He turned the screen to face her. It was obvious the hotel had made a mistake.

'I'm afraid your booking is for the ninth of March, Mr Barlow. Yes, I can see it here on our system too,' said Renata apologetically.

'Oh. Can we transfer the booking to today then?'

'I'm afraid not, Mr Barlow. We're fully booked. There's an exhibition at the GMEX. The only room I have available is a Junior Suite.'

'And how much is one of those?'

'Three hundred and fifty-five pounds. It does come with a riverside view, complimentary Wi-Fi and a walk-in shower.'

'For three hundred and fifty-five pounds, I'd expect a jacuzzi filled with ass's milk,' he said.

Marcus considered the alternative. A night in a Holiday Inn packed with a bunch of exhibition demonstrators in shiny suits trying to get their leg over one of their colleagues after a big night in the bar. The thought filled him with dread.

'I'll take it,' he said ruefully, aware that a Junior Suite at The Lowry was certainly not on Travel Centre's approved list. It was becoming an expensive day. He secured the booking with his Gold Amex card and took the lift to the fifth floor along with a porter, who wheeled his luggage for him.

Everything Renata promised him about his Junior Suite was true. It was bigger than his flat. Luxuriously furnished and decorated in warm, neutral colours, he could see why José Mourinho had stayed for so long. The interior designer knew what they were doing. All the ornaments, plants and pictures came in threes. He unpacked his clothes and put his toilet bag in the bathroom which came with complimentary Jo Malone toiletries. He made a mental note to take them when he left, he would give them to Libby. He had fifteen minutes before James was due to arrive so he lay on his king-size bed and texted Alice to say he had arrived safely.

James called him at seven o'clock precisely. He was usually late.

'Hi Dad. It's me. I'm in reception. Shall I come up to your room or meet you in the bar?'

'Hi! I'll meet you in the bar and we can have a drink and then go straight out for dinner. I'll be down in five minutes.'

He was excited to see his son and immediately recognised him from behind. He was taller than he was and with a broader physique. He walked up behind him, tapped him on one shoulder and ducked behind the other. It was a childish joke but James had been falling for it since he was small. He turned around and hugged his father. His dark beard had grown bushier since Christmas and Marcus felt he was being gripped by a bear. He kissed his son on a hairy cheek.

'Hi mate. Great to see you. You're looking good. How's everything?'

'You're looking very casual, Dad. Are you sure you're okay without a tie? Not going to have a breakdown or anything?' James laughed and gave his father another hug.

'Ha-fucking-ha! What would you like to drink?'

'Already ordered, hope you don't mind. Two large Bombay Sapphires with tonic. Also ordered some olives and spicy nuts.'

'Since when did you start drinking gin and tonic?'

'Since now!' said James and he laughed again.

The barman brought the bill and gave it to James, who passed it sideways to his father.

'I think this is for you. We should probably open a tab?'

'You can put it on Room 5.04,' Marcus said to the barman and signed the bill.

They took their drinks and snacks to one of the sofas and sat down.

'Cheers. Nice place, Dad,' said James looking around the bar, 'very swanky. I suppose you've got a decent room then?'

'Cheers. Yes, it's quite nice. So how's everything with you? Course going okay?' He decided not to tell James about his Junior Suite.

'Not too bad. Working on my dissertation but I'm on top of things. How's everything at home? Mum and Libby okay?'

It was James's usual tactic: minimal information followed by a diversion.

'Libby is working like a Trojan and your mum is doing her usual things. The vegan regime shows no signs of weakening. You could have done more to support me.'

James laughed.

'That's why I suggested going for a steak tonight. I thought you might be in need of one. How's everything with you, Dad? Still making mega bucks?'

'I'm busy enough. Got a big meeting tomorrow but I'm not enjoying it anymore. Everything's so serious now. The Firm has become one big machine.'

'I thought you loved it? Flying around the world on expenses, making loads of money. What's not to enjoy about that?'

'Pretty much everything. It's all just smoke and mirrors. Drink up, we'll have another. Same again?'

Marcus was drinking quicker than his son, which was unusual. He called the barman over and ordered another round.

'More spicy nuts?' he said to James.

'Definitely. These are five-star nuts.'

Marcus told James about Spearmint, Gerard, the Wonderwall, Kelvin and his meeting with Colin in the churchyard. James listened closely. Normally, he just took the piss.

'So, let's see the photo then!'

Marcus opened the email and showed him his photograph. James almost choked on a spicy nut.

'Oh Dad, that's just so bad! You really do look like a knob.'

'Thanks for the vote of confidence, son. We should probably be going. Drink up.'

They left the hotel by the rear entrance, crossed the bridge over the canal and walked up to Hawksmoor on Deansgate. The Bombay Sapphires had slipped down easily and Marcus was feeling good. They walked through the front doors of Hawksmoor into the dimly lit dining room, stained wooden panels and floors. It was busy for a Sunday evening and the waiter showed them to their table.

'Can I get you any drinks while you look at the menu?'

'Would you like a cocktail, James?' said Marcus.

'Sure. What are you thinking of having?'

Marcus scanned down the menu.

'We'll have two Reformed Pornstars, please.'

The waiter took the drinks order and James laughed at his father's choice.

'Thinking of yourself in your hard hat?'

'Not in the slightest. Your mother described my body as nondescript last week so I don't think I'm cut out for a career in porn.'

The two men looked at the menu.

'I assume we're going through the card, since you're paying?' said James.

'Well, I wasn't expecting your student loan to cover it, so I guess I'll have to. What are you having?'

'I'll have the pork belly ribs followed by the rib eye steak and peppercorn sauce with dripping fries,' said James, massaging his stomach.

'Great choice. I'm having the scallops, sirloin steak and Béarnaise sauce. Same fries as you and some spinach.'

The waiter returned with their cocktails and took their order. Marcus ordered a decent bottle of Malbec from a region in Argentina he had visited with Alice en route to their holiday in Patagonia. Marcus returned to the subject of his son's studies.

'So, tell me about the course. How's it really going? And no bullshit this time.'

Marcus had always felt James was uncomfortable at university, that he had only gone to please his parents. He would have been happier becoming a ski instructor.

'I'm not gonna lie to you Dad ...'

This was usually a phrase James used before he lied.

'... I think getting a 2:1 is going to be a push. I am working a lot harder this term. Not going out as much and getting up earlier.'

Marcus remembered the pictures on Instagram showing James with his arms around his friends, always with a drink in hand. Olivia was one of James's 'followers' and she always showed him.

'And are you still dabbling with recreational substances?'

'Bit of weed occasionally, mushrooms every now and then. Maybe an ecstasy tab if I go clubbing. It's nothing, Dad. Honestly, don't worry. I don't have a crack habit if that's what you're thinking!'

The waiter brought their starters and poured the wine. Both were delicious and James tucked into his ribs as if he hadn't eaten for a week.

'Bit better than our curry night in Rusholme last year?' said Marcus, cutting into a scallop.

'Absolutely Dad. I'm sorry about that. Must have been a dodgy samosa or something.'

Father and son relaxed in each other's company. Another bottle of Malbec was ordered in time for their steaks, which came complete with sauces and dripping chips that were fat, juicy and golden. James took out his phone and took pictures of their seared slabs of meat, oozing with blood.

'Must take a picture of this,' he said. 'I'll post it on Instagram so my flatmates get jealous.'

Their conversation moved on to football, women, politics, fast food, music, jobs. The second bottle of Malbec had slipped down nicely, so they ordered a third.

'So what are you going to do with a degree in Economics once it's over?' said Marcus. 'You could get a job somewhere like The Firm?'

James put down his cutlery and took another slurp of wine.

'Are you serious, Dad? Working late nights, weekends, cancelling things just to satisfy The Firm. That's all bollocks. I want to live my life now when I'm young, not be a slave to the money. It's good you're feeling as you do. It's about time.'

'*It's about time*,' he heard Colin's words in his head.

It was almost 10.30 by the time they finished. They decided a dessert wouldn't be a good idea but settled on two coffees and the bill. It was £350 including service. They left the restaurant and stepped out on to Deansgate.

'Are you going back to the hotel now or do you fancy going on somewhere?' said James.

'Going on somewhere? Like where? I should get back to the hotel. I need a good night's sleep before the meeting tomorrow. It's important.'

'Come on! I know a great club, Prism, it's not far from here. Bit of a student place, but not bad. We can get a drink and it won't be busy on a Sunday. We won't stay long. Just a couple of drinks.'

Marcus knew the sensible option was to go back to The Lowry, where his Junior Suite and Jo Malone body milk were waiting for him.

'Okay, fine. But I can't stay too late.'

Marcus wasn't a good dancer and couldn't remember the last time he'd been in a nightclub. About fifty yards before the entrance, James pulled Marcus into a narrow side street.

'I've got a few 'shrooms leftover from a night out last week. We'll split them, there's only a few.'

'What?' said Marcus.

'A few magic mushrooms. Shrooms! It will be a laugh, sharing a few with my dad. Don't worry, you won't think you can fly or anything, no thinking you're Batman. They'll just relax you, make you feel good before your meeting tomorrow.'

'James, I don't think this is a good idea. I think I might be a bit pissed already.'

'You'll be fine, Dad. Trust me,' said James, as he delved into his backpack and pulled out a small plastic bag containing some shrivelled fungi. He split the contents in two and handed half to Marcus.

'They look like some Chinese cure for eczema,' he said disdainfully. 'What do I do now? Rub them on my skin?'

'Drink them with this.' James took a bottle of water out of his backpack, put his share of the mushrooms into his mouth, took a swig of water, chewed and swallowed. He gestured to Marcus to do the same.

'Yuck, they taste disgusting,' he said, swallowing the contents in one. 'What happens now?'

'Wait and see. Don't worry, it'll be fine. You'll just feel very relaxed. I'm here with you.'

There was a short queue at the door to Prism, it wasn't a busy night. A few girls dressed in short skirts and high heels, cleavage pushed upwards and outwards, with their phones and fags in one hand together with some boys of a similar age, trimmed beards and gelled hair. Most of them had tattoos. The queue moved quickly. It took them five minutes to reach the entrance to the nightclub, where they were greeted by two large men. They were like the publicity poster for *Men in Black*, wearing sunglasses in winter, and at eleven o'clock at night. The slightly smaller one spoke to James in a nasal Mancunian snarl.

'You can come in mate but the old geezer can't,' and he pointed at Marcus.

Marcus felt insulted. He was a British Airways Executive Club Gold cardholder and had a membership with Leading Hotels of the World, and yet he was being denied entry to some shitty nightclub in Manchester by a Tommy Lee Jones lookalike.

'What's the problem?' said Marcus.

'We have problems with old geezers getting pervy with the girls. Touching them up and that sort of thing. So we don't let anyone over forty in,' said the Man in Black.

'I wouldn't do anything of the sort,' protested Marcus loudly. 'I'm married and I've got an eighteen-year-old daughter. I don't feel the need to touch young women up.'

The two bouncers bristled and stretched their neck muscles in a way that suggested they were limbering up to physically paste Marcus all over Deansgate. James intervened quickly.

'Look guys, I appreciate the age limit but he's my dad and he's come up from London to visit me. Nothing's going to happen. He's pretty respectable and not much of a perv.' James took two twenty-pound notes out of his pocket and handed them to the bouncers. 'Go on, let him in.'

The strategy worked. The bouncers put the money in their pockets, shrugged and waved them both through. James grabbed his father by the arm and pulled him into the entrance to the nightclub.

'What did you mean, "not much of a perv"? I'm not a perv at all,' said Marcus indignantly.

'Shut up, Dad. We're in aren't we? And you can pay me back for the bribe to the bouncers. I'm not loaded like you are.'

Marcus paid the entrance fee and the receptionist branded 'Prism' on the back of his hand in black ink. He reimbursed James for the bribe. He was £100 down and hadn't even had a drink. He left his Burberry raincoat with the girl in the cloakroom and took a ticket.

They descended the stairs into the nightclub and he could already feel the bass from the music reverberating through his body. His liver was vibrating. He recognised 'Duality' by Paul van Dyk from his 'Trance Anthems' playlist. James found them a small table away from the dance floor which was half-full with young people gyrating and pumping their arms in the air. Marcus felt like a fish so far out of water he was almost desiccated.

'Are you going to the bar then?' said James, shouting above the music. 'May as well stick to large Bombay Sapphires. Don't want to mix our drinks do we?'

Marcus thought it was a bit late in the day for restraint, following hot on the heels of the 'Reformed Pornstars' and three bottles of Malbec. Not to mention the consumption of an illegal substance.

'Fine. How stupid of me to think you might pay for something.' He went off to the bar and returned with the drinks and some water. 'I thought we might need some hydration after all the alcohol.'

'Smart move, Dad,' said James who was distracted by two girls sitting on the next table.

After the second round of Bombay Sapphires, Marcus needed to go to the toilet. James was engaged in conversation with the two girls, so he decided to find the toilets on his own. The interior of Prism was starting to get bigger. The dancefloor was now the size of a football pitch and the dancers were the size of ants. The closer he got to the walls, the further away they got. People were staring at him, walking forward with his arms outstretched.

He made it to the men's toilet, navigated his way past a couple of people to the stainless steel urinal and looked down. The yellow deodoriser blocks were a mile below him, he felt like he was standing on the edge of a precipice. He fumbled inside his trousers, steadying himself with one hand against the dirty mirror in front of him. He looked at himself. He was turning green and his eyes were spinning like saucers. Men were coming and going on either side of him as he stood, waiting for something to happen. His undiagnosed prostate issues had brought on performance anxiety as he looked at his mutating face and with a non-functioning penis in his hand. He finally managed to send clear signals from his brain to his bladder. His flow was like Niagara Falls, crashing and splashing into the trough below and over his beige chinos.

It took him ten minutes to return to the dancefloor which was now even bigger than before. He walked forward, hands in front of him, looking around for James but couldn't see him. The break from Dash Berlin's *'We Don't Belong'* kicked in and the lights in the club started to spin at the same speed as his head. He called out.

'James, where the fuck are you? I'm trapped, I can't get out.'

But James couldn't hear him. Marcus walked forward like a robot on acid, which was what he was. A group of girls were coming off the dancefloor, laughing and smiling. Not looking in front of her, one of them collided with Marcus's outstretched hands.

'Hey, fuck off you dirty bastard. You just touched my tits.'

He was quickly surrounded by a group of intoxicated girls, convinced he had groped their friend. He stared around, bewildered as a circle of angry, contorted faces pressed into his. Alerted by the disturbance, two more Men in Black were quickly on the scene.

'What the fuck is going on here?'

'This dirty old pervert just grabbed my mate's tits,' said one of the girls, pointing at Marcus. 'It was a sexual assault.'

'I didn't, I didn't,' slurred Marcus. 'It was an accident. She bumped into my hands. I've done nothing wrong.'

The Men in Black didn't need to gather witness statements. They took one look at Marcus's piss-stained chinos and his glazed expression and decided his evening was over. One grabbed him by the neck and the other by the arm, and together they frogmarched him towards the exit. Like the room, everything was spinning out of control. James looked up from exchanging phone numbers to see his father being manhandled to the exit. He jumped up and ran over.

'Dad, what's going on? What the hell have you done now?'

Marcus stared blankly at his son's face, which was turning into a grizzly bear.

'Is this your dad?' said one of the Men in Black.

'Yes, why? What's he done?'

'Touched a young girl up on the dancefloor, that's what. Grabbed her tits.'

'Dad, for fuck's sake, what did you do that for?'

Marcus was incapable of replying, his speech neurones had gone AWOL, the mushrooms were attacking every synapse in his body. James ran back to the table, picked up his bag, made apologies to the girls and made it upstairs just in time to see his father being ejected from Prism on to the pavement. Unable to break his fall, his nose hit the ground first, splitting like an overripe tomato. James ran to help his father whose nose was now bleeding profusely.

'That's why we don't let old geezers in,' said one of the bouncers. 'Perverts.'

James took out his phone and took a picture of Marcus lying face down on the pavement. He took a T-shirt out of his backpack to stem the flow of blood. Marcus looked at the T-shirt and felt faint. He hated the sight of blood, especially his own. The lights from the cars on Deansgate were blinding him as James got him upright.

'Jesus Christ, Dad. Look at the state of you. What a mess. Let's get you back to the hotel and cleaned up.'

He put his father's arm around his neck and they set off through the backstreets behind Deansgate and into the reception of The Lowry Hotel.

'What's your room number, Dad? Have you got your room key?'

Marcus stared blankly at his son. His mouth was opening but no sound was coming out. James walked over to the reception where a night porter was on duty.

'Can I help you sir?' He looked up at Marcus from behind the desk. He was shocked at the sight of the blood-soaked T-shirt underneath his nose. 'Jesus, is he okay? Has he been in a fight or something?'

'Yes, with himself,' said James. 'Marcus Barlow, he has a room in the hotel tonight. I think he's lost his key. I'm his son.'

The night porter checked the computer.

'Ah, yes. Mr Barlow. A Junior Suite for one night. Fifth floor, Room 5.04.' He made a new key and handed it to James. 'I think he needs to get a good night's sleep. That nose looks pretty sore to me. Goodnight, sir.'

James helped his father into the lift and got out at the fifth floor. The room was close by and James opened the door to the Junior Suite and guided his father into the bedroom. He looked around.

'Fucking hell, Dad! You're not exactly slumming it are you? Pretty palatial.'

He laid Marcus down on the bed, went to the bathroom and rinsed a flannel. He returned and wiped his father's face. The flow of blood had stopped and James cleaned the blood stains from his face.

'Where am I?' said Marcus staring around him. 'What happened? I feel really sick.'

'Back in your shitty room at The Lowry. Bit of a big night Dad. Nothing too bad, you'll be okay.'

It wasn't the time to tell Marcus he had been accused of a sexual assault and was lucky the police hadn't been called. He could have been spending the night in a less salubrious place. Marcus looked up at the expensive but tasteful light fitting which was flashing in a way that would give him a seizure.

'James, I'm really going to be—'

Marcus retched and James dived for the nearest receptacle. He picked up the

TuffTogs hard hat and stuck it under his father's mouth, just in time for Marcus to empty the semi-digested meat fest into the bowl. The spicy nuts were proving highly resistant to stomach acid.

James sat next to his father on the bed for the next fifteen minutes before emptying the contents of the hat down the toilet and rinsing it under the tap. When he returned, Marcus was lying on his back, eyes wide open but asleep.

'It's okay, Dad. I'll stay with you. Don't worry, you're going to be fine. Trust me.'

He took off his father's shoes, removed his blood-stained jacket and trousers, rolled him under the luxury goose-down duvet and pulled it over him. He got undressed and got into bed next to him and put his hand on his shoulder.

'Night, Dad. Fantastic evening. Avicii would have been proud of you. Maybe not the groping bit.'

He switched out the lights. It was 2.30 a.m. on Monday, 10 February 2020. The Project Spearmint pitch to Espina was seven hours away.

Chapter 14

THE DAY THE WALL CAME DOWN

It was the snore in his ear that woke him. Marcus opened his eyes to unfamiliar surroundings. He rolled over to see James lying on the pillow next to him, mouth open. Dog breath. He instinctively reached for his phone but it wasn't next to his bed. He felt for his wristwatch and checked the time. It was 8.15.

'Fuck me!' he shouted loudly and jumped out of bed. He was still in a blood-stained shirt and his underpants. 'Jesus Christ, what happened?'

He reached into his jacket pocket for his phone. It was dead and he took the charger out of his suitcase and plugged it in. He looked at James who was in a coma and shook him.

'James! James! Wake up. I've overslept. I'll be late for my meeting. Get up now!'

James stirred but didn't move. Marcus shuffled into the bathroom, turned on the light and stared at himself in the mirror. Blood from his plum-like nose had dried in his stubble, his eyes were sunken and bloodshot and his skin felt like sandpaper. From the bedroom, he heard his phone pinging multiple times. Ten new messages on WhatsApp, five from Mason, two each from Alice and Olivia and one from Gavin. He had three missed calls from Mason. He checked Mason's messages which increased in urgency and decreased in length.

Hope you had a nice night. On the train with the others. Want to have a short call about the meeting. Call me back asap?

Tried calling you. Please call me back. Would be good to speak.

Called again. Give me a call will you?!

Really unprofessional behaviour.

Selfish prick.

He didn't have time to explain something he couldn't remember, so sent a holding reply.

Sorry. Phone was dead. All okay. See you at Safewear. Raring to go! M.

It was 8.30 and he had 45 minutes to arrive at Espina's offices to deliver the pitch that could possibly save the team. He didn't shave. It would save ten minutes and he needed every second. Some stubble might make him look more like David Gandy. He entered the walk-in shower, turned it on and looked at the black, inky 'Prism' stain on the back of his right hand.

What the fuck is Prism? he thought.

The water cascading on his head felt like pebbles pummelling his brain. He washed himself thoroughly, making sure every trace of blood was removed. The stain on the back of his hand was proving harder to remove. His nose felt tender, like a giant abscess in the middle of his face.

He put on a fresh set of clothes and threw the carnage of the previous evening into his case. If explaining a ketchup stain to Alice had been difficult, evidence of an apparent knife crime would be much harder to conceal. He put on his high-vis jacket and looked for his hat. It was on the floor and he picked it up. It stank of vomit and there were little pieces of nut in the lining. Another mystery. He sprayed the inside with aftershave. He looked down at James, still asleep and snoring in bed. He hadn't moved an inch.

You can bloody well stay there, he thought.

He picked up his suitcase, laptop bag and hard hat and made his way to the door. He stopped. 'Where's my raincoat? I can't walk out of The Lowry in this stupid jacket,' he said to himself.

He checked the room but it was nowhere to be seen. He was short on time. He would call James after the meeting. He approached reception and was greeted by Renata who was staring at him with a confused frown.

'Good morning, Mr Barlow. How was your stay with us?'

He had spent six hours in his Junior Suite and could only remember the last forty-five minutes.

'It was great. Thank you.'

Renata printed a copy of his bill and handed it to him. Three hundred and fifty pounds for the Junior Suite plus an eighty-three-pound bar tab. He paid with his Amex card, thanked Renata and walked out of the door to a waiting taxi.

'Can you take me to Wythenshawe Business Park in Sale, please? And I'm in a bit of a rush.'

'I'll do my best,' said the taxi driver. 'Traffic is pretty bad. It's Monday morning.'

The traffic moved slowly through central Manchester. He kept checking his watch as the minutes ticked by. His phone rang, it was Mason.

'Marcus, where the hell are you? We're waiting in reception. I thought you would be here by now?' There was more than a hint of panic in his voice.

'I'm on my way, just stuck in traffic. Let me ask the driver.'

The driver held up a chubby hand to indicate they were five minutes away.

'I'm five minutes away. I know it's cutting it fine but don't worry, I'll make it.'

'Not a great start, Marcus. Get here as soon as you can.'

The taxi pulled up outside Safewear's offices with three minutes to spare. The concrete building was built in the 1970s. It was joined to a series of warehouses and, as Marcus approached, he could see a fleet of white delivery vans being loaded with Safewear's products. He rushed into the reception where the other members of The Dream Team were waiting in full costume. They looked like they were ready to repair a gas main rather than present their case to win a multi-million-pound project. At least Gerard was wearing long trousers, and Loder's and Snelling's uniforms fitted.

'What happened to you?' said Mason, looking at his face. 'Did you get mugged last night?'

He wanted to say he'd been the victim of a hate crime but came up with the most plausible excuse he could think of.

'I slipped over in the shower. Bashed my face against the screen. I stayed in the hotel, crashed out and didn't see my son. Really sorry I'm late. Are we all set to go?' As lies went, it was believable enough and nobody asked any awkward questions.

'I've signed you in. Just waiting for them to call us,' said Mason.

Gerard gave Marcus a reassuring hug and massaged his shoulders. He felt like a prize-fighter being prepared to enter the ring.

'Love the stubble, Marcus. Really good to see you getting into character. What's that funny smell?'

A small, middle-aged woman with thick-rimmed spectacles on a lanyard came into reception and invited them upstairs to the meeting room.

'Mr Ibbotson and the other directors are ready for you now. You're in the Altrincham Room today.'

The internal decor was little better than outside. Scuffed and peeling paintwork with faded pictures of masks, gowns and rubber gloves hanging on the walls. The stair well was cold and damp. The meeting room was stuffy and hot, the radiators were on full. There was silence as the team entered the room and the Espina directors eyed them up and down. They were expecting expensive City suits, ties and cufflinks.

Marcus broke the ice and extended a hand.

'Jim, Derek, good to see you again. Great to be back in Manchester. We thought we would give you a little surprise first thing on a Monday morning!'

'I thought I recognised you from your CV photo, Marcus! What's happened to your nose?' said Derek Bentley, the CEO.

Marcus thought Jim and Derek had probably pissed themselves laughing when they saw his photo.

'I fell over in the shower in my hotel room last night. Thank you for your concern. Please don't let this affect your judgement of our ability to support you.'

Introductions were made, hands were shaken and pleasantries exchanged. Everyone had to shake hands with everyone else before they could sit down.

'Can I offer anyone any tea, coffee, water?' said Jim Ibbotson. 'Help yourself to biscuits.'

The team took their seats in their rehearsed formation. Gerard in the middle, Marcus and Mason on either side and Loder and Snelling on the flanks. Refreshments were placed on the table and Marcus took four biscuits from the plate. The team had eaten breakfast in First Class, but his stomach felt empty.

'I think we can take our hats off now!' said Gerard enthusiastically.

Gerard passed around copies of the presentation in the form of the house bricks. Everyone on the Espina side nodded appreciatively. It was a nice touch and it had started well. Sarah Appleberry started taking notes as Jim Ibbotson set the scene.

'Firstly, thank you for coming to Manchester on a Monday morning and thank you for sending through all the templates on time. A very comprehensive response in most areas. We do have some questions, particularly on the proposed fees, but we'll come to them later. You have the next forty-five minutes to tell us why you should be our partner for the next phase of Spearmint.'

'A comprehensive response in most areas' and 'the proposed fees'. Just a couple of warning shots but nothing to derail things yet. Marcus replied.

'Thank you Jim and good morning to everyone. Thank you for giving us the opportunity to demonstrate how proud we are to be considered as your partner for this exciting project. We are proud of ourselves for the skills and experience we bring as your partner. Proud we have been able to support you with the first phase of this project and proud of the relationships we have built with you. Most importantly of all, we are proud to be here, right at the start of a bold and brilliant new future for TuffTogs.'

It was exactly as they had rehearsed in Communication Zone 2. Word for word. The Espina directors nodded in unison. Gerard took Brick Number 1 out of the box and placed it on the table to start building the Wonderwall. 'Pride'. Marcus continued.

'We're not going to waste your time going through slide after slide of PowerPoint. You've seen the slides, you know what they say.'

Only one person, Sarah Appleberry, had read the proposal. The others had skimmed the executive summary and looked at the fees. They all nodded appreciatively, as if they had read it from cover to cover.

'What we want to do this morning is bring this document to life, show you what we can really do for you, to make it live and breathe.'

Gary Chambers, the Safewear MD, cut in.

'I'm sorry to interrupt you Marcus, but can anyone smell something? It's pretty rank. Shall I open a window?'

'Yes, I can smell it too,' said Sarah. 'It's a bit like sick. Must be coming from the warehouse. Let's open a window and get some fresh air in here.'

Gary stood up and opened a window. Marcus knew where the smell was coming from.

'Before we continue, our hats are probably cluttering up the table. Perhaps we should put them on the floor?' He leaned forward to pick up his hat and gestured to the others to do the same.

It was Tony Brampton, the TuffTogs MD, who noticed it first.

'Marcus, is that some kind of stamp on the back of your hand? What does it say? Prison? I can't read it upside down.'

Suddenly, a gun went off in his head. The events of the previous evening started to flood into his consciousness. It was time to lie on his feet.

'Oh that? My daughter belongs to a Christian youth group. They had a dance in the village hall on Saturday night and I was helping out on the door. Went a bit heavy with the ink.'

For the next thirty minutes, The Dream Team continued to hit winners down the line. Mason made all the right points about the deal's complexity and risk as Gerard built the Wonderwall in front of them. Even Jim Ibbotson was paying attention. Simon Loder was concise and clear about data segregation, application consolidation and infrastructure separation. Sarah Appleberry wrote 'Spaghetti' on her pad. The Wonderwall was getting taller.

Brian Snelling frightened the pants off them, convincing Espina that weak links in their supply chain data integrity would be magnified if Spearmint went ahead, rendering them vulnerable to phishing and social engineering attacks. By the time he had finished, Espina was convinced it was 'cyber unhygienic'. Even the smell of vomit had evaporated. It was all going well, only two slides to go, 'Fees' and 'Key Messages'. Marcus turned to the penultimate slide.

'We believe we have put together a compelling commercial proposition. Each component in our scope has been crafted specifically to ensure the right balance of skills and experience to deliver the right outcome for you. It's really about two things.'

Marcus gave Gerard the signal to place two of the remaining three bricks at the top of the wall. 'Success' and 'Value'. As Marcus turned his head, Gerard's outstretched elbow hit him full on the nose. It was a direct hit and Marcus screamed in pain, lashing out with his arm into the Wonderwall, scattering the carefully choreographed bricks all over the meeting table. It was like the final scene from *The Dam Busters*.

'Jesus Christ, my fucking nose!' cried Marcus, as blood immediately started to spurt from both nostrils.

Gerard and Mason leapt up from the table, grabbed some tissues from the refreshment table and handed them to him. Sarah Appleberry ran around from the other side, pulled some paper towel from a roll and poured water on to it.

'Tilt your head back. My son gets nosebleeds so I know what to do,' she said, applying a cold compress to Marcus's nose.

With expert first aid assistance from Espina's Chief Procurement Officer, it took fifteen minutes for his nose to stop bleeding and for everyone to return to their seats. Gerard had hurriedly tried to rebuild the Wonderwall but, in the confusion, some of the bricks were out of sequence, presenting Espina with 'Unhygienic Spaghetti' and 'Trust Breakdown'. Nobody seemed to care anymore. Jim Ibbotson reconvened the meeting.

'I hope you're okay now, Marcus? Where were we?'

Marcus composed himself for the final soliloquy of the drama.

'Thanks Jim and apologies for that. So, in summary, everything we have presented today has been with one aim in mind. To be your partners in the next phase of Spearmint. This will lead to one thing.' Marcus paused for dramatic effect as Gerard had instructed him. 'Winning. Thank you for listening. We would be happy to answer any of your questions.'

Gerard placed the final brick on the top of the reassembled wall and The Dream Team sat back in their chairs. There was a period of silence. It was Sarah Appleberry who spoke first.

'Given what's happened, time for questions is limited so we probably only have fifteen minutes. Who wants to go first?' she said, turning to the Espina team.

The two business MDs asked sensible questions about managing redundancies and relocations. The team answered their questions easily. Jim Ibbotson didn't give a hoot about the employees and doodled on his presentation until it was his turn to speak.

'Loved the presentation, the jackets, the hats and the wall, until the accident. Certainly very entertaining. You made some great points ...' The bad tempered CFO didn't hand out compliments very often. It was only a matter of time before the 'but' came. '... but were you guys smoking something when you came up with the fees? Ten point three million pounds! You've got to be joking me!'

Sarah Appleberry waded in.

'I've been looking at your day rates, and frankly, I was astonished. Twelve thousand pounds a day for a partner and seven thousand pounds a day for a senior manager. I didn't think we were hiring brain surgeons here.'

She had hit the nail right on the head. The Firm's rates existed in some parallel universe. Mason responded defensively.

'I think you're taking that a little out of context Sarah. Because we value you so highly as a client, we have applied a significant reduction, as you can see from the graduated discount plan.'

His answer didn't satisfy the Chief Procurement Officer, who replied immediately.

'So how much discount have you applied?'

'Well, it's blended across different grades. It's very competitive I can assure you.'

'Give me a number.'

'That's quite difficult.'

'Have a go.'

'Thirty per cent?'

'Try harder.'

'Forty per cent.'

'Not even warm.'

Marcus could see the way the conversation was going and intervened.

'Sarah, Jim, what I think you're saying is you want us to go away and sharpen our pencils a little?'

'Bit more than a little,' said Sarah snappily.

'We get your point completely,' said Marcus. 'Let's take it away and look at the commercials again. What are the next steps from your side?'

'As you know, we're speaking with three other suppliers, all of whom we're seeing today. I expect there'll be some follow-up conversations and we hope to make a decision by the end of the week. Work to start a couple of weeks after that,' said Jim.

The Espina team stood up from the table indicating the meeting was over. The handshake ritual was repeated and the secretary escorted them downstairs where another group was waiting. Expensive City suits, ties, cufflinks, Tumi bags containing their insights.

The receptionist called two taxis to take them to the station. Mason and Marcus went in one, Gerard, Loder and Snelling in the other.

'How do you think that went?' said Mason.

'Great until Gerard elbowed me in the bloody nose,' said Marcus. 'They seemed engaged. Everything up to the Q&A on fees was great. Then it all went a bit tits up.'

'Sarah was a bitch, wasn't she? Must have gone through our rate card with a microscope.'

'It's her job. We need to go through the fees with a hatchet if we're going to win this.'

'What about Kelvin and his budget?' said Mason.

'Screw Kelvin.'

Marcus opened his phone and read the messages from Olivia, Alice and Gavin. His daughter's didn't make easy reading. A picture of his sirloin steak at Hawksmoor, oozing blood surrounded by dripping chips. James had posted it on Instagram and she had seen it.

Dad. How could you do this? Killing innocent animals is disgusting. So disappointed with you.

He opened the message from Alice. It didn't get better. A grainy picture of a man lying face down on the pavement looking distressed, and with blood streaming from his nose.

M. WTF r u doing? Is this u? J posted this lst nite. Where were u?

He looked at the fading 'Prism' stamp on his hand and closed his eyes. The taxi drew up at Piccadilly Station. They had fifteen minutes before their train to London, so he called James. It took a while for him to answer.

'Hello,' said a sleepy voice.

'James, it's Dad. Where the fuck are you?'

'In bed in the hotel. What time is it?'

'Almost 11.30. Get up right now! I've already checked out. The chambermaid has probably been in three times already, you lazy little shit. You've got some explaining to do, but now isn't the time. I think I've left my Burberry raincoat in that fucking hellhole you took me to last night. Get down there now and get it back. I'm on my way back to London. I'll call you later.'

'How did the meeting go, Dad?'

'Just get up.'

The team spent the journey dissecting the pitch, what went well and what didn't. Gerard apologised for elbowing Marcus on the nose and Marcus returned the apology for destroying the Wonderwall. There wasn't much else to talk about.

He took a taxi from Euston back to the flat. He was exhausted and only managed a short greeting to Eric who was arranging some lilies on the reception coffee table. He went into the bedroom and lay down on the bed, trying to piece together the events of the previous evening. He hadn't come up with an explanation for Alice, and it needed to be a good one. He would sleep on it, so he took a nap.

It was dark outside when he woke and Beirut was quiet. He had slept through the noise of drilling and piling. He took a shower and prepared himself for confession. He checked his phone. He had a missed call from James and called him first.

'I assume you're up now?'

'Yeah, hi Dad. I got up straight after you rang me. How was your meeting? Are you back at home now?'

'No, I'm at the flat. The meeting didn't go that well. Did you get my raincoat back from that nightclub?'

There was a silence.

'Erm, bit of bad news on that one, Dad. They said they didn't have it. I think it's probably been nicked as you didn't collect it, what with your unplanned exit and all that.'

The bill had gone up. A £1,500 Burberry trench coat had just been added to the tab. It was probably being flogged in some backstreet pub in Moss Side as he spoke.

'That's just fucking great. This gets worse by the hour. I've got your sister in tears because I had a steak, your mother is furious because she saw a photo of me lying face down in a gutter and now my raincoat has been nicked!'

'How did they find out?'

'Because you post your whole fucking life on Instagram, that's how!'

More silence.

'Shit. I'm really sorry, Dad. I didn't think of that. It was all fine until you groped that girl and got thrown out by the bouncers.'

'Groped what girl?'

'Some girl in the nightclub. She said you groped her when she came off the dance floor. She wanted to call the police. You were probably lucky you only got thrown out.'

It was now all about damage limitation.

'There's no way your mum can ever learn about this. Our story is that I did get a bit drunk and tripped over. No mushrooms, no club, no alleged groping, no bouncers. Just a fall. Are you with me on this, James? This is all your bloody fault.'

'Scout's honour, Dad. Trust me.'

'Fine. We just have to stick to the same story. I'd better call your mother now and explain.'

'Good luck with that. And thanks for an epic night by the way. Absolute stunner.'

He ended the call and sat on the end of the bed rehearsing his story before he called Alice. She answered within two rings.

'Marcus, what on earth has been going on? Are you okay? Where are you now?'

He took her concern as a positive sign.

'I'm at the flat. James and I probably had a few drinks too many. I tripped up coming out of a pub. Fell flat on my face. It probably looked a lot worse than it was.'

'At 1.30 in the morning? What kind of pub was it?'

'Some student place James knew.'

'You looked like you were in a coma. I want the truth, Marcus, and don't fucking lie to me.'

'I don't remember the name, honestly. I think I mixed my drinks and it all went to my head. And then I fell over.'

'On your face? How pissed were you, Marcus? I thought you had a big meeting today?'

'I was okay by the time I got back to the hotel, James was with me.'

'You need to grow up, Marcus. You're not a kid anymore. You've got some explaining to do to your daughter as well. She's pretty upset.'

'She's my next call.'

'Get an early night and try to stay out of trouble.'

He thought it had gone well. Alice had calmed down and he had got away with a telling off for being infantile. He rang Olivia.

'I want to apologise. I didn't mean to upset you, having a steak.'

'That's okay, Dad. I was just very shocked to see it, that's all. You seemed so up for the vegan thing. I know you're only doing this for me and Mum.'

'I know, I'm really sorry. Are we okay now?'

'Yes, we're fine. Better get on with my homework. Love you.'

'Love you too. Speak soon.'

The confessions hadn't gone badly. He gave it a B+, some room for improvement but not a complete disaster either. He walked across the hall and rang the doorbell to Gavin's flat.

'Hi Marcus. It's not Tuesday already, is it? Good God, what's happened to your face?' said Gavin.

'Long story, can I come in?'

They walked into the kitchen which was pristine as ever.

'Gin and tonic?' said Gavin.

'Best not. Can I have a sparkling water?'

'That bad?' Gavin took a bottle of San Pellegrino out of the fridge and poured a glass for his friend.

Marcus recounted the horror story of the past two days, from the burst tyre to his confession to Alice. Gavin listened with astonishment as each element unfolded.

'So, that's what happened. A total fucking disaster from start to finish. The past two days have cost me the best part of £3,000 and I've still got to get the tyre fixed. God knows what's going to happen at work tomorrow.'

'Well, taking hallucinogenic substances and being accused of a sexual assault that you can't remember, at fifty-five, is pretty spectacular. When I said, "it's about time", you did something different, that wasn't exactly what I meant. It's very funny though, you have to admit?'

'I didn't sexually assault anyone, but I get your point. Certainly not something to forget in a hurry. So, what's the plan for tomorrow night? Probably best not to tell Claire about my weekend?'

'Agreed. Not on a first date anyway.'

Gavin explained the menu. Marcus was on starters, burrata with Parma ham, and dessert, apple tarte Tatin. He was on petits fours, mains, herb-crusted lamb, a cheese course and mints.

'I'll get everything in The Temple tomorrow. We'll prepare as much as we can here before we head off. We'll go in my car. I said we'll be there around 7 p.m. That work for you? Claire is looking forward to meeting you.'

'I'm sure she is. A sex pest with a nose like Rudolph the Reindeer. I'll get back here around five.' Marcus stood up to leave and Gavin walked him to the door.

'You did the right thing, Marcus. About time you took a few risks. Take care and don't forget, it's dinner jackets tomorrow.' Gavin squeezed Marcus on the arm again and his friend walked back to his flat.

It was Monday, 10 February 2020.

Chapter 15

READY, STEADY, COOK!!

He looked in the bathroom mirror. His face was like a chameleon. The bruising had spread to his cheeks which were now a purplish yellow colour. His thoughts turned to dinner and the logistics of cooking in a kitchen that was unlikely to have the same facilities as the flat. He would have to leave work early and make the tarte tatin at the flat.

At the office, he went straight to Communication Zone 1, where Chloe was setting out the papers for the pipeline meeting.

'Jesus, Marcus. What have you done? Your face looks a right old state!'

'Thank you very much, Chloe. I slipped over in the shower in my hotel room on Sunday night. And I agree, it does look "a right old state".'

He imitated her Essex twang, sat down and waited for the others to arrive. The same conversation was repeated several times.

Mason sat next to him which he thought was odd. Kelvin entered the room with Izzy Majewska. Both of them looked serious. Izzy gave her usual update which nobody understood, except the bit at the end which everyone knew: the hole was getting deeper.

Twenty minutes into the meeting, the robotic conference call voice announced, 'Grant Bremner-Walker ... has joined the meeting,' followed by Grant's cheery greeting.

'Morning Kelvin, morning everyone. Sorry I'm a bit late.'

Kelvin's face took on the colour of Marcus's nose. The broken, red veins in his cheeks flared and throbbed.

'Grant, you're twenty minutes late. Either join at the start or don't fucking bother joining at all.' Kelvin leaned forward and disconnected the call, cutting off two other partners who had also dialled in. They didn't re-join either. 'Right, now where were we? Mason, Marcus, do you want to give us an update on the Spearmint pitch? How did it go yesterday?'

Mason turned to Marcus implying he should give the update.

'The pitch went very well. Gerard's format amazingly worked really well.

We're up against three other firms, and they gave us very clear direction that our fees were too high. They need a big haircut if we want to win.'

'How big a haircut?' said Kelvin, disapprovingly.

'Somewhere between a Vin Diesel and a Bruce Willis. What do you think Mason?'

Mason looked sheepish. Delivering bad news to Kelvin was never easy.

'They had some rottweiler from procurement who had been through our rate card with a toothcomb. Tried to pick holes in everything.'

'So, what sort of number are they looking at?' said Kelvin impatiently.

Mason tried to sweeten the pill.

'Somewhere between six and seven million pounds.'

Marcus intervened, lying to Kelvin wasn't a smart move.

'More like somewhere between three and four million pounds. It's still a good win if we can get the fees right.'

Kelvin clicked the lid on his fountain pen. He knew the client had them by the balls like they always did. It just depended on how hard they wanted to squeeze.

'I fucking hate clients,' said Kelvin. 'Do the best you can to win this without giving them the shirt off our backs.'

He got up and left the room before the rest of the updates.

* * *

At the same time as the pipeline meeting was closing, Gavin was knocking on the door of No. 11, Kensal Mansions. Claire opened the door with a smile, she was feeling good.

'No coffee and cakes this week?' she said, switching on the kettle and turning the radio down.

'I'm trying to finish early today. Got to get to The Temple, buy some things and start preparing a meal. And, just to be pedantic, panettone is technically a sweet bread and not a cake.'

'Ooh, sorry! So what are you cooking for us tonight?'

'It's a surprise but I need to check a couple of things. Can I see your roasting tins before I go? I'm sure they're fine.'

Claire opened a cupboard and invited him to look. He got up, walked over, took out a few pots and pans, and put them back.

'They'll do the job. Very adequate,' he said.

'I'm sorry it's not the *MasterChef* kitchen. Then again, you're not Gregg Wallace either.'

'That's lucky. So, tell me about your week. How's everything going?'

'Feeling really positive, actually. Coffee with Beverley was great. She's offered me some part-time work, two mornings a week, to help get her business up and running. It's just admin work and she's giving me my own laptop.'

'That's fantastic. I'm really pleased for you. Cash in hand, I assume?'

'Of course.'

Gavin laughed. As benefit fraud went, it was pretty small beer.

'The kids are great. Doing really well at school. Kyle is starting to come out of himself a lot more. Big day tomorrow. The result of the "Who Looks After Biscuit?" draw is announced. He's down to the last three. He's very excited.'

'Why is he excited about biscuits?'

'Biscuit. The class hamster. It's half-term next week and the winner gets to look after Biscuit for the whole week.'

'Oh, I see. Important stuff!'

'I'm not that keen but it will be good for Kyle.'

They went through their usual agenda. It had been a long time since Claire had been so upbeat. She was confident and assured. It had been a while coming.

'So, tell me again about your friend, Marcus? What does he like, not like? Any topics I should avoid? I'm quite nervous about meeting him.'

'He had a bit of an accident at the weekend, self-inflicted too. You won't be able to avoid noticing when you see him. Probably best not to raise that one, he's not very proud of it. I think you two will get on well. Anyway, I should be going now.'

She walked him to the door.

'Don't go too mad dressing up tonight. Leggings will do just fine. We'll be here around seven.'

'I won't. You can be sure of that. See you later.'

* * *

After lunch, Marcus entered Collaboration Pod 5. It was themed in a Moorish style, like the Alhambra Palace, all mosaics and murals. The seven partners who were included in the proposal to Espina joined him. It was the type of meeting known in The Firm as a 'no pain, no gain' session. A fist fight to reduce the scope, cut resources and slash fees to resemble a reality the client might recognise. Everyone had to take some pain, some more than others. Compromise and good reason would be essential.

Marcus opened the meeting.

'Thanks everyone for joining. To recap, the feedback we got from Espina is they really liked our proposal and we hit most of their key points out of the park. There are two things we need to address today. Reducing the scope and our rates. We need to be coming in around four to five million pounds max and preferably less.'

Everyone looked around the table suspiciously. The turkeys were being asked to vote for Christmas. Simon Loder went on the attack immediately.

'Well, I was there and didn't see any appetite for all this People and Culture stuff. Jim Ibbotson looked bored shitless. I think we should get rid of that whole piece and save £1.5 million. Not that I don't think it's important, of course it is. Maybe we keep one person in to do all the redundancy stuff?'

Compromise and good reason in action. Carole Parker, who led The Firm's Talent Management practice, responded immediately.

'That's total bollocks, Simon, and you know it is. This is a very sensitive area. If they fuck up the stuff on redundancies, the unions will be all over them. No way.'

It was the turn of Richard Davis, from Data Solutions, to go on the attack.

'Well, I don't know why Cyber has £2.5 million in there. I suggest we cut Snelling's piece down to £1 million, give me another £250,000 and we could probably cover the same scope. That's another £1.25 million saved easily.'

'Brian's piece on Cyber did go down very well,' piped up Gerard. 'They seemed very worried about being cyber unhygienic.'

'Total nonsense. Brainwashing,' said Richard Davis. 'Cyber is just like the Millennium Bug, same bollocks all over again. Safewear makes bloody hand sanitiser, not ballistic missiles.'

In the room, alliances were forming and enemies being made. It was whoever was prepared to give ground first. Compromise and good reason.

'I'm not sure about this "Retail Insight" workstream. Exactly what "insights" are we bringing to Espina?' said Carole Parker, sneeringly.

Joel Streeter, the Retail Lead for The Firm, leapt to defend his turf and his fees.

'It's not just about traditional B2B channels, Carole. It's also about convergence. Proliferation of choice is leading to more customers looking to marketplaces that provide curated experiences that no single supplier can offer. TuffTogs will need to factor this into their growth plans. It's about putting purpose at the core of everything they do.'

It was a weak argument, lots of meaningless words. The other partners could smell fear instantly. The pride attacked the weakling.

'I agree with Carole,' said Simon Loder. 'This insight stuff is much further downstream. We can bring you in later Joel if we need to.'

Sensing alignment, Mason went in for the kill.

'So, I think we're all agreed that retail insight goes?'

'Completely agree,' said Richard Davis. 'That's another £900,000 saved.'

Compromise and good reason. For the next hour, partners stabbed each other in the back and traded horses until they reached a number which everyone was happy with. Or, which they weren't unhappy with. £4.85 million.

'That's great everyone,' said Mason. 'Thank you for all your help and compromise. I think we all had to give a bit.'

This was little consolation to Joel Streeter who watched on helplessly as his retail insights and fees were thrown in the bin.

'I'll set up the call with Sarah Appleberry to set out the new fees and scope. I just hope we're not out of the frame.'

* * *

The front page of the *Evening Standard* confirmed the same fears as *Metro*.

UK VIRUS SPREADERS: IMMINENT THREAT

It was getting closer and now it had a new name, Covid-19. It sounded like a boy band. He knocked on Gavin's door and his friend invited him in.

'Hi Marcus. Ooh, nice colour scheme with the face. Very colourful. How are you feeling? I've been to The Temple and got everything we need. Anything you want right now?'

'Thanks for the compliment, not helpful. I'll take the puff pastry and the apples and I'll make the tarte tatin before we go. Otherwise, I'm fine. I'll come back around 6.30. Everything all right with you?'

'Yes, fine. Just making the herb crust for the lamb and a Madeira reduction. All on track. Don't forget the black tie.'

Marcus picked up the ingredients and walked to the front door.

'See you at 6.30 then.'

Making the tarte tatin was easy. A pastry brush was probably a gadget Claire didn't have. He put the pan in the oven. He had thirty-five minutes, time for a quick shave and a shower.

By the time he returned to the kitchen, there was the comforting smell of apples and toffee. The pastry had risen to a brown puffy crust. It looked perfect. He took it out of the oven and left it to cool on the hob. He had enough time to ring Alice. She answered immediately.

'Hi Marcus. How's the nose?'

She sounded stressed.

'Yes, I'm okay. Nose isn't so sore now. What about you, you don't sound very happy? Something wrong?'

'Not really. Theresa's found out Mike's definitely having an affair. Seems her suspicions were right all along.'

'How did she find out? Lack of sex?'

'Almost. She hired a private detective. Seems he wasn't playing as much golf as he said he was. He's been playing around with one of the lady golfers at the club. Theresa is devastated.'

Marcus thought about cracking a 'hole in one' joke, but it wasn't the right time.

'Any chance of a reconciliation? Can they patch things up?'

'Not at the moment. She only found out at the weekend. Confronted him with the photographs yesterday. She's in meltdown, wants a divorce.'

'Ooh, that's going to be messy. Mike's minted since he sold his business. He could lose a fortune. If I were him, I'd crawl back and beg for mercy.'

'Do you have to be so bloody mercenary, Marcus? It's not always about the money. It's the deception, the lies that hurt most.'

'Yes, of course it is. Sorry.'

'What are you up to this evening? Dinner with Gavin?'

'Yes, our usual arrangement.'

He wanted to tell her the truth but something stopped him. It was another deception and he felt guilty. He was only digging a small hole, he would be able to climb out of it.

'Okay, enjoy your dinner.'

'We're okay aren't we, Al?' he said, seeking her reassurance.

'Yes, of course we are.'

He went to the kitchen. The upturned dessert looked exactly as it should. Concentric circles of caramelised apples on a crispy pastry base. Perfect. He put it in a Tupperware container.

He changed into his dress shirt and bow tie. It had been a few months since Marcus had last worn his dinner jacket. He tightened the waistband although the jacket still looked like it had been borrowed from someone three stone heavier. It would have to do.

Gavin was ready at the door. They took the lift to the underground car park, walked to the Nissan Micra and loaded the bags into the boot. The two men squeezed themselves into the front seats and exited on to Westbourne Grove. Evening traffic was heavy as they passed the smart boutiques, fashionable restaurants and stucco-fronted houses before turning right on to Ladbroke Grove.

'Not feeling faint or anything?' said Gavin, teasing him. 'No drive-by shootings going on tonight.'

'Ha-bloody-ha,' said Marcus. 'Growing up in Staines wasn't exactly Mayfair, you know?'

They drove underneath the Westway and took a couple of turnings before parking in a side road next to Kensal Mansions. Marcus looked up at the brick Lego blocks.

'So this is local authority housing?'

'The Royal Borough of Kensington and Chelsea's finest. Try not to say it so disdainfully, Marcus. Real people do live here,' said Gavin. 'Help me get the things out of the boot.'

They walked through the alleyway, across the courtyard and climbed the four flights of stairs. Gavin knocked and they heard the sound of little voices running to the door. Gavin looked at Marcus and smiled.

'Alexa and Kyle. Don't forget their names, they're nice kids.'

Claire opened the door wearing a midi-length, black cocktail dress from Karen Millen. A £10 steal from a charity shop on Portobello Road. She had put her hair up and was wearing makeup, mascara and lipstick. Kyle and Alexa hid behind her legs, little pixies in pyjamas.

'Hi kids, how are you? Remember me? I'm Mummy's friend, Gavin.' He bent down to kiss Claire on the cheek. 'Well, don't you scrub up well?'

'I could say the same about you too,' said Claire, looking him up and down. 'Very smart, come in.'

Gavin turned right into the kitchen leaving Claire and Marcus facing each other.

'And you must be Marcus?' she said. 'I've heard a lot about you.'

She leaned forward, offering him her cheek. After the incident in Prism, Marcus was wary of getting it wrong. He kissed her on the cheek and recognised her perfume instantly. Hypnose, the same as Alice wore.

'Hello, I'm Marcus, Marcus Barlow. I've heard a lot about you too,' he said stiffly. He looked down at the two little pixies who were still clinging to their mother's legs. 'And I guess you must be Kyle and you must be Alexa?'

'What's wrong with your nose?' said Alexa. 'Why is it a funny colour?'

Overhearing from the kitchen, Gavin laughed. Claire looked embarrassed but Marcus answered immediately.

'I bashed it in the shower but it's getting better now. It looks funny doesn't it?'

Alexa nodded. Awkward moment number one, and the evening was only three minutes old.

'Kids, why don't you go and watch some TV and Mummy will be in to see you in a minute?'

The children ran into the living room as Claire and Marcus joined Gavin in the kitchen.

'Sorry about that. She just comes out with things. It's quite embarrassing sometimes.'

'Don't worry about it. I've got two older children and they're both still embarrassing me. It goes with the territory.'

He looked around her kitchen. Small and compact with its little, square laminated table and four chairs. It reminded him of his parents' kitchen in Staines. He looked at the pieces of art stuck to the walls with Blu-tack, little handprints and scrawls, people with big heads and small bodies, and pasta hedgehogs. Gavin broke his thoughts by popping a bottle of champagne and pouring three flutes.

'You didn't have to bring your own glasses!' said Claire indignantly.

'I didn't want to run the risk of drinking Bollinger out of plastic beakers,' he said and handed a glass to Claire and Marcus. 'Here's to a great evening. Cheers.'

'Cheers. So, what's the plan now?' said Claire.

'You get the children ready for bed, read them a story or whatever you need to do. Give me and Marcus half an hour and we'll call you when it's ready. That okay?'

'Sounds perfect. Thank you both so much for this. If you don't know where something is, just call me.'

'We'll be fine. Don't worry. Just go and do what you need to do.'

Gavin laid the table with a white linen tablecloth and napkins, and put two, long, gold candles into holders. Marcus prepared the starter, toasting the crostini and preparing the burrata and Parma ham. Her plates were all different patterns but it didn't matter. Gavin warmed blinis and spread cream cheese and smoked salmon on them.

'Take these in to Claire and top up her champagne,' said Gavin, handing him the plate of little canapés. 'I'll sear the lamb racks, crust them and prepare the vegetables.'

'Yes, chef,' said Marcus obediently.

He picked up the plate and bottle of Bollinger and walked along the hall to the living room where Claire was sitting on the sofa with her children watching *Toy Story* for the umpteenth time.

'Canapés? Smoked salmon blinis. Top-up?'

'Oh, thank you. I don't think I've ever had a blini. This is all a bit posh.'

Marcus looked around the small living room. It was tidy and tastefully decorated. He was surprised by its warmth and cosiness. He looked at the chair in the corner.

'Is that an Arne Jacobsen chair?' he said.

She looked surprised.

'Yes it is, well spotted. Do you know much about furniture?'

'No, not really, but I recognise his designs. It's a great chair.'

'It's my sanctuary. I found it in a skip on Cornwall Crescent and brought it back to life, gave it a new home. Someone obviously didn't know its value.'

Marcus looked at the television. Rex, the dinosaur, was introducing himself to Buzz.

'I'm from Mattel. Well, actually I'm from a smaller company that was purchased by Mattel in a leveraged buyout,' said Rex.

'That's the sort of crap I do for a living,' said Marcus.

'What is?'

'Leveraged buyouts.'

'What's a leveraged buyout?'

'Don't worry, you don't need to know. It's all bollocks. Have another blini.'

He returned to the kitchen where Gavin had finished searing and crusting the lamb. The vegetables were prepared and the Madeira jus was reducing.

'How's it going, chef? What time are we sitting down?' said Marcus, topping up Gavin's glass.

'Twenty-five minutes. Everything's under control.'

Gavin rinsed a few dishes and wiped the surfaces. Even in her tiny kitchen, a four-course meal looked effortless for him. Claire walked back into the kitchen to see the table laid and the candles lit, two men in dinner jackets and bow ties drinking champagne and preparing food.

'This is so beautiful. Thank you, both of you.'

'We've got a little present for you,' said Gavin. He reached into one of the bags and pulled out a beautifully wrapped package and handed it to her. She opened it carefully and burst into laughter.

'Mr Muscle spray! You do know how to spoil a girl, Dr Douglas.'

'I'm sorry but I couldn't bring myself to let you use an inferior surface cleaner.'

Claire gave the plastic bottle pride of place next to the taps and turned to Marcus.

'The children have asked if you would read them a bedtime story? They love your impressions of Woody.'

Marcus looked at Gavin who shrugged.

'Go ahead. I can manage everything here. I wouldn't want to come between a performer and his audience.'

Marcus followed Claire to her bedroom where Kyle and Alexa were sitting up waiting. He looked at the two small children in their pyjamas, hair still damp from bath time. It reminded him of his family. He sat down at the end of the bed.

'Sorry, but you have to sit in the middle,' said Claire, 'so they can both see the pictures and follow the words.'

There was no formality. She was completely natural, trusting him. He took off his jacket and shoes before sliding into the channel between the two children.

'So, what would you like me to—'

He hadn't finished his sentence before Alexa thrust her favourite book, *More Animal Stories*, into his hand. He knew it, opened the book and read the inscription on the front page, 'This Book Belongs to Claire Louise Carter'. He smiled.

'I used to read this to my children,' he said, looking up at her. 'They loved it too. Which story would you like me to read?'

'Dumpling!' yelled Alexa excitedly at the top of her voice.

'No! We always have Dumpling,' said Kyle dejectedly.

'I'll choose then?' said Marcus.

The children looked up at him and nodded their approval. He flicked through the pages, each story bringing back memories. 'I think we'll read "Dinosaur School".'

'I'll leave you to it. I'll come back when you're done. I don't expect you to put them to bed as well,' said Claire, winking at him.

Kyle and Alexa were wide-eyed and captivated as Marcus did different voices for Basil the Brontosaurus, Basil's parents Herb and Araminta, and Basil's teacher who was a stegosaurus. In return, he loved the bath time smell of the children lying next to him, little hands and heads resting on his arms, asking questions and laughing at his voices. He finished the story and closed the book. Alexa was almost asleep. He took it as a sign that his storytelling hadn't lost any of its magic. He levered himself off the bed, said goodnight and went to the kitchen where Gavin and Claire were discussing her first day with Beverley Cheng tomorrow.

'I think that did the trick. Alexa is asleep and Kyle won't be far behind. Over to you now, I think.'

'Thank you. It was really kind of you. I hope you didn't mind?'

'Not at all. I should probably be helping our chef get some food on the table now.'

Claire put the children to bed. Marcus assembled the starter as Gavin was putting the lamb in the oven. By the time she returned, the starter was on the table. Gavin switched the kitchen light off, leaving only the candles to light the room. They took their seats, with Claire between the two of them. Gavin poured three glasses of Sancerre.

'So, what do we have here?' said Claire.

'Burrata with pesto, served on crostini with Parma ham and vine-ripened tomatoes, and finished with a drizzle of truffle oil and black pepper,' said Marcus.

'I don't think you can get burrata in Tesco Express,' she said.

'It's like an immature mozzarella. You can always get it in The Temple.'

Claire laughed and put down her cutlery.

'Why do you call Waitrose, The Temple?'

'Because it's a shrine to decent food. A great fresh meat and fish counter, almost any ingredient you need and a better class of customer.'

'You mean, no people like me on Universal Credit?'

'Exactly,' said Marcus. 'It's all about standards.'

The conversation came to an abrupt halt followed by a silence. Awkward moment number two. It was Marcus who laughed first.

'Come on, I'm only teasing. They have an "Essential" range for poor people.'

It was an inappropriate thing to say but she laughed. There was a sparkle in his eye. He was being deliberately provocative.

'I know my place. I'll make sure I stick to Tesco Express. This tastes delicious, thank you. Tell me about your children, Marcus. How old are they again?'

Marcus told her about James and Olivia, what they did and what they were like. He showed her the photograph on his phone, on holiday in the Maldives.

'Beautiful children, and your wife is beautiful too. What's her name?'

'Alice, but I call her Al. She still calls me Marcus, especially when she is upset with me, which happens quite a lot. We've been together for almost twenty-five years.'

'What does she do?'

'She was a lawyer and had a good job but gave it up to look after the children and run the home.'

'A lady of leisure then? Bit like me.'

'More so now the children are grown up, empty nest syndrome and all that. You should make the most of every second of Kyle and Alexa while you can. It will go very quickly, believe me.'

Gavin declined another glass of wine, leaving Marcus and Claire to finish the bottle. Claire stood up to clear the plates but Marcus put his hand on her shoulder.

'I'll clear away while Gavin gets the main course ready.' He looked around the units.

She read his thoughts immediately.

'I'm afraid it's the kitchen sink, Fairy Liquid and a dish cloth.'

'Don't worry. My parents never had one either and we managed. I haven't forgotten how to wash a plate.'

Gavin took the lamb out of the oven and left it to rest while he strained the vegetables. He plated up and put them down on the table as if he were presenting them to Marcus Wareing.

'I have made for you herb-crusted rack of lamb dipping its toes in a Madeira reduction, snoozing on a bed of lightly crushed, minted new potatoes served with maple-glazed carrots and purple sprouting broccoli.'

'This looks amazing, Gavin. Thank you,' said Claire.

Marcus filled their glasses with red wine and resumed their conversation.

'So, Clarice. Quid pro quo. I tell you things, you tell me things. Yes or no, Clarice?' he said in an accent.

She responded immediately.

'*Silence of the Lambs*. One of my favourite films. So, what do you want to know, Dr Lecter?'

'Very good. I'm impressed,' he said. 'So how did you end up living here in Kensal Mansions on your own with two little ones?'

The main course lasted long enough for her to give Marcus the condensed version, from Walsall to Central Saint Martins and Jack's departure. Gavin knew it all already and stayed silent.

'Do you ever hear from him?' said Marcus. 'The STI was a nice touch, if I might say?'

'Yes, a prescription for antibiotics was my lasting memory of him. Last I heard, he was making his way around Australia. We didn't even get a Christmas card this year. He's just a total cunt in my opinion.' The C-word came out in anger, exaggerated by alcohol and she apologised immediately.

'Oh, no need to apologise. It's a great word. Sometimes, it's the only word which fits. The Firm is full of them,' said Marcus.

'What's The Firm?'

'It's where I work. Twenty years doing something worthless. The lamb was fantastic, Gavin.'

Marcus stood up and cleared away the plates. Gavin ran some hot water into the sink and began washing up. Two domesticated penguins. He put the tarte tatin in the oven to warm as Gavin prepared a small cheeseboard with crackers and quince jelly.

'Cheese for dessert?' said Claire.

'Always cheese before dessert,' said Gavin.

Marcus cut a piece of Époisse. It was runny and very smelly. 'Try this,' he said, offering it to her on a cracker.

'Oh my God! It smells like a blocked drain. Thanks, but no thanks!'

Marcus looked at her laughing in the flickering candlelight. The wine had flushed her cheeks. Her features caught the light and she looked very pretty. She had beautiful teeth and full lips like pink pillows. He thought she looked a bit like Emilia Fox but with darker hair. It was the same feeling he had when he first dated Alice, candlelight had magnified her beauty. He served the upside-down apple tart.

'Do you get lonely, living here on your own?' he said.

'Not so much during the day. The children keep me busy and I'm starting a part-time job tomorrow. It's the evenings that are the worst, especially long winter nights. I can't afford to heat the flat constantly, so sometimes it's cold. I've felt like giving up so many times. Gavin has been fantastic. Always supporting me, keeping me going. I couldn't have carried on without him. I only think of committing suicide once a week now.' She smiled.

Marcus admired her tenacity as much as her beauty.

'Can I ask you a question? I hope you don't think I'm being rude?'

'And why would I think that, Marcus?' she said sarcastically.

'How much do you have to live on every week?'

Awkward moment number three, but she didn't hesitate to answer.

'After I've paid all my bills, rent and council tax, probably around £90 a week. Universal Credit doesn't stretch very far. It's why this new job is so important to me.'

In Marcus's world, £90 was a very average lunch for two, a few drinks after work, a facial at the Refinery. She lived on less than the cost of a new tie. He put down his spoon and looked around the kitchen.

'Sometimes, I wonder if I'm living in a parallel universe. The Firm distorts reality. I hope you didn't think I was being impertinent?' He looked pensive.

'Come on, Marcus, don't get all morose now. It's not your fault for making the most of the chances that came your way. Making money isn't a crime. You've earned it,' said Gavin.

'For doing what?'

'Have another glass of wine and let's change the subject. I'll make some coffee and we can have some pralines. Maybe we could have them in the living room?'

'Great idea,' said Claire. 'I'm feeling a bit tipsy. I don't drink alcohol very often and all this wine has gone to my head. I need to sit down.'

'You go through too, Marcus. It's only a few plates. I'll clear away.'

Gavin started to clear away the plates and picked up the Mr Muscle spray. Marcus and Claire went to the living room. She stopped to look at her children who were fast asleep. She opened the door wide enough for Marcus to see.

'They're beautiful,' he said, and he walked into the living room. He looked down at the turntable and her collection of vinyl. 'Do you mind if I take a look? You can tell a lot about a person from their record collection. I've still kept all my vinyl since I was a teenager. Never sold a thing.'

'Must be worth a bit now,' she said, sitting in her chair. 'Original vinyl in good condition is very collectable. I love it.'

'Now I have Spotify on my phone which has everything. Do you have it?'

She picked up her phone from the coffee table. It was an old Nokia given to her by Judith.

'This is my phone. It just about makes calls and sends texts. It's on pay-as-you-go. I only keep it for emergencies. I can't even afford broadband.'

'So you don't have Wi-Fi?'

'No. We just about have heating.'

He flicked through her record collection, nodding approvingly in places and shaking his head in others.

'Anything you want to listen to?' she said.

'Yes, this,' said Marcus, pulling out *Frank Sinatra: The Ultimate Collection*. 'I haven't listened to him for years. I'll put it on.'

She admired the way he took the vinyl out of its sleeve, careful not to touch the grooves, spanning it with his fingers. He placed it on the turntable and placed the stylus gently on the first track. The undulating orchestral introduction to 'Strangers in the Night' started before Frank began to sing. Claire and Marcus were two lonely strangers but now they had said their first hello.

Ol' Blue Eyes was interrupted by Gavin returning with a tray of coffees and chocolates and he put them on the coffee table.

'So that's a Buzz Lightyear mug for you, Marcus, Dora the Explorer for Claire and Spiderman for me,' he said triumphantly. 'The pralines are great. I've already had two.'

For the next hour, the three of them sat around chatting. It was Claire who first talked about the virus.

'I'm starting to get really concerned. Beverley was telling me how bad it is in China.'

Gavin looked straight at Marcus. 'She's just as worried about it as you are. I think both of you are overthinking this. It could just be like flu. I'm not that worried about it personally.'

Marcus looked at her and nodded. 'I agree with you. There's no cure and I think we're only seeing the tip of the iceberg. This is going to get much worse.'

'Especially for me. I'm an asthma sufferer since I was a kid.' She picked up the inhaler from the coffee table and waved it at them.

'Best not to speculate when we don't really know,' said Gavin, trying to calm his anxious dinner companions.

It was getting close to eleven o'clock when Marcus looked at his watch.

'I think we should be going,' he said, turning to Gavin. 'Claire's got work in the morning.'

Gavin picked up the mugs and put them on the tray.

'Leave those,' said Claire, 'I can wash up a few mugs. You've done everything this evening and it's been a wonderful, wonderful time. I've loved every second of it. Thank you.'

'I really enjoyed meeting you, Claire,' said Marcus, putting on his dinner jacket. 'I hope we get to meet again sometime?'

'I hope so too,' said Claire.

They returned to the kitchen and Gavin blew out the candles. They said goodbye and Gavin and Marcus walked back to the car.

'Still got all its wheels, that's a bonus!' said Gavin.

Marcus laughed. His first trip north of the Westway hadn't ended with him being murdered or gang-raped.

'Great night for all of us, a really nice idea. I really enjoyed it. Claire's lovely. I think you should ask her out, she definitely fancies you.'

'Possibly, but not really my thing. Professional distance and all that?'

Gavin parked his car. Marcus inspected the flat tyre on the M5. He would have to call the RAC in the morning. They stopped outside Gavin's flat as he opened the door.

'Do you want to come in for a nightcap?'

'Probably best not. I'm still not fully recovered from Sunday's debacle and I drank quite a lot tonight too. I wasn't rude or anything, was I?'

'You were just yourself Marcus. It was great to see you like that. Goodnight then.'

Claire washed the coffee mugs and left them on the drainer. She looked out on to the courtyard and at the shrouded tower in the distance. She thought about the two men who had given her a memorable night. She thought about Marcus, posh, provocative, quirky, funny and kind. He was old enough to be her father but she felt more in common with him than she had done with anyone for a long time. Quid pro quo, Dr Lecter.

It was Tuesday, 11 February 2020.

Chapter 16

Horse Trading

Marcus was the main topic of conversation on the walk to school. Claire had thought he would be full of himself, but he had been anything but. He was funny, provocative, did good dinosaur voices and made a great tarte tatin.

It was her first day working for Beverley Cheng. She opted for a pair of jeans and a jumper. It was also a big day for Kyle. The winner of the draw to foster Biscuit the hamster during half-term was to be announced. Beverley looked smart in a Max Mara jacket and skirt, with bottle-green suede boots.

'Hi Claire. How are you?' she said. 'Ready for your first day?'

'Bit nervous but I'm fine.'

'Not of me I hope? I'm really looking forward to it. Give me two minutes.'

Beverley kissed Bruce goodbye and the two women walked back to her flat. More packing crates had arrived and the hall was crammed.

'Come through and I'll make us a coffee.' The Quooker spat its instant hot water into two mugs as Beverley sat down on a stool next to Claire. 'So how's everything been with you?'

'I've had a really good week so far. I even hosted a dinner party last night. First time ever.'

'Tell me more,' said Beverley excitedly. 'So who was the lucky man?'

'Men actually. Two of them, dressed in dinner jackets. Shouldn't we be starting work?' said Claire.

'Oh, that can wait. Gossip comes first. Tell me everything.'

Claire told her about Gavin's idea and the fantastic meal with Marcus. She described the menu in detail.

'Sounds amazing. What a great idea. Maybe Gavin fancies you?'

'Hardly,' said Claire dismissively. 'If he did, he wouldn't have brought his strange friend along as his chaperone. Anyway, I think Gavin might be gay or celibate. He's very handsome but he's never mentioned other women, or men for that matter. I don't think he's interested in me at all.'

'But you're interested in him, yes? Just too scared to find out? And what was his friend like? Marcus?'

'Much older than Gavin. Mid-fifties I would say. He's a partner in a firm in the City. He was nothing like I imagined he would be. Definitely odd but I really liked him. He's very outspoken and amusing.'

'Bit of an odd mix but sounds like you had a great time. I'm very jealous. It's just been me and Bruce here on our own all week.'

'Welcome to the lonely mothers' club. Shouldn't we be making a start?'

She was conscious of time and being paid to gossip wasn't part of their arrangement. They went through to a small room overlooking the garden, which was cluttered with files and half-opened boxes.

For the rest of the morning, Claire helped Beverley sort files and papers into separate piles: customers, suppliers, invoices to be paid, invoices already paid. It was like paid chatting with regular coffee breaks. Claire thought Beverley was probably more interested in her company than in any help. Beverley took a call and went into the kitchen. Claire could hear her speaking loudly and quickly in Cantonese. She carried on punching holes and stapling until Beverley returned.

'I'm sorry. That was Edward. He doesn't think he'll be coming back until March at the earliest. Things out there are in chaos. The situation is getting really bad. More cities are in lockdown and it's spreading fast. Supermarkets in Hong Kong are almost empty. People are stockpiling. I'm starting to get worried about him.'

'Yes, I would be too. Nobody in this country seems to be taking the virus seriously at all. All we seem to care about is Brexit and Prince Harry.'

By lunchtime, they had emptied half of the boxes in the office and Beverley seemed happy with their progress.

'It's lunchtime now and I'm getting tired of looking at boxes. Would you like to stay for lunch or do you have to go?'

Her tone suggested she wanted Claire to stay. It was only *Bargain Hunt* and *Loose Women* waiting for her at home.

'I don't want to put you to any trouble?'

'It's no trouble at all. Look on it as a perk of the job.'

* * *

Marcus and Mason had sharpened their pencils and sent a revised proposal to Sarah Appleberry, together with some smarmy words which proved they had 'listened to her concerns', and 'reflected their commitment to Espina'. Sarah had requested a call. It was a positive sign. The most likely scenario would be that one firm had messed up and were out of the running. The other three were now in a horse trade.

The two partners gathered in Communication Zone 6, a smaller room dominated by a picture of a group of employees standing on the summit of Mount Kilimanjaro in brand-compliant climbing gear. The picture carried the slogan 'Putting Something Back'. Marcus wasn't sure what was being 'put back'. Probably the lives of the people in the local Tanzanian village who had been sequestered to assemble the twenty-tent village complete with full catering facilities and a Wi-Fi network to keep the team up to date with their emails.

They announced their arrival on the call and waited for Sarah to join. With the small talk over quickly, Mason was keen to find out Sarah's view.

'You've obviously seen our revised proposal, Sarah? Can I assume you're much happier now? It's closer to what you and Jim were looking for?'

'Not sure I understand you, Mason? Happier and closer to what?'

'Our, our, our f-f-f-f-feeees,' stuttered Mason nervously.

'If you mean, am I happy to see you have drastically reduced the scope of work and included more junior resources, no I'm not that happy. Reducing your ludicrous rates a little, that's a positive.'

'Reduced them a little?' said Mason meekly. 'We thought it was a significant discount.'

'What was it? The discount percentage.'

'Sixty-five per cent, the lowest we can possibly go.'

'Well, let's see about that, shall we?' said Sarah, bullishly.

Mason turned to Marcus for support. Marcus was still looking up at the poster, wondering what 'Putting Something Back' meant.

'Marcus, do you want to come in here?'

It seemed like a good time to intervene before Sarah destroyed Mason.

'Sarah, hi, it's Marcus. Can I ask you a straight question?'

'Sure, go ahead. It would make a change.'

'Let's cut to the chase. In terms of the scope and our team, are we your preferred partner on Spearmint? Because, if we're not, let's end this call right now and stop wasting each other's time.'

It was a big punch to land, a right uppercut which hit the assertive Chief Procurement Officer flush on the jaw. She fell back against the ropes.

'Well, that's very bold of you, Marcus. I admire your honesty. Actually, it's between you and one other firm. Of course, I can't tell you who that is.'

It was down to two. Marcus backed her up with a series of jabs.

'That's okay. I don't need to know. So, what is it going to take to be your recommended partner? Give me something I can work with? Is there something in the scope you want us to change or is it just about the fees?'

'Well, there are a few minor changes to the scope, phasing, et cetera …'

She paused and Marcus anticipated it. He gave her a push.

'But …'

'It's your fees. They're still far too high. Your competition is coming in significantly lower. Your proposal is stronger, but it's a trade-off. Cost versus value. You know that, Marcus.'

'So, if we can prune our fees a bit more, you'd feel comfortable recommending us to Jim and Derek?'

'Bit more than a prune. Some big branches I would say.'

'Give me a figure we can both agree on.'

In the end, this was what it came down to. All the insights, thought pieces, methodologies, relationships, case studies, credentials, slides, CVs and appendices that had taken weeks to prepare, review, agree, produce and present. In the end it all came down to one thing: the money.

'Three point five million pounds.'

'Four point five.'

'Three point eight.'

'Four point two.'

It was like haggling for a rug in a bazaar, only with bigger numbers. Mason looked across nervously at Marcus. He wasn't only giving away Kelvin's shirt but his underpants and socks as well. Marcus went for the closing shot.

'Four million pounds and we're happy to confirm in writing straight after this call.'

There was silence at the end of the line. Sarah Appleberry knew she had done her job. She had got the best proposal for less than half the price even if the original number had been a work of fiction. She wrapped it up.

'Fine, that would be great if you could. I'm speaking to Jim and Derek later this afternoon. I'll confirm by the end of the day? That okay?'

'That's fantastic, thank you. I hope we've demonstrated our commitment to Espina on this one? Speak later.'

Mason hit the red button and the line went dead. He looked at Marcus and shook his head.

'Kelvin isn't going to be happy. We've just given away almost another million. What discount are we giving on this?'

'Probably somewhere between 70% and 72%. Look on it this way, it's four million we weren't going to get unless we did something. Sarah just wanted us to make her life easier. And coming back with nothing isn't going to make life any easier for you, is it, with your cock on the block?'

Mason knew Marcus was right. They had aimed for the stars and landed on Venus. It was better than blowing up on re-entry, and might just save his career.

* * *

Beverley walked with Claire and Alexa to school. They were early and waited in the playground along with the other mothers, nannies, au pairs and the odd father. The school bell rang, followed by a cacophony of excited little voices and the sound of chair legs scraping on wooden floors.

Helena Mistakidis led her class into the playground in her gold moon shoes. Kyle was holding her hand, but he broke free when he saw his mother and ran towards her. His face was illuminated.

'I won Mummy! I won! I'm keeping Biscuit for a week!'

He whirled round and round like a sycamore seed in the wind. Claire looked down at him. She hadn't seen him so happy for a long time. She looked at his teacher who was just as happy as Kyle.

'I'm really pleased for him. You can collect Biscuit tomorrow or Friday, whichever is easiest for you? I'm afraid his home isn't that small. It's more of a hamster palace. You'll need a car to get it home.'

Claire hesitated.

'I could give you a lift if you want?' said Beverley, instantly sensing her friend's dilemma.

Her offer put Claire in a more difficult situation. Nobody in Kyle's class had ever been to Kensal Mansions. She was too embarrassed to invite people to her home, worried about what they might think. She looked at Kyle who was still spinning joyously around the playground. She had little choice but to accept.

'Thanks Beverley. That's really kind of you. Maybe Bruce would like to have his tea with Kyle and help him settle Biscuit in?'

It was another massive step forward.

* * *

Marcus left the office early. There was nothing more to do apart from waiting for Sarah Appleberry's confirmation. Dusk was approaching but it was still warm. Since his raincoat had been stolen, he had been without a coat. He looked at the front page of the *Evening Standard* as he descended the escalator.

A picture of a fifty-three-year-old man dressed in a Scout's uniform, complete with yellow woggle, revealed him to be the super spreader believed to be responsible for infecting eleven others after returning from a conference in Singapore via a ski chalet in France. He had then gone to his local pub and a group yoga class. He was making a full recovery in hospital and had shown no visible symptoms.

Two things concerned Marcus. Firstly, surely the man was too old to be in the Scouts? Maybe he would get a badge with an image of the virus on it and have it sewn on his shirt, along with ones for map-reading and lighting a fire? His second concern was that Alice did yoga. She could be putting herself in danger. Someone on the next mat could be coughing on her while she was defenceless in the bird of paradise position?

He looked up at David Gandy advertising his vitamins. He felt he had let David down badly. He wanted to look like him, to be like him, but he knew it was impossible. He had a nondescript body and a traumatised nose. He moved further along the platform, the shame was too great.

The newspaper was full of adverts promoting three-course meals for two for £15, including a bottle of wine. St Valentine's Day was on Friday and he hadn't planned anything for Alice. They had given up on grand gestures years ago. Now it was a delicate balancing act between remembering and not going over the top, doing something simple which wouldn't arouse her suspicions. In the wake of Theresa and Mike's problems, he didn't want Alice getting suspicious about anything. A nice card and some flowers would suffice.

Beirut was still in full swing when he got home, diggers shifting piles of earth and cranes swinging steel girders around. He looked up at a man in the cabin of one of the cranes and wondered what he did when he needed a wee? Did he come all the way down or did he have a bottle in the cabin? Did he use his Thermos flask? He rang Alice, who was on her way to collect Olivia from her hockey match.

'How was dinner with Gavin last night? Did you cook? What did you have to eat?'

It was an avalanche of questions.

'Dinner was fine. He offered to cook, which was kind. Just a quiet night, good to chat and catch up.'

It was half the truth. Gavin had cooked and he had spent the evening chatting to him. He had only omitted the other half about Claire and their candlelit dinner in Kensal Mansions. Like Beirut, a hole in the ground was getting deeper and he was doing the digging.

'What are you doing tonight?' said Alice.

He remembered her seeing his dinner jacket.

'I've got this bloody charity dinner. I'm not really looking forward to it.'

'Prostate Cancer Awareness?'

'Yes.'

'Got the right audience then. A bunch of overweight, middle-aged men with bladder problems. Anyway, I've got to pick Libby up now. Have a nice night and try not to buy anything stupid unless it's a spa day or a tennis lesson with Roger Federer.'

'I won't. Speak tomorrow. Give my love to Libby. Oh, by the way—'

The call ended. He wanted to warn her about the danger from the virus in group yoga classes. She was probably still safe in Pilates. He received a WhatsApp message from Gavin.

Hi Marcus. Hope you enjoyed last night. Your turn next week. Enjoy the rest of the week and see you soon. G

He replied.

Hi Gavin. Yes, all good. Great night and I really liked Claire. She is very sweet. Thanks for organising. See you soon. M

It was ten minutes until the six o'clock news. There would probably be an item on the virus-carrying man-scout, and he wanted to see it. He was watching the closing action on *Pointless*, a programme he thought was pointless, when Outlook pinged. It was an email from Sarah Appleberry.

Subject: Project Spearmint – Phase II Support Confirmation
From: Sarah Appleberry
To: Marcus Barlow, Mason Sherwin

Thank you both for your time earlier.
I have now debriefed Jim and Derek and would like to confirm your
appointment to support Espina with the next phase of Project Spearmint.
We would like work to commence on Monday, 2 March 2020, based
here in Manchester. Thought you would like to know at the earliest. Look
forward to speaking soon.
Best regards
  Sarah Appleberry
  Chief Procurement Officer, Espina Plc.

The Firm had won. In the past, an email like Sarah's would have had him on his feet, fist pumping and beating his chest like a silverback gorilla. He stared at *Pointless*, as Sean and Katie from Bath were trying to guess pointless number one singles by Oasis.

'"The Hindu Times", he muttered under his breath.

He was right. It was a pointless answer, but Sean and Katie went with 'Don't Look Back In Anger', which everyone in the world knew, and they lost. Outlook pinged. It was Mason.

M. Great news. Always knew we would win this. Will drop a note to Kelvin to give him the good news. See you in the office tomorrow. M

Marcus didn't feel like a winner. He felt like Sean and Katie. It was all pointless. He was facing three months in Manchester, being bullied by Jim Ibbotson and avoiding another night out with James. Maybe he could spend his evenings scouring the streets looking for someone in a Burberry raincoat that was too big for them? He had missed the rest of the news, so he made himself some scrambled eggs on toast and flicked through the channels. There was nothing he wanted to watch so he switched to Netflix which had a message for him.

Marcus, recommended for you: Schitt's Creek

Just about sums up my life, he thought.

The front page of *Metro* on Thursday morning raised his mood.

ALL CLEAR

Along with the recovering man-scout, all eighty-three Britons who had been kept in isolation after returning from China had tested negative.

Maybe it's not so contagious after all? he thought and he felt better.

The office was busy. As expected, Mason had emailed Kelvin to tell him the news about Spearmint. There had been no reply. He looked up from his porridge to see Kelvin arrive. Marcus gave him time to open another packet of Nicorettes before he knocked on the door. Kelvin looked up and beckoned him in.

'Hi Marcus, how are you?' His head stayed down, looking at his screen.

'Good, thank you. I see Mason has given you the good news about Spearmint?'

'What's good about it? Six million pounds left on the table and we're giving the rest away for a song. Pretty shit news, if you ask me.'

His cursory reply caught Marcus off guard. It took him a moment to respond. Maybe the nicotine hadn't hit his bloodstream or Vanessa hadn't wanked him off for a few days?

'Well, thanks for that, Kelvin. Can I point something out? I did try to tell you that it was over-scoped weeks ago, and the fees were delusional, but you wouldn't listen, would you? You kept banging on about that "deliver The Firm" shit. What a load of bollocks!'

Kelvin finally looked up, sat back in his seat and started fiddling with his pen. People didn't say things like that to him. He threw his pen at the monitor.

'Who the fuck do you think you're talking to? Get out!' he yelled.

Marcus remained seated and looked straight at him.

'I'm not going anywhere because I haven't finished speaking. At least we sold something instead of sitting behind a desk manipulating numbers and playing politics. It may be only £4 million, but it was £4 million we didn't have before. So, screw you. And yes, I have finished now so I will get out.'

'Marcus, sit down …'

But Marcus had already opened the door. Outside in the pool area, a sea of faces were turned towards the glass partition. It was the grown-up equivalent of a fight in the school playground, except a teacher didn't come to break it up.

Marcus sat down at his desk. Chloe approached him. Like everyone else, she had witnessed what had just happened.

'Everything all right, Marcus? This has come through from Risk and Compliance.'

She handed him a small, brown envelope. He opened it and shook the contents on to the desk. It was a piece of brand-compliant ribbon with 'Doing It With You' printed on it, with a plastic security pass holder attached. It was his new lanyard. He looked up at her and smiled. He reached into his box of stationery, took out a pair of scissors and cut the ribbon into small pieces, stuffed them back in the envelope and handed it to her.

'Put that in the internal post to Risk and Compliance will you, Chloe? Thanks a lot.'

* * *

Claire and Beverley spent Thursday morning sorting, punching, stapling and shredding more paper. They had created twenty-three files which Claire had labelled in her stylish handwriting. The files sat on two shelves in pristine uniformity, like a display in Rymans.

'Lunch?' said Beverley. 'I think we're done here for the day. I'll give you a lift to the nursery and then pick up the boys and the hamster.'

'Biscuit,' said Claire.

Beverley prepared two pieces of poached salmon with a noodle salad and the two women discussed work over lunch. Beverley opened her purse and took out five twenty-pound notes.

'Here you go. Your first week's wages plus a little extra for being a great listener.'

Claire looked at the money and felt embarrassed. It felt like she'd been paid to chat and eat lunch, and now she was getting a lift to collect her children and a pampered hamster.

'I can't accept that. You've been more than kind, Beverley. I don't think I've helped that much. Really.'

'And you've been more than helpful, Claire. Don't upset me by arguing. We should be going soon.'

They arrived at the school early enough to get a parking space before the nanny armada arrived. Helena Mistakidis moon-stepped into the playground and approached the two women.

'Shall we go inside and get Biscuit now?'

Kyle's classroom was the third one along the corridor, a bright airy room with a high ceiling and eight pods of four desks. Bruce and Kyle showed their mummies where they sat. On the teacher's desk stood a towering, plastic structure, built on three levels including a penthouse suite, with interconnecting tubes, ladders and slides. Everything a playboy hamster could want. A sleep zone, a play zone, a food zone. Biscuit wasn't suffering from anxiety issues due to being bored.

'Wow, that's an impressive house,' said Claire.

The children stared into the cage but Biscuit was snoozing in the sleep zone and didn't wake up.

'Here's all the food and bedding he'll need,' said Helena. 'I've put all the instructions on how to look after him in Kyle's bag. Biscuit's pretty low maintenance. Just bring him back safely after half-term.'

'That's great. We'll take good care of him, won't we Kyle?'

Claire carried the high-rise hamster palace to Beverley's car. It was too tall to fit in the boot and went on the back seat with Kyle and Bruce. Alexa sat in the front seat with her mum. Claire directed her from the school, underneath the Westway, towards Kensal Mansions.

'I would park here,' she said, pointing to a vacant space in a row of parked cars. 'It's as close as we can get.' She was already starting to feel nervous.

Beverley looked out of the windscreen at the blocks of flats.

'Which is the one that caught fire?'

'Grenfell Tower? About half a mile away,' said Claire. 'Don't worry, it will take more than that to bring Kensal Mansions to the ground.'

They reached the stairs as Mr Mahoney was locking away Ian's mobility scooter.

'Well, what do we have here?' he said.

Claire poked her head around the tower.

'Mr Mahoney, this is my friend Beverley and her son, Bruce.'

The caretaker extended a rough, giant's hand and enveloped Beverley's small and delicate palm in it.

'Nice to meet you, Beverley.' He smiled to reveal his pitted tombstones and she responded in kind with her perfect, white smile.

'Good to meet you too. Claire has told me all about your cakes.'

'Kyle has won the competition to look after the class hamster during the school holiday. This is his house,' said Claire.

'His name is Biscuit,' said Kyle proudly.

'He's a hapster,' said Alexa.

'An impressive house, very impressive indeed,' said Mr Mahoney. 'I won't come up today as you're busy. I'll see you tomorrow.'

Claire, Beverley and the children climbed the stairs. She stopped at the front door and took several puffs on her inhaler.

'Come in,' she said, her anxiety kicking in. 'Children, shoes and coats off please! I'm afraid it's very small and—'

Beverley stopped her in mid-sentence.

'Don't be silly. It's lovely of you to invite us. It's good for Bruce. Let's get Biscuit settled in.'

Claire carried Biscuit to the bedroom and placed the tower on the chest of drawers facing Kyle's bed. He was still sleeping and hadn't noticed the change of scenery.

'I guess that's it then?' said Claire. 'I'll get the children some tea. Let's go through to the kitchen. Kids, why don't you watch some TV?'

The children went into the living room and switched on CBeebies. It was *Andy's Aquatic Adventures* and the eponymous hero was in his safari suit exploring a flooded forest. Claire made three glasses of Ribena and a plate of cow biscuits and took them into the living room. The children had gone into the bedroom to check on the new guest.

'Come on, leave him alone. He'll wake up when he's ready. Back in the living room now.'

Claire returned to the kitchen where Beverley was making tea.

'I hope you didn't mind? I thought these teabags looked interesting. Beautiful box.'

Claire laughed.

'Not at all, a present from Gavin. He thinks my normal tea is poisonous so he buys these for our weekly meetings. He's got very refined tastes.'

'He's very important to you, isn't he?'

'He is. When my GP referred me to social services, I could have got anyone, but I lucked out when I got him. After Jack left, I used to have suicidal thoughts, feeling like I couldn't cope, but he's helped put me in a much better place.'

Beverley looked concerned.

'Do you still have those thoughts?'

'Sometimes. Something small can trigger them but not as often now.'

Beverley squeezed her friend's hand across the table. 'Can I help you to make dinner?'

'No, it's okay. I made a shepherd's pie last night. It only needs to go in the oven and I'll heat up some peas and sweetcorn.'

'I don't think Bruce has ever had shepherd's pie,' said Beverley curiously.

'First time for everything. It's Alexa's favourite.'

Thirty minutes later, Claire called the children to the table. With five of them in the kitchen, it was cramped and the two mothers had to stand. Bruce loved his new meal, and Kyle and Alexa loved having a new playmate to join them. Beverley and Bruce got ready to leave.

'Thank you for the lift and the lovely day at work. I've had two fantastic days, enjoyed them so much. Do you want me to see you to your car?' said Claire.

'Why, do I need an escort?' said Beverley. 'I think I can remember my way back!'

'No, it's quite safe.'

The two women hugged, and Kyle and Bruce wrestled with each other.

'See you at school tomorrow morning,' said Claire.

'Yes, see you then. Enjoy the rest of your evening. Thank you for having us. Your flat is cute. It's very you.'

It was almost ten o'clock and Claire was sitting in her chair with a blanket waiting for the news to come on, when the living room door opened slowly. It was Kyle in his pyjamas.

'Hi sweetie. What's the matter? Can't you sleep?'

Kyle shook his head.

'It's Biscuit. He's making so much noise, he woke me up. He keeps playing on his wheel and with his ball. He won't go to sleep.'

Claire went into Kyle's bedroom where Biscuit was enjoying all the facilities of his luxury pad. He was very noisy.

'Maybe we'll keep Biscuit in the living room?' she said.

Kyle nodded sleepily and got back into bed.

Fiona Bruce was the newsreader which meant things were getting serious. The first case of the virus had arrived in London: a Chinese national, who was now isolating in St Thomas' Hospital. An expert in infectious diseases told the BBC reporter: '*It is important, of course, that people remain vigilant and minimise their own risk of being infected, but at this stage it is too early to say the extent of the risk of onward transmission as a result of this new case.*'

Too early? It made her feel anxious immediately. Vigilant about what? How could she be vigilant when she didn't know what she was looking for? The only one who wasn't worried was Biscuit, who was happily spinning. The virus hadn't killed any hamsters and he felt safe.

* * *

Marcus was drinking coffee and watching the lorry drivers waiting for the gates to Beirut to open. He wondered what they were doing for their partners on Valentine's Day? He decided to work from the flat and drive to Weybridge in the afternoon. He called the RAC, who responded quickly. Someone would be with him within the hour.

His phone rang forty-five minutes later. The RAC man had arrived and was parked on the ramp to the underground car park. Marcus went to the basement in his slippers and opened the gates.

'Not sure if you'll get your van down there? It's very tight. That's how I burst my tyre.'

The driver looked at him blankly, shook his head and accelerated down the ramp. He cleared the wall and the tyre-shredding kerb with millimetres to spare.

'Where's your car?' said the RAC man.

'How did you just do that?' said Marcus.

'Do what?'

'Drive your van down the ramp at that speed without bashing into the wall?'

'Got to know the width of your vehicle mate. Show me where your car is?'

Marcus felt humiliated. He pointed to the M5 and the driver pulled up alongside. The job was over in fifteen minutes, the spare tyre was on and the damaged tyre was in the boot. The mechanic filled out the paperwork and Marcus signed his electronic screen.

'Those low-profile tyres are shit. They look great but they're useless,' said the mechanic.

'Couldn't agree more. Thanks a lot. I'll get a new one this afternoon.'

Marcus returned to the flat and rang Alice.

'Hi, Al. Happy Valentine's Day.'

'Hi Marcus. Same to you too. Just on the school run. Was it anything important?'

'Not really. Just happy Valentine's Day. I'll be home sometime mid-afternoon, I want to avoid the Friday afternoon traffic.'

'Great. See you at home later. Bye then.'

Just as the RAC man had instructed, Marcus kept his speed below 50 miles per hour on the motorway to Weybridge. Having a temporary tyre on a BMW M5 was like having a racing bike with stabilisers. It told other motorists that he couldn't drive properly. Kwik Fit had a replacement tyre and could fit it that afternoon. Two hundred and eighty-five pounds added further insult to injury.

He dropped the car at the garage and walked to WHSmith to choose a Valentine's Day card for Alice. It wouldn't be easy, he had got it wrong on several occasions. Humour was fine as long as it wasn't smutty. Romance was good as long as it wasn't gushing. Size was important too. Alice hated cards that were too big, and she wasn't a fan of hearts, bows, cherubs or kisses. This narrowed his options. He settled on a card with two owls on a branch with a suitable pun about 'loving you-hoo-hoo'. It was perfect for the occasion. Alice liked owls.

He walked into the florist in the same parade of shops. Almost all the pots and buckets were empty. It was only mid-afternoon. He approached the counter.

'Yes sir. How can I help you?'

'I'd like a bouquet of red roses, please?' said Marcus.

The florist shook his head ruefully.

'I'm sorry but we've sold out completely. There's been a massive demand this year. I've pretty much sold out of everything. All I have left is some houseplants. Not that romantic, I'm afraid.'

Marcus could see for himself. No flowers. Houseplants weren't an option, Alice always killed them within weeks.

'Don't you have anything at all?'

'I've got one bouquet out the back that a customer ordered this morning and was due to collect at twelve, but they haven't come back for it yet.'

The florist looked at his watch. 'It's almost three now.'

'I've got to collect my car from Kwik Fit. I'll call in again on my way home. If it hasn't gone, could I take it?'

'You could try other florists or there's the supermarkets. Last resort, there's always a garage.'

He knew Alice would spot garage flowers immediately. They didn't come in the little cellophane bubble, filled with water and tied with raffia. It would signal 'cheap' and show a lack of thought.

'I'll call back,' Marcus said with a hint of panic.

He wrote her card in the waiting area of the garage, careful not to get grease on the envelope.

To my special Valentine. Always owls together. M. xx

He drove back to the florist and went in.

'Hi. I was here about an hour ago. You said you had an unclaimed bouquet? Has it been claimed yet?'

'No. It's still out the back. Do you really want it?' said the florist.

'Definitely. I can't go home with nothing. How much do you want for it?'

'It was £60. I suppose I could let you have it for £40?'

'Done.'

Marcus didn't have time for haggling. The florist went to the back of the shop and returned with a bouquet. They weren't red roses, but they were flowers in a mixture of colours. More importantly, they had the cellophane bubble, filled with water and tied with raffia. That's all Alice would care about. Marcus paid, left the shop, put the bouquet on the back seat and drove home.

Alice was getting out of her car with Olivia.

'Hi Marcus. How are you? Been keeping out of the gutters?' She leaned forward to kiss him and he could smell her perfume. It made him feel safe.

'Very funny. Yes, I'm glad to be home. Tough week all round. We sold the work on Spearmint.'

'Did you? That's great. You don't sound very happy?'

'Not sure if I care that much. I told Kelvin to fuck off yesterday.'

'Mmm … maybe not your smartest move, Marcus? He is your boss. Come on, let's get inside.'

He dumped his bags in the hall and returned to the car to pick up the flowers and the card. He walked into the kitchen where Alice was making tea.

'Here you go. It's just a little something. Happy Valentine's Day, Al.' He put the flowers on the island and handed his wife the card. She opened it.

'That's very sweet of you, Marcus, thank you.' She looked happy even if her tone was slightly patronising. 'I like owls. I thought Valentine cards were meant to be anonymous but I suppose I would recognise your writing after all these years? Anyway, it's the thought that counts. Yours is upstairs, I'll get it for you later.'

His card had gone down well. The prospect of Valentine's Day sex was going up. Alice walked around the island to smell the flowers.

'Oh! Another card. You've gone over the top this year, Marcus.'

Another card? What other card? he thought to himself and looked at her.

She was opening a small envelope buried in the middle of the bouquet. She stared at it and looked up at him.

'"*To Elsie and family. Our thoughts are with you at this difficult time. Richard and Barbara*".' She paused. 'Well, thank you for that Marcus. I thought our marriage was in better health but obviously not. So, what did you do? Stop off at the crematorium on the way home and steal them?'

After a week of lies and half-truths, he was fresh out of excuses. It was time to stop digging and start being honest, even if it was only about the flowers. At least Alice laughed.

'You are such a tosser, Marcus. I'm surprised you didn't turn up with a wreath of lilies. At least the card was nice. Yours, not Elsie's. Go and get changed and you can tell me about your week. We're having lentil bake tonight. I'll give you your card later.'

She put her arms around him and hugged him. It was everything he needed at that moment. Even lentil bake sounded good.

* * *

Claire sat in her chair with her blanket and a cup of tea. It had been a nothing day. She held out for the postman bringing her an anonymous Valentine card from a secret admirer, or even one who wasn't secret. All she got was a letter from Npower informing her of new tariff changes.

On the coffee table was the champagne cork from Tuesday night. She picked it up and played with it between her fingers. Her best night in years. She thought about her guests. Gavin, alone in his flat, playing his piano and wiping surfaces with Mr Muscle. Marcus, his big house, happy marriage, beautiful wife, perfect children and a job that paid for it all. He had everything.

In the corner of the room, Biscuit was waking up and rolling around the penthouse suite in his little ball. She looked at him.

'Maybe you've got everything too?'

It was Friday, 14 February 2020.

Chapter 17

TAKING THE BISCUIT

Half-term signalled The Great Exodus as partners jetted off with their families to Europe's most expensive ski resorts. Kelvin was in Verbier burning his nose again. So was Vanessa Briggs.

Bit of a coincidence? thought Marcus.

Partners were never far from their email. Jacob Mauser had broken his ankle the year before in Zermatt; taking a conference call on a red run. He had lost concentration trying to review a PowerPoint slide and had been wiped out by an out-of-control snowboarder. Alice had never been a keen skier and family skiing holidays had lapsed. Marcus missed them. They were one of the few times a year when he got to enjoy the company of his children.

The office was a calmer place, no egos clashing or stags rutting. The pipeline call had been cancelled. Kelvin had left Izzy Majewska in charge. There was no reason for anything to go wrong. Marcus opened SCAR. It stood for Secure Client Approval and Recognition. Every project went through its interrogation. It didn't make a difference if the client was a FTSE 100 behemoth or a Nigerian start-up with a dodgy financial history, everything went through SCAR.

To input all the data SCAR required and to chase the numerous approvals at multiple levels, Marcus enlisted the support of Angela Rust, the bright, young associate who had pointed out the flaws in the Wonderwall. She would ensure Project Spearmint was SCAR compliant.

Marcus received an email from Tyler Payton.

Subject: Greetings from Dubai
From: Tyler Payton

Hi Marcus
Heard the news about Spearmint. Well done.
All well here in Dubai. Back on Thursday night. I plan to tell Kelvin next

Monday. Wouldn't mind some advice on how to handle him? Any chance of a chat this week?

    Tyler

Marcus replied immediately proposing a call the next day. He knew Kelvin wouldn't take Tyler's news well. In fact, he would take it very personally. His departure would leave a hole in his plan. Holes in his plans didn't go down well with Kelvin.

* * *

Claire's week had got off to a bad start. The death of the *Love Island* presenter Caroline Flack in an apparent suicide had stirred up emotions in her that had lain dormant for a few months. The weather at the weekend had been awful, as Storm Dennis wreaked chaos across the country. It had subsided long enough to take the children to Kensington Memorial Park. They loved it there. It had a children's playground and a water play area. The previous summer, Claire pretended they were all going on holiday and took picnics and swimming things to the park every day. They weren't in the Algarve or Barbados, but it was a proper summer holiday to them.

The children put on their Wellington boots and coats, and the three of them set off for some fresh air. Ian's mobility scooter was out of its shed.

'Maybe I'll see Ian at the park?' said Kyle. 'I haven't seen him for a long time.'

'Maybe,' she said.

Alexa looked up at Claire.

'Mummy, can we see Marcus? He was funny.'

It came from nowhere and Claire was taken by surprise. Since the arrival of Biscuit, there had been talk of little else.

'I don't know sweetie. He's Gavin's friend. I'll ask Gavin tomorrow and see if Marcus wants to come to see us again?'

Alexa nodded and ran off with her brother to the play area. Claire wasn't sure if Marcus would want to come back to Kensal Mansions.

* * *

With email traffic from the slopes reduced to a trickle, Marcus cleared his inbox, approved all outstanding expenses and completed his pre-joining questionnaire for the upcoming 'Living Our Values' partner conference. Answers were meant to be anonymous. By the time he had given his age, sex, grade and department, it wouldn't have taken a data mining genius long to identify the person who described The Firm's leadership as 'the most talentless bunch of overpaid morons I have ever encountered'. Which is why he gave his age as forty, his sex as female and ethnicity as Asian.

He received a text from Gavin.

Hi Marcus. Hope you had a good weekend. Still on for tomorrow night? Your turn I think? Let me know. G

He replied immediately.

Yes, definitely. See you normal time. M.

His last meeting of the day was with Izzy Majewska to discuss resources for Project Spearmint. He needed a team of eight, excluding Technology and Cyber.

'I want Steve Pettigrew, a couple of senior managers, three managers and two or three juniors.'

She scanned her spreadsheet. Lots of people were available.

'Take your pick. Laila Saetang is available too,' said Izzy.

'That's okay. Steve will be fine and he knows the client.'

'It would help Laila's partner case.'

'I would rather have my teeth removed with an ice pick.'

On his way home, the front page of the *Evening Standard* alarmed him.

NOW CORONAVIRUS HITS WESTMINSTER

Someone linked to a super spreader, presumably the man-scout, had tested positive and attended a conference which was also attended by over 250 people, including several MPs. The virus was now running around in the capital.

Eric the concierge greeted him in reception. He was looking even smarter than usual, dressed in a black blazer with a military crest and matching tie.

'You look very dapper this evening, Eric. Going somewhere?'

'Good evening, Marcus. Yes, I have a retired Corps of Commissionaires dinner this evening at Fishmongers' Hall. We all meet up twice a year.'

'Do you take it in turns to hold the door open for each other?'

'Ha ha! Jolly good, Marcus. Very droll.'

'Only teasing. Have a nice evening, Eric.'

'You too, Marcus.'

By the time he was starting to fall asleep, he had binge-watched five episodes of *Schitt's Creek*. He was becoming infatuated with the Rose family. He wondered what would happen if he and Alice lost it all? They would have to move into a B&B in Staines, he would sell the M5, buy a Toyota Prius and get a job with Ace Cars.

* * *

It was just after ten and Claire was listening to the start of *Woman's Hour,* when the knock on the door came. Kyle ran to the door and stood on tiptoes but couldn't reach the latch. She opened the door.

'Good morning, Dr Douglas. How are you?'

'Hi Claire. Hi Kyle. I'm fine. How are you both? It's half-term this week isn't it?'

'Would you like to see Biscuit?' said Kyle excitedly.

Gavin looked at her blankly.

'You had better go and see Biscuit, the class hamster,' she said. 'He's probably asleep. He only comes out at night. Tea or coffee?'

'Coffee please. Didn't go to the Panettone Palace this morning.'

Gavin was gone for over five minutes. Claire suspected Kyle was giving him a detailed description of Biscuit's sleeping and feeding habits. He returned to the kitchen.

'Biscuit was asleep. Impressive accommodation for a hamster. How have you been this week? Work go well?'

'Really good. Beverley is so nice. I'm not sure I helped that much but she said I did. She even gave me an extra £20. Her husband is still stuck in Hong Kong.'

'What does he do?'

'I think she said he's a banker. She's quite worried about him. The cases of the virus are going up and there's been a couple of deaths already.'

'It's really bad on that cruise ship, nobody can get off. It must be like counting down the minutes to get infected, a floating time bomb.'

'Actually, I've got something to tell you. I think you'll be proud of me.'

'I'm always proud of you. What have you done?'

She told him about inviting Beverley and Bruce to the flat and cooking for them. Another big step.

'I'm really pleased. It's good to see you not locking yourself away. I really enjoyed our dinner last week.'

'Me too. What about Marcus, did he enjoy himself? He's quite strange isn't he? I liked him and the kids think he's great at bedtime stories.'

'He said he really enjoyed himself. The evening was good for him too.'

'To see how the other half live?'

'In a way. He lives in a bubble of comfort. In spite of his wealth, deep down, Marcus is a good guy who has lost his way. I know he's struggling, just like you do, like we all do. The evening was good for all of us, in lots of ways.'

'Well, I really liked him. Are you seeing him soon?'

'Tonight. It's our Tuesday date night, his turn to cook.'

'Say hello to him for me.'

* * *

The atmosphere in the office was calm and subdued. It was somebody's birthday and a large box of Krispy Kreme doughnuts had been left on one of the drop-in desks. It was fortunate that Tom Irons and Simon Loder were stuffing their faces with fondue in some Alpine restaurant. Marcus chose a glazed raspberry doughnut and watched from his desk as Chloe chose a chocolate custard one. She didn't seem her normal, chirpy self. He went over to her desk and pulled up a chair.

'Everything all right, Chloe?'

'Hiya Marcus. Yeah, I'm okay. What can I do for you?'

'Sit with me and eat our doughnuts together? What's going on?'

Chloe took a bite out of her doughnut and caught the ejected custard in the palm of her hand.

'Oops! Not much actually. Everyone's away at the moment. Ain't got much to do. Can't say I mind that much.'

'How are things at home? Your mum and dad well?'

'Yeah, they're okay. Muddlin' along. It's what you do, ain't it? Thanks for asking.'

He looked at his secretary, happily scoffing her squirting doughnut. He thought about Fernando in OnYouGo, making coffees and salads for people who earned ten times what he did but smiled half as much. He thought about Claire, existing on £95 a week but never giving up. What did they know that he didn't? What did they have that he couldn't buy?

At midday, he went to one of the Chilling Eggs and waited for Tyler to call.

'Hi Marcus. How y'all doin'?'

'Great, thanks Tyler. All quiet here. Everyone's gone skiing for the week. It's perfect. How are things in Dubai?'

'Pretty damn hot. By the time I've walked from the office to the hotel, I'm sweating like a hog on a spit.'

Marcus thought Texans had a unique way with words.

'So, you're planning on telling Kelvin on Monday?'

'Thought I would get it over and done with as soon as possible.'

'No second thoughts then?'

'None. Hopefully, I'll leave as soon as the schools have finished. We'll be back in Houston by the end of June. How do you think I should handle it with Kelvin? You've known him much longer than I have.'

'Well, I wouldn't do it on Monday. It's his first day back and he'll have a lot to catch up on. Things aren't great and your news will only make things worse. I'd go for Tuesday. He will take this news really badly. Personally.'

'So, how do you think I should position it?'

'Tell him you're going back to Houston to take a great job with an oil major. New career challenge and all that good stuff. It's a perfectly legitimate reason.'

'And you think that will go down okay?'

'No, not in the slightest, but it's better than telling him he runs a shit-show. He'll bribe you to stay, offer you more units, more responsibility, blow smoke up your arse because he needs the money you bring in.'

'Then what?'

'When that doesn't work? Verbal or physical assault and possibly both. You might want to consider body armour.'

'Should I call him and ask for the meeting?'

'No, definitely not! Just get his secretary to put it in his diary. If he smells a problem, he'll beat it out of you and blame you for ruining his holiday. Trust me.'

'Thanks a lot, Marcus. Really helpful. Can't say I'm looking forward to it.'

'No problem. Look forward to hearing how it goes when you're in hospital. Good luck!'

'By the way, well done on Spearmint. How are you feeling at the moment?'

'Probably not that different to you but without the new job offer.'

'Well, maybe it's time for you to think of other things too?'

They had all said the same thing. Colin, Gavin, Libby and now Tyler.

'Something will come up, I'm sure. Have a safe flight back. See you next week.'

Marcus was preparing pak choi when the doorbell rang just before eight. Gavin was as punctual as ever and he welcomed him in. He looked immaculate, always the right amount of stubble to look fashionable but not unshaven. Gavin squeezed his shoulder.

'Hi Marcus. How are you? Seems like I haven't seen you for ages. The nose is looking much better now.'

'I'm surviving. Come on through. Gin and tonic or Campari?'

'Ha ha! G&T is perfect.'

Marcus led his friend into the kitchen, made the drinks and they toasted each other's health.

'So, what's on the menu tonight?' said Gavin.

'Salmon roulades, teriyaki chicken with rice noodles, followed by lemon syllabub. I'm afraid the roulades aren't homemade. From The Temple. Sorry.'

'Sounds great. So, what's the latest in "Marcus World" then?'

'Not that much. Alice and the children are fine. Amazingly, we won Spearmint. Maybe I'll start taking class A drugs before every pitch in future?'

'So Gerard came good in the end?'

'Looks that way, although taking a chainsaw to our fees probably had more to do with it.'

Marcus took the roulades out of the fridge and set them down on the table. They took their usual places.

'So the win must be good for you? An even bigger bonus this year?'

'Probably. To be honest, I didn't even get excited when we won. I told Kelvin to fuck off last week.'

'Kelvin is your boss, right?'

'Probably my ex-boss if he has his way!'

Marcus replayed the conversation and Gavin laughed.

'Love it. Good for you. He sounds like a complete thug. How did you feel afterwards?'

'Better than I have done for ages. Telling your boss to fuck off is pretty cathartic.'

As he strained the noodles, he told Gavin the story of the Valentine's Day flowers debacle.

'And you didn't think to check they might be for another occasion?'

'Why would I? I thought the florist would have told me, given me a few clues or at least taken the bloody card out. Alice wasn't massively impressed but she saw the funny side of it. Just about.'

'So typical of you, Marcus. Great idea but piss poor execution.'

'Thanks a lot. How has your week been?'

'Things are fine at work but I'm worried about my mother. I spoke to her at the weekend. She's got Alzheimer's and is almost crippled by arthritis. My dad isn't much better. They're stuck in the middle of nowhere and managing the estate is too much for them.'

'Do they have help?'

'Yes, there are the estate workers, but my parents still do everything themselves. They're much too old but there's no chance of them stopping. They'll die there, for sure.'

'Why don't you go home and see them? I'm sure they would be pleased to see you, wouldn't they?'

Gavin put down his cutlery.

'It brings back a lot of painful memories. Addiction, rehab, addiction, rehab. I hurt them a lot when I was younger. The golden boy whose halo slipped.'

'You have a younger brother, don't you?'

'Yes, Rory. He's a dentist in Perth. Never put a foot wrong in his life. Unlike me who has put both feet wrong, but I'm still the golden boy. He helps when he can but he's got his own life. In a way, I envy him, just like I envy you. Family, stability, support. They count for a lot.'

It was the first time Marcus had seen his friend's vulnerability. Always so assured and confident in his minimalistic world of tidiness, with his piano and his music. Loneliness wasn't something Marcus associated with Gavin.

'Sounds like they could do with a visit. You should go.'

They cleared away and Marcus brought two coffees to the living room area.

'I saw Claire today. She was in good spirits, better than I've seen for a long time. Kyle won the competition to look after the class hamster over the holiday. He's chuffed,' said Gavin.

'They're nice children. I really liked them.'

'They liked you too. Good at reading stories apparently?'

Marcus shrugged his shoulders showing false humility.

'You never lose it. I just wish I'd had more practice when James and Olivia were younger. I missed out on a lot of bedtime stories.'

'Claire liked you as well. Told me to say hello. I think you would be welcome anytime. Especially if you turned up with another tarte tatin.'

Marcus laughed. 'That's sweet of her. She hasn't got it easy, for sure.'

'And there are plenty of people worse off than Claire, believe me. I see them every day. Life can be a real struggle for some.'

Marcus thought of his colleagues, sitting in steaming hot tubs, drinking champagne or Aperol spritz in a luxury chalet overlooking white mountains. Life wasn't much of a struggle for them.

'Yes, I'm sure it is.'

They talked until just after 11.00, when Gavin stood up to leave. They stopped at the front door.

'You've got a lot going for you, Marcus.'

'Thanks. See you next week. Hope your mum gets better.'

Marcus set off for Twin Gates early on Friday evening. It had been a quiet week, enjoyable without the politics and fighting. Earlier in the day, he had taken Chloe to lunch, and enjoyed her company. Naïve and innocent, her honesty was a breath of fresh air in a climate at The Firm that was stuffy with lies and politics.

'I bet you have a cleaner, don't you, Marcus? And a gardener? In that big house of yours.'

'We've got Jacinda who does the cleaning and washing, and Jorge who does the garden. We've had them both for years.'

'Why don't you do the garden yourself? My dad does ours. It's a Japanese water garden.'

'Because I don't have the time. I'm always too busy. And your dad is a landscaper!'

'That's rubbish, Marcus. You could make time if you really wanted to. You should, you'd enjoy it.'

If Chloe's knowledge of Greek mythology was lacking, she more than made up for it with common sense. She said it how she saw it, and she was right, his excuse was rubbish. His father had died digging the garden. There were worse ways to go.

'Maybe I should, Chloe. Thank you.'

Sarah Appleberry hadn't replied to his emails. Her job was done, she had sharpened their pencils for them. He was sure it was nothing to worry about.

He opened the front door at Twin Gates, walked through the kitchen to the office where Alice was painting. He liked the smell of turpentine, it reminded him of the garage at the house in Staines.

'Hi Al, how are you?'

'Hi, Marcus, I'm okay. Trying to avoid a mauling from Belinda Churchill at the next art class.' She put down her paintbrush. She seemed to have thousands of them. She leaned forward to kiss him. 'I don't want to get paint on your suit.'

Marcus walked behind the canvas.

'How are Tony's thighs coming on? Happier with them now?'

'Not really. I'm not sure if I'm cut out for life class. Perhaps I should stick to bowls of fruit and landscapes? It's easier to get a banana right.'

'I think Tony looks good. I hope I look that good when I'm sixty-three.'

'You look good now, Marcus. It's all that moisturising you do!'

'Thank you. You look good too. And bananas aren't easy things either, getting the bend right. I'll go and get changed.'

'Any plans this weekend?'

'Apart from spending time with you and Libby, not really. I thought we might go to the garden centre together and buy some plants? I'd like to go in the garden.'

Alice stared at him and shook her head.

'Marcus, you never go in the garden. That's why we have Jorge. What's brought this on, the sudden urge to go in the garden?'

'Just something Chloe said to me today. That's all.'

He went upstairs to get changed. He checked the row of neatly ironed shirts in his wardrobe. Jacinda and Vanish had worked their magic. All traces of 'The Nightmare on Deansgate' had gone. The only stains left were on his memory.

* * *

The credits rolled at the end of *EastEnders*. Keanu had left Sharon crying in hospital with his baby and was last seen kissing his weeping mum and entering Walford Station.

At least he didn't leave in a taxi looking back at the Square. They always do that. Keanu will probably be appearing in Casualty *soon*, thought Claire.

The children were asleep and, apart from the television, the flat was eerily quiet. Something seemed odd but she couldn't work it out. And then it came to her. Every night that week, Biscuit had emerged from his nest to entertain himself noisily in the food and play zones of his hamster mansion. Except tonight, he hadn't. She gave it until *News at Ten*, but there was still no activity.

She unclipped the upper floors. Biscuit slept in the basement. She poked her finger into the bedding, expecting him to wake sleepily, rub his eyes with his tiny paws and look around for a sunflower seed. But he didn't move. Claire opened the ball of tissue paper. Biscuit's eyes were closed and his little furry body remained stiff and motionless.

'Jesus-fucking-Christ!'

Biscuit was dead. The fallout would be massive. He was due back in school on Monday morning, where thirty children were expecting his arrival in the same condition in which he had left. Kyle would be a pariah, shunned in the playground. She had Gavin's number for emergencies, like when she was having suicidal thoughts or felt depressed. She had only called it three times before.

'Hi Gavin. It's Claire. I'm sorry to call you at this time on a Friday night but it's an emergency. I don't know what to do.' Gavin turned his music down. He was listening to Verdi's Requiem.

'What's happened? Are you okay?'

'I'm fine, the kids are fine. It's Biscuit, the fucking hamster. He's dead. I've just discovered him. He was fine last night and now he's stiff with his eyes shut.'

'Hamsters do sleep a lot. Are you sure he's dead?'

'Gavin, I just shook him. He's stiff as a board, not taking a nap. He's due back in school on Monday, and preferably alive. What the hell am I going to do?'

Her breathing grew shorter and she ran to the kitchen to find her inhaler. He heard her squirting two puffs.

'Calm down and sit down. Put Biscuit back in the bed and wrap him up like you found him. Don't tell the kids anything. Pretend he's still asleep. I'll come round in the morning, take him away, find a pet shop and buy a new hamster. I'll bring the new one back and swap it over. You can keep the kids distracted while I do it.'

'But what if we can't find a hamster that looks like Biscuit? He's very distinctive. Where will we get one?'

'Don't be ridiculous, hamsters all look the same. We'll find one. I'll be round in the morning at 9.30. Leave it with me.'

He had witnessed the aftermath of drug overdoses, wife beatings and numerous assaults in his time as a social worker, but this was his first death.

'Gavin, you're a star. I'll make you a bacon sandwich when you get here. You've saved my life.'

'Coffee's fine. I don't eat processed meat. It's not good for you. See you in the morning. I'm glad it was nothing trivial.'

'You must think I'm completely mad?'

'I've always thought that. Put Biscuit back in his bed and we'll deal with it in the morning. Get some sleep.'

'You too.'

Gavin parked his car in the road next to Kensal Mansions and walked through the alleyway where Mr Mahoney was sweeping away the debris from Friday night. More boxes of KFC bones to feed the giant rats. He climbed the stairs to No. 11 and knocked on the door. He could hear excited voices from within and Claire opened the door.

'Detective Sergeant Douglas. I believe there has been an incident? May I come in, Madam?'

'Very funny. Come in.'

The children were having breakfast. Claire switched on the kettle and the two adults spoke in code.

'Any developments since last night?' he said.

'No, all quiet, luckily. I said he was asleep. So what's the plan?'

'I'll remove the B-O-D-Y. I've looked online and there's a P-E-T superstore in Camden. I'll go there straight from here and meet you back around lunchtime. Is that okay?'

'You have to get one that looks the same.'

'I'll do my best. Maybe he has a twin?'

He excused himself to go to the toilet while Claire created a distraction with more toast and Marmite. He went into the living room, opened the cage and removed Biscuit. He rearranged the bedding and closed the cage. He stopped in the bathroom to wrap Biscuit in some toilet roll and put him in his laptop bag. He came back into the kitchen and finished his coffee. Claire widened her eyes for an update.

'Okay, I think I've got everything. I'll see you all later. I'll call you when I'm on my way back.'

'Thanks. Say goodbye to Gavin, kids.'

He had just over two hours to complete his mission, and set off along Westbourne Grove, through Maida Vale and Swiss Cottage, until he arrived at the pet superstore in Camden. It was virtually empty, just a couple of people looking at cat toys and someone bringing their dog in to be groomed. He was approached by an assistant who was stacking shelves with bags of dog food.

'Can I help you, sir?'

'I hope so. Do you sell hamsters?'

'Yes, please come with me.'

He followed her to the rodents section, which had rows of glass boxes containing mice, rats, gerbils and hamsters.

'Is there a particular type of hamster you're looking for?'

He didn't understand her question but unzipped his laptop bag, unfurled the roll of toilet paper and held out the deceased Biscuit in front of her.

'I'd like one that looks like this,' he said. 'His name is Biscuit. It's a long story.'

'Is it dead?' The girl looked like she was about to burst into tears.

'I'm afraid so. We didn't want to upset the children by telling them he had died.'

'I remember when my first gerbil died. I cried for days.'

'Then you know the feeling. I'm sure you can help me?'

They inspected the different cages of hamsters for a suitable replacement. It wasn't easy. Right colour, wrong size. Right size, wrong colour. They settled on a compromise, somewhere between a ginger nut and a rich tea.

'Do you need a cage as well? Food, bedding?' said the assistant, placing the new hamster in a small box.

'Oh, no thank you,' said Gavin. 'This hamster has just landed on its little paws. Its home is The Savoy for hamsters.'

'Would you like me to take Biscuit away for you?'

He wondered if Biscuit deserved something more ceremonial. A little plot in Kensington Gardens and a memorial service.

'If you wouldn't mind? That's very kind of you.' He handed her the roll of toilet paper containing Biscuit's rigor mortised body. It wasn't a glorious end to his life, but his spirit lived on in the form of his new namesake, whom Gavin carried back to the car and placed on the front seat.

By 11.45, he was outside Kensal Mansions. He called Claire, who answered immediately.

'Hi there. Did you get it?' she said anxiously.

'Yes. I have Biscuit II with me. I'm parked in the road. Take the children out and leave the front door on the latch. I'll come up, settle him in and leave. Come back in fifteen minutes and it will all be done.'

'Are you sure they look the same?'

'I think so. You'll have to trust me.'

'How much do I owe you?'

'Twenty pounds, but don't worry. You don't need to pay me back.'

'We'll talk about it when I see you. I'll be out of here in ten minutes. Thanks so much, you're a saint.'

'Don't worry, I was only planning on giving myself a face mask this morning. Finding a replica hamster will be the highlight of my weekend.'

'What did you do with dead Biscuit? Have you still got him?'

'No. Trust me, he's in a much better place now.'

A few minutes later, Gavin watched them turn left out of the alleyway and head off in the direction of the park. He picked up the box and in three minutes was in the living room of No. 11.

Biscuit II seemed to adjust well to the bed of his predecessor, even if the sheets weren't clean and the previous occupant had left the room in a bit of a mess. He made sure the new resident was comfortable, closed the cage and left the flat, flicking the latch on the way out. He planned to spend the rest of his day playing the piano to calm his nerves. It wasn't every Saturday he was called upon to dispose of a dead body.

Claire called time on the walk pretty swiftly, saying she didn't feel well, which was partly true. She had already taken a Xanax to calm her nerves. The children kicked off their shoes and ran into the living room. She was switching the kettle on when Kyle came running down the hall.

'Mummy, Mummy! Biscuit is awake. He is playing in his wheel. Can we get him out and stroke him?'

Biscuit II had significantly more energy than his predecessor. Claire stared into the cage.

- 244 -

'Maybe he knows it's the weekend? He probably has more energy on a Saturday.'

Kyle nodded in agreement.

Claire looked at the hyperactive hamster.

'Keep your mouth shut,' she muttered to herself.

It was Saturday, 22 February 2020.

Chapter 18

MELTDOWN

Claire and the children were waiting for Beverley to arrive. She was giving them a lift to school, along with Biscuit II and his high-rise home. The impostor had been active all weekend, much to the children's delight.

'Morning Claire. Hi kids. Did you have a good weekend?' said Beverley.

'Yes, great thanks. All good. How about you? Any news from Edward?'

'I spoke to him yesterday. Things are getting worse in Hong Kong.' Beverley looked worried, her husband on the other side of the world, caught in the eye of the viral storm.

They arrived before the nanny armada and parked close to the gates. Claire carried Biscuit II into the playground where Helena Mistakidis was already on duty. She saw them coming.

'Hi everyone, welcome back. Did you all have a great half-term?'

Kyle and Bruce nodded. She could see Claire struggling with the hamster tower.

'Come on. Let's get Biscuit inside. How was everything, no problems?'

Biscuit II was moving around energetically.

'Just put him down over here,' said Helena, pointing to a space at the back of the classroom next to a glass tank containing stick insects.

Why couldn't Kyle have won the draw to look after those? thought Claire. *Nobody would know if they were dead or not.*

On the wall above the table was a big sign, '*Biscuit, Our Class Hamster*', together with photos taken when he wasn't asleep. She placed the cage on the table and hurriedly left the classroom.

'Thanks for looking after Biscuit, Claire. Well done Kyle!!' said his teacher. Kyle beamed and ran off to play with Bruce and Liam.

'Would you like a lift?' said Beverley.

'That's very kind of you but, if it's okay, I'd like to walk? I could do with some fresh air and so could Alexa.'

'No problem. See you later. Have a nice day.'

'Thank you. You too.'

* * *

Marcus hadn't had a great weekend. His trip to the garden centre had been unsuccessful. He was advised that planting a herbaceous border in February wasn't a good idea, better to wait until warmer weather. He returned home empty-handed with his newly discovered enthusiasm squashed. Alice had avoided any 'I did try to tell you' comments. He reverted to Project Garage, which was unaffected by seasonal temperatures.

The 7.38 train was busy, even in First Class. The red-faced, sweating man with the Brompton sat opposite him, sprayed in black Lycra, which accentuated the curves of his moobs and his bulbous genitals as he sat open-legged on the seat. He was still reading *Wolf Hall*, which was looking more dog-eared and tatty.

Monday morning's edition of *Metro* was the usual mixture of sport, fluff and adverts. A headline on an inside page caught his attention.

VENICE CARNIVAL CANCELLED AS ITALY HIT BY KILLER VIRUS

Cases of Covid-19 in two regions of northern Italy had risen dramatically. There had now been four deaths. A number of municipalities had been locked down, with schools, restaurants and businesses being forced to close. Cases were also rising fast in South Korea and Iran. Marcus looked at the sweaty cyclist.

He's probably just unfit, he thought, but moved to another seat as a precaution.

The office was busy. All the chatter was of 'great powder', 'superb moguls', 'going off-piste' and 'amazing chalets'. Snow bores in action. Everyone had arrived back in one piece apart from David Prince, who had dislocated his shoulder on a button lift and had his arm in a sling. They all carried the same distinctive branding, red noses, panda eyes and talking loudly about their holiday to anyone within earshot. He had just finished his breakfast when Mason approached him.

'Morning, Marcus. Good weekend? Everything go okay last week?'

'Hi Mason. Yes, fine. How was Chamonix?'

'Brilliant. Big dump of snow at the start of the week then perfect sunshine and powder. Couldn't have been better. How's Spearmint?'

'Appears to be fine. Sent some things to Sarah Appleberry but haven't heard back. Will chase her again today.'

Kelvin was in his office. He had been locked away with Izzy Majewska and Jenny Moffatt all morning. His nose was peeling again and he looked stressed.

Marcus took a route past the empty Collaboration Zones and bumped into Tyler Payton who was back from Dubai with a proper tan.

'Hi Marcus. How you doin'?'

'Hi Tyler. Good flight back?'

'Yeah, Emirates business class is a joy. Even had time to go to the cigar room before the flight.'

'When is your meeting with Kelvin?'

'Tomorrow. Straight after the pipeline meeting. I've got my body armour ready.'

'Good luck, you'll need it. Come and find me afterwards, if you're not in hospital by then!'

Marcus checked The Sequence. Stockwatch was having a big red day. Already 130 points down and a sea of scarlet across the board. The virus was now starting to infect financial markets too. He tried to call Sarah Appleberry but went straight to voicemail. He sent another email. He was curious about why she hadn't returned his calls?

He left the office just after 6.30. He put in his AirPods and chose David Bowie's Greatest Hits. 'Heroes' would be in his Desert Island Discs for sure. He was staring at the advertisements on the wall of the escalator. It was the usual collage of West End musicals, hair-loss treatments and the latest mobile phone, when he noticed something different about two passengers on the escalator going up. They were wearing face masks and they weren't Japanese tourists. He thought it was odd.

By the time he got off at Queensway, he had read more about the worsening situation in Italy. The number of cases had risen above 300. Eight people were dead. Italy was now third in the league table behind China and South Korea. He checked Stockwatch again. It had closed 247 points down, its biggest fall for weeks. It made him feel anxious and he called Alice as soon as he got to the flat.

'Hi, Al. Have you seen what's going on in Italy? It's getting really bad.'

'Yes, it was on the news tonight. Some places are going into total lockdown. Do you think it could happen here?'

'I don't know what we can do to stop it. The stock market took a real hit today. Traders are starting to get really jumpy. As if bloody Brexit wasn't bad enough, now this. It couldn't have come at a worse time. It could ruin everything.'

His anxiety was going into hyperdrive.

'Calm down, Marcus. The number of cases here is still very low. Let's hope we can contain it.'

She had always been the voice of stability in their relationship, the epitome of 'Keep Calm and Carry On'.

'Yes, I guess you're probably right.'

* * *

There was a full attendance for the pipeline meeting. Everyone was back from skiing. Marcus sat next to Chloe and opposite Tyler. He gave him an 'Everything all right?' look and Tyler nodded. Kelvin arrived and took his seat at the head of the table.

'Good morning everyone.'

They were the first words Kelvin had uttered to him since their spat two weeks earlier. Izzy gave the financial update.

'With four days left to the end of February, we are forecasting a worsening position against plan. We have yet to see any positive signals on when things will pick up. On the plus side, the sale of the next phase of Spearmint will shift the dial positively in March and April, although not by as much as the £10 million we needed.'

It was Tyler Payton who spoke first.

'Well, I think we should all say well done to Mason and Marcus on a great win. Great stuff you guys!'

Tyler looked directly at Kelvin who muttered under his breath from the end of the table. Everyone else nodded their approval.

Izzy continued.

'So, allowing for the slight revenue uplift from Spearmint, we are forecasting a negative variance of between five and six million pounds by the end of the financial year. As a direct consequence of our performance this year, we are having to take steps to realign our cost base for next year.'

Everyone in the room knew what 'realign our cost base' meant. Redundancies.

So that's what Kelvin was discussing with Izzy and Jenny Moffatt yesterday? thought Marcus.

For once, Izzy's update was crystal clear. The team was going to miss target. Simple as that. Everyone was now aligned and singing off the same hymn sheet. Kelvin wasn't going to let the moment pass.

'I just want to say, this is the first time in my life that I have missed a fucking revenue target. Some people around this table will bear the consequences of that. I just hope that realigning our cost base will limit some of the damage.'

It was Kelvin's way of saying when the ship went down, some partners would be joining the staff overboard. The room was eerily silent. There were some very concerned faces around the table as the meeting closed early.

It was 11.30 when Tyler came to find him.

'Do you fancy going for a coffee?' he said.

He looked shaken. Marcus inspected Tyler's face for evidence of a headbutt but there was nothing.

'Meet you in OnYouGo in ten minutes?'

They bought two coffees from Fernando and sat in the corner of the restaurant. It was the same spot where Arabella had interviewed him for his bio.

'So, how did it go with Kelvin? I presume you've spoken to him?'

Tyler nodded.

'Just now. Went pretty much as you said it would. He was shocked that I've decided to go to a corporate and return to the US. Said it was a backward step and that I'd regret it.'

'That's just him believing there isn't another life outside The Firm. It's all he's ever known. What did he offer you?'

'A shed load more units and to be "Oil & Gas Sector M&A SME Coordinator for EMEA".'

The number of acronyms in a job title was the way to tell if a role in The Firm was meaningless. This one had them all.

'That's just crap. It's a made-up title to keep you happy.'

'I know, which is why I turned him down. There are enough people in this place with roles that mean nothing without me adding to them.'

'How did he react when you didn't even say you would consider it?'

'His mood changed immediately. He got very angry and started doing that weird thing with his pen. Said he was really disappointed with my attitude. That I had never been a team player, only out for myself.'

'Was he looking in the mirror at the time?'

Tyler laughed.

'So was that it?' said Marcus.

'Not exactly. He finished the meeting by calling me a selfish American cunt.'

'Mmmm … impressive. So what happens now?'

'I leave on Friday. I'll hand everything back this week, return my laptop and phone and ride off into the sunset.'

'Well, I'll miss you for sure. Let's have dinner together once you've gone.'

'I'll miss you too, Marcus. Don't leave it too long before you make a decision too. Who knows what's around the corner?'

* * *

Gavin had bought two coffees from the Panettone Palace and they were discussing the weekend's events.

'So, can you imagine how I felt when I poked him and he didn't move? I don't even know how long he'd been dead. Lucky the kids didn't see him,' said Claire.

'Must have been a bit of a shock. How was it when you took Biscuit II back to school? Everything go okay?'

'The new hamster is much more active. He was playing in his house all weekend, he didn't stop. Kyle and Alexa thought it was great.'

'Probably because he wasn't dead!'

She ignored him and continued.

'I just hope none of the children at school start asking awkward questions.'

'I did my best to get a perfect match. I think I did a pretty good job, even if I say so myself.'

'What did you do with the body?'

'Buried it in a shallow grave in some woods and covered it with wet leaves, where it will be discovered by a woman walking her dog, who sees a little pink paw sticking out of the ground and calls the police.' Gavin laughed.

Claire imagined Biscuit's decaying little body, shrouded in a tent and cordoned off by police tape as Dr Nikki Alexander in *Silent Witness* determined the time and cause of death.

'Don't be awful. That's disgusting.'

'To be honest, when I got your call, I thought you'd had a meltdown and done something stupid.'

'I was having a meltdown but I'm okay thanks. Nothing like you're thinking of.'

'Well, that's all good then.'

Gavin told her about his mother's illness and their conversation moved on to their relationships with their parents, and the ways they had influenced them, good and bad.

'I always remember the Philip Larkin poem when I think about my mum and dad,' said Claire. '"*They fuck you up, your mum and dad. They may not mean to, but they do.*" Well, my dad definitely fucked me up. He never accepted me for what I was. Always wanted me to be different. I don't want to be like that with Kyle and Alexa.'

'You won't be. You're a great mum to the children.'

She stared out of the kitchen window. She was deep in thought.

'Gavin, can I ask you a question?'

'Sure. That's what I'm here for.'

'What would happen to Kyle and Alexa if something happened to me?'

'Depends on whether you've made a will or not. Do you have one?'

Claire laughed. She wasn't even divorced. Technically, she was still married to Jack.

'No, of course I don't. Promise me something, Gavin? If something did happen to me, don't let my parents take them. They'll ruin them like they ruined me.'

'What about Jack? He's still your husband.'

'What about him? He's a selfish wanker.'

Gavin reached across the table, held her hand in his and squeezed.

'Nothing bad is going to happen. Stop worrying and getting anxious. I'll see you next week. Glad the job is going well.'

'Thanks. Say hello to Marcus for me.'

* * *

Marcus and Chloe confirmed arrangements for the team to arrive in Manchester the following Monday morning. In accordance with Travel Centre policy, the team would be staying at the Holiday Inn and catching the 8.30 train from Euston. Everyone would be travelling Standard Class.

He called Sarah Appleberry again. It went straight to voicemail. Something didn't feel right. It had been another red day on Stockwatch, things were getting worse. He opened RAPID and submitted his expenses and timesheet. He claimed for the train, the Travel Centre approved rate for one night in a hotel and a couple of taxis. He put The Debacle in Deansgate down to a bad experience. Even clients couldn't be expected to pay for that.

* * *

Claire walked into Tesco Express. Lester Primus was helping an elderly lady separate two wire shopping baskets. He saw Claire and approached her. His bald head reflected the fluorescent lights as if it had been freshly polished.

'Hi Mr Primus. We didn't see you last week. They told me you had to go to head office. Everything go okay?'

'Yes, sorry I wasn't here. It was fine. We were getting a briefing on the coronavirus, how we may have to run the stores, protective equipment, looking after our staff and our customers, that sort of thing. It's just in case. Head office calls it "risk mitigation".'

'Are you expecting things to get worse then?'

'Nobody has a clue, but you only have to watch the news to see what's happening elsewhere. We shouldn't start getting alarmed just yet.'

She was relieved that head office hadn't discovered their little arrangement, but his news about preparing for the worst worried her. He interrupted her thoughts.

'Come through. There's not that much this week, I'm afraid. A few things left over from Valentine's Day, some chocolates and biscuits. Thought the kids might like them? You don't have to take them but they're a fraction of the price. Mrs Primus liked them.'

She imagined Lester and his wife enjoying the fifteen-pound Valentine meal deal, washed down with a bottle of Prosecco blush and followed by the chocolates. She followed him to his office. His tight grey suit hugged his stocky frame.

'Here you go,' he said, handing the two half-empty bags to her. 'Sorry it's not that much this week.'

'Really, Mr Primus. You don't have to apologise. You've been more than kind to us.'

He smiled and gave the children their Starbursts, warm from his trouser pocket. They walked back into the store, said goodbye. Claire finished her shopping, feeling good that she was able to pay.

* * *

The financial impact of the virus hit the front page of the *Evening Standard*.

BILLIONS WIPED OFF WORLDWIDE VALUE OF SHARES AS PANDEMIC FEARS RISE

Stockwatch had tumbled by 400 points in the past two days. One hundred billion pounds had been wiped off the FTSE 100. It was starting to feel like 2008 all over again and Marcus was feeling anxious. He rubbed his thighs as he sat on the Tube. Cases of the virus in Italy were rising exponentially. Even the filming of *Mission: Impossible 7* in Venice had been brought to a halt. Tom Cruise was 'holed up' in the Hotel Gritti Palace for another five days. Marcus googled it.

A palazzo dripping with precious fabrics, antiques and art, one that truly encapsulates the spirit of the City, the grande dame par excellence.

Marcus could think of worse places to be holed up. Tom would always be welcome to sit it out at Twin Gates. Alice had fancied the pants off him since

Top Gun and would make allowances for his wacky religious beliefs. Maybe Tom would become a fan of 'veggie lasagne' with a random ingredient?

Marcus rang the doorbell to Gavin's flat at ten to eight. He was early.

'Hi Gavin. Sorry I'm a bit early. Not been a great day and just wanted some company. Is it okay to come in?'

'Of course, come through. What's happened? Are you all right?'

They went through to the kitchen and Gavin made two gin and tonics. Marcus took a big gulp.

'Have you seen the latest news about stock markets? They've crashed in the past two days. Billions wiped off the value of shares.'

'No, I haven't. I don't read the financial news and haven't watched TV this evening. What's going on?'

'Fears about a pandemic, although they won't call it one. I can't think why not, it's everywhere. This could be a meltdown as bad, if not worse, than the crash of 2008. Remember how bad that was?'

'I was probably in rehab Marcus. I don't remember much about it. I didn't remember much about anything at that time. Is it bad?'

'I think it could get much worse. Have you seen what's happening in Italy? If this virus spreads, it could get really nasty. Nobody seems to be taking it seriously at all, more worried about floods and Harry and Meghan's fucking security bill.'

Gavin sipped his drink and looked concerned.

'Some of my cases will really struggle to cope with being locked down. Staying indoors is worse than going out for some of them.' He got up, took two poached pear and Roquefort salads out of the fridge and put them on the table. 'If you thought things were bad, at least you didn't have to hide a dead body at the weekend?'

'Hide what?'

Gavin told him the story of Biscuit's final hours and the dash to swap in his replacement without detection.

'Jesus!' said Marcus. 'That's bloody brilliant. The perfect crime. Any problems at school?'

'Apparently not. Biscuit II was returned yesterday with no complications.'

'When I murder Kelvin McBride, which could be any day now, I know I can count on you to help me dispose of his body.'

Gavin lifted an orange Moroccan tagine out of the oven and placed it on a trivet. 'Lamb, sweet potato and apricot tagine,' he announced, lifting the lid and disappearing behind a veil of steam.

'Very impressive,' said Marcus. 'Great food theatre. Tonight could be our last meal together for a while. I'm going to Manchester on Monday and I'll probably be up there for three days a week for the next few months. I'm really sorry.'

'That's a shame but I guess it's your job. Our dinners are the highlight of my week.'

'Mine too. Hopefully, Spearmint will settle down quickly and I won't need to be up there so much.'

By the time they had finished and Marcus had got up to leave, he felt a lot better. Gavin had calmed him down, just like Alice had done. There wasn't anything he could do about the virus, just take it in his stride.

Marcus was knocked out of his stride as soon as he picked up a copy of *Metro* the next morning.

CORONAVIRUS GRIPS EUROPE

Eleven deaths from the virus in Italy and rising. Pictures of people in masks and empty shelves in supermarkets. A thousand guests at a hotel in Tenerife had been placed under lockdown after an Italian doctor who had stayed there had been diagnosed with the virus.

Puts a new slant on an all-inclusive holiday, thought Marcus.

Thirteen schools in the UK had been forced to close or send pupils home to self-isolate.

By the time he had finished his breakfast and scrolled through the news websites, he was more convinced than ever that Armageddon was on its way. It was time to break the silence with Kelvin and he knocked on the door. Kelvin looked up from his laptop and waved him in.

'Hi Kelvin. How are you? How was your skiing trip?'

'Great thanks, Marcus. Family had a great time. Have you calmed down now?'

Kelvin obviously thought Marcus had been in the wrong, but he didn't seem to be bearing a grudge.

'Have you seen the news about the markets plummeting? What's The Firm's position if the virus hits the UK?'

'Yes, of course I've seen it. Risk and Compliance haven't issued anything yet, so I'm waiting to hear. It's being discussed at a global level.'

Risk and Compliance were hot on people wearing brand-compliant lanyards but considerably slower off the mark when it came to dealing with pandemics.

'This could get very nasty,' said Marcus. 'This could screw our business in a big way.'

'As if it wasn't screwed enough already,' sighed Kelvin with an air of resignation. 'Everything okay with Spearmint? When are you off to Manchester?'

'Monday morning.'

'Good luck.'

Kelvin looked down at his laptop, a signal that Marcus's time was up. Marcus returned to his desk and checked The Sequence. Stockwatch was stable, slightly green. The step count on his health app was way below target but he ignored it. Beating himself up for not taking the stairs seemed irrelevant with the virus on its way. It was late in the afternoon when he received a reply from Sarah Appleberry.

Subject: Project Spearmint – Phase II Mobilisation
From: Sarah Appleberry
To: Marcus Barlow, Mason Sherwin

Hi both
Sorry I haven't been in contact. Quite a few things going on here at the moment. Jim and I would like a call with both of you on Friday if that's possible? Will discuss more when we speak. Let me know if 12.30 works for you?
Regards
S

Within minutes, his phone rang. It was Mason.

'Have you seen the note from Sarah?'

'Yes, I have. Seems a bit cryptic, bit vague?'

'What do you think they want to discuss? Not more money off our fees, surely?'

'I really don't know. I'm sure they'll tell us on Friday. I'll go back to her and confirm. In the meantime, I'll get the team briefed for Monday.'

Her note was cryptic and didn't give anything away. 'Things going on here'. He wondered what it meant?

Morale in the office on Friday lunchtime was upbeat. Pizza Friday had come around again. At the same time as the team was gorging itself on slices of pepperoni and mushroom, Kelvin was locked in a room with Izzy Majewska and Jenny Moffatt deciding which people in the team would be realigned. No more Pizza Fridays for them. Marcus sat down at his desk with two slices of quattro stagioni and checked Stockwatch. Another fall was in progress. The FTSE 100 had dropped to 6,460, its lowest point for a year. His retirement plans were starting to look shaky. He joined Mason in Communication Zone 2. He had already dialled in and pressed hash. Sarah Appleberry and Jim Ibbotson joined immediately.

'Afternoon Marcus, afternoon Mason,' said Jim. 'Thanks for joining the call.'

'Afternoon,' said Mason nervously.

'I'll get straight to the point,' said the CFO, dispensing with any conference call foreplay. 'We're not going to be moving ahead with the next phase of Spearmint. I'm sure you'll both be disappointed with the news.'

Mason looked at Marcus, eyes wide open. It was as if he had just been told he had two weeks to live. Jim continued.

'As both of you have seen in the news, the coronavirus is taking a hold in more and more countries. In the past two weeks, we have seen a massive upsurge in demand for Safewear products, gloves, masks, sanitiser, face shields and gowns, both domestically and in export markets. We're getting orders from as far afield as Iran, UAE, Turkey. Our warehouse is virtually empty and Gary Chambers, the Safewear MD, is putting together a plan to run twenty-four-hour shifts from next Monday. We're even taking on more staff. Orders have simply gone through the roof. Right now, we don't think it's the right time to disrupt the business by selling it.'

The Ethical Dilemma had finally been resolved. Not by reason and logic, but by the virus. After all the analysis, options, scenarios and politics, Espina had made the right decision. Selling Safewear was a madness before the virus and would be an even bigger one now. The Firm would take the credit for helping them come to the right decision. It was only Mason who didn't see the logic. He was only thinking of himself and Kelvin's threat.

'Jim, if I could just play devil's advocate here. Surely now is exactly the right time to be selling Safewear? Full order book, factory running at full capacity, motivated workforce. Why would you want to pull the plug on Spearmint now?'

The Firm was always playing devil's advocate with its clients. It was a polite euphemism for saying 'you're all idiots and we fundamentally disagree with you'. Jim Ibbotson wasn't in the mood for advocates of anything apart from his point of view.

'Because there's too much fucking money to be made out of this coronavirus crisis. We think there will be a global shortage of PPE, demand will go through the roof and so will prices. There will always be winners out of this virus shit. Selling Safewear now would be stupid.'

Sarah Appleberry cut in.

'I'm sorry we've left it so late in the day to tell you. We wanted to see how things panned out before making a final decision. Maybe we'll revisit it again later in the year once things have calmed down?'

'But if I could just—'

Marcus swept his hand across his throat in a gesture which said to Mason, *'Shut the fuck up!'*

Marcus continued.

'Jim, we fully understand your decision and thanks for letting us know. Obviously, we're disappointed. We were really looking forward to working with you.' It was a lie, but it was the polite thing to say.

'We were too, Marcus. If it's any consolation, yours was the best pitch by a country mile. That wall thing and the costumes? Outstanding. Anyway, got to go now.'

Marcus pressed the red button and ended the call. Mason looked like he was about to cry. He was now at the mercy of Kelvin who was busy realigning the cost base, a realignment that would now include him.

'Don't worry, Mason. I'll tell Kelvin the bad news. It might be better coming from me?'

'Thanks Marcus. You're a mate.'

Marcus sent Kelvin an email repeating what Jim Ibbotson had told them. It would ruin his weekend, and an even bigger realignment of the cost base would be needed. He gathered the team in Collaboration Pod 3, the place where they had first built the Wonderwall. It seemed fitting. The team was disappointed. They were now back on the bench. More internal innovation and insight-building lay in wait, if they managed to escape from being 'realigned'. Trains were cancelled and hotels un-booked. Project Spearmint was now officially dead.

It was Friday, 28 February 2020.

Chapter 19

The Immaculate Conception

Marcus was sitting in his mother's armchair in the garage. His weekend had been spent taking more boxes of their possessions to local charity shops. He didn't share his parents' love of Nana Mouskouri, Val Doonican and Glen Campbell. 'Easy listening' didn't sit well alongside the Ramones.

The *Sunday Times* had depressed him. The financial world was in turmoil. Economists were falling over themselves to slash their forecasts, describing the impacts of the virus as 'a known unknown'. Marcus didn't like uncertainty any more than they did. Alice came into the garage.

'Just came to see if you wanted a coffee?'

He didn't hear her and continued staring at the wall.

'Marcus, are you okay? Would you like a coffee?'

'Sorry, Al. I was miles away. Got a lot on my mind at the moment.'

'Why, what's the matter?'

She pulled up a threadbare footstool and sat in front of him.

'The virus, collapsing stock markets, work, Spearmint, Kelvin, you, the kids. How many more things do you want?'

'Well, you can take me and the kids off your list of worries for a start. We're fine. Is it Spearmint? That wasn't your fault, you did win it.'

'Spearmint was just the tip of the iceberg, another nail in my coffin.'

'The straw that broke the camel's back then?'

Alice giggled and it made him smile.

'Al, I'm trying to be serious here!'

'I know, I know. I was trying to cheer you up, I'm sorry.' She squeezed his hand. 'What's really wrong, Marcus?'

'It's that place, The Firm, all the bullshit, the back-stabbing and politics. It's why Tyler got out. Lucky bastard.'

'So why don't you get out too if you hate it so much?'

'Because I'm fucking scared, Al. Really scared. The Firm has given me ... given *us* everything. What else can I do? I've spent twenty years of my life doing this shit.'

'Perhaps you could start by being yourself? Doing something you really want to do.'

He ignored her and carried on with his rant.

'And now this virus is threatening to destroy everything. Everything I've worked for. For us, for the children.'

'Okay Marcus, that's enough self-pity for a Sunday morning. Yes, things might get a bit tough but we are hardly on the streets, are we? We have plenty of money and how much do we really need? And, if the worst comes to the worst, I'll go back to being a lawyer.'

'Things would never get that bad, would they?' he said, raising his eyebrows and smiling.

'Piss off, Marcus. You know what I mean. If you want to leave, then leave. You don't have to prove anything to anyone. Doing something more practical might be good for you?'

He shook his head. 'Mmm, I'm not so sure that's a viable option is it? I haven't exactly got a great track record.'

'No, perhaps you're right,' said Alice who sighed.

His attempts at DIY had always ended in disaster, requiring the services of local tradesmen to repair the damage at a significantly higher cost than the original problem.

'Anything has to be better than being unhappy,' Alice said. 'Think about it. So, would you like that coffee?'

'Yes, that would be great. Thanks for the chat, Al.'

'I have my uses.'

She returned a few minutes later with a cup of coffee. He was sorting out more boxes of memories.

'Feeling better now?'

'A little. Not looking forward to the office tomorrow. I'll have to find something to keep me busy before Kelvin realigns me!'

'That's not going to happen but, if it does, we'll deal with it together.'

He watched her leave the garage. She had been his rock throughout their marriage. If she chose to eat tofu instead of roast beef, he would go along with it.

* * *

Marcus walked to the station on Monday morning. It was sunny and spring was on its way. *The Mamas and the Papas' Greatest Hits* were raising his spirits. He imagined him and Alice cruising down Highway 1 in California in a beaten-up

VW camper van, surfboards tied to the roof, staring out at the Pacific Ocean on their way to Santa Monica. *Metro* shattered his dream.

VIRUS CASES JUMP IN THE UK

It was now official. It was a crisis. Each page in the newspaper had a little red logo saying it was a crisis. Britain was climbing the infection league table. The country's response was being led by Matt Hancock, the Health Secretary. Marcus had never heard of him. He thought he looked like a chinless baby but felt sorry for him. A global pandemic had landed in his in tray and he was clearly floundering. He thought Matt was probably wishing he'd been Transport Secretary instead.

The prime minister was chairing an emergency meeting of the COBRA committee that morning. If COBRA was involved, it showed things were really serious. The press on Sunday had been full of stories about Boris getting divorced, getting engaged and becoming a father again, all in the space of a couple of months.

Lucky that a pandemic and a global economic meltdown won't distract him too much then? thought Marcus.

The office was busier than usual, free desks were at a premium. He found one next to Steve Pettigrew, near to the EcoPod. He was greeted by the IT department's blue screen. Another batch of software updates. It was time to go and see Kelvin.

For a man facing a big hole in his plan, Kelvin was looking remarkably relaxed. He welcomed Marcus into his office and even smiled at him.

'Come in Marcus, sit down. How was your weekend?'

'It was okay, thanks. How about yours?'

'Yes, it was great. I played golf. Great round, few drinks afterwards. Pretty chilled really.'

'You saw my note about Spearmint? Turned out Safewear was the jewel in the Espina crown all along.'

'Yes, you always said it was. These things happen. We'll just have to find something new, won't we? Something will turn up.'

There were a number of reasons why Kelvin was in such an amenable mood. He had overdosed on Nicorettes, Vanessa had given him a blow job on the way to work or he had bought a new car. Or perhaps he had something else up his sleeve?

'How are the cost base realignments coming along?' said Marcus.

'I can't answer that one right now. Conversations will need to be had in the next couple of weeks.'

There was a pause.

'At all levels.'

Marcus knew what he meant. 'At all levels' meant partners. Kelvin was going to chop out some dead wood and now he had the perfect excuse to do it.

'Any communication from Risk and Compliance on our position on Covid-19?'

'More discussions are taking place at a global level. We'll have to wait and see.'

If discussions were taking place at a global level, the virus would have come, gone away and returned again before any decisions were made. Marcus changed the subject.

'Are you speaking at the "Living Our Values" conference next week?'

'Absolutely. I'm facilitating one of the sessions. Why? Are you going?'

'Of course. Wouldn't miss it for the world. I've even done my pre-joining questionnaire.'

'I'll see you there then.'

Kelvin gave Marcus his 'time's up' stare, and Marcus stood up and left the office.

After the collapse of Spearmint, Marcus spent the rest of the day 'networking'. It was a form of grovelling, knocking on doors, sending emails and making calls to partners he hadn't spoken to for years. When times were good, everyone was your friend. When they were bad, you might as well be wearing a badge saying, '*I've got the virus*'. It had been a tough day. By the end of it, he felt like a young offender trying to sell dusters and tea towels to people who had cupboards full of them. It was one rejection after another.

He decided to walk to Waterloo Station. The nights were getting longer and it had started to drizzle. He crossed the river at Waterloo Bridge and looked back towards the City. It was like a giant Christmas tree, illuminated by millions of lights, but was shedding its money like needles. It was hard to believe that an invisible virus could turn the lights out. The 18.05 was delayed by ten minutes and he sent Gavin a message.

Hi Gavin. Change of plan. Spearmint got canned! Not going to Manchester now. Will be at the flat tomorrow if you would like dinner? My turn. Let me know. M

Gavin replied immediately.

Yes sure! Sorry to hear about Spearmint. Normal time? See you then. G

The news must have made Gavin happy. He had used smiley yellow faces. He texted Alice.

Getting the 18.15. Will get a cab from the station. Should be home between 7.15 and 7.30. See you soon. M

She answered immediately too. Everyone in the world was using their phones. *No prb. C u wen u home.*

Her smiley, yellow faces weren't as happy as Gavin's. His were big smiles, hers were more like a grin. He still didn't understand them.

It was still raining when he got out of the station and there was a queue at Ace Cars. He decided to wait outside. If the virus was looking for a base to launch an attack on Weybridge, Ace Cars was an obvious choice. Marcus knew the drill and followed Kareem to the waiting Prius, which accelerated away silently. Smooth FM was playing 'Everything I Do' by Bryan Adams.

I bet this is on ten times a day, thought Marcus.

Kareem hummed along to the 'Groover from Vancouver'. Marcus wasn't in the mood for silence and opened the conversation.

'Have you got a family, Kareem?'

Kareem looked at Marcus in his rear-view mirror.

'Yes I do. A wife and two small boys, eight and five. They're a handful but they are nice boys. I'm very proud of them.'

'Do you spend much time with them? It can't be easy, doing the job you do.'

'I take them to school every morning, and I try to get home in time to see them before they go to bed. Not always. Sometimes I have to work late.'

Marcus thought it was a nice thing to say, that he was proud of his family. Kareem swung the Prius on to the drive at Twin Gates.

'You have a very beautiful house. I would like to own a house like this one day.'

Unless he won the Lottery, the reality was that Kareem would never own a house like Twin Gates. Marcus wondered why he was so well rewarded for doing something which added no value to anyone's lives.

'Goodnight Kareem. It was nice chatting with you. Hope you get home in time to see your boys.'

'Have a good evening, sir.'

Alice was in the kitchen with Olivia. Marcus could overhear them talking. Art class had obviously not gone well.

'Hi everyone. How are we?' he said, trying to lift the mood.

'Mum's slagging off Belinda Churchill!' said Olivia. 'Said she thought Mum was better suited to still life.'

Marcus looked at Alice. He could tell she was upset.

'So, Tony's thighs didn't get Belinda's seal of approval then?'

'Fucking bitch. After all the hard work I put in last week. She said my painting reminded her of Picasso.'

'She probably meant it as a compliment.'

'Did she fuck? She humiliated me in front of the whole class and Tony. I'm never going back.'

Marcus looked at Olivia who raised her eyebrows. No words of encouragement were going to work. When Alice used the F-word, it was time to give her space. They left her to take out her frustrations on the courgettes and went upstairs.

'How are you doing, Libby?' he said to his daughter.

'I'm okay. School is going well. Mum told me about Spearmint. Are you disappointed?'

'Not really, but thanks for the concern. I'm more worried about the virus, things are getting pretty bad. I think the worst is yet to come.'

'Yes, that's what Boris said too,' said Olivia.

Although he had voted Conservative in the November election, Marcus had serious misgivings about the prime minister's ability to lead the country in a crisis. The fact he was known ubiquitously by his first name summed up his lack of gravitas. Clowns were also known by their first names.

'Oh, that's okay then. Everything must be under control. No need to panic,' he said sarcastically. 'I'm going to get changed.'

* * *

He was on the train when an email from Izzy Majewska pinged in his inbox.

Subject: Project Spearmint – Marketing Costs
From: Izzy Majewska
To: Marcus Barlow, Mason Sherwin

Hi both
Have just seen the charges for the Spearmint pitch. £75k!!! We're trying to control costs, so this is a major negative variance. Am trying to head this off before Kelvin sees it. Can we catch up before the pipeline meeting?
Best wishes
    Izzy

With Spearmint dead and buried, the inquest was now starting. If it had gone ahead, nobody would have given a toss. The cost of the Wonderwall, the costumes, the bios, the photos, the brick-shaped pitch documents, would have been lost in the fees. Compared to the millions The Firm wasted on its 'insights' and 'thought pieces', it was a drop in the ocean. They met with Izzy at 8.45 outside Communication Zone 1.

'So what do you want us to say, Izzy?' said Marcus.

Mason stayed silent.

'How on earth did the costs come to seventy-five grand? What was it printed on? Gold leaf?'

'Bricks actually,' said Marcus. 'It's Gerard and the CIC team, plus the costs of using DP and their stupid fucking icons. It's only wooden dollars.'

'But seventy-five grand of wooden dollars, Marcus? Charged to our team.'

'I agree with Izzy, it is a bit excessive,' said Mason reverting to being slippery. 'I suppose things did get a little out of hand with CIC. We should have kept them on a tighter rein.'

Typical Mason. The boy who dobbed his mates in for smoking to avoid getting the cane himself.

'Mason, as I recall, it was you and Kelvin who wanted to get Gerard and his lunatics involved from the start? I went along with it, against my better judgement. However, it worked and the client loved it. We tell Gerard to halve the recharges. The rest of it, we'll have to do something with. Izzy, any bright ideas?'

'I suppose I could write it off to an old client code?'

'Sounds like a plan, I'll leave it with you.'

The other partners arrived for the pipeline meeting. Izzy gave her update, including the news on Spearmint, which had significantly worsened the out-turn for the year. Everyone waited for Kelvin to say something but it never came. Storm Kelvin had blown out.

* * *

Claire got back to the flat in time to hear the closing headlines on the *Today* programme. The number of cases of the virus in the UK had risen to thirty-nine. The government had set out its four-part strategy to fight the virus, '*Contain, Delay, Mitigate and Research*'. It sounded impressive, straight out of COBRA. Boris was telling everyone to wash their hands frequently with soap and hot water. It seemed like a feeble response to a pandemic, but she went to the sink and washed her hands anyway.

Gavin arrived at the usual time. She was pleased to see him. Apart from a brief chat with Beverley and Monday's episode of *The Chase* with Mr Mahoney, adult conversation had been in short supply. He sat down at the kitchen table as she switched the kettle on.

'How have you been?' he said.

'Okay. I managed to pay for Kyle's school trip to the urban farm at the end of March. The money from Beverley has been really useful. I've even managed to buy the kids a few things, some new clothes.'

'And how's the work going?'

'I really enjoy it. We've been going through boxes of fabric samples and my skills with a PC are improving.'

'Good for you. You okay in yourself?'

'I am. Bit lonely, but miles better than I have been for a while. Do you think you should wash your hands?'

'Why? Aren't you using the Mr Muscle spray I gave you?' He wiped his finger on the kitchen table and pulled a face.

'Ha-ha! Very funny. No, I mean what Boris said about us all washing our hands to stop the virus.'

He reached into his laptop bag, pulled out a small bottle of hand sanitiser and squirted a blob on to his hand.

'I use it all the time anyway. I'm probably immune.'

She wondered if aftershave and smelling nice could make you immune from the virus. It was an Eau Sauvage day. It would certainly make him bullet-proof.

'Aren't you worried about the virus?' she said.

'I'm concerned for sure. If we end up locked down like people in China and Italy, it's going to be really hard for some.'

'Like me, you mean? I don't know what I'm going to do, cooped up in this flat with two small children. We'll all go mental. What about their school and nursery? What do I do if they close?'

He shrugged his shoulders and shook his head.

'We've just got to wait and see. It might not get that bad.'

* * *

Marcus dropped his laptop off at the flat, picked up some plastic bags and headed to The Temple. His day hadn't been too bad, networking had unearthed a new opportunity, Project Medusa. For a Tuesday evening, the supermarket was busy. A shopper leaving the store passed him at the top of the escalator. She was carrying six jumbo packs of toilet roll.

Must have a stomach upset, he thought.

He turned right into the fresh fruit and vegetable aisles to be met with rows of empty shelves and packing crates.

'What's going on here?' he asked himself.

He parked his trolley and walked up and down the aisles. Where there was normally a choice that would satisfy the most demanding of chefs, now there were empty spaces. The same was true in the bakery, and at the meat and fish counter. 'Pasta, rice and pulses' was a desert. It was as if a plague of locusts had descended on Waitrose. A harassed store manager was busy directing staff to replenish shelves with anything and Marcus approached him.

'Excuse me, I can see you're busy. Can I ask what's happened? Have you had delivery problems or something?'

'Panic buying, hoarding. People have gone mad today. Toilet rolls, pasta, medicines, hand wash, cleaning stuff, tinned soups. It's all because of the virus.'

'But the virus doesn't give you the shits,' said Marcus. 'Why are people hoarding bog rolls?'

'Haven't got a clue,' said the manager. 'It's just mental.'

Now the virus had changed his menu too. He wasn't worried about wiping his arse but having no fresh ginger or Thai basil had put a dent in his plans for Asian pesto chicken with rice noodles. He managed to assemble enough bits and pieces to make a stir-fry and left the store. He got back to the flat and called Alice in a panic.

'Hi Al. I've just got back from The Temple. The world's gone fucking mad. The shelves were almost empty. People are stockpiling food, cleaning materials, pasta. Is it the same in Weybridge?'

'Marcus, slow down. I have no idea. I haven't been shopping this week. We had our delivery from the Organic Delivery Company yesterday. Seemed fine. Why, what's happening at your end?'

He was relieved to know the panic-stricken masses hadn't started hoarding meat substitutes as well. At least his family would be able to survive on vegan protein.

'How many rolls of toilet paper do we have at home?' he said.

'I have absolutely no idea. I don't keep count. Why?'

'Try to get more if you can. There could be a shortage looming. And get more hand sanitiser too.'

With six toilets in Twin Gates, it was unlikely his family would have to resort to using old copies of *Metro*.

'Fine, Marcus. I'll go online and place an order with Ocado tomorrow.'

'It would be better if you went to The Temple in person. That way you're guaranteed to get some.'

'I'm playing tennis in the morning. Will you stop panicking about bloody bog roll, Marcus? I'll get more if it makes you happy?'

'Preferably Andrex Quilts if you can. Don't go for an inferior brand unless absolutely necessary.'

'For goodness' sake, Marcus! Aren't you having dinner with Gavin tonight?'

'Yes, I am.'

'Well get on with cooking it then. I'm going. Bye.'

Two days earlier, she had been the voice of good reason and support. He couldn't understand how she could have changed so quickly?

By the time Gavin arrived, everything was prepared. It was an eclectic menu. Duck pâté on warm wholemeal flatbreads, then beef stir-fry, followed by mini-Black Forest gateaux. Marcus explained what had happened.

'I didn't realise things had got so bad so quickly,' said Gavin.

Marcus decided not to enquire about Gavin's stock of toilet roll and they sat down to the pâté and flatbreads. The bottle of Chassagne-Montrachet that Gavin had brought was far too good for a stir-fry made up of less-than-perfect ingredients, but he insisted they drank it.

'So, what happened to the infamous Spearmint then?' said Gavin.

'Turns out, Espina was sitting on a goldmine all along. If you own a dull, boring business making protective gloves and face masks, what do you need to make it successful?'

'A global pandemic?'

'Exactly,' said Marcus. 'Orders flooding in, shifts working twenty-four seven, hiring more people. Why would you sell it? Right place, right time. They'll make a killing.'

'Hopefully not.'

Marcus made the stir-fry in his Ken Hom wok and brought it sizzling to the table. By the time he had coated the ingredients in some yellow bean sauce, even the manky vegetables looked edible.

'If there are going to be food shortages, maybe we'll be forced to trawl the depths of our larders and use things that have sat there for years,' said Marcus.

'Like what?'

'Like this.' Marcus got up, went to the cupboard, rummaged around and produced a small, flat tin. He handed it to Gavin.

Fray Bentos Steak & Kidney pie. Topped with our signature puff pastry crust.

'It looks disgusting,' said Gavin.

'Absolutely delicious. Has a shelf life measured in decades. Best with baked beans. I used to live on them when I was a student. Alice won't let me have them in the house now.'

'I can't say I blame her. Full of mystery meat, no doubt?'

Marcus served their desserts straight from the plastic pots. They were a throwback to his mother's birthday meals at the local Berni Inn. Prawn cocktail, rump steak and Black Forest gateau. It was a fond memory.

'I haven't had this for years,' said Gavin, taking a spoonful. 'It's pretty good.'

'Now we have the virus to thank for something after all, reuniting us with our culinary pasts.'

'Maybe I'll make Spam fritters next week? My mum always used to make them for Rory and me!'

The two friends laughed and scrolled through their memories of childhood food from a time when kumquats and balsamic glaze hadn't entered their consciousness. Marcus told Gavin about his conversation with Alice in the garage. He nodded in agreement.

'She's right. How much money do you need? I know it's your safety net but don't be scared. You are talented in lots of ways, Marcus.'

'Like what?'

'Reading bedtime stories and serving retro desserts.'

Marcus laughed.

'Maybe I could work for Ace Cars? I could drive around all day listening to Planet Rock.'

Gavin looked baffled so he told him about Kareem and Smooth FM.

'At least he's happy, and that's what counts. Anyway, I should be going,' said Gavin as he stood up to leave. 'Great meal Marcus. Definitely one of your best!'

At the front door, Gavin put his arms around Marcus and hugged him. Marcus didn't usually hug men, it made him feel awkward. His father had never kissed him.

'We will get through it, Marcus. It might get worse before it gets better. But it will get better.'

'It could get worse too. If I end up using toilet paper like we had at school! Tore my arsehole to ribbons.'

* * *

The two women sat at opposite ends of the desk in Beverley's study. Claire screamed at the laptop in exasperation.

'Why is it called Excel when I obviously don't?'

Beverley looked at her and laughed. Claire was frowning at her screen.

'Are you staying for lunch? It's only last night's leftovers but there's more than enough for us. It's five minutes in the microwave. Please stay?'

Apart from another gripping instalment of *Escape to the Chateau*, there was no reason for Claire to rush back to Kensal Mansions.

'That's very kind. I'd love to.'

Beverley put a bowl of noodles in the invisible microwave which started to hum quietly. She switched on the TV on the wall behind them. It was the *News at One*. The number of cases in Italy had risen to over 3,000, with 100 deaths. Beautiful historic cities were deserted and tourist hotspots were now only inhabited by pigeons. In the UK, shoppers were filmed in supermarkets fighting over bottles of disinfectant.

'How are things in Hong Kong? Any news from Edward?' said Claire.

'Getting more stable. A hundred or so cases and only a couple of deaths. Nothing like Italy or Wuhan. I spoke with him on Tuesday. He's trying to get back next week.'

'That's great news.'

Alexa wanted to walk and held hands with her mum and Beverley, who swung her between them. They arrived just in time to hear the school bell ring followed by the pandemonium of screaming children. Kyle ran straight up to his mummy, closely followed by Bruce.

'Mummy, Mummy, guess what happened today?'

It could have been any one of a thousand things.

'I don't know, darling. What did happen?'

'Biscuit's had babies, five of them! They look like little jelly beans. When we looked in his cage this morning, we could see them. They are really small and their eyes aren't open yet.'

It took a while for the news to sink in. Biscuit II had had babies. But Biscuit was male. Male hamsters didn't have babies. Biscuit hadn't adopted like Elton John did either. Helena Mistakidis came up to them.

'Has Kyle told you the good news about Biscuit? He, or more accurately, *she* has had a litter overnight. One of the children noticed them this morning. It's incredible, we always thought Biscuit was a boy!'

'So how did Biscuit get pregnant?' said Beverley. 'Presumably by playing with another hamster? Have you got any other hamsters in school?'

'No, that's the weirdest thing. We only have stick insects and two gerbils in

Year 3. We can't work out how it's happened. It's a complete mystery.'

That's the thing about fibs. They turn into lies, bigger lies and then whoppers. Claire tried to look amazed too. It was hard to believe that God had chosen Biscuit II, as the living vehicle to demonstrate his divine powers by sending the angel Gabriel to impregnate him. Claire had to come clean.

'Kyle, Bruce, do you want to go and play? Mummy needs to talk with Miss Mistakidis and Beverley for a moment.' Kyle and Bruce ran off to play as Claire pulled the two women close to her. She lowered her voice to a whisper.

'I think I might be able to explain how this has happened.'

Claire revealed the circumstances behind Biscuit's death and resurrection in the form of Gavin's carefully chosen body double. One thing had been overlooked which had led to the 'miracle'. It wasn't a miracle at all. Biscuit II was already up the duff and Gavin had screwed up. Big time. Helena and Beverley stared at her for a second and then burst into fits of laughter.

'I'm really sorry but I couldn't bring myself to confess to killing Biscuit. He probably died of natural causes. That's why he slept so much. I couldn't turn up after half-term with an empty cage. It would have been awful for Kyle.'

'Stop, stop!' said Helena, hysterically. 'I think I'm going to wet myself! And you went through with the whole charade of returning Biscuit to school last week?'

'I had to. What are you going to do?' said Claire to the teacher.

'What can I do? Not much we can do now,' said Helena. 'We'll just have to pretend that Biscuit was a girl all along.'

'And explaining how Biscuit had babies?'

'I don't think five-year-olds are concerned about that, do you? Looks like we'll be needing to find some new homes for the babies though.'

'Well, you can leave me out of that one! I'm done with hamsters.'

'Don't worry. It'll remain a secret between us. I'd better get on. See you both tomorrow,' said Helena.

'I'm not sure I can trust you anymore!' said Beverley, as she laughed again. 'See you tomorrow.'

Claire put Alexa in the pushchair and they walked back to Kensal Mansions.

'What were you talking to Miss Takidis and Bruce's mummy about?' said Kyle.

'Oh, just grown-up stuff. Nothing serious. Let's go home.'

It was Thursday, 5 March 2020.

Chapter 20

Simply the Worst

His annual medical was an event he had been dreading. The masked receptionist directed him to Room 3 where the doctor was waiting. Dr Saira Gupta was a diminutive young woman, dressed in a white lab coat with a stethoscope draped around her neck. She was also wearing a mask. She greeted him warmly. He liked her more than his family GP, a grumpy old git who possessed none of Dr Gupta's bedside manners.

'Nice to see you again, Mr Barlow. Please sit down. Please excuse the mask, we can't be too careful. So, how have you been over the past twelve months? Generally?'

'I think I'm doing well, doctor. Lost a couple of stone and trying to walk a lot more. I'm also cutting down on red meat. My body mass index is 23.1, which I think is quite good.'

'Yes, I've read your responses to the questionnaires. You've mentioned anxiety and stress quite a few times? Do you want to tell me a little more about that?'

He explained recent events at The Firm, that he felt scared of the future, and the virus had made his anxiety worse. She listened sympathetically and nodded.

'Although we don't know what will happen with Covid-19, events like this make all of us feel anxious at times. We question things more and question ourselves. It's like a giant magnifying glass; it takes all our insecurities and makes them bigger.'

Marcus nodded.

'That's it exactly. Last week I got anxious we didn't have enough toilet roll, now that everyone is hoarding!'

Dr Gupta laughed. Toilet roll induced anxiety was a new one, although she had seen plenty of middle-aged, professional men going through a similar crisis.

'Well, maybe it's about time you considered a different lifestyle? Slowing down, doing something different.'

How many more people are going to say this? he thought.

He went to the toilet to produce a urine sample. He screwed the lid on the pot and held it up to the fluorescent light. He thought it was a good colour. He left it in the little cabinet where there was a sample left by another patient. It was the colour of golden syrup.

'Mmm … that's not looking so good,' he said to himself.

He re-joined Dr Gupta and got undressed. All the basic tests were normal and she confirmed his BMI as 23.1. She was pleased and said the probability of a heart attack was low. He lay on his back as she inserted a needle into a vein in his arm.

'You will feel a little prick.'

He wanted to crack the obvious joke. *'I feel that all the time, doctor.'*

He didn't. He guessed she had heard it before and would only laugh out of politeness. All of this was delaying the inevitable, the moment Marcus had spent the weekend dreading.

'Okay, Mr Barlow. If you could pull down your underpants, roll over and face the wall, and bring your knees up to your chest.' Dr Gupta snapped on a pair of rubber gloves.

Just as working for The Firm wasn't all mega-deals and expensive restaurants, Marcus appreciated that being a doctor wasn't all organ transplants and micro-surgery. As he turned to face the wall, he could see Dr Gupta squirting a blob of lubricant on to her middle finger. Last year, he had told Alice about his prostate test, that he had felt violated but she had no sympathy.

'Try sitting in a pair of stirrups while someone sticks a speculum in your fanny. That's violation, Marcus!'

Dr Gupta performed the procedure swiftly. All over for another year.

'Well, that seems fine,' she said, removing her rubber gloves. 'Let's see what the PSA test comes back with. I'll forward the results to the urologist to see if any follow up is needed. Now, let's do your ECG. If you want to get changed into your gym kit?'

The ECG was the second most unpleasant thing about his medical. The removal of the electrodes at the end of the procedure caused pain. It was like having a chest wax. Dr Gupta went for the quick approach, and she apologised. Even private healthcare didn't prevent the pain. He got dressed as she entered more details on her computer.

'Great to see you again, Mr Barlow. The results will be online within the next week. If there's anything unusual or needing a referral, I'll be in touch. See you again next year. Remember what I said about the anxiety and lifestyle. Give it some thought, eh?'

'Thanks a lot doctor, I will. Hope to see you next year.'

He decided to stop off in Caffè Nero for a macchiato and a pain au raisin. He deserved some reward for being violated. Somebody had left a copy of *Metro* on the table and he picked it up. The headline writer was clearly having an off day.

According to the article, people had been hoarding prawns, scallops and mussels. He thought it was a weak pun. The prime minister had paid a surprise visit to the *This Morning* studios to face a grilling about the pandemic from Holly Willoughby and Phillip Schofield, fresh from another arduous season hosting *Dancing on Ice*. Boris reassured the nation there wouldn't be food shortages and the UK economy would survive the pandemic. The UK had suffered its third death and the number of cases had risen to 273.

He thought Holly and Phil should have pressed Boris a bit harder on the Government's plans to tackle the virus but there probably wasn't enough time before the next item on how to make moussaka.

He opened Stockwatch and immediately felt nauseous. If the previous week had been bad, today it was falling off a cliff. People were selling stocks in droves. He crossed the river at London Bridge and walked up towards Monument, the tower commemorating the Great Fire of London. It seemed appropriate. His retirement plans were going up in flames too.

The office was busy and Marcus set himself up in one of the Chilling Eggs and logged on. It was Monday morning and there were bound to be system updates. IT didn't disappoint, a blue screen. He checked WhatsApp. Messages from Alice and Gavin. He read Alice's first.

Hi M. Got loo roll. Hd 2 go 2 Aldi 2 get it. 64 rolls. Happy?

He had never set foot in an Aldi store. He wasn't brand promiscuous and saving money on food wasn't important to him. He hoped she hadn't bought 'own label'. It would be vastly inferior to Andrex Quilts. He opened the message from Gavin.

Hi Marcus. Sorry, won't make dinner tomorrow. Mum not well. Going to Scotland this afternoon. Will be gone all week. Hope you are ok? See you soon. G

The news unsettled him. He had planned to stay at the flat all week and was looking forward to their dinner. Speaking to Gavin made him feel less anxious. He replied.

Sorry to hear about your mum. Fully understand. Have a safe journey and hope all goes well. See you soon. M

The blue screen ended and Marcus opened Outlook. Risk and Compliance had finally woken up to the pandemic and had issued guidelines and a list of measures The Firm was taking to protect its employees and clients. All offices would remain open, internal and client meetings would continue as normal, and people would have to wash their hands more frequently. That was it. The Firm was washing its hands of the virus in the name of business continuity.

Not wanting to be on his own, he decided to go home, leaving his overnight bag in his locker. He texted Alice to say he was coming home and took the Drain to Waterloo. It seemed less full than usual. He picked up a copy of the *Evening Standard*.

The country was at the start of an epidemic which had begun to kill people. He checked Stockwatch for the closing position. A hundred and forty-four billion pounds had been wiped off the face of shares in a single day. People were selling their shares and buying toilet rolls instead. He wondered if it could get much worse?

The journey passed in a blur as he stared out of the window and wondered if the people in the houses next to the railway line were feeling as anxious as he was? He decided not to take a taxi and walked home in the dark. He walked along the tree-lined avenues of large mock-Georgian houses, protected behind their security gates.

Those won't keep you safe, he thought.

It was almost 7.30 by the time he put the key in the lock and stepped into the hall. The house was warm and he could hear Alice and Olivia chatting in the kitchen. Olivia had got the results from her mocks and was excited. He put on a happy face and entered the kitchen with a smile.

'Someone sounds excited?'

'Hi Dad.' Olivia put her arms around him. 'I got my results today. An A in biology, A in chemistry and a B in maths. Bit disappointed with my maths but it was a hard paper. Hopefully I'll improve a bit by the summer.'

'Well done, I'm really proud of you. You always work so hard. All to play for now.'

Olivia ran upstairs and Marcus looked at his wife. She was crying.

'Don't be upset, Al, a B in Maths isn't so bad. She's done really well.'

'I know, Marcus. I'm chopping onions. So why didn't you stay at the flat tonight?'

'Gavin's gone back to Scotland. His mum's quite ill. I'll probably stay in London on Thursday night. I've got this stupid "Living Our Values" conference all day followed by dinner.'

'What's "Living Our Values"?' she said, scornfully.

'A pile of bollocks to show The Firm cares. It's just window dressing. Every organisation has to have "values" now.'

'So what *are* The Firm's new values?'

'No idea. All will be revealed on Thursday. Probably not that different to the ones we've got already. Anyway, how was your day?'

'It was okay. You saw my text about loo roll? None in The Temple. I ended up going to Aldi in Chertsey.'

It wasn't the time to question her brand selection. He would have to hoard a few rolls of Andrex Quilts for his own use.

'How did your medical go this morning?'

'Well, I think. Dr Gupta seemed happy. I think I'm in pretty good condition for a man of my age. Just got to wait for the blood test results.'

'You do look good, Marcus. I'm sure you'll be fine.'

He went upstairs and got changed. His chest looked like the surface of the moon with its shaved craters. He checked the cupboard in the en suite. Four rolls of Andrex Quilts. Not enough to last a pandemic but sufficient until reinforcements arrived. He hid a couple in his wardrobe.

After dinner, they went to the living room and Alice picked up her copy of the *Daily Mail*. He saw the front page from his chair.

THIRD VIRUS VICTIM IN THE UK

'I don't suppose you saw the news today about the stock market, did you?' he said.

'No.'

'It's crashed again. Lowest it's been since 2012. A hundred and forty-four billion pounds wiped off in a single day. I'm starting to get very worried about this, Al. Really worried.'

She heard him but carried on reading. Feeling ignored, he switched on the TV. It was *MasterChef* where John and Gregg were introducing the next batch of hopefuls.

'*One hour, fifteen minutes, one great plate of food. Let's cook,*' said John.

Gregg beamed sadistically at the contestants.

She looked over the top of her newspaper. 'You should go on *MasterChef*, Marcus. You'd be good at it.'

He was still upset she hadn't appreciated how a financial meltdown would impact on their lives.

'Of course, great idea. I could show them my signature dish. Baked beans on fucking toast, because that's what we'll be living on soon. I'm going to bed.'

* * *

Unusually, Kelvin McBride was the first person to take his seat in Communication Zone 1 for the pipeline meeting. Vanessa Briggs arrived with Mason, just ahead of Marcus who was talking to Chloe. The other partners arrived one by one, poured refreshments and took their seats. There were three empty chairs around the table. Marcus did a quick roll call. Tyler had already gone, but Tom Irons and Grant Bremner-Walker were missing.

Perhaps they're dialling in? he thought. He leaned forward to open the conference call but Kelvin stopped him.

'No need to open the call, Marcus. We're all here.' Kelvin brought the room to order. 'Okay everyone, I have an announcement to make. As everyone knows, this year has been tough. I've said before, we have to use this as an opportunity to realign our cost base. Consequently, Tom Irons and Grant Bremner-Walker will be leaving at the end of June. They are on gardening leave with immediate effect. Izzy, do you want to update everyone on the rest of the cost base realignment?'

Three partners had gone in the space of two weeks. Somebody was always going to pay and, in the end, it was Tom and Grant. Marcus thought restaurant owners all over London would be weeping into their lobster bisques over the demise of Tom Irons and his gold Corporate Amex card. Grant had always been dead wood.

Izzy picked up the thread.

'Thanks Kelvin. In line with a reduction in partners, we will be further realigning our cost base and reducing staff headcount by twelve FTEs. These people will all leave at the end of the month. Here is the list. Discussions with the individuals concerned will take place this week.'

A piece of paper with twelve names on it went through pairs of hands. It was a done deal.

'Can I ask how these people were chosen?' said Marcus, scanning down the list.

'Based on the interim performance review and other metrics,' said Izzy dispassionately.

'But some of these people were rated as "outstanding" or "over-performing" weren't they?'

'Just not as over-performing as others,' said Izzy.

Marcus looked at Kelvin who stared back at him blankly.

'Not great timing is it?' said Marcus. 'There's a lot of uncertainty with the pandemic. Is it really essential we do this now?'

Kelvin grinned sadistically.

'Perhaps if you'd sold Spearmint, you might have saved a few of them?'

It was a typically insensitive comment which angered Marcus, who responded in kind.

'I'm sorry, Kelvin. I didn't realise we were running Schindler's fucking List here. Spearmint not happening wasn't down to me. And what about these people's bonuses? We're just a few months away from year end.'

Izzy intervened immediately.

'As you know very well, Marcus, all bonuses are discretionary. You can't be paid a bonus if you're on notice. They will all get three months' pay. This has been agreed with our HR Business Partner.'

'So what's happening to partner promotions this year?' said Marcus.

'Laila will be going through,' said Kelvin.

Marcus spent the rest of the meeting staring out of the window at the City. Behind every window, on every floor of every glass tower, there would be people staring at screens wondering how their world would change. Kelvin had found his way.

Marcus was sitting alone in the Chilling Egg when Mason walked past.

'Hi Marcus, you look deep in thought?'

'Just thinking about the meeting this morning. All a bit brutal if you ask me.'

'Feeling bad about Tom and Grant?'

'Not really, they'll be fine. It's the twelve people in the team I feel sorry for. Shit timing all round.'

'I was next on the list, you know? Kelvin had me in his office yesterday. Told me that if Tyler hadn't gone, I would have. I'd better have a bloody good year, next year.'

Twelve months with the sword of Damocles hanging over his head, Mason's behaviour would become even more dysfunctional. It was time for some plain speaking.

'Mason, have you ever thought about playing with a straight bat for once and not being a conniving cock?'

Mason recoiled. Marcus was being more than direct.

'Is that what you think of me, Marcus? A conniving cock?'

'Pretty much. You're very talented, Mason. And enthusiastic. You don't need to behave like you do. Try showing a bit of integrity for once, it might pay off.'

He looked down at his laptop and Mason skulked off with his tail between his legs. Marcus had just broken one of the golden rules of being a partner. He had spoken the truth.

* * *

Gavin's cancelled visit had left a hole in Claire's day. Apart from Christmas and holidays, she couldn't remember a week when she hadn't seen him. The revelation about Biscuit II's pregnancy would have to wait. She collected the children and they walked to Tesco Express. Panic buying had emptied the shelves. Lester Primus was at the front of the store looking stressed. He looked up from tidying the depleted shelves of fruit and vegetables.

'Hi Claire, hi kids. How are we all?'

'Hi Mr Primus. Looks like I've come a bit too late today.'

'Tell me about it. People are stocking up on anything and everything because of the virus. We're having to limit people to two items. We can't fill the shelves quickly enough. I'm trying to keep some stuff back for my older customers. Is there anything specific you need? I've got a couple of bags for you in my office, just basics, but nothing reduced.'

The store manager went to his office and returned a couple of minutes later with a couple of carrier bags. He looked guilty.

'Just take what you need and give me the rest back. It will all go.'

She peered into the bags. There was enough to keep them going until the end of the week. She looked at him and smiled, and he returned the compliment.

'Thank you, Mr Primus. You're the kindest man in the world. You didn't have to do this.'

She wanted to kiss him. He reached into his trouser pocket and produced a packet of Starburst and gave one each to the children.

'I hope it helps. It's only basic stuff. Come back later in the week. I'll put some toilet roll aside for you, it's like gold dust at the moment!'

Claire pushed her trolley around the aisles and found enough to supplement Lester Primus's jamboree bag of kindness.

* * *

Marcus walked into the kitchen at Twin Gates and put the copy of the *Evening Standard* on the island.

'Have you seen this?'

He turned the newspaper to face his wife who was washing some leeks in the sink.

VIRUS 'SET TO HIT MANY THOUSANDS' IN UK CRISIS

It was a big shift in the rhetoric. The deputy chief medical officer was bracing the country for a dramatic change in public perception. It was a slap around the face of the nation, a big wake up call. Alice dried her hands and came to look.

'Yes, the *Daily Mail* said pretty much the same thing. It's starting to get bad, although nothing as bad as Italy. They've had thousands of deaths.'

'It will be the same here, I'm certain of it. We're just a few weeks behind them.'

'What have they said at work?'

'Bugger all apart from being told to wash our hands more. By the way, Kelvin fired Tom Irons and Grant Bremner-Walker yesterday. Twelve members of staff are going as well.'

The names meant little to her. They were simply characters in the daily drama of Marcus's life at The Firm.

'Why did he fire them?'

'Bad year, didn't sell enough and someone has to carry the can for failure. It was never going to be Kelvin, he doesn't carry cans. I wish I was on the list, pushed instead of jumping. Except I haven't got the balls to jump. What's for dinner tonight?'

'Leek, spinach and Quorn bake with sweet potato topping, with vegan cheese. One of Libby's recipes from *Women's Health*.'

'Sounds delicious. I'll go and get changed.'

It was a poor substitute for one of Gavin's culinary specials but he wasn't in the mood to be picky. His mind was on other things.

Marcus left the house early on Thursday morning and drove to the flat. The 'Living Our Values' conference wasn't starting until 9.30 and he had time to drop his bags and take a taxi to the Mandarin Oriental hotel in Knightsbridge. The previous passenger had left a copy of *Metro* on the back seat and he picked it up.

PM: 'I DID NOT GO NEAR HER'

A health minister, Nadine Dorries, had tested positive for coronavirus and the prime minister, who had attended the same event, was refusing to take a test, as he hadn't been within two metres of her.

Boris must be a bit off his game, thought Marcus.

The newspaper had devoted six pages, each one emblazoned with the red 'Coronavirus Crisis' logo, to report how the country was tackling the virus. It was now officially a pandemic, no longer a mere outbreak or an epidemic. The Chancellor of the Exchequer had announced a £30 billion support package in Parliament.

Paying for this little lot is going to make The Deficit seem like pocket change, thought Marcus.

As the taxi turned in to Hyde Park, Marcus checked The Sequence. Jenny Moffatt had sent an email with a ten-point communications plan to improve team morale. Pizza Fridays were being stepped up to every two weeks. He opened Stockwatch. The markets had been open for little more than an hour and Black Monday was turning into Black Thursday. The FTSE 100 was plummeting again, almost 400 points down already. He closed the app and stared out of the window into Hyde Park. Crocuses and daffodils were flowering. Early signs of spring, but it felt like the darkest days of winter.

His taxi driver dropped him outside Harvey Nichols opposite the grand façade of the hotel. He crossed Knightsbridge and walked up the steps where he was greeted by a liveried doorman in a red morning coat and black top hat with gold braid. It was the sort of job that would have suited Eric. The lobby was impressive, polished marble floors and walls, high ornate ceilings and expensive chandeliers. He was directed to one of the hotel's banqueting rooms by one of the many smartly uniformed members of staff. When he arrived, most of his colleagues were clustered in small groups outside the main meeting room having refreshments.

He had been to many similar events and knew what to expect: 85% men, 90% over forty, 40% clinically obese and almost exclusively white. And they weren't having mere 'refreshments'. Smoked salmon kedgeree, eggs Benedict and waffles with caramelised bananas didn't fall into that category. A team of four baristas were making coffee, and Marcus collected a double macchiato and a croissant and joined a group standing at one of the high tables. Simon Loder was wiping a blob of hollandaise from his tie with a linen napkin. All the talk was of falling partner units.

'We were planning on having our basement extended underground into the garden to accommodate a swimming pool, cinema and gym. We had to fight bloody hard to get planning permission from Westminster Council but it looks like that might have to go on hold for a year,' said one partner.

Multiple heads nodded in sympathy.

'I know,' said another. 'I had to call Aston Martin and delay my order for the new DB11. Dropping down the queue and losing my place is a real pain. I'll have to keep the Maserati for now.'

It wasn't the smell of the kedgeree or a stock market that was falling into oblivion that was making Marcus feel queasy.

These people are living in a parallel universe, he thought to himself.

At 9.55, a member of the events team walked around, ringing a little bell to signal an end to refreshments and the hand-wringing over imminent poverty. Partners gathered around the seating plan and took their seats in the main auditorium which had been set out in 'cabaret style'. Twenty-five tables of ten. With everyone seated, the lights dimmed and the audience hushed. Marcus wondered if Shirley Bassey was going to come out from behind a curtain in a sequinned dress and an ostrich feather bower and belt out 'Big Spender'. He was close. It was another corporate anthem.

'You're simply the best ... Better than all the rest ... Better than anyone ... Anyone I've ever met.'

Marcus thought Tina Turner had probably made millions in royalties from having her signature tune played at similar corporate events. It probably kept her in wigs. A single spotlight shone on the stage and The Firm's CEO and Senior Partner, David Ellington, walked on. He was nicknamed 'The Duke', and he absolutely loved it. Arms aloft and waving to his disciples, he stood at the front of the stage, bathing in the applause and the spotlight, pleading for it to stop. Just not that quickly.

'Partners! Partners! Please!' he begged.

The clapping died down and the Duke continued.

'Welcome to the Mandarin Oriental and the first of our "Living Our Values" presentations. As we have read and witnessed with our own eyes, our world is going through tough and challenging times. We face uncertainty at every turn. That's why now, in these difficult moments, we need solid foundations, pillars of strength we can lean on. Our Values. And that is what today is all about, introducing you to our new values.'

Marcus wondered if the Duke had let Gerard and the CIClets loose on his showpiece event? Perhaps a giant Wall of Values was going to appear from behind a curtain.

He was relieved to find the Duke had opted for plain old PowerPoint. He flipped up the opening slide and presented the agenda for the day. Another spotlight illuminated the right of the stage to reveal his co-presenters: six, male partners sitting on high bar stools like backing singers, each one with a headset and lapel microphone. Four of them were wearing brown shoes and no ties, trying to show informality. One of them was Kelvin McBride who was chewing on a Nicorette. He was clearly nervous alongside the other top bods.

The first session was devoted to explaining The Firm's new Values. Each of the partners on the stage would explain what the Values meant to them personally. The Duke said it would be 'deep, sincere, touching and meaningful'.

After a break for coffee, there would be a Q&A session until lunch. In the afternoon, there would be a series of breakout sessions, carefully timed around afternoon tea. Drinks and dinner would be at 7.30 for 'networking and idea sharing'.

For the next hour, each partner on the stage presented one of the six new Values, along with how they were going to 'live and breathe them in everything they said and did'. Marcus read down the list.

Endlessly pursuing a Better World
Always showing we Care
Placing no boundaries on The Impossible
Integrity is in our Bloodstream
Embracing Differences between us
Humility above Pride

Apart from the sloppy use of capitals, Marcus wondered if the Values had been devised using the same process as the draw for the World Cup? One random word from Pool 1, one from Pool 2 and, hey presto, a new Value. They were meaningless twaddle. The Duke closed the session and the lights went up as Queen's 'We Are the Champions' blasted out of the PA.

Nothing like a bit of humility to bring the session to a close, thought Marcus.

The kedgeree had been cleared away and replaced with a selection of freshly baked pastries and biscuits. The partners were very excited. Their new Values were like a new toy. That is, until a newer toy came along; then they would be discarded in a cupboard along with all the other old toys. Kelvin was mingling, still wearing his headset. He had presented the value *'Always showing we Care'*, and he approached Marcus.

'Hi Marcus. What did you think of the first session? Good?'

Kelvin was answering his own question. Marcus didn't feel it was the time to burst his party balloon.

'Yes, it was great, Kelvin. Well done you. Very sincere and touching, I could tell it came straight from the heart.'

'Thanks Marcus. That means a lot coming from you.'

'Meaning what?'

'That you can be very cynical about these things. Not taking them seriously. The Firm's leadership has put a lot of thought into our Values. It's up to us to live them now, to lead by example.'

'Yes, I can see that.'

Like a bee in a rose garden, Kelvin buzzed off to network and mingle, receiving more pats on the back, the pollen of praise. Marcus checked Stockwatch. Down by another 200 points. The partners were stuffing their faces with palmiers and madeleines while the world outside was going into meltdown. He felt very uneasy.

The bell rang for the audience to reassemble and the partners took their seats for a ninety-minute Q&A session. Two people from the events team circulated the room with microphones, as partners raised their hands as if they were in an opulent classroom. The onstage team strolled around clarifying definitions, explaining behaviours and putting accountability into the hands of the partners. Nobody challenged anything because nothing needed to change. The rules of the game would stay the same.

It was getting close to lunch as Marcus checked Stockwatch again. It had fallen another 100 points. He started to shift in his seat as the Duke gave his personal slant on how integrity was in his bloodstream. It came across with the sincerity of a TV evangelist asking for donations for a new roof on the church. Marcus's arm shot up in the air. One of the events team rushed to his table and handed him the microphone. He stood up.

'David. Thank you for this morning. Very insightful. I have a question about always showing we care.'

The Duke nodded sincerely.

'Of course, absolutely fundamental. Core to our business. What's your question, Marcus?'

The Duke knew Marcus by name, but that was all. He didn't know who he was or what he did. He didn't care much either. All he knew was that he made money for The Firm.

'As you said in your opening speech, we are indeed living in tough and challenging times. So challenging that earlier this week our team made twelve people and two partners redundant in the name of realigning our cost base. I don't know how much events like today are costing, but that money could probably have saved the jobs and careers of some of those people. How does that align with a value of "always showing we care"?'

Two hundred glasses of Voss sparkling water hit the tables simultaneously. The noise was silently deafening. The Duke looked to his onstage team for help. When it came to hecklers, he was no Jimmy Carr. Marcus's question was like a grenade with the pin pulled out, and it was about to explode in somebody's hand.

'Kelvin, I think you were leading on "Caring"? Do you want to take this one?' said the Duke, lobbing him the grenade.

Kelvin stood up from his stool and squinted into the spotlight.

'Good question, Marcus. As you know very well, all organisations have to take tough decisions to protect their business. The Firm is no different. Of course, we're sad to let people go, but sometimes you have to make the big calls. It doesn't mean we don't care.'

Kelvin sat down but Marcus remained standing with the microphone in his hand.

'Can I ask how many of these events we are holding?'

'Five,' said the Duke, proudly. 'But this is the only one at this hotel. The others are at Claridge's.'

Marcus handed the microphone back, sat down and looked at his notepad. He had scrawled 'Wankers!' on it. He tore it off, crumpled it up and stuffed it in his trouser pocket.

'Okay everyone, let's break for lunch. Back in here at two,' said the Duke.

David Bowie's 'Heroes' ushered the partners out of the room. Outside the meeting room, the hotel's banqueting team had set out a dim sum lunch, roast suckling pig and a Maine lobster salad. Marcus was queuing with Simon Loder when Kelvin grabbed him by the elbow.

'Marcus, can I have a quick word?'

They walked into an adjoining corridor. Kelvin was chewing furiously on a Nicorette, a little river of saliva was running down his chin. He was red in the face.

'What the fuck did you think you were doing in there? Asking that question? If you had a problem with our decision, we should have discussed it offline. Not in front of the Duke and 250 other fucking partners!'

Marcus wiped a little ball of spit from his cheek.

'I thought it was a valid question, Kelvin. You should take it as a compliment. An early example of me living our values. Honesty and integrity and all that.'

'Don't be a smart cunt with me, Marcus. You did that deliberately to humiliate me, David and the leadership. Of course we care … up to a point.'

'Really? You don't think you've humiliated yourselves? Coming up with another load of bollocks that nobody in that room truly believes in. It's garbage and you know it. And how much money have we spunked on this event? A hundred and fifty grand? Two hundred grand? The sad thing is, you don't realise what a bunch of pricks you look. Always doing it for yourselves.'

Kelvin shook his head and looked at him.

'Well, if you really think that, maybe there's not much point in you being here, is there?'

Marcus wasn't sure what he meant. Was he firing him or excusing him from an afternoon of more hypocrisy? He didn't stick around to qualify the question.

'Couldn't agree with you more! Hope it goes well. Probably another load of bollocks.'

Marcus turned away, walked back into the dining area, picked up a pork and prawn dumpling from the buffet and headed for the cloakroom. Fortunately, his raincoat hadn't been stolen and he walked through the lobby and into the fresh air of Knightsbridge.

It was Thursday, 12 March 2020.

Chapter 21

QUID PRO QUO, DR LECTER

The cool breeze rejuvenated him after the suffocating air of back-slapping and arse-kissing. He turned in to Hyde Park where the wind was whipping across the Serpentine. He walked slowly around the lake, lost in his thoughts. He had pushed the detonator button with both hands. He wanted to call Alice but she was probably having coffee with Theresa, listening to her latest plan to make Mike homeless and strip him of his millions.

He continued walking into Kensington Gardens and around the pond, once, twice, three times. The geese and ducks were flocking around an old woman who was feeding them stale bread.

It was a short walk, across Bayswater Road and down Queensway, but he didn't want to go home. There would be nobody to talk to and he was feeling lonely. It would soon be rush hour and he couldn't face driving back to Weybridge. He carried on walking along the Bayswater Road until he reached Notting Hill Gate. He was starting to feel hungry, so he went into Caffè Nero and ordered a large cappuccino. There wasn't much left on the shelves. His roasted mushroom and mascarpone tostati melt was a poor substitute for roast suckling pig and Maine lobster.

He checked The Sequence again. It was definitely worse than Black Monday. His retirement plans were in tatters and he had just signed his death warrant. He crossed Notting Hill Gate and walked along Ladbroke Grove until he reached Westbourne Grove. Things were starting to look familiar. Ahead of him, he recognised the flyover for the Westway, busy with rush hour traffic. He carried on walking until he reached the Underground station. He was thinking about the events of the day. If they had brought an end to his career, he didn't want to spend the evening alone staring at Beirut. He needed company.

He remembered her flat was a few roads beyond the Westway, and the council estate had stood out like a sore thumb. It wasn't hard to find Kensal Mansions but finding her flat was more difficult.

Was it on the second or the third floor? he asked himself.

He tried to remember how many flights of stairs he and Gavin had climbed that night. At the time, he had been preoccupied with not dropping the tarte tatin. He knocked on a few doors and was viewed suspiciously by the residents, who clearly thought he was a bailiff, denying any knowledge of Claire or her children. He and Alice knew everyone in their road from Neighbourhood Watch meetings. In Kensal Mansions, people didn't seem to know who lived next door. Eventually, he reached No. 9, where the smells of spices were wafting out of the window. He rang the doorbell. Mrs Hassan opened the door wearing a cream and turquoise shalwar kameez.

'Hello. I'm sorry to disturb you but I'm looking for Claire's flat. She has two small children, Kyle and Alexa? Kyle likes Buzz Lightyear?' He tried to describe Claire's height with a vague flapping of his hand. The Buzz Lightyear information was superfluous.

'No. 11, two doors down,' said Mrs Hassan, pointing along the balcony.

'Thank you. Very helpful.'

She closed the door and Marcus walked along the balcony. It was 5.30 in the evening and the lights in the flat were on. He rang the doorbell and from inside he could hear children's excited voices.

The Governess had just destroyed the ambitions of Graham, a bus driver from Grimsby. His over-confidence in going for the bigger prize had been his undoing and she had done him up like a kipper. His dream trip to Florida remained a dream.

'There was no way, no way, he was going to beat her,' said Mr Mahoney. 'She's really hot tonight.'

The children snuggled into his musty, maroon cardigan, the smell of old man. Claire was flicking through *Excel for Dummies*.

'The lemon drizzle cake is very good, Mr Mahoney,' she said, trying not to spit crumbs everywhere. 'Just the right amount of icing.'

There was a knock at the door and the children jumped up. It was too early for Judith, and Ian never knocked. The Kensal Warrior would be joining forces with someone from Alabama, wiping out Taliban insurgents. It might be Mrs Hassan with some samosas? Claire got up and walked to the door. The silhouette suggested it was someone tall. Gavin? Certainly not Mrs Hassan. She opened the door.

'Hi Claire. I hope you don't mind me calling round like this. Have I caught you at a bad time?'

She was lost for words. Marcus was the last person she expected. She stuttered and gave a gabbled answer that he didn't understand.

'I was watching *The Chase* with Mr Mahoney. We do it every evening, except weekends, because that's when he bakes.'

They stared at each other, as if they had never met. Strangers in the night. He looked different in a suit from how he'd looked in a tuxedo. Stiffer, more professional.

'So, is that a yes or a no then?'

'Sorry, of course. Come in, come in. It's raining.'

She beckoned him in. Kyle and Alexa had come to see who was at the door. They recognised him and Claire filled in the gaps.

'Kids, you remember Marcus don't you? He's Gavin's friend, he read you a story?'

She hung his wet raincoat over the back of the kitchen door.

'Come through to the East Wing. I'll introduce you to Mr Mahoney. He's the caretaker and my friend. He brings us cake, it's lemon drizzle today.'

Marcus walked into the living room where Mr Mahoney was already standing. He was struck by the size of the man and extended his hand.

'Hello. I'm Marcus. Marcus Barlow. Good to meet you.'

'Nice to meet you. Phelan Mahoney.'

The caretaker grasped Marcus's soft and manicured hand in his calloused grip and shook it firmly. Claire stared at both men. They had known each other seconds and were already on first-name terms. It had taken her eighteen months to reach that level of informality.

'Would you like a cup of tea and a slice of Mr Mahoney's cake? It's one of his best,' she said.

'That would be fantastic, thank you.'

Mr Mahoney turned to the new arrival and pointed at the television.

'Are you a fan of *The Chase*, Marcus?'

'I can't say that I am, Phelan. I don't usually get to watch TV at this time. If I do, I'm probably more of a *Pointless* man.'

'A greatly inferior quiz in my opinion,' said Mr Mahoney. 'The big fella with the glasses knows a thing or two but he isn't in the same league as The Governess or The Beast.'

Marcus thought they sounded like names from a wrestling contest. He was about to ask a question, when Claire returned with a mug of tea and a piece of cake and put them on the coffee table. Twenty years of working at The Firm had taught Marcus how to read the mood of the room. It was clear the only people allowed to speak were Bradley, the contestant and The Governess, with occasional exclamations from Mr Mahoney. He looked at Claire and smiled, took a bite of cake and stared at the television. She was right, the cake was delicious. A few miles away, the 'Living Our Values' conference would have ended and his colleagues would be in the bar drinking vintage champagne. He didn't regret not being there.

As the credits started to roll, Mr Mahoney got up.

'Well, I must be going. Nice to meet you Marcus and hope we meet again. *Eggheads* is on BBC2 next and that's worth watching too.'

Marcus stood up and shook Mr Mahoney's hand. 'Nice to meet you too, Phelan.'

The caretaker said goodnight and Claire hugged him at the front door.

'Don't worry. He's just a friend of a friend. He is nice though.'

'Yes, he's very well dressed. See you tomorrow.'

Claire returned to the living room, where Alexa was showing Marcus how to draw mice.

'So, to what do I owe the honour of this visit?' she said.

'I'm really sorry to turn up like this. I've had one of the shittiest days in living memory. Gavin's in Scotland and I couldn't face driving home. I didn't want to be on my own. I've been walking around for hours and sort of ended up here? I'm sorry.'

'No need to apologise. I know the feeling. You can have a Xanax if you're feeling anxious!'

'What's a Xanax?'

'Prescription medication for anxiety, but only for serious nutters like me.'

Marcus laughed.

'I'm going to make dinner. You're welcome to stay and you can tell me what made it one of the shittiest days in living memory!'

'Are you sure? I didn't come here to get fed. I just wanted to talk to someone and didn't want to be in the flat on my own.'

'It's only sausage casserole with mash. There's enough for four.'

'Will you read us a story?' said Alexa, looking up from her drawing.

'"Dinosaur School" has become a bit of a hit!' said Claire.

'Doesn't look like I've got much choice, does it?'

They left the children playing in the living room and went to the kitchen.

'What can I do to help?' said Marcus

Claire reached into a cupboard and took out an onion, a few carrots and some potatoes. She placed them on the kitchen table with a peeler and a chopping board.

'You can peel and chop those. I think you should take off the Ferragamo tie and cufflinks. Probably get in the way.'

'How finely do you want these onions chopped?'

Claire cut a string of sausages and started to fry them. Marcus thought the smell was fantastic. It reminded him of Wednesday nights in Staines. It was always Wall's pork sausages on Wednesdays. He started to peel potatoes as Claire fried the onions.

'Come on then, what made today so bad you took your life in your hands and came to the darker side of Ladbroke Grove?'

'Actually, Ladbroke Grove is very nice. I walked from Notting Hill. Some very nice houses and probably very expensive ones too. Just a shame they come to an end halfway down. It all gets a bit grotty after that. Do you have an Oxo cube and some Worcester sauce? And why are you adding baked beans and sweetcorn?'

'Because it fills my children up and we don't have anything else. I probably have an Oxo cube somewhere. Is that why you came here, to criticise my cooking?'

'Add the Oxo cube and a few squirts of Worcester sauce, they will add more flavour. Beans and sweetcorn? Never seen that before, very odd. Do you have any fresh herbs?'

She burst out laughing. There was something very strange about the man sitting at her kitchen table in a pinstripe suit giving her tips on how to make a sausage casserole.

'I think I have some dried sage. Are you going to tell me what went wrong today or not?'

'Sorry, I was only trying to help.'

She put the casserole in the oven as Marcus told her about the events of the morning, the 'Living Our Values' debacle and his row with Kelvin.

'How much did you say they spent on the event?' she said, incredulously.

'Probably somewhere between two hundred thousand and two hundred and fifty thousand pounds. And there's four more to come.'

'Jesus Christ, Marcus. How do you justify spending that? A million quid for something nobody gives a shit about. That's just a joke.'

He shrugged.

'That's the way it works. One rule for partners and lots of rules for everyone else. People will sacrifice everything to join a club with only one rule.'

'So, do they all end up like you? Bitter, resentful and burnt out?'

Ouch! That one stung. He had never seen himself like that.

'Is that how you see me? Bitter and resentful?'

'Bit harsh, sorry. Can you really walk away from all that just because of one bad day? Seems hasty to me. I'm going to bath the kids. Keep an eye on the casserole and mash the potatoes for me?'

'Have you got a potato ricer?'

'What the heck is one of those?'

'Don't worry. I'll cope.'

She returned twenty minutes later with two freshly bathed children in pyjamas and dressing gowns, flushed little faces and damp hair. She served the casserole and Marcus spooned the mashed potato on to the plates.

'I'm afraid it's Ribena or tap water, I can't afford wine.'

Marcus laughed.

'Tap water's fine, thanks.'

At the Mandarin Oriental, 250 people were sitting down to a starter of smoked confit chicken with roast marrowbone and pickled walnuts, accompanied by bottles of 2013 Louis Jadot Domaine des Heritiers Les Demoiselles Chevalier-Montrachet Grand Cru. It would ease the pain of putting the new ski chalet in Whistler on hold for another year.

He loved the conversation around the kitchen table. The stories about their days, the silly giggles between brother and sister, the digs, pokes and nudges.

'Miss Takidis says we have to find homes for Biscuit's babies,' said Kyle.

Claire translated.

'Miss Mistakidis is Kyle's teacher. Biscuit is the class hamster who everyone thought was a boy but turned out to be female and had babies. It's a long story, I'll tell you more later.'

'Is this the hamster that Gavin had to find at short notice? The replacement for the dea—'

She shook her head vigorously and changed the subject.

'Dinner okay? Hope it's up to your usual standards.'

'Very tasty actually. The baked beans were a good addition. I'll remember that one.'

Claire started to clear away the plates. 'It's probably bedtime for you two. Go and brush your teeth. I think Marcus is going to read you a story?'

The children left the table and ran to the bathroom.

Five minutes later, Kyle and Alexa were sat up in Claire's bed waiting for him. Alexa handed him the book.

'Perhaps we'll read another story tonight, not "Dinosaur School"?' he said.

Alexa looked up and frowned at him. This was not the plan.

'How about "Norty Boy". It's about a very naughty hedgehog. Just like the one you have in your kitchen.'

Alexa frowned again. She was highly sceptical. By the time he had finished the story, his repertoire of voices had worked their magic. Claire came into the bedroom as he was closing the book.

'I think we should give Marcus a cuddle to say thank you?'

Kyle gave him a hug but Alexa went for the full-on smacker. It made him think of Olivia, and he felt slightly guilty.

'My pleasure. Sleep well both of you.'

Claire returned to the kitchen after putting the children to bed. Marcus had the Mr Muscle spray in his hand.

'That's all done. They said you were better at funny voices than me.' She looked at him. 'You and Gavin are very similar, always wiping!'

'Maybe that's what we have in common? A love of clean surfaces.'

'Have you heard from him?'

'No, I haven't. I didn't want to disturb him in Scotland. Have you?'

'No, but I wanted to strangle him after what happened with Biscuit II, the transgender hamster who turned out to be pregnant.'

'I thought it had been the perfect crime? At least, that's what Gavin told me?'

'It was, until Biscuit II had babies!'

Claire explained how their deception had been uncovered, and her subsequent confession and humiliation. Marcus roared with laughter.

'So he still doesn't know a thing?'

'Not a bloody clue. And apart from me, Kyle's teacher and Beverley, nobody else knows either. And now you do.'

'So you and Biscuit II are in the same situation?' said Marcus.

She wondered what he meant.

'How come?'

'Both single parent families, raising offspring without a dad.'

She looked at him and shook her head. He was extraordinary.

'You don't do empathy very well, do you, Marcus? Did you not think that comparing my circumstances to a hamster's might upset me?'

'I'm very sorry. I was being flippant. I didn't mean to be rude. Alice is always telling me that I open my mouth first and think later. I'm sorry if I offended you.'

She looked over the brim of her mug at the man who was looking like Kyle when she told him off. Her face creased into a smile.

'Got you worried, didn't I? Thought you'd upset me, did you?'

'Have I?'

'As if. Man up and let's go and sit in the living room.'

Marcus sat on the sofa and took his phone out of his pocket. There was a message from Alice.

Hi M. Hope 2dy was ok and not 2 pnful. Njoy the dnr. All gd here. Spk soon. Al.

Happy yellow faces. Sent just after six. He didn't reply. Like Beirut, the hole was getting deeper and he was still digging.

He started to relax, sitting in his socks, collar open and shirt sleeves rolled up. Claire was certainly better company than some boring arsehole bragging about his wine investments being held *en primeur* by Berry Bros. & Rudd.

'So what are you going to do? Do you think Kevin will fire you?'

'Kelvin, not Kevin. No, I think I'll probably survive his wrath but he'll get his own back one way or another. To be honest, I'm more worried about the crash in the stock market.' He started to rub his thighs.

'Can I ask you a question, Marcus?'

'Sure. Fire away.'

'Do you remember when you asked me how much I had to live on each week?'

'Yes, around £100 a week, if I remember?'

'Yes. Bit more now I have my part-time job. How much money do you need to live on?'

'I don't know. I couldn't even tell you how much money is in our bank account.'

'Then you're a very lucky man, aren't you? You're not even close to rock bottom. There were nights after Jack left, sitting here on my own, knackered, lonely, skint, staring at packets of tablets, thinking about killing myself.'

'So what stopped you?'

'No alcohol. I didn't want to commit suicide on Ribena.'

He laughed.

'Of course, it was the kids that stopped me. I couldn't see anyone else taking care of them in the way they deserve. My parents did a shit job with me and Jack walked away. Leaving the kids to them? I couldn't do that. What I'm trying to say, Marcus, is that money is the least of your worries.'

He took a sip of tea and stared down at the carpet. He felt embarrassed.

'I'm sorry, you're absolutely right. But, that's what The Firm does to you. Makes it all about the money.'

'And what does your wife say? She must know you pretty well, how long have you been together?'

'Nearly twenty-five years. She understands me as well as anyone. I don't want to let anyone down.'

'Isn't it letting them down even more to live a life where you aren't happy?'

Marcus looked across the room at Claire. She was curled in her chair, a blanket over her legs and her mug cupped in her hands. The warm light from the table lamp was casting a shadow across her pretty face. She was only seven years older than Olivia, but her struggle to survive had given her a wisdom that was way ahead of her years. Instead of having fun in a Shoreditch bar with friends, she was living in a small council flat in Ladbroke Grove giving advice to a fifty-five-year-old man. Knowing she was right made him feel worse.

'So how is your job going? Enjoying it?'

Claire held up her book, *Excel for Dummies*, and he laughed.

'So what do you use Excel for?'

'Lists of customers, suppliers, fabrics, invoices. Basic stuff I suppose. I'm the original Excel dummy!'

'Show me.'

Claire picked up her laptop and sat next to him on the sofa. She opened one of her files. He looked at it and pursed his lips.

'Mmmm…'

'It's not very good, is it?' she said defensively.

He took the laptop from her and started to move his fingers across the mousepad and keyboard. In minutes, he had inserted rows, merged columns, changed fonts, inserted formulas and coloured cells.

'There, that looks better,' he said, handing her the laptop back. 'Much more consistent.'

'Looks bloody amazing. How did you do that?'

'I've spent thirty years staring at spreadsheets, so I know what looks good and what doesn't. That's what I do, I make the ordinary look fantastic. Smoke and mirrors. It's easy when you know how.'

For the next thirty minutes, he taught her more than an evening reading *Excel for Dummies* would have done.

'Thank you so much,' she said, closing her laptop.

'Quid pro quo, Dr Lecter,' he said.

In the background, the *BBC News at Ten* came on. Claire reached for the remote and turned up the volume. The prime minister entered a wood-panelled room, flanked by two men Marcus didn't recognise. They were obviously friends of Boris because he called them by their first names, Chris and Patrick. Boris had come from chairing a meeting of the COBRA Committee.

'It's always serious when they have a COBRA meeting,' said Marcus.

Boris levelled with the British people.

'More families are going to lose loved ones before their time,' he said.

The first element of the Government's strategy to contain the virus had failed. It was moving into the next phase, delaying its spread.

'At all stages, we have been guided by *The Science*,' said Boris, looking across nervously at Chris and Patrick.

'What does that mean?' said Claire, looking at Marcus.

'It means he hasn't got a bloody clue what's going on. That's why they are there. To tell him what's going on and what to do next.'

Boris handed over to The Science and Chris and Patrick flashed up a series of graphs. They needed to 'flatten the sombrero' and protect the NHS. The Science said Britain was four weeks behind Italy. The Government had responded swiftly and decisively, advising the over-seventies to avoid going on cruises, and telling everyone to keep washing their hands.

'What do you think is going to happen next?' said Claire when the news had ended.

'If we're four weeks behind Italy, we should start locking things down now. It will be the same catastrophe here unless we do something quickly. Boris is burying his head in the sand if he thinks it won't take off here in the same way. In the end, it will come down to a trade-off between saving lives and making sure the economy doesn't go through the floor.'

'If they shut the schools and lock us down, I don't know what I'll do. Having two kids cooped up in here will drive us all mental.'

'Would you go and stay with your parents?'

'Not a chance in hell. I'd rather be cooped up here than stuck in a house with my dad. He's probably already banned my mum from ordering Chinese takeaways. What about you?'

'We'll have to keep going into the office. We'll have a bank of ventilators complete with a row of laptops so any staff with the virus can still check their emails!'

He stood up and picked up his jacket from the back of the sofa.

'I should be going. I've abused your hospitality enough already.' He took a business card out of his wallet and gave it to her. 'Here you go, if you need to contact me, my numbers are on here. Don't feel you're on your own. If you need help, don't be shy to call. Being here tonight got me out of a place I didn't want to be?'

'The Mandarin Oriental?' she said.

'Well, that too but you know what I meant.'

'Aww, is that Marcus Barlow, Partner, being a bit sensitive?' she said, looking down at his business card.

'Might be.'

'What the fuck is "Doing It With You" meant to mean?' she said.

'Don't ask.'

He walked down the hall, put on his shoes and raincoat and opened the front door. He turned to face her.

'Thanks for putting up with my over-emotional ramblings. I hope I didn't spoil your evening?'

'Don't be daft. You enhanced my sausage casserole and improved my Excel skills. Quid pro quo, Dr Lecter.'

He leaned forward and kissed her on the cheek.

'Thanks again, Claire.'

She put his business card on the window ledge in the kitchen and stared at it again. *'Marcus Barlow, Partner.'* She smiled.

It was Thursday, 12 March 2020.

Chapter 22

CLOSING THE STABLE DOOR ...

He left the flat and drove along the M3. He was thinking about the previous evening with Claire. He was feeling guilty and turned the music off.

He pulled on to the drive at Twin Gates. Alice was out and he had the house to himself. He put his washing in the laundry basket and hung up his suits. Her dressing gown was left on the bed. He picked it up and smelled it. He went downstairs to the kitchen. The *Daily Mail* was folded on the island.

MANY LOVED ONES WILL DIE

Boris's words to the nation from the night before. The paper devoted thirteen pages to, '*Corona: What you and your family need to know now*'. He made a coffee and sat down to read what he needed to know now. The 596 confirmed cases were a drop in the ocean compared to the 10,000 that The Science estimated were already circulating in the population. The horse hadn't bolted, it was ten miles down the road and almost out of sight. The editor of *The Lancet* put things into perspective.

The UK is on the edge of an avoidable calamity.

He looked out into the garden. It was hard to believe that its laurel-lined borders could be breached. He checked WhatsApp. Messages from Gavin and James.

Hi M. Hope you are well. Things here not so good. Mum struggling. Home at the weekend but may have to come back. Dinner next week? G.

Hi Dad. Things getting very weird here at uni. Lectures cancelled. Catch up over the weekend?

He replied to Gavin.

Sorry to hear your mum isn't better. Yes to dinner. See you soon and safe travels. M.

Gavin already had enough on his plate. Telling him about his spontaneous visit to Kensal Mansions could wait. He heard the front door open and Alice called out.

'Marcus, could you give me a hand with the shopping?'

She was unloading bags from the back of the X5 and dumping them in the hall.

'Hi, Al,' he said as he kissed her and picked up some bags.

'Hi Marcus. Didn't expect you home before me? Everything okay?'

'Yes fine. It's good to see you.'

Some multi-coloured bags from Aldi stood out against the green ones from The Temple.

'I'm surprised they let you in,' he said, pointing to the offending bags. 'Did people shun you like a leper?'

'No, of course they didn't, Marcus. Stop being a pathetic snob and help me.'

They carried fifteen bags in to the kitchen.

'Did you empty The Temple on your own?'

'I couldn't get an Ocado delivery for three weeks and the Organic Delivery Company is the same. Rachel Hepworth's mum is giving Libby a lift home from hockey so I thought I'd do a big shop before we all starve.'

Karen Hepworth was Alice's tennis partner. She was also partial to drinking during the day.

Let's hope she doesn't get breathalysed at the school gates, he thought.

He emptied the bags while Alice put things away.

'So, how was your conference yesterday? Feeling pumped up and motivated by your new Values?'

'Yes, all those things and more. Ready to live and breathe them for another year.'

Alice was stacking tins of chickpeas and borlotti beans. It wasn't the time for multiple confessions. They would have to wait.

'How have you been? How's the tennis going?'

'Karen and I are through to the final of the over-fifties ladies' doubles. It's next Wednesday.'

'That's great, Al. Well done. I hope you win.'

'Do you have any plans for the weekend, Marcus?'

'Bit more work on Project Garage. The apprentice is coming over to pick up my dad's old tools tomorrow. How about going out for dinner?'

'Do you think it's safe? Have you read the paper? Even I'm starting to get worried now.'

It was the first time she had shown any concern about the pandemic. He resisted the temptation to say, 'I told you so.'

'Maybe we should give the meal a miss then? Did you watch Boris's press conference?'

'Yes, Libby and I watched it together. Do you think lockdown is coming?'

'It's inevitable. Ten thousand estimated cases in the UK already. People on the Underground are wearing masks now.'

'What are they saying at The Firm?'

'Bugger all.'

A car drew up. Olivia got out and waved goodbye to Rachel and her mum. The front door opened and she came into the hall like a Sherpa, school bags, sports kit, hockey stick, saxophone. She dropped her things and came into the kitchen.

'Hi Mum, hi Dad.' She kissed Alice and hugged Marcus, she was still flushed and sweaty from her match. 'How are you, Dad? How's Gerard?'

Gerard Cornelius fascinated his daughter. He had become a technicolour cult figure in a world of grey and blue suits.

'I haven't seen him for a while but I'll pass on your regards when I do. Did you win?'

'Yes, 3–1. I scored twice. I'm going for a shower. I feel pretty sticky downstairs.'

'Lovely. Thanks for that,' said Marcus.

Marcus helped Alice to prepare dinner, butternut squash curry with cauliflower rice. He considered suggesting baked beans and sweetcorn as the random ingredients but Alice had already done that herself. Pomegranate seeds.

He left her blitzing a cauliflower into grains. The lights in Olivia's room were on and he knocked on the door.

'Come in.' She was lying on the bed in her pyjamas, swiping through Instagram and listening to Chris Brown. 'Hi Dad. What's up?'

'Nothing sweetie. Just wondered, do you still have your old phone or did you give it away?'

They had bought her a new iPhone 11 for Christmas to replace her Samsung, which was now obsolete being two years old.

'No, I've still got it. It's in in my desk. Why?'

'Would you mind if I had it? My friend at the flat in London, Gavin, the social worker, knows someone who doesn't earn a lot of money and has a crappy old Nokia. Would you mind if I gave it to Gavin, so he could give it to her?'

'Sure, I don't mind at all. Let me check first to make sure it hasn't got anything incriminating on it.'

'Incriminating, like what?'

'Pictures of my boobs, my fanny. Normal stuff I send to boys.'

Olivia's school had sent a letter to parents warning about the dangers of cyberbullying and photo shaming, after a student had sent intimate pictures of her private parts to a boy which had then gone viral across Surrey.

Marcus had asked Alice at the time, 'Would you have liked it if I'd sent you pictures of my penis when we started dating?'

'Not in the slightest, Marcus,' she had responded, 'I would have dumped you immediately.'

He was shocked by his daughter's admission.

'Do you really send pictures like that to boys? Or girls?'

'Don't be ridiculous, Dad. Of course I don't, I was joking. Just old texts, phone numbers and stuff on it. I'll go through it.'

'Thanks a lot, Libby. See you downstairs.'

After dinner, Alice was reading everything she needed to know now about the virus in the *Daily Mail*. *Sport Relief 2020* was on television, the biennial charity-fest for highly paid sports stars and comedians to goof around and raise money for good causes. Marcus didn't recognise any of the presenters apart from the anchor-man, Gary Lineker.

'I see Gary's still got that horrible beard,' said Marcus enviously. 'It's more like grey bum-fluff. He looked much better without it.'

Alice looked up from her newspaper.

'I think he looks rather distinguished. He's a very attractive man for his age. He's almost sixty, you know? I think he still looks pretty horny. I'd do him for sure.'

Marcus was four years younger than Gary but felt four years older. Alice never said he looked horny. 'Nondescript' was the word she had used. Gary put on his serious face and looked to camera, ready to pull the nation's heartstrings.

'Now, let's not forget what all of this is for,' said Gary.

'I'm going to make a cup of tea. These bits make me vomit,' said Marcus. 'Do you want one?'

He returned in time for the *BBC News at Ten*, where the story of the day was the Premier League's decision to suspend all fixtures until April.

'Good news for James,' said Marcus.

'Really? Why's that?' said Alice.

'He won't be able to spend all weekend in the pub watching football. Might improve his chances of getting a decent degree.'

Gary didn't return for the second half. He'd done his job, played well, looked horny and set the team on the way to a new record total. He was substituted at half-time by a small, camp man who looked like an egg in a suit. Alice didn't think he was horny and decided it was time for bed.

Marcus was in the garage when Steven, the young apprentice, arrived with his father. He was wearing a navy-blue polo shirt and had tattoos on both arms. His left ear was pierced several times. He picked up one of the wood planes in the box and caressed it like it was a piece of antique porcelain.

'Beautiful tools, Mr Barlow. Your dad looked after them very well. You can't get tools like these anymore. Are you sure you don't want anything for them?' Steven ran his fingers along the blade of a wood chisel, feeling the sharpness of its edge.

'No, I'm glad you'll put them to good use. I can just about wire a plug. I was always a source of disappointment to my dad!'

Steven's father looked at the outside of the house and the cars parked on the drive.

'Doesn't look as if you've done too badly for yourself,' he said.

'No, I suppose not.'

He helped Steven and his father load the boxes of tools into the back of their van. On the top of one of the boxes was a saw. The varnish on the handle had been rubbed away by the sweat from his father's hands. His initials, 'SB', were engraved on it. Marcus picked it up.

'Would you mind if I kept this? I'll never use it, just sentimental value.'

'Please, keep it. We use power saws now,' said Steven.

Marcus sat down in his mother's armchair and decided to call James. It took a few rings for him to answer. Marcus could hear a lot of noise in the background.

'Hi James, it's Dad. Where are you?'

'Hi Dad. I'm in the pub with some mates.'

'What are you doing there? You can't be watching football, it's all been cancelled.'

'Netball. Sky Sports are showing netball. There are some pretty fit women on the court.'

Marcus laughed. The Premier League's loss had been netball's gain. He admired his son's dedication. Not even a pandemic seemed to blow him off course.

'So, what's happening with the lectures?'

'They're saying if we go into lockdown, everything will be shut down and lectures and tutorials will be done online. Some people have gone home already.'

'What are you going to do? Stay in Manchester or come home?'

'Dunno yet. I'll see what everyone else wants to do. I don't fancy being locked down in Rusholme on my own. Being looked after by Mum seems more appealing.'

'Probably a lot safer too. That George Foreman grill is a breeding ground for germs.'

'I'll decide over the weekend and give Mum a call.'

'Remember you'll be returning to Veganopolis. No lamb chops or steaks here anymore. Factor that in too. How's the course going?'

'It's okay. I'm a bit up against it but I am doing *some* work now.'

He didn't like James's emphasis on the word 'some'.

'I'll let your mother know you might be coming home, but you should give her a call. You know she hates surprises.'

'Sure, will do. Everything all right with you, Dad?'

'Yes, I'm fine. Enjoy the netball.'

He wasn't fine but interrupting his son's Saturday afternoon letching wasn't going to change that.

It was the opening words to *The Andrew Marr Show* which set the tone for Marcus's Sunday morning.

'This is going to change how we behave on the street and to one another, certainly for the rest of this year and maybe for years to come,' said Andrew.

Marcus was reading the business section of the *Sunday Times*. He felt worse with every article. He stopped eating his porridge and stared out of the kitchen window.

'Are you all right, Marcus?' said Alice. 'You're deep in thought?'

'Have you spoken to James?'

'Not since last week. Have you spoken with him? Is he okay?'

'I spoke to him yesterday. University may be closing because of the virus. He's thinking of coming back home.'

'I'd be much happier with him here and not in that dreadful house.'

'He said he'll call you and let you know. Do you fancy going for a walk later? I can't face another day in the garage.'

'Sure. Let's go after lunch.'

Marcus was walking past Olivia's room when she called out and came to the door.

'Here you go, Dad,' she said, handing him her old phone. 'All wiped clean, no pictures of my nipples.'

'Thanks a lot sweetie.'

'Hope Gavin's friend gets some use out of it.'

The weather was warm as Marcus and Alice left the house and turned on to the footpath leading to the farmland backing on to their garden. They linked arms as they walked together. In their matching Le Chameau boots, they looked like an advert for a Saga holiday catalogue.

'So, tell me, what's on your mind, Marcus? You never ask me to go for a walk unless there's a problem. Come on, spit it out.'

The things on his mind were like a giant fur ball in the back of his throat.

'Actually, there are three things I would like to discuss today,' he said, formally. 'Item one …'

She stared at him blankly and shook her head. 'Marcus, I'm your wife not a bloody agenda. Can't we talk like two normal people?'

'Sorry, force of habit. Work first then. Something pretty bad happened last Thursday.'

He gave her a truncated version of the events at the 'Living Our Values' conference and his bust-up with Kelvin. He omitted the bit where he left and turned up at Claire's flat. Alice shook her head.

'Marcus, you can't keep having fights with everyone. Especially Kelvin. What made you say that stuff?'

'It was the fucking hypocrisy. Kelvin and David Ellington standing on a stage saying they cared, straight after two partners had been fired and twelve people in the team made redundant. And then stuffing their faces on lobster and champagne. It made me feel sick.'

'But we both know how The Firm works, Marcus. It's never going to change. If it's making you so unhappy, just leave.'

'It's not that simple, Al. Which brings me to my second point. Did you see what happened to the stock market last week, the biggest fall since 2007? Our investments have been hammered, I can't just leave now!'

Alice remained calm.

'Of course I read it, Marcus. Speak to Stuart and see what he says. We live in a £3 million house with no mortgage, you have that flat in London plus our investments. We're hardly on the streets, are we? But I don't think this little outburst is about money, is it?'

'Oh, really? Tell me Dr Freud, what is it about?'

Alice raised her eyebrows and sighed.

'Don't be childish and spiteful. It's blindingly obvious to me.'

'What is?'

Alice was smart enough to see through his bluster and cut to the chase.

'You're shit scared of a life outside The Firm. Could you survive without your life-support machine? Well, millions of people do, every single day.'

He turned to face her.

'I'm sorry and you're absolutely right. This has been coming for a while, but with the uncertainty over Covid, maybe now isn't the time to be taking any risks? I suppose I'll have to kiss Kelvin's arse and knuckle down.'

'Marcus, do what you think is best but there is a world outside The Firm. It is a real one, not a fantasyland. And personally, I wouldn't kiss Kelvin McBride's arse if you paid me.'

'But you'd kiss Gary Lineker's, wouldn't you?'

'Definitely. What was the third thing you wanted to discuss?'

'Don't know. I've forgotten.'

It was time to quit while he was ahead.

For a Monday morning, something felt different. Fewer people on the train and on the pavements around Bank station. The atmosphere in the office was subdued. News of the redundancies had leaked and not even doubling up on Pizza Fridays had raised spirits. David Ellington had sent an email to every member of staff. The successful launch of the 'Living Our Values' programme was 'a landmark moment in The Firm's history'. The email was emblazoned with the new Values, together with photographs of the Duke on stage, and partners networking and 'idea sharing'. Humility over Pride.

He was eating his porridge when he was approached by David Prince, the youngest partner in the team. His arm was still in a sling.

'Morning Marcus. Good weekend?'

David was attending the third 'Living Our Values' conference at Claridge's on Wednesday. He was keen to make a good impression on the top bods and wanted some advice.

'Don't be afraid to challenge and question but always do it in a positive way. And remember to nod. Nodding is very important,' said Marcus.

David nodded.

'The Firm loves challenge, as long as you don't expect anything to change. Do that and you'll be fine.'

David nodded again.

'Thanks a lot, Marcus. Really helpful advice.'

'Enjoy Claridge's.'

He sent an email to Stuart Fielder, his financial advisor. Marcus and Stuart had been friends at university and, after graduating, Stuart had set up his own investment business and done very well. Stuart replied quickly. They would have a call on Wednesday morning and he told Marcus not to panic. It made him feel better until his newfound confidence was dashed as he checked The Sequence. More selling off, another big red day was looming.

It was late afternoon as he was reviewing the final proposal for Project Medusa, when Outlook alerted him to a voicemail from David Ellington. It was addressed to all partners and headed 'URGENT – Coronavirus Alert'. He opened it and listened. Two partners attending the previous Thursday's 'Living Our Values' conference had tested positive for Covid-19 and were now self-isolating at home. Both had been on a ski trip to Méribel the previous week. The Duke stressed there was no need to alarm staff, and they should continue following The Firm's guidance, as set out by Risk and Compliance.

So leaving the conference early had been a blessing in disguise, Marcus thought.

David Ellington lowered his voice to a funereal register.

'I also have to inform partners that, regrettably, we have taken the decision to cancel the rest of our "Living Our Values" events in line with the new Government policy on mass gatherings. We will reconvene them at a later date. In the meantime, please stay safe partners.'

Marcus felt sorry for the Head Chef at Claridge's who was now left with 250 portions of turbot ceviche and loins of venison on his hands.

Maybe 250 of the capital's homeless will be eating well this evening, he thought. Telling Alice he had been in the vicinity of the virus the previous week would need to be handled delicately. He texted Gavin.

Hi G. Hope you got back ok. Will be at the flat tonight if you want a drink? M.

It wasn't long before Gavin replied.

Back okay thx. Big meeting at work to discuss C-19. Sorry. See you tomorrow. Hope you're okay too. G.

His last meeting finished at 5.45, and he met Chloe in the lift lobby.

'Alright Marcus? Everything going okay?'

'I'm fine, Chloe. Family are all well, how about you?'

'Yeah, all good thanks. I'm starting to get worried about this Covid thingy. Do you think we'll all have to work from home?'

'Probably, although God knows how we're meant to speak to each other?'

'Didn't you read the email from IT? We're all getting Zoom.'

'I never read emails from IT. What the hell is Zoom?'

'It's like Skype but loads better. It's like a giant conference call but with video. I think we're all getting it this week. It would be cool if I didn't have to come in from Gants Hill every day. I can stay in me pyjamas or me Tigger onesie!'

'Sounds great, Chloe, I'd go for it. What about your mum and dad? How would lockdown affect them?'

'Mum's a midwife at Whipps Cross Hospital and Dad has his landscaping business. No way they can work from home! I'll have the house to myself. Apart from Natalie, my little sister. She's nineteen and works in a jewellers in Chigwell. Safe journey home, Marcus. You staying in the flat tonight?'

'Yes. Have a safe journey too.'

Chloe headed to Liverpool Street to join the Essex diaspora and Marcus went to St Paul's. He wanted some fresh air and hoped to see Colin again. He wanted to tell him to get down to Claridge's and get himself a decent meal for nothing.

He got a seat on the Tube immediately. It was hard to find any comfort in the news in the *Evening Standard*. Doing his best impression of an ostrich, Boris was doing all he could to avoid placing the nation under lockdown. Everyone else was doing it for him. Theatres were closing, sporting events were being cancelled, schools and universities were likely to shut before the Easter holiday. Boris responded by invoking the spirit of Dunkirk and the thousands of plucky Brits who would be rallying round to help the elderly and vulnerable. Manufacturers of everything from vacuum cleaners to Formula One cars were stepping forward with offers to design and build the extra ventilators that would be needed to support the underfunded and under-resourced NHS.

If I get the virus, I want to be on a McLaren ventilator, thought Marcus. *Not one from a company that makes food mixers.*

* * *

The mothers standing outside Little Acorns Nursery were engulfed in clouds of smoke and looking worried.

'What's happened?' Claire asked Zoe. 'The other mums don't look happy?'

'We might be closing the nursery on Thursday afternoon. We don't know for certain, we'll know more tomorrow.'

'But what's everyone going to do? People who rely on childcare? What's happening to you and the rest of the staff?'

Zoe shrugged her shoulders, she was close to tears.

'We don't know yet. Nothing is clear at the moment. Our manager told us yesterday.'

Claire put her arms around Zoe and hugged her. She was a second mum to Alexa, and Claire felt like her big sister.

'Not the greatest news. Thanks for letting me know. What are you doing today?'

'Making Mother's Day cards. Glue and paint everywhere!'

Beverley and Bruce were already in the playground. Beverley was talking with Helena Mistakidis.

'Morning Claire, how are you?' said Beverley.

'Not very happy. I've just been told that the nursery is likely to close this week. What's happening to the school?' she said to Helena.

The teacher shook her head and shrugged her shoulders.

'Probably the same. We're waiting to hear as well. There's a staff meeting tomorrow lunchtime. Mrs Lindsay will let us know what's happening then.'

'But they can't just close the schools can they? What about the children's lessons? Kyle and Alexa will go mental stuck in our flat all day.'

The teacher shook her head again.

'The restaurant where my husband works is closing and he may lose his job. Everyone's worried how the virus is going to affect us. I'm sorry, I have to go.'

Helena walked away to speak to other concerned parents.

'Do you want to come back to mine for a coffee?' said Beverley.

'I'm sorry, I can't. Gavin's coming today and I haven't seen him for a couple of weeks. With all of this stuff going on, I really need to talk to him. Hope you don't mind? See you tomorrow as usual?'

'Of course, see you tomorrow.'

Jane Steel was reading the news headlines on Radio 4 when Claire got back to the flat. The headlines were dominated by the virus. The number of cases in the UK had risen to 1,572 and 55 people had now died. Reports estimated the actual number of cases to be closer to 50,000.

She tidied the flat before Gavin arrived. She opened the door and was shocked to see him wearing a mask.

'Jesus, have you come to mug me?'

'New policy, I'm afraid. We have to wear them in enclosed spaces with strangers. It's to protect you as well as me.'

'Have you got the virus then?'

'I don't think so.'

'Then take it off, for goodness' sake. You're frightening me.'

They went into the kitchen. He wasn't his normal, cheerful self.

'How are you? How was Scotland?'

'Not much fun. Mum isn't well at all and Dad is struggling too. I'll probably have to go back. On top of that, we had a meeting at work last night. From the end of this week, all site visits are suspended. No face-to-face contact.'

'So what does that mean? We won't be seeing each other anymore?'

She put a teabag in each mug and added hot water. She was silent and pensive.

'What's the matter?' he said. 'I thought you'd be glad to have a break from me!' He laughed, but she didn't.

'That's not funny. I found out this morning that nursery and school might be closing this week. I'm dreading being locked down in this flat. Have you seen what they're going through in Italy and Spain? I'm not sure how I'm going to cope with that.'

'And you won't consider going back to your parents?'

'Fuck that. No way.'

'It's not going to be easy for any of us, Claire. I think we should make a list of everything you might need, to prepare for the worst, if lockdown happens.'

For the next hour, they made a list of everything she might need to survive lockdown. Paracetamol, food, tampons, cleaning products, toilet roll, batteries, candles, writing and drawing materials for the children. She called them out and Gavin wrote them down.

'Razor blades, Gillette Venus,' she said.

'Bit random. Are they really essential?'

'Definitely. I'm not going through lockdown with hairy armpits and hairy legs. I'd rather get the virus than have hairy legs.'

He laughed and wrote it down.

'There's a pound store in Queensway. I can get a lot of this stuff there for next to nothing. I'll drop it round later in the week. It's the least I can do. How are you off for money?'

'I'm okay. I'm not stealing food anymore. This is coming at the worst possible time, just as things were starting to come good.'

'I know. I'm really worried what lockdown could do to people.'

They stared into their mugs until Gavin broke the silence.

'So what else is new?'

She had been waiting for the right moment.

'Not much, apart from finding out I was looking after a miracle of nature.'

He looked baffled.

'What are you going on about?'

'You know Biscuit? That butch, macho, horny male hamster you got for me?'

'Yes.'

'Well, it turns out that just over a week after returning him to school, he went and had babies.'

'How did that happen?'

'Because you bought a bloody female hamster, you idiot! Even worse, she was pregnant too.'

Colour and size had been the only selection criteria, sex never came into it.

'How the hell was I to know? All I was told to do was find one that looked like Biscuit. So I did. What happened at school?'

'Well, it was pretty hard to explain it as a miracle. The angel Gabriel didn't put in a visit, so I had to own up to Kyle's teacher.'

'Did you mention my role in it?' he said defensively.

'No, it's okay, I didn't grass you up. I just said a "friend" helped me. Some friend!'

Gavin broke into a giggle.

'I don't know what's funnier, you having to confess or finding out Biscuit II was pregnant.'

'Don't worry, I've forgiven you.'

She took the mugs to the sink. On the window ledge was Marcus's business card. She picked it up and turned around to Gavin.

'Oh, and I had a personal visit from this man last Thursday,' she said, handing him the card.

It took him a few seconds to work it out.

'Marcus? What was he doing here?'

'Had a meltdown at some conference. Insulted his boss, stormed out and kept on walking until he reached Ladbroke Grove and then here.'

'Was he okay? Had he been drinking?'

'No, he was completely sober. He stayed for dinner, improved my sausage casserole and Excel skills and left about 10.45. He's a very sweet guy, even if he is an acquired taste. When are you seeing him next?'

'Tonight for dinner.'

Gavin wondered what could have happened, and why Marcus hadn't said anything to him?

* * *

Kelvin McBride asked the partners to remain in Communication Zone 1 after the pipeline meeting. He was in a good mood.

'Partners, we're about to enter an extended period of uncertainty, as Covid-19 unravels. Yesterday, I met with the top bods over tea at Claridge's. We've decided to make some one-off adjustments this year to take account of the impact of Covid on the business. Izzy, do you want to give more details?'

'Thanks Kelvin. The Executive has agreed to split this year into two. Nine months up to December, pre-Covid, when we were basically on track, and three months up to the end of March, which have been difficult, and which have caused the shortfall against plan. So, in a nutshell, we have hit target this year. Well done everyone!'

Kelvin and the top bods had used the pandemic to their advantage. The virus had saved their partner units. He continued.

'There will be a general communication to all staff later today but I wanted to tell you all personally. As of five o'clock this Thursday, all offices will be closed, apart from essential IT and technical support staff and Document Production. People will be told to work from home until further notice. Zoom will be rolled out over the next couple of days to enable us to collaborate with our clients and our teams. Thursday will be the last day in the office for all of us for some time.'

Marcus thought Kelvin was about to burst into the Vera Lynn wartime anthem, 'We'll Meet Again'. Nobody looked surprised, everyone had seen it coming. David Prince was the first to ask a question.

'Kelvin, how are we going to support people working from home? Not everyone will have the same facilities as they have here in the office.'

It was a good question. Nobody had Chilling Eggs or an Amazon-themed breakout zone in their house or flat. Most of the staff were lucky if they had a desk. Kelvin had an oak-panelled library in his London apartment and a fully functioning office in his Cornwall bolthole.

'Thanks for raising that, David. Good question. The honest answer is, they'll simply have to make do. We don't know how long lockdown will last so there's no point in incurring any unnecessary expenses. Izzy will be issuing guidelines on what can be claimed or not. It's basically nothing.'

Oliver Rankin piped up.

'Obviously, people will miss the buzz of the office. How are we going to maintain morale during lockdown, if it comes to that?'

'Another good question, Oliver,' said Kelvin. 'We'll certainly need something to replace Pizza Fridays. I've asked Jenny Moffatt to help us put together a programme of events to keep team spirits up. Perhaps you could lead on that one?'

Oliver nodded. He agreed with everything Kelvin asked him to do. Kelvin closed the meeting and the partners filed out. He asked Marcus to stay behind. He came straight to the point.

'So, what do you want to do, Marcus? Stay or go?'

Marcus expected Kelvin to make his mind up for him and produce a letter from his breast pocket. Before he had a chance to reply, Kelvin continued.

'Because let me make it absolutely clear, if you do want to stay, there will be no more fucking moments like last Thursday. Right? The Duke was livid. He said you had "undermined the entire spirit of the event".'

'But I was only telling the truth, and you know I was. Do you want me to leave?'

'No, I don't. But you know the rules of the game. You've been here long enough. Surviving here isn't about telling the truth all the time. It's about putting up with the shit for long enough to make enough money to fuck off and enjoy the rest of your life. You know it and I know it. Think about what you want to do, Marcus. But don't take too long about it.'

The afternoon passed quickly. The proposal for Project Medusa was sent to the client. A call had been arranged for the following Monday. The email from David Ellington had gone out to all staff and the floor was buzzing with chatter about closing the office and working from home. Opinions were mixed.

'My flatmate and her boyfriend are always shagging. If I'm locked down with them, I'll never get any work done.'

'My wife hates me enough already. We're only still married because I travel all the time. Lockdown will cause a divorce.'

'I'm thinking of emptying my wardrobe and using it as a desk.'

People began to throw things in bags and boxes ready to take home. Pairs of shoes and creased items of clothing left in lockers for months were packed up. Partners directed their secretaries to courier boxes to their homes or their second homes. Or, in some cases, to their third homes.

When he got back to the flat, he called Alice and told her the news.

'So, when do you think you'll start working from home?'

'Friday probably. Maybe Thursday. It all felt a bit weird in the office. A bit like getting ready for Christmas.'

'I've heard from James. He's decided not to stay in Manchester. One of his friends is giving him a lift back on Friday. It will be good to have the four of us all together for Mother's Day.'

'Sounds great. I'd better go now. I'm having dinner with Gavin tonight. Good luck with the tennis tomorrow.'

'Thanks a lot. Enjoy your dinner.'

He walked across the hall in his slippers and knocked on the door. Gavin took a while to answer.

'Sorry Marcus, just taking some venison steaks out of a marinade. I brought them back with me from the estate. Come in. Do we hug or not?'

'Probably best not to,' said Marcus. Music was playing in the background. 'Chopin?'

'Rachmaninov,' said Gavin, making two gin and tonics.

'I'll get it right one day, never mind. Cheers. How are things at home?'

'Not great. Mum's Alzheimer's is getting worse. With the virus, both of them are high risk. Luckily, they're in the middle of nowhere so pretty well isolated. They're probably in more danger of shooting themselves than catching it.'

'What are you going to do?'

'I'm driving back up to Perth this Friday. We've been told to work from home, no more site visits. Believe me Marcus, lockdown will screw people up more than the bloody virus. What about you?'

Gavin served minestrone soup as Marcus told him about closing the office.

'But that's okay for you, isn't it? You can work from home, can't you?'

'Easily. I hate it that's all. I worked from home a few weeks ago and it was bloody awful. Alice doesn't like me being under her feet either. My son's coming home from university so it will be the four of us at home.'

Gavin cleared away and took the venison steaks out of the oven.

'It's your birthday soon, isn't it?'

With everything that had been going on, Marcus hadn't given it a thought.

'Yes, the twenty-second. Same day as Mother's Day this year.'

Gavin stood up, went to the other side of the room and returned with an immaculately wrapped box and a gift card, beautiful handwriting in turquoise ink.

To Marcus. I think David Gandy would approve. Happy Birthday. G.

'That's really kind of you. Thank you. Shall I open it now?' said Marcus.

'No, save it for the day. I'm sorry I won't be here to celebrate with you.'

They were having coffee when Gavin raised the subject of Marcus's visit to Claire.

'I called on Claire today. She told me about your impromptu visit. What happened? Unlike you, just turning up on a whim like that?'

Marcus recounted the events of the 'Living Our Values' conference leading up to the bust-up with Kelvin.

'I couldn't face coming back here on my own. I was lonely and ended up there. I don't know why. It just happened.'

'I'm a bit surprised you didn't tell me about it earlier?'

'I'm sorry. I haven't even told Alice. I don't know why either, guilt I suppose? She would probably feel betrayed.'

'And who could blame her? For God's sake, Marcus, you're digging a hole and you keep digging. You must tell Alice, unless of course …'

Marcus spotted the innuendo immediately and got angry.

'Don't be ridiculous! It was nothing like that. She was a friendly voice when I needed one. That's all it was. I'm old enough to be her dad. I'm stuck between a rock and a hard place. I want to leave The Firm but can't afford to.'

Gavin got angry too.

'Why is it always about money with you, Marcus? Why is it never about being content with what you have?'

'Because I don't know anything else, for fuck's sake! It's always been about the money. That's what that place has done to me. I'm trapped in a living hell!'

The last time he'd cried had been at his mother's funeral. Gavin saw his distress, got up from his seat and put his arm around him.

'I'm sorry, Marcus. I'm really trying to help you, but you can't go on like this. This will mess you up badly unless you start making some changes.'

Marcus put his hand in his pocket for his handkerchief. He had left it on the desk in the flat.

'Can I have a tissue, please? I've forgotten my handkerchief.'

It broke the ice, and Marcus looked up and smiled at his friend.

'I didn't mean to get angry. Not with you, of all people. I'm sorry.'

Gavin handed him a box of tissues and sat next to him.

'Promise me you'll speak to Alice. Don't keep secrets from her. Tell her about going to see Claire. It's not worth lying about.'

'I know you're right. I will. So today was your last visit? How was she?'

'Apprehensive, anxious of being locked down in her flat. I said I would take some things round on Thursday before I go to Scotland.'

'You've just reminded me of something. I'll be back in a minute.'

Marcus got up and returned two minutes later.

'If you're seeing her this week, give her this from me. It was Libby's old phone. It's got to be better than that shitty one she's got at the moment.'

Gavin looked at him, smiled and prodded his chest with a finger.

'There's a really good man in there, Marcus. We both know it.'

Marcus smiled and the two men hugged each other.

'I should really be going. Early start tomorrow, last couple of days in the office for a while. Have a safe trip and I hope things improve for your parents.'

It was Gavin's turn to show his emotions and his eyes watered.

'You take care too, Marcus. You're a great friend and I hope our dinners return before too long. I'll certainly miss them. Remember what I said, talk to Alice.'

'I promise. Keep in touch.'

Marcus walked along the corridor to Apartment 2.3. Gavin poked his head around the doorframe.

'And by the way, Marcus. Happy Birthday next week!'

It was Tuesday, 17 March 2020.

Chapter 23

... After the Horse Has Bolted

Claire pushed Alexa through the clouds of smoke at the gates to the nursery.
'Any news, Zoe?' said Claire.

'No, none. We'll find out at the end of the day or tomorrow. I'll let you know as soon as I do, don't worry.'

Zoe looked worried. If the nursery closed, they would all have problems. She kissed Alexa goodbye and walked with Kyle to school. Mrs Lindsay was in the playground. She was worried too, surrounded by parents eager to know what was going on. She joined the circle around the headmistress.

'The Education Secretary is making a statement in Parliament this afternoon. I have been told by the local authority to expect the school to close on Friday afternoon. I'm sorry I can't say more but I will be here this afternoon and tomorrow if any of you need to talk to me. I should know more then.'

Beverley arrived with Bruce, and Claire told her what Mrs Lindsay had said.

'I heard from Edward last night. He's got a flight to Dubai tomorrow and lands in London on Friday morning.'

'That's great news. You must be very happy?'

'Bruce is very excited. Edward will need to quarantine for two weeks but at least he will be home. Shall we go then?'

The two mothers said goodbye to their boys who were oblivious to anything other than playing football. The hall in Beverley's flat was even more congested. More packing crates had arrived from Hong Kong.

'I'm really sorry about the mess,' said Beverley. 'I'll have to clear some of this before Edward gets back but I haven't got the energy right now. Come on, let's have a coffee. You said you had things to tell me. I'm excited!'

As the Quooker whooshed, Claire told Beverley about Marcus's visit, turning up in the middle of *The Chase*.

'Are you sure he doesn't fancy you? Older man, younger woman? It happens, you know?'

'No, don't be stupid! It was nothing like that. I think he wanted some company. If he wanted an affair, he could pick someone with more going for her than me! I think he might be slightly autistic. He's definitely strange, but he's very kind. The kids think he's great.'

'You're very attractive. Don't put yourself down.'

Claire scoffed at her.

'Oh yes, and candidates are queuing up at my door, aren't they? A caretaker with no teeth, an asexual social worker and a Marxist neighbour with size ten feet. No thanks, I'm better off on my own.'

They took their drinks into the study and sat on either side of the desk.

'I've got something to show you,' said Claire proudly. She opened the Excel files she had been working on and turned the laptop to face Beverley.

'Wow! Impressive. *Excel for Dummies* helped then?' said Beverley.

'Mmm ... not quite.'

'What do you mean?'

'It was Marcus. He showed me what to do. He's a bit of a whiz with Excel. Taught me loads of things.'

Beverley moved the cursor over the cells in the spreadsheet. 'He certainly knows how to write a formula! Cooks well and does bedtime stories too. His wife is a lucky woman. Let's get on, we've got a lot of emails to send.'

Rishi Sunak, the Chancellor of the Exchequer, was in a generous mood. A £350 billion support package was announced to keep the economy afloat. The government had gone on a spending spree with a sack of grants, subsidies and bailouts to fight the virus. Rishi said it was a package to reflect unprecedented times and the prime minister said he was leading a 'wartime government'. Marcus knew it was only a matter of time before Boris donned a homburg and went around the country giving V-signs and puffing on a cigar. While he waited for another batch of IT updates to download, he checked The Sequence. The FTSE 100 was on the slide again, heading for another big red day. He found a vacant Chilling Egg and called his financial advisor.

'Have you seen the markets this morning, Stuart? In freefall again. This couldn't have come at a worse time.'

'It's turbulent but I don't think it will be as bad as 2008. We just have to hold our nerve, sit tight and ride this out. Everyone is down at the moment.'

'I think Covid has just blown a fucking big hole in my retirement plans.'

'You're being a bit over-dramatic, Marcus. You've got plenty of cash to ride this storm out. Look on it this way, if we get locked down, you won't need anything because you won't be able to go anywhere and you won't be able to spend your money on anything. So sit tight and don't panic.'

Stuart's advice made him feel better. He got a text from Alice.

Hi M. Nmare at tennis. Can u gv me a call? A.

No yellow faces. He thought she may have injured herself and rang her. She answered immediately.

'Hi Al. It's me. Where are you? Everything okay?'

'No, I'm not okay actually. I'm at the tennis club. Today was the final of the over-fifties ladies' doubles, remember?'

'Yes, I wished you good luck.'

'Well, we've just been fucking disqualified!'

Marcus found it hard to believe a bastion of middle-class decorum like the tennis club would disqualify anyone.

'Why? Have you or Karen tested positive for a banned anabolic steroid in a random drug test?'

'Oh, piss off, Marcus. I don't need this right now. Anyway, we're both pumped up to the eyeballs with HRT anyway. No, Karen must have been a bit tipsy before the match started, and she swore at one of our opponents at the changeover. Called her a "fucking cheating bitch" for calling one of her shots out. The umpire overheard and disqualified us for being unsportsmanlike. We were one set up as well.'

'Bit harsh. It's not exactly Wimbledon, is it? Where is Karen now?'

'I put her in a taxi. There was no way I was going to let her drive. And to make it worse, the tennis club is closing tomorrow due to the virus. It's been a bloody nightmare.'

Having a partner with a forehand like Serena Williams was all well and good provided she was sober enough to use it.

'I'm really sorry, Al. I know you were looking forward to it. Maybe Karen will have sobered up by the end of lockdown? And there's always next year?'

After lunch, Chloe came to find Marcus, who was going through his locker for anything he needed before the office closed. He picked up some framed photographs of Olivia and James, taken on holiday in Sardinia a few years earlier. James hadn't started shaving and Olivia was wearing braces. Personal photographs were not brand compliant and were banned from the new building. He found a box of nutrition bars at the back of the locker and checked the expiry date. June 2017. He was interrupted by Chloe.

'Hiya Marcus. Wanna try Zoom now? I've booked us a room.'

He threw the nutrition bars back in the locker and joined her in Communication Zone 6. The team at the summit of Mount Kilimanjaro were still 'Putting Something Back'. She set up his account details in Zoom. If Chloe's spelling had some issues, her typing skills were outstanding. He admired the way her fingers danced across the keyboard like pink ballerinas.

'Right, Marcus, let's have a go shall we? I'll send you an invite now.'

Outlook pinged and he clicked on the link. Zoom opened.

'Can you see me, Marcus?'

'Of course I can. You're sitting next to me.'

'No, on your screen. Have you got your camera turned on?'

He stared blankly at the screen. She clicked on some buttons.

'Try now.'

'Oh yes, I can see you.'

'Wait a minute, I'll go out of the room.' She left the room and walked down the corridor. 'Can you hear me now, Marcus?'

'Yes I can. Loud and clear. Do we need to say "over" when we've stopped talking?'

'No, Marcus. We ain't flying a plane.' She returned to the room. 'There you go. All set up. You can switch your video off like this if you don't want people seeing you in your jimmy-jams first thing in the morning.'

He didn't want to tell Chloe that he hadn't worn pyjamas since he was fourteen. The virus was closing the office but it had given him Zoom instead.

* * *

Claire was talking to Zoe when a woman in a dark blue uniform approached them. It was Carole, the nursery manager. She was shaking her head.

'Hi Claire. We're still waiting to hear officially but I'm planning on the nursery closing on Friday. I'm really sorry.'

'So everything is closing?'

'Apart from the children of essential workers or vulnerable kids. Probably no more than a handful. I am so sorry.'

'I understand, Carole. I don't think I'm an essential worker somehow.'

'But you are an essential mum, don't forget that. Hopefully, it won't be long before we can have the children back. I'm here all day tomorrow.'

The news from school was no better. Helena Mistakidis was in the playground talking to concerned parents. She beckoned them over.

'Hi there. Still waiting for official confirmation but I think we'll be closing on Friday.'

'What's happening to the children's lessons?' said Beverley.

'Every child will get a set of workbooks. I was up until four in the morning preparing them. They'll be ready to collect tomorrow.'

She looked tired and drawn, the natural glow of her skin was dimmed. Claire admired her. Totally dedicated to her children, always doing her best to help them.

'Couldn't lessons be done online?' said Beverley.

'I wish we could,' said Helena. 'Some of the children in the class don't have access to the internet. We can't run different lessons, I'm afraid. We'll do our best to support parents.'

It reminded Claire that she was one of the 'digital poor'. She didn't have broadband. Another reminder of how she was failing her children.

'How are the children taking it?' said Claire.

'We haven't told them. We thought it would be best coming from you. The trip to the urban farm has been cancelled. All your deposits will be returned.'

Claire knew Kyle would be disappointed. He had been going on about piglets for the past week.

'See you both tomorrow,' said the teacher.

Helena shuffled away. Her moon shoes lacked their usual bounce. They were like diving boots on the end of her legs.

* * *

It was almost four o'clock in the afternoon when Outlook pinged. A message from Izzy Majewska informing him that Kelvin and Vanessa had recommended Laila Saetang to support him on Project Medusa.

Three minutes later, he received an invite from Laila proposing a meeting that evening at 7.30. He declined, and his phone rang immediately. Laila wasn't used to rejection.

'Hi Marcus. I'm just looking at your online diary and you don't seem to have anything on tonight. Are you sure we can't meet later? It would work well for me.'

'Absolutely certain. I'll be out of the office.'

'Oh, do you have a client meeting offsite?'

'No, it's a new thing I'm trying. It's called having a life. You should try it sometime. What's wrong with tomorrow morning?'

Like Mason, Laila was missing the gene which detected sarcasm.

'Sorry, but I have a clash with the "Are Millennials a Threat to Your Business Paradigm?" webinar. Are you not joining it?'

'No.'

'How about 10.45 tomorrow morning? I'll move some things around.'

'Great. See you then.'

Some people in the office were saying goodbye to their colleagues as if they would never see them again. The stationery cupboard looked like the Vikings had passed through. Stocks of highlighter pens and Post-it notes would keep everyone safe from the virus. Marcus picked up his belongings and said goodnight.

* * *

Mr Mahoney had just left when Claire switched over to BBC One to watch the six o'clock news. The lead story was the closure of schools and nurseries. Boris said he had been guided by The Science. It was the same science that had said a few weeks earlier that closing schools wouldn't slow the spread of the epidemic. The Science had changed its mind and so had Boris who wanted to flatten the sombrero. He needed to. The virus had scored a century of deaths in quick time and was looking good for a big score. The number of cases had risen to 2,626.

Claire sat down on the sofa with the children and explained that the Easter holidays were starting earlier, and that school would be closed from Friday.

'Is this because of the virus Mummy?' said Kyle.

Even five-year-olds listen to playground gossip.

'What's a virus?' said Alexa.

'It's like having a very bad cold,' said Claire. 'It's not good for old people if they catch it.'

'Like Mr Moany?' said Alexa.

'Yes, like Mr Mahoney. We don't want him to catch it, do we? So we're going to stay at home next week and Mummy is going to be your teacher!'

'Where will we have our lessons?' said Kyle.

'In the kitchen. And any naughty behaviour will be punished by ...'

Claire jumped on both of them and started to tickle them. They screamed, begging their mummy to stop.

'Come on you two. Bath time.'

Marcus was sitting on the sofa in the flat. The *News at Six* had just ended when Olivia called him.

'Hi Dad. Have you seen the news there won't be any exams this year? What do you think?'

She sounded worried.

'Hi Libby. Yes, I've just seen it. Not really a shock about schools closing. What have they said about lessons for the rest of the year?'

'All our lessons will be online. Only thing we may have difficulty with will be practicals. Luckily, most of the coursework is done. It's more about revision. What I'm really worried about is not having any exams.'

'What have they said?'

'There's no information yet on how A levels will be graded if we don't have exams. Maybe they will go on the results of the Mocks? I only got a B in Maths. If I don't get into Bristol because of that, I'll be fucking annoyed. I might as well give up now and go and work in bloody Aldi.'

Like him, she was always getting things out of proportion.

'Well, you could aim a bit higher! Maybe you could get a job on the meat and fish counter at The Temple? You'd still be working with animals, just dead ones.'

Olivia laughed.

'Thanks, Dad. Maybe I'll become an estate agent or a traffic warden instead, just to spite you!'

Estate agents and traffic wardens were the two jobs he rated less than his own. He had made his children promise they would never be either, or risk disinheritance.

'I'm sure the Government has a plan. Universities will surely need more than a photograph and some fake ID?'

She started to calm down.

'How are things with you anyway, Dad?'

'They're all fine. Last day in the office tomorrow before it closes. Don't forget it's Mother's Day on Sunday.'

'Already got the card and present. Did it last weekend. I've got your birthday card and present too.'

'How's Mum?'

'Still really upset about the tennis. I thought it was very funny, Karen turning up pissed at 9.30 in the morning.'

'Yes, me too. Best not tell her that.'

* * *

It was his last day in the office. He was walking up Queensway on the way to the station when his phone rang. It was Alice. It was unusual for her to ring him so early in the morning.

Surely she can't still be upset about the tennis? he thought. He answered.

'Marcus, have you seen the BBC website this morning? Libby's just showed it to me.'

'No. Why?'

'There's a story about two partners at The Firm testing positive for coronavirus. They attended some conference in London last week and are now self-isolating. It wasn't the same conference you attended, was it?'

He wondered how the press had got hold of the story? It was hardly headline news. He attempted to play it down.

'I was aware of it. And yes, it was the same conference. As I didn't come within 100 yards of them, I didn't think it was important to say anything. They work in Data Solutions, I never mix with those people.'

'And you didn't think to mention this to me? You thought that an outbreak of the virus at the place where you work was trivial?'

'Why would I mention it? I haven't got any symptoms and I didn't come into contact with either of them.'

'Have you read anything about this virus, Marcus? Some people are asymptomatic, which means they don't show symptoms. I'm not asking if you snogged the face off them, I'm just asking whether you might have come into contact with them? Do you think that's unreasonable?'

Telling Alice he had only been at the conference for three hours might have placated her but might have led to other questions he didn't have answers to.

'Alice, I'm fine. Fit as a butcher's dog.'

'Well there's no way you're coming home this weekend until you've self-isolated. I'm not taking any risks. You'll have to stay at the flat until we're certain.'

'Certain about what?'

'Certain you haven't got it.'

'But it's my birthday on Sunday, and it's Mother's Day! All four of us together. I booked a table at Pennyhill Park for lunch on Sunday.'

'Well I'm sorry about that but we're all having to make sacrifices now. It's a nice thought, Marcus, but I'm not taking any chances.'

'So, I'll cancel the booking then?'

'No, don't do that. We'll speak later. Have you got much on today?'

'Nothing much apart from infecting the rest of The Firm.'

* * *

Alexa was excited about her last day at nursery. As they walked along Ladbroke Grove, she was telling Claire all the things she was going to do.

'I'm making you a card. It's princess dinosaur card.'

Claire thought princess dinosaur cards would be in a minority on Mothering Sunday.

When they arrived, Carole, the nursery manager, handed Claire a piece of paper confirming the closure. No date had been set for it to reopen.

'I'm so sorry, Claire. The staff are all very upset.'

'What's going to happen to them?'

'We'll keep them on the payroll for as long as we can but that won't be for more than a couple of months. Hopefully, we'll be able to open again soon.'

Zoe came up to them and bent down to hug Alexa.

'At least it's shepherd's pie today,' she said.

Claire could see Zoe was tearful and stroked her arm.

'See you later.'

Helena Mistakidis looked exhausted. She shook her head as Claire got closer. It said everything.

'I told the children last night and said the Easter holidays had come early and I would be teaching them.'

'What did they say?' said Helena, laughing.

'They think it's funny but the novelty will soon wear off. What about you, what's happening to all the teachers?'

'We're on a rotation to keep the school open for the children of key workers, but it's little more than day care. Sorry Claire, I've got more families to speak to. See you later.'

Beverley arrived with Bruce. Her hair was tied up in a bun and she wasn't wearing any makeup.

'Are you okay?' said Claire.

'Not really. I've been up all night trying to get the flat sorted before Edward gets back. I've still got so much to do.'

'Do you want to skip work today, if you're too busy?'

'No, I need someone to talk to. Bruce is quite upset the school is closing. He's only just settling in, so it's not great timing. Says he'll miss Kyle.'

'A little bromance,' said Claire. 'Kyle seemed fine about it. I don't think it's sunk in yet.'

Beverley's flat was in disarray. The hall was littered with cardboard boxes, brown paper and bubble wrap which popped like Chinese firecrackers as they walked over it.

'Excuse the mess.'

Beverley made two mugs of coffee and they sat at the desk in the office. Something wasn't right.

'Are you sure everything's okay? You don't seem yourself today?' said Claire.

Beverley looked over her laptop and across the desk.

'I'm worried that if we go into lockdown we won't see each other. I really look forward to these two days. Today could be our last one for a while.'

'But Edward will be back tomorrow and you must have missed him?'

Beverley smiled and sipped her coffee.

'Edward and I met at university when we were nineteen, and we married when we were twenty-four. A lot has changed for both of us. Of course, I still love him, just in a different way. We almost lead separate lives, connected by Bruce.'

'At least he didn't run off with someone else and give you an STI,' said Claire.

'No, that's true. But our Wednesdays and Thursdays are special to me. They've given me a new lease of life.'

'Yes, me too,' said Claire.

* * *

Marcus heard her before he saw her. He had bought two coffees in OnYouGo and was sitting at one of the small tables in the meeting area. Laila was wearing a pair of black and white Jimmy Choo stilettos which clacked on the wooden floor. She was wearing a Bluetooth headset and talking loudly into space. She sat down at the table, still talking and stuck her index finger in the air, indicating she would be finished in one minute. She mouthed 'sorry' to him, although she clearly wasn't. She repeated it four times and, four minutes later, she spoke.

'Morning Marcus, sorry about that. Client stuff, you know how it is? Couldn't get them off the phone.'

'Yes, I guessed,' he said. 'I got you a flat white. Hope that's okay?'

'Yes, perfect. Thank you.'

Marcus and Laila discussed the proposal for Project Medusa. It was the first time Laila had worked with him and she was keen to impress. The Golden Carrot was within touching distance. She did a lot of nodding.

'Looking at it, I think Project Medusa is a many-headed monster?' said Marcus, pointing to a sketch on his pad.

'What do you mean by that?'

'Greek mythology? Medusa the Gorgon, the many-headed monster, slain by Perseus?'

'Sorry, I did astrophysics at Cambridge.'

'Did you now? Of course you did,' said Marcus, trying not to be patronising. 'I meant the project might not be as straightforward as it seems. More complicated. Maybe that's why the client called it Medusa?'

'Well, that's good for us then, isn't it?' said Laila enthusiastically.

'In what way?'

'Complication is good. The more complicated we make it, the more difficult it looks, the more frightened the client will be of screwing it up. They'll be more likely to use us to keep them out of the shit.'

He took a sip of his double macchiato.

'Well, that's one way of looking at it,' said Marcus. 'Or there's another way.'

'What's that?' said Laila, sounding surprised.

'We could try to do the right thing for the client and go from there. Let's have the call with them on Monday and see how we get on.'

'Okay, we'll play it your way. One last thing, Marcus?'

'What's that?'

'How much contact with me on a daily basis do you want?' said Laila, earnestly.

He was slightly taken aback.

'What level of contact were you thinking of?'

'A morning briefing for the team at seven thirty, a progress update at lunchtime for just you and me, and then a wrap up with everyone at the end of the day around eight. How does that sound?'

'Once a day around five will be fine.'

* * *

Zoe cried when Claire collected Alexa from Little Acorns. She handed Claire a folder containing her daughter's latest artistic creations. Alexa had blue paint in her hair.

'Your Mother's Day card is in here,' said Zoe, pointing to the folder. 'You're not allowed to see it until Sunday, is she Alexa?'

Alexa shook her head.

'It's quite special,' said Zoe. 'Very unique.'

'Say goodbye to Zoe then, sweetie,' said Claire. 'Thank you for everything you've done for Alexa this term. See you soon. Stay safe.'

Alexa didn't want to walk, so Claire put her in the buggy. At school, the bell had gone and excited children were running into the playground. Helena Mistakidis and her teaching assistant followed her class carrying two boxes. Claire and Beverley waited for the queue of worried parents to go down before approaching them.

'Here are Kyle and Bruce's folders with their workbooks. If you can do two to three hours a day with them, it would be great. I'll be calling you to find out how everything is going.'

'Thanks Helena. Have you got much left to do?' said Beverley.

'Not really.'

Claire said goodbye to Beverley and walked home. She was pleased Biscuit II had found a good home for lockdown. Sebastian and Desdemona lived in a big house near Notting Hill; Biscuit and her babies had moved upmarket, more in keeping with her luxury residence. Gavin was due later that evening, so *The Chase* had been cancelled. Mr Mahoney understood. His coffee and walnut cake would last for another day. Gavin knocked on the door shortly after five and came in carrying four carrier bags. He put them down on the kitchen table.

'The pound shop came up trumps!' he said as he started to unpack the bags, announcing each item, like guests being introduced to the Queen at a garden party. 'Razor blades, pens and pencils, triple A and double A batteries, shampoo, deodorant, drawing books, paracetamol ...'

By the time he had finished, the table was littered with the items.

'There you go,' he said proudly. 'Your Covid-19 survival kit.'

'Amazing, thanks a lot, Gavin. How much do I owe you?'

'One pound.' He laughed and paused. 'You don't owe me anything, it's the least I can do. How are you and the kids feeling?'

Claire told him about her conversation with the children the previous evening, how they didn't seem concerned by it.

'Make sure you take it slowly,' he said. 'Don't put pressure on yourself to be a teacher, a carer and a mum all at once. If you think things are getting on top of you, take a break, watch TV or go for a walk.'

She made him a mug of green tea and they went into the living room. The children were watching *Blue Peter*. One of the young-looking presenters was demonstrating how to make a Mother's Day card.

'Jesus, I haven't seen this programme in years. I had a Blue Peter badge once,' said Gavin. 'It might still be in my bedroom at home. They were a prized possession for a ten-year-old.'

'What did you get yours for?' said Claire. 'Gutting a stag on a windswept moor?'

'Ha ha! Very funny. My friend Angus and I rescued a sheep that had fallen into a stream. My mum wrote in to the BBC. I treasured that badge. Did you get one?'

She shook her head.

'No, we didn't have many drowning sheep in Walsall.'

The *BBC News at Six* came on and the first item was the prime minister's latest press conference. Boris was in a target setting mood. Numbers were flying around like a murmuration of starlings. The tide against the virus would be turned in twelve weeks. Testing would be ramped up from 5,000 a day to 10,000 and eventually 250,000 a day. It was impressive stuff, all the time guided by The Science.

'All over in twelve weeks then?' said Claire. 'Do you believe him? Judith says Boris wouldn't know the truth if it bit him on the cock.'

'Not an image I care to think about, but who knows? What I do know is I must be going. Still got to pack. I'm setting off early in the morning.'

'Will you see Marcus before you go?'

'Possibly. I saw him on Tuesday for dinner. It's his birthday on Sunday so I gave him his card and present.'

'That's sweet of you. He's lucky to have you as a friend.'

She shouted to the children, who ran into Gavin's arms. He scooped them up and spun them around as he walked to the front door.

'Look after your mum and be good. I'll try to call on Tuesday around the normal time.' He stopped in his tracks. 'Shit, I'd almost forgotten. I've got something for you. It's from Marcus.'

He opened his satchel, took out the phone and handed it to her.

'It was his daughter's old one, but he thought you might get some use out of it. At least you can take decent pictures and we can WhatsApp each other!'

She looked at the phone. Apart from a few scratches, it looked brand new.

'That's very kind of him. Why did he do that?'

'He was just being Marcus, thought it would help. I'll be off then. Remember what I said, don't take on too much. Any problems, give me a call.'

He gave her a hug and kissed her on the cheek. It was against all the protocols but they were both consenting adults.

'Look after your mum and dad,' she said.

He walked along the balcony to the stairs and turned around to look at her.

'Stay strong. You'll be okay.'

Marcus said goodbye to Chloe and the few people left in the office. All the other partners had gone by lunchtime. Simon Loder and Jacob Mauser had booked a 'lockdown lunch' at Tamarind in Mayfair and hadn't returned. They were feasting on the gourmet tasting menu before the famine of lockdown kicked in. The memory of crispy lobster with spiced red chilli jam might have to last a while.

The pavements outside the office were empty. The worker bees were back in their hives, money-pollen collecting was over for the day. Possibly for months. It was almost seven o'clock by the time he got to his flat. He had walked the entire journey home, almost six miles. He had listened to Pink Floyd's 'Dark Side of the Moon' and 'Wish You Were Here' as well. Eric the concierge was handing over to George.

'Evening, Marcus. Off to Weybridge tonight?'

'Not tonight Eric. I'm here tomorrow for sure. Maybe for longer, I don't know yet.'

Eric looked baffled, but discretion was a quality he had in spades. As long as the residents used the correct waste bins, he never asked questions.

'See you tomorrow then, Marcus. Have a good evening.'

Marcus heard music from Gavin's flat and rang the doorbell. The music was turned down and he came to the door.

'Hi Marcus. Want to come in for a drink?'

'That's kind but no, thank you. You probably have a lot to do. I just thought I'd say have a safe journey. And thanks again for the birthday present.'

'My pleasure. You back to Weybridge tonight?'

'No, I've got some things to do tomorrow with work so I'll set off in the afternoon. What time are you leaving?'

'Six thirty. I want to get there by mid-afternoon, if I can.'

'Drive safely. Hope all goes well with your mum and dad. Speak soon.'

'You too. Oh, by the way, I gave the phone to Claire. She was really grateful. I'll keep in touch.'

Beirut was quiet, the chains from the cranes hung vertically, still and motionless. He sat down on the sofa in his raincoat and rang Alice.

'Hi Al. It's me. How's everything?'

'We're all okay, Marcus. How are you?'

'I'm fine. Last day in the office. It was all a bit weird. A lot of people were already working from home. It was almost deserted.'

'Yes, I can imagine.'

'Al, can we talk about me coming home tomorrow, please? I'm absolutely fine. No symptoms at all.'

From showing little interest in the pandemic, Alice had now become an authority on the virus, obsessed with the daily press conference and what Boris and The Science were telling her.

'Marcus, could you be a little less selfish for once and think of others? You were in the close proximity of two people who have subsequently tested positive. You are a risk. You need to self-isolate for at least a week to be safe rather than sorry.'

'But it's my birthday on Sunday. What am I meant to do, celebrate it on my own?' he whimpered.

'Stop behaving like a spoilt child. If we get locked down, there will be plenty of time to celebrate when you come back.'

Those bloody Data Solutions wankers! he thought to himself. Alice's logic was faultless, he just didn't want to accept it.

'So, have you asked Jacinda to stop coming to the house, then? She could be mixing with anyone and you wouldn't know it. Have you taken her temperature? Asked her to do a test?'

It was a lame and petulant retaliation.

'No, and that's not going to happen either. Jacinda is sixty-three and lives on her own. She has been with us since we moved to Twin Gates and is completely trustworthy, unlike you. Stop being pathetic and accept you'll need to stay at the flat for a few more days. Go for a walk in Kensington Gardens with Gavin or something.'

'He's going to Scotland tomorrow. I'll be here on my own.'

'Well, you're always going on about enjoying your own company, now's the perfect opportunity. Speak tomorrow.'

Karen's drunken outburst may have cost her the over-fifties' ladies doubles title, but Alice had just beaten Marcus in straight sets.

He looked in the fridge. Just a few shrivelled tomatoes and a couple of out-of-date yoghurts. Even for someone with his laissez-faire attitude to 'best before' dates, it was pushing it. He left the flat and walked along Queensway to KFC, which was busy.

'I'll have the ten-piece Wicked Variety Bucket please, plus a side of coleslaw and a side of beans. And extra ketchup and salt.'

Back at the flat, he laid the feast out on the sofa next to him and, still in his raincoat, devoured the lot in an act of finger-licking defiance.

'Fuck you, Alice,' he said to himself, as he wiped a fallen baked bean off his raincoat.

It was Thursday, 19 March 2020.

Chapter 24

Zooming into Lockdown

Marcus sat at the breakfast bar drinking black coffee. The milk in the fridge had turned to sludge. His KFC feast had given him indigestion requiring a swig of Gaviscon in the middle of the night. He switched on the television. There was optimism and upbeat chatter on the BBC Breakfast red sofa. The Queen had addressed the nation, lending her support and evoking more memories of WWII spirit. The virus didn't share the same spirit. There had been another 144 deaths and 3,000 cases.

He showered and checked his wardrobe. One clean shirt, one pair of underpants and some casual clothes. Learning to use the washing machine was becoming urgent. He kept his one clean shirt in reserve and opted for business casual.

He joined the Zoom call with Laila. She appeared on his screen against the backdrop of an expensively furnished living room, reflected in a large silver-gilt mirror.

'Morning Laila. How are you?'

She pointed to her ears. She was wearing a pair of diamond earrings that were like small pebbles, tasteful rather than ostentatious. She pointed to her ears again. A message appeared on his screen.

Turn your audio on.

He looked for the microphone button and clicked on it.

'Can you hear me now?'

'Perfectly. Good morning,' said Laila.

'And to you too. You were up early this morning, weren't you?'

'I go for an 8 kilometre run every morning. I try to do at least an hour's work before I get dressed. No commuting will give me another two hours at each end of the day.'

He imagined her dripping sweat all over her keyboard as she powered into her morning.

'That's very inspiring. You wanted to discuss Medusa?'

'Yes, the chat we had yesterday was very helpful. I did more work on it last night and have come up with a new leveraged value proposition. Can we discuss at eleven?'

He loathed the term 'value proposition'. It meant nothing. She had also combined it with 'leveraged'. Double bollocks.

'Do you want to give me a clue or keep me in suspense?'

'Let me do more work on it and I'll send it across later.'

'Fine. Try to get some breakfast.'

'Already have. I have a spinach and kiwi fruit smoothie every morning.'

'Speak at eleven then.'

With sour milk and an empty fridge, a trip to The Temple was his first priority. A long queue went around the corner. He approached the security guard.

'What's the problem? Why such a big queue this morning?'

'We're only allowing fifty people in at a time. It's to stop people hoarding and panic buying.'

'I'm a Waitrose loyalty cardholder. Does that count for anything?'

The security guard shook his head and Marcus joined the back of the queue. Young men and women squeezed into Lycra were coming out of 1Rebel, their faces red and sweating, their hair damp from spinning or boxercising, getting in a final session before the gym closed. It took him forty-five minutes to enter The Temple.

The in-store experience was how Marcus imagined it might be if Fortnum & Mason gave the Queen her own private slot at Christmas. No trolleys being rammed into his ankles, no shoppers clogging up the aisle, staring at the cheese wondering which cheddar was on special offer. An elderly lady passed him.

'Anyone over seventy gets let in as a priority, you know? It's lovely now it's not so crowded, isn't it?' she said.

Marcus smiled politely. He thought Waitrose should consider lowering the priority threshold to fifty-five or at least give cardholders preferential treatment.

'Yes, it's great isn't it? So much nicer.'

He filled his bags with as much as he could carry. If he was spending his birthday on his own, a ribeye steak and some lamb chops would bring some comfort. It wasn't Sunday lunch at Pennyhill Park, but it was the next best thing. Nobody was hoarding Fray Bentos pies either. He bought four.

Back at the flat, he dialled in to his next Zoom call, the first meeting of the Lockdown Social Committee. Marcus looked at the six faces on the screen. Everyone seemed happy. It was like the first morning of a summer holiday, no sunburn or upset tummies yet. Oliver Rankin opened the call.

'Morning everyone. Thanks for joining. Hopefully the technology won't be a problem and we can all "Zoom" along.'

Only one person laughed. That was Oliver himself. He was in the middle of introducing Jenny Moffatt when he was interrupted by a ping, and a new face appeared. Hannah Blake had joined.

'Sorry, I'm a bit late,' said Hannah. 'The dog has just been sick and I had to clear it up.'

'No problem,' said Oliver. 'I was just introducing Jenny Moffatt from HR and how she will be supporting us with—'

He was interrupted by another ping and another new face. Graham Wilder had joined. Graham was wearing a T-shirt and shorts. He was leaning back in his chair with his hairy legs on the table.

'Sorry Oliver, I'd forgotten it was recycling day. Just had to put the bins out. All yours now.'

Oliver made another attempt to start the meeting but was interrupted by more pings from Angela Rust, who had just got back from the chemist, and David Barker, who had been dealing with the arrival of a plumber. David was taking the call in his kitchen.

'Who's that in the background, David?' said Hannah.

'That's Matt from Matt's Taps. He's come to fix my sink.'

Matt turned around and waved to everyone.

'You might want to turn your video off and go on mute, David?' said Oliver. 'We don't want to disturb Matt.'

'I'm fine,' said Matt. 'Don't mind me.'

'Have you just come from the beach, Graham?' said David.

'No, just chillin' here in the flat. No point in wearing a suit anymore, if we're all working from home.'

It had taken fifteen minutes for everyone to join, leave and join again, then make their excuses for being late and indulge in small talk.

If this is the new way of working, we're going to be here forever, thought Marcus.

Finally, Oliver introduced Jenny and explained the role of the Lockdown Social Committee. There was lots of nodding. Everyone agreed it was a good idea to keep morale up during lockdown. They would take soundings and come up with a list of ideas for the next meeting. Everyone was upbeat.

Marcus got up from his desk and dashed to the toilet, two cups of coffee were having an effect. He was in mid-flow when he heard Zoom calling him from the bedroom. He looked at the clock in the bathroom. It was 11.05. He had forgotten about Laila and her leveraged value proposition. He quickly washed his hands and joined Zoom. Laila was waiting.

'Sorry I'm late, Laila. Had to take a quick loo break.'

Laila didn't do empathy and got straight to the point.

'Have you had a chance to look at the presentation I sent earlier?'

'No, I'm sorry I haven't.'

'Not a problem. I'll share my screen and walk you through it.'

Laila shrunk to the size of a postage stamp as PowerPoint replaced her. Her new idea was nothing new, it was the usual tactic to frighten the client shitless.

'They need a three to four month diagnostic phase to assess the current state in both organisations and develop a completely new TOOL, from front-end customer segmentation to back-end processes and infrastructure landscape,' she said confidently.

TOOL was The Firm's all-singing, all-dancing, diagnostic and design capability. Insight-led, data-driven and fact-based, it stood for Target Organisation and Operating Lifecycle. It was a cloud-based sledgehammer to crack a nut.

'What makes you think that?' said Marcus sceptically.

'Yeast Feast is a wholesale artisan baker right? Fresh bread, sourdoughs, pastries, wraps, flatbreads? Sold through high street supermarkets, specialist health food retailers, organic home delivery companies?'

'With you so far.'

'And it's buying Make 'n' Bake, the UK's largest manufacturer of cake and bread mixes. Since *Bake Off*, its sales have rocketed.'

'Still with you. Although a cake mix isn't really the same thing as baking your own but carry on.'

'Well, different products, target markets, routes to market, sales channels, marketing strategies and back-end systems all add up to one thing?'

'What's that?'

'This is a lot more complex than they think.'

Marcus started getting flashbacks to the Wonderwall. This had all the same ingredients.

'You haven't been speaking to Gerard Cornelius from Client Ideation have you?'

'No, why? Is he a TOOL expert?'

He's an expert tool, thought Marcus.

'No, just wondered. So what's next?'

'Let's have another call on Sunday morning to update our proposal and send it to Yeast Feast before the call on Monday.'

'I'm afraid it's my birthday on Sunday.'

'What, all day?'

'They usually are,' said Marcus, starting to get irritated.

'Have you got a big day with your family planned then?'

A family lunch at Pennyhill Park was the plan before the virus and Alice intervened. Now, he was on his own with a ribeye steak.

'Don't worry, let's have the call. How about 10.30?' suggested Marcus.

'Great, thanks Marcus. Appreciate it.'

'Are you doing anything special on Mother's Day?'

'My mum died last year and I don't have kids. Speak on Sunday.'

***

Claire and Alexa were waiting in the playground for Kyle. She saw Beverley approaching and smiled.

'Edward flew in from Dubai this morning. I've left him at home. He's very tired and has to quarantine now.'

'Does Bruce know his dad's waiting at home for him?'

'No, it's a surprise. I didn't know for definite myself until last night.'

Helena Mistakidis walked over to them. She tapped the two boys on their heads, as if she were anointing them.

'Now, both of you be good for your mums, won't you? Behave like you do for me and listen to what they tell you. I'll be checking up on you. And don't forget to do your schoolwork.' She turned to the two mothers. 'Try not to put me out of a job in the meantime!'

The three women stared at each other. They said goodbye by looking and not touching. Helena walked away as Claire turned to Beverley.

'I guess we might not be seeing each other for a while either?'

As they were leaving the school, Claire saw Biscuit II and her multi-level emporium being loaded into the back seat of an Audi A7. She was on her way to Notting Hill with her babies.

No lockdown slumming it for you, she thought. *Stay safe. Hope they don't kill you.*

Mr Mahoney was putting away Ian's mobility scooter when Claire got back to the flat after stopping off at Tesco Express.

'Let me give you a hand,' he said, taking four bags of shopping in one meaty hand. They climbed the four flights of stairs together. Claire paused at the top.

'I just need to catch my breath,' she said, taking a puff on her inhaler. She opened the front door and Mr Mahoney put the shopping bags on the kitchen table.

'Is it okay if I come up just before *The Chase* starts? I don't mind if you're busy.'

'No, it's fine, Mr Mahoney. See you soon.'

The caretaker returned twenty minutes later with a coffee and walnut cake, as Claire made two cups of builder's tea. They assumed their normal positions in the living room, and Bradley Walsh was his usual cheerful self. The Dark Destroyer eliminated two contestants, but Susan (a call centre operator from Warrington) and Lionel (a music teacher from Bath) joined forces to pocket £12,000 between them.

'The Dark Destroyer had a nightmare today. A total nightmare,' said Mr Mahoney. 'The producers won't be very happy with him.'

Claire switched over to BBC One for the *News at Six*. There was only one story: lockdown. Boris was joined by Rishi and Jenny Harries, who was looking considerably perkier than last time. Chris and Patrick were probably in the local Wetherspoons grabbing a last-minute pint before the pubs shut. Each lectern had a new message: 'Stay at Home', 'Protect the NHS' and 'Save Lives'.

Boris had followed The Science and confirmed what everyone knew was coming: the country was going into lockdown, everything was closing and everyone had to stay indoors. Rishi said the government would pay 80% of people's salaries if they were unable to work.

Well, he won't be paying mine, for sure, thought Claire. Mr Mahoney stood up to go.

'Well, I guess that's it for a while? That's sad, very sad.'

'It looks that way, Mr Mahoney. We'll still be able to say hello to each other and I'll check on you every day. Promise.'

'I don't think baking cakes is banned, is it? I'll still make one for you and the children.'

'The virus probably doesn't live on coffee and walnut, so I guess that's okay.'

He hugged Claire and the children and left.

* * *

Straight after the news, Marcus called Alice.

'Did you hear what Boris had to say?'

'Hi, Marcus. Yes I did. James is back, his friend dropped him off this afternoon. He's upstairs with Libby at the moment catching up. It's nice to have him home. What did you think of what the Chancellor had to say?'

'Looks like the Government is paying for everything. The bill for this is going to be huge. Have you got everything you need at home?'

'I think so. I've managed to book an Ocado delivery for next Tuesday and the Organic Delivery Company finally came yesterday. Are you okay? Have you calmed down now?'

'I'm a bit lonely, but I'm fine. Gavin left for Scotland this morning and I went to The Temple. Long queue but I've got enough food for a few days.'

'I bet you bought some of those awful Fray Bentos pies, didn't you?'

'No.'

What are you doing tonight?'

'Having something to eat and watching Netflix. I'm watching *Schitt's Creek*. It's very funny. It could be us one day if lockdown carries on.'

Marcus knew Alice would never watch a programme like *Schitt's Creek*. He said goodbye to her, lay down on the sofa and stared at the ceiling.

'So this is lockdown? Fucking great.'

It was Friday, 20 March 2020.

Chapter 25

The Mother of all Sundays

Marcus was woken by the ping of a message on his phone. He knew it would be Libby wishing him a happy birthday. She was always first. He opened WhatsApp. Libby had a new rival. It was from Laila Saetang.

Have sent slides to you. Can you look before our call at 10.30? L.

The woman's a bloody machine, he thought.

He made a coffee, poured a glass of orange juice and proposed a toast to himself.

'Happy fifty-fifth birthday, Marcus. Hope you have a wonderful day. Much planned? Oh, pretty quiet really. Spending it on my own. Didn't want to make a fuss, put people to any trouble.'

He looked out of the window. A woman was taking her French bulldog for its early morning walk. It paused, arched its back, quivered and did a poo on the pavement. She stared at it and walked on.

Maybe I'll come into your living room and shit on your carpet, he thought.

By the time he had shaved and showered, WhatsApp had been busy. Libby was first, followed by Alice.

Happy Birthday, Dad. Sorry we're not with you today. Let's have a video call later. About 12.30? Giving Mum her present now. Give you yours when I see you. Love youuuu.

Her message came with lots of emojis of birthday cakes, banners and balloons. He only had one card.

Hi M. Happy Birthday. We'll celebrate when we're all together. Have a nice day and speak later. Love you. A.

Her message came with lots of emojis too. At least she had used proper words instead of txtspk for her message. He thought of her, sitting up in bed with a glass of champagne and the *Mail on Sunday*, being waited on by her devoted children for Mother's Day. And then he realised James wouldn't even be awake. He replied.

Thanks Al. Happy Mother's Day to you as well. Sorry PHP got cancelled. We'll do it another time. Have a nice day and speak later. Love you too. M xx

Their joint celebration lunch at Pennyhill Park had been another casualty of lockdown. The hotel had called to cancel. Alice was very upset.

'Well, in these difficult times, we all have to make sacrifices, Al,' he had said with only a slight tinge of sarcasm.

He went for a walk around Kensington Gardens to clear his head. It was a strange atmosphere, people avoiding eye contact, keeping their distance. A couple of policemen were strolling in the park wearing stab vests. He didn't think social distancing could be that dangerous.

He bought a copy of the *Sunday Times* and returned to the flat in time to review the presentation Laila had spent the night working on. Document Production wasn't locked down, and they had sprinkled it with their magic icons. He Zoomed. Laila was looking intense and she got straight down to business.

'Morning Marcus. Have you had a chance to look at the materials?'

'Morning Laila. How are you? Good weekend so far?'

'Yes, great,' she said impatiently. 'What do you think of it?'

For the next half an hour, Laila explained her logic and, most importantly, how much money The Firm would make. She had answers to all his questions.

'So who's going to present the new piece on TOOL?'

'Me. I'm all over it,' she said confidently.

What Laila lacked in empathy she made up for in self-confidence. He wasn't in the mood to argue, not on a Sunday morning and not on his birthday.

'Fine. What do you need from me?'

'Nothing. I really want to prove I can lead on this.'

He admired her honesty and balls.

'Fair enough. It's your show.'

'Thanks a lot, Marcus. I'm glad we're aligned on this now.'

'Alignment' was everything and everyone had to be aligned. And now they were. Laila had got what she wanted.

'Well done on this, Laila. It's good stuff. Speak tomorrow.'

He was about to un-Zoom when she interrupted.

'By the way, Marcus?'

'Yes?'

'Happy birthday.'

'Thank you.'

Even robots have a heart, he thought as he closed his laptop.

* * *

Claire's Mother's Day had got off to a bad start. Kyle had woken in the middle of the night with a nightmare. The disturbance had woken Alexa, and the three of them had all slept in her bed. She had been awake since 5.30 with a small elbow in her back, overthinking and getting anxious about lockdown.

So much for a lie in and breakfast in bed, she thought.

Over breakfast, the children gave her their cards. She had already seen them but pretended to be surprised.

'Alexa, that's beautiful. And you made this all yourself? Thank you, my darling.'

Alexa explained the story of the blue princess dinosaur, who had once been green, but had eaten magic Rice Krispies which had made her blue, so she could marry a prince. It was high on imagination, even if it was a significant departure from the traditional Mother's Day theme. Kyle had stuck closer to the script and gone for flowers and a big spiky sun. He had almost written the message himself, tracing over his teacher's writing.

'And did you write all of this yourself?' said Claire.

Kyle nodded.

'"*To Mummy. Thank you for being the best Mummy in the world. Love from Kyle*". It's beautiful, sweetie. Thank you.'

Kyle beamed and Claire put her cards on the window ledge. Next to them was another card. '*Marcus Barlow, Partner*'.

She thought about him. He was probably sitting in his big house, surrounded by his beautiful wife and family, celebrating his birthday with champagne and a full English breakfast. She picked up the phone he had given her. Ian had replaced the SIM card for her and showed her how to use it. She wanted to text Marcus, to wish him a happy birthday but she thought he would be preoccupied with his perfect family. Her thoughts turned to her mother, probably waiting hand-on-foot on her father, and she felt guilty. She opened the phone and sent a text.

Happy Mother's Day, Mum. Hope you are well. Thinking of you today. Kids are well but off school now. Thought you might like to see this? Love Claire. xx

She attached a picture of Kyle and Alexa taken in the Memorial Park the day before. They were both smiling and waving. She pressed 'Send', and it was gone. She had done her bit for Mother's Day.

* * *

Marcus only had one card and one present. He took Gavin's immaculately wrapped gift and card out of the cupboard and sat on the sofa. He opened the card. It was a cartoon image of an inebriated chef, slumped over a cooker drinking a glass of wine. He read the message, written in ink in beautiful handwriting.

To my best friend Marcus. Have a wonderful birthday. Looking forward to many more dinners. Make it a year to remember. Best wishes always. Gavin.

A year to remember. The virus was doing its best to make it a year to forget. He opened the present. It seemed a pity to spoil the wrapping paper, so he peeled the Sellotape carefully. He opened the box. It was a pair of brown suede Tod's driving shoes, just like the ones Gavin wore. He tried them on and they fitted perfectly. Gavin always got things right. He sent him a message to thank him. WhatsApp pinged. James had woken up.

Hi Dad. Happy Birthday. Sorry you're not here with us. Speak at 12.30. Btw the food at home is shit! We need to talk. Get back soon. James. xx

He felt better knowing James was feeling the full force of the oppressive vegan regime. He went to the fridge and took out his ribeye steak to admire it. Spending his birthday alone came with some upsides. The business section of the newspaper was full of doom and gloom. Not even the sport section brought any respite. Every match and event had been cancelled. All the debate was when the Premier League would start again, if it ever would. Marcus was happy for them to call time on the season now. At least Crystal Palace would be safe for another year.

At lunchtime, his phone rang. FaceTime. He answered to see the three Barlows sitting at the kitchen table. They started singing 'Happy Birthday' as soon as he answered.

'Hi Dad. How are you? Any symptoms yet?' said Olivia, waving.

'Hi everyone. Thanks a lot, I'm fine. No headaches, no cough, not even a sniffle. You all look well too. How's everything at home?'

'We're all fine here, Marcus,' said Alice. 'James and Libby are looking after me. Breakfast in bed, glass of champagne, read the paper, had a long bath, and look at these!' Alice panned the camera round to reveal a large bouquet of flowers and a box of truffles on the island. 'Aren't they beautiful?'

'Yes, very,' said Marcus.

'And not stolen from a grave either.'

'Ha ha! Very funny.'

Alice couldn't resist another dig about Valentine's Day.

'So what exciting things are you all doing today?' he said.

'Having lunch soon, then we're going for a walk, and in the afternoon we might play Cluedo,' said Alice.

At the mention of lunch, Marcus looked at James who was raising his eyes to the ceiling, a look of desperation. It was time to twist the knife.

'Sounds great. What are you all having?'

'Red lentil ragu with Camargue rice,' said Olivia excitedly. 'It's one of Mum's favourites. It's from my *Women's Health* magazine.'

'Wow, how delicious. I so wish I was with you all.'

He looked at his son who carried the look of a man pining for his George Foreman grill, now languishing in a puddle of cold grease in an empty house in Rusholme.

Serves you right for those fucking magic mushrooms and Prism, he thought.

'Sorry, no Colin the Caterpillar cake this year, Dad,' said Olivia. 'We'll have one when you come home and we do the candles thing. Do you have anything in the flat to celebrate with?'

'I have these,' he said, opening the food cupboard and taking out a box of Mr Kipling Bakewell Slices and holding them up to the camera. 'They'll be fine.'

'So what have you got planned for the rest of the day?' said Alice.

'I thought I might do a base jump off the top of the Shard this afternoon. Failing that, I will learn how to use the washing machine. I only have one clean shirt and one pair of underpants. I hadn't planned on being here, remember?'

Alice ignored his little dig.

'Well, at fifty-five, it's probably a good time to learn.'

It was easy for her to say, having the services of Jacinda on call, but he decided not to be spiky.

'Yes, you're probably right.'

They chatted for another ten minutes and the call ended. His birthday celebrations were over for another year. He made another coffee, sat on the sofa with a Bakewell Slice and picked up the newspaper. He wasn't a big fan of Cluedo anyway.

Professor Plum, lead piping, ballroom, he thought as he turned the pages devoted to another killer, one that was doing it by the thousand.

* * *

Claire and the children returned from their walk in the Memorial Park. The children were disappointed. The play areas had been cordoned off by the council, a protection against the virus, which obviously thrived on see-saws and roundabouts. She spoke to a workman who said it was to prevent adults and children getting close to each other in a confined space.

'What a load of bollocks,' she said.

He shrugged his shoulders and walked away.

She knocked on Mr Mahoney's door.

'Hi Mr Mahoney,' she said, standing back from the door. 'Just wanted to check you're okay?'

'Hi Claire, hi kids. I'm okay. Thanks for checking on me. I'm baking at the moment. I'll bring it up later, it's a tea loaf. It's in the oven. I'll leave it outside your front door when it's cooled down. How was your walk?'

'They've closed the children's play area but I can't keep them cooped up indoors all day. Home school starts tomorrow. I'd better get going. I'll check in on Ian as well. Bye, Mr Mahoney.' They climbed the stairs and walked along the balcony. She let the children into the flat.

'Take your shoes off. I'll be in in a minute. I'm just going to check on Ian.'

She knocked on the door to No. 12. There was no answer and she knocked again. She knew the Kensal Warrior would be locked down in a cyber world, headphones on, hands glued to a console. She was starting to get worried when Ian finally came to the door, headphones around his neck. He looked bleached from being locked in a darkened room all day, his eyes were bloodshot.

'Hi Claire. Everything all right?'

'I was going to ask you that. You took ages to answer.'

'Sorry. I was playing *Call of Duty*.'

'Are you okay? Have you got enough food and drink? Do you need me to get you anything from the shops?'

'No, I'm alright, thanks. Mrs Hassan brought me some samosas earlier. And I've got loads of Pepsi Max. I'm fine.'

'You need to look after yourself, Ian. Eat properly and try to get out once a day.'

The gap in the door was closing already. Claire sensed he wanted to get back to the Taliban. Shock and awe.

'Let me know if you need anything. Don't be afraid to ask, we're just next door.'

She returned to her flat, thinking about him, his twisted body trapped in his fantasy world. It was the ultimate lockdown.

* * *

Marcus had binge-watched three episodes of *Schitt's Creek* before deciding to confront the washing machine. He sorted his laundry into two piles, shirts and other stuff. He stared at the dials on the control panel. It was more complicated than the dashboard on a fighter jet.

If Jacinda can do it, it can't be that hard, he thought to himself.

He threw the shirts in the machine, added a detergent pod and turned the dial to 'Cottons' which seemed logical, since that's what they were made of. The machine remained silent. He pressed 'Start'. Silence. He called Alice.

'Hi Marcus. What's the matter? We're in the middle of Cluedo.'

'Sorry to interrupt you. I'm trying to get the washing machine to work but nothing's happening. What am I doing wrong?'

'Have you got it switched on? Is there a light on?'

He looked at the machine.

'Yes, it's on and showing me lots of symbols and numbers. I don't know what any of them mean.'

'Have you checked the manual?'

'I don't know where it is. It probably didn't come with one.'

'Don't be ridiculous, Marcus. Of course it came with instructions. You probably threw them away. Is water going into it?'

He thought about their machine in the utility room at Twin Gates, how it made a noise when Jacinda turned it on.

'Mmm … maybe not. What do I do?'

He followed her instructions, turning the little taps at the back of the machine. Water surged into the drum.

'Brilliant, thanks a lot, Al. Seems to be working fine now.'

'Pleased you've got it working. I'll get back to our game of Cluedo now.'

'Thanks. Bet it's Miss Scarlett, spanner in the library.'

'Bye Marcus, and happy birthday.'

The prime minister was making another statement to the nation. He had a new friend, Robert Jenrick, who did something with communities. Chris and Patrick were still missing. Their drink in Wetherspoons before lockdown had probably turned into a complete bender and destroyed their weekend. Jenny stepped in to do The Science. Boris thanked everyone for their sacrifices, particularly those who didn't visit their mothers.

Mother's Day could be a tricky one for Boris, thought Marcus. *All those lunches to go to. Bet he's glad to see the back of it.*

Robert was also being guided by The Science. Everyone now had to remain two metres apart. He called it 'social distancing'.

Sounds a bit like ethnic cleansing, thought Marcus.

The virus thought so too. Deaths had jumped by 100 in the previous two days. Jenny assured the public there would be sufficient protective equipment and ventilators to cope when the surge came as it inevitably would.

The washing machine was beeping, indicating that its job was done. He opened the door and removed his shirts which were damp and smelled nice. Success.

* * *

Claire was in the kitchen preparing dinner. She was chopping an onion when there was a knock at the door. It would be Mr Mahoney with his tea loaf. She put down her knife, dried her hands and went to the door.

'Hi Claire. Happy Mother's Day. How are you?'

A man in a blue checked shirt and a Barbour jacket stood in front of her. He was tanned and his brown, wavy hair fell over the collar of his jacket. He had the stubble of someone who hadn't shaved for a couple of days. He stared at her with piercing green eyes and smiled, almost sadistically. In his right hand, he held a bunch of cheap chrysanthemums, garage flowers. Her hand trembled as she held the door.

'Aren't you going to invite me in? Nice place.'

It had been almost two years. His hair had been much shorter, his skin paler. It was Jack.

'What are you doing here, Jack? How did you find us?' Her voice was faltering. Shock and awe.

'I rang your mum last week when I got back from Oz. She gave me your address. I always got on well with your mum. She said she never hears from you, never sees her grandchildren.'

'Well, that's a fucking lie. Her and Dad never want to see us. I've tried loads of times.'

Her mother still believed the breakup of her marriage had been Claire's fault, that she trapped Jack by getting pregnant and got what she deserved. She felt foolish for sending her the photograph of the children. She hadn't even had the decency to tell her that Jack was back.

'Aren't you going to invite me in then?' he said.

'You're not coming in. It will upset the children. They barely remember you. You made your choice when you fucked off with your boss.'

She was about to add 'and left me with an infection and two babies' when she heard footsteps running down the hall. Jack moved to the side and looked around her.

'Hi Kyle. It's Daddy. Wow, you've grown up so much! Come here, little man.'

Kyle stopped in the hall, looked up at his mummy and at Jack. She could see his mind starting to scroll through its files of memories, piecing together clips to confirm the truth. He looked up at her again. Jack moved closer to the door with his arms outstretched. She wanted to slam the door in his face but it was too late. Jack stepped forward and scooped up his son, hugging him like he had been away for years.

'How are you my little man? You're so big now.'

As she closed the door, Jack handed her the flowers.

'These are for you. Happy Mother's Day.' He walked into the kitchen with Kyle still in his arms. 'Where's Alexa?'

'She's watching television. I'll go and get her.' She walked along the hall, a thousand thoughts in fifteen footsteps. Why had he come back? What did he want? Why now?

Alexa was watching one of her favourite cartoons, she was engrossed and didn't look up.

'Alexa? Come into the kitchen with Mummy. Someone has come to see you.'

Alexa's eyes didn't move from the screen and Claire repeated herself again.

'Is it Mr Moany or Judith?' said Alexa.

'No, it's your daddy. He's come back to see you.'

Alexa looked up from the sofa. She was confused, she didn't remember her daddy.

'The man who went away?'

'Yes, come with me and you can say hello to him.'

Claire picked up her daughter and carried her. Alexa clung to her like a tree frog. They walked into the kitchen, where Kyle and his father were talking. Jack looked up. The baby he had left behind was now a little girl. She looked like him, the same long brown hair, the same green eyes. He held his arms out but she squeezed her mother tightly. Claire shook her head. He waved.

'Hello Alexa. I'm Jack. I'm your daddy.'

Biologically you might be but that's all, thought Claire. She put Alexa down on her booster seat. 'So, what do you want? Tea or coffee?'

'Coffee would be good. Milk, no sugar. Same as always, I haven't changed.' He smiled at her again.

'Same as always.' Every word he uttered made her feel sick. His sleazy grin and the pretence of being a father. Things would never be the same. Since he left, almost everything in her world had changed. She made two mugs of coffee and put them on the table.

'Last I heard, you were in Australia? When did you get back?'

'I got back last week. Didn't want to be locked down there. The bar in Brisbane I was working in was shutting, so I managed to get a flight back. Came back via Doha.'

'Where are you staying? Shouldn't you be in quarantine or something?'

'I'm staying with my parents in Sevenoaks. I thought you'd want to know that I'm back in the country?'

Claire thought about her in-laws, Giles and Saskia Halford. They were both GPs. They disliked her and she hated them.

Pair of posh, self-righteous shits, she thought.

'So, you're locked down with them?' she said.

'Yes, it's not too bad. They're pleased to have me back.'

Claire watched as Jack talked and played with her children. It was too good to be true. It seemed he was on autopilot, following a script, '*How to be a Parent After Two Years in Nowhere*'. Alexa was the first to warm, showing him her pictures on the wall and explaining how Spiky had lost some of his spines. Kyle was quieter and sat still in his chair.

'I've just got to go to the toilet. Can you keep an eye on them for a minute?' she said.

Claire went to the bathroom and locked the door. She was starting to retch. She put her head over the bowl, put her fingers down her throat and tried to make herself sick. Her stomach lurched forward, waves of nausea breaking over her but nothing came up. She went to the basin, splashed water on her face, flushed the toilet and returned to the kitchen. Alexa was telling Jack about Zoe. Kyle remained silent.

'Are you okay, sweetie?' Claire said to him, stroking his head.

'I think I've done a wee-wee,' he said.

She picked him up and felt his bottom. His trousers were wet and warm. She stared at Jack and comforted the little boy.

'Don't worry, sweetie. It's not your fault. Let's go and change your trousers. Maybe we'll put your pyjamas on now?'

They left the kitchen and Alexa went too. She wanted to put her pyjamas on as well. Jack was left alone in the kitchen and he looked around, surrounded by things that were part of a family he wasn't part of.

Claire came back on her own, leaving the children in the living room watching television.

'I've got to make their dinner soon. Why don't you go and sit with them, get to know your kids?'

She couldn't stop herself. She wanted him to know they had moved on without him. Jack sat on the sofa with the children. Alexa told him how they watched television with Mr Moany every day.

'Does Mummy have a boyfriend?' he asked. 'Mr Moany?'

'He's very old and smells funny. He doesn't have teeth. But he makes us cakes,' said Alexa.

Jack looked around the living room. Under the coffee table, he recognised her portfolio and another book that looked familiar. He picked it up and read the cover. 'Jack and Claire, 15 July 2015'. He opened the album and stared at the first photograph, Claire in the wedding dress she had designed and made herself, skilfully cut to hide her pregnancy. He was about to turn the page when Claire came back into the room.

'Please can you put that back, Jack?'

'Why? I was only looking at it. I haven't seen these in a long time.'

'Why, did your parents burn theirs as a celebration? I'd prefer it if you didn't touch my things, so please put it back? I've made a fish pie for the children. Do you want to stay, there's enough for four?'

'Thanks. That's kind of you.'

'It'll be ready in ten minutes. Sit and watch TV with the children.'

The fish pie bubbled through its brown crust. She put it on the table with the broccoli and called everyone to the kitchen. Jack held Alexa's hand, but Kyle kept a distance, still trying to work things out in his little mind.

'What do you want to drink, Jack? Water or Ribena?'

'Water is fine, thanks.'

The talk over dinner was small. Schools, nursery, the children's friends, favourite things. Jack was engaging, charming and witty, all the things she'd liked about him when they got together. Some things about him hadn't changed.

'Okay both of you. Let's brush our teeth, wash our faces and get ready for bed. Say goodnight to Jack.' She made the point of not calling him Daddy. He had given up the right to that title.

'Can I read them a story?' he said. 'You don't mind, do you?'

'Best not. If you could wash up the plates, that would be a help? I'll be back soon.'

The children said goodnight. Alexa gave Jack one of her special kisses, but Kyle just said goodnight. Claire read them a short story and put Alexa to bed first before tucking Kyle under his duvet.

'Why has Daddy come back?' said the little boy.

That's a bloody good question, she thought to herself.

'Because he wanted to see you and Alexa. He's been away for a long time.'

'Is he going to stay with us now?'

'I don't know, sweetie. Mummy and Daddy have a lot to talk about. Would you like him to stay with us?'

Kyle looked confused. He shrugged his little shoulders in his Buzz Lightyear pyjamas.

'I don't know,' the little boy whispered.

She hugged him through the duvet and kissed him on top of his head.

'It will all be okay, Kyle. Don't worry, Mummy will always be here with you.'

By the time Claire returned to the kitchen, Jack had washed the plates and left them to drain. He turned towards her. His 'charm' face had changed.

'Shall we go and sit in the living room? You've made it look really nice. Love the chair, by the way. We need to discuss things. You and me, the children.'

'We can stay here and talk. What "things" did you want to discuss, Jack? Why have you come back?'

She didn't give him time to answer. What followed had been rehearsed in her mind hundreds of times on hundreds of nights spent alone, thinking about her life, thinking of ending it. It was like squeezing a big spot, anger and bitterness stored up inside her for nearly two years splattered over the kitchen table in a spray of pus.

'Because, if it's to say you're sorry for shagging around with your boss while I was pregnant with Alexa, or for giving me her shitty disease, or for walking out on me and your children to go off on some ego trip without even letting us know where you were, really, don't fucking bother! If it's just to say that you're sorry for not contributing a single penny to raising your children while we were all struggling here with hardly any food and no money, as you drank and fucked your way around Australia or wherever you were, save your regrets and apologies, Jack. I don't need them and the children don't need them either. We're all just fine as we are. So, what did you want to discuss, Jack?'

He had expected her onslaught and he stared straight at her.

'I want to be part of their lives. I have rights as their father. My mum and dad have spoken with a solicitor friend and he says I can apply for access and potentially shared custody.'

'Rights? What fucking rights do you have? You gave up those rights when you walked away with no conscience, without even thinking about whether or not we would cope. As for your parents, they haven't even sent a birthday or Christmas card in years. I know they hated me, but their grandchildren? Really?'

He didn't flinch.

'According to the law, I have rights as their biological father and I intend to use them. And don't point the accusing finger at me about my lifestyle. Who's this, your latest fuckbuddy? Some friend with benefits?'

He picked up the business card from the window ledge and threw it across the table at her.

'So, how many times has Marcus Barlow, Partner, "done it with you" then? I would have thought he was a bit out of your league, or maybe he just wanted a bit of council estate skank? Is that how you're coping? A bit of money on the side?'

She looked at the business card and thought of Marcus. She thought of his silly accents and voices, reading bedtime stories to the children and helping her. Jack had no right to judge Marcus, or her.

'He's just a friend. Well, not even a friend. I've only met him twice. He's a friend of my social worker, Gavin. He's everything you're not, Jack.'

He looked around the kitchen and turned his nose up like a bad smell had wafted by.

'And is this what you call coping? A shitty council flat on an estate in the arse end of London. Is this what you want for our children, the best you can give them?' he shouted, his anger rising.

She felt he was trying to demolish everything she was proud of, humiliating her, saying it was all valueless. The last two years of struggle had been for nothing. It wasn't perfect, but he was in no position to judge her. She reached to her right and picked up a saucepan from the draining board and swung it at his head.

'You fucking prick. I don't care what you think!'

He raised his arm just in time, as the saucepan crashed into his elbow, right on the funny bone. He screamed out in pain. He leaned across and grabbed her jumper by the collar and pulled her head down on to the table. He stood up and pressed on her face, pushing her cheek into her eye so she couldn't see. She could feel spit dribbling from the corner of her mouth as she tried to swallow. She struggled but he was much stronger. She tried to shout, to distract him, but he was dominating her.

The tea loaf had taken a while to cool. Mr Mahoney wrapped it in foil and climbed the stairs to Claire's flat. He could feel its warmth on his hands. He looked through the kitchen window. The lights were on and he could see the back of a man. Claire heard a banging on the window but Jack kept pushing her face into the table with both hands.

The frames on the front doors of the flats in Kensal Mansions had withstood many storms, but they were no match for the right shoulder of Phelan Mahoney.

The lock popped instantly and Jack suddenly felt his collar being grabbed by a giant hand. Like many of his generation and background, Phelan Mahoney was useful with his fists.

'Get off her, you dirty cunt!'

With a single swing of the caretaker's arm, Jack was lying on his back in the hall, slumped against the wall. Mr Mahoney hadn't punched him, it was just a swing of the arm. The punch was next as he stepped into the hall and stood over him.

'Mr Mahoney, stop! Don't hit him! It's Jack, my husband,' screamed Claire.

The caretaker turned to look at her, concern on his face.

'Are you okay, Claire? Has he hurt you?'

'I'm alright. He's only bruised my face. Just get him out of here.' She was shaking.

The caretaker picked Jack up with one hand around his neck and pinned him against the wall. Jack was now trembling too. One punch from Mr Mahoney and he would be joining Ian in the living room of No. 12.

'It's okay, it's okay, get off of me. I'm going.' He slid along the wall, keeping a safe distance from Mr Mahoney and his clenched fists. 'We'll be talking again, Claire. You'll hear from me again soon, you can count on that. Give me my coat, it's on the chair.'

Claire threw the coat to Mr Mahoney who had stepped out on to the balcony. He threw it over the balcony into the courtyard below.

'There's plenty of dog shit down there. Now fuck off!'

Jack skulked along the balcony and down the stairs, picking up his jacket and walking through the alleyway. Mr Mahoney watched him all the way and stepped back into the hall. Claire fell into his arms and sobbed, safe in the mustiness of his cardigan.

'I'm really sorry about your door. I'll fix it tomorrow. I don't think he's coming back anytime soon.'

He grinned a toothy grin. 'You okay now? I'm sorry I used the C-word.'

'You just beat me to it.'

'Why are you crying, Mummy?'

Claire looked down the hall. Kyle was standing outside his bedroom, nervously twisting his fingers. She went to comfort him.

'Mummy's fine, sweetie. Don't worry.'

'Did Daddy hurt you?'

'No, we were talking and he got angry. Mr Mahoney stopped him from getting very angry.'

'Why was he angry?'

'Let's talk about that tomorrow. Let me tuck you back into bed.'

Claire came back into the kitchen and looked for her inhaler. She was struggling to breathe. She took two puffs and breathed slowly. Mr Mahoney had made two mugs of tea and cut two slices of his tea loaf. They sat down together.

'I thought tea would be a good idea. And the cake is good too.'

She smiled at him.

'It's a great idea, Mr Mahoney. Thank you. I don't know how that would have ended if you hadn't come.' She stroked his hand. 'I don't think our social distancing is going that well, do you? It's only been one day. Boris won't be happy with us.'

'I expect he's busy enough for certain.'

* * *

He opened a bottle of 2010 Château La Dominique, Saint-Émilion, and let it breathe. He had been saving it for a dinner with Gavin. Marcus seasoned his steak, positioned it on the plate, took a picture and sent it to James.

Hi James. A birthday on your own has some benefits. Here's mine. Enjoy the tofu. Dad. x

He seared the steak to medium-rare perfection, poured a glass of wine and sat down to enjoy his birthday meal. WhatsApp pinged. He thought it would be James, aggrieved with meat envy, but it was from Gavin.

Happy Birthday M. Glad you liked the shoes. Hope you had a great day. Signal here not good. Parents don't have broadband! G.

He raised his glass in a toast to his absent friend. Gavin would have enjoyed the claret, it was very good. The steak and the large piece of Roquefort that followed proved to be great company for the wine and he finished the bottle, listening to 'Physical Graffiti', which he always thought was Led Zeppelin's best album. He was relaxing on the sofa when WhatsApp pinged multiple times. It was just a number that came up on the display. No name.

He opened the messages.

Hi Marcus. Thank you for the phone.
Really kind of you. Hope you had a good Birthday?
Thought you might like this from your biggest fans.
Take care. C.

He opened the photograph. Kyle and Alexa in the park waving. Jimmy Page's opening power chords to 'Kashmir' started and he stared out of the window. It took him a few minutes to work things out. Gavin must have told her. He realised he didn't know her surname and saved her number as 'Claire Ladbroke'. He replied.

Hi Claire. Thanks a lot. Glad the phone works. Spent my birthday in my flat on my own. Long story!! Hope you had a good Mother's Day.

He was loading the dishwasher when his phone pinged multiple times again.

Sorry you were on your own today

Not much fun!

My husband came back

Surprise visit. Two years too late.

Shit Mother's Day but sort of okay now

Mr Mahoney sorted him out!

Her multiple texts were irritating but at least she used whole words and punctuation. And no yellow faces. Marcus envisaged the scene in her flat. He didn't envy Claire's husband if Mr Mahoney had intervened. It had been a very firm handshake when they met. He replied again.

Doesn't sound good. Are you sure you're okay? Here if you need a chat.

She replied quickly with more texts.

Maybe another time?

Bit tired now

Might need some advice.

Thanks a lot.

By the time he had cleared away and tidied the kitchen, it was time for the *BBC News at Ten*, which said the same things the news had said four hours earlier. Lockdown was starting for real in the morning.

It was Sunday, 22 March 2020.

Chapter 26

IN THE COURT OF KING ZOOM

Marcus was sitting on the sofa checking The Sequence. Outlook was overheating. His diary was filling up with Zoom meetings quicker than the ballroom on the *Titanic*. Invites had the same titles, 'Catch up on', 'Briefing for', 'Pre-meet to discuss', 'Pre-pre-meet to discuss' or simply, 'Chat'. They were things that would previously have been sorted out in a corridor conversation, or over a coffee. That had gone. The office kingdom had been overthrown and a new monarch was on the throne, King Zoom, and he ruled in a different way.

King Zoom didn't commute, read *Metro* or have a double macchiato and porridge before he started. He didn't indulge in cheery office banter or tell any jokes before he opened his laptop. He started at 7.30, sometimes earlier, and didn't stop until late in the evening. He didn't need food or drink, he didn't even stop for a piss. He just kept working and working. Marcus looked at his diary and wondered when he would eat. King Zoom had stolen his day. Long live the king!

Fuck me, he thought. *What the hell's going on?*

The call with the joint CEOs of Yeast Feast was at 10.30. King Zoom would be summoning him soon. He shaved and showered, skipped his moisturising regime, and brushed his teeth for two minutes instead of three. His bowels were like his diary, congested. Ten minutes later, he was seated at his desk in a collar and tie, cufflinks and suit. Standards had to be maintained, even in lockdown.

His first call was at 8.30 with Steve Pettigrew. Steve was wearing a T-shirt and hadn't shaved. In the background, he could see Steve's wife loading the dishwasher.

'Morning Steve. How are you? Good weekend?'

'Not bad, Marcus. Mother's Day at home. How about you? You look very smart. Are you at home?'

Marcus explained the fiasco over his birthday. Steve commiserated.

'All because of those Data Solutions partners? Sounds like a pretty rubbish birthday. At least you don't have to put up with this.'

Steve picked up his laptop and panned around his new 'home office'. He lived in a two-bedroom flat in Kentish Town. He was working at the dining table, opposite his wife Laura, who was a hypnotherapist. Their son was reading a book at the end of the table.

'What happens when you have a client call, or when Laura has to speak to her clients?' said Marcus. 'If I was suffering from bulimia, I'm not sure I'd want you listening in.'

'We'll have to take private calls in the bedroom. Not ideal. Still, it's only the first day. I guess it's the same for everyone?'

'My diary has gone mental,' said Marcus. 'It's full of Zoom calls. I wonder when we'll ever do any bloody work?'

'How's it going with Laila?'

'Working with a power-hungry insomniac with no life? So far, so good. She thinks lockdown is great. More time to work.'

He grabbed five minutes to make a coffee before the Project Medusa call with Laila and the joint CEOs from Yeast Feast. Daniel Barelli and Joe Stern were ex-investment bankers who had got themselves some private equity funding to set up Yeast Feast. The business had ridden the wave of the artisan bread boom. Set up in a small factory in Wandsworth, the business had grown exponentially, moving to larger premises outside Kingston in 2018. Its products were in every supermarket and health food outlet in the country. Even Alice knew them; she liked their gluten-free, multi-seed flatbreads. They were buying Make 'n' Bake, the final piece in the jigsaw before they listed the business, cashed in their chips for squillions and buggered off into the sunset to enjoy the rest of their lives. That was the plan. He joined Zoom.

'Morning everyone. Marcus Barlow.'

Three other faces were on his screen. Laila was in her living room, Daniel and Joe were in their stylish apartment in Docklands. They had matching mugs and were obviously not isolating from each other. It was Joe Stern who spoke first.

'Nice work on the tie, Marcus. Are you wearing a suit as well?'

'Actually, no. My professional appearance only extends as far as my waist. Below that, I'm wearing stockings, suspenders and high heels. Lockdown has given me the freedom to finally express myself.'

Daniel and Joe laughed out loud. Laila's face remained frozen like she had been injected with Botox using a turkey baster.

'Sounds great,' said Daniel. 'Go for it.'

As icebreakers go, it was different and better than the weather or their journey. Nobody was going anywhere. Daniel and Joe confirmed they had read the documents, which was unusual. Laila opened the presentation and spent the next hour explaining what TOOL would do for them.

'You have to start with the end in mind, what you want this business to look like in two years' time, from front to back. That determines the value you can create which determines how much you should pay for Make 'n' Bake. Until you know the end game, you run the risk of making a colossal mistake. That's why TOOL is central to our proposal.'

'And potentially screwing up five years of hard work in the process?' said Daniel.

'Exactly,' said Marcus.

Laila was bold and confident, saying all the right things in all the right places. Yeast Feast was rising nicely.

'I'm loving this,' said Joe. 'It's exactly what we should be doing. How long did you say this TOOL thing would take?'

'Three months, approximately,' said Laila.

'Could you do it in two?'

It was a blatant buying signal.

'Absolutely,' said Marcus.

Daniel and Joe nodded in agreement. Marcus and Laila had stumbled across a rare breed of animal thought to be extinct. A client who didn't question the cost. They were known as 'blind cows'; they couldn't see and you milked them for everything.

'How much will the TOOL phase cost?' said Daniel. 'Ballpark figure?'

'Between £1.5 million and £2 million,' said Marcus.

'On a contingent fee basis?'

'Fifty per cent on time and materials and fifty per cent contingent on higher cost savings delivered,' said Marcus. The blind cows didn't take long to make a decision.

'Agreed. When can you start?' said Joe.

Laila was quick off the mark.

'Next week?'

'Great. Thanks for the call everyone. Really good,' said Daniel and they disappeared from the screen.

It took thirty seconds for Laila to call Marcus.

'That went pretty well, didn't it? Apart from your transvestite joke at the beginning which could have gone horribly wrong.'

'Do you think so? I thought they liked it. It broke the ice, didn't it? Maybe Daniel and Joe are cross-dressers too?'

'"Too"? What do you mean, "too"? Are you a cross-dresser, Marcus?'

'Only at weekends when I prefer to be called Melissa.'

She had had enough of Marcus's fantasies and wanted to get on.

'I'll start on SCAR and the Engagement Letter. Nobody's going anywhere, so we should get it all approved this week.'

'True. Good point. Speak later.'

* * *

Kyle was fidgeting. He was already bored after an hour practising his key words. It was only an hour into the day and home schooling was proving a challenge. Claire switched on the kettle and turned up the radio in time for the start of *Woman's Hour*. Jane Garvey introduced two 'experts' on home schooling. They made her feel a failure. Organised, disciplined and intelligent, they were the mothers who baked cakes and ran a thriving interior design business at the same time as teaching physics to their enthusiastic and diligent kids. They didn't live in a damp flat on a council estate either. It was the next item on the programme that disturbed her more. An increase in cases of domestic violence during the lockdowns in China and Italy. Jack's assault had only been stopped by Mr Mahoney's timely arrival. It could have been much worse than a bruised face. Beverley rang.

'Hi Claire. I just got your messages. What happened last night?'

'Hi Beverley. We're just taking a break from schoolwork. I'm still shaken, it was pretty awful.'

'Tell me. What happened?'

Claire gave her friend a cut-down version of Sunday's events. It made her feel sick again.

'What a bastard,' said Beverley. 'What right did he think he had, just turning up like that, after how long? You should tell the police.'

'I'm okay. I'm more upset by what it's done to Kyle. He wet the bed last night. I don't want to get the police involved. Jack would probably say Mr Mahoney assaulted him.'

'Do you want to meet up, go to the park maybe? Socially distanced support!'

'That would be great. Better than no support at all. How about 3.30? I'd better get back to lessons or Helena will be on my case! See you later.'

Claire called the children back into the kitchen. Following the advice of the two supermums on *Woman's Hour*, she took a decision: only one set of lessons, Alexa would do what Kyle did, only slower. She took some peas out of the freezer. Not exactly counting beans but they would do, at least for 30 minutes until they defrosted.

Kyle saw Bruce first and ran to hug him, despite protestations from their mothers. The boys didn't understand why they weren't allowed near each other. They didn't understand why the play area was shut either. The two women sat on a bench as the children ran around. Beverley could see the bruising to Claire's face and instinctively hugged her.

'Are you okay? Nothing broken?'

'No, I'm fine. I think I'm still in shock. Seeing him after two years was the biggest shock of all. Worse thing, he's still bloody good-looking.'

'He's a shit and he had no right to do that.' Beverley cupped Claire's face in her hands. 'You're a brilliant mum and he's a pig. I still think you should tell the police.'

Claire shook her head.

'How are you getting on with the schoolwork?' said Beverley.

'Not great. Probably only did a fraction of what Miss Mistakidis had in her timetable. It's really hard to keep their attention without getting distracted. I'm trying to stop myself from kicking them into the living room and putting the telly on. How about you?'

'Edward has already shouted at Bruce twice for not concentrating. He doesn't have any patience with him. It's not easy, but it's only the first day. You should check out the BBC website. It has some great stuff online.'

'I haven't got broadband, remember?'

'Shit. I'm sorry, I forgot.'

'How are things with Edward? Pleased to have him back?'

'Not as much as I'm going to miss seeing you. We were making so much progress.'

'I'll miss it too.'

The two women said goodbye and went in different directions. Claire checked on Mr Mahoney, who was pleased to see her. He was sad to watch *The Chase* on his own.

'It won't be the same without you and the children. Do you think they'll stop *The Chase* because of the virus? We don't want Bradley or The Governess catching it from one of the contestants.'

'I wouldn't worry, Mr Mahoney. I expect they've got enough shows recorded to keep us going for a few months.'

The virus was changing everyone's lives. At least Bradley Walsh was safe.

* * *

Marcus declined the Zoom invitation to the Risk and Compliance webinar, 'Covid-19 and Protecting Our Data: The Twin Threat'. It gave him time to have lunch. He turned on the television just before the *BBC News at One*. *Bargain Hunt* was coming to an end and he switched over to ITV, which was in the middle of an advert break. An advert for walk-in baths, followed by another for eco-friendly cremations.

Jesus, is this what I've got to look forward to in retirement? he thought.

He recognised Carol Vorderman. She was advertising an equity release scheme for over-fifty-fives. He thought she looked too good to be doing adverts, but after being replaced on *Countdown* by the younger Rachel Riley, she was probably grateful for the work.

Carol turned to the camera.

'*You could even give your children some of their inheritance money early.*'

Marcus thought of James, who was probably still in bed, and shouted at the screen.

'You can fuck off with that idea, Carol!'

Carol Vorderman's equity release offer was starting to look more appealing after he checked Stockwatch. Another massive red day. It had fallen below 5,000, the lowest it had been in years. Poverty was becoming more imminent by the day. Staying on at The Firm was his only option, even if he was on a ventilator. He got a message from James, who had seen his picture of the ribeye steak.

That's brutal, Dad. FFS get back here soon. Eggs are under threat now. I'm going back to Manchester!

It was a small consolation that James was struggling with the vegan regime. Although Marcus hated isolating on his own, it wasn't all bad. A Fray Bentos steak pie, oven chips and baked beans tonight. He replied.

Illegitimi non carborundum.

He knew James would need to Google it.

It was after burning his hand with the iron for the third time that Marcus decided to call Alice.

'Hi Al. It's me. How's lockdown going?'

'We're all fine here, Marcus. How are you doing at the flat?'

'Happy enough, apart from burning myself three times with the iron.'

Alice hadn't picked up an iron in years.

'Oh, well done, it's about time. I've started a new painting today. Gone back to watercolours and still life. I'm painting the garden, the view from the office. It's something to keep me busy. The children are fine but James seems to have changed since Christmas. He's been quite aggressive at times.'

'Do you want me to have a word with him? See if there's something on his mind?'

'No, leave it for now. He'll come around.'

Marcus guessed James was suffering from chronic meat withdrawal. After surviving at university on Deliveroo and Just Eat, going 'cold turkey' on pulses, nuts and grains was always going to be tough. He described his new working day and the dictatorial regime of King Zoom.

'Sounds horrific, if you ask me. What about those poor people who live in flats? And what about if they have kids, especially little ones?' said Alice.

'I'm living in a flat too, remember? Lockdown is the same for everyone.'

'Yes, with high-speed broadband and every creature comfort around you. There are loads of people far worse off than you, Marcus.'

Says the woman living in a six-bedroomed house with a cleaner, gardener, Ocado and the Organic Delivery Company, spending her time painting the fucking garden, he thought to himself.

'I'm thinking of coming home this weekend. I've had absolutely no symptoms at all.'

'I think you should wait, Marcus. You might be asymptomatic. This virus is very contagious. I don't want you bringing it into the house and infecting all of us.'

Thanks to the *Daily Mail*, Alice was now an expert on isolation protocol. He was tired and couldn't be bothered to argue.

'Fine. Speak soon.'

The prime minister's statement to the nation was later that evening. He had some serious things to say that could only be done after *EastEnders*. Boris appeared on his own, speaking from behind a desk, the gravitas turned up to eleven. Apart from essential shops, everything would be closing. Nobody could go out, except for shopping and one form of exercise a day. Nobody was allowed to meet anyone outside their home. Weddings and baptisms were cancelled, but funerals for the Covid dead were still going ahead. Boris made lots of promises about the race to find a vaccine and buying millions of test kits. He returned to wartime rhetoric to lift the nation's spirits.

'The people of this country will rise to this challenge. And we will come through it stronger than ever. We will beat the coronavirus and we will beat it together. And therefore I urge you, at this moment of national emergency, to stay at home, protect our NHS and save lives.'

We'll be fighting it on the beaches next! thought Marcus.

The situation had to be serious. The BBC had wheeled out Fiona Bruce for the post-statement analysis. Reeta Chakrabarti or Clive Myrie only got the fluffier stuff, and Huw Edwards was probably being kept up their sleeve for when a member of the Royal Family caught the virus and died.

Watching at the same time, Claire found Boris's statement depressing. Confined to the flat, apart from one form of exercise once a day, she was feeling more anxious. The first day of lockdown hadn't gone well. She took a Xanax to calm her and took two puffs on her inhaler. She put on an Ella Fitzgerald record and sat back in her chair with her blanket around her. Ella sang 'Someone to Watch Over Me'.

I wish they would, she thought, *because they've been doing a shit job so far.*

* * *

It was only tumbleweed that was missing as Marcus walked up Queensway to Kensington Gardens. He was taking his one form of exercise early in the day. He picked up a copy of *Metro* from outside the Underground station, which was also closed. The news that KFC, Nando's, Greggs, Subway and Costa Coffee were all closing made him think of James. Coming home had turned out to be a blessing in disguise; he could have starved in Manchester.

He scanned his diary. Eight Zoom calls, first one starting at 8.15 a.m. Eric the concierge was in reception, busy with a tape measure.

'Good morning, Eric. Early start today?'

'Good morning, Marcus. I didn't know you were still in the building? I thought you would be locked down with the family. I know Mr Douglas has gone to Scotland. Most of the apartments in the block are empty.'

'Long story Eric, but better not get too close. Two people at work have tested positive and Alice has asked me to stay here. I'm self-isolating. What are you doing?'

'We're having a Perspex screen put up in front of my desk.'

'To do what?'

'Stop people breathing on me.'

Marcus put on a suit and tie and ended his first Zoom call before joining the pipeline call at nine. Eleven faces appeared on his screen: Kelvin, Izzy, eight partners and Chloe who was wearing a onesie with Eeyore motifs. A Winnie the Pooh theme was emerging. Marcus looked at the backdrops to the faces of the partners. Bookshelves in studies, black and white family portraits in home offices and views of expansive gardens warmed by the morning sun. Kelvin opened the meeting in a good mood. He was wearing a striped Breton sweater.

'Morning everyone, welcome to our first Zoom pipeline call of lockdown. I hope everyone's getting used to Zoom now?'

There was lots of nodding. Marcus looked at Simon Loder, taking a bite out of a smoked salmon and cream cheese bagel. He took a drink from a crystal glass.

'What's that your drinking?' said Vanessa Briggs, who was wearing an aubergine-coloured jumpsuit with one button too many undone. She looked like an off-duty fighter pilot.

'Champagne,' said Simon. 'Goes well with the smoked salmon. Only Waitrose champagne though. Bit early in the day for Ruinart.'

Everyone laughed. Lockdown was much harder than anyone had anticipated. Izzy gave the performance update. The dial hadn't shifted, but it didn't matter, they had already fixed the numbers. Kelvin jumped back in.

'I think everyone should be aware of Project Medusa, which it looks like Laila Saetang has just sold for £2 million. Could be the blind cow we've been waiting all year for.'

As he was speaking, the sound of seagulls screeching loudly in the background interrupted his last words.

'What the hell was that?' said Oliver Rankin. 'It sounded like seagulls.'

'Yes, I heard it too,' said Jacob Mauser.

Kelvin went on mute and switched off his camera. He reappeared a couple of minutes later.

'Sorry about that. Just had to deal with something here. Where were we up to?'

Izzy was just about to invite partners to give their updates when Marcus interrupted.

'We were talking about mysterious seagull noises, Kelvin. They disappeared around the same time you did. Bit of a coincidence that? Does Hampstead have a large seagull population?'

'I'm not in Hampstead, Marcus. The family and I have decamped to our holiday home in Cornwall. We got away just before lockdown. I don't think the locals are that happy but sod them. It's our second homes that keep the local economy going.'

Marcus thought about Steve Pettigrew, working at his kitchen table and what he had said.

'I guess it's the same for everyone, Marcus?'

Except it wasn't.

* * *

Claire had spent the previous hour spinning a small globe to show Kyle and Alexa different countries and places in the world. She was getting better in her new role as a teacher. Her phone rang.

'Hi Claire. It's Gavin. How are you?'

It was good to hear his voice.

'Hello! Good to hear from you. The kids are both well. They're a bit bored and it's only the second day. Only going out once a day is going to be tough. I didn't have a great weekend.'

'Why? What happened?'

'Jack turned up out of the blue on Sunday afternoon. It didn't go well. In fact, it was bloody awful.' Her voice started to tremble as she told him what happened: the assault, Mr Mahoney arriving, Kyle wetting himself. 'Can he do that? Just barge back into our lives after two years. He left us, he didn't give a shit about us, and now he decides he wants to be a father. Can he do that, Gavin?'

The desperation in her voice grew. She wished Gavin wasn't so far away and she needed him. Jack's reappearance had come at the wrong time.

'Your mum should have let you know. Have you spoken to her?'

'No, not yet. I'm still too angry. But can he do that, Gavin? Can he barge back into our lives again, just like that?'

'Well, the law says he has a right as their biological father, unless you can prove he is an unsuitable parent and a threat to the children.'

'That's easy. He fucked off with someone else and left us on our own for two years without contributing a bean. Then he comes back and assaults me. Isn't that unsuitable enough?'

'I know, I know,' he said, trying to calm her down. 'I know it's upsetting but try not to get anxious. He hasn't actually done anything formal and getting violent on Sunday isn't going to help his case. Focus on the children and yourself and getting through lockdown. He probably won't do anything.'

'Oh, he will, I know him. His parents will be pushing him to take back what he thinks is his. It was the way he looked at our home, he resented everything about me. Like I was a failure and he could do so much better.'

He hadn't heard her speak like this for a long time.

'Stay calm, Claire. He won't be able to take the children away from you. That isn't going to happen. Trust me. Is Kyle okay?'

'He is, but he's very mixed up. He hasn't been himself since Sunday evening, and he wet the bed again last night. It's still going around in his little head.'

'That's so sad. I'm sorry Mother's Day was such a disaster. You deserved much better than that.'

'I felt so low. I texted Marcus on Sunday night to thank him for my phone. Turns out he was in his flat, celebrating his birthday on his own. Both of us had a crap Sunday.'

The news about Marcus took Gavin by surprise.

'Really? He never said anything to me about being on his own. Was he okay? I'll call him later.'

Gavin wondered what had happened? Why had Marcus spent his birthday on his own and not told him?

'Have you heard from him since?'

'No.'

Kyle came into the kitchen. The programme on dinosaurs had finished and he wanted a glass of Ribena.

'I'll have to go, Gavin. Back to lessons. Thanks for the call, it was great to hear from you. How are your mum and dad?'

'They're okay. Lockdown isn't so different; they've been self-isolating for years. Call me if you need anything and look after yourself and the children.'

The queue outside Tesco Express stretched along Ladbroke Grove. Andrew Coates was wearing sunglasses at five o'clock in the afternoon on a cloudy day. Policing the long queue was the latest in his growing list of duties.

'Sorry, only one person per family allowed in at a time,' he said, raising a hand and barring Claire's entry.

'What? What are you talking about?'

'Read the sign. Only one person per household allowed in at any one time. Social distancing. New policy.'

'And what do you suggest I do with my children? Tie them up to a rail?'

'How about leaving them at home with their father?'

After Sunday's events, he'd struck a raw nerve and she stepped out from behind Alexa's buggy when a familiar face appeared.

'Hello Claire, hi kids,' said Lester Primus, who was wearing a mask. 'Is there a problem?'

She pointed at the security guard.

'There is with him! He said I can't bring my children into the shop. Only one person per household or some bollocks like that.'

Lester looked at him and shook his head.

'For goodness' sake, Andy, use some common sense, will you? I'll speak to you afterwards. Claire, come in.' He beckoned her into the shop. 'I'm sorry about him. He gets a bit keen with all these new rules. The shop has been like a war zone these past couple of days.'

Claire looked at the shelves, which were bare and empty. It was like a scene from a Russian bakery during the Cold War.

'I've put a few things by, but even our food bank is empty. People have been stealing from it. On Mondays, Wednesdays and Fridays, between nine and ten, we are only open for people over seventy and the vulnerable. I'm happy to let you in then if it helps?'

'Thanks, Mr Primus. That's really kind of you. It's really difficult for me with lockdown and home schooling. I'll come back tomorrow. Hopefully there'll be something on the shelves by then.'

The store manager went to his office and returned a few minutes later with a plastic bag containing a few essential items, mainly tins and pasta. She bought as much as she could. It came to £24.65 and would keep her family fed for a couple of days. She walked past Andrew Coates on her way out.

'See you tomorrow morning, Andy.'

She winked at him and he scowled from behind his mask.

* * *

Marcus finished his seventh Zoom call and went to the toilet. King Zoom was playing havoc with his digestion. His day had become seamless. Morning had fused with afternoon which was blended with evening. He made a coffee and sat down to watch the daily coronavirus briefing.

Boris, Chris and Patrick were taking a break and had been replaced by their understudies: Matt Hancock, Jenny and a new chum named Stephen. Matt was wearing his rainbow NHS lapel badge, showing his solidarity with the frontline.

Once all this is over, he'll be the one freezing pay increases for NHS workers, thought Marcus. *Someone will have to pay for all of this and it won't be Matt.*

Matt looked into the camera and gave out the latest stats. Eighty-seven more people had died bringing the total to four hundred and twenty-two.

'Our hearts go out to their families and their friends,' said Matt solemnly.

He was launching a raft of new initiatives to fight the virus. Two hundred and fifty thousand volunteers were being recruited to help the NHS, and twelve thousand former doctors, nurses and ancillary staff had signed up to support the national effort.

Maybe if they hadn't been treated like shit, they wouldn't have left in the first place? he thought.

Hypocrisy and jingoism brought out the worst in Marcus. It was hard not to be cynical. Jenny and Stephen bailed Matt out when the journalists' questions got a bit too clever. On his debut for the first team, Matt hadn't played well. He looked out of his depth.

Marcus took a Fray Bentos steak and gravy pie out of the cupboard and was struck by the yellow banner on the lid. He hadn't noticed it before.

New Improved Recipe. 33% More Meat.

More filling wouldn't necessarily improve the taste, and the increase in the amount of meat was very precise. He hoped they hadn't tampered with a winning formula and put it in the oven. He was clearing away after dinner when his phone rang. It was Gavin.

'Hi Marcus. How are you?'

'Hi Gavin. For a second, I thought it was work so I'm glad it's you. Work is a total nightmare at the moment.'

'It's always been a nightmare, Marcus. So what's different?'

Marcus summarised his new life under King Zoom.

'Sounds horrendous.'

'How are things in Scotland?'

'They're okay. Spending most of my time looking after my mum. Her Alzheimer's is getting worse. Apart from that, it's pretty dull, playing the piano and having long walks with the dogs. The coffee here is awful and I miss the Panettone Palace. I spoke to Claire today. She said you spent your birthday on Sunday on your own in the flat? What happened?'

'Yes, I'm still here. I'm isolating.'

He told him the story of the infected Data Solutions partners, and Alice's discovery. Gavin roared with laughter.

'Why didn't you just tell her at the time?'

'Because I knew what she would say, I thought I would get away with it. I didn't go anywhere near those two people and I left the conference early, remember?'

'Why didn't you tell me you were celebrating on your own?'

'And what could you have done? I wanted to suffer on my own as punishment for my own stupidity.' He changed the subject. 'Did Claire tell you about her husband coming back? That all sounded a bit grim?'

'Yes, not good. I'm quite worried about her. She sounds pretty fragile at the moment. Something like this happening in lockdown could be a real setback for her.'

They talked about missing their Tuesday night dinners. Marcus didn't own up to his meal that evening. Even with its increased meat content and special puff pastry topping, he knew his friend would disapprove. They talked for almost an hour before Gavin had to go, his mother needed to take her tablets.

One word Gavin had said stuck in his mind. Fragile. He felt fragile too. Isolated by the virus and trapped in a world that was becoming more alien to him by the day. Alice wasn't fragile at all. She was safe in Twin Gates with James and Olivia to support her, her watercolours and the latest delivery from Ocado. He felt lonely, isolated and called another fragile soul.

Claire had just watched Jac Naylor, the brilliant and acerbic CT surgeon, perform miracles in *Holby City*. The credits were rolling as her phone rang. A name appeared on the screen of her phone. 'Posh Marcus'.

'Hi Marcus. I didn't expect to hear from you! Do you specialise in surprises?'

'Sorry, have I caught you at a bad time? I spoke with Gavin earlier this evening and he was concerned about what happened on Sunday. I thought I would call instead of texting. I'm not very good with my fingers.'

'I expect you prefer a quill?' she said.

'Ha ha. Very funny. So how is lockdown going?'

He listened to her for almost an hour, as her anxieties and frustrations poured out in a torrent. Gavin was right, she was fragile.

'Are you okay for money?' he said.

'Yes. I got paid last week but that's all stopped now. I can't work at Beverley's place anymore because of lockdown.'

'Why can't you work remotely? You have a laptop, don't you?'

'Yes, but I don't have broadband, remember? I can't afford it.'

He did remember and he felt bad for raising it again. Everyone in his world had high-speed, fibre optic broadband. In the real world, some people didn't.

'Then maybe I can help you? I can give you a Wi-Fi dongle. I've got a couple of them. At least you'll be able to connect to the internet from home, and maybe you could carry on working for Beverley during lockdown?'

He thought about Olivia, connected seamlessly to her online lessons and revision classes from her bedroom. Lockdown had found a way to make social inequality wider.

'Could you meet me on Thursday afternoon, somewhere near your flat? Back end of the day? I could give it to you then.'

'I take the kids to the park every day. Kensington Memorial Park. It's close to my flat. How about four o'clock? We can meet by the play area, there's some benches there.'

'Should be okay. If there's a problem, I'll call you. Bring your laptop with you too.'

There was a lull in their conversation.

'Marcus, can I ask you a question?'

'Fire away.'

'Why would you want to help me? You don't really know me. What do you want from me?'

It was a question he didn't have an immediate answer for. He gave her a flippant reply.

'I guess one good turn deserves another. A 'thank you' for the sausage casserole and the tip on the baked beans and sweetcorn.'

She laughed.

'See you on Thursday afternoon then?'

'Yes. Sleep well.'

It was Tuesday, 24 March 2020.

Chapter 27

I Am Legend

Westbourne Grove was quiet, the occasional car on a road that was normally busy. Marcus waited fifteen minutes before a taxi pulled up at the kerb.

'Can you take me to Bank, please?'

'Yes, mate. Are you going in to work?'

'Sort of. I have to go into my office to pick up something. I'm hoping I can get in.' He sat in the back seat and shouted through the glass partition. 'How's lockdown affecting you?'

'Fuckin' dead, mate. Not really worth me coming out but I need the money. Family to feed an' all that.'

Every London cabbie moaned. Things were always bad. Along with a hatred of cyclists, cycle lanes, the Mayor and Uber drivers, it was part of their normal conversation.

'The City is a fuckin' ghost town. Have you seen it?' said the cabbie.

'Not since before lockdown. Empty is it?'

'Everything's shut. No tourists, no office workers. It's like that film, *I Am Legend* with Will Smith, when Chicago got wiped out by a killer virus and was overrun with zombies.'

Marcus wanted to tell him it was New York, not Chicago, but he couldn't face a debate so early in the morning. He stared out of the window at the empty pavements and closed shops. The taxi breezed along the Marylebone Road, past Euston and King's Cross stations, normally busy with commuters. They were deserted too. The taxi entered the City at Holborn Circus. The driver was right, it was a ghost town. Sandwich bars and coffee shops closed, steel and glass towers empty with no lights on. The country's money tree had lost its leaves and its branches were bare.

Marcus paid the driver and walked across the pavement to his office. Lights were on in reception, suggesting the presence of life forms. The revolving doors were motionless and didn't move when he pushed against them. Michael and a colleague were sitting behind the reception desk. They were both wearing masks. He tapped on a window with a key until Michael eventually looked up and beckoned him to a side door, the entrance for disabled people. He unlocked it, top and bottom.

'Good morning, Marcus. What are you doing here? I thought you would be working from home like everyone else?'

'Good to see you, Michael. I've left something important in the office and had to come in to get it. Am I the only one in?'

'There's a skeleton staff on the IT helpdesk. And the Document Production people are in.'

Lockdown had closed the City, but Document Production was open twenty-four seven producing The Firm's insights. The espresso machines in OnYouGo were silent. Marcus took the only working lift to his floor. The motion sensors activated the lights, which flickered into life. Rows of abandoned desks, chairs and monitors, just as they had been left. The beaming faces of people in the 'Putting Something Back' posters stared out at nobody. Apart from the humming of the vending machines, the floor was eerily silent.

He went to his locker and opened it. He rifled through piles of old proposals, reports and insights accumulated over years. Paper milestones in his career, reminders of a time when working at The Firm had been all-consuming and fun. He found the 4G dongle and put it in his laptop bag. It had never been used.

I don't think The Firm is going to miss this, he thought.

He closed his locker and sat down at an empty desk. He checked The Sequence. He had missed an alignment call with Laila. He would call her later. There was an email from Izzy Majewska reminding the team about The Firm's lockdown dress code. Although King Zoom was more relaxed, some of his subjects had been bending the rules.

'T-shirts, singlets, vests, sleeveless tops and nightwear are not deemed appropriate business attire. If shorts are worn, bare legs should not be in view. Male members of the team should not allow facial hair to look unkempt. When on video calls with clients, staff should not be seen eating.'

Someone had complained that an assistant manager had joined a Zoom call bare-chested, applying deodorant while eating a bowl of Corn Flakes. Marcus thought about Chloe and her wardrobe of Winnie the Pooh-themed onesies. He hoped she wouldn't give in to sartorial fascism.

He sent texts to his family, letting them know he was still alive and had no symptoms. A return to Twin Gates by the end of the week was his plan.

He picked up his laptop bag and walked around the floor. More lights came on to illuminate the Chilling Eggs, Communication Zones, Collaboration Pods, and the walls festooned with brand-compliant 'Doing It With You' banners. Without its worker bees, the office was a dead hive. He wondered if it would ever make honey again. He picked up a couple of highlighter pens and some Post-it notes from the pillaged stationery cupboard. The staff might not have desks but at least they weren't short of staplers. He took the lift to the ground floor where Michael and his colleague were playing solitaire on their laptops.

'Are you leaving, Marcus? I'll have to let you out,' said Michael, getting up and walking to the door.

'Thanks Michael. Nice to see you. Stay safe.'

Marcus crossed the road to Poultry. There was no need to look up. Any suicidal traders would be doing it at home with pills and booze. He walked along Cheapside and looked ahead to the dome of St Paul's. He recognised a shabby figure sitting on a bench in the empty garden wearing a familiar brown trilby. He was smoking a cigarette. It was Colin.

'Hello there. It's Colin, isn't it?' he said. 'We met here a couple of months ago. I'm Marcus.'

Colin stared at him and screwed up his watery eyes. Many bottles of cider, and probably something stronger, had passed his lips since their last meeting. His memory wasn't good.

'Did we? Are you the police?'

'No, I'm not the police, Colin. We met here, in this garden and we talked about lots of things. You gave me some very good advice, actually.'

'Did I? I don't remember.' Colin looked down at his stained clothes, the holes in his dirty trainers had got bigger. He shook his head in an act of self-mockery. 'I don't think I should be handing out advice to anyone. Do you?'

Marcus laughed. 'Do you mind if I join you?'

Colin gestured with his hand and Marcus sat at the other end of the bench. The virus wasn't the only thing Marcus was scared of catching from Colin. Their first meeting had made a profound impact on him, and he was disappointed it hadn't been mutual.

'I've come past a few times, hoping to see you again. Are you still sleeping rough, Colin?'

Colin nodded. He coughed and spat a lump of green phlegm into the flower bed. It dangled from a shrub like a Christmas bauble.

'They've been trying to get us into hostels and off the streets. Figured I was safer on the streets, so I keep away from the places where they can find me. I don't like the hostels. Full of God-botherers and do-gooders.'

'Probably not a bad idea. The virus would love a nice warm hostel, full of people coughing on each other. It must be good, having the City all to yourself? Your own private kingdom?'

Colin smiled at the thought he was a monarch of the City, a pavement king who couldn't remember when he'd last had a shower or changed his clothes.

'It's much harder to get food now. Nothing's open, nobody around to give you anything. Can't even get a drink, all the pubs are shut. What are you doing here? Are you the police?'

'No, I'm not the police. I had to go into my office. The place is closed. It was bloody weird being in there on my own.'

'I used to work in the City.'

'I know, you told me. A trader with Merrill Lynch, right?'

'Were you there too? Did we work together?'

Marcus laughed.

'No, Colin. I didn't work with you. You told me, last time we met?'

'Did I? I don't remember.'

It was becoming clear their second conversation wasn't going to match their first. They talked about the cathedral, about London and its history. Then Colin paused and stared up at the dome.

'How old are you, Malcolm?'

'I'm fifty-five. It was my birthday last Sunday. Why?'

'The City is full of cunts and charlatans, you know? People who know fuck all about nothing. You should get out while you can. You've still got a few years left.'

'Maybe it's about time I did something different?'

'Yeah, damn fucking right you should,' said Colin, who had forgotten it was his idea.

Marcus stood up. He reached into his inside pocket, took out his wallet and gave Colin a twenty-pound note.

'Good to see you again. Look after yourself, Colin. Take this and buy some food and something to drink. There's a Tesco next to the station. Hope I see you again sometime.'

Colin didn't put up a fight this time and took the money. Life on the streets in lockdown wasn't an easy gig.

'Thanks a lot. See you, Malcolm.'

Marcus picked up a copy of *Metro* from the stand outside St Paul's station and scanned the front page.

CHARLES IS LATEST TO BE LAID LOW

Prince Charles was self-isolating at Balmoral with the Duchess of Cornwall after testing positive for the virus. His symptoms were mild.

Camilla might not be a looker but at least she sticks by him, he thought enviously.

Boris had smashed his first target. Over 400,000 people had signed up to be NHS volunteers. Another article reported that frontline NHS staff in some hospitals had been asked to share face masks and wear bin liners.

That's great. Volunteer to help the NHS and catch the virus, he thought.

He had walked to Holborn Circus before he saw a taxi. He flagged it down.

'Queensway, please.'

His phone rang. It was Laila.

'Morning, Marcus. You didn't make our alignment call? Where were you?'

'I had to do something personal. What did you want to align about?'

'To make sure we're on the same hymn sheet for the call with Yeast Feast this afternoon.'

'We were aligned at six o'clock last night. What happened to misalign us while we were asleep?'

His sarcasm bounced off. She was blinded by The Golden Carrot.

'Yeast Feast could be the difference between me making partner this year or not.'

He wanted to tell her it was already a done deal and to relax.

'It'll be fine, don't panic. It might come down to the money, but they didn't seem that fussed.'

'Blind cows?'

'Exactly. Speak at 12.30. Don't worry.'

'No cross-dressing ice breakers this time, please?'

He had thirty minutes before his next appointment with King Zoom. He made some toast and Marmite and switched on the television. His attention was grabbed by *Undercover Boss,* a US import, and gave it a try. It was a simple format. Out-of-touch CEO gets dressed up in a heavy disguise and goes on the road to meet frontline employees hampered by outdated procedures. It seemed the employees were all selected because of a disability, a terminal illness or had received a poor education. The employees point out the flaws in the organisation and, in return, the then-unmasked CEO hands out thousands of dollars to change their lives. Floods of tears and big hugs follow.

Probably a heck of a lot cheaper than hiring a bunch of consultants, thought Marcus.

He joined the Yeast Feast call early and waited for the others to arrive. Laila was late. She had been in the toilet being sick.

'Sorry I'm late. Just had to deal with something,' she said nervously.

She opened the call with the usual sycophantic nonsense, thanking Yeast Feast for the opportunity, delighted to respond, one-team approach, et cetera, et cetera. Daniel and Joe had read the six-page engagement letter, as well as the thirty pages of appendices.

'So how many people will you put on it?' said Daniel.

'Initially four, for two months,' said Laila, 'increasing to six as we move into the design phase.'

'How many people to do it quicker? Say, in a month? Ten, twenty?'

The blind cow was lactating. Marcus spotted the trap and stepped in.

'It's not a simple question of more people and less time. But you probably know that, don't you?'

Daniel and Joe smiled. They knew all about blind cows from their time as investment bankers. They were just testing Laila, seeing how much she wanted it.

'Of course,' said Joe. 'How about 40% of the fees on time and materials and 60% on contingent? A bit more skin in the game for you.'

Laila went for the close immediately.

'Agreed. Forty–sixty. When do you want us to start?'

'How about next Wednesday? Give us time to set things up on our side.'

'Perfect,' said Laila. 'We're looking forward to working with you.'

The call ended and seconds later, Laila called Marcus. She was in a good mood. The Golden Carrot was getting closer.

'That went well, didn't it? They didn't even ask for a bigger discount. Two million pounds for Phase One. How much more do you think to come?'

'Probably, at least the same again. They want to do this deal, IPO as quickly as they can, cash in their chips and go and sit on a beach somewhere. Our fees are peanuts in the big scheme of things.'

'Blind cows?' said Laila enthusiastically.

'Like Stevie Wonder with udders.'

* * *

Claire was wiping Alexa's nose as they sat on a bench opposite the cordoned off play area. It was Kyle who saw him first.

'Mummy, look it's Marcus,' he said, pointing along the footpath.

Marcus saw him at the same time and waved. He sat down on the other end of the bench. Neither of them knew what to do, hug, kiss, shake hands? They opted for a wave.

'Hi Claire, hi everyone. How are you all?'

'Say hello to Marcus, kids,' said Claire.

Alexa waved and Kyle said hello. Claire sent the children off to play together. She turned to look at Marcus and pointed to his suit.

'You'll get mugged around here looking like that. Luckily, all the villains are in lockdown too. So how's isolation going?'

'Oh, it's a laugh a minute. I haven't seen my family for almost two weeks because of my paranoid wife, celebrated my fifty-fifth birthday on my own and I now spend all my day staring at people's faces and interiors.'

'Sounds blissful. I'd love some time on my own. The only time I get to myself is when the children are in bed. By then I'm so knackered, I fall asleep in the chair.'

'How's the home schooling going?'

'Alexa is easy but Kyle needs constant attention. I've probably done a fraction of what his teacher asked us to do. I'm meant to be speaking to her tomorrow. I'm thinking of avoiding her call.'

Marcus laughed. 'Maybe you could say the dog ate your homework?'

'If only I had a dog to blame.'

'Heard any more from your husband?'

'No, nothing. Not a peep. His parents will be pushing him. They know all the right people, professionals. I think I've got to accept the children should know their father, even if he is a complete twat.'

Marcus looked at her hands, still holding the crumpled tissue she used to wipe Alexa's nose. They were shaking. Fragile.

'Would you have your husband back?'

'Never in a million years. Two years is plenty of time to fall out of love with someone. Especially someone who gives you chlamydia.'

He could see she was getting stressed and changed the subject.

'Did you bring your laptop with you?'

She reached into the back of the buggy, took out the laptop and handed it to him. He opened it, asked her to enter her password, and tapped away on the keyboard. He took the dongle box out of his raincoat pocket.

'Brand new, 4G. Never been used.'

He plugged it into the USB port, opened new menus, tapped more keys and suddenly the Google home page flashed up.

'There you go, your passport to the world of useless information.'

'And how much will this little gizmo cost me? I'm not exactly flush with cash.'

'Nothing. Think of it as a gift from The Firm. It's registered to me so try not to download porn. I don't want them thinking it's me.'

'How come it's free?'

'Online porn?'

'No! This dongle thingy.'

'Because I don't pay for anything. My phone, Wi-Fi, this thing. The Firm pays for everything, well almost.'

'And you're thinking of leaving? You must be mad.'

'That's the price they pay for stealing your soul.'

He told her about his second meeting with Colin, how he had gone downhill and his memory had deteriorated.

'Poor guy. Must be hard dealing with lockdown when you're sleeping on the streets. And I think I have it tough. At least we've got a roof over our heads and food in our stomachs,' said Claire.

'There's always someone worse off than you,' said Marcus philosophically.

'And there's millions of people worse off than you, Marcus.'

Kyle and Alexa had finished chasing each other and came running back to the bench. Their little cheeks were red.

'Is Marcus coming back to our house tonight, Mummy?' said Kyle.

'I'm afraid I can't. I've got more Zoom calls and you need to be getting back for *The Race.*'

'It's *The Chase* and Mr Mahoney and I have to watch it on our own now. We should be going too. Thanks for the dongle and the phone too. I hope you liked the photo on your birthday?'

'Loved it, thank you. Maybe using fewer texts but with longer sentences would be good? Thanks for not using the yellow faces. I hate them.'

He opened his phone and pointed to the stream of texts from Sunday evening.

'Who the hell is Claire Ladbroke? My surname is Halford.'

'Sorry. I didn't know your surname so I put something I could remember.'

She opened her phone and showed him.

'Marcus Posh?' he exclaimed.

'Actually, it's "Posh Marcus" and it's because you are.'

He laughed and they stood up together.

'If things get tough and you want someone to talk to, you can always call me. Anytime.'

'When are you going home to your family?'

'Hopefully tomorrow. That's a subject to be discussed tonight.' He shrugged his shoulders and smiled.

'Good luck with that one. Keep in touch if things get tough for you too. Thanks for everything. You're a legend, Marcus.'

* * *

Marcus had eaten and was deleting emails on his phone, when he was disturbed by the noise of whooping and clapping outside. Beirut was still. He opened the doors to the balcony and saw people in the adjacent flats clapping and banging on saucepans. He shouted across to a man in a vest who was hanging out of his window with a frying pan and a wooden spoon.

'What are you doing?' shouted Marcus.

'Clapping for carers. Supporting the NHS,' he said.

Marcus had forgotten, so he joined in the clapping, which went on for fifteen minutes. If the virus was killed by noise, lockdown would have been all over in one night. Nobody wanted to stop for fear of appearing unpatriotic or unappreciative. Gradually the ovation subsided and people closed their windows and went inside. National duty had been done and he rang Alice.

'Hi Al. Have you been clapping for the NHS?'

'Of course we have, Marcus. All three of us were outside doing our bit. Were you?'

'Yes, I was. It's very important to show we care, solidarity with frontline workers and all that good stuff.'

They were both being disingenuous. He had forgotten about it, and the houses in their road were so far apart that nobody would be able to hear anyone else. Their neighbour's house could have fallen into a sinkhole and Alice wouldn't have known.

He told her about his trip to the office and meeting Colin again in the garden of St Paul's. Alice sounded in a good mood, so he broached the subject of his return.

'I'm thinking of coming home tomorrow afternoon. It's been two weeks since the conference and I've not shown any symptoms whatsoever. I've got some Zoom calls in the afternoon and then I'll drive home ...'

She jumped straight in.

'The police are stopping people, you know? If it's not a journey that's strictly essential?'

'What? Being with my family during lockdown? I'd say that was pretty essential. I'll take the risk, just like you're taking a risk allowing Jacinda into our house.'

In the game of Lockdown Top Trumps, the 'Do You Really Need a Cleaner?'

card was a 10, and Alice knew it. She only had a 'Make Marcus Feel Guilty' card, which was an 8.

'Fine. If you're willing to take the risk of being stopped by the police, go ahead.'

'Great, I will. See you tomorrow evening. Probably around 6.30.'

* * *

He sat on a bench in Kensington Gardens watching two swans preening themselves in the morning sunshine. He wondered if swans really mated for life or stayed together out of convenience, possibly having the odd affair and producing illegitimate cygnets. He looked at the front page of *Metro*.

CHECKPOINT BRITAIN

Armed with new emergency powers, the police were using roadblocks to stop and question motorists about the necessity for their journeys, employing drones to provide aerial surveillance of illegal gatherings.

Maybe Alice was right? Going home tonight could be a bit risky, he thought.

He imagined a squadron of drones and police helicopters tracking him along the M3, arresting him as he pulled on to the drive at Twin Gates and carting him away to a cell in Esher police station. He would only be freed after a nationwide campaign by Amnesty International.

He was making his porridge and listening to *BBC Breakfast* in the background. Charlie and Naga were on the red sofa. They were discussing the shortage of protective equipment for the NHS heroes, when Marcus heard a voice he recognised.

'Safewear is doing everything we can to get vital PPE to the NHS front line, care homes and private hospitals throughout the UK. We are playing our part in the national effort to fight the virus in every way we can.'

It was Jim Ibbotson, the CFO of Espina, coming live from the Safewear factory in Manchester. Marcus turned around to see Jim and Derek Bentley sitting in the meeting room where the Wonderwall debacle had happened a few weeks earlier.

'We're running three eight-hour shifts every day of the week, including weekends, to meet demand, not just from the UK, but globally as well.'

Jim and Derek were beaming. Naga asked some prickly questions about the awarding of government contracts and profiteering in a national crisis but they had all the answers.

'We are living in unprecedented times, Naga,' said Jim piously. 'Of course, a business like Safewear will benefit in these circumstances, but we would like to think we're doing our bit too. We have taken on temporary labour in almost every part of our business to cope with increased demand. Creating jobs is what Espina and Safewear has always been about.'

'You lying bastard,' shouted Marcus at the television. 'Two months ago, you couldn't wait to sell Safewear and shit on everyone in the process. The virus saved your arses.'

Jim and Derek proudly showed Naga and Charlie examples of the products they were producing to protect the NHS heroes. The Espina shareholders thought Jim and Derek were heroes too. Espina's share price had rocketed by 50% in less than a month.

Three Zoom calls into his morning, Marcus joined the second meeting of the Lockdown Social Committee. Oliver Rankin had learned his lesson and allowed five minutes for people to join. Jenny Moffatt joined the call from her kitchen, which was a twee mishmash of Cath Kidston and Orla Kiely. Marcus had wondered if she would be calling in from her fantasy dungeon, complete with a man in a gimp mask strapped to a rack, but it was all flowers and patterns.

'Morning, everyone,' said Jenny. 'I hope everyone is bringing lots of ideas to keep morale up during lockdown?'

Oliver opened the floor to 'creative and exciting ideas'. Suggestions included a monthly quiz, breakfast clubs, hobby groups, bingo. It quickly became apparent that finding a single activity that suited everyone was impossible. Eighty people on a Zoom call was unmanageable. It would probably make morale worse.

'I don't know when we're going to find time to do any of these things anyway,' said Graham Wilder. 'I'm on Zoom calls until ten o'clock every night.'

'And I'm not sure Risk and Compliance will be supportive of an online tequila slammers contest,' said Jenny Moffatt, trying not to completely dismiss the idea from an enthusiastic Angela Rust.

They agreed to break the team into smaller groups. Marcus would be responsible for one.

'Any big ideas for your first event, Marcus?' said Oliver condescendingly.

Marcus thought the list of suggested ideas was devoid of creativity and anything but exciting.

'I've got two, actually, Oliver. The ideas came to me over the weekend. "Through the Zoomhole" and "Whose Deliveroo?" I think I'll start with "Through the Zoomhole".'

'What the hell is "Through the Zoomhole"?' said Oliver.

Marcus explained the concept. Members of the team would make a video of their home, show some personal possessions and provide some clues and hints, then people would have to guess whose home it was to win a prize.

'That sounds bloody brilliant!' said David Barker. 'Count me in for that one. I bet there's a few shockers. I'd better have a tidy up round here.'

Apart from Oliver, who thought the idea was intrusive, everyone else thought it was a good one.

'And what about "Whose Deliveroo?"' said Jenny Moffatt.

'Everyone orders a home delivery. We vote on whose is the best while we eat, drink and chat,' said Marcus.

'Is it just Deliveroo, or can it include Uber Eats as well?' said Graham Wilder.

Marcus had never heard of Uber Eats but got the point.

'Any home delivery will do. Starter, main and dessert.'

'Love it,' said Graham. 'Can we put them on expenses? We must be saving shedloads on staff entertainment during lockdown.'

'I can't see a problem with that,' said Marcus flippantly.

Oliver grimaced but said nothing. He had decided to organise a bingo evening with his group, and Jenny would do a quiz with hers. It was agreed Jenny would assign the groups, and the first events would take place the following Thursday.

'Great, I'll start planning "Through the Zoomhole" now,' said Marcus.

He loaded his bags into the boot of the M5 and started the car. It roared into life. He selected the Clash's 'London Calling' from Spotify. It seemed appropriate, with viral Armageddon heading towards the capital.

The roads to the M3 were almost empty. No roadblocks, drones or helicopters. He opened the door to Twin Gates at six o'clock precisely. His family was gathered in the living room watching television.

'Hi, everyone,' he said cheerily. 'I'm back.'

Olivia and James waved but Alice didn't look up. It was the *BBC News at Six* with Fiona Bruce. Something important had obviously happened.

'Ssshhh! It's Boris, Dad. He's got the virus. So has Matt Hancock and Chris Whitty,' said Olivia.

'Oh fuck!' said Marcus, dropping his bags and sitting down on the arm of the sofa. Boris appeared in a video from Downing Street to show the nation he was still alive and leading the fight. He looked grim, his hair was more dishevelled than usual. The Government's two main strikers and its attacking midfielder were now injured. It was up to a right back, Michael Gove, to lead the attack from now on.

'Maybe Boris and Matt Hancock haven't been keeping two metres apart?' said Marcus.

'I wouldn't get within two metres of Matt Hancock,' said Olivia. 'He gives me the creeps.'

'Goes to show the virus doesn't discriminate, doesn't it?' said Marcus.

'All the more reason for us to be careful then,' said Alice frostily. It was evident she wasn't entirely comfortable with his arrival.

They watched the highlights from Gove's press conference, delivered with gravitas for the 759 people who had now died from the virus. The rate of infection was doubling every three to four days.

'Poor Boris,' said Olivia. 'I feel so sorry for him. Isolated from his pregnant girlfriend. They leave his meals at the door to his apartment, you know?'

Marcus was tempted to point out he knew exactly how it felt to be isolated. Instead he tried to raise the mood in the room.

'Well, it's certainly good to see everyone! How has the first week of lockdown been?'

It had been fine. Olivia's school had delivered a full timetable of lessons online, including practicals and revision classes. It's what you got for £7,000 a term. James had been working on his dissertation, although getting hold of his tutor had been difficult. He seemed a little distracted. Alice had been fine too. Although yoga, Pilates, tennis and her art class had all been cancelled, she was pleased to have the children at home. All the birds were back in their nest.

'Glad everyone's well. Better go and get changed then,' he said, leaving the living room.

He was getting changed when James came in and sat on the end of the bed.

'So, what's it like being back at home? Mum waiting on you hand and foot, is she?' said Marcus.

'Yeah, it's pretty cushy. Bit strange being back in my old room, like being in a time capsule with the old Coldplay and Victoria's Secret posters on the wall. Libby seems to have grown up a lot, even in a few weeks. Food is shit now Mum and her have gone almost totally vegan. I'd give anything for a steak like we had in Manchester.'

'The less said about that bloody night the better. I don't think your mother believed my story and she knows nothing about that infernal nightclub. I think we need to keep it that way, don't we?'

'Prism? Don't worry, mum's the word.' James tapped his nose with his index finger.' But what are we going to do about the food? We can't go through lockdown on chickpeas and bulgur wheat. We need a strategy, Dad.'

'I agree, but it's not the time to rock any boats right now. I've just got back in the house and your mum wasn't that happy about it either.'

'No, she said. But at least you're here now. How's work?'

Marcus told James about his new life under King Zoom, aligning with Laila and his latest conversation with Colin. As he pulled a jumper over his head, James looked up at him.

'Do you really need the money, Dad? Or is it that you wouldn't know what to do if you stopped?'

His head was trapped inside the jumper and he paused to think.

'What would I do? I haven't got a fucking clue. Maybe it's not about the money at all?'

'You could always give some to me.'

Marcus remembered Carol Vorderman's advert for equity release. Maybe James had seen it too?

'Piss off and get a job first.'

'Oh yeah? Because everyone is hiring graduates in the middle of a pandemic, aren't they? I'll probably end up being a delivery driver for Amazon.'

Their conversation was broken by Alice shouting that food was on the table. They met Olivia on the landing and went into the kitchen together.

'So what's for dinner tonight, Mum?' said James in a tone of mock enthusiasm.

'Sweet potato and aubergine curry,' said Alice, 'followed by apricot crumble with gluten-free flour and oat milk custard.'

It was the first time the four of them had been together since Christmas and the conversation around the table was lively. Olivia amused them with a story about one of her classmates who had left her camera on while she changed her top in her bedroom, giving the chemistry teacher and the class a shock. Marcus explained his idea for 'Through the Zoomhole'. Alice wasn't keen on the idea of Twin Gates being filmed. The family cleared away and James and Olivia went to their bedrooms leaving their parents alone in the kitchen.

'So, how have you really been this week, Al?' said Marcus. 'You haven't said much?'

He could tell when she was anxious. She would twiddle her hair with her index finger, play with her earrings and breathe heavily through her nose. She started to twirl her hair nervously.

'If you want the truth, Marcus, I'm starting to get really scared. Scared of getting it, passing it on to the kids, to you. I haven't been out of the house all week. Stepping outside to clap for the NHS was my only exercise this week.'

He tried to empathise.

'I'm not exactly taking lockdown in my stride either. Work this week has been a nightmare with all this Zoom shit. Why don't we go for a long walk this weekend, have a chat about things and make each other feel better? We might even find time to celebrate my birthday?'

'I bet you had one of those horrible pies when you were on your own, didn't you?'

He laughed. The list of things he hadn't been honest about was growing.

'I'm afraid I did. Comfort food for the lonely. Hope you're not upset with me? They do have thirty-three per cent more meat in them now.'

She looked across the table, smiled and held his hand.

'Thirty-three per cent of bugger all is bugger all. I hope you enjoyed it? It's been so awful this week, there were times when I would have died for a bacon sandwich.'

The virus was testing everyone in different ways.

'I know, I get it completely. Brown sauce too?' He squeezed her hand. 'I am pleased to see you. Really. Glad to be back at home with you and the kids.'

It was Friday, 27 March 2020.

Chapter 28
TIME TO STOP DIGGING

Claire was lost in Google and the children were laughing at Mr Tumble on CBeebies. Beverley rang. She never called at weekends.

'Hi Beverley. Everything okay?'

'Hi Claire. Sorry to ring on a Saturday morning but I thought you should know. It's Edward, he's tested positive for Covid.'

'Shit! No way. How is he?'

'He started coughing on Wednesday night and had a high temperature on Thursday morning. The bank got him tested and it came back positive yesterday. Bruce and I have been tested too but we haven't got the results yet. We should know on Monday at the latest.'

'So where is Edward now? Are you and Bruce okay?'

'He's isolating in Bruce's room and Bruce is in with me. So far, we're both fine, no symptoms. I had to tell you. Apart from Amazon drivers, you and the children are the only people we have come into contact with. Are you okay?'

'Yes, we're all fine. The kids are watching TV and I'm on the laptop. I've got Wi-Fi here now, thanks to Marcus.'

She told Beverley about their meeting. There was a long pause.

'Claire, you have to tell Marcus that Edward has it and you've been in contact with me. Where is he now? Is he at his flat?'

'I don't think so. He said he was going home yesterday. But if you haven't had any symptoms and I haven't either, what's the point in worrying him over nothing?'

'Claire, this isn't nothing. It's very contagious. What if I have got it and you get it too? You could have passed it on to him. And what if he passes it on to his family and doesn't even know? You can't ignore it, you have to tell him!'

Claire imagined Marcus sitting in his kitchen with his perfect family.

'You're right, I'll contact him. Let me know if you or Bruce develop symptoms. I'll do the same.'

'Of course. I'm so sorry but I thought you had to know.'

She put her phone on the coffee table. Telling Marcus was one problem, getting the virus herself was a different ball game. She closed her laptop and got up.

'Mummy's going for a shower. Get out of your pyjamas and get dressed. I won't be long.'

As the water ran over her body, rinsing the shampoo from her hair, she was thinking about Beverley's news. How was she going to tell Marcus? She got out of the shower, put on her dressing gown and towel turban. She left the children playing, went into the living room and texted him.

Hi Marcus.
Please can you call me?
It's really important.

* * *

Olivia had got up early to decorate the kitchen. Birthday balloons and a banner with a big '55' in the middle welcomed him when he came downstairs. Alice was stirring porridge with almond milk. After admitting to her moment of weakness, Marcus hoped he would be greeted by the smell of sausages sizzling in a frying pan, but Alice had regathered her composure.

'Happy Birthday for last Sunday, Dad,' said Olivia, who hugged and kissed him like she was eight.

'Thanks, Libby. Great decorations, very colourful.'

Alice left the porridge for a moment to kiss him on the cheek.

'Happy Birthday, Marcus. Glass of champagne or Buck's Fizz?'

'Champagne, please. Buck's Fizz always reminds me of cheap weddings.'

She took a bottle of Bollinger out of the fridge. It was already open. She poured three glasses and they toasted his good health. She brought the porridge to the table where two cards and two presents were waiting.

'Do I open these now or after breakfast?' he said.

'Oh, do it now. They've been sitting in a drawer for two weeks,' said Alice.

And whose fault is that? thought Marcus.

'Great, thanks everyone.'

He opened Olivia's card first. He knew it would say 'World's Greatest Dad', as it had done every year for as long as he could remember. He was wrong. '*With age comes wisdom … and saggy balls*', said the card, with a picture of a wrinkled, hairy, pendulous scrotum. Olivia giggled as he read it.

'Thanks Libby, that's great. Have you been gossiping with your mother about me?'

Alice sighed and raised her eyes. She didn't like it when Marcus was smutty. He opened his daughter's present, a new shaving brush and a pot of coconut oil shaving cream.

'Thank you. That's great.'

'Mum said your shaving brush was disgusting. This one's synthetic. I didn't want badgers being culled so you could shave. Badgers are cute.'

'They also carry bovine TB, but it's a nice thought,' he said.

He opened Alice's card. It was a simple card, two small birds sitting on a branch. *'Even though you're a bit of a tit, I still love you. Happy Birthday.'* He read the message inside.

Marcus. Happy fifty-fifth birthday. Make it a year to remember. Love always. Al. xx

'Thanks Al. Nice card.'

He opened her present. It was a voucher for a five-day yoga and meditation retreat in Ibiza.

'I think it will be good for you, Marcus. Get your mind and body aligned.'

Why does everyone want to align with me? he thought.

'That's great, Al, thanks a lot. It will be good for both of us.'

'I thought you could go on your own? It will do you good to sort yourself out.'

'If you're in Ibiza, you could go clubbing, Dad. Go to Pacha or Amnesia, do some ecstasy or ketamine!'

After his disastrous night in Prism with James, his daughter's tease was closer to the truth than she knew.

'I don't think that's going to be very good for me, but thanks for the suggestion, sweetie.'

As Olivia and Alice giggled about Marcus 'Dad dancing' in Ibiza, his phone pinged three times. It was on the island. Alice picked it up and read the messages.

Hi Marcus.

Please can you call me?

It's really important.

'Claire Ladbroke? Seems urgent. Who is she?' Alice said, handing him the phone.

Marcus was thinking about Avicii and Amnesia. Alice caught him off guard.

'Oh, oh just someone from work. It will be about Project Medusa. I'll call her back later.'

He had never been a good liar. His mind was spinning, why did Claire need to speak to him so urgently? Perhaps her husband had returned and done something worse? It couldn't be because the dongle wasn't working.

As a former lawyer, Alice took a stance of guilty until proven innocent whenever she suspected him of not telling her the truth, which was frequently.

'You've never mentioned a "Claire Ladbroke", Marcus. I know most of the people in your team, you talk about them constantly. I've never heard of her.'

'She's new. Only joined a few weeks ago. It's her first project, she's probably a bit nervous.'

He sensed Alice wasn't convinced. He thought of Mike, now living in a one-bedroom flat in Chertsey instead of a nine-bedroom pile in St George's Hill. Theresa had thrown him out and had engaged a legal team ready to hang, draw and quarter him financially and emotionally. Marcus was only trying to help Claire and her children. He had nothing to hide. So why did he feel the need to keep hiding it from her?

'She probably just wanted to check something. I'll sort it. Just going to brush my teeth. Thanks for the voucher, Al.'

He went upstairs and read her messages again. It made him feel even more anxious. He returned to the kitchen where Alice was reading the newspaper.

CRISIS AS BIG THREE HIT BY VIRUS

It was the same story as the night before. Boris, Matt and Chris all had the virus. Someone hadn't been washing their hands properly.

'I'm going in the garage,' said Marcus. 'Thought I might clear out more of Mum and Dad's things.'

'None of the refuse centres are open. You won't be able to dump anything,' said Alice.

'Well, maybe I'll just sort things out for when they are.'

He put on an old pair of shoes, left the house through the utility room and walked along the patio. It was a sunny spring day and the tulips were flowering. The garage smelled of grass cuttings and petrol from the ride-on mower. Jorge, the gardener, had been that week. He sat in his mother's armchair and rang Claire.

'Claire? Hi, it's Marcus. I got your messages. Is everything okay?'

'Hi Marcus. Sorry if I interrupted your weekend? Yes, we're all okay but there's something I must tell you.'

She told him Beverley's news.

'Apart from seeing Beverley and Mr Mahoney, and going to Tesco, you're the only person I've met face to face this week. I thought you should know. Have you had any symptoms?'

'None. Not even a sniff.'

'Me too. But I think you should tell Alice. It's too risky not to. You don't have to mention that you came into contact with me.'

'But I didn't come into contact with you! We were socially distanced on a bench, outside in a park. Two metres apart.'

'We both touched my laptop and we didn't sanitise our hands afterwards.'

'Oh, for goodness' sake! We weren't breathing on each other, were we?'

'You have to tell her, Marcus.'

He tried to imagine how Alice was going to take this latest news.

'You're right, I'll have to tell her. She's terrified enough about the virus as it is. I'll think of something. Let me know if anything develops at your end. Take care and look after yourself.'

'Thanks Marcus. You too.'

He pottered around in the garage, filling black bags with junk, which bought him time to think. He returned to the kitchen where Alice was covered in flour.

'What are you doing?' he said.

'Making bread. I read an article in the *Daily Mail* about how people are returning to traditional skills in lockdown. Knitting, baking, making clothes. I managed to get some organic, gluten-free sourdough flour, so I thought I would bake some fresh bread. We have a bread maker in the cupboard under the stairs, don't we?'

'We do, and we haven't used it for fifteen years since the last home baking craze. It might need a clean. My new client, Yeast Feast, would love you. What's next, darning my socks?'

'Very funny. I've got to do something to occupy myself or I'll go mental. Did you ring Claire Ladbroke? What was so urgent?'

'No, not yet, but I will. It's probably not that urgent. Shall we go for a walk after lunch, get some fresh air and have a chat? We haven't had a proper chat for ages.'

'Sure. I'll see if Libby and James want to come too.'

'Would you mind if it's just the two of us? I feel we haven't spent any quality time together in the past few weeks. We have a lot to catch up on.'

'Do we? You're behaving a bit weirdly, Marcus. Are you okay?'

'Yes, I'm fine. Got a lot on my mind with work and that bloody Zoom thing.'

He sat down at the kitchen table and checked The Sequence. Laila was spewing out PowerPoint like a bilge pump. Six new emails and a Zoom invite for an alignment call at 9.30 on Sunday morning.

Lucky I'm not a part-time vicar, he thought, *I might've been preparing my sermon.*

He left Alice kneading dough and went upstairs. James had just surfaced, emerging from his bedroom like a caveman.

'Morning, Dad,' he grunted.

'Afternoon, James. Shame you weren't up earlier, you could have celebrated my birthday with the rest of us.'

'Sorry Dad. I needed some sleep. Sorry I didn't get you a card or present this year. Lockdown kinda screwed me on that one. I will get you one, promise.'

'Don't worry. There's always next year. I'm sure we won't be in lockdown then. How's the dissertation going? Working on it late last night, were you?'

'It's going okay. Been a nightmare getting hold of my tutor. He was hard enough to get hold of before lockdown.'

'What's happening with your exams?'

'Don't know. I'm a bit fucked, to be honest. If they get scrapped, it's not good for me. I was pinning my hopes on a last-minute push.'

'Meaning what exactly?'

James shifted nervously from side to side. He had done it since he was a child when he had done something wrong.

'I was hoping the final exams might get me out of a Third, which is where I am now. I've probably had too much of a good time in my first two years. You know how it is? Don't go mad at me, Dad.'

Marcus looked at his son. Since the age of sixteen, James had been on one long, uninterrupted bender. He was Weybridge's equivalent of Avicii, but without his millions or talent. Marcus wished he had some of his son's zest for enjoying himself. In a way, he envied him. He smiled and hugged him. Not even James's beard or dog breath put him off.

'It's your life, mate, and nobody's died have they? There's plenty of worse things than a Third. I'll leave you to tell your mother. That will be much harder.'

If James had one confession to make to his mother, Marcus had a list.

'We still need to come up with a plan on the food, Dad. I can't survive on this vegan shit for much longer.'

'Your mum was weakening last night. She's been fantasising over bacon sandwiches. We need to pick our moment. Timing is everything, trust me.'

Alice's first attempt in fifteen years at baking bread had turned out well. It had risen and browned in the right places, and it smelled good. She was pleased with herself and joined Marcus on their walk in a good mood. He held her left hand as they walked and felt the diamond of her engagement ring and her wedding band. They reached the halfway point, the oak tree struck by lightning.

'Can we sit down here on the bench for a bit?' he said. 'It would be nice to chat before we head home. I've been cooped up in the flat all week.'

He had been building up to the moment. They had discussed lockdown, Boris, PPE, NHS, testing, vaccines, deaths. Covid was the only thing to talk about. There were moments when he got ready to speak, breathed in and braced himself but nothing came out. He had sat in the boardrooms of some of the world's biggest organisations and dealt with some real bastards, but he had never been so lost for words.

'There's something I need to tell you, Al.'

'What's that?'

'Those messages this morning? Claire Ladbroke? Her name isn't Ladbroke, it's Halford and she doesn't work at The Firm. She's one of Gavin's social work cases. Struggling single mum and all that.'

'What's she doing texting you on a Saturday?' she said curiously.

'She wanted to let me know that she has been in contact with a friend of hers whose husband has tested positive for coronavirus.'

Alice shook her head.

'So what? She should probably self-isolate as a precaution. What's that got to do with you, Marcus? I don't understand. If she wants your advice, she's asking the wrong person. You're quite happy to mix with people who have the virus and not tell anyone, including your family.'

He ignored her sarcasm and continued.

'That's why I'm telling you now.'

'Telling me what?'

'I met her last Thursday, but it was in a park and we were two metres apart.'

'Why did you meet her in a park? What for?'

'I was giving her a Wi-Fi dongle. She can't afford broadband and I thought it would help her and Kyle with his schoolwork. The Firm gave me one but I've never used it because we have broadband at home and in the flat.'

It was a stream of facts that Alice was struggling to connect.

'Who's Kyle? Is that her husband? And what's her broadband got to do with you?'

'She isn't married. Well, she is, but she hasn't lived with her husband for two years. He ran off and they're separated now. Kyle is her son. He's five. She's also got a daughter, Alexa. She's three.'

Alice's patience was wearing thin.

'Marcus, you're not making any sense. I'm starting to feel really uneasy. What exactly are you trying to tell me? Who are all these people? Are you having some sort of relationship with her or something?'

'No, of course I'm not. Well, not in the way you're thinking. I've only met her three times and one of those was to give her a dongle.'

'Three times? When the fuck were the other two? Marcus, I'm starting to get very upset now. What's going on?'

Being economical with the truth was harder than lying. He was running out of road. It was time to get it all out on the table. For the next hour, he told her everything. Gavin, Claire, the children, the dinner, bedtime stories, refuge after the partner conference, sausage casserole …

'All I was trying to do was help her. Nothing else. She's not a bad person, Al. In fact, she's very smart. Her life could have been very different. Her kids are nice too, well mannered, funny. Living on a council estate in a tiny flat, on her own with two small kids …'

Alice was staring straight ahead, looking out over the fields, while Marcus explained his three meetings with a woman she had never heard of until an hour earlier. She finally snapped.

'Marcus, please will you shut up? I can't listen to any more of this shit. Do you know what really hurts me the most listening to all of this?'

'But I haven't done anything wro—'

'Fucking shut up will you! Don't say another word! What hurts me the most is that when I needed you, when your children needed you, where the fuck were you then? Flying around the world for The Firm, thinking you were the king of the fucking planet, that's where. Mr Billy Big-bollocks. Did you ever stop to think that I might have needed some support too? That James and Olivia might have wanted a bedtime story from their dad?'

It was a right hook that landed bang on his jaw and put him down for the count. He tried to get to his feet.

'But I always thought you were in control, that you loved looking after all of us, making the home run smoothly. You never said you were unhappy?'

'Did you ever stop to ask me if I was actually happy, Marcus? And now, just because you've recognised that your time at The Firm meant jack shit, you've suddenly become the Good Samaritan to some single mum you've only met three times. Well, fucking great for you, Marcus.'

Alice started to shake and cry. Anger and hurt. She got up from the bench and started to walk away.

'Al, please don't go. Let's talk this through. I didn't do anything wrong. Nothing is going on with Claire, I promise. I was only trying to help her.'

She turned to face him, tears running down her cheeks.

'This isn't about some squalid little affair, Marcus. You're too bloody awkward to have an affair. It's an infidelity, but of a different kind. It's a betrayal of us, your family. You can only blame The Firm for so much. Take some fucking responsibility and sort yourself out, for goodness' sake. I can't put up with any more of this shit. I'm going back home now and you've got to go to the flat.'

'Why? I've only just come home! I've got no symptoms and I've been isolated for two weeks already. What's the point in going back to the flat? I could isolate at home just as easily.'

'I'd prefer it if you went to the flat until we know for definite that this woman doesn't have it and you don't either. I'm anxious enough without worrying we might have it in the house. You can go this afternoon as soon as we get back.'

'But what am I going to tell the children? Don't you think it looks a bit odd, me shooting off again after one day?'

'How about telling the truth for once?'

'What? That I came into contact with someone who doesn't have the virus, who came into contact with someone who doesn't have the virus but who came into contact with someone who does? It's ridiculous.'

'Say whatever you want, I really don't care!' Alice turned away and started to walk back.

Marcus got up from the bench, caught up with her and tried to hold her hand but she shook him off.

'Sort yourself out, Marcus. You're out of control.'

Marcus went upstairs to pack and knocked on Olivia's bedroom door. She was lying on her bed.

'Hi Dad. Good walk?'

'Not really. I've just found out some bad news. There's a very small chance that someone I know has come into contact with someone who has the virus. I've told Mum and she thinks it's safer that I isolate at the flat.'

'How come? Who is it?'

'A friend of Gavin's. The guy who lives opposite me in the flat.'

'Has he got it then?'

'Not that I know of, he's in Scotland.' He couldn't face another detailed explanation. 'Your mum thinks it's best I go. I don't want any of you getting it.' She got up to give him a hug. He stepped away from the door. 'We probably shouldn't?'

'Bit late for that now. Mum's being a bit unfair, but she's terrified of the virus. Are you sure you're okay?'

'I'll be fine. It will only be for another week and then I'll be back. Thanks for the presents, they were great.'

'Happy birthday, Dad.'

He walked along the landing to James's room. He had his headphones on but looked up when he saw his father at the door.

'You okay, Dad?'

As he expected, James was more laid back about the news.

'That's a bit of a shitter. It's not as if you've actually come into direct contact with her. Mum's being a bit weird, like she always is.'

'Maybe, but you know your mum?'

'Yeah, I know. I'm dreading telling her about uni. Can't you do it for me, Dad?'

'Absolutely not. I think I've given her enough bad news for one day. And I'd leave it a couple of days, if I were you. Now isn't the right time.'

'When do you think you'll be back?'

'Probably in a week or so. Keep in touch. See you.'

Alice was in the living room watching the daily news conference. A small bespectacled man with immaculately groomed hair delivered an impressive array of statistics. Deaths had reached 1,019, an increase of 260, the highest in a single day.

'I think he might be the Business Secretary,' said Marcus. 'Anyway, I'm off now. I'll call you later.'

He moved towards her chair but she gave him a withering stare that stopped him in his tracks.

'Are you planning another mercy visit to Claire Ladbroke or are you leaving it to Gavin to do his job?'

'He's in Scotland, which is why I stepped in to help her. I wasn't aware helping people was a crime. Maybe spending a few minutes in the real world might be good for you too, Al? I'll get you a long weekend retreat on a council estate for your birthday. Might help you align with yourself. See you.'

Marcus walked away and closed the front door with enough force to show he was upset. Lockdown meant that the roads were clear and he got to the flat quickly. He opened the door, dumped his bags in the hall and immediately headed to The Temple. It was six o'clock on a Saturday evening, and there was still a queue. There was almost no food left. Even the Fray Bentos pies had all gone. Somewhere in Bayswater, there was a covert cell of 'signature puff pastry crust' devotees.

He heated a Charlie Bigham's moussaka for two, had it on a tray and switched on the television. It was *Pointless Celebrities*. Apart from Esther Rantzen, he didn't recognise any of them, which made them all pointless. He switched over to Netflix and re-joined *Schitt's Creek*, hoping it would cheer him up. The parallels between himself and Johnny Rose, the patriarch of the Rose family, were obvious. Both of them were dealing with histrionic and temperamental wives. Marcus didn't think Moira Rose would cope well with lockdown.

He looked again at the messages Claire had sent that morning.

I did nothing wrong, I was only trying to help, he thought.

Alice had been right about one thing: he had created a real mess on his own and the virus had given it a good stir. He had to sort it out. He sent Claire a message.

Hi Claire. I'm back at the flat now. Decided it would be safer for me to isolate here. I'm fine, no symptoms. Don't worry. M.

She replied immediately.

Sorry to hear that. Things not so good at home then? All okay here. Me and the kids are fine.

Not really. All my fault, not Alice's. Made a bit of a mess of things.

Sorry. I shouldn't have put you in this situation.

Not your fault either. How is your friend?

Not heard anything. Will let you know.

Thanks. Would be helpful. How's the dongle?

Fantastic. You've been really kind to us. You didn't need to be.

Quid pro quo, Dr Lecter. Bye now.

He ended the exchange and switched off his phone. He knew exactly why he had helped her. Another soul whose dreams had been ended and was trying to survive.

* * *

Marcus was sitting in front of his laptop at 9.30 on Sunday morning, when King Zoom called. He had spent an hour reading the latest documents for Project Medusa. Laila's face appeared on screen. She looked like an extra from *Shaun of the Dead*.

'Morning Laila,' he said chirpily. 'Another late one I see?'

'Hi Marcus. Yes, I didn't get to bed until five and was back online at eight. Have you seen the stuff I've sent through for Medusa?'

'Yes. Been through it all, very thorough.'

They flicked through endless pages explaining how TOOL would be launched to Yeast Feast and Make 'n' Bake. After an hour, they were aligned.

'I don't think Yeast Feast will be ready to start this week, but let's see. Send the materials and let's get confirmation on a start date from Daniel and Joe.'

'Do you need to see it again before I send it?' she said.

'No, get some sleep. We can speak to them tomorrow. Enjoy your Sunday.'

He knew he was asking the impossible. The Golden Carrot was getting closer by the day.

* * *

Claire and the children returned from the park and knocked on Mr Mahoney's front door. He was icing a carrot cake. She told him about Beverley's husband having the virus.

'The Chinese lady who came here one day with the mouse?'

'Yes, and it was a hamster, not a mouse. Anyway, I won't come any closer. How have you been doing?'

'Bit lonely. I miss our routine. The Governess was hot on Friday.'

She wondered what he meant by 'hot' but didn't want to pry.

'I know, we miss it too. Anyway, I'd better get home, give these two their dinner. See you soon, Mr Mahoney.'

By the time she had climbed the four flights of stairs, she was struggling to breathe. She took two puffs on her inhaler. The weather was fresh, it was unusual for her to feel so breathless. She sat down in the kitchen.

'Take your shoes off and put your slippers on. You can watch some TV.'

Kyle and Alexa ran to the living room leaving her alone in the kitchen. Anxiety usually made her asthma worse, but she was calm. She made a cup of tea and sat still for fifteen minutes. She put her tiredness down to PMT. Her period was due any day.

'Come on Claire. Pull yourself together,' she said to herself.

It was Sunday, 29 March 2020.

Chapter 29

TESTING TIMES

Claire woke in the middle of the night. Her bed was soaking wet. She shuffled to the bathroom and peeled off her pyjamas. She wrapped herself in a towel and looked at herself in the mirror. A bead of sweat ran down her neck and between her breasts. She felt the tickle of its fall. She took her temperature. It was 37.2. She was feeling feverish. Her period hadn't started. She put on her dressing gown and went to the living room. She sat in her chair and wrapped herself in a blanket.

She switched on the television. It was 5.30 and the round-the-clock BBC News channel was analysing the pandemic from every angle. The death toll in the UK had risen to 1,228 and the first frontline NHS worker had died from the virus. Dishevelled experts with bed hair were already awake and eager to give their opinion.

Dan and Louise are probably still in makeup, she thought.

She wondered if the two presenters looked like a sack of shit when their taxi picked them up in the early hours? She imagined the taxi driver going home to his wife.

'That Louise Minchin looks a state when she gets in my car. Doesn't look anything like she does on the telly.'

She shuffled to the kitchen and switched on the kettle and the radio. 'Thought for the Day' was ending and its soothing words made her feel better. Dawn was breaking as she stared out of the kitchen window at the shrouded tower in the distance. The *Today* programme reported that normality wouldn't be returning for at least six months. That's what The Science was saying too.

'Six more months of this shit,' she said to herself. 'October. Fuck me.'

A new research study had revealed increases in depression and anxiety since the start of lockdown.

'We found higher rates of anxiety and depression in those aged under thirty-five, living in a city, living alone or with children, with lower incomes, and with health conditions,' said a Professor of Clinical Psychology.

No shit, Sherlock, thought Claire.

One week of lockdown and she was already feeling the effects of isolation and anxiety. She went to the bathroom and took a Xanax. She was feeling shivery and took a shower to get some heat into her body. Bending over to pick up the shower gel, she felt a rush of blood to her head. She put one hand against the wall and grabbed the shower curtain with the other. She felt she was going to faint, so she sat down on the edge of the bath.

'Jesus Christ, I feel dreadful. What's the matter with me?'

It took her ten minutes to shower, sitting in the bath and letting the water cascade over her. She levered herself out of the bath. Drying was a struggle and she put on her dressing gown and went into Kyle's room. He was awake and was playing with Buzz and Woody.

'Good morning,' she said, sitting on the side of the bed, stroking his head. 'Did you sleep well?'

Kyle nodded. 'No wee-wees last night, Mummy.'

'That's great Kyle, well done. I'll get your sister up and we'll have breakfast. Stay here and play for a bit. I'll be back soon.'

Alexa was still asleep, an angel with her thumb in her mouth. Claire left her to sleep and turned to feel her bedclothes. They were damp after her night sweat. Removing a pillowcase exhausted her and she felt breathless. She picked up her inhaler from the bedside table, squirted two puffs and sat down.

It'll have to wait, she thought and put on yesterday's clothes. She woke Alexa and the three of them went through to the kitchen.

'Mummy isn't feeling very well this morning. I'll need you both to be good today. What do you want for breakfast?'

'Rice Krispies!' shouted Alexa excitedly.

'Weetabix!' said Kyle.

Claire put the bowls and boxes of cereal on the kitchen table and went to the fridge. There was just enough milk for breakfast. She hadn't been shopping since Thursday. Shopping was the last thing she felt like doing.

'Are we doing school today, Mummy?' said Kyle.

'Yes, of course, otherwise I'll get into trouble with Miss Mistakidis.'

Schoolwork was the second last thing she wanted to do. She really wanted to go back to bed and sleep. The children finished their breakfast and ran off to their bedrooms. Her phone rang. It was Beverley.

'Hi Claire. We've had our results back. Good and bad news. I'm positive but Bruce is negative. I wanted you to know as soon as possible.'

'You don't sound very ill?' said Claire.

'I don't feel ill at all. I've got a headache and my temperature is up slightly, but that's about it. No fever or shivering, no cough. Bruce is fine too.'

'So what are you going to do?'

'Not much I can do. Stay isolated until things get better. I'll try to shield Bruce as best as I can. I rang to check how you are?'

'We're all fine here. The children are bored not being able to go out.'

'And what about you?'

'Same. Time of the month, but I'm fine.'

Claire convinced herself it was probably a heavy period starting and she would feel better in a couple of days.

'As long as that's all it is? Keep well and say hello to the kids for me,' said Beverley.

Claire stared out of the kitchen window. Not telling Beverley how she really felt was stupid. She went to the living room, picked up the computer and googled 'symptoms of coronavirus'. She opened the NHS website and went through her self-diagnosis.

'Fever and high temperature. Definitely. Persistent cough. No.'

She thought about her breathlessness in the shower. The hot and cold flushes, the night sweat. The message in red was clear.

Use the NHS 111 online coronavirus service if:
You're worried about your symptoms.
You're not sure what to do.

She was certainly worried, and she wasn't sure what to do. What if she got worse? She called Gavin but only got his voicemail. She left a message.

'Hi Gavin, it's Claire. Can you call me when you get this? I'm not feeling well and I'm worried I may have the virus. Beverley Cheng has tested positive. I don't know what to do. I'm really worried. Bye.'

* * *

Marcus greeted Eric the concierge on his return from his early morning walk in Kensington Gardens.

'Morning, Eric. How are you?'

Eric stood to attention behind his new Perspex screen. He looked surprised.

'Good morning, Marcus. Didn't expect to see you back here so soon. I thought you were locking down in the country?'

Everything outside the M25 was 'the country' to Eric. Marcus didn't have the inclination to explain his premature return.

'Just work stuff, Eric. I need to be in London this week. Catch you later.'

He sat at his desk and opened Outlook. The Duke had sent an email to all employees informing them The Firm was *taking the opportunity to re-evaluate our business model in light of the extraordinary circumstances presented by the virus*.

Jenny Moffatt had allocated the groups for the social events taking place on Thursday. Marcus was happy with his group, which only had one other partner: Vanessa Briggs. He sent an email explaining the 'Through the Zoomhole' event and inviting volunteers to make videos of their homes. Within ten minutes, he had received two offers. One was from Graham Wilder and the other, surprisingly, was from Vanessa Briggs.

Great idea, Marcus. Love it. Looking forward to Thursday enormously. Will do my video today. V.

He was slightly worried by her enthusiasm but sent an encouraging reply thanking her for her support. He opened RAPID and submitted his timesheet, which was already late. Izzy Majewska's email threatening life-changing injuries for any further delay would be winging its way to him any second. He opened the tab marked 'Approval of Expenses'. His inbox was fuller than usual, fifteen new requests which alerted his curiosity.

What are people claiming for? he thought. *Nobody's going anywhere, everyone's working from home.*

The team was locked down but that hadn't stopped people from being inventive with The Firm's money.

One orthopaedic chair with lumbar support, £320.
Two additional monitors, £210.
Bombay Palace, home delivery curry, £64.80.
Walnut laminate corner desk, £199.
Canon Ink-Jet printer, £85.
Imperia Pasta Machine, £92.

He scanned down the list of claims. He was intrigued by the claim for the pasta machine. Not an essential piece of kit for producing PowerPoint and Excel spreadsheets. He approved it with a single click.

'If it brings a little relief from King Zoom, good luck to you.'

* * *

The children's interest in lessons, even on a computer, was flagging by 10.30, and Claire resorted to the television for relief. Gavin hadn't returned her call and she was feeling sleepy. She took her temperature, it was 37.4. Her forehead felt warm and she put a tea towel under the cold tap and placed it over her face. She called down the hall.

'Come on, we're going out. Let's get some fresh air. It will do us all good.'

Kyle and Alexa whooped, jumped off the sofa and ran down the hall.

'Can we go to the park, Mummy?' said Alexa.

'Yes, put your shoes on and a coat. It's chilly outside today. Come on, hurry up.'

She ushered the children out on to the balcony at the same time as Ian was emerging from No. 12. He looked like a ghost. He shuffled past the children, jerky, awkward movements caused by his distorted gait and atrophying muscles. Claire stepped back into the doorway.

'Hi Ian. How are you? Sorry, I don't want to get too close, I've got a bit of a temperature.'

Ian looked into the hallway.

'Hi Claire. I'm okay, but you look dreadful. Are you all right?'

If Ian, the Kensal Warrior, thought she looked dreadful, Claire knew things were bad.

'I think it's just a cold, but I won't get too close. You're the last person who needs to catch the virus.'

'Maybe, I'm not?' said Ian wistfully. 'I'm going to the shops, anything you need?'

'Would you mind getting me four pints of semi-skimmed milk? I'm almost out. That would be very helpful. Let me give you the money.'

'That's okay. I'll leave it by your front door. You can pay me later.'

He pointed to the ground and they both looked down. There was a small parcel wrapped in aluminium foil. Claire picked it up and opened it slightly. She smiled.

'Mr Mahoney's carrot cake,' she said. 'That's sweet of him.'

They looked along the balcony, there was a similar parcel outside all the doors.

Ian shuffled along the balcony, holding on to the handrail before twisting and arching his body to take the stairs. Claire and the children caught up with him before the third flight and he stopped in the stairwell to let them pass. He was wheezing like his lungs were tin cans.

'I'm sorry. I'm getting slower every day,' he said, looking back up the stairs, embarrassed to make them wait.

'Take your time, Ian. We're in no rush.'

Ian reached the bottom of the stairs, where his mobility scooter was waiting for him and he slid sideways on to the seat.

'Can I go on Ian's spaceship?' said Kyle.

'No sweetie, not today. Ian's going to the shops and we're going to the park.' Claire reached into her pocket for her inhaler. Four flights of stairs had exhausted her and she was breathing like Ian. 'Just give Mummy a minute to catch her breath.'

She was sitting on the same bench she had sat on with Marcus, when her phone rang. It was Gavin and she was pleased to hear his voice.

'Claire, hi, it's Gavin. I've just picked up your message. Sorry, the signal here isn't great. What's the matter? What's wrong?'

'Hi there. I'm worried I may have the virus. I haven't got a cough but my temperature is up, I'm getting hot and cold shivers and my breathing isn't great. I walked down the stairs at the flat just now and feel completely knackered. I'm in the park with the kids at the moment.'

'You said Beverley has it?'

'Yes, but her symptoms seem to be mild. No fever or headache, but I'm burning up here.'

'You must take a test, Claire. Don't take any chances, you have to find out for certain, especially with your asthma, and for the children's sake too.'

'How do I get a test? What do I do?'

'Ring 111 and they'll tell you where the nearest test centre is. Or go straight to a hospital.'

'But what if I have got it, how am I going to isolate from the children? It's impossible. And what if I have to go to hospital, like Boris? Who is going to look after them?'

She started to cry and licked the salty snot off her top lip. She looked at her children. They were chasing each other, happy and oblivious.

'One thing at a time. Get a test done first and we'll go from there. Don't worry about Kyle and Alexa, we'll make sure they're looked after if the worst comes to the worst. We have arrangements in place for this sort of situation.'

'What arrangements, Gavin?'

'Foster parents. They're used to stepping in at short notice, in difficult situations.'

'Like domestic violence or child abuse?'

'Special cases that need temporary care. Like the virus.'

She became angry. 'Sod that. No way. I'm not letting them go to complete strangers. Kyle's anxious enough as it is after Jack's latest visit. I'm shocked you're even suggesting it. Why aren't you here when I need you? You're meant to be my bloody social worker!' she shouted.

She knew she was simply lashing out, being unfair. He had been her rock for two years.

'I'm sorry I'm not there, Claire, but my parents need me too. Some days my mum doesn't even recognise me. She hit my dad with a wooden spoon yesterday.'

She imagined him in a Paul Smith pastel-coloured cashmere sweater, Armani jeans and suede Tods slippers, caring for his parents, doing his best. She missed the smell of his aftershave and his teasing. It made her cry even more.

'I'm sorry, Gavin. I didn't mean that. I was being selfish. I'm sorry. I just miss you.'

'I get it. These awful times are testing all of us in different ways. I'll text you later, but ring 111 as soon as you can. I miss you too. Even if you do think *Taxi Driver* is the best De Niro film.'

She laughed through her tears.

'I'll call 111 when I get back to the flat. I'll let you know how I get on. Good luck with your mum.'

She took her temperature again. It was still raised and she called 111. After navigating the complex menu, it took fifteen minutes for an operator to answer. The call centre was being overloaded by members of the public eager to find out why they suddenly felt like shit.

Maybe putting a few NHS volunteers on the phone lines might be a good idea! she thought.

Eventually, a woman's voice answered. Claire was speaking to Denise. They exchanged names and basic details. From her accent, Claire guessed Denise was from the North East. It was quickly evident she was new to her role on the NHS hotline.

'Are you displaying any Covid symptoms, Claire?' said Denise.

'Yes, I have a high temperature and feel feverish. My temperature is 37.5.'

'Is that high?' said Denise. 'I only know it in Fahrenheit when it goes over 100.'

Unfortunately for her, Claire had been put through to a retired school dinner lady who still used imperial measures.

'Yes, it is high. Very high.'

'And do you have a persistent dry cough, Claire?'

'No, I don't have a cough but I feel really unwell and want to have a Covid test. Can you tell me where I can get one?'

Denise wasn't going to be diverted from her script.

'I'm sorry, Claire, but I've got a few more questions to go through first. It won't take too long. How long have you been displaying symptoms, Claire?'

'This is probably my second day. I felt a bit off-colour yesterday.'

'And are you an essential worker, Claire?'

'I'm a single mum with two small children. Is that essential enough?'

'I know what you're saying pet, but that's not on my list of essential workers, Claire. I'm sorry. Just a few more questions. Now, have you recently returned from a country that has a high rate of Covid infection?'

'Like where?'

'Ooh, I don't know,' said Denise. 'Let me check my list.' There was a rustling of papers and a pause in the conversation. 'Here we are. China? Korea? Iran? Italy? Been to any of those, Claire?'

'I haven't been further than the end of Ladbroke Grove since Christmas. I don't even have a passport. If it helps, I have been in contact with someone from Hong Kong who has tested positive. That's why I'm calling you.'

More rustling of papers.

'Yes. Hong Kong is on my list, Claire,' said Denise triumphantly.

Denise's sickly over-familiarity and bureaucratic incompetence was beginning to grate. Claire's patience finally snapped like a frayed shoelace.

'Denise, I think I might have the virus and I need to take a test, and quickly, so I can protect my children and myself. I don't need you to keep calling me "Claire", as if you know me. You don't. What I want is a bloody test. Can you help me with that or not?'

There was silence at the end of the phone. Denise's fragile sensitivity had been shattered all over her desk at the call centre.

'I'm sorry, pet, I do understand. I'm only trying to help. My best advice would be to go to a hospital and see if you can get a test done there.'

'It would have been helpful if you had said that at the beginning. I'll do that then.'

'Do you know your local hospital, pet?'

'Yes, I do. Thanks for all your help.'

'Good luck, pet,' said Denise. 'I hope it all goes well for you.'

Claire sent a text to Gavin.

111 was useless. Going to hospital for a test.

* * *

Marcus took a break from zooming, put a hot cross bun under the grill and checked The Sequence. Stockwatch was green, which made him feel better.

Lockdown meant his step count was woeful, but his headphone audio levels were lower than they had been in February. At least he would be able to hear the ambulance coming when he had a heart attack.

He was disturbed by the screaming of the smoke alarm. The hot cross bun was on fire and clouds of black smoke were billowing from the grill like the Vatican conclave deciding on the next Pope. He grabbed the flaming bun, burning his fingers on a cremated sultana, and threw it in the sink. He opened the balcony doors and fanned smoke outside until the alarm stopped. His ears were ringing. There was a different ring in the background. He could hear King Zoom summoning him to align with Laila.

'Bollocks to that.'

He let King Zoom go silent. He put another bun under the grill and diligently watched it brown, before applying an unhealthy amount of butter. It was time for the daily coronavirus briefing. Boris and Matt were still in the sick bay. The Government had turned to the reserves. Dominic Raab was making his first appearance, and he was joined by Patrick and Yvonne from The Science.

I wonder what's happened to Jenny? thought Marcus. *I hope she is okay?*

Dominic gave out the latest stats. 1,408 people had now died. He passed on his condolences to their families and friends. The Government was pulling out all the stops to get British nationals, who were stranded abroad, back home.

If I was stranded in the Maldives, I wouldn't be in a rush to get back, Marcus thought. *Probably a lot safer than London.*

Patrick presented the charts, which showed the UK's death count was gaining quickly on Italy's and Spain's. The next two weeks would be critical. WhatsApp pinged. It was Gavin.

Hi Marcus. How's lockdown going in Weybridge?

He had forgotten to tell him about his expulsion from Twin Gates.

Back at the flat! Long story. Give me a call when you can. Will explain when we speak. I'm okay and hope you are too. M.

He returned to his desk and waited for Laila to call. She hated not being aligned. His phone rang. It was Gavin and not Laila.

'Marcus, hi, it's me. What are you doing back at the flat? I thought you were going back to Weybridge to be with the family? Is everything okay?'

'Yes, I'm fine. Things went a bit tits up at the weekend.'

Marcus told him the whole story. Meeting Claire in the park, Claire texting him, his confession to Alice and his subsequent exile to the flat. Gavin didn't show him much sympathy.

'Well, you didn't handle it very well with Alice, I must say. Why the hell didn't you tell her the truth earlier? I can understand completely why she felt angry. There was no reason to keep it from her.'

'But I was only trying to help Claire and the kids! My dongle intentions were all good.'

'Keeping it from Alice wasn't very smart, was it? She's your wife, for goodness' sake! As it's turned out, she was probably right to kick you out.'

'And what do you mean by that?' said Marcus.

Gavin filled in the gaps for him.

'I spoke to Claire this morning. She called me in a panic. Her friend, Beverley, has tested positive and now Claire's feeling feverish. I've told her to get a test as soon as possible. She's going to hospital.'

'Why didn't she tell me?' said Marcus. 'Is she all right? How are the children?' He was slightly put out Claire hadn't told him. She was the reason he was estranged from Alice, even if he had made it worse all by himself.

'I don't think she's feeling up to calling anyone right now. She's pretty fragile and I'm worried about her. She said the kids are fine,' said Gavin.

'I'll call her. See if there's anything I can do to help?'

Gavin and Marcus rarely crossed swords. Their weekly dinners had been all about good food, good company and conversation. Gavin's tone changed instantly.

'That's not a good idea, Marcus. I know you mean well but getting more involved isn't going to help anyone. Let's see what her test shows, if she can get one. If she tests positive, I'll let you know. Stop interfering and trying to fix everything.'

He knew Gavin was right. He had always been a 'fixer'. It was what he did for his family and his clients. King Zoom was ringing again. He let it ring off.

'Maybe, you're right? I thought she would have told me, that's all. Let me know as soon as you hear anything.'

'Of course. And Marcus?'

'What?'

'If Claire does test positive, you must tell Alice. Don't dig another hole by lying over something as serious as this.'

'I will, I will. Stop lecturing me, will you? How's everything in Scotland, by the way? Shot any beaters recently?'

'The grouse season is over, Marcus, and things are okay, thanks. We'll probably have to cull my mum soon.'

Marcus sat at his desk thinking about their conversation. Gavin may have been right but acting on his instincts was one of his biggest skills. It had taken him to The Golden Carrot. He texted Claire immediately.

Hi Claire. Gavin told me about your symptoms. How are you feeling?

Her reply came quickly.

Feel like shit. High temperature and fever. Going to hospital tomorrow to get tested.

Are the children all right?

Yes, they're fine. Checked their temperature, both normal.

Anything I can do to help? Let me know how the test goes?

Thank you.

He felt impotent. Marcus Barlow was used to fixing things, even viruses.

* * *

Kensington Gardens contained the usual smattering of Day-Glo joggers and dog walkers taking their daily ration of exercise early. On his second lap of the pond, his phone rang. It was Laila.

'Morning, Marcus. You missed our alignment calls last night. I've sent you a couple of emails.'

'Yes, I saw, more like ten. Everything okay with Medusa?'

'I haven't heard back from them. Do you think something's wrong?'

'I doubt it. They're probably trying to get their team together. Can't be easy when everyone's in lockdown. Give them a couple of days.'

'Medusa is really important to me, Marcus. You know that. I don't want to fuck up now. I'm quite anxious.'

'How about trying mindfulness?'

It was an off-the-shelf solution plucked out of thin air. Alice said mindfulness was about being 'conscious of the present moment'. It sounded like the sort of bollocks Paul McKenna would come out with.

'Marcus, I don't even sleep, let alone having time for that bollocks!' said Laila dismissively.

They had found something on which they were both aligned. Mindfulness was bollocks. The real reason for her anxiety was The Golden Carrot. It was so close, she could almost taste it.

'If we haven't heard back by close of play, I'll give them a call. In the meantime, perhaps go for a run?'

'Thanks Marcus. Truly helpful. Speak later,' she said sarcastically.

The partners were waiting for Kelvin to join the pipeline call. They were chattering about their struggles to cope with lockdown.

'We can't get an Ocado delivery for at least another two weeks,' said Simon Loder.

Jacob Mauser empathised with his colleague.

'I know. We've had the same problem. Luckily, I managed to get an Asda delivery last Saturday. Just for basic essentials, of course.'

There was an awkward silence. Amongst the partners, there was a hierarchy of supermarkets. Ocado and Waitrose were in Tier 1, along with niche organic suppliers. Sainsburys and M&S were acceptable as Tier 2, but only the 'Taste the Difference' and 'Not Just Any Food' ranges. All the others were swear words and Mauser had crossed the line.

'Gosh, that's dreadful, Jacob,' empathised Vanessa Briggs, 'where do you live?' she said as if she was about to alert the air ambulance to fly in some supplies from Waitrose to save him.

Marcus laughed out loud which was heard by everyone. He had forgotten to go on mute.

'Something amusing you, Marcus?' said Mason sneeringly.

'No, nothing. Just wondering when The Firm was going to get Bear Grylls to give us lessons on how to survive lockdown without Ocado. Maybe learn how to skin and roast a squirrel?'

Their conversation was interrupted by Kelvin's arrival.

'Morning everyone. Sorry I'm late. Just been on a call with the Duke and some of the other top bods about our business model.'

Saying 'other top bods' was Kelvin's way of letting everyone know he was a 'top bod' too. Izzy Majewska gave the performance update. Everything was on track now the virus had moved the goalposts. From his glass-fronted sun terrace overlooking the estuary in Padstow, Kelvin glowed. The virus had made his life even better than it was before.

'So how is morale in the team?' he said in a concerned tone.

'Patchy,' said Jenny Moffatt. 'People living in flats or with families are struggling. It's not easy being out of the office and working longer hours.'

'We have the social events this week, don't we?' said Kelvin, as if Zoom bingo was going to make everything better.

'We do,' said Jenny. 'I was thinking we should do a weekly temperature check, to see how people are feeling and what more we could be doing?'

It was a good idea. There was only one flaw. It came from HR.

'Not sure that's a great idea, Jenny,' said Kelvin, plonking his ample arse squarely on top of it. 'We probably know the answers already without asking the questions. Any other bright ideas, anyone?'

'What about doing *Undercover Boss*, Kelvin?' piped up Marcus.

Kelvin stared into his camera over a glass of freshly squeezed orange juice.

'What the fuck are you going on about, Marcus?'

'You know, like the TV show in the US? You put on a heavy disguise, a wig, makeup, maybe even get a disability. Nobody knows who you are and you spend a day working with different members of the team to see what their working days are really like.'

'And doing what exactly?'

'Pretending you're a new joiner, helping with PowerPoint slides, formatting Excel tables, adding icons, processing SCAR requests, updating the benchmarking database, that sort of thing. You could do it all remotely from Cornwall too.'

Kelvin wasn't alone in thinking that Marcus had finally lost the plot. Apart from Chloe, none of the partners had watched the show.

'And then what?' said Kelvin, showing his irritation.

'You reveal your true identity and reward the best ideas with a large sum of money. Then they break down and weep all over their screens.'

A wallpaper of stunned faces waited for Kelvin's reaction.

'Have you gone completely mental, Marcus, or are you just taking the piss?' Kelvin looked at his watch. 'I'm checking it's not April Fool's Day!'

'I think it would be a great thing. Maybe the disability bit would be hard to pull off on Zoom,' said Marcus with the stony face of a gunslinger in a shoot-out.

Three messages appeared in his inbox within seconds.

Marcus, you're a legend. I love that show. (Chloe)

Genius idea. Hysterical!! (David Prince)

You are so dead. (Mason Sherwin)

Kelvin left his pistol in its holster and walked back into the saloon for a whisky.

'Well, thanks for that one, Marcus. Any more bright ideas on how to improve team morale from watching daytime television, please feel free to pass them on to Jenny.'

Marcus was approving more 'living' expenses when Kelvin called him. He had drunk a few whiskies in the saloon and was now ready for the gunfight.

'I suppose you thought that was funny this morning? Your little *Undercover Boss* joke?'

'Honestly, I was being serious, Kelvin. I think the idea has some merit. A top bod finding out at first-hand how people are feeling can't be a bad thing?'

'Are you suggesting I'm not close to the team?'

'Well, it's probably quite difficult from Padstow.'

Kelvin went for his gun.

'What is it with you, Marcus? Do you want to be part of this partner team or not?'

'I'm not sure. Perhaps you should make me an offer I can't refuse?'

Marcus did his best Don Corleone impression. Kelvin fired straight back as if he was expecting it.

'Leave it with me.'

The phone went dead. Marcus leaned back in his chair. He had finally fired the bullet. It was time to see if the sheriff wanted him to get on his horse and ride out of town.

* * *

It had been another night of fever, wrapped in a towel to absorb the sweat. Her temperature had risen to 38.6 and she was taking paracetamol like Smarties. The children were watching CBeebies when she called Beverley.

'Just calling to see how you are?'

'Hi Claire. You sound dreadful. Are you really all right?'

Claire told her about the call to 111.

'But you told me you were okay? Why didn't you say anything? It's probably my fault if you've got it. I feel terrible. When are you having a test?'

'It could have been anyone, and I might not have it. There's nothing you can do, so don't blame yourself. Hopefully, I'll get a test today or tomorrow and get the results back in forty-eight hours. That's according to the NHS website. Are you and Bruce all right?'

'Yes, we're still isolating from Edward. Bruce is fine. How about your two?'

'They're both fine. Happy watching television. I haven't got the energy to do schoolwork.'

'That's the least of your worries. Focus on keeping yourself dosed up and stay indoors. Keep in touch and let me know if you need anything?'

'Yes, you too.'

* * *

It had been two days since he had spoken to Alice. He called her on FaceTime.

'Hi Al, it's me. Thought you might like to see I'm not displaying any symptoms and am as fit as a fiddle.'

'I can certainly see you Marcus and I'm pleased to hear it. You could be asymptomatic, you know? Why are you wearing a suit and tie? Aren't you meant to be working from home?'

'You know me, old habits dying hard and all that? Things here are all fine.'

Things weren't fine. He had just provoked Kelvin McBride into making him an offer he couldn't refuse. It wasn't the time for another confession.

'How's your friend, Kate?' said Alice in a sarcastic tone.

He knew she had got her name wrong on purpose. The emphasis on the word 'friend' was meant to be ironic. He ignored her.

'She's not well, if you want to know. She's got a fever, breathless and she suffers from asthma too, which makes it worse. She's going to hospital tomorrow to get a test.'

He was waiting for another spiteful remark but she took him by surprise.

'Shit, that's terrible. I feel so sorry for her. It can't be easy, coping with lockdown, feeling unwell and with two little children to look after. How old are they?'

'Five and three.'

'That's tough. I wouldn't want that with two little ones. When is her test?'

'Tomorrow, I think she said.'

'And how are you, Marcus? Are you sure you're not showing any symptoms? You're fifty-five which puts you in a higher risk category. Tell me the truth.'

'Thanks for reminding me. I'm fine. I would tell you if I had any symptoms. Honestly.'

It had been his lack of honesty which had locked them down in separate places but Alice didn't need to point it out.

'I think you should definitely have a test too. And we may need to have them as well?'

'If Claire tests positive, I'll have to, even if I haven't been in close contact with her.'

'Well, we only have your word for that, don't we?'

'I know. I'm sorry if I've let you down.'

'You haven't let me down, Marcus. It's just you being you. Always thinking you have to fix things on your own. It's one of the things I've always loved about you. Do you want to speak to the children?'

'No, it's okay. I'll call them later. Thanks again, it was good to see you.'

'It was good to see you too. Bye Marcus.'

* * *

Claire sat in her chair, she was exhausted after making dinner. Fish fingers, oven chips and beans. Lazy food. She didn't feel hungry and didn't eat. She was thinking about her test. Who would look after the children? Her options came down to two, Judith or Mr Mahoney.

'Mummy's popping next door to see Judith. I'll be back in five minutes. Just sit and watch television.'

Kyle and Alexa were engrossed in *Waffle the Wonder Dog* and didn't look up. Claire put on her coat and walked along the balcony, rang Judith's doorbell and stood back. By the time Judith opened the door, she was already starting to shiver.

'Hi Claire. Jesus Christ, you look terrible! What's the matter?'

Judith stepped forward and Claire raised her hand.

'Don't come too close, Judith. My friend, Beverley, has tested positive for Covid and I'm feeling feverish now. I'm going to the hospital tomorrow to have a test. Any chance you could look after the children while I go? It should only be for a couple of hours. I'm really sorry to ask.'

'How long have you been feeling like this?'

'Last couple of days. I've got a temperature and keep getting hot and cold shivers. I'm even getting night sweats.'

Judith ran her hands through her black wavy hair and shook her head.

'Claire, you know I would love to help you, if I could? But what if Kyle and Alexa have it too? I've got a really busy day of conference calls tomorrow. The result of the leadership contest is on Saturday and I'm preparing press releases and statements.'

'But the children will just sit quietly. They won't disturb you,' said Claire desperately.

'I've got a call with Lisa Nandy at midday, Sir Keir Starmer at two and Rebecca Long-Bailey at four. It just won't work. I can't have Alexa asking to have her nose wiped while I'm on a call with the next leader of Her Majesty's Opposition. I'm so sorry. Any other time, you know I would? Is there anyone else who can help?'

Claire thought helping a struggling single mum at a time of crisis was exactly the sort of thing that a future Labour leader would admire.

'Don't worry, I'll ask Mr Mahoney. After that, I'm out of options. I guess I'll have to take them with me.'

'You could get a taxi? Do you have the money?'

She knew she had a twenty-pound note in her purse. It was all that was left from her wages. It would get her one way to the hospital at least. 'I'm sorry I asked. I'll ask Mr Mahoney now. Would you mind keeping an eye on the children for five minutes while I go downstairs?'

'Sure. Let me get my mask.'

Each flight of stairs to the ground floor got harder. She thought about how long it was going to take her to get back up. She knocked on the caretaker's front door. She knew he would be watching *The Chase*. He came to the door. He was unshaven and looked tired.

'Hi Claire. Everything all right?'

She was almost standing on the grass.

'Not really, Mr Mahoney. I've got a real problem. I'm worried I may have the virus. I'm going for a test at the hospital tomorrow. Any chance you could look after the children for me? Only for a couple of hours.'

Enveloped in the folds of her puffer coat, she was starting to shrink.

'Claire, you know I'd do anything to help you, but what if the children have it too? I can't risk catching it, not at my age. Are they all right?'

'They're fine but we're all cooped up in our flat, so who knows?' She knew she was putting him in the worst position and started to cry. 'I'm really sorry, Mr Mahoney. I shouldn't be asking you but I didn't know who else to turn to. Judith can't do it.'

'What about social services, can't they help? What about your social worker?'

'Gavin? He's in Scotland and the last thing I want is social services poking their noses in, thinking I'm not coping. I'm sorry Mr Mahoney, I shouldn't be asking you, but you're my best friend.'

Their relationship was more than just friendship and a love of Bradley Walsh. She was the daughter he'd never had, and Kyle and Alexa were his grandchildren. The caretaker's eyes were watery too.

'And you're my best friend too, Claire, but I'm no use to you if I end up dead. Maybe you'll have to take them with you?'

'Looks like it's my only option. I'd better get back before Judith frightens the kids to death with her mask. See you soon.'

She turned and started to climb the stairs. She paused on every landing, her breath getting shorter with every step. It took her five minutes to get to her flat. She went straight to the kitchen and puffed on her inhaler.

'Any joy?' said Judith.

'No. I should never have asked him. I was being selfish. I'll have to take them with me. Thanks for looking after them, Judith.'

'Least I can do. I'm so sorry about tomorrow. If things get worse, ring 111 and get a doctor to come out. You really don't look good.'

'Let me see how I feel in the morning. Good luck tomorrow with Rebecca Long-Something.'

'Bailey,' said Judith and she laughed from behind her mask. 'She's very nice actually.'

Claire made a cup of tea, returned to the living room and wrapped herself in a blanket. The children were watching *Clangers*. She looked around the living room and at her battered portfolio beneath the coffee table. She felt humiliated, begging her neighbours to look after her children while she had a test to determine whether or not she had a killer virus.

Fuck you, Jack. Just fuck you.

* * *

Marcus had finished his last Zoom call. He called Olivia and James. Olivia was still fretting over the grading for her A levels. He knew her world would collapse if she didn't get into veterinary college. James was still plucking up the courage to tell his mother about his degree. His son was like him, always struggling to confront the truth, putting off giving Alice bad news. That evening's dinner, asparagus and lemon spaghetti with peas, hadn't given James much backbone either.

Marcus put a pizza in the oven. Lazy food for lockdown. He thought about Gavin's advice.

'*Getting more involved isn't going to help anyone.*'

He ignored Gavin's advice and called her.

'Hi Marcus. How are you?'

'Just rang to see how you are. Still feeling feverish?'

'Yes. My temperature isn't coming down and I'm having trouble breathing. It's like someone's kneeling on my chest. I'm using my inhaler all the time.'

'How are the children? Are they okay?'

'They seem to be. I've just put them to bed. I couldn't manage a story, haven't got the energy. They'll fall asleep eventually.'

He thought of the children on the night of their dinner, both of them lying on either side of him as he read 'Dinosaur School'.

'Where do you have to go for your test?'

'St Mary's. Paddington.'

'Who's looking after the kids?'

'Judith, my neighbour, can't do it. Some important Labour Party thing. I asked Mr Mahoney but he's meant to be shielding. That's about it.'

'So, what are you going to do?'

'I'll get a taxi and take the children with me. I've got no other choice.'

'I'll take you,' he said.

'What?'

'I've got a car. I'll pick you up, take you to the hospital and wait with the children while you have your test, then I'll bring you all home.'

'But what about your work? And what if I have got it, I don't want you to get it. Think of your wife and children.'

'I wouldn't worry about work. After today, I might not be there for much longer. Soon I might be getting an offer I can't refuse!'

'What have you done now?'

'Nothing that should concern you. Well, do you want a lift or not? My car does have a fourteen-speaker sound system.'

'Well that obviously seals it! You sure know how to woo a girl, don't you Marcus?' she said sarcastically. 'Seriously, I don't want to get you into trouble at work or with your wife.'

He told her what Alice had said earlier. He didn't say she had called her 'Kate'.

'That's very sweet of her.'

'Don't forget, she's a mother too. What time do you want to go tomorrow?'

'Around three o'clock? Would that work for you?'

'Perfect. I'll call when I'm outside your flat. I'll get there around 2.30. Should give us plenty of time to get to Paddington. My pizza is probably done now, I'd better rescue it before it becomes a crisp. See you tomorrow.'

'It's really kind of you, Marcus. Thank you.'

It was Tuesday, 31 March 2020.

Chapter 30

THROUGH THE ZOOMHOLE

It had been another restless night in Kensal Mansions, more sweats and a suffocating feeling, like a tombstone crushing her rib cage. The children had squabbled over breakfast and her temper was short. Enthusiasm for home schooling was waning on all sides.

'It's not like school,' said Kyle defiantly. 'It's not fun. I miss Bruce and Liam.'

'I know Kyle, but we have to work at home like Miss Mistakidis told you. Would you like to do something on the computer?'

'I want to see Zoe,' chipped in Alexa.

'Soon, sweetie, soon.'

Claire didn't know when 'soon' would be, but it couldn't come soon enough. She scrolled through *BBC Bitesize* for something more interesting than letters and counting frozen peas.

'What about learning about a real spaceman called Neil Armstrong?' she said, scrolling through the pages. 'He was a spaceman too, like Buzz Lightyear. He was the first man to walk on the moon.'

The word 'spaceman' grabbed Kyle's attention immediately, and they sat in front of the computer reading his story together. Kyle was amazed that Neil's footprints would be on the moon for millions of years.

'Will they stay there forever?'

'They will. There's no wind or rain on the moon to wash them away,' said Claire knowledgeably.

She had scrolled ahead. Alexa wanted to know what space food was like.

'Did the spaceman have shepherd's pie on the moon?'

'Probably not. I don't think his spaceship had an oven.'

Alexa screwed up her face in disapproval. It wasn't much of a giant leap for mankind without proper shepherd's pie.

Claire saw the postman walk past her kitchen window and heard the noise from the letterbox clattering and envelopes falling on the doormat. She waited until the children were watching television before picking up the letters. One envelope had 'UK Government' on the front and was addressed to 'The Occupier, 11 Kensal Mansions'. The other envelope was of a higher quality, heavier, embossed paper in an ivory colour. It was addressed to Mrs C. L. Halford. Not many people used her middle initial.

She opened the envelope from the UK Government. It was a letter from the prime minister on headed notepaper bearing the royal crest and his address. Boris had written to her personally to let her know what he was doing about the virus.

'It's important for me to level with you …' wrote Boris.

That's a first then, thought Claire.

'… We know things will get worse before they get better, but it is with that great British spirit that we will beat coronavirus and we will beat it together.'

Boris had signed the letter. His signature was legible but scrawly.

His arm must be dropping off, having to sign millions of these, she thought. *No wonder he's poorly.*

She opened the second envelope. The letter was from Talbot Bailey Moss Solicitors, with an address in the City. An expensive address on expensive headed paper. The heading on the first page was in bold.

PETITION FOR DIVORCE
Mr J. A. N. Halford (Petitioner)
Mrs C. L. Halford (Respondent)

She read the two-page letter. She was shaking before she got to the end. Jack had initiated divorce proceedings on the grounds of her 'unreasonable behaviour'.

My unreasonable behaviour! she thought. *He committed adultery with some old slapper and then deserted us. Giving me an infection as a parting gift seems pretty fucking unreasonable to me.*

The letter continued, *'Our client wishes to play a full and participative role in the upbringing and education of his children, Kyle and Alexa, and will be seeking agreement to a shared access arrangement as part of the divorce settlement. We would advise you to seek legal representation in advance of the next steps in the process.'*

The letter was signed by Ms Erica Studden.

I wonder what pack of lies he's told you, Erica? she thought.

She picked up her mug and threw it at the wall. It smashed, and dregs of tea splattered all over Spiky, the balding pasta hedgehog. Boris was right, things had got worse before they got better. She threw the letters on the worktop and picked up a cloth to wipe the wall. A few more of Spiky's pasta quills had fallen off. She swept them up with the shards of the shattered mug.

She sent a text to Gavin.

Jack's filed for divorce. Got a letter today. Wants shared access to the kids. Help.

As usual, Jack's timing was impeccable. Every time she had been down, he was always on hand to kick her in the teeth. She started to feel hot as anxiety kicked in, waves of nausea rising from the pit of her stomach. She ran to the bathroom, put her fingers down her throat and retched. It splattered into the bowl. Tea, pieces of toast, the remnants of a fish finger and some peas. Peas always seemed to stick around for longer than they should. She flushed the toilet, rinsed her face and brushed her teeth. The toothpaste had lost its 'minty freshness', it could have been custard.

* * *

There was only one story on the front pages as he looked at the stand outside the newsagent in Queensway.

GREEN SHOOTS HOPE IN VIRUS BATTLE
FIX TESTING FIASCO NOW
NHS PLANS ROUTE OUT OF VIRUS LOCKDOWN
PSYCHO SEAGULLS CORONA RAMPAGE

Maybe the coronavirus will turn out to be a giant April Fool's Day prank? he thought.

The *Daily Telegraph* reported that the NHS had announced plans to develop a world-class 'test and trace' app that would pave the way to ending lockdown.

That's probably the April Fool's joke this year, he thought.

Laila interrupted his porridge with the news that Yeast Feast wanted to delay the launch of Project Medusa until the following Monday. There had been a disagreement with Make 'n' Bake about which online collaboration tool to use.

'Are you okay with topping and tailing the kick-off meeting?' said Laila.

'Topping and tailing' was one of the key competences needed to be a partner. It involved saying a few well-practised words at the start of key meetings and closing with sycophantic gratitude.

'Of course I am,' he said.

Marcus checked Outlook. Risk and Compliance had sent him a third reminder for the mandatory online training course, 'Avoiding Micro-Aggressions During a Pandemic'. Three videos for tomorrow night's 'Through the Zoomhole' event had arrived. Vanessa Briggs and Graham Wilder, plus a surprise one from Chloe.

Hi Marcus. Thought you might need something a bit different so I've done a video of my mum and dad's house. Hope it's okay!

He opened her video. The internal decor of Mr and Mrs Bulmer's three-bedroom semi in Gants Hill reminded him of a DFS advert. A large red leather L-shaped sofa dominated the living room, matched in size by a gigantic television. Marcus imagined the Bulmer family sitting down to watch *I'm a Celebrity ... Get Me Out of Here!*, hiding their faces behind giant bowls of popcorn as another pointless celebrity ate the dehydrated genitals of a marsupial. Mr Bulmer was clearly useful with his hands and had set about renovating the family home and its garden to a standard that the man on *Grand Designs* would be creaming himself over. There weren't many houses in Gants Hill that came with a Japanese water garden complete with koi carp, waterfalls and mock-Shinto artefacts.

Nobody is going to get this one, he thought and sent a reply.

Great video, Chloe. Thanks a lot. Will be surprised if anyone gets this! Lovely garden too. Ask your dad if he wants to come and do mine!

He browsed the two other videos. Graham Wilder's contribution was clever. The video was made with the camera at different angles. Graham shared a first-floor, two-bedroom flat in Clapham with Seb, a friend from university. It looked like it hadn't seen a vacuum cleaner since Christmas. It was a typical boys' flat, complete with gaming corner, big sound system and a few electric guitars. The George Foreman grill in the kitchen was a bit of a giveaway, and Marcus thought his son would approve. Grease was probably a boy thing. He sent Graham an email.

Thanks for the video, Graham. Nice camera angles. The pile of beer cans by the bin might be too big a clue? Liked the underpants under the bed too. Have they been there long? Hope all okay. Marcus.

He opened the video from Vanessa Briggs. It was quickly apparent why she had volunteered so readily: she had a beautiful home and wanted everyone to know it. Six-bedroomed, stucco-fronted houses in St John's Wood didn't come cheap, and Vanessa's home was anything but cheap. With her hedge fund manager husband Lawrence, they had a disposable income which put every luxury within their grasp. The interior was a head-on collision between Venetian palazzo and Danish minimalism. But it was the picture hanging in the dining room, above the white Statuario marble fireplace, that caught his eye.

What the hell is that? he thought.

He paused the video and zoomed in. It was like a scene from *A Midsummer Night's Dream* on acid. Woodland animals in human form wearing sexy lingerie, and with erect cocks ready to enter exposed anuses.

The team are going to love this when they see it! he thought.

He sent a note to Vanessa.

Beautiful house, Vanessa. Loved the picture in the dining room. Very provocative.

She was online and replied immediately.

Thank you, Marcus. It's an original David Harmison. See you tomorrow. Looking forward to it. V.

He sent a Zoom invitation to the group, reminding them of the start time, the teams and the rules. Drinks and a catch-up at 7.30, a short break to clap for carers, and the game would start at 8.15.

At 2.15 in the afternoon, Westbourne Grove was almost empty. He gave way to a number 7 bus coming from the opposite direction. It was empty. Its bored driver forgot to flash his lights in gratitude.

At least they're probably running on time during lockdown, he thought as he turned up 'Divas of Country' on the M5's fourteen-speaker sound system. He turned right on to Ladbroke Grove and headed north towards the Westway. He called Claire from the car.

'I'm five minutes away. I'll park in the road next to the flats. See you soon.'

She could hear the voice of Patsy Cline singing 'Crazy' in the background.

'I'll get the children ready. They're very excited, they don't go in many cars.'

'I'm sorry, I haven't got any children's car seats. Will they be okay in the back?'

'They'll have to be, won't they? See you in a few minutes.'

Claire and the kids slowly descended the four flights of stairs, walked across the courtyard and through the alley. It was littered with discarded 'wraps' and beer cans. Addicts taking their single form of daily exercise.

Marcus was standing next to the passenger door. He wasn't hard to spot. There weren't many cars in the road like his, and there weren't many people wearing a pinstripe suit, tie and face mask either. He waved to them and Kyle and Alexa waved back. Claire put on her face mask and looked at him.

'Bloody hell, Marcus. Do you sleep in a suit? Do you lose your superpowers if you're not in pinstripes?'

'Hi, Marcus, nice to see you!' he said with a hint of irony. 'Thanks for putting your life on the line for me. How are all of you?'

'Sorry. I didn't mean to be rude. Just a bit overwhelmed by all of this to be honest,' said Claire.

'How are you feeling?'

'Bloody awful. I've still got a high temperature. I'm going from hot to freezing and finding it hard to breathe. This bloody thing doesn't help either,' she said pointing to her face mask. Her eyes, normally so bright and alert, were sunken, bags behind bags caused by broken sleep and sweats.

'No, they're not the most comfortable things are they? Come on, let's get you all in.'

He opened the back door and the children climbed in.

'I can see your children are grown up,' said Claire, pointing to the car's interior.

'What do you mean?'

'Cream leather. You'd never have chosen that with small ones. All those sticky fingers.'

'No, probably not.'

The M5 accelerated away. It had a bit more horsepower than Ian's mobility scooter, and Kyle was impressed as he was pushed back into his seat.

They had turned on to Westbourne Park Road when Marcus sniffed.

'Can you smell something? Smells pretty rank in here.'

'I can't smell anything,' said Claire.

She turned around and looked at the children. Alexa's pink Wellington boot was the source of the pong. It was also on the backseat, the back of the front seat and the cream carpet. Alexa had stepped in a dog turd in the courtyard and had smeared it all over the car's interior.

'I'm really sorry, Marcus. It's dog poo on Alexa's boot. I've got some wet wipes in my bag. We'll wipe it off when we stop. Alexa, sit still and don't wave your feet around.'

He put a brave face on it and smiled. Inside he was in turmoil.

'Stepping in dog shit is meant to be lucky, you know?' said Claire, trying to be positive.

'Is it?'

The satnav directed them to the hospital where Marcus found a parking space in a side street. Claire walked slowly towards the entrance of A&E as Marcus was removing Alexa's offending boot. The leather seat wiped clean, but the carpet would need something more professional.

The scene inside the hospital was chaotic. The A&E department had been divided into two zones: a red zone for coronavirus cases and a green zone for everything else. Chairs in the waiting areas were separated; even sprained ankles and sliced fingers were socially distanced.

The signs directed Claire to the red area. There were seven people waiting, different ages, sexes and ethnicities. The virus was embracing diversity. Two nurses in plastic aprons, gloves, face masks and face shields were scurrying around. Claire approached a desk where a small woman dressed in blue PPE was sitting. She was wearing a pair of reading glasses behind a pair of large Perspex safety goggles behind a plastic shield. Triple protection. She pointed to a line of yellow tape on the floor, two metres away from the desk, and held up her hand, indicating that she was to wait. Claire read her name badge. She was called Ann.

'Have you come about a Covid test?' said Ann. Claire could barely hear her muffled question through her mask.

'Yes, I don't have an appointment. My name is Claire Halford.'

'Please can you sanitise your hands?' said Ann, pointing to a bottle of gel on the table. Claire squirted the gel on her hands and rubbed them together. 'Do you know your NHS number or have a form of ID?'

'Will a Tesco Clubcard do?'

'Not really. I need something to prove your identity and address.'

Claire rummaged around in her bag and found an old bill from Npower.

'Will this do?' she said, offering up the crumpled piece of paper. Ann inspected the bill and nodded.

'We've got a bit of a backlog, I'm afraid. There will be a bit of a wait, probably around half an hour. We ran out of test kits earlier today and that's put us behind. It's all a bit of a mess. You can come back tomorrow, if you want?' said Ann apologetically.

'I can't come back. I need someone to look after my children. It has to be today.'

'Are you displaying any symptoms of Covid?'

'Yes, I think so. I've got a fever, my temperature is high and I'm not breathing well. I suffer from asthma too. I really need to have a test today.'

She sounded desperate and Ann nodded sympathetically.

'We've been turning people away all week, telling them to go home and isolate. Let me take your details. Maybe go for a walk and come back in half an hour. Probably better you're not in here for longer than you need to be.'

Ann took some details and Claire walked slowly out of the hospital to the car where Marcus and the children were playing 'I spy'. He saw her coming and got out.

'That was quick. All done?'

'No. I've got to go back in thirty minutes. There's a backlog, ran out of test kits apparently. You can go if you have to get back to work? I'll take the kids in with me and get a taxi home.'

'I think "Avoiding Micro-Aggressions in a Pandemic" can wait.'

'What?'

'Don't ask. Let's go for a walk, probably better than sitting in the car.'

Marcus put Alexa's wellingtons on and got the children out of the car. She watched him; he hadn't lost the knack of being a dad. Kyle walked ahead and Alexa reached up to hold Marcus's hand. The pavements were empty as she told him about the letter from Talbot Bailey Moss Solicitors.

'Talk about picking your moment,' she said. 'I could have the bloody virus, and he thinks my behaviour was unreasonable.'

'They are right you know, Jack's solicitors? You should get yourself a decent solicitor. You will need one.'

'And, of course, I can afford a solicitor on Universal Credit, can't I? Don't be stupid, Marcus. Jack knows I'll never be able to afford a good solicitor. That's why he's done it.'

Claire returned to A&E. Ann recognised her.

'We still have a twenty-minute wait, I'm afraid. Are you happy to wait?'

Claire nodded and Ann handed her some paperwork.

'Take a seat over there,' she said, pointing to the chairs. 'If you could sanitise your hands, please?'

Eventually, she was called by a nurse who escorted her to one of the partitioned areas.

'Hi Claire. I'm Bernadette.' She explained the throat and nasal swab procedure and laid out the test kit on the table in front of her.

'Aren't you going to do it?' said Claire.

'It's very easy, you can do it yourself. Or would you prefer me to do it for you?'

Claire nodded.

Bernadette removed the swab from the wrapper, it was like a giant cotton bud, and swabbed the back of Claire's throat.

'I'm going back as far as your tonsils.'

Claire tried to explain she didn't have tonsils but it got lost in translation. The tickling made her gag.

'Right, now I have to do your nose,' said Bernadette. 'Both nostrils.'

She completed the swabbing, put the stick in the plastic tube and sealed it in an envelope. Claire put her mask back on.

'When will I get the results back?'

'Hopefully in forty-eight hours, but some are taking longer. If you haven't heard in seventy-two hours, call 111. In the meantime, you must self-isolate until you get the result.'

Calling 111 was obviously the solution to everything.

'Can I ask a question? Should I be wearing a face mask at home? I suffer from asthma and I'm finding it hard to breathe, but I'm worried about my children.'

'How old are they?' said Bernadette.

'Five and three.'

'From the little we know so far, the effects on small children are much less severe. If a mask makes it harder for you to breathe, then I wouldn't.'

'Thanks a lot. I'll try to keep it on.'

Claire shuffled back to the car and got in.

'How was it?' said Marcus, rubbing sanitiser on his hands and offering the bottle to Claire.

'Thrill of a lifetime,' she said, applying gel for the third time in an hour.

Marcus started the car. Tammy Wynette was singing 'D.I.V.O.R.C.E'.

'Not sure that's appropriate right now, is it?' said Marcus, turning the sound system off.

They were back at Kensal Mansions in twenty minutes. Marcus switched the engine off and she turned to face him.

'Thanks, Marcus. I know I'm being selfish but I couldn't have done it on my own. Probably best you don't come in.'

'Have you got food in the flat?'

'Enough. I can't face shopping. Hopefully I'll start to feel better soon.'

'Call me if you need anything. Oh, one more thing?'

'What's that?'

'I'd rather you didn't tell Gavin about today. He got a bit defensive when I told him about the dongle. Told me quite strongly not to get involved. I don't want to upset him again.'

'He's only being protective. I'm sorry if I've put you in an awkward situation. I really am.'

'No need to apologise. I offered, but best you don't tell him? Call me when you get the result?'

'Sure. Of course.'

The television was on in Mr Mahoney's living room. She started to climb the stairs. Even Alexa was climbing quicker than her.

'Wait a minute, kids, Mummy needs to catch her breath.'

More puffs on her inhaler before making the final assault to the summit.

No wonder they need oxygen to climb Everest, she thought.

Mrs Hassan was straining rice at the kitchen sink, clouds of steam billowing out of the open window. She waved as Claire passed. There were lights on in Judith's flat and Claire assumed she was busy writing Rebecca Long-Something's press release. She wondered how Boris was getting on in hospital. At least he didn't have to take his kids with him to get a test. He would have needed a minibus.

* * *

Marcus was back in the flat in time for the press conference. It was the usual script. Restate the three-step action plan, guided by The Science. Report the number of cases and deaths and show remorse. Thank the 'wonderful NHS' and other frontline workers and give out some big numbers. Show some graphs. Take questions. Leave.

Everything was going in the wrong direction. Hospital admissions were rising and the number of deaths had increased to 2,352. All the questions were about the record on testing and the shortage of PPE and ventilators.

He checked WhatsApp, a new message from James.

Hi Dad. Thanks for the chat on Sunday. Decided to talk to Mum today. Didn't go well. Give me a call sometime.

He thought his son might be in need of moral support and called him.

'What happened?' said Marcus.

'Well, you know you said, "timing is everything"?'

'Yes.'

'I obviously got it wrong. I got up late, came downstairs and was getting myself some breakfast. Mum was in the kitchen making bread. It's her new hobby.'

'Yes, I know,' said Marcus. 'It was her new hobby fifteen years ago too.'

'She asked why I never seemed to be working, like Libby. Then she went on about how hard Libby has always worked. She was like a dog with a bone, wanted to know how I'm doing, what I was working on? Eventually I had to fess up.'

'How did she take it? Not well, I presume?'

'She threw a set of measuring spoons at my head and told me I'd never get a decent job with a Third.'

'A 2:2 or a Third isn't the end of the world. You'll be fine, James.'

'Mum asked me if you knew?'

Suddenly, panic set in. Alice would be livid if she knew he'd kept this news to himself. His list of confessions to Alice was growing. Another shock could send her rushing to bed with a box of Nurofen and an eye mask.

'What did you say?' he said nervously.

'I said you didn't know but I'd call you later.'

'Thanks, that was smart. Don't worry, she'll come round eventually.'

'I hope so. I'm going for double lockdown, staying in my room until she cools off. I walked into town this afternoon and stocked up on pasties, scotch eggs and sausage rolls from Costcutter. They'll keep me going for a few days. I'll pretend I'm off my food and that will make her feel guilty!'

Marcus laughed. 'And where are you storing these contraband items?'

'In plastic bags, hanging out of my bedroom window.'

Marcus imagined the shame of Costcutter bags hanging from one of the upstairs windows at Twin Gates. It would certainly get raised at Neighbourhood Watch.

'Do you feel better? Now you've confessed and got it out in the open?'

'Sort of. I didn't want to let you and Mum down.'

'You haven't. When you emerge from your room and have finished gorging yourself on sausage rolls, tell Mum that I know now and I'll call her tomorrow.'

* * *

Kyle and Alexa were euphoric. Lessons were abandoned before *Woman's Hour* started. Claire had another sweaty night and her temperature was up to 38.4. All she wanted was some sleep. She didn't have the energy to change her bed. It would have to stay damp. She turned on the radio. Jenni Murray was interviewing a woman from the Isle of Lewis in the Outer Hebrides, which had just recorded its third case of the virus. Even the most isolated places weren't safe.

'*When you look out of your window, what do you see?*' said Jenni.

'*Straight in front of our house, in one direction is a loch,*' said the woman in a soft, lilting Scottish accent, '*and in the other is the Atlantic Ocean.*'

Claire wondered what she would have said if Jenni had been interviewing her.

'*Well, Jenni, in one direction is the derelict Grenfell Tower, one of London's most impressive landmarks, and in the other is the Hammersmith & City Line.*'

Her fantasy of being interviewed on *Woman's Hour* was interrupted by a text from Gavin.

Hi Claire. Just got your message about Jack? Not helpful. Wait until I'm back and we'll deal with it together. Don't worry. How did your test go?

Waiting for the result. Tomorrow or Saturday. Feel awful. I think I've got it. Very scared.

I'm here for you. Don't worry. Things will be fine.

Alexa came into the kitchen wanting her nose wiped.

Thanks G. Will let you know.

* * *

King Zoom had been demanding. It was late afternoon before Marcus got the chance to eat. He made a bagel with smoked salmon and sat down to watch the press conference. With public confidence plummeting, Boris, *in absentia*, had put his strongest team on the pitch: Matt Hancock and two professors from The Science.

'At each point, we've been following scientific and medical advice, and we've been deliberate in our actions, taking the right steps at the right time,' said Matt.

It was a strategy straight out of The Firm's partner handbook. 'If the shit's gonna hit the fan, always make sure there's someone else's face in front of yours'.

Matt was writing off £13.4 billion of historical NHS debt. The virus could now make debt and lives disappear simultaneously. Manipulating the number of people who had died wasn't so easy. There had been 569 deaths in the previous 24 hours.

It was time to start preparing for the team's social evening. He replayed the three videos and made notes, clues and hints about the owner's identities. He practised his Loyd Grossman impression. Loyd was the original host of *Through the Keyhole*, before Keith Lemon got the gig.

If we let Keith Lemon into Twin Gates on his own, I'd be worried about him going through the laundry basket to sniff Alice's knickers, he thought.

The running order would be Graham Wilder's flat, then Vanessa's mansion, leaving his trump card, Chloe's house, until last. With thirty minutes to kill, Marcus prepared some snacks and opened a bottle of wine.

At 7.30, he opened Zoom and multiple faces began to appear on his screen. It was a full turnout. He was pleased people had forgotten about work for one night. He set the scene, everything that happened on the night would be under Chatham House rules.

'Whose house is that?' said Angela Rust, who thought the game had already started. 'Is Chatham a new joiner?'

Some people had made a special effort. Chloe was dressed as an Easter bunny, complete with floppy ears and fake tan. She introduced the team to her little sister, Natalie, who was dressed identically. There was a face on screen that Marcus didn't recognise. He had a long, blonde mullet, earrings, full moustache and was wearing a red baseball cap, sunglasses and a loud Hawaiian shirt.

'I saw a tiger and the tiger saw a man,' said the face in an accent which came straight out of a Louisiana swamp. The younger members of the team started laughing. Tim Cooper, a new joiner, had come as Joe Exotic, the hero of the popular Netflix series, *Tiger King*.

'Carole Baskin is a fucking bitch!' said Angela, who was getting louder.

Marcus didn't know who Carole Baskin was.

Vanessa had hired a purple, sequinned, strapless flapper dress, complete with ostrich feather bower and headband. She was smoking a cigarette from a long holder and drinking an espresso martini. An arm appeared on screen and she looked up. A fresh cocktail appeared.

'Who's that, Vanessa?' said Graham Wilder. 'Is that your butler?'

'It's my husband, Lawrence. He's keeping me supplied with espresso martinis,' she said, dragging seductively on her cigarette and blowing smoke into the camera in a vampish way.

The chatter moved on to lockdown and how people were coping. It was different for everyone. Those who didn't have to commute loved it, those at home with children were hating it. Some were living on 'ping meals', while others were practising for *MasterChef*. What everyone agreed was they missed each other, having personal contact with their colleagues.

Just before 8 p.m., Marcus announced the break to clap for carers, and to refill glasses and replenish food. Lawrence Briggs appeared right on cue with a bottle of Louis Roederer Cristal champagne in an ice bucket and a selection of canapés.

'Did your husband make those?' said Hannah Blake.

'No, the caterers were in earlier. Lawrence just put them on a plate,' said Vanessa nonchalantly.

The team left their screens to step out of their houses and lean out of windows to show their support for the NHS and frontline workers. Marcus clapped for a few minutes until it was safe to stop without seeming like a killjoy. He waited for faces to appear on the screen again. People were feeling upbeat, they had done their bit. He explained the rules again. Everyone had to watch each video which he would narrate. The three teams would ask three questions each and, after that, their captain would submit their answer to Marcus via a message. Each member of the winning team would get a bottle of wine. He pressed play to start the first video: Graham Wilder's flat in Clapham.

'So, who could live in a house like this?' said Marcus in his strongest Loyd Grossman accent.

Nobody laughed, most people didn't know who Loyd was.

'When was the last time the sink in the bathroom was cleaned?' asked Angela. 'And the toilet looks disgusting.'

Graham sent Marcus a message. *'Probably Christmas.'*

'It's clearly owned by a man,' said Hannah. 'No woman could exist with so little wardrobe space.'

The X-Box, gaming chair and pile of size 11 trainers were obvious clues but the posters of Adam Lambert on the living room wall threw people off the scent. Graham's flatmate, Seb, was gay and Adam was a gay icon. Only Angela's team guessed correctly as Graham stepped 'Through the Zoomhole' to reveal his identity. Angela's team were in the lead after round one, and she downed two more glasses of wine to celebrate. Everyone took five minutes to replenish their glasses before Marcus introduced the second video.

'Join me as I take you … Through the Zoomhole,' he said as he pressed play.

People stared at their monitors in awe as Marcus gave them the guided tour of Vanessa's stunning palazzo palace in St John's Wood. She had started at the top of her four-storey house and worked her way down.

'So now we enter the master bedroom which comes with two adjoining walk-in dressing rooms and an en suite bathroom with "his and hers" toilets, a marble hot tub and twin washbasins. This is a room big enough for an army to bathe in.'

After an excursion into each of the five exquisitely decorated bedrooms, Marcus moved downstairs via the grand central staircase.

'This is a house built for entertaining. From its sixteen-seat dining table to its welcoming and warming fireplace, this is a room that simply screams out, "great company, great food and great wines".'

Vanessa remained impassive, eating another canapé and sipping her champagne. Inside, she was elated. The hours, weekends, holidays sacrificed for The Firm, this was what it was all for. Power, prestige and recognition. The camera panned up to the picture above the fireplace.

'And all of this splendour is presided over by this original and stunning piece of art,' said Marcus.

People stared at their screens, leaning forward for closer inspection. Marcus was moving into the expansive and expensive Kesseler kitchen when a voice called out.

'Whoa! Sorry Marcus, can you pause a minute, rewind and go back to the dining room? I want to see that picture again,' said Hannah.

'Yes, me too,' echoed a number of others.

'Sure.'

He backtracked the video and paused it. 'I'm reliably informed by the owner that it's an original David Harmison,' he said.

People were leaning forward to scrutinise the image.

'Holy shit! Take a look at that ringpiece,' said Angela. 'The kestrel is just about to shag the rabbit up the arse.'

'That would definitely put me off my dinner,' said Graham.

Crowd trouble was breaking out.

'Where are we going next, Marcus? Into the S&M dungeon?'

'I bet there's a sex swing in the basement,' said Tim Cooper.

Marcus pressed play and moved through the kitchen, passing the spiral, temperature-controlled wine cellar and finishing in the nanny's suite in the basement.

'So, who could live in a house like this?' he said, coming to the end of the video.

'Someone with fetish for kinky pictures of bum holes and boners,' said Angela who was opening another bottle of wine.

Vanessa had never planned on her twenty-thousand-pound original piece of art being derided as a 'kinky picture'. Marcus responded to the team's questions trying not to reveal Vanessa's identity.

'It's obviously a partner,' said David. 'My entire flat would fit inside one of those wardrobes. Someone who is clearly married too.'

'And someone with a liking for bum sex,' said Angela who was getting louder.

Like a game of 'Guess Who?', the teams narrowed it down with binary questions. Two teams went for Simon Loder and one for Mason Sherwin. They weren't even close. Marcus revealed the answer.

'So, who could live in a house like this? It is ... Vanessa Briggs!'

Vanessa did an embarrassed form of 'jazz hands' on screen and downed her champagne in one. The damage had been done. The multiple gasps of disbelief and shaking of heads said it all.

'So nobody guessed correctly, which leaves Angela's team in the lead after two rounds. Let's take a short break to refill our glasses. Back in 5 minutes for our third and final video.'

Screens went blank as people left to replenish drinks, check on children and go to the toilet. When he returned, Marcus had two messages. The first was from David Barker.

This is brilliant, Marcus. Loving it. Would never have guessed the anal fan was Vanessa!

The second was from Vanessa.

You f*cker! Completely humiliated. Never supporting one of your stupid ideas again.

Those who live by the sword, die by the sword, thought Marcus.

The team reassembled on Zoom. Angela was looking worse for wear, a blob of salsa was dripping down her chin.

'Everything okay, Angela?' said Marcus.

She gave him a thumbs up and he pressed on.

'Okay, now we come to our third and final video, join me as I take you ...

Through the Zoomhole.' He pressed play and the camera entered the Bulmer household in Gants Hill.

'This is a house designed around comfort and relaxation, the family is placed right at the heart of this home.'

The camera panned to the red leather L-shaped sofa and the eighty-two-inch QLED television with its surround-sound cinema system.

'Everything one needs for a night in with a bottle of wine and a great DVD.'

'Now that's what I call a fuck-off television!' said Tim Cooper.

The camera moved seamlessly from the living room into the kitchen and into the extended conservatory, which Chloe's dad had turned into a replica of an East End boozer, complete with bar, taps and optics. A pool table dominated the centre of the room.

'This house says have fun and party. Someone who hasn't lost touch with their roots,' said Marcus.

'Looks like a brilliant place for lockdown,' said Hannah.

The camera moved through the large bifold doors and into the Japanese water garden. The acers and cherry blossom trees were showing their new foliage, and the koi carp were feeding on the surface of the pond.

'But this person also has an affinity with the Land of the Rising Sun,' said Marcus.

'That's an impressive garden,' interrupted David. 'Bet those fish aren't cheap either. This is a seriously classy place.'

The camera moved back inside and upstairs. Both girls' bedrooms were a sea of pink. Fluffy, pink toys occupied every surface, bunnies, bears, ducks, lions.

'What child wouldn't be happy in this room?' said Marcus.

'One that was locked in there with a paedo and a bag of sweets,' shouted David.

Graham Wilder remained quiet. He had a one-night stand with Chloe after a team night out when her parents and sister were away on holiday in Alicante. She had insisted her favourite teddies sat at the end of the bed to watch them having sex which he thought was a bit weird.

The three teams asked their questions which Marcus did his best to answer. Thoughts were gravitating towards Lucy West, who everyone knew had two small daughters.

'It has to be her. Her daughters are something like ten and seven. That fits with all the fluffy toys and the dolls,' said Hannah.

All three teams went for Lucy West.

'So, who could live in a house like this? It is ... Chloe and Natalie Bulmer!'

Chloe and Natalie jumped up and down and whooped, their bunny ears flapping.

'So, it looks like the winners on the night are Angela's team. Well done to you all,' said Marcus.

People stared at their screens but could only see the top of Angela's head. She was slumped over her keyboard.

'Angela? Angela? Oh dear, we seem to have lost Angela for the moment,' said Marcus. 'Well done to everyone else in the team. Chloe will be arranging for bottles of wine to be delivered to you, although Angela might not be needing it any day soon.'

Apart from Vanessa Briggs, and a slightly anxious moment for Graham Wilder, everyone in the team had loved the evening. 'Through the Zoomhole' had been a resounding success.

'Okay, in two weeks' time, we'll be playing "Whose Deliveroo?". More about that to follow in the next week or so. In the meantime, I hope everyone remains safe and well,' said Marcus.

He exited Zoom, closed his laptop and finished his glass of wine. It was 10.30 and he thought about calling Alice. If she was already in bed, she wouldn't thank him for disturbing her. He was also feeling tipsy, which was not a good state to be in for making more confessions. It would have to wait until morning.

It was Thursday, 2 April 2020.

Chapter 31

'FELLOW FEELING'

The early banter on the Project Medusa team alignment call was all about the previous evening's social events. Jenny Moffatt's quiz had descended into farce over illegal googling, and Oliver Rankin's online bingo had caused a diversity disaster.

'It all kicked off when Oliver called out, "two fat ladies, eighty-eight", and Katie Hayman objected, saying it was sizeist and made fun of fat people,' said Steve Pettigrew. 'Oliver tried to diffuse it by saying it was just a bingo call, but Katie was having none of it. She's very sensitive after her gastric band surgery. She's reported Oliver to HR.'

An Assistant Manager chipped in.

'It happened straight after Oliver called "dancing queen, number seventeen" and made a gesture which upset Giles and Matt. Everyone knows they're both gay.'

Laila didn't do banter and was getting frustrated. The Golden Carrot was calling.

'Please can we get started? I want to make sure we're all aligned for Monday's kick-off meeting.'

After three hours of flipping through PowerPoint slides, responsibilities were assigned and accountabilities allocated. Laila was stressed, she was biting her bottom lip.

'And you're fine with the topping and tailing bit, Marcus? I think it needs to be really crisp,' said Laila.

The team giggled, unleashing a series of baking puns.

'Yeah, no soggy bottoms, Marcus.'

'No loafing around or we'll be toast.'

Laila remained stony-faced. It was the day before launching a project which could shape her destiny. She didn't need jokes.

'I'm sure I'll rise to the occasion. You can crust me on that,' said Marcus, which provoked cheers of approval from the team. 'Don't worry, Laila, it will be fine. The materials look great, first-class job.'

He made a coffee and checked The Sequence. Another red day on Stockwatch. He called Alice. She was in the car.

'Hi, Al. You sound as if you're out and about?'

'Yes, I'm in the car park at Waitrose. I can't get an Ocado delivery for two weeks. How are you?'

'I'm okay. Stuck in front of Zoom for most of the day. I had a good night yesterday though.'

He told her about 'Through the Zoomhole' and Vanessa's piece of erotic art.

'I hope you're not planning on making a video of our house, are you? I don't want people laughing at my pictures!'

'Tony the Fireman's thighs weren't that bad. Everything all right at home? How are the kids?'

'Yes, we're all fine. Have you spoken to James?'

'Yes, he told me about his conversation with you. Did you really need to throw the measuring spoons at him?'

'He was bloody lucky it wasn't the rolling pin. It's just so typical of him, all that money spent on his education and he blows it on having a good time. What do you think?'

'Come on, a Third isn't the worst thing in the world! He hasn't killed anyone, has he? And the money doesn't come into it, it was our choice. In a way, I envy him. I bloody wish I was twenty-one again.'

'I'm sure you do. I think I've upset him. Since our row, he's not been eating. Just comes down to the kitchen, picks at things and goes back upstairs. I'm a bit worried.'

Marcus thought about James's stash of contraband processed meat products stored outside his bedroom window, sustaining him in isolation from his mother.

'Don't worry, I'm sure he'll be fine. He's probably just feeling a bit bruised.'

'How are you feeling and how is Claire?'

Marcus decided to deal with his confessions one at a time.

'I'm absolutely fine, no symptoms at all. Just a bit of a hangover from last night. Claire's not so good. She went for a test at the hospital on Wednesday. She's waiting for the result.'

'She was very lucky to get a test from what I see on the news,' said Alice.

He decided to go for it. Timing was everything.

'Yes. In the end, I had to take her to hospital. She had no option unless she took the children with her in a taxi. That wasn't an option, as I saw it. Please don't be angry, Al? She had no choice. God knows, we all need some help in these bloody awful times. I took every precaution, mask, sanitiser, social distance.'

He braced himself for the explosion or snide remark.

'I'm not angry, Marcus. Actually, I'm proud of you. You're a much nicer person than me. I'm too selfish, always thinking about myself. I wouldn't have done it.'

She started to get upset. Life under lockdown had cranked up everyone's emotions.

'Don't get upset Al, you would have done the same. Isolation and lockdown where she lives is no joke, believe me. Hopefully, she'll get the results today.'

'And if she tests positive? What then?'

'I'll have to get a test obviously.'

'Yes, obviously Marcus. But I was referring to her. What will she do if she gets worse? We've all seen what this virus does to people, it's frightening.'

'I know. Gavin will get her some support, I suppose. They won't leave her to deal with it on her own.'

'I wouldn't be too sure about that.'

One confession down, one more to go. He quit while he was ahead.

* * *

Kensington Gardens was crowded with people taking advantage of the lockdown sunshine. Every bench was occupied, nobody was keeping their distance. Clusters of swans and ducks were gathered on the path around the pond, being fed by small children.

By the time lockdown ends, we'll have a population of obese ducks. Maybe Joe Wicks can come up with a routine for fat swans? he thought.

He walked back to the flat and picked up an early edition of the *Evening Standard* outside Bayswater Station.

FREE FALL: VIRUS DEALS RECORD BATTERING TO ECONOMY

The economy was falling through the floor faster than the 2008 financial crisis. He looked at the rows of shops and restaurants, all apologising to their customers for being 'closed until further notice'. Not everything was going down, the number of deaths in London had passed 1,000. It had been two days since he had taken Claire for her test. He wondered why he hadn't heard and called her.

'Hi Claire, it's Marcus. Any news?'

'No, nothing. They did say forty-eight to seventy-two hours.'

She sounded despondent.

'Well, that could be a good thing,' he said, trying to be positive. 'No news is good news and all that. This whole testing thing seems to be a shambles. How are you feeling?'

'Like absolute shit. I think I'm getting worse. I just want to go to bed and sleep but I can't. I've got the kids to look after. I've stuck them in front of the telly all day.'

'Are you eating? You need to keep your strength up.'

'I've got no appetite. I can't taste or smell anything.'

'You should eat something, even if it's just soup and a slice of toast.'

'I haven't got any soup. We're running low on everything. We can get by for another day on pasta, baked beans and sweetcorn. Hopefully, I'll feel better tomorrow.'

'Okay. Let me know as soon as you hear anything, will you?'

'Of course. Thanks for calling, Marcus.'

He was going to make himself a tuna salad niçoise for dinner. It was her 'pasta, beans and sweetcorn' comment that did it.

Nobody should have to live on pasta, baked beans and sweetcorn, not in an epidemic, he thought.

He jumped up from the sofa, put on his shoes, grabbed some bags from the cupboard and headed for The Temple. There was a lull before the early evening rush. He took the escalator to the first floor and grabbed a trolley. It was like a scene from *Supermarket Sweep* as he moved swiftly up and down the aisles, loading his trolley with as many essentials as he could. At the checkout, he had filled six bags.

'Do you have a myWaitrose card?' said Sandra from behind her screen.

'Is the Pope a Catholic?' said Marcus, scanning his card.

He paid for the shopping and, laden down like a pack mule, struggled back to the flat. Eric the concierge was polishing the brass door handles, keeping them free from the virus, and opened the door for him.

'Let me give you a hand with those, Marcus,' said Eric with his usual tone of military deference. 'Stocking up for another weekend of lockdown?'

'If you could get the lift for me please, Eric? I'm going straight to the basement. Mission of mercy!'

Eric leapt into action at the double, summoned the lift and held the door, as Marcus struggled with his bags. He loaded the boot with the shopping, started the car and accelerated up the ramp and on to Westbourne Grove. The radio was playing the Bill Withers song 'Lean on Me'.

It was a great song and he sang along with Bill.

'Bill Withers, the great American soul singer who died in Los Angeles on Monday,' said the presenter mournfully.

That's bloody sad, thought Marcus. *He was a great.*

He pulled up in the road next to Kensal Mansions, unloaded the bags and struggled to the alleyway, where Mr Mahoney was sweeping away the usual detritus.

'Hello. It's Phelan isn't it? I'm Marcus, we met a few weeks ago? We watched *The Race* together. Sorry, I can't shake your hand at the moment. I'm taking these to Claire.'

Even with a mask on, Mr Mahoney recognised him instantly. Waitrose bags and pinstripes weren't that common in Kensal Mansions.

'Nice to see you again, Marcus. Let me give you a hand.'

'If you don't mind? That would be a great help, thank you.'

The caretaker's sausage fingers picked up four of the bags with ease. Calloused palms from years of holding a pneumatic drill. He walked across the courtyard to the steps and carried the bags to the door of No. 11.

It took a while for Claire to answer. She was wrapped in a blanket.

'Marcus! What the hell are you doing here?' she croaked.

'Pasta, baked beans and sweetcorn is not a proper meal. I've been to The Temple and bought you some decent food.'

Claire stepped aside as Marcus put the shopping on the kitchen table. She looked down at the six shiny green bags.

'I've never shopped in a Waitrose. Nice bags. Very stylish.'

'Bags for life,' said Marcus. 'You can have them, I've got loads. I've only bought things I thought you might need, mostly basics but with a few extras.'

'Like what?'

'Sun-dried tomatoes, Kalamata olives, sea bass fillets, on special offer from the fish counter, rosemary and garlic focaccia—'

She stopped him in mid-sentence.

'I get it, Marcus. Thank you, very thoughtful of you.'

Kyle and Alexa had finished watching *Waffle the Wonder Dog* and came into the kitchen. They were pleased to see him.

'Can I have a glass of Ribena and a cow biscuit, please Mummy?' said Alexa.

Claire looked at Marcus.

'Don't suppose you bought any cow biscuits, did you? Malted milks. They have a cow on them.'

'No, I'm sorry. But I did get these, they are very nice too.' He took a packet of Bourbon Creams out of one of the bags and opened them. He removed his mask, broke off one of the biscuit layers and scraped off the chocolate cream with his front teeth. The children loved it.

'That's disgusting,' said Claire. 'Teaching my children bad habits. You've only been here ten minutes. Do you want a coffee?'

'I can make it. Go and sit down. I'll bring it through. You don't look great at all.'

He finished putting the shopping away, put the kettle on and looked at the pile of dirty plates in the sink. He hated mess but knew it wasn't her fault. He hung his jacket on the back of the chair, removed his cufflinks and watch, rolled up his sleeves and washed up. He wiped all the surfaces with Mr Muscle.

By the time he went into the living room, she was asleep in her chair, wrapped in a blanket. He looked at her, her head on one side, resting on a cushion, legs tucked up to her chest. She looked safe and he let her sleep. It was almost six o'clock.

'Would you mind if I watched something?' he whispered to the children.

They both nodded and he sat between them and switched channels to BBC One. There was a new man from The Science: Professor Jonathan Van-Tam. Marcus thought he looked a bit of a gangster with his buzz cut and grey pinstripe suit.

Sounds a bit like Jean-Claude Van Damme, he thought.

The peak in deaths was forecast to come on Easter Sunday. It was a journalist's question that aroused Marcus's interest.

'Can I just ask, is there any benefit in wearing a face mask? Should the public wear face masks when they go outside?'

Matt Hancock side-stepped the question and talked about something irrelevant. He left it to the professor to answer.

'There is no evidence that the general wearing of face masks by the public who are well affects the spread of the disease in our society. In terms of the hard evidence and what the UK government recommends, we do not recommend face masks for general wearing by the public.'

I think you might have that one a bit wrong, professor, thought Marcus.

He handed the controls to Kyle and looked at Claire. She was still fast asleep. The children needed to eat and he was hungry too.

'Would you like something to eat?' he whispered to the children.

They both looked up and nodded.

'How about sausages and mashed potatoes?'

They nodded again.

'Special onion gravy?'

He looked into the bedrooms. Unmade beds, undrawn curtains and piles of dirty clothes on the floor. He put the potatoes on to boil and returned, making the beds, opening the curtains and folding the clothes. It felt odd, handling a stranger's underwear, but he reconciled it in his mind believing he was being kind.

Thirty minutes later, dinner was ready and the table laid. He made four glasses of Ribena. A decent Côtes du Rhône would have gone down well. He shook Claire gently on the shoulder. She awoke and looked startled, a tall, masked man standing over her. She rubbed her eyes.

'What time is it?' she said sleepily.

'Almost seven. I've made dinner for us. It's only bangers and mash with purple sprouting broccoli, but I've made onion gravy too. Better than pasta with sweetcorn and beans. How are you feeling?'

'Better for a sleep. Are the children okay?'

'They're fine. They're in the kitchen, Kyle is stirring the gravy.'

Claire uncurled herself, wrapped the blanket around her shoulders and shuffled into the hall. She noticed the bedrooms.

'You've made the beds and tidied up? That's very kind of you.'

On a normal Friday night, Marcus would have been getting ready to go out to dinner with Alice. Now he was making beds and cooking dinner for a family that wasn't his. After dinner, Marcus cleared the table.

'Was that okay?'

'It looked really nice. Sorry, I didn't eat very much. I can't taste anything. The kids liked the gravy,' said Claire.

'Shall I get them ready for bed? I don't mind.'

She reached for her inhaler and puffed. 'You don't need to. They can go for another day and you're not exactly dressed for bath time. I don't want you to ruin your suit.'

'It's okay, I've got lots of them and it's only a suit.'

They all got up and Marcus walked behind her as she shuffled along the narrow hall in her slippers.

'Have you taken your temperature?'

'No, but I will.'

Bath time was exactly as Claire had feared. Marcus emerged dripping wet with two children in pyjamas. He read 'Zap!', the story of Kenneth the Chameleon who couldn't change colour until he met Kiki and started to blush.

'I bet you were a good dad,' said Claire, when he returned to the living room.

'I'd like to think I still am,' he said, taking mock offence.

'No, when they were smaller. You enjoy it, don't you?'

'I always did when I got the chance. I just didn't get the chance very often.' The conversation had touched a nerve and he changed the subject. 'Did you take your temperature?'

'It's 38.6. Highest it's been, I'm really worried, Marcus. I feel dreadful.'

'Let's hope you get the result tomorrow. Are you going to be okay, do you need me to do anything before I go?'

'No, I'll go to bed and hope I start to feel better soon. You've been amazing, Marcus. I'm sorry I'm dumping all my crap on you. I'm sure you've got enough crap of your own?'

'Everyone's got crap to deal with in this lockdown.' He got his things together and stood at the door of the living room. 'Call me if you feel worse and let me know the result.'

'Sure. You're a star, Marcus.'

Fifteen minutes later he was back in the flat. The roads were deserted on a Friday night in lockdown. He kicked off his shoes, poured a glass of wine and switched on the television. A new series of *Have I Got News for You* had started and it made him laugh. There was only one item of news.

* * *

The first hour of Saturday morning was devoted to his body. He shaved, exfoliated, cleansed and moisturised before setting off for Kensington Gardens. Boris's request for people to stay at home was being ignored, and the park was crowded. Pairs of policemen were patrolling to ensure social distancing was being observed. Serious crime in the capital had plummeted leaving plenty of resources to maintain the two-metre rule. He bought a copy of *The Times* and sat propped up against the trunk of a fallen tree. He liked the Saturday edition, it came with a jumbo crossword which would occupy him for most of the day. The banner headline on the front page caught his eye.

LOVE IN ISOLATION: SEX AND INTIMACY IN QUARANTINE

The article came with the customary picture of two pairs of entwined, presumably heterosexual legs, in the missionary position, soles of feet poking out from beneath a crisp, white duvet.

Why can't picture editors be a bit more imaginative? he thought. *It doesn't have to be reverse cowgirl, but they could try harder.*

He turned to the article. It promised to give him 'strategies to get through quarantine with a renewed sense of self-love and a deeper understanding of your sexual and intimate needs'. Ten minutes of reading and all the article had done was leave him feeling frustrated. The realisation it had been a long time since he had been intimate with Alice. The article suggested spicing up telephone conversations for couples parted by lockdown. He made a mental note to suggest phone sex when they spoke. He received a WhatsApp from James. It was early for him.

Hi Dad. Big news! Was hiding my pasty wrappers in the bin this morning. Found empty packaging for bacon hidden at the bottom. Looks like Mum's finally cracked.

Tempted by the serpent in the form of three rashers of crispy bacon and HP sauce, all the evidence pointed to Alice succumbing. He replied.

What have you done with it?

Kept it.

Excellent. Speak later.

* * *

The postman didn't ring twice, he didn't even ring once. It had been three days and she still hadn't received her result. Her temperature was 38.7. She was flickering between hot and cold like a dying light bulb. Kyle and Alexa were restless, imprisoned in the flat for two days. Summoning up all her energy, she decided to go out. The fresh spring air was invigorating and she felt better being able to breathe without wheezing through her mask.

At the entrance to the alleyway, she met Judith coming from the opposite direction. She seemed distracted and gabbled excitedly. 'Have you seen the news, Claire? Keir Starmer is our new leader. I've just been to HQ making sure the press releases and videos went out on time.'

'I haven't seen anything,' said Claire. 'Is that good news?'

'Well, personally I voted for Rebecca, but it's important the Party now puts aside our differences, unites behind our new leader and gives him our fullest support.'

She sounded like the press release she had just issued. Claire had seen the new leader interviewed on television and thought he looked sensible.

'How are you feeling now?' said Judith. 'Should you be outside?'

'I haven't had the result yet. It was due yesterday but I can't keep the children locked up all day. I'm going to call 111 when I get back.'

Judith went on the attack immediately.

'Another Tory clusterfuck, testing and PPE! Couldn't manage a shag in a brothel that bunch of public school tossers.'

'What would Labour have done differently?' asked Claire innocently.

'That's not the point,' said Judith dismissively. 'As the Opposition, our role is to oppose. Constructively.'

Judith walked ahead of her. After a single flight, Claire had to stop.

'Judith, hang on. I need to get my breath. You go on with the children. I'll get there.' She stopped and put her hand against the wall to steady herself and reached into her coat pocket.

'Bloody hell, Claire, are you all right? You're like a ghost,' said Judith looking down from the next flight.

It took them five minutes to climb the remaining flights and reach the balcony where they parted.

'Make sure you ring 111 and get your result. It's all the fault of those Tory wankers.'

'I will. See you, Judith.'

Although the government's testing programme had been heavily criticised, not many people realised it was telepathic. As Claire was preparing to call 111, her phone pinged with a text message.

'*Your Covid-19 test result is POSITIVE. You MUST complete 14 days of isolation immediately. We will contact you shortly. For clinical advice, please call 111.*'

It was official. She had the virus. If certainty brought relief, her thoughts quickly turned to the consequences. She sent texts to Gavin, Marcus and Beverley.

Got my test result. Positive. Have to isolate now for 14 days. Feeling pretty shit.

Beverley was the first to reply.

OMG! Poor you. So sorry if you got this from me. Let me know what I can do. Will call you later. xx

It didn't have to be Beverley. It could have been anyone, someone passing too closely in Tesco Express, leaning into the freezer at the same time. Chicken nuggets and oven chips could have been equally to blame. Claire was now in an elite group, one of only 40,000 people to have tested positive for the virus.

* * *

Her text had woken him. He had fallen asleep after lunch, struggling to digest his chicken and chorizo ravioli and the anagram for thirteen across. He opened her message and replied immediately.

Sorry to hear that. At least you know. Call me if you need anything. M.

He remembered the headline in the *Evening Standard* in January.

China reports first death from mysterious outbreak in Wuhan

It had taken three months and a few detours but the virus had finally caught up with him. He needed a test too.

He picked up his phone and called Partner Matters, a 'Concierge' service dedicated to making the lives of The Firm's partners run smoothly. Every partner mattered. They made the money for The Firm It was an arse-wiping service for those who couldn't wipe their own. It was on call, twenty-four seven, three hundred and sixty-five days a year. He called the exclusive number. It was answered on the second ring.

'Good afternoon, Mr Barlow, you're through to Partner Matters. You're speaking to Stephanie, how may I help you?'

Partner Matters' intelligent telephone system had recognised his number and his photograph had appeared in front of Stephanie. His profile contained his credit card numbers, loyalty card numbers, BUPA membership, favourite restaurants, preferred seats on an aeroplane and the names of his wife and children.

'I would like to arrange a Covid-19 test, please? Can you arrange that?'

'Certainly, Mr Barlow. I have all your medical details in front of me. When would you like to have it?'

'When can I have it?'

'Today?' said Stephanie efficiently. 'Somewhere close to Weybridge?'

'Actually, no. Somewhere in central London would be better.'

'Even easier. We have a number of private GPs on call offering a Covid testing service. Can you leave this with me and I'll call you back within thirty minutes?'

'Perfect. Thank you, Stephanie.'

If Kelvin made him an offer he couldn't refuse, Partner Matters would be one of the few things he would miss. Fifteen minutes later, Stephanie called him back with an appointment at 3.30 with a private GP in Devonshire Place, just off the Marylebone Road. Two hundred and fifty pounds was a small price to pay for certainty. He thought about the testing process Claire had been through. Partner Matters versus Nobody Matters. No contest.

* * *

Claire was feeling worse. The news she had tested positive hadn't helped. Her temperature was 38.8. The paracetamol and ibuprofen tablets she was taking by the handful weren't helping.

'Are you feeling better, Mummy?' said Kyle who had got up from the sofa and was standing in front of her. She looked at him. His jumper was on back to front and he had odd socks on but he had wanted to dress himself. She wanted to hug him, her special little boy.

'I'm trying sweetie. I want to feel better, I really do.'

'Have you got the virus, Mummy?' he said. His bottom lip was quivering.

'Yes, I have but you mustn't worry. Lots of people get it and get better. Mummy's going to get better too. We're all going to be fine.'

'Is Marcus coming to see us today?'

'No, not today. He's busy. We'll see him soon.'

She went to the kitchen to make a mug of tea. Teapigs lemon and ginger would make her feel better. She filled the sink with hot water and put the lunch plates in to soak. The letter from Talbot Bailey Moss Solicitors was on the worktop and she removed it from the envelope.

Our client wishes to play a full and participative role in the upbringing and education of his children.

Over my dead body, she thought. She stared out of the kitchen window at Grenfell Tower. She thought about what Gavin had said.

'Let me know if you need support. We have processes in place to deal with this scenario.'

Processes. Scenarios. Kyle and Alexa were now part of a 'scenario'. She picked up her phone and dialled a number. A woman's voice answered.

'Hello.'

'Hi Mum. It's Claire, how are you?'

The tension in her mother's voice was detectable immediately, anxiety brought on by a lifetime playing dogsbody to Arthur Carter. Her mother's first words whisked her back to Walsall in a flash.

'Oh, hi Claire. We're all okay, same old, same old. Your father and brother are both on furlough now. I'm still working in the bakery. Otherwise, we're locked down like everyone else. How are you and the children?'

'They're fine. Going a bit mad with lockdown and missing school. They're growing up quickly but you haven't seen them for over a year, have you?'

'I got the pictures you sent the other week. They look beautiful. You look good too, dressed up a bit.'

'I've got a job now. Well, I had a job until lockdown. Working for another mum from Kyle's school. It's just admin work but we get on well. She's very nice. She's called Beverley.'

Her mother made a series of embarrassed grunts, trying to sound interested. She seemed nervous, wanting to get off the phone before the inevitable argument kicked off.

'That's good. I'm sure a bit of extra money comes in handy.'

She had given Claire the perfect opening.

'Well, it does seeing as Jack doesn't contribute a penny. How is Jack by the way? Have you spoken to him recently?'

'You know I did. He called me and wanted your address. He wanted to see his children.'

If her mother had stopped at this point, there was a chance the conversation might have turned out differently. But she didn't.

'As he has every right to,' she continued, 'he is their father.'

The pain of disloyalty hurt more than her aching body.

'Oh really. Is that the same "right" he used to assault me in my flat with his children sitting in the living room? The same "right" that made his son start wetting the bed again?'

'As I heard it, you assaulted him first? Hit him with a saucepan, didn't you?'

'So you've spoken to him again?'

'Yes, he rang me after he came to see you. Told me what happened.'

'And gave you his version, which, of course, you believed? You didn't think to ring me to see if I was okay? If it wasn't for my neighbour, God knows what he would have done.'

'He didn't tell me that.'

'Well, of course he wouldn't. It takes more balls than he's got to own up to assaulting his wife.'

'It sounds like six of one and half a dozen of the other to me.'

She thought about what Gavin had said. Maybe it would be better for Kyle and Alexa to be part of a 'process' than being with people who couldn't care less.

'Okay Mum, I get it. You still think everything is my fault. Let's stop now, shall we?'

'Are you all right, Claire? You don't sound very well?'

'I'm fine, just a bad cold. Say hello to Dad and Anthony for me. Bye now.'

* * *

Marcus walked from Beirut to Devonshire Place. He passed Madame Tussauds and the green dome, which used to be the Planetarium before it was converted to accommodate more waxworks. Children and tourists were more interested in posing for selfies alongside One Direction than they were in the solar system.

The waiting room of the surgery was typical of those around Harley Street. High, ornate ceilings, replica antique furniture and old copies of *Country Life* and *The Field*. He picked up a copy of *Country Life* and flicked to the 'Girl in Pearls', a full-page, black and white portrait of a winsome beauty from the Shires. Tinder for the upper classes. Octavia, from Lincolnshire, was the eldest daughter of a brigadier and had recently begun a fledgling career in PR, which she would obviously give up once she had found a suitable husband.

Octavia probably comes with a few hundred acres too, he thought to himself.

The receptionist called him and escorted him to a room on the second floor, where he was greeted by Dr Alan Guthrie, an ENT Registrar at a large NHS hospital in East London. Marcus explained his recent contact with Claire and lack of symptoms. Dr Guthrie nodded.

'Strictly speaking, that's against the rules, entering the premises of an infected person who isn't a family member in your immediate support bubble.'

'I did what I thought was right for someone who needed help.'

'Unfortunately Mr Barlow, kindness is what gets people killed, but I do understand. I suggest you keep an eye on her? Anyway, shall we do your test now?'

He took Marcus's temperature and blood pressure. Both normal. The doctor opened the test kit and swabbed Marcus's throat and nostrils before sealing it in the two tubes and placing them in the envelope.

'When will I get the results, doctor?'

'With a bit of luck, by lunchtime tomorrow. We have a private lab doing our tests. In the meantime, I would stay isolated until you get the result. The receptionist will take payment downstairs. Good luck, Mr Barlow, I hope your friend is okay.'

Marcus called Alice as he walked home along the Marylebone Road. She was sitting in the garden.

'Hi Marcus. How are you?'

'I'm fine. I wanted to let you know that I've just had my Covid test. I had it done at some place near Harley Street. I should get the result tomorrow.'

'That was quick!'

'Partner Matters. They're very efficient.'

'Of course they are. What about Claire? Has she had her result?'

'Yes, she's tested positive.'

Alice sat up on the recliner, her newspaper fell on the patio.

'Oh shit, no! Are you sure you're okay, Marcus? You're in a high-risk category. Look at Kate Garraway's husband. He's in intensive care with the virus. He's in a bad way.'

Marcus didn't know who Kate Garraway was. She was obviously better known than Mr Garraway.

'Is she a mum at Libby's school?'

'No, Kate Garraway, the TV presenter on *Good Morning Britain*? She was also on *I'm A Celebrity* this year. Her husband is in a critical condition with it.'

'You know I never watch *Good Morning Britain*.'

'So, how is Claire?'

'Not great. She's got a very high temperature. Aches all over.'

'What about her children, how are they?'

'They seem okay. I did some shopping for her yesterday. She had no food. All she had was pasta, sweetcorn and baked beans. That's no way to live. I looked after the children while she got some sleep.'

There were no eruptions, no shouting.

'That was kind of you. Not very sensible, exposing yourself to the virus?'

'Someone had to help. I took all the necessary precautions. If you and the children were in the same situation, I'd want someone to help you.'

'I think that's unlikely. It was a bit reckless. But that's you all over, Marcus, act first, think later.'

'I'll call you tomorrow once I get my results.'

Boris was still sick. Michael Gove was doing the daily briefing. It had a Saturday feel to it.

Can't be much happening today, thought Marcus as he sat down with a hot cross bun and a cup of coffee. Seven hundred and eight people had died in the previous twenty-four hours. Gove did a good job of delivering the bad news. Gravitas was turned up high.

They should give him that slot permanently, he thought.

The conference was over quickly and Marcus returned to the crossword. He was still struggling with thirteen across and it was starting to irritate him. He called Claire. He could hear her wheezing, short pulsating breaths.

'I had my test done today. I'll get the result tomorrow. Have you heard from Gavin?'

'No, not a word but I did ring my mum this afternoon.'

'I'm sure she was pleased to hear from you?'

She told him what happened.

'Oh, I see. That's not helpful. You didn't need that crap, not at this time.'

She sounded fragile, about to crack at any moment.

'Do you want me to come over? I really don't mind. I'm only sitting here doing the crossword.'

'No, it's okay. You've done more than enough for us. I'll call you if I need anything. Good luck with the crossword.'

* * *

Sunday was going to be hot and the British public were getting ready to make the most of it. The virus was going to be spread on the beaches, in the fields and in the streets. Matt Hancock was on *The Andrew Marr Show* and he was talking tough, promising severe measures if people didn't comply with the lockdown restrictions. Sunbathing and barbecues were out. Marcus thought about Kelvin and his family, locked down in Cornwall, walking his dogs on the beach and drinking a glass of chilled Chablis on the sun terrace. Severe measures indeed.

Andrew Marr challenged Matt's bold objective of 100,000 tests a day by the end of April. Matt screwed up his eyes and looked intense.

'I didn't say it would be easy to get to 100,000 a day, I said that we need to get to 100,000 a day, and I'm absolutely determined that we get there.'

No doubt it will be the fault of The Science when it all goes wrong, thought Marcus.

He was preparing to go for his walk when his phone rang. It was Gavin.

'I've just got off the phone to Claire,' he said. 'She didn't sound good at all. Her situation is getting worse. I'm going to make some calls to get her some proper help.'

The word 'proper' jarred. Buying a few bags of shopping and cooking bangers and mash hadn't made him Mother Teresa, but he had done his best.

'I did some shopping and helped with the children on Thursday.'

'Yes, I know. She told me. I did ask you not to get more involved, Marcus. Social services has well-defined processes in place for this scenario. As I said, I'll be making some calls now.'

Marcus thought Gavin sounded like someone from Risk and Compliance. 'Well-defined processes'. Everything had to have a 'process' now.

'Is that from the *Distressed Single Parents With Covid-19 Support Manual*, version 3.1?' said Marcus, sarcastically.

'Don't be ridiculous. You know what I mean, Marcus. It's about doing the right things in the right way at the right time.'

'Fuck me, Gavin. You sound like Matt Hancock. You'll be telling me that it's all being guided by The Science next.'

Gavin took offence with that.

'Marcus, I suggest you focus on you and your family and let me support Claire and her family in the best ways I can. That's what I'm paid to do. I understand you've had a test as well? Any news?'

'Still waiting for the result. Should get it today.'

'Let me know how it goes? I've got to go now, calls to make. Trying to support people from here isn't easy, you know?'

'No, I'm sure it's not. I'll let you know my result. Bye.'

* * *

Lunch had been a struggle. Claire was still in her dressing gown and pyjamas as she made a salad and boiled some new potatoes. She looked in the fridge. She still had a Moroccan vegetable tagine and a Thai green chicken noodle soup. Marcus's idea of 'basic essentials'. She was straining the potatoes when the saucepan lid slipped. Boiling, starchy water scalded her hand and she dropped the saucepan into the sink, spilling its contents into the soapy water.

'Shit!' She ran her hand under the cold tap and wrapped it in a wet tea towel. It was quickly becoming red and inflamed.

'Have you hurt your hand, Mummy?' said Alexa who saw the makeshift bandage.

'Yes, sweetie. I poured some very hot water on it. It was an accident.'

'Is it sore?'

'It is sore. I'll probably get a blister.'

'What's a blister?'

'It's what happens when you burn your skin on something hot.'

'Like the sun?'

Alexa's interrogation was like a runaway train, questions followed questions. Claire slammed on the brakes.

'Alexa, just eat your lunch, please!' she shouted.

Little heads went down. Lunch with soapy potatoes was eaten in silence and the children returned to *Toy Story 2* for the umpteenth time. Claire left the dirty plates on the draining board and shuffled back to the living room. Her temperature was high and her breaths were getting shorter. All she wanted was some sleep as she wrapped her blanket around her to stop the shivering.

* * *

Marcus was reading the *Sunday Times*. The newspapers had printed excerpts from the Queen's broadcast message to the nation going out that evening.

'And those who come after us will say that the Britons of this generation were as strong as any.'

His phone rang.

'Good afternoon, Mr Barlow. I'm calling on behalf of Dr Alan Guthrie. We have the result of your Covid-19 test.'

'Yes?' he said hesitantly.

'Good news. It's negative. All clear.'

It seemed too simple, too binary.

'Is that a definite "all clear" or a "probably all clear"?' he said.

'It's a definite "all clear". I would recommend you inform your GP that you have had a test and that it's negative,' said the doctor's secretary. 'We will send you an email with the confirmation, but we thought you would like to know.'

'Thank you for letting me know so quickly. It's a relief, for certain.'

'Not a problem. Have a good afternoon Mr Barlow.'

'Negative' was a great word. Every partner mattered. He sent messages to everyone who mattered to him. They all replied quickly. One person didn't.

With sporting fixtures cancelled and TV schedules decimated by the virus, the networks had resorted to repeats of old comedy shows and war films to raise the nation's spirits. He settled down to watch *Battle of Britain*. He had seen it many times. A stellar cast of Britain's finest acting talent: Sir Laurence Olivier, Trevor Howard, Michael Caine, Kenneth More, and Susannah York as the love interest. If Spitfires and Hurricanes could defeat the Luftwaffe, the British attributes of 'self-discipline, good-humoured resolve and fellow feeling', highlighted by the Queen, would surely defeat the virus.

With the German airborne invasion repelled and Churchill's immortal words ringing in Marcus's ears, it was time for Matt Hancock to take the stage for the daily briefing. Marcus wondered if it would be Matt's finest hour too. It had been a busy Sunday for him. Matt was wearing the same outfit he had worn on *The Andrew Marr Show* in the morning. He said all the same things too, getting tough on people who broke the rules. The Scottish chief medical officer had been caught out already, visiting her holiday home twice during lockdown.

I wonder how tough they will be on her? thought Marcus. With another 621 people dying from the virus, there was every reason to get tough on people who flouted the rules.

* * *

It was Kyle who woke her. *Toy Story 2* had finished.

'Mummy, can I have a glass of Ribena? I'm thirsty.'

Claire stirred. She tried to speak but couldn't get her breath. She put her blistered hand to her chest to steady herself and tried to respond. Her words came out in a dribble.

'Just … give … Mummy … a … minute … sweetie.'

She felt inside her dressing gown, her pyjamas were damp, more sweats. She puffed on her inhaler and levered herself out of the chair. The living room was a tip. She walked slowly to the kitchen. Her mouth was dry and she picked up a glass from the worktop, pushed some dirty plates aside in the sink and filled the glass from the tap. She ran her tongue over her lips to moisten them, they felt dry and cracked. It was hard to swallow. She sat down and opened her phone. A message from Posh Marcus.

Got my result. Negative. Hope you're okay? M

She imagined Marcus like Robert Duvall as Colonel Kilgore in *Apocalypse Now*, striding across a bombed beach with dead bodies all around him. She had seen it many times and knew the script.

'*He was one of those guys that had that weird light around him. You just knew he wasn't gonna get so much as a scratch here.*'

In the war against the virus, Marcus was Kilgore in pinstripes with a 14-speaker BMW M5 for a helicopter gunship. She replied.

Great news.

Marcus opened her message and replied.

Are you sure you're okay?

He waited and waited. There was no reply, nothing that indicated Claire was typing. He called her and it rang until it cut off. He jumped up, put on his new Tods and grabbed his jacket.

'Wallet, phone, keys, mask, sanitiser,' he said to himself.

In fifteen minutes he was parked next to Kensal Mansions and sprinted through the alleyway, taking the stairs two at a time. He ran along the balcony and looked through the kitchen window. She was slumped over the kitchen table.

'Shit!'

He banged on the window but she didn't stir. He knocked on the door and kept knocking. The noise disturbed Judith, who was watching the news and shouting abuse at Matt Hancock. She opened her front door and stepped on to the balcony in a billowing, turquoise kaftan.

'What's going on?' she said.

He thought she looked like Demis Roussos.

'It's Claire. She's not answering the door. It looks like she's passed out in the kitchen. She might even be …'

Judith looked in through the window.

'Oh my God!' Judith banged on the window.

'Do you have a key?' he said.

'No, I don't. Mr Mahoney, the caretaker, does. He lives on the—'

Marcus pushed past her, ran down the stairs and knocked on Mr Mahoney's door. The caretaker answered the door and recognised the masked man who was doubled over and panting in front of him.

'It's Claire. She's passed out in her flat. Have you got a key?' he said breathlessly.

'I have, I have. Let me get it.' He pulled a key off a rack of hooks in the hallway and handed it to him. 'This is hers.'

Marcus snatched it and turned for the stairs, the caretaker closed his door and followed him. Marcus brushed past Judith who was still trying to rouse Claire and opened the door. He turned right into the kitchen, pushed a chair out of the way, put his hands on her shoulders and shook her. Her body stirred. He felt a wave of relief. Judith was standing in the doorway to the kitchen.

'Sorry, can I ask, who are you?'

'I'm Marcus Barlow, a friend of Claire and Gavin, her social worker.'

'She's never mentioned you to me,' said Judith, shaking her head.

Much as he appreciated Judith's sense of citizenship, now wasn't the time for a Neighbourhood Watch meeting.

'I'm hardly a bloody burglar, am I? Call a fucking doctor!'

'Don't you think we should call 111? That's what they advise,' said Judith.

Marcus reached into his jacket pocket, took out his phone and dialled 999. He had never used 111 and wasn't in the mood for experimentation. An operator answered immediately and within five minutes an ambulance was on its way. He put his arms around Claire's body and lifted her gently into the upright position. She felt so light and frail, like a rag doll. She stirred and murmured and Marcus looked up at Judith and Mr Mahoney who had appeared at the doorway. He nodded to them. He put his arm around her and gently stroked her face. It felt hot, she was burning up.

'Claire, Claire, it's me, Marcus. An ambulance is coming.'

He watched her chest start to move. Short, pulsating, repeating breaths. He held the glass of water up to her lips and she felt its moisture. He turned to Mr Mahoney.

'Phelan, could you go down and meet the ambulance, show them where to go? It'll be quicker.'

The caretaker nodded and left. Kyle and Alexa saw Judith standing in the doorway to the kitchen.

'It's okay kids. Mummy's not very well. A doctor is coming to see her. Do you want to come with me and we can go next door and wait together?'

Kyle and Alexa shook their heads and they walked nervously along the hall. Judith stepped back and they looked into the kitchen. They saw Marcus with his arm around their mother. Claire was coming round, she opened her eyes slightly and smiled.

'Mummy's okay. Don't worry.'

She brought her hand up to her head. He noticed the scald and the blister.

'Jesus, what have you been doing to yourself? That looks very sore. Let's get you back to the living room, it's more comfortable.'

'I'll go back next door then,' said Judith. 'Let me know if you need anything.'

'Thank you,' said Marcus. 'I'll let you know what happens.'

He picked Claire up in his arms, carried her through to the living room and laid her on the sofa. The children sat on the floor next to her, Alexa played with the hem of her mummy's dressing gown nervously. Ten minutes later, there was a knock at the front door and a man and a woman in green uniforms entered. They were wearing surgical masks, face shields and gloves.

'Emergency call for Claire Halford? Covid case who has collapsed?'

'Hi, I'm Marcus Barlow, a friend of Claire's. I made the 999 call. She's in here.' Marcus showed the ambulance crew into the living room.

'Hello Claire, I'm Graham and this is Stacy. We're here to look after you. How are you feeling?'

She looked up and smiled weakly. She struggled to speak. 'Not so good. I've got Covid.'

'Yes, your friend Marcus has told us,' said Graham. 'We'll try not to ask you too many questions. How long have you been feeling like this?'

'About a week, much worse in the last three days. My temperature is very high.'

'Yes, we'll do all that in a minute,' said Graham as Stacy was powering up a box of electronics.

Graham took some basic details. Marcus never knew her birthday was the sixth of September. There was no reason for him to know. He hardly knew her.

'We're going to do a few tests now,' said Graham. 'Do you want to take the children into the kitchen? We'll let you know when we're done.'

Mr Mahoney was waiting outside on the balcony. He looked worried.

'How is she?'

'They're doing some tests now. I'll let you know what happens.'

'What if she has to go to hospital?'

'I'll let Gavin, her social worker, know. We spoke together yesterday. I know he's looking at options for worst-case scenarios.'

The caretaker left and Marcus sat the children down in the kitchen. It looked like a bomb site and he filled the sink and wiped the surfaces. Graham came to find him.

'Can I just have a quick word?'

Marcus stepped out of the kitchen.

'Stacy and I both agree that Claire should be admitted to hospital. She's not in a good way.'

'What tests have you done?' said Marcus.

'Her temperature is 38.8 and I'm very concerned about her breathing. Her blood oxygen is 93%, which is low. Does she live here on her own?'

'Yes, with the two children.'

'Next of kin, other relatives?'

'Her parents, I suppose. They live in the Midlands. They're not close and she's separated from the children's father. I don't have contact details for any of them.'

'Relatives or friends nearby?'

'Probably just me and the caretaker Mr Mahoney, from downstairs. She's friends with another mum from school but she's tested positive too. I'm best friends with her social worker, Gavin Douglas. Obviously I'll let him know what's happened. You can take my number as the first point of contact.'

Graham entered Marcus's contact details into the tablet, turned around and the two men returned to the living room. Stacy was removing the electrodes from Claire's chest and pulling her dressing gown across her. She was now wearing a plastic mask and had a small cylinder by her side.

'Claire, I've spoken with Marcus and we're taking you to hospital. Your fever is very high and your blood oxygen level is a concern. Hospital is the best place for you right now. Leaving you here isn't an option, I'm afraid. Do you understand me?' said Graham.

Claire nodded weakly. 'What about the children?'

'They're in the kitchen having beans on toast. I've told Graham that I'll stay here with them tonight and call Gavin to let him know. He'll probably contact your parents to tell them what's happened,' said Marcus.

She shook her head.

'Don't.'

'I'm going to get a wheelchair from the ambulance. We'll be back in five minutes. Marcus, perhaps you could get a few things together for her?' said Graham.

'Of course.'

He returned to the kitchen and squatted between the children who had finished their yoghurts. He put his arms around them.

'Mummy is going to hospital so the doctors can make her better. I'm going to look after you tonight. Would you like that?'

The children both nodded.

'Can we have "Dinosaur School"?' said Alexa.

'Of course,' said Marcus. 'Go and sit with your mummy.'

Claire was dozing but woke as they sat next to her on the sofa. She hugged them and stroked their hair.

'Why are you wearing that mask, Mummy?' said Kyle.

'To help me breathe, sweetie.' Her words were muffled. 'Just cuddle me.'

Marcus looked around her bedroom for a bag or a small suitcase but couldn't find one. He went to the kitchen and picked up a Waitrose bag for life and went to the bathroom. He opened the cabinet and took out some essentials. Toothbrush, toothpaste, shampoo, nail scissors. He wasn't used to packing for women.

Tampons? he thought to himself. *I'm sure they have them in hospitals?*

He looked at the photograph on the bedside table of the three of them, taken the previous summer in the water park. The children were in their swimming costumes, squinting into the sun. Claire was in a white dress, sitting on the grass. By the time Graham and Stacy returned, he had packed the bag and left it in the hall.

'Where are you taking her?' said Marcus.

'The ED at St Mary's, Paddington,' said Graham. 'At least it's local. We've been taking people as far away as South East London. Right now, there's a shortage of emergency beds across London.'

'What about the new Nightingale Hospital in Docklands? Doesn't that have thousands of beds?'

Graham shrugged.

'Lots of beds, no staff.'

The ambulance team pushed the alloy wheelchair down the hall to the doorway of the living room. Claire was hugging her children on the sofa.

'All right, Claire, do you think you can walk with us to the wheelchair?'

She nodded as Graham and Stacy lifted her off the sofa and across the room. They strapped her in like an astronaut and wrapped a blanket around her. Graham pushed the wheelchair down the hall, manoeuvred it over the threshold and pushed her along the balcony to the stairs. Marcus carried Alexa in his arms and held Kyle by the hand. Judith was watching out of her kitchen window and waved. At the bottom of the stairs, Mr Mahoney was waiting outside his flat. Claire looked across and the caretaker started to cry. Graham lowered the tailgate to the ambulance as Stacy pushed the wheelchair on to it. She turned it to face Marcus and the children. They all waved to Claire as Graham closed the doors.

The ambulance pulled away. No flashing blue lights or sirens and Marcus took that to be a good sign. They walked back through the alley where Mr Mahoney was waiting.

'Where are they taking her?'

'St Mary's. Paddington. I'll call the hospital later and let you know anything as soon as I do.'

* * *

Going back into her flat without her presence felt odd. He felt like a burglar.

I need to make things as normal as possible, he thought and immediately picked up the pace.

'Okay, both of you. Go and watch television while I tidy up in here. We don't want Mummy coming back to a mess, do we? Then we'll have a bath and read our stories. That sound good?'

Alexa whooped and Kyle skipped to the lounge. He marvelled at their resilience, an ability to live in the moment and not overthink things. Children had mindfulness nailed. He made a start in the kitchen, finished the washing up and put everything away. He was sanitising his hands when he saw the open letter from Talbot Bailey Moss Solicitors on the worktop.

PETITION FOR DIVORCE
Mr J. A. N. Halford (Petitioner)
Mrs C. L. Halford (Respondent)

Jack, you're a cunt. You should have been here, he thought.

Her bedroom smelled of her. Damp and fetid with sweat and faint traces of her perfume. He opened the small window to let in some fresh air. He made the beds, folded more clothes and put some in the laundry basket. It was already full but he crammed more in. He tidied the living room, clearing away the evidence of her illness, empty packets of paracetamol, half-full glasses of stale water, her thermometer, her blanket.

'All right you two, bath time!'

An hour later, he was sitting in her chair looking around the living room. He had never seen it from that angle and it looked different, bigger. He relaxed into her chair and could see why she loved it. He was exhausted. Telling Alice what had happened could wait until morning. There was nothing she could do now.

He turned on the television. The *BBC News* was five minutes later than normal. Everything had been pushed back for the Queen's message but it wasn't the lead story. The main headline was the prime minister had been admitted to hospital; he was still suffering from the virus ten days after testing positive. Number 10 was putting out the message that the move was 'purely precautionary'.

He wondered if Boris had been taken to St Mary's too? Maybe he was lying in the bed next to Claire surrounded by books by Homer and Cicero.

Maybe he'll try to hit on her? he thought.

He found the number for the hospital switchboard and called. It was late on a Sunday evening and it took fifteen minutes for someone to answer.

'Hello, I'm ringing to enquire about a patient brought in earlier this evening? Her name is Claire Halford.'

'How are you spelling that?' said the operator.

'Halford.' He spelt it out. 'Like the cycle shop.'

'Sorry, I don't know what you mean?' said the operator. He heard the tapping of a keyboard in the background. 'Halford, yes. Claire? Are you a relative?'

At that moment, he was the closest thing she had to a friend, let alone a relative.

'Yes, I'm her father, Marcus Halford.'

'Would you like to be put through to the ward, Mr Halford?'

'Yes please.'

Five minutes later Marcus was speaking to Linda Cross, a staff nurse on the ward. He could hear lots of voices in the background, instructions being shouted, people moving around.

'Good evening, Mr Halford. I'm Linda. Claire has been seen by a doctor and has had another Covid test. We should get the result back by morning. Her temperature is still very high and she is on supplementary oxygen. She is sleeping at the moment. We've also treated her hand for a nasty burn.'

'Thank you. She suffers from asthma, you know?'

'Yes, we are aware of that. That was in her notes. She is stable, being on oxygen and resting is the best thing for her right now.'

He sensed Linda was needed elsewhere.

'Okay, thank you for your help, Linda. I'll call again in the morning.'

He put his phone on the coffee table. 'Stable' was good. He looked at the record turntable and Claire's vinyl collection stacked in front of it. For someone in their twenties, she had built a great collection. A tune came into his mind. He took Duran Duran's *Wedding Album* out of its cover. He wiped the vinyl with the special cloth, raised the lid and placed it carefully on the turntable. He lifted the arm and placed the stylus gently on the second track. The speakers popped as it hit the groove. 'Ordinary World.'

Except the world wasn't ordinary anymore. Where was the life he recognised? The record ended and he made up a makeshift bed on the sofa with a blanket and some cushions. He couldn't be bothered to get undressed and got underneath the blanket in his clothes. The launch of Project Medusa was ten hours away.

It was Sunday, 5 April 2020.

Chapter 32

FOSTERING PROBLEMS

Marcus had woken early. He stared in the bathroom mirror, compromises would be needed. He stripped to his underpants. Like the rest of his clothes, they would have to do for another day. Packing an overnight bag with his moisturising regime and shaving kit had been the last thing on his mind.

She must have a razor somewhere? he thought.

He found something in the cabinet that looked like a hybrid, something between a razor and a dildo. 'Gillette Venus, mmm ...' he said to himself as he inspected the pink object. 'Looks like this will have to do.'

Ten minutes later, deprived of his George Trumper sandalwood shaving cream and Clinique post-shave moisturising balm, his face looked like it had met Freddie Krueger on the way home from the pub after a big night. He removed his underpants and gave them a cursory inspection, turned on the shower and stepped behind the curtain. The shower made rivulets of blood from his lacerated face run down his neck and into his chest hair. He picked up a plastic bottle, 'Radox Feel Uplifted Shower Gel'. The last time he had seen a Radox product, it was a box of purple bath salts in the bathroom in Staines. His mother believed it helped her sciatica.

He was drying himself with Kyle's Power Rangers towel, still damp after last night's bath, when he was interrupted by Alexa appearing from behind the door.

'I need to do a wee-wee.' It was more of an announcement than a request as she pulled down her pyjamas and sat on the toilet. She stared at him drying himself. 'Do you have a willy, like Kyle?'

He opted for a short answer followed by a diversion.

'Yes, I do. Is Kyle awake? Let's go and get him up? We should be having breakfast soon.'

He stuck pieces of toilet roll on his cuts, scooped up his clothes and with Trini, the yellow Power Ranger, covering his genitals, headed to the living room to get dressed. His shirt was crumpled and he decided to keep his jacket on for the Zoom call with Yeast Feast. By the time he had finished dressing, Kyle was awake and he and Alexa were in the kitchen.

'What would you like for breakfast?' he said, trying to be upbeat.

'Rice Krispies!' said Alexa.

'Weetabix for me,' said Kyle quietly.

'Coming right up. Are you all right, Kyle?' said Marcus.

'Is my mummy coming home today?'

'I don't know. We'll have to see. I called the hospital last night and they said she was sleeping, so that's good.'

He poured three glasses of orange juice and the cereals. He hadn't had Rice Krispies for years and poured a bowl for himself.

'Have we got school today?' said Kyle.

'No, not today. It's the holidays. I've got to call my work soon. Will you two be okay watching television for a bit? I won't be long.'

'What work do you have to do?' said Kyle.

'Nothing important,' said Marcus.

Time meant nothing to Kyle and Alexa who escaped into the world of *Octonauts*, a bunch of underwater heroes in a race against time to save sea turtles. He made himself a coffee. And then it dawned on him.

'Fuck, I've left it at the flat.'

He had forgotten his laptop. It was 8.45, no time to go home and get it. 'Topping and tailing' would have to be done from his phone. It wasn't ideal. He opened Outlook. He had already received four emails from Laila, panicking about alignment and her quest for The Golden Carrot. He sipped his coffee and propped his phone against a saucepan on the table with his back to the window. The online launch of Project Medusa didn't have the same feel as pre-lockdown workshops at The Firm. No pastries, bacon rolls, smoothies and cappuccinos.

At 8.55, he joined the meeting with a ping. Lots more pings followed, a cast of thousands. Most of the chatter was about Boris being taken to hospital. Apparently, he was in St Thomas'. Marcus was pleased Claire had been spared his bedside lecture on Aristotle.

It was Joe Stern from Yeast Feast who noticed it first.

'Hiya Marcus. What's happened to your face this morning?'

Fifty people stared at his window and the five pieces of blood-stained tissue stuck to his face. Laila messaged him immediately.

'You've got bog roll stuck on your face!'

He was in the process of peeling them off beneath the kitchen table when somebody asked a question.

'Marcus, why have you got a picture of Grenfell Tower as your wallpaper?'

Marcus sat up, turned and looked behind him. He had never noticed it before.

'Err, that's not my wallpaper,' he said. 'I think that's the real thing.'

Laila was looking professional. A navy Missoni suit with a white shirt. She had already been for an 8 kilometre run, read through the presentation twice and thrown up her kelp and blueberry smoothie. She brought the meeting to order and shared the agenda. Marcus was up first and started 'topping'. He was halfway through his introduction when he heard a scream from the living room. He leapt up, threw his AirPods on the table and ran down the hall. Kyle had tossed the remote control to Alexa who had caught it with her face and was sitting on the floor crying. He picked her up and consoled her, wiping her cheeks with his handkerchief. He carried her to the kitchen and sat down with her on his lap. Everyone on screen was looking bemused.

'Sorry about that, just a collision between a remote control and a little girl's lips. This is Alexa. Now, where was I?'

For the next fifteen minutes, Marcus delivered an impressive piece of 'topping'. 'So, in summary, we're looking forward to working with both of your teams on this exciting first phase of Project Medusa. Thank you.'

Laila breathed a sigh of relief. Marcus had gone down really well. It was like watching Pavarotti sing 'Nessun Dorma' for the last time. She sent him a quick message.

Thx Marcus. Great session. Really good. Maybe time to buy a new razor?
Good luck with the rest of the day. Back at 4.30 for tailing.

With the topping over, in his head, he made a list of all the things he had to do. He had four missed calls from Gavin and called him back.

'Gavin, sorry I've had four missed calls from you?'

'I've been trying to call you for the past hour! Work has just informed me Claire is in St Mary's? What's going on?'

'Sorry, I was on a Zoom call for Project Medusa. I was doing the opening session. It went pretty well, even if I say so myself.'

Gavin ignored him. 'Where are you at the moment?'

'Claire's flat. She went downhill rapidly yesterday. I found her collapsed on the kitchen table and dialled 999 immediately. Lucky I did, or she might be dead now.'

'Jesus. What about the children? Who's looking after them?'

'I am. They're both absolutely fine.'

There was a long silence before Gavin spoke again.

'I can't understand how this has happened? The ambulance crew should never have left them with you. Social services should have been informed immediately. I only found out this morning. It's a major process failure.'

Marcus resented his efforts being described as a 'major process failure'.

'Well, try looking at it another way, Gavin? Perhaps it was obvious to the ambulance crew that I was perfectly capable of looking after two children who were very happy to be looked after by me.'

'So you've had a DBS check, have you?'

'What's that?'

'A Disclosure and Barring Service check.'

'Is that some kind of paedophile register? I've got two grown-up kids of my own who will reassure anyone that I'm not some kind of kiddy fiddler. Anyway, it was an emergency and you should be happy I was on hand to save the day.'

'Marcus, this is not about "kiddy fiddling" as you put it. It's there to protect children, and it's the law. There are proper procedures to be followed.'

'Claire was very happy to leave the children with me. If she'd had any objections, she would have raised them at the time.'

'She was probably delirious. You said she'd passed out?'

'Actually, I think you're delirious, Gavin. So, what are you going to do now? Get to the point.'

'I'll obviously have to notify her parents as next of kin, and probably her husband too, but I don't have his contact number. In the meantime, until Claire comes out of hospital, we'll have to use a fostering arrangement. There's a foster home in Enfield that's fully Covid-compliant and can take Kyle and Alexa today. Hopefully, it's only an interim measure until we can sort out something more permanent until Claire recovers.'

Marcus paced around the tiny kitchen table.

'Enfield? You mean Enfield in North London? You may as well put them on Mars. Is that what you people call "caring"? Putting them in a strange place that you've never seen and with people you've never met? Frightening them half to death with their mother in hospital? Get a fucking grip, Gavin!'

'It's called complying with the law, Marcus. I know how you struggle with that concept. The foster parents are on an approved register with full DBS checks in place.'

'Really? That's just bullshit and you know it is. You're letting Claire down in the biggest way possible at a time when she needs all the support she can get. Can't you see that?'

Marcus was shouting with anger and frustration.

'Marcus, it's my job. For goodness' sake, stop being unreasonable! Someone from the children's team will be there around 2.30. Her name is Julie Miller and she's very experienced in this sort of thing. I'm happy for you to stay to look after them until Julie gets there.'

'Of course I'll stay to look after them. I'm not going to leave them on their own, am I? Just do whatever you have to do, Gavin.'

He threw his phone on the table and looked at his watch. It was eleven. He still had to ring the hospital and had to call Alice. He cleared away the breakfast things and started to build a plan in his mind. He sent Claire a text.

Hope you are feeling better and got some sleep. All well here. Children are fine and send their love. Call when you can. M.

He went to the living room. 'Shall we send a picture to Mummy to cheer her up?'

He sat between them on the sofa. The children pulled cheesy grins and Marcus did his best enigmatic 'David Gandy' smile. Except David never had cuts on his face.

'I need to go home. Would you like to see where Gavin and I live? We can go in my car again for an adventure.'

Kyle and Alexa jumped up and down on the sofa.

'I just need to get some things together, I'll be back soon.'

He picked up the Waitrose bags and filled them with children's clothes, some toys, including Buzz and Woody, and the Dick King-Smith book. He picked up the photograph of Claire and the children taken in the park. He put the bags by the front door.

'Okay, let's get our shoes and coats on.'

He looked around the living room. It was their home, the place where they felt safe. He closed the door. He felt in the pockets of Claire's coat, took out her keys and purse, and ushered the children on to the balcony. He closed the front door behind him and locked it. There wasn't much to steal in No. 11, Kensal Mansions, but he locked it anyway.

'I must speak to Mr Mahoney,' he said to the children. 'Don't run on the grass.'

Mr Mahoney was making a sandwich. He saw Marcus through the kitchen window and came to the front door.

'Hello, Marcus. Have you spoken to Claire?'

'Hi Phelan. No, I haven't spoken to her, but I called the hospital last night. She's on oxygen and was sleeping, which is good. They said she was "stable". Must be a good thing?'

'That's good. She looked awful yesterday, awful.' Mr Mahoney looked down at the bags. 'Going somewhere?'

'Yes, I'm going back to my flat. It's only in Queensway, not far. I thought I would do some washing to help Claire out. Bit of a change of scenery for the children too, bit of an adventure.'

'That's good of you. It will take their minds off missing their mum.'

'See you later.'

Marcus strapped the children in the backseat of the M5. Fifteen minutes later, he had parked in the underground car park and switched off the engine. He left the bags in the boot.

'Okay, we're here. This is where Gavin and I live.'

'Do you live in here?' said Kyle, looking at the rows of parked cars. Marcus laughed.

'No, we have to go in a lift. Come with me.'

They took the lift to the second floor and walked along the corridor. Marcus pointed to a door on the right.

'This is where Gavin lives.'

'Is he there now? Can we see him?' said Kyle.

'He isn't here at the moment. He's in Scotland.'

'Is that a long way away?'

'Quite a long way. And this is where I live,' he said, opening the front door. 'Go through to the living room.'

The children took their shoes off like their mother had taught them. Kyle walked nervously into the living room, looking around him. He walked over to the balcony window and stared out at the diggers moving piles of earth around in Beirut.

'Wow! Lots of diggers,' he said, pointing out of the window.

'Yes there are,' said Marcus. 'Would you like a drink and something to eat? You must be hungry?'

The children nodded.

'Sit down, I'll put the television on for you.'

He turned on the television and the children's eyes popped.

'What a big television!' said Kyle. 'Is it the biggest television in the world?'

'No, I don't think so. I think there are probably lots bigger. What would you like to watch? CBeebies?'

'Yes, please,' said Kyle.

Waffle the Wonder Dog in Ultra HD with full Sonos surround sound was a new experience for the children. Alexa jumped when Waffle barked.

'Do you like lasagne?' said Marcus.

The children nodded.

'It'll be ready in about twenty minutes. Not long. I've just got to make a phone call.'

He left the children watching Waffle, went to the bedroom and called the hospital. The switchboard answered quickly and he was put through to Jasmit.

'Hello, I'm Claire Halford's father. I'm calling to see how she is?'

Jasmit put him on hold and returned a few minutes later.

'Hi Mr Halford. I've just spoken to one of the nurses looking after her. She had a quiet night and is still sleeping. Her test result has come back, it's confirmed positive, I'm afraid.'

'That's not a surprise. She was very ill yesterday.'

'Her temperature is still much higher than we would like. Her arterial blood gas results still show a need for additional oxygen. That's more of a concern to us right now.'

'Can we speak to her? Her children would like to talk to her. We sent a photo this morning.'

'When she wakes up, I'll pass on your message. Sending photos is always a nice way to keep in contact. Anyway, I have to go now, Mr Halford.'

'Thank you, I'm sure you're very busy. Goodbye, Jasmit.'

He had hoped for more news, better news, to know she was sitting up in bed eating grapes and listening to hospital radio, some enthusiastic young DJ playing easy listening hits that would please everyone. He returned to the living room.

'I've just spoken to the hospital and they say Mummy is still very tired and resting.'

'Can we see her?' said Alexa.

'Maybe tomorrow, sweetie, let's see.'

He realised he had called her 'sweetie'. It felt a natural thing to do. Lunch passed quickly, the usual mixture of random thoughts and questions.

'I have to ring my wife,' said Marcus. 'I won't be long. Is that okay? You can carry on watching television.'

'What's her name?' said Kyle. 'Is she nice?'

'Alice. Yes, she is very nice,' he said. 'Most of the time,' he muttered under his breath.

Marcus sat on the edge of the bed and called Alice on FaceTime. She was in the garden and was shocked to see his face.

'Goodness me Marcus, what have you been doing to yourself? You haven't been drinking again, have you?'

'No, I haven't. Anyway, all the pubs are shut. My face is the end of a long story. I've had quite a chaotic twenty-four hours. You probably need to sit down?'

'I am sitting down, Marcus. I can sense you're about to tell me something bad. Don't tell me they got your result wrong? You're positive?'

'No, it's nothing like that. I'm fine, just listen.'

- 465 -

He told her about Sunday, Claire's collapse, the ambulance, hospital and spending the night at her flat.

'Fucking hell, Marcus. How did you get so involved in all of this? You were meant to be safe, isolating on your own, stuffing your face with those shitty pies. Now I find out you're rescuing people and looking after children that aren't yours.'

'I'm sorry, Al, but I had to do something. What was I meant to do? Watch *The Dam Busters* for the twentieth time and hope she would be okay?'

'How is she now?'

'I called the hospital earlier. She's stable. Still has a high temperature and she's on oxygen. I haven't spoken to her.'

'Poor woman. I've seen the pictures on the news. It looks so horrific. Where are her children now?'

Marcus paused. 'Here in Beirut with me.'

'Presumably until her parents can look after them?'

'That can't happen. She hates her parents and her husband's a complete wanker. Gavin's arranging for them to go to a foster home in Enfield.'

'Where's Enfield?'

'Some place in North London. A foster home run by people who don't even know the children.' There was a pause in their conversation. 'I'm not going to let it happen, Al. I saw Claire's face as she was being put in the ambulance. She wouldn't want me to hand them over to strangers. Think about it, would we have wanted this for James and Libby?'

'Well, that would never have happened, would it?'

'Well, aren't we lucky then? Nobody predicted the damage this virus would cause?'

'What are you trying to tell me, Marcus?'

'I want to bring Kyle and Alexa back to Twin Gates with me this afternoon. They can stay with us until Claire gets better. They'll be happier and safer than in some foster home in Enfield.'

'Whoa, stop right there! And what about us, Marcus? Have you stopped to think of your own family in your ludicrous scheme? This isn't just about you and your little crusade. There's James, Olivia and me to consider. How do you know her children aren't infectious? Their mother is in hospital with the bloody virus, for God's sake!'

'I know where you're coming from Al, I really do, but we can't sit back and simply do nothing. These little children have nobody in their world apart from their mum, who is sick in hospital. We can wear masks and take precautions at home but they're not showing any symptoms. It doesn't affect little ones in the same way as adults.'

'And what about their clothes, things they need? Have you thought of that, Marcus?'

He put all his chips on the table.

'I've got them in the boot of the car. All packed, enough for a week at least. If they need more, we'll buy them. Can't be that hard?'

'Of course, you've got so much experience of buying children's clothes, haven't you? And what about Gavin, what have you told him? You can't simply drive off with someone's children. It's called kidnapping. If he calls the police, you could get all of us into big trouble.'

'Don't worry. I'll deal with him, persuade him this is the best option. We have to try. It's the best thing for the children, trust me. They'll be happier and safer with us. I know it's what Claire would want. You can always say no.'

She sensed there was a real passion and urgency in his voice.

'What time are you planning on leaving the flat?'

'As soon as I've finished speaking to you. I won't do this without your support. It's up to you, if they have to go to foster parents, then so be it.'

Alice looked around the garden, memories of James and Olivia growing up flashed through her mind. Paddling pools, swings, trampolines, tree houses. She stood up.

'I don't like the thought of foster parents any more than you do. I'm only saying yes for the children's sake. They shouldn't be with total strangers. I'll make up the guest bedroom next to Libby's. If they're going to stay with us, they should both sleep in the same room. I must be bloody mental going along with this, Marcus.'

'It's the right thing.'

'I'm sure it is. I'll see you later. Is there anything we need to get for them? I'll send James to the shops.'

Marcus went through a short list off the top of his head.

'Sugar-free Ribena, Rice Krispies, Weetabix, proper milk, yoghurts, cow biscuits, baked beans. That would be great. Everything else we probably have or can get later.' Alice knew what cow biscuits were.

Marcus returned to the living room, sat between the children on the sofa and put his arms around them.

'While your mummy is in hospital getting better, how would you like to stay with me, Alice and my children in my house?'

'Isn't this your house?' said Kyle, looking around the living room.

'Yes, it is, but I've got another house. It's much bigger. It's not very far away and it has a big garden to play in. I have two children but they're older than you.

Their names are James and Olivia. We will look after you until your mummy gets better. Would you like that?'

'Is your television at your other house bigger than this one?' said Kyle.

'Much bigger, and we have four televisions. Would you like to come?'

The children both nodded, four Samsung QLEDs swung it. Marcus tidied the flat and put the dishwasher on. He didn't know when he would be returning, so he cleared the fridge and the recycling bin and left them by the front door.

'Okay, let's switch the television off and get our shoes on. We're off now.'

Eric the concierge was watering the plants in reception. The smell of hyacinths was strong and lingering.

'Hi Eric. I'm off now, going back to Weybridge. Got the all-clear yesterday. I've put a couple of rubbish bags by my front door, would you mind putting them out for me?'

Eric looked down at the children.

'Of course, Marcus. Good news on the test. And who do we have here then?'

'This is Kyle and Alexa. Children of a friend of mine. They're coming to stay with me and Alice for a few days. I'll see you in a few weeks, Eric. Hopefully, once lockdown has ended.'

'I'll look forward to getting back to normal. See you soon. I'll keep an eye on the flat in the meantime.'

'Thank you, Eric. Stay safe and see you soon.'

He was just past Sunbury on the M3 when Gavin called. He had been expecting it.

'Hi Gavin. I know what you're going to say but I can't talk right now. I'm driving and I've got the children with me. I'll call you as soon as I get home. They're perfectly safe, don't worry.'

Gavin was in no mood to be fobbed off.

'Have you lost your bloody marbles, Marcus? I've just had a call from Julie Miller. She said she got to Claire's flat and it was locked up, no sign of anyone. Mr Mahoney told her the children had left with you.'

'Yes, I guessed that might happen. I'm sorry, Gavin, but I had no choice. Give me an hour and I'll call you back. We'll sort this out. Promise.'

He switched his phone off. Thirty minutes later he swung the car on to the drive of Twin Gates.

'Here we are! This is my house.'

He turned around and unclipped their seat belts and they sat up and stared out of the window.

'Wow!' said Kyle. 'It's a very big house.'

The front door opened. Alice had seen him arrive and was waiting in the hall with James and Olivia.

'This is Kyle and this is Alexa,' he said. 'And this is Alice, my wife.'

Alice instinctively crouched down to their height and touched them both on the arm.

'Hello, it's nice to meet you. Marcus has told me a lot about you. Come in.' She stepped to one side to allow Kyle and Alexa into the hall. 'And these are my children. This is James and this is Olivia, but we call her Libby.'

Kyle and Alexa looked up shyly. They weren't used to meeting so many grown-ups at once.

'Come through. Let's get you both a drink and a biscuit. Marcus, why don't you get their things in from the car? James, give your dad a hand,' said Alice.

The children stopped in the hall to take off their shoes. Alice looked at them and smiled.

'That's okay, you can keep them on for now. Let's get in and wash our hands.'

Marcus gave James a hug.

'Well, this is a new one, even for you, Dad. Rent-a-kid. Mum sent me out earlier to buy a whole load of stuff. Managed to buy myself a few more sausage rolls at the same time. How long are they staying with us?'

'Until their mum is better, I suppose. I don't know when that will be.'

'How's she doing?'

'Stable, on oxygen, but not great.' He picked up three of the Waitrose bags and handed them to James. 'If you could take these in, I'll bring the rest. Your mum's put them in the room next to Libby. Sorry, I didn't ask, how are you, mate?'

'I'm okay, surviving. Things have calmed down a bit with Mum. Getting pretty fed up with the vegan thing, but it's bearable.' He paused. 'With my illegal stash.'

Marcus went into the kitchen. Kyle and Alexa were already sitting at the table with cups of Ribena. The cups looked familiar. One said, 'Best Brother on the Planet', the other said, 'Little Miss Bossy'.

'They've been in the back of the cupboard for years,' said Alice, looking up. 'Never plucked up the courage to throw them out.'

'Come on, Mum, admit it, you've been saving them for your grandchildren haven't you?' said Olivia who was drinking a cup of tea.

Marcus hugged his daughter. 'And how are you, Libby? I've missed you.'

'I'm fine, missed you too Dad. Trying not to get too stressed about exams and university.'

'Still no news?'

'None.'

Alice was telling Kyle and Alexa why Olivia was called 'Little Miss Bossy', and they were all laughing together. Marcus signalled to her.

'I've just got to make a call.' He mouthed Gavin's name.

Alice nodded.

Gavin answered immediately.

'That was quick,' said Marcus. 'Where are you?'

'Sitting in the garden of my brother's house in Perth. At least they have decent Wi-Fi here. I've been dealing with a lot today. Did you get back okay?'

'Yes, no problem. The children are in the kitchen with Alice and Olivia. Look, I'm really sorry if I've caused you a problem. I apologise, and to Julie Miller as well. I'm sure she's a very nice person.'

'Yes, she is. So, before I call the police, how are we going to resolve this mess, Marcus?'

Gavin had started the negotiations. Marcus had spent twenty years of his life negotiating.

'It's not a mess and it's not for *us* to resolve. It's really up to *you* to resolve. As I see it, you've got two choices. You can follow your procedures, call the police or some authority who will come here and take the children away, causing them more distress and upset, so they can go to your process-compliant foster home in Enfield. That's one option.'

'Which is exactly the right thing to do,' said Gavin curtly.

'Or there's option two, which is what Claire would want. You tell your bosses that it's all been sorted and the children are both safe with their grandparents.'

'So you want me to lie for you?'

'Yes and no. I want you to use some common sense and decide what's best for the children. Give us some time until Claire can decide for herself. It should only be for a couple of days.'

Marcus knew Gavin wouldn't call the police. He had invested too much supporting Claire to blow it all now. Marcus sensed him weighing up his options and didn't break the silence. It was Gavin who broke first.

'You've put me in a bloody difficult situation, Marcus. It doesn't look like you're giving me much choice, stuck between a rock and a hard place. Looks like I'll have to deal with things at my end. I don't know how, but I'll think of something.'

'It's the right thing to do, Gavin. I'm only thinking of the children and Claire.'

'I hope so. These are people's lives you're playing with, not numbers on a spreadsheet.'

'And you think I don't know that? That's exactly why I'm doing it. Just give us a few days for Claire to get better. I'll keep you updated on how things are and you can call anytime.'

'I'll stall things at my end for a couple of days, but that's all. Say thank you to Alice from me. She's the saint in all of this, going along with your insane ideas.'

'Probably. Thanks Gavin, I know this isn't easy for you.'

Marcus returned to the kitchen. Alice looked up and he gave her a look of reassurance. Everything was going to be okay. He looked at the children.

'Would you like to see your room? We can show you the garden too, if you want?'

'One thing at a time,' said Alice. 'Don't rush them.'

They left the kitchen together and went upstairs. Alexa held Alice's hand.

'This is your room. Both of you will sleep in here. It's a big bed. You have your own toilet and bathroom, it's through here. And from this window, you can see the garden.'

The children looked around their room and stared into the garden. It was a big room with a view.

'Is this your garden?' said Kyle. 'Are they your horses over there?'

'It's our garden up to the bushes. The horses in the field belong to the farmer. We can go and stroke them later, if you want to. Would you like that?'

'Yes please,' said Alexa.

Marcus unpacked the children's clothes from the plastic bags.

'I'm not sure what's clean and what's dirty,' said Marcus. 'I didn't have much time. I left in a bit of a hurry.'

'I'll ask Jacinda to wash everything tomorrow. Start with everything clean.'

He put the photograph of Claire and the children on one of the bedside tables. Alice picked it up and looked at it.

'That's a lovely picture.'

They settled them in the TV room, which had an even bigger television.

'Do you want a cup of tea?' Marcus said to Alice.

'I'd love one. Lemon and ginger, please. They're very sweet children. Alexa is really pretty, such beautiful hair.'

Marcus looked at the front page of the *Daily Mail* which was folded on the island.

'The Queen looks nice,' he said. 'Always very well co-ordinated. A matching brooch for every occasion.'

'Did you watch her message last night?'

'No, I missed it. I was putting the children to bed. I had read most of the speech in the paper. All very Vera Lynn, meeting again, don't know where, don't know when.'

'Don't be cynical, Marcus. She means well.' Alice looked at the clock on the wall and jumped up. 'I want to watch the daily briefing. I'm addicted to it now. That Jonathan Van-Tam is a real hunk.'

'Bit different to Gary Lineker and his silly beard.'

Alice ignored him and turned on the television in the kitchen. The captain's armband had been passed to Dominic Raab.

'No Jonathan today, then?' said Marcus, trying to commiserate with her. Dominic followed team orders and didn't try any new moves. The death toll had risen by 439, which was a neat segue into the prime minister's health. Dominic told the country that Boris was leading the government from his hospital bed.

One thing was certain. Nobody on the team had the faintest clue when lockdown would be eased or what the exit strategy would be. Marcus opened his phone. Still no word from Claire, but four missed calls from Laila and two texts.

Marcus, where the fuck are you? You're meant to be 'tailing' the closing session for Medusa.

Don't worry, I've done it now. Thanks for nothing.

In his rush to abscond with the children, he had forgotten to 'tail' the workshop. He called her immediately.

'Laila, hi, it's Marcus. I'm really sorry about this afternoon. Bit of a family crisis here. I simply lost track of time. I'm so sorry.'

'Pretty unprofessional, Marcus. Nobody knew where you were, or whether or not you were joining. In the end, I did it on my own.'

She was right. It was unprofessional and he should have called her. A year ago, it would never have happened.

'I didn't mean to drop you in it. Did it all go okay, I'm sure it did?'

'Yes, no thanks to you.'

No damage had been done. For Laila, The Golden Carrot was getting closer. He returned to the kitchen where Alice was chopping peppers.

'We didn't discuss what sort of things they eat. What do they have at home?' she said.

'Pretty normal stuff, I think? Sausages, shepherd's pie, roast chicken, casserole, fish fingers, pasta bakes. Same stuff we used to have, I suppose. Claire feeds them pretty well, she doesn't give them takeaways or crap. It's not easy feeding them healthily on Universal Credit.'

'What's that?' said Alice innocently.

'It's like a "super benefit", everything all rolled into one. Just looks like a colossal fuck-up if you ask me?'

'So the children do eat meat and fish?'

'They do. Why, is that going to cause a problem with the vegan thing? It should only be for a few days. I can go to The Temple in the morning and get some extra things if we need them.'

If Alice wanted to play hardball, he still had 'Bacongate' up his sleeve. She came up with a compromise.

'I've got plenty of stuff for us four. Buy what they normally have. I don't want them going hungry while they're staying with us.'

'What are we having tonight?'

'Mediterranean pasta bake. I've found some tins of tuna in the cupboard. They can have that. Why don't you take them for a walk before dinner? It's a nice evening. Alexa wanted to see the horses.'

'Great idea.'

Marcus had left Alexa's buggy in Kensal Mansions but she was happy to walk and they turned on to the path leading to the farmland backing on to the garden. They stopped at the wire fence and called to the horses, who ambled across the field to greet them. Olivia picked Alexa up and showed her how to stroke the horse. She felt it's soft, velvety muzzle.

'His nose is tickly,' she said and pulled her hand away.

Olivia put a piece of carrot on her hand and held it still.

'Keep your hand flat like this,' said Olivia as the horse snuffled the carrot and started to chomp.

'He doesn't brush his teeth!' said Kyle. 'He's like Mr Mahoney.'

James picked Kyle up and the two children grew in confidence, feeding the horses until the bag was empty. James put Alexa on his shoulders and she gripped his beard tightly. Kyle held Olivia's hand as they walked back to the house.

Two pasta bakes were bubbling on the kitchen table with a bowl of salad and the table laid for six. Two small plastic plates with little cutlery indicated where Kyle and Alexa were sitting. There were two glasses of Ribena next to the plates.

'Jesus, Mum, did you keep all this stuff from when we were kids?' said James, picking up a tiny fork. Alice shrugged and smiled.

'Wash your hands if you've been feeding the horses. Did you two enjoy that?' she said, looking down at the children.

'One horse was naughty and tried to bite my fingers,' said Kyle.

'They had nasty teeth,' said Alexa.

They sat the children on cushions as Alice explained the two dishes.

'This one has tuna and this one has vegan chorizo,' she said. 'The children can try a bit of both. I'm sure they'll like it.'

Dinner passed off without incident. The children entertained them, talking about their school and nursery, Miss Takidis and Zoe, Bruce and Liam, Biscuit. Marcus and Alice were clearing away.

'Well, at least they're not fussy eaters,' said Alice. 'They've got very good table manners, very polite little children.'

Good manners mattered to Alice.

'They're sweet kids, aren't they? They must be very confused by what's going on. I'll ring the hospital soon, see if there is any news on Claire.'

'I do feel for her, being there on her own with no visitors.'

He walked around the island to the dishwasher where Alice was bending over, stacking plates. He put his arms around her waist and pulled her up, turned her towards him and kissed her on the lips. She pulled away.

'What are you doing? This isn't some cheap 1970s German porn film, Marcus? "Oh madam, your machine is broken and my trousers seem to have fallen down",' said Alice in a decent German accent.

'Funny you should say that. I read an article in *The Times* last Saturday about increasing intimacy during lockdown. If I was still isolating, I was going to suggest the idea of us having phone sex.'

Alice laughed out loud. 'Do you think you've got the imagination for dirty talk, Marcus? Go and ring the hospital.' She kissed him on the lips.

It took a long time for the phone on the ward to be answered. Jasmit was coming to the end of another energy-sapping twelve-hour shift, another day swimming against the tide.

'Hi Mr Halford. It's Jasmit, we spoke yesterday?'

'Yes, I just wanted to check on how Claire is doing? Is she any better this evening?'

'Still struggling, I'm afraid. Her oxygen levels are still low but her temperature has stabilised. It's down to 38.2 now, still higher than we would like.'

'Has she been awake?'

'Briefly, for a short time this afternoon, but she's very drained. She's receiving intravenous fluids and we are monitoring her closely.'

'Is it possible to speak to her when she wakes up? Her children are missing her and would love to speak to her. You have my number, don't you?'

'Of course. It was on her notes when she was admitted. There is an email address you can send messages and photographs to. We'll do our best to show them to her when she wakes up.'

Jasmit gave Marcus an email address and he wrote it on a pad.

'That's very helpful, Jasmit. It must be bloody hard for you and the other nurses?'

'It is, Mr Halford. Believe me.'

His words felt meaningless. What Jasmit wanted was some sleep, not hollow words or more clapping. He ended the call and went to the TV room. They were all watching *Finding Nemo*.

'I've just spoken to the nurse who is looking after Mummy. She is still sleeping but she did wake up for a short time this afternoon. She sends you her love. We'll try to speak to her tomorrow.'

Alice looked up at Marcus but he closed his eyes and shook his head. There was more to be said but at the right time. Alice jumped up.

'Right, who would like to have a bath and a bedtime story? You can watch the rest of *Finding Nemo* tomorrow.'

'Me!' shouted Alexa.

Alice picked her up. It could have been her and Olivia at a similar age. The years had gone by in a blink.

'Say goodnight to Libby and James,' said Alice.

Everyone waved to each other and they went upstairs. Thirty minutes later, two little bodies were in their pyjamas. Alice was drying Alexa's hair with her Dyson Supersonic. She held her long tresses and brushed them gently.

'We don't want any tangles, do we?'

Alexa shook her head.

'Are you reading us a story tonight, Marcus?' said Kyle.

'Of course.'

He picked up the book from the bedside table and showed it to Alice. He showed her the inscription. She looked at him and smiled.

'Works every time,' he said.

Alice finished brushing Alexa's hair and brushed Kyle's. 'Okay, let's get you both into bed.'

It was a king-size bed, and their little bodies hardly ruffled the duvet. They sat up against the pillows and Marcus sat between them.

'If you wake in the night, you know where our bedroom is, don't you? Just at the end of the landing,' said Alice.

The two children nodded.

'I'll say goodnight then. Sleep tight.' She leaned over and kissed Kyle on the head, walked around the other side of the bed to kiss Alexa. She gave Alice one of her special kisses.

The children had fallen asleep before Marcus had reached the end of 'Dinosaur School'. It had been an exhausting day for everyone. All three Halfords were sleeping. He poked his head into Olivia's room. She was lying on her bed swiping through Instagram. She looked up.

'Kyle and Alexa asleep, Dad?'

'Yes, they were whacked out. Listen out for them in case one of them wakes up, would you? Strange place, new surroundings and all that.'

'They're nice kids, very funny. I heard you reading 'Dinosaur School', doing all your voices! Works every time, eh, Dad?'

'Seems to.'

'James and I were chatting downstairs. We think you've done an amazing thing, bringing them here. How's their mum?'

'No real improvement since yesterday, but some people don't recover quickly. Look at Boris. We'll have to wait and see.' He sat down on her bed. 'Can I ask you something?'

'Sure.'

'You don't resent me for doing this, do you? Putting them first, bringing them into our home with all the other shit that's going on?'

'No, of course not, why would I?'

'Just wondered. All the nights I was away, not being here with you and James. Did I do the wrong thing?'

'We can't go back, Dad. You did what you thought was right at the time. And we've turned out okay, haven't we?' She hugged him. 'You've done a good thing Dad, we're really proud of you.'

Alice was sitting in the living room reading the paper when Marcus came downstairs. *EastEnders* was on in the background. Sharon was looking upset, floods of tears and mascara, and Phil was looking like an angry snooker ball. They snogged and the 'doof, doof' theme tune kicked in.

'Are those two still beating the shit out of each other and then making up?' said Marcus, glancing at the television. 'They'll be fighting each other in their wheelchairs.'

'I don't know. I never watch it,' said Alice, looking up from the newspaper.

It was a fib. She knew every plot and storyline.

'How's Claire?'

Marcus gave her a precis version of his conversation with Jasmit.

'Let's hope the next twenty-four hours bring better news. It must be awful for her. We'll get the children to draw some pictures tomorrow. We can take some photos and send them to her. It might cheer her up.'

'That's a nice idea.'

* * *

It was the feel of a rubber glove against her cheek that woke her from her dream. She was in a charity shop in Walsall, the other girls from her class were laughing at her. Her father and brother were standing outside, and they were laughing too. Her eyes flickered as she felt hands on her face and heard a voice.

'Claire? Claire, can you hear me?'

It was a woman's voice, but not one she recognised. She opened her eyes to a crack, scared to discover she was back in Walsall. Blurred images of three masked faces were watching over her. They were hidden behind plastic shields, wearing blue plastic aprons and gowns. Her dream had morphed into an episode of Holby City and Jac Naylor was about to open up her chest. She waited for her words.

'*She's bleeding out. I need more suction here. Get me four units of cross-matched, now!*'

But it was a different voice.

'Claire, I'm Liz, one of the nurses. Try to open your eyes and nod if you can hear me?'

In the background, she could hear the beeping and whirring of machines. Her head felt like it was in a vice, something was squeezing on it. She opened her eyes and felt the pressure of a mask on her nose, her mouth was dry and her tongue was stuck to her teeth. Liz held her hand and spoke again.

'You were having trouble breathing so you're receiving supplemental oxygen through this mask. Is it too tight?'

Claire nodded and one of the nurses leaned over to adjust it.

'We've taken your temperature, we're trying to get the fever down. We want to do an ECG and take some blood. Are you okay for us to do that?'

Claire went to raise her arm but felt a snagging pull.

'You've got cannulas in your hand, try to keep it still. Is there anything I can get you?'

Claire pointed to her mouth and whispered. 'Some water please?'

A gloved hand raised a plastic cup to her mouth and removed the mask. She sipped through a straw. The water was lukewarm, but it unglued her mouth and moistened her lips. A nurse rolled back her bedsheets as another unfastened her gown. She could feel the cool air on her breasts. They wheeled a machine alongside her bed as a nurse began attaching the sticky circles to her chest and limbs.

'Attach the chest leads first, then the limbs. It's easier,' said Liz.

'I'm trying to remember my training. I don't use one of these very often,' said the nurse.

'Where were you working before all this kicked off?'

'Ophthalmology.'

The machine whirred into life, regurgitating paper with its multiple traces of waves and rhythms. She stopped the machine after a couple of minutes and tore off the strip of paper.

'That's it, all done now.' The nurse peeled off the clips and sticky circles. 'Lucky women don't have hairy chests,' she said.

Claire smiled.

'I'm going to take some blood now, Claire. Try to keep your arm still,' said Liz.

She watched as Liz filled a series of tubes with her blood. She was amazed by how quickly they filled. At least her blood was still flowing.

'The doctor wants to look at your blood cell count again. Do you need to go to the toilet?'

Claire shook her head. The nurses were wiping her skin with a moist wipe and it cooled her, she felt fresher. Liz was looking at Claire's notes on a tablet.

'Looks like your father has called to see how you are.'

Was it another dream? How had her father found out? He wouldn't even see her at Christmas let alone call a hospital.

'My father?' she said weakly.

'Yes. Next of kin, Marcus Halford.' Liz read out a number. 'Called twice.'

Posh Marcus. She smiled.

'Can I see my phone?'

Liz reached into a small cupboard and handed it to her. She switched it on and it came to life.

There were texts from Marcus, Gavin and Beverley. She opened Marcus's first message and looked at the photograph. She recognised the living room in Kensal Mansions. The children looked happy and she noticed the cuts on his face.

What the fuck have you been doing to yourself? she thought. She opened his second message.

Hi Claire. Hope you are feeling better? K&A are with me and Alice. They are safe and happy. They send their love. I did what I thought was best. We are all thinking of you. Get better soon. M x

Another photo. Her children asleep in a strange bed, Alexa sucking her thumb and Kyle with Buzz and Woody on a table next to him. She recognised the photo of the three of them taken in the park. Tears started to run down the side of her mask. She looked at the time, it was 2.38 in the morning, too late to call him. She waited for her tears to stop and sent a reply.

Thank you. C xx.

It was Tuesday, 7 April 2020.

Chapter 33

Adagio for Strings

He had fallen asleep spooning against the warmth of Alice's back. It felt good until she complained of being too hot and banished him to his side of the bed. More work on intimacy during lockdown was definitely needed.

He got up, sat down for a pee, then put on his dressing gown and went downstairs. It was a sunny morning and the garden looked beautiful, stripes in the lawn and tulips in flower. He took his coffee on to the patio, sitting on one of the recliners. A solitary magpie bounced across the lawn. He saluted it for good luck.

He was on his way upstairs when he saw the paperboy delivering the newspaper. He waved to him and picked it up from the doormat.

PREMIER IN HOSPITAL DRAMA: NOW STRICKEN BORIS TAKEN TO INTENSIVE CARE

The prime minister's health had deteriorated overnight. Boris wasn't going to be playing for the first team anytime soon. Dominic was the stand-in captain. 'Get well' messages from all sides of the political spectrum were flooding in. It was left to a junior Foreign Office minister, to win the award for class toady.

'Take care boss. Get well. Come back fighting. But for now rest, look after yourself and let the others do the heavy lifting.'

'What a creep,' Marcus muttered to himself. 'Matt Hancock couldn't lift a ping pong ball on his own.'

Alice was awake and sitting up in bed. He handed her the newspaper.

'Boris is in intensive care now. Dominic Raab is in charge.'

'Shit. That's awful, poor Boris.' She took the paper from him and put her reading glasses on. 'Apparently he's in good spirits,' she said, scanning the front page. 'It's Carrie I feel sorry for.'

'I do too. Living with Boris can't be easy, never knowing if he's coming home or not. At least she knows where he is now.'

'Don't be so unkind, Marcus. Any news from Claire?'

'I got a text last night. Didn't say much, just a thank you.'

'If she's anything like Boris, she's probably not up to doing anything. We'll do those pictures today and send them. They will cheer her up.'

'I'm going for a shower. I'm not shaving today, not after yesterday's butchery. My face is still raw.'

'I forgot to ask you, what did you do to your face?'

'Well, obviously I didn't have my razor when I stayed at Claire's flat. So I had to improvise.'

'What with? A potato peeler?'

'A Gillette Venus ladies' razor. She must have been pruning roses with it. It cut me to ribbons.'

Alice waved him away. 'Enough information, Marcus. She probably can't afford a laser. Go and have a shower, I'll get up now.'

Being reunited with his portfolio of exfoliating and skin conditioning products invigorated him. He opted for his version of business casual and went to the children's bedroom. They weren't there and he panicked. They had only been in his care for one day and had gone missing. As he rushed downstairs, he heard a conversation that brought instant relief.

'And Jesus lives in space,' said Kyle earnestly. 'He has a special rocket so he can go to all the planets and be kind to people.'

'Really?' said Alice, showing a healthy interest in an intergalactic messiah. Faith was a wonderful thing. 'Do you know the names of any of the planets, Kyle?'

Kyle nodded again and looked to the ceiling.

'Saturn, Jupiter ...' he paused, '... Mars, the Moon.'

'That's very good,' said Alice, as Marcus came into the kitchen. 'Kyle has been telling me about Jesus and the universe. He knows lots of planets.'

'Big stuff for eight o'clock in the morning. Did you sleep well?' he said to the children.

They both nodded.

'I've had a message from your mummy, she sends you her love.'

'Can we see her?' said Alexa.

'I'm sorry, sweetie. It's not safe in hospital, but we will try to call her later.'

Alice put the boxes of cereal on the table along with a carton of milk. Cow's milk.

'Do you want a cup of coffee?' she said.

'Yes please. You know, technically it's not a planet?'

'What isn't?'

'The moon, it's not a planet. It's more of a satellite of earth, which it orbits. It doesn't orbit the sun independently, so it's not a planet.'

The Quooker whooshed. Alice put the mug down and stared at him.

'And you are telling me this because …?'

'I don't think we should be giving the children incorrect information while they're in our care. Just saying, that's all.'

'Sometimes Marcus, you're such a prat. Why don't you do the breakfast and dispense some factually correct information at the same time? Obviously, you know more about Jesus being a spaceman than I do. I'm going for a shower.'

She swept out of the kitchen, her silk dressing gown billowing behind her like a wizard. It left Marcus to dispense cereals and facts. The children were none the wiser, they were staring at the garden.

'Can we play in the garden today, please Marcus?' said Alexa.

'Of course, after breakfast when you're dressed. Come on, let's eat our Rice Krispies.'

Marcus joined the pipeline call at nine. It was a very subdued affair. In a flagging market, partner spirits were starting to flag too. Kelvin had the look of a Cornish lobster fisherman, tanned and weather-beaten. He asked Izzy Majewska to give the financial update. It was the same as it had been for months.

Too many people doing nothing, might have to get rid of more, keeping them busy on internal crap, thought Marcus.

The updates were flat and uninspiring too. Chloe, who was wearing her Tigger onesie, messaged Marcus.

Project Siclops?

He replied.

Cyclops. One-eyed creatures. Greek.

Thx M.

He thought it was an ill-considered project name for a takeover of a chain of opticians, but, in the land of the blind, the one-eyed man is king. Kelvin moved on to the next agenda item. Team morale.

'From the feedback I've received, it seems last Thursday's social events were a bit of a mixed bag. I'm sorry I wasn't able to join any myself. I was on a Zoom meeting with the Duke and some other top bods. All I want to say is, in the current climate, we need to be super vigilant about people's sensitivities and the language we use. We don't want to come across as micro-aggressive. Do you want to say anything, Jenny?'

'Thanks Kelvin. I agree completely. HR has received three complaints about the team bingo event and one about the "Through the Zoomhole" event.'

'Can you elaborate, Jenny?' said Kelvin.

'Of course. With regard to the bingo event, one complaint concerned an inappropriate use of "sizeist" language, and two related to homophobic gestures and phrases.'

Oliver Rankin visibly winced. He had never anticipated that 'two fat ladies, eighty-eight' and 'Dancing Queen, seventeen' would cause such problems.

'Thoughts on consequences?' said Kelvin.

'Bit early to say. It's obviously confidential while investigations are ongoing. Probably a commitment from the offending individual to undertake further one-to-one micro-aggression training and an apology to the individuals.'

'What about "Through the Zoomhole"?' said Marcus. 'This is news to me, everyone seemed to enjoy it?'

'Almost everyone,' interrupted Vanessa Briggs.

Jenny came back in.

'It was brought to my attention that a junior member of staff passed out drunk at the end? We really shouldn't be encouraging that sort of behaviour at company events.'

Behaviour at company events! Marcus remembered the incident of the partner who had groped one of the topless loaders at a client hospitality clay pigeon shooting event. She had retaliated by hitting him in the scrotum with the butt of a twelve-bore, and he'd ended up in hospital with a testicular contusion.

'If you're referring to Angela, she was in her own flat and simply had a little too much alcohol. Surely that's up to her?' protested Marcus.

'I'm afraid not, Marcus. From now on, all lockdown social events will need to be vetted and approved by Risk and Compliance. A new template will need to be approved before any more events can go ahead.'

Marcus got up from his desk and went to the kitchen where Alice was preparing a banana, avocado and spinach smoothie in her Nutribullet. He slammed his empty mug down on the granite worktop.

'What's the matter now?' said Alice.

He recounted the discussion, shouting over the noise from the processor.

'But that's ridiculous. Oliver Rankin wouldn't upset anyone. How much does this woman weigh?'

'Well over 20 stone,' said Marcus. 'Probably more before her gastric band surgery?'

'Sounds like a bit of fat-shaming might just save her life. She's being slightly ungrateful if you ask me.' Alice was bored with the latest outrage at The Firm and changed the subject. 'I think we should get the children doing their pictures. I'll clear some space in the office.'

The children were watching *Teletubbies* with Olivia, who was lying on the sofa in her pyjamas. Olivia had loved *Teletubbies* too when she was their age. The format hadn't changed.

'Are they still speaking like morons?' said Marcus, pointing at the television.

'Of course,' said Olivia, in an accent honed by her posh, all-girls school in Surrey. 'I think it's still the same baby as the sun.'

'Probably worth millions now with all those royalties,' he said. 'Shall we go and draw some pictures to send to Mummy to make her feel better?' he said to the children.

Alice had made space at the end of the office, moving her easel and paints to a corner. She brought in two stools from the kitchen and laid out some colouring pencils and paper on the desk.

'What would you like to draw?' she said. 'Maybe a nice picture to cheer your Mummy up.'

Alexa started instantly, a yellow, spidery sun in the top left corner, with a horizontal blue sky. A classical style for a three-year-old. Kyle took longer to start, different ideas going through his mind. He played with his pencil, twiddling it between his small fingers, before making some strokes, square shapes, strong images. Belinda Churchill would have been impressed.

'What are you drawing, Kyle?' said Alice, looking over his shoulder.

'It's our house. These are the stairs and this is the grass where we play. It's always got dog poo on it. We live up here.' He pointed to a door somewhere between the ground and the sky.

'And who is this?' said Alice, pointing to a face with black teeth.

'Mr Mahoney. He watches TV with us every day.'

'He's the caretaker in the flats,' said Marcus, looking across from his laptop. 'Nice guy, massive hands.'

'And who is this?' said Alice, pointing to a number of images.

'That's Mummy and Alexa and me. And this is you and Marcus and Olivia and James,' said Kyle.

'Well, they're both beautiful pictures. Shall we write your names on them?'

'Marcus, take some photos and send them to Claire. We'll put them up in the kitchen. Let's have a drink and go in the garden? It's a nice day.'

The children jumped up and ran into the kitchen leaving Marcus alone to look at the two pictures on the desk. Different styles, same love. The children were putting their shoes on when James sauntered into the kitchen carrying a large box covered in dust.

'What have you got there?' said Alice.

'Just been up in the loft and found it. My old Scalextric. Don't know if it still works but thought I'd set it up in the TV room. I thought Kyle might like to play with it? I could show him my video games too?'

'He might be a bit young for *Grand Theft Auto*, don't you think?' said Alice.

'Probably. I found some of my old PlayStation games, I bet they still work. No gang rape or drive-by shootings in *Spyro the Dragon*. What are you all doing now?'

'Your dad and I are going to take them in the garden. Let them get some fresh air and run around. Might tire them out.'

The children loved the garden. Lockdown hadn't cordoned off the swing, trampoline and the tree house. They had the freedom to explore its boundaries in safety. From her bedroom, Olivia heard their screams as they were chased by James, the big, bearded giant, and she decided to join them. They played football and frisbee until they were exhausted and lay down on the recliners, out of breath and with little flushed cheeks.

'Put your arms around your sister, Kyle. Look at me, smile both of you.' Marcus took more pictures. 'We'll send these to Mummy as well.'

Alice called everyone in for lunch. 'Wash your hands please and sit up at the table?'

The same places as the previous evening, routines were being established. James sat next to Kyle.

'Do you support a football team?' said James.

The little boy looked up at him and shook his head.

'I think my friend Bruce supports Liverpool. Who do you support?'

'Crystal Palace. Marcus supports them as well. Would you like to support them too?'

Alice intervened quickly.

'I think that's enough, James. Kyle is only five. It's not your job to indoctrinate him while he is here.'

James laughed and protested.

'Oh really? I didn't see that stopping Dad taking me to the barbers when I was four and telling him to give me a number one so I looked like Andy Johnson. What's that if it's not indoctrination?'

'It's gender stereotyping too,' said Olivia. 'What about Alexa?'

James turned to both children.

'Do you both want to be Crystal Palace fans?'

James nodded and the children nodded back.

'There you go. All sorted. Two new Eagles fans,' he said, arms held aloft, outstretched in triumph.

Alice and Olivia shook their heads in despair.

After lunch, the children helped to assemble the Scalextric after fifteen years of obsolescence and gathering dust. It still worked. Marcus stayed at the kitchen table and sent messages to Claire.

Hi Claire. Hope you are feeling better? Kyle and Alexa are happy, no problems here. Sending some pictures they have drawn and some photos taken in the garden. They send their love. M. x

He wondered how many people were sending messages of support to their loved ones lying in hospital. Carrie Symonds was probably doing the same, sending Boris pictures of her tummy.

It was mid-afternoon when Jacinda arrived. Marcus bumped into her coming in the front door. He was on his way to The Temple. He hadn't seen her for months and could have sworn she had shrunk.

Maybe she's been on a boil wash? he thought.

Jacinda always wore sparkling white trainers and leggings which were too tight. She walked at a frenetic pace, short chubby legs pumping her tiny feet.

'Hello Mr Marcus,' she said in her Brazilian accent. 'I not see you in a long time.'

Her formality hadn't changed in ten years.

'Hi Jacinda. Yes, it's been a while. How have you been keeping? Coping with lockdown okay?'

'Yes, busy but always happy!'

Jacinda was employed by three other houses in their road and three more in the next. Not one had relinquished her services during lockdown.

'Jacinda, Mrs Alice and I have two little children staying with us. They are staying in the guest room next to Olivia's. Would you mind washing and ironing their clothes? Mrs Alice will pay you, of course.'

'Yes, that is good. Not a problem,' said Jacinda, who was en route to the utility room to get her domestic toolkit. 'Is Mrs Alice at home today?'

'Yes, she's in the office. I've got to go shopping now. Maybe see you later?'

Marcus set off for The Temple with a shopping list that Alice had written and a handful of bags for life. He took her BMW X5 and called Gavin from the car. It went straight to voicemail. He switched on the sound system.

'Oh no, sweet Jesus. Not fucking Adele,' he shouted, as the opening lines of 'Rolling in the Deep' pumped out. His taste in music rarely overlapped with his wife's. His taste was rooted in 1970s' rock and punk, hers was almost exclusively drawn from the 'why did he leave me, he's such a fucking bastard' catalogue. The high priestess of this genre was Adele, and Alice loved her.

'If anyone ever rang me up and said, "Hello, it's me," in that creepy voice, I'd put the phone down immediately and call the police,' he had said to Alice. He switched to the radio. Even the phone-in on LBC was better than Adele.

The queue at The Temple was short, and people were in good spirits. He sanitised his hands and his trolley and put on his mask before walking the aisles. He stopped at the butcher's counter and peered at the twenty-eight-day-aged Aberdeen Angus sirloin on display. It looked delicious and triggered a Pavlovian response.

'I'll take four of those steaks, please,' he said to the man behind the counter, who was sharpening his knife at the ready.

'Certainly, sir.'

Marcus looked at his green name badge. 'Ben, Partner'. You didn't need The Golden Carrot to be a partner at The Temple.

'Anything else, sir?' said Ben politely, sticking the label on the bag.

'No, that's great. Thank you.'

He was driving back to Twin Gates when Gavin returned his call. He pulled over and turned the engine off.

'Hi Marcus. Sorry I missed your call earlier. Bit of a crisis here. Mum went missing for two hours this afternoon.' He sounded distressed.

'Shit. Sorry to hear that. Is she okay?'

'Sort of. One of the estate workers found her walking in the woods in her nightie, slippers and a Barbour jacket. As if that wasn't bad enough, she'd taken a gun from the gun cupboard.'

'How on earth did she do that? Isn't it locked?'

'Yes, but she knows where the keys are kept. We've moved the keys now but it frightened the hell out of all of us.'

'Do you think she intended to use it?'

'No idea. I don't think she knows what she's doing most of the time. I've spent most of this morning on the phone to social services in Perth.'

'Bit of a busman's holiday then, still sorting other people's problems.'

Gavin saw the irony and laughed.

'Indeed. How are things with you? Have you heard from Claire? I sent her a text but I've heard nothing.'

'The children are fine. Everyone is making a fuss of them. I'll send you some photos. I got a text from Claire last night but it just said, "thank you". I haven't spoken to her.'

He still felt guilty about compromising his friend and tried to make amends.

'Gavin, I'm really sorry. I know I've put you in a shit position at a difficult time.'

'I know, Marcus. And I know you're only trying to do the right thing. I've told work that the children are with their grandparents. There's so much shit going on, you and Alice looking after the children is the least of my problems.'

'Are things bad?'

'Staff shortages, fear of the virus, domestic violence going through the roof, alcohol and drug abuse rocketing, the elderly and disabled starving because nobody does their shopping. Do you want me to go on?'

'No, I get the picture. So much for all of us being in it together?'

'Oh don't worry, this is just the start. It's only going to get worse.'

Marcus felt sympathy for him, dealing with other people's crap as well as his own. 'When we get back to normality, we'll celebrate in style.'

'Normal sounds perfect right now. Let me know when you hear from the hospital? Take care of yourself and thank Alice for me.'

'Will do. Take care too. Bye now.'

Ten minutes later, he was unloading the shopping. Alice came out to help. They carried the bags into the kitchen and started putting things away together.

'What the hell are these?' she said.

He knew immediately what she was referring to.

'They're for the children. Just in case they didn't like the vegetarian options,' he said defensively.

'Four twenty-eight-day-aged Aberdeen Angus sirloin steaks? So that's making them feel at home is it? I'm not a complete idiot, Marcus. I thought they lived on pasta, baked beans and sweetcorn! Fine, they can go in the freezer for now and we'll need to talk about this.'

'I thought we could transition them gradually to meat substitutes, rather than going completely cold turkey.' It wasn't his best choice of words. 'Don't you miss it?'

'Miss what?'

'Meat. A bacon sandwich, crispy bacon, fresh bread, HP sauce?'

He watched for any tell-tale signs, but she never flinched.

'Not in the slightest.'

* * *

The two doctors stepped through the makeshift doors. Two months earlier, it had been a children's ward. Now it had been converted into a specialist unit to accommodate the growing numbers being admitted with the virus. Dr Mike Hughes and Dr Sandeep Anand were halfway through another gruelling twelve-hour shift. Sandeep hadn't had a day off in almost two weeks. They removed their face shields and threw their masks, plastic aprons and gloves in the bin. They were sweating from the heat on the ward. They were joined by Jasmit and three other nurses who all slumped down on the chairs in the staff area.

They looked up at the white board on the wall, its hand-drawn grid containing the names of the forty-eight patients in the six bays on the ward. Every row was filled with a name. Names were smeared away, either dead or recovered, but always replaced with a new name. Two names had been erased that morning leaving a dirty smudge.

'Claire Halford? Admitted on Sunday night,' said Sandeep, looking at Jasmit.

'Temperature is down a little but still running a fever at 38.5. Heart rate is 105 bpm and respiratory rate is high, 32. We have increased the oxygen flow, but her blood oxygen level has never gone above 88%,' said Jasmit. 'She's really struggling.'

'She's tachycardic on her ECG,' said Mike. 'Her heart is working overtime. Has she been alert since she was admitted?'

'Briefly, last night for a couple of hours, but she was very weak. She struggled to talk.'

'Maybe we should consider transferring her to ICU?' said Sandeep.

'It's full. Beds don't even go cold before someone new gets in them. Let's see how the next twenty-four hours go and see if she makes any improvement? Right now, there's probably four or five cases ahead of her. Have we spoken to her relatives?' said Mike.

'Her father has called a couple of times,' said Jasmit. 'Wants to know everything. Another internet expert.'

They all laughed and finished their review of the names on the whiteboard. The team was now aligned as they equipped themselves with a fresh set of PPE and stepped behind the plastic curtain.

* * *

Kyle and James were playing with the Scalextric in the TV room. It was a welcome distraction from his dissertation. Marcus and Alice stayed in the kitchen to watch the press briefing. It was the big event in her day. Tea and gluten-free Bakewell slices were prepared in readiness.

'You take this pretty seriously, don't you?' said Marcus.

'I've got bugger all else going on. Of course I take it seriously! What about you? You haven't done much work today. Aren't you meant to be busy Zooming?'

'Not that much going on. New project kicked off yesterday, got a power-crazy director in charge. Pipeline Call this morning. Bugger all going on, bit like you.'

'How's Kelvin?'

'Looking tanned and relaxed, sitting on his sun terrace in Cornwall, drinking champagne and counting his money.'

'You haven't upset him again, have you?'

'No, it's all fine. BFFs.'

The offer he couldn't refuse still hadn't arrived.

Escape to the Country was ending and their conversation was halted by the start of the afternoon's *BBC News Bulletin*. The headlines concentrated on Boris who was 'stable' and 'not requiring mechanical ventilation or non-invasive respiratory support'.

'Why are they telling us that?' said Alice.

'To show he's not at death's door yet. Ventilation is the start of a slippery slope, I suspect.'

Dominic Raab rallied the troops. '*I can reassure the prime minister, and we can reassure the public, that his team will not blink, and we will not flinch from the task at hand at this crucial moment.*'

Seven hundred and eighty-six people had died in the previous twenty-four hours. Dominic delivered the 'thoughts and prayers' bit.

'Michael Gove does it much better.'

'Does what much better?' said Alice.

'The condolences bit. Gove puts in big pauses for reflection and sincerity. Ups the game massively on gravitas. Raab doesn't come close.'

'How many people do you think will die?'

'Didn't the Government say anything below 20,000 would be a good result? It's probably too early to tell. If Italy and Spain are anything to go by, we're nowhere near the peak yet.'

Patrick from The Science presented the graphs.

'*It's possible we're beginning to see the beginning of change in terms of the curve flattening a little bit, but we won't know that for a week or so. What we're not seeing is an acceleration in the number of new cases.'*

'That's good then, isn't it?' said Alice. 'Shows lockdown is having a positive effect.'

'Possibly,' said Marcus, but his mind was elsewhere. 'I wish I knew how Claire is doing.'

'Still no news?'

'Just a text last night. I'll call again later.'

* * *

As they lifted her head from the pillow, her eyelids flickered.

'Hello, Claire,' said Jasmit. 'We're just making you more comfortable. Can you sit up for me?'

Claire leaned forward slowly. The nurse adjusted the straps on her mask.

'Is that too tight?' she said, checking the seal against her cheeks.

Claire shook her head.

'Is there anything I can get you?'

'I need a wee.' Every word was a struggle.

'It's a bedpan I'm afraid, you're wired up to all of this!' Jasmit showed her the spaghetti of tubes and wires that were monitoring and beeping. 'I'll be back in a minute.' A nurse soothed her limbs with a surgical wipe, the coolness against her skin refreshed her. Jasmit returned with a bedpan and helped her. She drew the screens around the bed. 'Sorry, I hope you don't mind us carrying on?'

Having spectators while she was having a wee was nothing new. Kyle and Alexa had little respect for her privacy either.

'Can I ring my children?'

The nurse handed her the phone from the bedside cupboard and it came to life. Messages from Beverley and Gavin, and three from Marcus. She opened them first and started to cry.

'What's the matter, Claire?' said Jasmit, putting an arm around her. Claire scrolled through the images on her phone with the nurse.

'Pictures from my children.'

'That's so sweet,' said Jasmit.

Digital compassion had replaced grapes and flowers. Photos of the children sitting in the garden. Flushed faces, rosy cheeks, Kyle smiling with his arm around his little sister. They were both safe and that was all she cared about. She pressed the video button and called Posh Marcus.

He was sitting at his desk replying to Laila's emails when his phone rang. It was probably Laila wanting to align. 'Claire Ladbroke' appeared on the screen and he called out.

'Alice, quick, get the children, Claire is on the phone!' He turned around to the screen as her face appeared. 'Claire, great to see you, how are you?'

He waved and she waved back feebly. A weak smile behind her mask didn't conceal she was still in the grip of the virus. Against her white pillow, her skin looked grey, her hair flat and uncombed. She struggled to reply.

'I'm okay. I'm very tired. How are the children?'

'They're good, they're good. Don't worry about anything, they're absolutely fine. They're just coming. Hang on.'

Alice ushered the excited children into the office. Claire could see her behind Marcus. She wasn't how she had imagined her. Much taller and more elegant, with longer hair. Her complexion was faultless, like polished ivory. Alice looked over her husband's shoulder and waved.

'Hello, Claire. Your children are beautiful. They're a credit to you, they're no trouble at all. Here they are.'

Claire waved feebly and whispered, 'thank you'. Marcus let Kyle and Alexa sit down and knelt by their side.

'Look, here's Mummy. Say hello.' He held the phone in front of them.

The children competed excitedly with each other to tell Claire their news. The house, their bedroom, the size of the television, the garden, James, Olivia, horses, Ribena and cow biscuits. Claire leaned back against her pillow, watching the joy on their faces. Little cameos of the life she had always wanted for them.

'Are you being good for Marcus and Alice?'

The children nodded.

'When are you going to be better, Mummy?' said Kyle.

'Soon sweetie, soon. I will see you soon. Love you so much.' She waved to them and they waved back. The words were draining her.

'Don't worry about anything. Just focus on getting yourself better,' said Marcus.

She looked at him, the man in the tuxedo who came from a world that was completely different to hers. Now their worlds were joined.

'Thank you, you're so kind.' She started to cry again.

'And when you come out, there will be a new razor waiting for you. I had to borrow yours and it sliced my face to ribbons.' He pointed to his face and laughed.

She managed a smile and waved goodbye. She handed the phone to Jasmit who ended the call.

'Was that your dad with your children?' said Jasmit. 'He seems very funny.'

'Yes, he is.'

* * *

Marcus and Alice made sure both children were asleep before coming downstairs and making a cup of tea.

'How do you think Claire looked?' said Alice. 'I didn't want to intrude. I didn't think it was my place to stay. Felt a bit awkward. It was her time with her children.'

'You weren't intruding, Al. You're doing more than I could ever expect, but I know what you mean. She didn't look good, did she? Everything was a strain, she was struggling to speak. I'm so pleased she spoke to the children and they saw her.'

'Poor little things. They don't have a clue what's going on, do they?'

'Probably best they don't right now.'

She took a sip of her tea and reached across the table.

'Have you thought about what happens if Claire gets worse? What if she doesn't get better or even ...'

He couldn't look at her. He stood up and walked across the kitchen, staring straight ahead into the garden. It was dusk and the setting sun was casting shadows of the oak trees across the lawn.

'I haven't given it a thought for a second, why would I? I'm just making sure the children are protected from all of this shit. That's all we can do.'

Alice got up from the table and joined him. She put her arm around his shoulders.

'I'll support you in any way I can. Let's pray for the best.'

* * *

Claire had drifted in and out of sleep. The pressure of the air being forced into her lungs was uncomfortable. The noise of machines whirring and beeping was constant, and the blurred blue images of the medical staff moving from bed to bed disturbed her. There was no night or day on the ward. Her last time in hospital was when Alexa was born, sitting up in bed, Kyle with his hand on his sister's new-born head. Jack took the photograph. It was one of the happiest moments in her life.

Her mind started to wander, playing tricks, flashbacks from her past; random, unconnected incidents glued together in a collage of hallucinations. The

Carter family holiday to the caravan park in Devon, her Jean Muir dress, her first day at Central Saint Martins, the opera with Jack, Mr Mahoney shouting at the television, Kyle counting steps, Spiky the pasta hedgehog.

It started quietly at the back of her mind. The undulating, rhythmic sound of cellos and violins, the silences, the crescendos. She was sitting in the Arne Jacobsen chair, her blanket wrapped around her and a mug of tea in her hands. Samuel Barber's *Adagio for Strings* was playing on the turntable.

It was Tuesday, 7 April 2020.

Chapter 34

THE GOOD FRIDAY AGREEMENT

Marcus finished his alignment call with Laila. Yeast Feast and Make 'n' Bake were playing nicely. Kyle and Alexa weren't. Kyle had sat next to Olivia at the kitchen table. Alexa objected and tried to bite him. Kyle retaliated by whacking her with his spoon.

Marcus came into the kitchen to find Alexa sobbing.

'What's going on? Why is Alexa crying?' he said, protectively picking her up. Kyle shrugged, he hadn't seen anything. The only material witness was Olivia. 'What happened?'

Olivia was having a bowl of muesli with oatmilk and trying to read *My Brilliant Friend* by Elena Ferrante. She put down her book and sighed.

'Six of one and half a dozen of the other. Alexa bit Kyle and he hit her back with a spoon. Don't make a big fuss, Dad. James was always beating the shit out of me when we were small.' She returned to her book.

'Be careful, Libby, little ears are listening,' he said.

She didn't look up. 'That never stopped you and Mum when we were kids. I was only four when I learned the word "bellend".'

'Well, we don't like fighting, do we?' said Marcus, looking at the children.

They shook their heads.

'Your mummy wouldn't like it either. Say sorry to each other and let's have our breakfast.'

The children apologised and Marcus poured himself a bowl of Rice Krispies. Olivia was putting her cereal bowl in the dishwasher.

'We would have got a smack if that had been us. James and I should have called Childline about you and Mum.' She laughed, picked up her book and left the kitchen, passing Alice on the way.

'Who's calling Childline? What's happened?'

'According to our daughter, we were only a phone call away from having Esther Rantzen turning up on our doorstep accusing us of beating our kids.'

Everything in the kitchen was now calm. Alice set the Nutribullet to work, pulverising some celery and carrots.

'You know what the children need, don't you, Marcus?' she said.

'What's that?'

'A routine. I know it's half-term, they're on holiday and we're in lockdown, but they need some structure, more things to do.'

'Like what?'

'Baking. Bake some bread, make some jam tarts, something to keep them occupied.'

'Great idea,' he said enthusiastically. He turned away, put two slices of bread in the toaster and took the Marmite out of the cupboard.

'So what activities are you going to do with them today?'

Her question took him by surprise.

'I'm very happy to do my bit, Marcus, but I'm not doing everything on my own. We've been down this route once before, remember?'

'Sorry, I get it. I'll take them for a walk to see the horses and maybe they could help me with Project Garage this afternoon? I'll get them dressed, then I'll ring the hospital.'

'Haven't you got any proper work to do?'

'Not really.'

* * *

Two more patients had died overnight, two more calls to relatives to be made that morning. Some bright spark had suggested using WhatsApp to inform the next of kin.

We'll be sending sad face emojis with a text message next, thought Dr Hughes.

He had sent Dr Anand home to get some sleep before he collapsed or did something stupid. The unstirred milk powder in his coffee stuck to his teeth. He spat it out, threw the cup in the bin and returned to the ward.

You are entering a COVID AREA – keep doors closed at all times. Masks must be worn.

Thanks for reminding me, he thought.

He gathered his team together. It was like a scene from *The Dirty Dozen.* Three final year medical students accelerated to the front line, two junior doctors from Neurology and Obstetrics and a registrar from Paediatrics. He was joined by Liz and a nursing team assembled from wherever they could get them. Liz was trying to update the whiteboard.

'Why do people always use the wrong fucking pens?'

She threw the pen across the room in frustration. A young nurse picked it up and tried to clean the whiteboard.

'How many beds are coming free in ICU today?' said Aaron, the Paediatric Registrar.

'Probably two, maybe three if someone dies? I'm waiting for confirmation,' said Liz.

'What about spare beds on the ward?' said Mike.

'Already filled. I'll write the new names when I can find a bloody pen that works. We're turning people away. They'll have to go to the Nightingale instead.'

Everyone laughed at the irony. Four thousand empty beds and no staff.

'Maybe Matt Hancock can draft in the Cubs and the Brownies?' said Aaron.

The team laughed again. Liz was updating the whiteboard when his call was put through to her.

'Good morning, it's Marcus Halford, Claire's father. I'm ringing to see how she is?'

'Oh, that's a bit disappointing. I thought you were ringing to see how I am,' said Liz. 'Apart from working with total morons who don't use the correct whiteboard pens, I'm fine.'

Marcus laughed too.

'We spoke to Claire yesterday but she didn't look good to me. How is she doing?'

'Well, she's stable but I guess you've heard that before? Truth is, Mr Halford, she's not out of the woods by any measure. We have increased the flow of oxygen to get her airways to open more, but she's struggling. Not much that's positive news to tell you, I'm afraid.'

'Should she be in intensive care?'

'Possibly but ICU beds are like gold dust. There are worse cases ahead of your daughter. At least she was awake yesterday which is always a good sign. Try to stay positive.'

After The Great Barlow Bake Off, the rest of the day passed quickly. Marcus and Alice were alone in the TV room watching the news conference. Two mugs of tea sat on either side of a plate of freshly baked jam tarts.

'It's a bit like that programme where they film people watching television. They always have mugs of tea and cakes on the table,' he said.

'Do you mean Gogglebox, Marcus?'

'Is that what it's called? I've only watched it a couple of times. They always seem to be eating.'

Sophie Raworth was interviewing a woman whose hair looked like it had had 20,000 volts passed through it. She was talking excitably about keeping children fit during lockdown.

'Wasn't she the Green Goddess?' said Marcus.

'No, this is Mad Lizzie. She was on ITV. The Green Goddess was on the BBC. She was much posher,' said Alice.

'She certainly looks mad to me,' said Marcus, taking a bite out of a strawberry jam tart. 'These are very good. What about Mr Motivator? Is he still alive?'

'Yes, he's back on TV too. He looks good as well. Certainly better than you will if you don't stop stuffing your face with jam tarts.'

She hushed him as the programme cut to the Chancellor who was approaching the lectern accompanied by The Science.

'Do you think Rishi Sunak has big ears?' said Marcus, staring at the Chancellor.

'Marcus, shut up, I'm trying to listen.'

The Chancellor had just given out the stats. Alice had missed it.

'See, I've missed the death total now. Please shut up, Marcus.'

They watched the rest of the press conference in silence. Rishi was giving away lots more money, £750 million to charities who were struggling.

'Yes, that's exactly what's happened,' exclaimed Alice. 'All the charity shops in the high street are closed.'

Marcus imagined the houses in their neighbourhood full to the brim with black bin liners full of last season's outfits, unable to be passed down to the needy poor of Weybridge. He sent a text to Gavin.

All fine here. Children well and happy. Spoke to Claire last night. Not great. Keeping our fingers crossed. Call anytime. M.

* * *

It was the buzzer on the oximeter which brought the medical team running. Claire's oxygen level had fallen dramatically, triggering a rise in her heart rate. The machines next to her bed were beeping and flashing. Jasmit arrived first, followed by Aaron.

'She's hypoxic,' said Jasmit. 'Her sats have dropped to 85%, pulse 110, resps are 38.'

'Let's get her on her front. Increase the oxygen flow rate and concentration,' said Aaron. 'Let's get a new set of bloods too. Call Mike, she's deteriorating.'

Fifteen minutes later, Mike arrived in full battle dress.

'It's happened very quickly, Mike,' said Aaron. 'She was semi-awake earlier in the afternoon but she's gone downhill in the past hour. I'm really concerned about the hypoxia and what it's doing to her heart. Her pulse is 140.'

Mike looked at the latest data hoping it would give him some options.

'Do you think we need to intubate, Mike?' said Liz.

'Let's hold off for now. Increase the pressure and see if that helps the airflow to her lungs. We need more time. Monitor her sats and heart rate every half an hour. Liz, can you call ICU and see what the situation is up there? If she gets any worse, we'll have to get her into ICU, although fuck knows if there'll be a bed?'

* * *

The medical team was gathered around the whiteboard. Spirits were higher than they had been for days. Four patients had been discharged and only one death. Three beds had already been filled. The Coronavirus Conveyor Belt was running at full speed. Mike thanked his team.

'Can I just say thank you to everyone? I know what you are all doing, every single day, to cope with this. I know this is coming at a cost, not just to you, but also to your families and loved ones, who are having to cope without you. Watching people die every day isn't easy but we simply have to keep going and support each other through this.'

Mike had appointed a nurse as the ward's 'PPE Tsar' and she updated everyone on the latest situation.

'We narrowly avoided another crisis yesterday. A delivery arrived in the nick of time. Can I remind everyone to label their face shields, they are like gold dust at the moment and we can't have them going missing. The situation with gloves and aprons is just about okay for now.'

The team went through the list of patients on the whiteboard; it was like results night at the Eurovision Song Contest. The winner with the highest Early Warning Score got to go to ICU. Liz gave the update on Claire.

'Really not good. Sats are very low and her resp and heart rates are high. Her latest bloods show her white blood cell count is up significantly. Nothing is going in the right direction.'

She looked at Mike and he knew what she was about to say.

'I think we've given it as long as we can. The ICU team need to review her. Agree?'

The virus was forcing everyone to make choices they didn't want to make. A twenty-five-year-old mother of two with the best years of her life ahead of her, or an eighty-three-year-old man with emphysema. Mike looked at the data on his tablet but the numbers didn't give him an answer. He stared at the floor and rubbed his unshaven chin.

'Fine. Contact ICU and let's get someone down here to look at her.' He stared back at the whiteboard. 'Who's next?'

* * *

It was Caroline who answered the phone. She was a theatre nurse from Orthopaedics, who had recently been transferred to the Covid ward. People needing new hips and knees would have to limp along for a little longer.

'Good evening. It's Claire Halford's father. Is that Liz or Jasmit?'

'No, I'm sorry. Liz is still on the ward and Jasmit has a night off. This is Caroline. How can I help you?'

'Hi Caroline. I'm ringing to see how Claire is?'

'Just bear with me, Mr Halford, I'll check. Are you all right to hold?'

In the background, he could hear the hubbub of the medical team making the thousands of decisions they made every day. Five minutes later, she returned.

'Hi Mr Halford, sorry to keep you waiting. Claire is still struggling I'm afraid. She is going to be reviewed by the ICU team as soon as a bed becomes available.'

He didn't know what to say. His rose-tinted view of hospital was *Carry on Doctor*, patients sitting up in bed in striped pyjamas, eating grapes and waiting for Hattie Jacques to do her ward round. Nobody ever died in *Carry on Doctor*.

'Is that good or bad?'

'We'll have to see what the ICU team say. It might be the best thing for her right now. She isn't showing any signs of recovery.'

'So what are her chances?'

'Probably best not to think like that, right now. Just focus on Claire getting better and thinking positively.'

'Has she been conscious at all? Did she get the messages we sent today?'

'She's asleep at the moment, but keep sending them, we always show them to patients. It's a good thing, both for her and for you.'

It was the first time he had realised the messages and videos were as much for his benefit as they were for Claire's.

'Yes, you're probably right. I'll call again tomorrow. Thank you.'

'Have a good evening, Mr Halford.'

Olivia helped Alice to bath the children and soon they were in their pyjamas and slippers standing in the hall. They had saucepans and wooden spoons in their hands.

'Coming out to clap for carers, Dad?' said Olivia.

He wondered what the doctors and nurses looking after Claire and thousands of others across the country thought about the national display of gratitude. A well-intended and heartfelt gesture that raised morale or sentimental claptrap that glossed over a national crisis?

'Sure. Come on, let's all go outside.'

They stepped on to the drive and whooped, cheered and banged their saucepans. Alice wolf-whistled. He was jealous of her. He couldn't wolf-whistle, just air and wet fingers. He lost himself in the clapping and whistling, staring up at the darkening evening sky. He thought of Claire, on her own, fighting for her life. He turned his face away, not wanting to show his tears.

It was just the two of them in the living room. Alice sensed a tension in him. He was distracted and she switched the television off.

'What's the matter, Marcus? You're somewhere else, aren't you?'

'I rang the hospital tonight before the clap for carers thing. They might be transferring Claire to ICU if she doesn't improve. Sounds like she's getting worse.'

'Why didn't you mention it earlier?'

'I'm still trying to get my head around it, thinking of different scenarios, possible outcomes.'

'Such as?'

'Such as what happens if she dies? What happens if she pulls through and needs time to convalesce and recover? What if she has to stay in hospital for a long time? Those sort of scenarios.'

He had spent his career assessing risk. Probability and impact. Every scenario he thought of would have a high impact. He hadn't got a clue about probability, or what to do if they happened.

'We can carry on looking after the children, for as long as it takes. But I really think you should speak to Gavin about this, Marcus. Her family has to be told. This isn't about whether she hates them or not. It's the right thing to do.'

He put his hands to his face and stroked his cheeks.

'I know, you're right. I'll talk to Gavin tomorrow.'

'As always, we'll do what we have to do, face things when we come to them. That's all we can do. Let's watch the news.'

The opening story was the prime minister coming out of intensive care and back on to the ward.

'That's great news, isn't it?' said Alice. 'Boris is on the mend. Gives us all some hope, doesn't it?'

'Yes, of course it does.'

* * *

It was Good Friday. Dan and Louise had handed the *BBC Breakfast* reins over to Charlie and Naga. Marcus walked into the bedroom with a cup of tea for Alice.

'Marcus, come and sit down and watch this,' said Alice, pointing to the television. 'This man is ninety-nine years old and he wants to walk a hundred lengths of his garden before he is a hundred to raise money for the NHS. He's incredible.'

Marcus watched the footage of the army veteran pushing his walking frame along the patio of his back garden. Slow, measured steps.

'That's impressive,' said Marcus, looking at the elderly gentleman, resplendent in his blazer and military medals. 'Good to see him wearing a tie as well. I hope I look that good at ninety-nine.'

Naga flushed and gushed as Captain Tom Moore flirted with her from his armchair.

'Tomorrow will be a good day,' said Captain Tom at the end of the interview.

'Let's hope so,' said Marcus.

Marcus went to the office to call Gavin. It went straight to voicemail and he left a message.

'Hi Gavin, it's Marcus. Can you give me a call when you get this? I called the hospital last night. They may be transferring Claire to the intensive care unit. She's not improving. We need to discuss informing her parents. Children are fine. Speak soon.'

Olivia came into the kitchen. Her father was deep in thought and staring into the garden with a coffee in his hand.

'Morning Dad. How are you?'

He turned around.

'I'm okay, Libby. Did you sleep well?' He sounded flat and drained.

'Yes, I'm fine. What's up?'

'They might be admitting Claire to ICU. It's obviously not good news.'

She put her arm around him.

'That's not great. I'm so sorry for her. I guess we've got to put our faith in the doctors. I think I've come up with a great idea for today!'

'What's that?'

'Olympics in the garden! It's going to be a nice day. I'm sure we can find plenty of things to play with the children. There's loads of our old stuff in the garage.'

He put his arm around her. 'Sounds like a great idea, sweetie. Is James joining us?'

'Definitely! I'll get him up now.'

Olivia rounded up the children and took them upstairs to James's bedroom. She opened the door and they ran in and jumped on the bed. The bearded giant awoke from his deep sleep and fended off the little pixies who were bouncing on him.

'Good God, James, what have you been doing in here?' said Olivia. 'This room stinks.'

It was a stale, musty smell of sweaty trainers infused with dog breath. She looked down on the floor and saw the pile of empty wrappers for sausage rolls and scotch eggs lying on top of his dirty clothes.

'What the hell are these?' she shouted.

James was trying to protect his genitals as Kyle and Alexa jumped up and down on him. 'What does it look like, shit-for-brains? Food wrappers. Pork to be exact. Little piggies that go "oink, oink, oink", all minced up! Now will you get out of my room!'

Alice appeared at the door.

'What's going on? What's all the shouting about?'

Olivia opened the door wider and pointed to the floor to show the offending packaging to her mother. 'James has a secret stash of sausage rolls and pasties. He's been secretly scoffing them on his own.'

'They're not pasties, you little vegan twat, they're Scotch eggs actually.'

'Where did you get them from?' said Alice.

'Costcutter. When I went shopping the other day.'

'But that was on Sunday, almost a week ago. Where have you been keeping them, for goodness' sake?'

James leaned across to his bedroom window, unhooked a Costcutter bag from the fitting and lifted it in.

'James, that's disgusting! Throw them all away immediately. You could have been honest about it.'

James got out of bed and was standing in the middle of his room in his underpants and T-shirt, surrounded by the contraband wrappers.

'What do you mean by "honest", Mum? "Honest" as in hiding empty packets at the bottom of the waste bin because you had a craving for a bacon sarnie? That sort of "honest"? Maybe people who live in glass houses shouldn't throw stones?'

Olivia looked confused. 'What are you two going on about? Empty packets of bacon? I don't understand.'

'Speak to Mum. She knows what I'm going on about. Now piss off and let me have a shower.'

Olivia ushered the children out of the room and went downstairs with her mother. Marcus was sitting at the kitchen table reading the newspaper.

'What was all that shouting about upstairs?' said Marcus.

'James has been keeping a secret stash of sausage rolls and other crap in his room. It's disgusting. And what did he mean by bacon sarnies, Mum?' said Olivia.

Marcus twigged what had happened but remained silent. The Vegan Empire was coming under attack.

'I haven't got a clue what James was going on about. He was just being spiteful because he got caught red-handed. Shameful.' Alice said it with the face of a poker player. Not a flicker of an eye or a flinch of a muscle. Olivia bought it.

'James always gets defensive like that when he's in the wrong. He's so childish.'

Marcus admired the way his wife could tell a blatant lie with total conviction. Alice took control.

'After this latest incident, I think we need a family conference to discuss food in this house. As you say at The Firm, Marcus, we all need to be aligned.'

'Great. I'll look forward to that,' he said.

* * *

Claire was transferred to the hospital's intensive care unit at ten o'clock the previous evening. It had been a military operation to move her, along with the spaghetti of wires and tubes that were keeping her alive. There were fourteen beds in ICU, all surrounded by banks of machines and screens displaying fluorescent numbers and repeating squiggles. The atmosphere was calm and quiet apart from the metronomic beeping of the machines. There were ten men and four women, all of various ages. Claire was the youngest by some distance. In the next bed was a Polish man in his early forties who had been overweight long before the virus had left Wuhan. He was on a ventilator, a machine doing the work of his lungs.

The consultant was Dr Thijs Mulder, originally from Rotterdam, supported by Dr Sarah Girton, his Senior Registrar. Together with three junior doctors, the Senior ICU Sister Siobhan Doyle and a team of eight nurses, they held the lives of the fourteen patients in their hands. Mike and Liz gave Sarah and Siobhan a full debrief at the handover.

'Has she been conscious at all in the past twenty-four hours?' said Sarah.

'Very briefly. In and out,' said Liz. 'Very sporadic. Hasn't eaten anything by mouth since yesterday.'

'Closest relatives?' said Siobhan.

'Her father calls every day. He called earlier. The grandparents are looking after the children. No mention of a husband. Contact details are in her notes. Her social worker and a friend send text messages regularly. Her phone is in her bag of things.'

Thijs Mulder spent ten minutes in the donning station putting on his PPE before entering ICU. His name on his gown was unnecessary. Standing at six foot, six inches tall, and with his face shield on, he looked like a giant blue lighthouse. He came on to the unit at 8.30 to begin his handover with Sarah. He had given her the Easter weekend off to be with her family. She had worked six consecutive days, fourteen-hour shifts. He was divorced and his children lived with their mother in a small town on the outskirts of Rotterdam. He hadn't seen them since Christmas. Sarah and two nurses were with one of the patients, a seventy-three-year-old woman, changing her catheter and adjusting the flow of fluids in her drips. Thijs tapped her on the shoulder and she turned and craned her neck to look up at him.

'Morning Sarah. Busy night?'

'Hi Thijs. Usual. We lost Mr Francis and returned one patient, Ellen Price, to the ward. I'll be surprised if Mr Marek lasts to the end of the weekend.'

'New arrivals?'

'Mr Maddison, bed 3. Seventy-six, history of ischaemic heart disease, CCF. I've contacted Dr Liebman in Cardiology. He's coming down this morning.'

'Double whammy,' said Thijs. 'CCF and now coronavirus, that's bad luck. Who else?'

Sarah turned and pointed to Bed 11. 'Claire Halford, twenty-five. Brought in on Sunday. History of asthma. Declined rapidly in the past twenty-four hours. Sats have never gone above 90% and heart rate and resps are very high. Probably need to discuss intubation.'

Thijs turned to look at Bed 11. A small young woman, propped up but asleep. The two doctors did a round of the fourteen patients before Sarah prepared to leave.

'Anything good planned for the weekend?' he said.

'Sleep, sleep and more sleep!'

'The weather is supposed to be nice. Spend some time with the family in the fresh air. The air is pretty rank in here!'

The Barlow Olympics had been a big success. Hula-hooping, egg and spoon races, dressing up races, ball catching and three-a-side football had occupied them for three hours. Alice was delighted she had won the hula-hooping contest with a hip-swinging eighty-five seconds. Five years of reformer Pilates had been worth it. Marcus was upset that James had gone over the top of the ball with a tackle that had left him clutching his shin in agony.

'What the fuck did you do that for?' he said, looking up at his son who was standing over him like a demented Roy Keane.

'Don't be such a pussy, Dad. It was a fair challenge.'

Lunch was outside and they were finishing their key lime pies when Alice announced the convening of the family conference. Family conferences were the constitutional process that Alice used to get her own way. The agenda was set by her and she had the casting vote on any split decisions.

She switched into 'lawyer mode'.

'Okay everyone, in light of this morning's unpleasant events and James's secretive behaviour with sausage rolls and pasties—'

James interrupted immediately.

'How many more times? They were Scotch eggs, not pasties.'

Alice ignored him and continued.

'I think we need to reassess this family's position on the eating of meat and meat-based products.' She called on Olivia to set out the case for the prosecution.

'Thanks Mum. At Christmas, I thought we had all agreed to be vegetarian or vegan on the basis of the benefits to our health, avoiding bowel cancer, reducing cruelty to animals and reducing greenhouse gases?'

'What's climate change got to do with it?' said James, shaking his head.

'Farting and belching livestock, plus all their manure, contribute somewhere between 20% and 50% of all global greenhouse gas emissions. Methane is far worse than carbon dioxide. Plus, a plant-based diet leads to better land use, lower water consumption and stops us poisoning our rivers and oceans.'

James set out his case for the defence. It wasn't as well constructed as his sister's.

'But meat tastes so bloody good! Don't tell me you don't miss a good roast chicken dinner.'

After much discussion back and forth, the debate came down to two arguments. The first was proposed by Marcus.

'I think what this is boiling down to is that we should have more of a balance. James and I are happy to go with a predominantly vegetarian diet, but with some flexibility for fish, chicken and, occasionally, red meat. We're not forcing you two to join us. You can both eat what you want.'

Olivia set out the counter proposal.

'I don't think this is a half-in, half-out option. You can't be semi-vegetarian. We have to do this as a family, make a conscious decision to do what's best for ourselves and the planet. I thought that's what we'd agreed at Christmas?'

'I never agreed to anything. I've been at university, remember?' James sneered at his sister.

Having heard the closing arguments, Alice became Judge Judy.

'Fine, let's put it to a vote, then. Those in favour of a vegetarian or vegan diet?' Olivia and Alice raised their hands.

'Those in favour of a balanced diet including red meat?'

James and Marcus raised their hands. Everyone knew what was coming next.

'It appears the vote is split. So, as I do the majority of the shopping and cooking here, I have the casting vote. We're sticking to the policy we agreed at Christmas.' Alice stood up from the table and started to collect the plates.

'Er, just a minute, Al. I think you're forgetting two votes that haven't been counted?' said Marcus, looking across the table at Kyle and Alexa, who had been listening without understanding a word.

'What are you going on about, Marcus? Don't be absurd. They're far too young to make decisions like that. Anyway, they're guests.'

'That's a bit undemocratic, don't you think? While they're under our roof, they should have a say.' Marcus played his trump cards. 'Kyle, how much do you like sausages and mashed potato with special onion gravy? Big, fat juicy sausages?'

Kyle licked his lips and nodded.

'A lot!'

'Alexa, what's your favourite dinner? Something you would have every day if you could?'

'Shepherd's pie.'

He looked across the table at his wife and daughter who were in shock. 'I would say it's more like 4-2 in favour of a more balanced diet. Shall we clear away then?'

Stacking the dishwasher was done in frosty silence. Although Alice believed in compromise, she hated losing. The Good Friday Agreement hadn't gone the way she planned. Olivia went upstairs to her room to sulk and Alice went to the living room to read the newspaper.

'Well played, Dad,' said James, patting his father on the back. 'Did you see Mum's face? Didn't even need to use this.' From beneath his hoodie, James produced the incriminating evidence, 'Waitrose Dry-Cured Smoked Streaky

Bacon'. 'Doesn't look like we'll be needing this now,' he said as he put it at the bottom of the bin. 'As you said, timing is everything.'

Marcus sent the videos of the Barlow Olympics to Claire.

Everything going well here. K&A are both happy but miss you. All of our thoughts are with you. Get better soon and we're here waiting for you. M. x

It was soon after he sent the message that Gavin returned his call.

'Is Claire in intensive care now?'

'I don't know for certain, I haven't called the hospital today. They seemed pretty sure she would be transferred if a bed became available.'

'Shit. How are the children?'

'They're fine, kids are very adaptable. They're playing in the garden now.'

'That's good, at least they're happy. I've been thinking about what you said about letting her parents and husband know. You've changed your tune, haven't you?'

'Alice persuaded me. Claire might hate them but we have to consider them in all this. I can't pretend to be her father indefinitely.'

There was a pause.

'Her father?'

'Of course. What was I meant to say when I rang the hospital? I'm a casual acquaintance who met her at a dinner party and kidnapped her children? I had to say something. Hopefully, she'll get better and we won't have to worry about lying for much longer.'

'Yes, you're getting very good at it. How's Alice and things at home?'

'Bit frosty, but okay.' Marcus told his friend about the family conference.

Gavin laughed.

'The Good Friday Disagreement by the sounds of it. At least it's out in the open now, no need to be a closet carnivore. Well done on coming out.'

Marcus wanted to ask him if he had considered doing the same, but it wasn't the right time.

'I'll call you after I've spoken to the hospital. Speak soon.'

Matt Hancock was starting the daily press conference. Alice was excited.

'It's Jonathan Van-Tam today. He's so good, I just love him.'

Matt gave out the numbers.

'Of those who've contracted the virus, 8,958 have sadly died, an increase of 980 since yesterday.' He was keen to explain his 'three-strand' strategy for tackling the PPE crisis. It was different to his 'five-pillar' strategy for testing.

'What's the difference between a pillar and strand?' said Alice.

'Haven't got a clue. I wouldn't trust a word that comes out of that man's mouth.'

Matt picked up the ball on the halfway line, dribbled past three defenders, closed in on the penalty area before smashing it into the roof of the net from twenty yards. Unfortunately, he was going in the wrong direction and scored one of the own goals of the season.

'We need everyone to treat PPE like the precious resource that it is. That means only using it when there is a clinical need, and not using more than is needed,' said Matt piously.

'Oh dear, that's a bit unfortunate,' said Alice. 'Accusing NHS staff of wasting PPE. Bit clumsy, especially when their own lives are at risk.'

Matt gave special mention to Burberry who had offered to reconfigure their production lines to make PPE.

'Do you really think the NHS will be getting gowns with the Burberry detail on the cuffs, belt and neck?' said Alice.

'Possibly,' said Marcus. 'Staff will soon be fighting over who gets the Armani aprons or the Versace gloves.'

* * *

Thijs Mulder slumped on a plastic chair outside the PPE Room. He was stretched out with his long legs in front of him, like a giraffe at a watering hole. Sarah had been right, Mr Marek hadn't lasted the weekend. He hadn't lasted past Friday and died at 4.35 in the afternoon. The nurses had disconnected the wires and tubes and pulled a sheet over his body, waiting for the porters to take him to the mortuary. He had died thirty minutes after a video call with his wife and three daughters. They were sitting in the living room of their house in Ealing, saying their goodbyes in Polish to a husband and father who couldn't say goodbye to them.

Thijs was joined by Sally Dawson, Siobhan's number two, who was deciding whether to go outside for a cigarette or not. The stress from fighting the virus had kickstarted a habit she had kicked six years ago.

'What's up, Thijs? You're miles away.'

'I'm okay. Thinking about what I've got to do next. Ring Mr Marek's family, and I need to ring Claire Halford's father too. We'll need to intubate her now. I'm worried about the strain it's putting on her heart and organs. There's a real possibility of renal failure.'

'Do you want me to get you his number?' said Sally.

'If you wouldn't mind? It's best that her family speaks to her before she is sedated. She has children, right?'

'Two small ones judging by the videos they send her.'

'That's a fucker.'

Sally went for a cigarette. Smoking was banned on hospital property but the doctors and nurses knew the secret corners, behind waste bins or down alleys that were littered with butts. She returned to ICU and gave him the phone numbers. He could smell the cigarette on her breath, but nobody was judging.

'Thanks, Sally.'

Mr Marek's wife broke down in tears and he could hear the sobs of her daughters in the background. He had been in hospital for two weeks and on a ventilator for the past five days. Nothing had prepared his family for his death in isolation from them. Thijs ended the call, composed himself and called Marcus.

Marcus was chopping onions when his phone rang. It came up on his phone as a 'No Caller ID' which made him anxious.

'Hello?' he said cautiously.

'Hello, Mr Halford? This is Dr Thijs Mulder, lead ICU Consultant. I'm calling about your daughter, Claire?'

Marcus put down the knife.

'Yes, doctor? Has something happened?'

'Claire was transferred to ICU last night. She was admitted because she is still struggling with breathing, which is putting considerable strain on her other organs, particularly her heart and kidneys.'

'How is she now?'

'Not good, I'm afraid. The CPAP treatment hasn't been as effective as we had hoped.'

'CPAP?' said Marcus.

'Continuous positive airway pressure, I'm sorry. In severe cases, like your daughter's, it's not been enough to fight the infection, to give her lungs a chance to repair and to breathe on their own. We now have to take further steps, which is why I am calling you.'

Marcus looked across the kitchen at Alice. The look on his face made her stop chopping the sun-dried tomatoes.

'I'm afraid, we're going to sedate her and put her on a ventilator. This will hopefully reduce some of the strain on her heart and other organs. I'm calling you now as I thought you and her children might want to speak to her before we intubate? She won't be sedated and possibly be a little more conscious.'

'Is she going to die, doctor?' said Marcus, nervously.

'That's certainly not something we're thinking about at this time, Mr Halford. My team is totally focused on doing everything we can for your daughter. How about we call you back in thirty minutes?'

Marcus was relieved the doctor hadn't given him a straight answer.

'Of course. We'll get the children ready. Speak in half an hour. Thank you for your call and your honesty, doctor.'

'I wish I had better news.'

* * *

Thijs entered the PPE room and went through the same routine he repeated numerous times a day. Drink water, sanitise hands, put on gown, apron, mask, face shield, gloves. Ready for battle. He entered the ICU ward through the set of double doors, ready to brief his team.

'Sally, I've spoken to Claire's father. We're going to call him back in thirty minutes so her children can speak to her before we intubate. Can you get her ready?'

The nurse nodded and the team moved to Claire's bed. Two nurses cleansed her skin with surgical wipes, adjusted her mask and brushed her hair. Claire stirred and opened her eyes.

'Hello, Claire,' said Sally, leaning over her. 'Sorry we're pulling you around a bit. We'll have you more comfortable in a minute.'

A nurse held a straw up to her mouth and she sucked gently on it. The fluid unlocked her mouth, parched and dry from the constant flow of gas.

'We're going to call your family soon, we thought you would like to see them?'

The nurses adjusted the spaghetti of wires and tubes, setting the bed to a position where Claire was able to sit more upright.

'This video came through from your father earlier. We thought you would like to see it?'

The nurse pressed play on the tablet and held it in front of her face. Blurred images of her children playing in a garden, a young man with a beard helping Kyle with an egg and spoon. A pretty, athletic girl showing Alexa how to hula-hoop. And she recognised him, Posh Marcus and heard the words at the back of her mind.

'Hello, I'm Marcus, Marcus Barlow. I've heard a lot about you.'

* * *

Marcus put his phone on the island and looked down. He didn't move.

'What's the matter? Bad news?' said Alice, warily.

'Sort of. Claire has been moved to ICU. I've just spoken to the consultant. They're going to sedate her and put her on a ventilator. They think it's a good idea for the children to speak to her before they do. I'd better go and get them ready.'

Alice stepped around the island and hugged him. 'We have to be strong now, Marcus. It will be okay.'

He could smell her perfume. Hypnose. The same smell when he met Claire for the first time.

'We'll do the call in their bedroom. Do you think we need to bath them first, make sure they're clean?'

Alice smiled at him. 'No. I don't think that's a priority right now.'

The children were excited when Marcus told them they were going to speak to their mummy. They ran upstairs and he sat them on their bed, backs against the headboard, chatting about all the things they wanted to tell her.

'Mummy might not be able to speak very much so we will do most of the talking. She's still not very well, but the doctors and nurses are doing their best to make her better.'

It was fifteen minutes before the phone rang and Claire appeared on the screen. It hit him immediately. She looked so frail; her skin was like parchment, translucent and drained of colour, almost blue.

'Hello! How are you?' he said, hiding his shock behind the question. 'We're all really pleased to see you. Everything's fine here. Let me give you to the children.'

He handed the phone to Kyle and stood by the side of the bed as the children told Claire all their news, a cocktail of truth and exaggeration. They talked for almost twenty minutes, with little offstage prompts from Marcus. Claire didn't speak.

'We're all thinking of you, Claire,' said Marcus. 'Get better and we'll see you soon. You're in safe hands. We'll send more pictures tomorrow.'

They all waved to the camera.

'I love you Mummy,' said Kyle.

'Love you Mummy,' said Alexa, pursing her lips and kissing the screen.

The screen went blank as Sally ended the call.

Marcus was rinsing Alexa's hair, trying not to get shampoo in her eyes. Kyle was sitting behind her. Two little pink prawns sitting in tandem.

'Is my mummy still sick?' said Kyle.

Marcus remembered what Thijs Mulder had said earlier.

'We all want Mummy to get better, don't we? The doctors and nurses are looking after her.'

He sprayed the shower in Kyle's face, and Kyle responded by splashing water over him.

Conversation over dinner was subdued. Alice had updated James and Olivia. Everyone was trying to keep things as normal as possible, talking about the Easter egg hunt on Sunday and the arrival of the Easter bunny. Kyle told them about looking after Biscuit.

'There's a bit more to that story,' said Marcus to Alice as they cleared away. He told her the story of Biscuit's resurrection as a pregnant female.

'Noooo! Poor Gavin!' said Alice. 'He was only doing his best. He wasn't to know, was he?'

They put the children to bed and sat down to watch TV. The virus was playing havoc with the schedules, even the guests on *The Graham Norton Show* were appearing courtesy of King Zoom.

'Are you watching this?' said Alice.

'Not really. I'm thinking about the call with Claire. She looked dreadful. It was as if life was draining out of her through all those tubes. She was just lying there, unable to speak. I'm confused why the doctors wanted to have the call?'

She switched the television off and turned to face him. 'What makes you say that?'

'It's just a weird feeling. I'm thinking, if she does die, tonight might be the last time the children speak to their mother. Fuck me, I can't get my head around that, Al. It's too brutal.'

She moved along the sofa to be next to him and held his hand.

'Come on, stay positive. The children are safe and the doctors are doing everything they can.'

'What if she doesn't come through this, what then?'

'We'll cross that bridge if and when we come to it.'

He rested his head on her shoulder and she stroked his hair.

* * *

The ICU team were assembled around the bed. The team checked the list of equipment, confirmed roles and ensured Claire was as pre-oxygenated as possible.

'Everyone ready?' said Thijs.

The team checked the monitors and the equipment again.

'Ready,' said Sally.

Everyone confirmed their agreement.

The anaesthetic was given through one of the cannulas in Claire's arm. She was sedated within a minute, her breathing reflex numbed by the drug. Thijs stood behind her and positioned her head. He inserted the laryngoscope into her mouth opening the way for the endotracheal tube to pass her vocal chords. It was a tricky procedure, but one he had done hundreds of times. Sally passed him the endotracheal tube and he passed it to the side of the laryngoscope and into the trachea.

'Okay, can you inflate the cuff please, Sally?'

The monitors confirmed intubation had been successful. The team secured the tube in place and connected it to the ventilator. Claire was in a different world now.

It was Friday, 10 April 2020.

Chapter 35

RESURRECTION

Dr Thijs Mulder walked from his house in Queens Park, through Maida Vale and Little Venice to the hospital. It was a route he took most days. Saturday morning was sunny, his walk along the towpath was a world away from the asylum he was about to enter. Some owners of the canal boats moored in Paddington Basin were sitting on the open decks drinking coffee. There were worse places to be locked down.

He sat in the locker room thinking about the day ahead. Ben Wong, the most junior doctor in his team, was finishing his shift. The past three months had been a baptism of fire, learning on the job in the biggest health crisis for generations.

'How are you doing, Ben?' said Thijs, looking up from the bench.

'Pretty fucked to be honest, Thijs. I feel like I'm drowning.'

'Well, it's up to our nostrils and we're treading water, that's for sure. How was it last night?'

Ben gave him the elevator pitch. Half of the patients had been in ICU for two weeks with little or no change, stable but with no signs of getting better. The good news was there had been no deaths overnight.

'We had the cardio guys in this morning looking at the young woman in Bed 11?'

'Claire Halford?'

'Yes. They're very concerned about her low BP, and her latest ECG is very arrhythmic. They think it could be myocarditis. We've sent off a new set of bloods and requested an echo. We should get the results back later this afternoon.'

'Myocarditis? Shit, that's all she needs on top of everything else. What are you doing this afternoon? It's a nice day out there.'

'Sleeping.'

Thijs changed into a fresh set of scrubs and entered the ward. Siobhan Doyle was back and he was pleased to see her. Things always went smoothly when Siobhan was there. They went through each of the patients, prioritising those most at risk and agreeing a plan. He gripped her shoulders in his hands and turned around.

'Er is werk aan de winkel,' he said.

She had heard him say it many times, 'there is work to be done'. They came to Bed 11.

'So, how is Claire doing?' said Thijs to one of the other doctors. He looked down at her through his face shield. She was lying on her back, peaceful with her eyes closed, disturbed only by the rhythmic noise of the ventilator and the beeping of the machines.

'The pneumonia is getting worse. Her immune system has gone into overdrive. Her sats are 87%. We're giving her as much oxygen as she can take. Here are the latest chest X-ray results. The cardio team has been down. Their concern is—'

'Myocarditis. This might be spreading to her heart?'

'Exactly.'

The team discussed what more they could do, but their options were limited. It was like being in a fight with both hands tied behind their backs.

'Okay, let's monitor her very closely,' said Thijs. 'These next few hours could be critical.'

* * *

After lunch, Marcus and Alice took the children for a walk to feed the horses. Alexa wasn't scared of feeding the horses anymore and Kyle enjoyed the freedom to run in the fields. It was one of the warmest Easters on record.

'I expect the papers tomorrow will be full of stories about how the UK is hotter than Sudan or Saudi Arabia,' said Marcus.

What the papers would be full of was pictures of deserted motorways and beaches. Lockdown had stopped the traditional Easter getaway in its tracks, forcing families to stay at home. Some were getting their rusty bikes out of the garage, putting on helmets the size of breadbins and heading for the cycle paths.

'I think we need to buy the children some new clothes. They can't keep wearing the same ones. If it stays hot like this, they'll need more summer things,' said Alice.

'I'm afraid I packed in a bit of a hurry. Sorry, if I did the wrong thing?'

'Don't get defensive, Marcus. You did nothing wrong. I'm just saying. I'm sure Claire wouldn't mind. Buying them a few things isn't going to hurt. Come on, let's head back, it's too hot.'

By the time they got back, James was in the kitchen, making himself a cheese and pickle sandwich.

'Up late last night working, were you? Burning the midnight oil?' said Marcus with a hint of sarcasm.

'Yeah, bit of a late one,' he grunted. 'I partnered up with this awesome dude on *Call of Duty*. I've seen him online loads of times but it's the first time I've played with him. The Kensal Warrior. He's a complete legend, a total killing machine.'

Alice was in the living room waiting for her daily fix. Reeta Chakrabarti read the headlines, which featured the ninety-nine-year-old gentleman walking lengths of his garden to raise money for the NHS.

'Do you see that, Marcus? He's raised £120,000 so far. That's amazing.'

The briefing was being led by the Home Secretary, Priti Patel.

'There must have been a bit of a revolt in the Cabinet this week,' said Marcus. 'I expect people were pointing their fingers, saying Priti hadn't done her bit yet.'

Priti was also in a rush to spend public money. She announced £2 million to support helpline services for victims of domestic abuse, a growing problem during lockdown.

'Probably the only reason some couples stay together is because they get a break from each other when they go to work. Lock them down and they're at each other's throats,' said Marcus.

Alice stared at the television. 'I couldn't agree more.'

'I think I'll ring the hospital, see how Claire is doing.'

'Don't forget, you've got to do the Easter eggs before it gets dark. It will be nice for the children to wake up and see them in the garden. I'll prepare dinner after this is over.'

'What are we having?'

'We've got loads of eggs to use up. I was going to make a Mediterranean vegetable frittata with some salad?'

Although the Good Friday Agreement had gone his way, Marcus didn't want to gloat.

'Sounds great,' he said and went to the office.

The hospital switchboard was busy and it took ten minutes for his call to be answered. Siobhan had returned from her coffee break and answered the telephone.

'Hello, this is Claire Halford's father. I'm calling to see how she is doing.'

'Hi Mr Halford. This is Siobhan, the Senior ICU Sister. I don't think we've spoken before?'

'No, I don't think so either. Although I have spoken to Jasmit, Liz, Dr Hughes and Dr Mulder!'

'Well, that's certainly a cast of thousands!'

He guessed her accent as coming from Dublin or somewhere close. At least she sounded cheerful.

'So how is Claire doing? She was put on a ventilator yesterday?'

Siobhan's tone changed, the momentary cheeriness had gone.

'Yes, she was intubated last night. Dr Mulder and I have been with her today. I wish I could say she's improved, but unfortunately she has deteriorated further overnight. The pneumonia has provoked an extreme immune reaction in her lungs. The build-up of fluid is what's causing her breathing problems, which is why we took the decision to put her on a ventilator. Unfortunately, added to this, we think the infection may be affecting her heart.'

'So what can you do for her?'

'We're working closely with the cardiology team to stabilise her heart rhythm, and she's receiving drugs to raise her blood pressure, as well as anti-inflammatory drugs to reduce swelling in the heart. Our team is doing everything we can, but she is struggling. I have to be honest with you, Mr Halford.'

'We keep sending her messages and pictures. That's okay, isn't it?'

'Of course it is. We've printed some off and put them by her bed. It's the least we can do. Would you like me to get Dr Mulder to call you? He is working today.'

'No, that's okay, Siobhan. I expect everyone's busy and you've been very helpful. I'll call again later, thanks again.'

'No problem at all, Mr Halford. Goodbye.'

He returned to the kitchen where Olivia was laying the table. He updated them with the latest news.

'Poor woman,' said Olivia. 'It's so awful. She's only a few years older than me. Puts a few things into perspective, doesn't it? Here I am fretting about my stupid exams and she's lying in intensive care. It's so unfair.' She started to cry.

He put his arm around her and cuddled her. 'They're different things, sweetie. This virus is challenging all of us, just in different ways. Why don't you get Kyle and Alexa, wash their hands and bring them to the table?'

Alice took two frittatas out of the oven and placed them on the island to cool.

'She's very sensitive, you know, Marcus? I think she's very upset by what's happening to Claire. She's become very attached to Alexa since she's been here.'

'Yes, I can see that.'

They took their seats at the kitchen table. James sat next to Kyle, unaware he was sitting next to the boy who had ridden on the Kensal Warrior's spaceship.

They were five minutes into dinner when Alexa dropped her fork and spoon.

'I feel sick,' she said.

Marcus turned to look at her.

'What's the matter, Alexa?'

'I feel si—'

Alexa retched and vomited frittata over her plate and the kitchen table.

'Oh my God!' said Marcus.

Alice leapt up immediately and grabbed handfuls of kitchen towel.

'Marcus, wipe her face and take her plate away.' Alice wiped up the puke, scooped Alexa from her chair and hugged her. 'It's okay sweetie, don't be frightened. You've just been sick, don't worry.'

Alexa began to cry and Alice comforted her, walking her around the island and stroking her head until she was calmer. Kyle carried on eating. With the drama over and Alexa nibbling on a rice cake, family conversation resumed.

'I thought the omelette was okay, Mum!' said James. 'Could have done with some chorizo in there, but it was fine.'

'It was a frittata not an omelette, and the eggs were still in date,' said Alice defensively. 'They were Duchy Organic not Essentials. There must have been something in it that disagreed with her.'

'She hates eggs,' said Kyle who hadn't raised his head from his plate. 'My mum never gives them to her because she's always sick.'

'That would have been good to know,' said Alice.

* * *

Marcus had forgotten his duties as the Easter bunny and was walking around the garden early on Sunday morning in his dressing gown and slippers with a bag of chocolate eggs. He hid them in bushes, in flowerbeds, on the bird table and in the greenhouse. Alice was up and making a cup of tea.

'You could have put some clothes on to do that. I do hope you've got pants on? Happy Easter, Marcus. Cup of tea?'

'Sorry, I forgot to do it last night. No pants I'm afraid. Happy Easter to you too. Coffee for me, if that's okay? Are the children awake yet?'

'No. Leave them for now, they'll wake up soon. How are you feeling?'

'Frightened. The ICU nurse I spoke to didn't pull any punches. Claire's in a bad way.'

'Any news from Gavin on contacting her parents?'

'Probably not until after the holiday when he can get to their numbers.'

The newspaper clattered the letterbox and Marcus went to collect it. He scanned the front page as he returned to the kitchen.

'Anything interesting in the paper?' said Alice.

'Boris is on the mend and Julian Assange has apparently fathered two children while he was holed up in the Ecuadorean embassy.'

'Blimey! That takes some doing. He must have been very discreet.'

'Yes, although I think being indiscreet is what put him in there in the first place. I'm going for a "3S". I'll get the children up when I'm done.'

Alice winced, she hated his euphemism for morning ablutions.

'I wish you wouldn't say that, Marcus. It's so vulgar, especially on Easter Sunday.'

'Sorry. I bet Jesus had a dump too.'

By mid-morning, everyone was dressed and in the kitchen.

'Has the Easter bunny come to our garden?' said Alexa excitedly.

'We'll have to go and find out,' said Marcus. 'He's quite sneaky, he hides his eggs so they aren't easy to find.'

Alice gave the children plastic bags to collect their eggs and they ran into the garden, running from fence to fence in a frenzy of chocolate-induced hysteria. An hour later most of the eggs had been discovered. They returned to the kitchen where Alice had left four big Easter eggs on the kitchen table.

'This one is for Alexa, and this one is for Kyle. Happy Easter.' She kissed them both. 'And this one is for Olivia, and this one is for James. Happy Easter to you too.' She kissed her children.

'Brilliant, Smarties!' said James, caressing his egg protectively like the big kid he was.

'Remember, no chocolate until after lunch,' said Alice.

* * *

The drive from Finchley to Paddington took twenty-five minutes instead of over an hour. Lockdown and Easter Sunday had some benefits. Dr David Liebman, Consultant Cardiologist, was enjoying *Rhapsody on a Theme of Paganini* by Rachmaninov. It was one of Classic FM's most popular choices. He parked his Lexus in his reserved space in the small car park behind the hospital and entered through a back entrance.

'You're needed in ICU as soon as possible,' said his secretary. 'They've got three patients with severe heart complications and they need you there urgently. Dr Datta is already in ICU. I've told them you'll be down as soon as you get in.'

'Fine, thanks Joyce. I'll get changed down there.'

David Liebman wasn't used to wearing scrubs. He normally spent most of his time at his private practice in Harley Street, looking at ECGs and scans for overweight businessmen concerned about chest pains. The virus had changed all that. Fifteen minutes later, he was in the room outside ICU being helped into his PPE by one of the ICU nurses.

'Is Thijs in yet?' he said to her.

'Not yet. We're expecting him sometime this afternoon.'

'How have things been over the holiday so far?'

'Pretty relentless. As soon as one goes out, another comes in. Another death last night, Mr Maddison.'

'The COPD patient?'

'Yes.'

Activity in ICU was frenetic, two cars had pitted at the same time. Their pit crews were turning their patients, rolling and manoeuvring them into position, rearranging the tubes and wires. More cars would be coming into the pits soon. He recognised his colleague, Sunil 'Sunny' Datta, by the drawing on the back of his gown, a giant sun drawn in red marker pen.

'Morning Sunny,' he said, tapping him on the shoulder. 'What's going on?'

Sunny pointed to a bed in the corner.

'Bed 11. Claire Halford, twenty-five years old, admitted a week ago. Previous history of asthma. Transferred to ICU late on Thursday evening and intubated. Declining rapidly.'

He handed the consultant the tablet containing all the data and they moved to the end of her bed. They spent twenty minutes discussing the results of her most recent ECG, chest X-ray and blood tests, poring over them in the stifling, suffocating atmosphere.

'Looks pretty conclusive to me,' said David Liebman. 'Everything points to myocarditis. The fluid around the heart, the arrythmia and the elevated troponin levels. Even if her lungs start to recover, her heart is going to need time to recover too. This could do more damage to her other organs than her lungs.'

He spoke to one of the doctors on the ICU team.

'Can you get Thijs to call me as soon as he gets in? Claire Halford, Bed 11? We need to discuss her urgently. Dr Datta is staying with you in the meantime.'

* * *

Marcus and Alice were in the living room. *Garden Rescue* was ending. A couple were crying with joy over their new barbecue and alfresco dining area.

'All these makeover programmes are the same. Some lucky bugger gets a renovated house or a landscaped garden for doing nothing more than pissing off on holiday and letting Alan Titchmarsh or that Lawrence Llewellyn-Bowen loose on their property,' said Marcus dismissively.

'Did you know, Charlie Dimmock is back on *Garden Rescue* now? Making a bit of a comeback with her water features,' said Alice.

'Well, I hope she's wearing a bra now.'

The BBC had given Clive Myrie the bank holiday shift. News that the prime minister was out of hospital and recuperating at Chequers wasn't the top story. As the UK's death toll exceeded 10,000, a leading government advisor warned that, 'The UK is likely to be one of the worst, if not the worst, affected country in Europe.'

'Oh, that's all good then,' said Marcus cynically. 'At least we're ahead of the rest of Europe in something.'

Matt Hancock had drawn the short straw for the Easter Sunday slot.

'Has he only got one tie?' said Marcus. 'It's always that shitty pink one.'

'Maybe he has a wardrobe of pink ties?' said Alice. 'Maybe Mrs Hancock fancies him in pink ties.'

'She'd have to be blind to fancy him.'

Matt didn't have anything new to say. Critical care beds, PPE, testing, volunteers, everything was going in the right direction. All the country had to do was stay at home.

'I'm going to call the hospital now,' said Marcus.

* * *

Thijs Mulder arrived in ICU just before three o'clock. He had fallen asleep on the sofa at home after bingeing on his latest Netflix box set and half a bottle of Macallan. He arrived at the entrance at the same time as Sally Dawson, who was having a last drag on her cigarette. He smiled.

'Those things will kill you. Bad for your lungs.'

She threw it on the ground and stubbed it out with her foot.

'I think my lungs should be more frightened of other things, don't you?'

The ICU team were assembled in the staff area. There had been no more deaths since Mr Maddison. Twenty-four hours without having to take pictures or videos of the dying or play tearful farewell messages to patients who couldn't hear them.

'So, who are our biggest concerns right now?' said Thijs.

'Lee Blake, Bed 4, Doreen Fitzgerald, Bed 7, and Claire Halford, Bed 11,' said a junior doctor.

Thijs was shocked by how quickly Claire had gone downhill.

'And you need to call Dr Liebman in Cardio as soon as possible.'

Thijs gave a pep talk to his team, knowing they were drawing on reserves that were running dangerously low. Lukewarm coffees were drunk and stale sandwiches eaten before the team re-equipped themselves and returned to the battlefield. He called David Liebman.

'David? Hi, it's Thijs. How are you?'

'Afternoon Thijs, not too bad. Wish I was at home with the family on Easter Sunday, but never mind.'

'I didn't think Easter was a big thing for you?'

'It's not, but I'll take any free holiday that's going right now. Thanks for getting back to me. I was in ICU this morning with Sunny Datta, my registrar. We're both really concerned about the young woman, Claire Halford. The tests have confirmed myocarditis. I think it's a toss-up which one gives up first, her heart or her lungs.'

The two doctors discussed the different permutations. They were running out of options.

'If things carry on, I would say the risk of arrest is high,' said David. 'The next twenty-four hours will be critical. Are you on call tonight?'

'Yes. Until tomorrow morning.'

'If anything happens, call me. I can be here in half an hour. Dr Datta will be here for a few more hours.'

'Thanks, David.'

Thijs was on his way to the PPE room when one of the nurses stopped him.

'Thijs, I have Claire Halford's father on the phone wanting to know how she is. Do you want to speak to him?'

'Yes, put him through to my office, will you?'

The doctor returned to his office and took the call.

'Mr Halford, this is Thijs Mulder. Good afternoon.'

'Happy Easter, Dr Mulder. I just wanted to know how Claire is doing? I spoke to Siobhan yesterday. Has there been any improvement overnight?'

'Happy Easter to you too. You've called at a good time. I've just come off the phone with Dr Liebman, the consultant cardiologist who is also looking after her. He has confirmed myocarditis, a heart complication caused by the virus. Basically, it's attacking her heart muscle. I'm going to be frank with you, Mr Halford ...'

'I'm going to be frank with you.' As soon as he said it, Marcus knew it wasn't good news. When people were frank, it never was. Thijs gave him the bottom

line, the next twenty-four hours would decide which way it went. Marcus stared into the garden, Alexa and Kyle were playing with James and Olivia.

'Do you think the children should speak to her this evening, doctor?'

'She won't be able to speak to them, Mr Halford. She is sedated but it's a good idea that you and your grandchildren talk to her. My team is doing all we can. I really hope we can turn her around, but the next day will be critical. Around seven o'clock tonight? I'll get one of my team to call you.'

'That's fine, doctor. Thank you. Let's speak later.'

Marcus walked back into the kitchen where Alice was peeling sweet potatoes. He felt numb. Claire was meant to be like Boris, feeling a bit poorly, off to hospital, a short time in intensive care and then discharged to recuperate and be comforted by her happy children. Knock, knock, knockin' on heaven's door wasn't part of the plan. He repeated what Dr Mulder had told him.

'The next twenty-four hours will be critical. He thinks the children should speak to her. They're going to call us at seven tonight.' He paused for thought. 'What the fuck do I tell the children, Al? That their mum might die and this could be their last chance to say goodbye, even though she won't be able to say goodbye to them? Just what do I tell them?' He shouted, getting angry with the frustration of not being able to fix things. Marcus Barlow had spent his life fixing things.

'Just be as normal as you can, Marcus. Don't mention Claire being very ill. Tell them she is sleeping but she can hear them and wants to hear their voices. Take things one step at a time.'

Alice was always at her best in a crisis.

'You're right. Let's get them in and bathed. Would you help me talk to them? This has to be handled very delicately. I'd better let Gavin know the latest too.'

'Of course. You're not very good at "delicate", are you Marcus?' She smiled and pinched his arm.

Kyle and Alexa were washed, dried and polished in their pyjamas, sitting on the end of their bed. Alice had blow-dried Alexa's hair and she looked beautiful. Kyle had his arm around his little sister. Everyone was ready at seven and the call from the ward came through ten minutes later. Alice stood in the doorway of the bedroom watching as Marcus sat on the floor, back propped against the bed and held the phone in front of the three of them.

Claire was lying on her back, eyes closed, the breathing tube connected to the ventilator taped to her face. Sally stood next to her, one hand on her shoulder and the other holding the tablet in front of her.

'Hello everyone! Happy Easter!' said Sally, looking cheerful and waving. Putting on a brave face for relatives was an essential. 'Hello children. I'm Sally and I'm looking after your mummy.'

The children waved back. The children told Claire about the Easter bunny and the egg hunt in the garden. They spoke excitedly and uninterrupted for fifteen minutes, short stories and tall tales, the things they had done and the things they missed. Marcus was choking with their innocence, their unwavering faith Claire would get better and return to Kensal Mansions. He was struggling to look at her, lying motionless on the bed. There were four adults listening to the conversation. One was asleep and the other three were all crying. Alice stood at the doorway, gripping the door frame tightly, Sally stroked Claire's shoulder and Marcus held the phone with both hands.

'I think we should be going so say goodnight to Mummy now?' he said to the children. 'Sally probably has lots of work to do as well.'

'No rush this end,' she said sympathetically. 'Really, take as long as you need.'

'Is there anything else you want to say to Mummy?' he asked the children.

'Get better, Mummy. I love you,' said Kyle.

Alexa kissed the screen, a Cupid's bow of moist love.

The call ended and Alice came into the bedroom and lifted the mood. 'Okay Marcus, you go and get cleaned up and I'll take Alexa and Kyle downstairs with me. It's a surprise dinner tonight.'

'What is it?' said Marcus.

'It's a surprise.'

He went to the bathroom and washed his face. He looked at himself in the mirror. Apart from the puffy eyes, he thought he looked okay. He knocked on James's door. He was lying on his bed, listening to music.

'Fancy coming downstairs for a glass of wine? I could do with one.'

'Sure.'

James needed no invitation to drink his father's wine and leapt off the bed.

'Everything okay, Dad?'

Marcus told him the latest news.

'That's such a shitter. Her kids are pretty cool little dudes.'

They collected Olivia on the way and entered the kitchen where Alice was showing Kyle and Alexa how to lay the table.

'So what's this surprise meal then?' said Marcus. She picked up a chopping board and turned around.

'I took those sirloin steaks out of the freezer. Olivia and I are having vegan chicken steaks. Thought a bit of red meat might cheer you up?'

Marcus and James looked at each other and nodded, the Good Friday Agreement was working in practice. Marcus went to the cupboard and returned with a bottle of 2014 Château Giscours, Margaux.

'I think this should go well,' he said, pulling the cork.

Alice showed she hadn't forgotten how to cook a medium-rare steak and Olivia didn't faint at the sight of blood oozing on their plates. Marcus raised his glass.

'Happy Easter, everyone. Here's to Claire getting better.'

Glasses clinked and Marcus looked at the faces around the table. There was an elephant in the room but, for a few minutes, everyone pretended it wasn't there.

Alice was reading in the living room when he sat down next to her. *Antiques Roadshow* was on in the background. She handed him his phone.

'Gavin's been texting you. He's sent a few messages. I've made you a cup of tea as well.'

Marcus opened his phone and replied.

Will let you know as soon as I do. Kids are fine. Keeping things as normal as possible. Speak tomorrow. M.

Antiques Roadshow was the usual formula. Filmed in a Grade I listed stately home on a perfect summer's day, gaudily dressed experts inspected family heirlooms and gave a valuation which made their owners gasp with shock.

'It's not exactly a great advert for diversity is it?' said Marcus, pointing to the television.

'What do you mean?' said Alice, staring at the screen over the top of her reading glasses.

'White, middle-class, middle-aged British people finding out that the ceramic pot that held the kitchen door open for years is worth a small fortune.'

'I thought you liked Fiona Bruce?' said Alice. 'Presenting *Antiques Roadshow* hardly makes her a racist, does it?'

'I do like Fiona Bruce, I just think the format could do with being a little more up to date, that's all. Just saying.'

Alice started to watch the fourth episode of *The Nest*, a drama about a troubled teenager offering to be a surrogate mother for an infertile couple. Marcus had missed the first three episodes and Alice quickly grew tired of his endless questions. Troubled and unable to concentrate, he left her to it and went to bed.

He had a library of unfinished books on his bedside table, and he picked one up and turned the pages, hoping to find his place and remember the plot. It was pointless and he closed it again. He lay on his back, closed his eyes and did something he never did, said a silent prayer before falling asleep, not noticing the warmth of Alice getting into bed next to him.

* * *

It was 2.05 when one of the ICU nurses knocked on the door of the room where Thijs Mulder was trying to steal a few hours of precious sleep.

'Dr Mulder, it's Claire Halford. Her condition is deteriorating. I think you need to come quickly.'

He sat up, threw the duvet to one side and rubbed his eyes. He had bed hair and his mouth was dry. He had slept in his scrubs and was out of the door in less than a minute.

'Can you get hold of Dr Liebman or Dr Datta and get one of them here as soon as possible?'

The nurse nodded. He ran to the ICU where one of the team helped him into his PPE, and ten minutes later he was standing next to Bed 11. Claire was lying face down on the mattress, eyes closed. The virus had come out fighting and was throwing all its punches. She was unable to respond, her organs were being starved of oxygen. He looked at the latest ECG. Her heart was taking a beating.

'How long until Dr Liebman gets here?' he shouted to one of the nurses.

She looked at the clock on the wall. 'Thirty minutes. He's on his way.'

Just over half an hour later, Dr Liebman was standing next to Thijs beside Claire's bed. He reviewed the latest ECG, checked the numbers and squiggles on the monitors.

'We have to raise her blood pressure somehow or she'll arrest; let's add aspirin and milrinone.'

The nursing team reacted immediately and pumped the drugs straight into her cannula.

'Unless her lungs start giving some support to her organs, her heart could give up very soon.'

'Without blowing her lungs completely, we're giving her as much oxygen as she can take,' said Thijs.

The cardiologist shrugged his shoulders. 'I know,' he said.

Woken prematurely, the two doctors did the rounds of the other patients in ICU. Everyone was stable and the ward was quiet apart from the hushed conversations of the medical team going about their work. The tranquility was suddenly shattered by the high-pitched tone coming from one of the monitors next to Claire's bed. The numbers were flashing red and the squiggles were behaving erratically. They ran to her bed. David Liebman looked at her monitors.

'She's in VF. Get her on her back and start CPR immediately,' he shouted.

The ICU team turned her quickly as a nurse undid her gown and pulled it down, exposing her chest. A junior doctor applied his hands to her sternum and applied downward pressure on her rib cage, short, staccato pumps. He counted as the team looked nervously at the monitors for any signs of response.

'Get me the defibrillator,' said David.

A nurse tore off the backing on two pads and slapped them on Claire's chest. He charged the defibrillator.

'Shocking. Stand clear.'

He pressed the buttons, sending the voltage through her chest. No change. The junior doctor recommenced CPR. No change. David charged again.

'Shocking. Stand clear.'

The sequence was repeated for the next half an hour. No change. Nobody wanted to look at each other. Thijs looked around at their faces, they all said the same thing.

'I'm calling it, I think we should stop now. Are we all agreed?'

The team bowed their heads and nodded.

He looked up at the clock on the wall.

'Time of death, 4.48 a.m.'

He looked down at her face and her motionless body which concealed the microscopic killer. The team all looked at each other. They had been actors in the same drama almost every day for the past month. Each new death was as painful as the others. Sarah put her arm around a young nurse who was crying.

Thijs and David Liebman left the ward and were being helped out of their gowns. Thijs threw his face shield on to a chair and sanitised his hands. He looked at the cardiologist.

'It never gets easier, does it? And the worst part is the peak of this pandemic is yet to come. This is just the start. They think standing on their doorsteps clapping once a week keeps us all going in here. It's a fucking joke.'

Sally Dawson came into the room and removed her face shield. 'I'm going for a fag, I need one. Do you want me to call Claire's father when I get back?'

'No, it's okay. I'll do it,' said Thijs. 'I only spoke to him a few hours ago. It's probably a bit early. I'll freshen up and do it later. Nobody wants to be woken in the middle of the night to be told their daughter is dead.'

'Can I offer you a lift?' said David Liebman. 'I'm going home now. I'll try to get a few hours' sleep before I come back.'

'No thanks, David. I think I'll walk home. Some fresh air will do me good.'
David nodded. 'Sure.'

* * *

Marcus was sitting on the patio in his dressing gown, drinking a coffee. It was cooler than the day before and there was a mirror of dew on the lawn. Something glinting in the magnolia tree caught his eye. It was an undiscovered Easter egg. He stood up and removed it from the forked branches. He unwrapped the foil and took a bite. His phone on the patio table rang. 'No Caller ID'. He answered immediately.

'Hello.'

'Hello, Mr Halford. It's Thijs Mulder here. I'm sorry to call you so early in the morning. I've left it as long as I could. There is no easy way to say this but I'm afraid I have some very bad news. Claire died earlier this morning. She deteriorated rapidly overnight and, despite the best efforts of my team …'

The doctor carried on talking, explaining the clinical reasons for Claire's death but Marcus was only catching odd words. A solitary magpie cackled and flew across the garden.

'Your daughter's body did all it could but her immune system was being swamped. This virus is an awful thing. We're learning about it all the time but we couldn't save her. The damage to her heart and lungs was too great. I am so sorry to give you this awful news so early in the day.'

It took a while for him to respond. It was a strange question.

'So, what happens now, doctor?'

'In terms of what, Mr Halford?'

'Claire? Her body? What happens to it?'

'Oh, I see. Her body will remain here in the mortuary until we receive instructions to release it to a funeral director. We will issue the medical certificate today so you'll be able to register your daughter's death after the bank holiday.'

'What time did you say she died?'

'4.48. I am so sorry for your loss, Mr Halford. My team are devastated too. My condolences to you and your family.'

'Thank you, doctor, and thank you and your team for everything they did for Claire. Goodbye.'

He remained motionless on the chair. The past week had been a blur, the virus had changed everything. He tried to get his thoughts in order, just as The Firm had trained him, identifying the key issues and prioritising the solutions.

He texted Gavin immediately.

CALL ME. URGENT. M.

He went inside, made two cups of coffee and carried them upstairs to his bedroom. The radio alarm was on and Alice was waking up.

'You're up early, everything okay?'

He sat next to her on the bed and held her hand. 'I've just spoken to the consultant. Claire died at 4.48 this morning. Cardiorespiratory failure caused by Covid-19.'

He said it in a very 'matter of fact' way, the key information. She sat upright immediately.

'Oh no! That can't be true. So quickly?'

'I've texted Gavin. I'm waiting for him to call me back. We should tell James and Olivia, but I don't think we should tell Kyle and Alexa until I've spoken with Gavin. Officially, I'm not her next of kin. I probably shouldn't be the one to tell them.'

'So who should?'

'God knows. I'd better get dressed. There's a lot to do.'

'I'll get up and get the children their breakfast,' said Alice. 'It's dreadful.'

Gavin was two miles outside his parents' estate before he got a signal. His phone pinged with multiple messages. He opened the messages from Marcus. Something had happened. He pulled over to the side of the road to call him.

Marcus was getting dressed when he got the call.

'Hi Marcus. It's Gavin. I've just picked up your messages. What's happened?'

Marcus sat down on the end of the bed.

'Hi Gavin. The hospital called me about an hour ago. Claire died in the early hours of the morning. Well, 4.48 to be exact. Cardiorespiratory failure caused by the virus. Seemingly, she went downhill very quickly overnight and they couldn't save her. It was her heart as well as her lungs.'

Gavin stared out of the car window at the moorland that rose above the stream to his right, a stark but beautiful landscape. He gripped the steering wheel hard and started to shake.

'But ... but ... she can't have died! She was so good the last time I saw her. She was getting stronger, things were getting better for her. Surely, this can't have happened?'

'I know. It hasn't sunk in for me either. I know she was more than "a case" to you. You meant a lot to her too? If it wasn't for you, we would never have met. It's fucking awful. I'm going to need your help to get things sorted at this end?'

'Yes, of course, anything. What do you need from me?'

'We need to agree who's going to tell the children. I'm not their next of kin, Gavin. Maybe, it should come from her husband or her parents? They do need to know. We can't keep it a secret.'

Gavin took time to reply.

'You and Alice should tell them, Marcus. The children must come first and you are closest to them right now. I know you and Alice will do the right thing. We both know what Claire thought about her parents and Jack. It's what she would have wanted. What do you think?'

'I agree the children have to come first. That's why I brought them here. But I don't want to get you into more trouble doing something I shouldn't do.'

Gavin exhaled, a wry laugh from his snotty nose.

'I think it's a bit late for that, don't you? We have to do what we think is best now. I'll call her parents tomorrow. There will be some explaining to do but this has to be dealt with now. It can't be left. I'll leave it up to you and Alice to decide how best to handle it.'

'Can we speak again later? I need time to think this through.'

'Sure. Do you want me to come back to London?'

'What about your mum and dad, don't they need you?'

'Rory will have to step up. Dentists are doing bugger all right now. I was on my way over to see him when I got your message. I'll tell him what's happened. He'll understand.'

Marcus had already started to draw up a to-do list in his mind. He knew he couldn't do it all on his own, and Alice was already doing more than he could expect.

'If you could, that would be great. Let me know when you're coming back. Perhaps we can meet up at the flat later in the week to agree what needs to be done? I can think of a thousand things.'

'I'll call you later. Are you okay, Marcus? I'm sorry, I didn't ask.'

'Still hasn't sunk in. I'm in "fix" mode at the moment. Take care of yourself, Gavin. Speak later.'

'You too, Marcus.'

By the time he got down to the kitchen, the children were finishing their breakfast. Alice had made porridge and Olivia was up. He could tell Olivia had been crying.

'There's some porridge in the saucepan for you, Marcus,' said Alice. 'It might need warming up a bit. Add some more milk to it.'

Marcus looked at the children. 'Did you like your porridge? It's my favourite,' he said.

'More than Rice Krispies?' said Alexa with a frown.

'Even more than Rice Krispies.'

'Shall we go and get dressed?' said Olivia to the children.

Marcus sat down next to Alice.

'I've just spoken to Gavin.'

'How was he?'

'Shocked, upset, disbelief. Like all of us. He's trying to get back to London this week, if his brother can look after his parents? He thinks *we* should tell the children.'

'And what do you think?'

'I think I agree with him. Claire had no time for her husband or her parents. What do you think, Al? I trust you.'

'If that's what you think is best? I think the children feel safe here. I keep thinking of her, dying alone in hospital.'

'I suppose we have to hope that, at some point in the last few days, she was able to remember happy times, the three of them together? I guess we'll never know. It's what I'd like to think happened.'

His spoon started to shake, tapping against the rim of his bowl. Alice reached across the table to steady him.

'I hope so too. When do you want to tell them?'

'I thought we might go for a walk this afternoon, just the four of us? Maybe the bench by the oak tree? Or we could tell them here? What do you think?'

'Let's go for a walk after lunch. In the meantime, let's keep everything as normal as we can. We need to be strong for them and for Claire.' She held his hand to her lips and kissed it.

* * *

Gavin left his brother's house in one of Perth's nicest neighbourhoods. His brother had agreed to take some responsibility for their parents. He would return to London on Wednesday.

At the Friarton Bridge where the A90 crosses the River Tay, he turned left towards Dundee, following the river until it widened into the Firth of Tay and the road cut inland. He turned in to a back street near the football ground and parked outside a small, dingy semi-detached house. It hadn't changed much in four years. The windows were dirtier and more of the render had fallen off the walls. He moved the overflowing wheelie bins to one side and walked up the weedy path. The bell didn't work and he knocked. A fat woman in her sixties with a pinched, ruddy face and her hair tied back in a bun answered the door.

'Hello Annie. Is Robbie in?'

The woman looked him up and down. He was too well dressed to be the police. She ushered him into the hall and shut the front door behind them. The house stank of cat piss and stale cigarette smoke. Robbie was even fatter than his wife, dressed in dirty track suit bottoms and a polo shirt. He was sitting on a threadbare armchair in the back room, the cushions were sticky from the Brylcreem he slapped on his wispy hair every day. He was smoking a cigarette and reading the *Daily Record*. He looked up and recognised Gavin immediately.

'Mr Douglas, we've no' had the pleasure of your company for a while. You're looking good, I must say. What can I do for you? I dare say this is no' a social visit?'

'No, it's not. I want some coke. A gram.'

Robbie didn't ask questions. He got out of his armchair and went to another room. He returned a couple of minutes later with a small plastic bag and handed it to him with stubby, yellow, nicotine-stained fingers.

'How much?' said Gavin.

'Forty pounds.'

Gavin took two twenty-pound notes out of his wallet and gave it to him. He put the small plastic bag in his inside coat pocket and walked to the door.

'Annie will see you out. Nice to see you again, Mr Douglas,' said Robbie, slumping back into his greasy chair. 'Drop by anytime you're in the area. And next time?'

'What?'

'Wear a fucking mask. Have you no' heard? There's a virus going around.'

* * *

Alexa held Alice's hand as they left the drive of Twin Gates. Kyle ran ahead. It was Easter Monday in lockdown, not a car on the road. They turned left into the fields and Marcus guided them through the kissing gate. There were some rabbits on the path ahead.

'Did they give us our eggs?' said Alexa, pointing to them.

'Possibly,' said Alice.

The rabbits dived into the hedgerows as they approached the field where the horses were grazing lazily. Alice wolf-whistled to attract their attention and they looked up and ambled towards them. Kyle had named one of the horses 'Mr Mahoney' because of his teeth. It reminded Marcus of another thing to add to his to-do list. Telling the caretaker of Kensal Mansions wouldn't be easy.

He rehearsed what he was going to say to the children, going over it again and again in his mind. He didn't have a clue. Images of angels, clouds, stars, heaven and God all flashed through his mind. Telling fibs about the Easter bunny was one thing. As they approached the bench by the burned-out oak tree, Alice looked at him and he nodded.

'Why don't we take a rest and sit down for a little bit?' said Alice. 'There's something Marcus and I want to tell you.'

They sat the children between them, holding their hands. They felt sticky from the apples and horse dribble. Marcus turned to face them.

'Kyle, Alexa, you know that your mummy has been very ill in hospital since you've been staying with us, don't you?'

The children nodded.

'And she was finding it very hard to breathe because of the virus?'

They nodded again.

'The doctor who was looking after her spoke to me today. He told me that your mummy didn't get better. She wasn't able to breathe properly and her heart stopped beating. She died this morning.'

He stopped and waited for them to process the news in their own way. Nothing was said for an eternity. It was Kyle who spoke first.

'Why didn't the doctors make my mummy better?'

'The doctors did everything they could to help your mummy. They tried very hard, but they couldn't make her better. She was very sick and that's why she died.'

'Has she gone to heaven?' said Alexa.

Marcus looked at Alice. It was the day of the Messiah's resurrection. It wasn't the time for atheism.

'Yes, she has. Your mummy was a very good and kind person who loved both of you so much. Wherever she is, you know she will always love you.'

'When will we see her again?' said Kyle.

Marcus could feel the weight of responsibility piling up on top of him. His resolve was starting to crumble

'Mummy isn't being hurt or feeling ill anymore. We won't see her again but we will always remember her in lots of ways.'

It was Kyle who broke first. Big fat tears started to run down his cheeks, his little shoulders shaking with each sob. Marcus pulled him to his chest and squeezed him as hard as he could, stroking his head. He looked over Kyle's shoulder and could see Alice crying too as she hugged his sister. Except Alexa wasn't crying. She was looking at her brother and the two grown-ups, confused by their tears. Marcus took his handkerchief out of his pocket to wipe Kyle's eyes. Alice shook her head and reached into the pocket of her gilet to produce some tissues. She always had tissues. Marcus took them and dried Kyle's eyes. It took five minutes for the little boy's tears to stop. Alexa continued to stare at her brother.

'Who will look after us if Mummy isn't here?' said Kyle.

'Marcus and I are going to look after you for as long as you want. You are going to stay with us. With Olivia and James too,' said Alice. 'Marcus is going to speak to Gavin and he will tell us what to do. Is that okay?'

'Do we have to go back to our house?' said Kyle.

'You can stay with us for as long as you want,' said Marcus. 'We will go back to your house soon and see Mr Mahoney, Ian and Judith. Let's walk back home now. Maybe you can watch some television with Olivia or play video games with James?'

The children both nodded.

'Can we have Ribena and cow biscuits?' said Alexa.

'Of course you can, sweetie,' said Alice.

She picked Alexa up and carried her in her arms. Marcus put his hands around Kyle's waist and hoisted him up on his shoulders. He felt the damp warmth of the little boy's trousers on his neck.

'Come on, let's go home now,' he said.

* * *

Gavin put on his walking boots and shooting jacket. He called out to his parents that he was going for a walk.

'I won't be long,' he shouted. 'I'll take the dogs with me.'

He called out to Wallace, the black Labrador, and Timmy, the pick 'n' mix mongrel. The dogs came running and they set off through the woods which surrounded the house on three sides. After twenty minutes, he came to a small, wooden hut used by the beaters and estate workers during the shooting season. It was never locked and he stepped inside. It hadn't been used in months and there was dried mud on the floor from the last shoot. He filled the kettle from the tap and lit the single-ring gas burner with a match. There was a box of stale teabags next to the kettle and some stained mugs. He rinsed one under the tap but it changed nothing. The kettle boiled and he threw a teabag in the mug and added the hot water. He found a dirty tea towel, wet it under the tap and wiped the table, smearing the grime.

He opened the windows and could smell the scent of the damp pine forest; it was a natural diffuser. He reached into his inside pocket and took out the tiny plastic bag he had bought from Greasy Robbie. He tipped some of the white powder on to the grubby table and opened his wallet. He took out his my Waitrose card and a ten-pound note. He chopped and diced the white powder, moving it around on the table into little lines. He rolled the ten-pound note into a tube and held it between his thumb and forefinger. He stopped for a moment to look at the four tramlines before pushing the tube up his nose, squeezing his other nostril and hoovering up one line of the powder.

He sat back in the chair and stared out of the window. He could feel the burn of the powder against his septum and the bitter taste at the back of his throat. Wallace looked up at him dolefully. He had seen it before.

'I'm sorry, Wallace,' he said. 'I just needed it. Fucking shit day.' He hoovered up another line. He looked out into the woods but couldn't see the trees. All he could see was Claire sitting in her kitchen, crying, laughing, arguing with him about all the things they talked about. The dopamine level in his brain was surging and he felt better and happier. The cocaine helped him to remember her as she was, funny, goofy, engaging and smart. He saw her in the Karen Millen cocktail dress, laughing with him and Marcus, the dinner that brought them all together on a magical evening.

'I'll miss you. And *Raging Bull* was definitely the best De Niro film.'

He wet his finger and wiped the remaining residue from the table.

'Come on you two, let's get back.'

* * *

Olivia and James were in the kitchen. The island was full of tins and packets.

'What are you two doing?' said Alice.

'Making a trifle,' said James. 'We always had trifle on Easter Monday. Sherry trifle. Grandma used to make it. It was my idea.'

'Where did you get the ingredients?' said Alice, looking at the sponge fingers and tins of mandarin segments.

'I nipped out to Costcutter while you were out.'

He knew what his mother was thinking.

'How was the walk?' said Olivia.

'We fed the horses, didn't we?' said Alice, looking down at the children. 'Mr Mahoney was very hungry.'

Marcus and Alice left the children in the kitchen, helping Olivia and James with the trifle. Normal was good for everyone.

'Would you mind if I watched the briefing?' said Alice.

'Why would I mind?' said Marcus.

'Thought you might be sick of Covid after all that's happened today?'

'No, you're okay. Switch it on.'

Another 717 people had died overnight.

'Every one of them is a tragedy, and our hearts go out to all of the loved ones who are grieving their loss at such a difficult time,' said Dominic Raab.

His intention was good but Marcus didn't want Dominic's heart going out to him or to Kyle and Alexa. It wasn't going to bring Claire back. He picked up the empty mugs and took them to the kitchen. Olivia was holding Alexa's hands as she whipped the cream and James was stirring custard with Kyle. The topic of conversation was sharks. Five minutes earlier, it had been volcanos. Normal was good.

'I'm just going in the office,' said Marcus. 'I've got a bit of work to do.'

He sat down at his desk, opened his laptop and logged on to the network. His screen went blue immediately.

Your machine is receiving critical software updates. Please restart your machine after completion.

The little cursor began its journey across his screen.

'You have got to be kidding me!' he said to himself. 'It's Easter-fucking-Monday.'

He waited fifteen minutes to achieve '100% completion' and restarted his computer. He opened a new Word document and typed the heading, bold and underlined.

CLAIRE HALFORD: TO-DO LIST

Even post-mortem actions needed a plan. It was what The Firm had trained him to do.

Inform relatives (parents, husband) and friends/neighbours (Beverley, Mr Mahoney, Judith, Ian)
Register death and obtain death certificate
Find a funeral director
Make funeral arrangements (parents?)
Discuss interim care arrangements (Gavin)
Collect children's clothes from flat
Collect CH personal effects from hospital
Inform council and utilities
Funding/Universal Credit – stop

Inform school and nursery
Schooling arrangements for K&A
Contents of CH flat – what to do?

He scanned down the list. It was a big project, one that would need dedicated resources for certain. He closed his laptop and returned to the kitchen. The trifle was chilling in the fridge and the children were chilling in the television room. Alice was chopping some peppers.

'What have you been doing?' she said.

'Just some work. Answering a few emails, nothing important. How are the children?'

'They seem okay, they're with James and Olivia watching TV. It hasn't hit them yet, it will take time.' She looked straight at him. 'You were really great on the walk, Marcus. You couldn't have done it any better. I know it wasn't easy.'

'Thanks, Al. That means a lot. I tried to avoid all that angels, stars and special places shit. I didn't want to lie to them.'

'Poor little things, I feel so sorry for them. All of this has brought back feelings of when ours were that age. What would you have done if I'd died?'

'Given up work and looked after them, probably. It's what you would have wanted me to do, isn't it?'

'Really? And left The Firm?'

'I guess so. What's for dinner?'

'Ratatouille with vegan meatballs followed by trifle. That okay?'

'Sounds great.'

Marcus and Olivia bathed the children and put them in their pyjamas. They wanted to talk about their home, their mother, Mr Mahoney, Ian and Judith.

'Shall we go back to your house this week?' said Marcus. 'Maybe get some more of your things? We could see Mr Mahoney too.'

The children nodded.

'Will Mummy be there?' said Kyle.

'No, Mummy isn't at home anymore,' said Marcus.

'Where is she then?'

'She's in heaven,' said Alexa.

The children wanted Olivia to read them a bedtime story and Marcus and Alice returned to find them both almost asleep. They kissed them goodnight, covered them with the duvet and went downstairs.

'What are you doing now?' he said.

'I thought I'd watch the final episode of *The Nest*, it's quite good. But if you want to talk, I can watch it another time. I don't mind. What do you want to do?'

'You watch it. I've got something I need to do for work. I didn't finish it earlier. It won't take me long.'

He got up and walked to the office, opened his laptop and connected to the network. Thirty-eight new emails had accumulated over the weekend. Reminders for expenses that needed approval, fifteen emails from Laila Saetang and an invite for an online training course for partners, 'Bullying During Lockdown: Controlling Our Behaviours'.

That'll be fun, he thought. Kelvin still hadn't made him an offer he couldn't refuse. He opened a new message and began to type.

Subject: Retirement
From: Marcus Barlow
To: Kelvin McBride
Cc: Jenny Moffatt

Dear Kelvin
I am writing to confirm my decision to retire from The Firm with immediate effect. As you are aware, in recent months I have become more disenchanted with the direction The Firm is taking. It is no longer the same place I joined twenty years ago. During my time at The Firm, I have enjoyed many wonderful experiences, but I now feel it is time for me to move on.

Recent events, both within and outside The Firm, have forced me to take stock of the things that are most important to me. I have reached the conclusion that these are incompatible with continuing a career at The Firm.

I do not want any interim arrangements to smooth my departure. I've never been very good at gardening, so I will be leaving immediately. I am certain all my responsibilities can be handled by other partners or members of the team. I will ensure that any company assets and property are returned immediately. I will not be retaining any intellectual property belonging to The Firm. You're welcome to it.

I wish you and the team every success and hope that we get a chance to meet once lockdown has ended. I have no idea what I am going to do next but, after twenty years, maybe it's about time I did something for me? With my best wishes,
Marcus

He read the email to make sure he'd said everything he wanted to say. Then he read it again. The cursor hovered over the 'Send' button. He thought about his meeting with Colin in the garden of St Paul's. He clicked 'Send' and the message disappeared. He closed his laptop, switched off the light in the office and went through to the kitchen. It was almost ten o'clock. He made two mugs of tea and took them through to the living room where Alice's TV drama was ending.

'I've made you a cup of tea,' he said, putting it down on the nest of tables next to her.

'Oh, that's very sweet of you, thank you. Did you get your work done?'

'Yes, all done now. Just had to send a few emails. It's been a stressful day, hasn't it? I certainly don't want to go through that one again. Are you okay?'

He held her hand. It felt soft. She had just moisturised.

'Yes I'm fine. I'm still thinking about Claire and those little ones upstairs. It's awful.'

'I know, Al. The virus is changing all our lives. None of our worlds look like they did a few months ago. We've just got to deal with it as best as we can. One day at a time. Maybe nothing will ever be the same again?'

It was Monday, 13 April 2020.

ACKNOWLEDGEMENTS

One of the skills needed in my previous career was the ability to make the simple seem complicated. In the world of professional services, it's how money is made and I was good at it too. Now, in retirement as a writer, the opposite is true. A talent for making the complex seem simple is needed, guiding the reader through a range of emotions designed to make the book a memorable experience. I hope I have learned some new skills now.

Some people deserve special mention. Nicky Taylor for her sensitive and thoughtful editorial advice in the early stages; Dr. Guy Parsons for his insights on what life on the frontline during the pandemic was really like; Tim Bulmer for the unique cover design, the team at Matador for turning my manuscript into reality and Ben Cameron and his PR team for helping me bring the book to an audience.

I should also like to thank my former employers for giving me some of the experiences which form the foundations to parts of this book. Without you, none of this would have been possible!

Lastly, to my family and friends, who encouraged me to keep going through endless months of lockdown and isolation. You all know who you are. To the people who attempted to distract me, you only made me more determined. So, thank you too.

NEIL BOSS is a former partner at a large professional services organisation.

He retired from the world of Mergers & Acquisitions in November 2019. The coronavirus pandemic put on hold his plans to fly fish around the world and be a better guitar player.

Maybe It's About Time is his first novel.

He lives in Hertfordshire, England.

Photograph: Jennifer Gillam